Case Studies in Conten

SERIES EDITOR: Ross C Murfi

JAMES JOYCE
A Portrait of the Artist as a Young Man

Complete, Authoritative Text with Biographical and Historical Contexts, Critical History, and Essays from Five Contemporary Critical Perspectives

EDITED BY

R. B. Kershner

University of Florida

Bedford Books *of* St. Martin's Press

BOSTON • NEW YORK

For Bedford Books
President and Publisher: Charles H. Christensen
Associate Publisher/General Manager: Joan E. Feinberg
Managing Editor: Elizabeth M. Schaaf
Developmental Editor: Stephen A. Scipione
Production Editor: Theresa L. Walton
Copyeditor: Deborah Fogel
Text Design: Sandra Rigney, The Book Department
Cover Design: Richard Emery Design, Inc.

Library of Congress Catalog Card Number: 92–52515

Manufactured in the United States of America.

7
f

For information, write: Bedford Books, 75 Arlington Street, Boston, MA 02116 (617–426–7440)

ISBN: 0–312–06170–6 (paperback)
ISBN: 0–312–08987–2 (hardcover)

Published and distributed outside North America by:

MACMILLAN PRESS LTD.
Houndmills, Basingstoke, Hampshire RG21 2XS and London
Companies and representatives throughout the world.

ISBN: 0–333–59490–8

Acknowledgments

The text of *A Portrait of the Artist as a Young Man* is based on the version corrected from the Dublin holograph by Chester G. Anderson, reviewed by Richard Ellmann, and first published in the United States of America in 1964 by Viking Penguin Inc.

"Stephen Dedalus and Women: A Feminist Reading of *Portrait*" by Suzette Henke is a substantially revised version of an essay that appeared in *Women in Joyce,* ed. Suzette Henke and Elaine Unkeless (Urbana: U of Illinois P, 1982; © 1982 by the Board of Trustees of the University of Illinois) and *James Joyce and the Politics of Desire* by Suzette A. Henke (New York and London: Routledge, 1990; copyright © 1990 by Routledge, Chapman, and Hall, Inc.).

About the Series

Case Studies in Contemporary Criticism provide college students with an entrée into the current critical and theoretical ferment in literary studies. Each volume reprints the complete text of a classic literary work and presents critical essays that approach the work from different theoretical perspectives, together with the editors' introductions to both the literary work and the critics' theoretical perspectives.

The volume editor of each *Case Study* has selected and prepared an authoritative text of the classic work, written an introduction to the work's biographical and historical contexts, and surveyed the critical responses to the work since its initial publication. Thus situated biographically, historically, and critically, the work is examined in five critical essays, each representing a theoretical perspective of importance to contemporary literary studies. These essays, prepared especially for undergraduates by exemplary critics, show theory in praxis; whether written by established scholars or exceptional young critics, they demonstrate how current theoretical approaches can generate compelling readings of great literature.

As series editor, I have prepared introductions, with bibliographies, to the theoretical perspectives represented in the five critical essays. Each introduction presents the principal concepts of a particular theory in their historical context, and discusses the major figures and key works that have influenced their formulation. It is my hope that these introductions will reveal to students that good criticism is informed by a set of coherent assumptions, and will encourage them to recognize and examine their own assumptions about literature. Finally, I have compiled a glossary of key terms that recur in these volumes and in the discourse of contemporary theory and criticism. We hope that the *Case Studies in Contemporary Criticism* series will reaffirm the richness of its literary works, even as it introduces invigorating new ways to mine their apparently inexhaustible wealth.

Ross C Murfin
Series Editor
University of Miami

About This Volume

Until the present volume, the edition of *A Portrait of the Artist as a Young Man* most generally regarded as authoritative was the Viking Press edition "corrected from the Dublin holograph by Chester G. Anderson and edited by Richard Ellmann" in 1964. The present text includes over two hundred fifty additional emendations by Professor Anderson—most of them minor, but a number of them significant.

The editing of Joyce's books has become a controversial and hotly debated topic in recent years, not only among scholars but in the popular press as well. Without joining that debate or making any ultimate claims for the authority of the text below, I will say that I believe Part One of the present volume to be the best text of *Portrait* currently available. I have provided brief explanatory notes for the text, mostly in cases where Joyce's use of words is apt to cause trouble for the general reader. Readers who wish further information about any of the numerous allusions in the book should check either standard references or specialized ones such as Don Gifford's *Joyce Annotated,* Second Edition (Berkeley: U of California P, 1982).

Part Two includes five critical essays exemplifying different current critical approaches to Joyce's *Portrait.* Choosing and commissioning these essays was a difficult task because of the wealth of material available; Joyceans have been among the earliest critics to adopt fresh approaches, and American Joyceans in particular have generally welcomed the variety of European critical perspectives that have developed since the 1960s. All of the contributors here are well known for their work on Joyce, with one exception: Norman Holland, one of the founders of reader-response criticism, has not previously written on Joyce. Given the critical orientation he is exemplifying here, this inexperience is all to the good, since his essay shows an immediate sense of discovery as well as a variety of kinds of resistance to Joyce's novel.

Suzette Henke, co-editor of the ground-breaking volume *Women in Joyce* (1982) and author of *James Joyce and the Politics of Desire* (1990), has provided an article condensed and adapted from her feminist discussions of *Portrait* in those two books. Sheldon Brivic's psychoanalytic essay is adapted from one in his book *Joyce Between Freud and Jung* (1980); he has since published *Joyce the Creator* (1985) and *The Veil of Signs* (1991), a psychological study emphasizing the thought of Jacques Lacan. Cheryl Herr is probably best known for her work on the popular culture of Joyce's time in *Joyce's Anatomy of Culture* (1986). In that volume and in subsequent work, she has combined semiotic, poststructuralist, feminist, and Marxist literary methods in distinctive ways, but in the essay specially written for this volume she has chosen to ring imaginative changes on a more narrowly deconstructive approach. My own essay, which appears here for the first time, is an attempt to view *Portrait* as an element in the cultural structures and tensions of its time; in representing the New Historicist approach I have read the book more broadly and with less concentration on details of the text than I do in the Bakhtinian interpretations I offered in *Joyce, Bakhtin, and Popular Literature* (1989).

In reading over the four interpretations—my own set aside for the moment—I am struck by the variety of questions and the sorts of knowledge that are brought to bear on Joyce's novel. While each essay clearly illustrates one dominant critical approach, there is also considerable overlap in them, so that, for example, not only Brivic but also Holland and Henke at times use psychoanalytic terminology. Rather surprisingly, both Holland and Herr make important use of Robert Graves's guides to Greek mythology; and all the critics at some point mull over the meaning of a word or the intonation of a voice from Joyce's text. These coincidences, though, should not really be surprising: like all good critics, the contributors here are responding to James Joyce's work, not merely applying a critical template. It would be more surprising if a critic of whatever persuasion were to read *Portrait* without being drawn to a minute examination of words or to a meditation on myth. Whatever else it may be, the critical process at its best is a dialogue. I hope the second section of this book will be approached as a conversation—and a conversation that the student is cordially invited to join.

Acknowledgments

I first conceived this project after using Ross Murfin's fine edition of Conrad's *Heart of Darkness* in a graduate seminar and wishing that a similar edition were available for Joyce's *Portrait.* Once we had established the fact that such an edition would be possible, Ross Murfin's enthusiasm, efficiency, and expertise showed him to be the editor everyone hopes for but few find. At Bedford Books, Charles Christensen and Joan Feinberg approached the project with intelligence and courtesy, as did Steve Scipione, who among his other responsibilities in developing the book put in countless hours over the question of the text. Terri Walton gracefully shepherded the book through production, while Deborah Fogel not only copyedited the manuscript with great skill but also caught several errors in the 1964 text.

I would like specifically to thank the contributors to this volume, who are friends as well as colleagues. Norman Holland proved to be just as gracious a contributor as he has been a colleague at Florida; and through their unselfish cooperation as well as the quality of their work, Chester Anderson, Suzette Henke, Sheldon Brivic, and Cheryl Herr showed me once again why Joyceans are especially fortunate in their fellows. Among Joyceans elsewhere, I am indebted for various sorts of help and encouragement to Zack Bowen, Bernard Benstock, Morris Beja, Walton Litz, and Robert Spoo; and among my colleagues at Florida I especially want to thank Dan Cottom for critical discussions in less than critical situations. I first read Joyce with Richard Macksey; I want to thank him for showing me a glimpse of what critical sophistication might look like. Over the years my students have probably had more influence on my thinking about Joyce than has anyone else. Some of them, such as Garry Leonard and M. Keith Booker, have now joined the larger discussion of Joyce outside the walls of my classroom. I owe them all my thanks for many ideas that I now think of as my own. Finally, my thanks and dedication, once again, to Rhonda Riley.

R. Brandon Kershner
University of Florida

About This Text

The text used here corrects the edition of *A Portrait* which I did as my doctoral dissertation at Columbia University and which was printed in 1964 and thereafter by the Viking Press, though with some changes vetoed by Richard Ellmann. That edition was based on Joyce's own faircopy holograph (now at the National Library of Ireland) and on corrections made by him to the *Egoist* serial and to the first edition. The rationale for the 1964 edition, which restored several hundred words and made many other corrections following Joyce's clear intention, can be found in *Neuphilologische Mitteilungen* (LXV, 2, Helsinki, 1964).

However, there were errors made in carrying out that rationale—most of them my own, though Mr. Ellmann's vetoes added to them substantially. With the help of Jill Whenmouth as my research assistant in 1971, I found these errors as best I could and corrected them. But even though Marshall Best, then the pleasant executive vice president at Viking, was willing to make the changes, Mr. Ellmann was not. When I visited him in New College, Oxford, in 1972, he scolded me with his usual cheeriness for not being Hans Walter Gabler (later to become well known as the textual editor of *Ulysses*), who had found some of the typescript pages made from the manuscript in Trieste in 1913 and 1914 and who would have other news about the text.

I corresponded with Professor Gabler in Munich that year and talked with him in Zurich in 1973. He then published two articles on the text: "Towards a Critical Text of *A Portrait* . . . ," in *Studies in Bibliography* 27 (1974) and "The Seven Lost Years of *A Portrait* . . . ," in *Approaches to Joyce's "Portrait": Ten Essays,* edited by Thomas E. Staley and Bernard Benstock (U of Pittsburgh P, 1976). He may one day fulfill the late Richard Ellmann's expectations and bring out a text more "scientific" than this one.

However that may be, I am most grateful to R. B. Kershner and Bedford Books of St. Martin's Press for enabling me to get these corrections into print for the first time—not least the most striking of them all, the change from *green* to *geen* in Stephen's song on the opening page.

Chester G. Anderson
University of Minnesota

Contents

About the Series iii

About This Volume v

About This Text ix

PART ONE

A Portrait of the Artist as a Young Man: The Complete Text

Introduction: Biographical and Historical Contexts 3

The Complete Text 19

PART TWO

A Portrait of the Artist as a Young Man: A Case Study in Contemporary Criticism

A Critical History of *A Portrait of the Artist as a Young Man* 221

Psychoanalytic Criticism and *A Portrait of the Artist as a Young Man* 235

What Is Psychoanalytic Criticism? 235

Psychoanalytic Criticism: A Selected Bibliography 246

A Psychoanalytic Perspective:
SHELDON BRIVIC, The Disjunctive Structure of Joyce's *Portrait* 251

Reader-Response Criticism and *A Portrait of the Artist as a Young Man* 268

What Is Reader-Response Criticism? 268
Reader-Response Criticism: A Selected Bibliography 275
A Reader-Response Perspective:
NORMAN N. HOLLAND, *A Portrait* as Rebellion 279

Feminist Criticism and *A Portrait of the Artist as a Young Man* 295

What Is Feminist Criticism? 295
Feminist Criticism: A Selected Bibliography 302
A Feminist Perspective:
SUZETTE HENKE, Stephen Dedalus and Women: A Feminist Reading of *Portrait* 307

Deconstruction and *A Portrait of the Artist as a Young Man* 326

What Is Deconstruction? 326
Deconstruction: A Selected Bibliography 335
A Deconstructionist Perspective:
CHERYL HERR, Deconstructing Dedalus 338

The New Historicism and *A Portrait of the Artist as a Young Man* 361

What Is the New Historicism? 361
The New Historicism: A Selected Bibliography 369
A New Historicist Perspective:
R. B. KERSHNER, Genius, Degeneration, and the Panopticon 373

Glossary of Critical and Theoretical Terms 391

About the Contributors 403

PART ONE

A Portrait of the Artist as a Young Man: The Complete Text

Introduction: Biographical and Historical Contexts

James Augustine Aloysius Joyce was born on February 2, 1882, in Rathgar, a fairly prosperous southern suburb of Dublin, Ireland. His father, John Stanislaus Joyce, was from Cork, where the Joyce family had been merchants for some generations, and where they had married into the O'Connell family, who claimed a connection with the famous Irish nationalist, Daniel O'Connell, "the Liberator." The earliest Joyces were Norman but later established themselves in the west of Ireland near Galway, where a large area is known as "the Joyce Country." As the critic Edmund Epstein stresses (1984, 4–5), John Joyce insisted upon the family's noble descent, and indeed a Joyce coat of arms is registered, with the motto, *Mors aut honorabilis vita* ("An honorable life or death"). According to Colbert Kearney (1989), who has researched the Cork background, family myth asserted that the gentlemanly Joyces of Cork, including John Joyce's father, James Augustine, were dragged down by the shopkeeping O'Connells.

Like all Irish Catholics, the Joyces inherited a tradition of legal and cultural repression. Having suffered invasions by Vikings and by Normans in medieval times, Ireland was more systematically conquered by the British, beginning in the Elizabethan period; successive waves of invasion and settlement established an "Anglo-Irish" aristocracy that controlled much of the land, while during the eighteenth century the "penal laws" effectively barred Catholics from social advancement.

Even the Irish language spoken by Joyce's ancestors was prohibited. A series of reforms culminating in the Emancipation Act of 1829 allowed the growth of a Catholic middle class, but the hopes of the Catholic peasantry—and many of the middle class as well—remained firmly tied to the establishment of an independent Irish nation (Lyons, 1973).

When John Joyce moved from Cork to Dublin in his mid-twenties, he was a man of some means, including property in Cork; by the age of forty he had lost his final job as tax collector and was never again regularly employed. He was a man of considerable charm, a fine tenor and storyteller, but also an improvident spendthrift and drinker. A friend, Constantine Curran, described him as "a man of unparalleled vituperative power, a virtuoso in speech with unique control of the vernacular" (1968, 69). In many ways a disastrous parent, he nevertheless fathered eleven children, of whom eight survived to adulthood. Whatever strain this may have put on his resources, a pregnancy virtually every year following her marriage proved a far greater strain for May Joyce, who died at forty-four. James Joyce was the eldest surviving child; two of his siblings died of typhoid, a disease encouraged by the family's poverty.

But in 1888, when James Joyce was sent to board and study at Clongowes Wood College, most of these embarrassments and tragedies lay in the future. Clongowes, run by the influential Jesuit order, was perhaps the best preparatory school in Ireland (sons of the wealthier Anglo-Irish families were often sent to still better schools in England). Despite the repressive picture he paints of the school in *Portrait,* Joyce later spoke warmly of his experience there; unlike Stephen, whom we only see unjustly punished, Joyce received punishment that he admitted he deserved on several occasions, including once for bad language. Joyce was a good student at Clongowes despite his youth, and in some ways he never abandoned the habits of thought with which the Jesuits inculcated him. But public events in Ireland were equally important to him, at least as they reached him through the talk of his parents and their friends.

The two and a half years that Joyce attended Clongowes happened to coincide with the climax of the Parnell affair, which seized the young boy's imagination. (The scholar Malcolm Brown [1972, 326–47] has presented the story most vividly.) Charles Stewart Parnell, a Protestant landholder, entered the British House of Commons as an Irish member of Parliament in 1875. Along with the former Fenian, or Irish revolutionary, Michael Davitt, he founded the predominantly Catholic Land League to redistribute farmland. Gradually he became head of a political group that included nationalists of all sorts, from moderates to militant revolutionaries. By 1879 he had become leader of the Irish home rule movement, which insisted that the Irish be allowed a measure of self-government. He managed to unite the Irish vote in the House of Commons, and by threatening various tactics of parliamentary obstruction, he was able to bargain for the support of the prime minister, Gladstone, for home rule. His cause suffered a setback in 1882, when a radical group called the Invincibles assassinated two British officials in Phoenix Park, northwest of Dublin. Although Parnell publicly condemned the assassination, in 1887 the London *Times* ran a series of articles based on information supplied by a former Nationalist named Piggott, accusing Parnell of supporting the Invincibles. A trial showed that the letters supposedly written by Parnell were forgeries, but the ruthlessness of Parnell's conservative opposition was made clear. Then in 1890 Parnell was accused of adultery in a divorce suit brought by Captain William O'Shea, a former member of the Home Rule party, against his wife Katharine.

The trial made headlines. Parnell's ten-year liaison with Mrs. O'Shea, to which the captain had given tacit assent, was the stuff of scandal, and the intimate details that emerged were embarrassing for all concerned. For instance, Katharine and Parnell addressed one another as "King" and "Queen" in private. One of Parnell's code names in communicating with his lover, "Mr. Fox," became widely known, while Mrs. O'Shea was universally referred to as "Kitty," which was coincidentally a slang term for a prostitute. Parnell was a man of enormous pride and rather cold, aristocratic demeanor. He refused to defend himself against the charge and wished simply to marry Mrs. O'Shea, who for ten years had remained legally married to her husband only in hopes of a legacy. Gladstone decided that his Liberal party's home rule policy could not withstand association with a man of such questionable moral character, and the Irish party, at the urging of Davitt and Parnell's former supporter, Tim Healy, removed Parnell from leadership. Parnell refused to capitulate, and the party split; he was denounced by Catholic churchmen, whose leaders hoped to regain influence over the Nationalist movement. Among his attackers was Archbishop William Walsh, whom Simon Dedalus characterizes as "Billy with the lip."

As his power diminished, Parnell was accused of outrageous things, such as embezzling the Land League's "Paris funds" to subsidize his love life. Following his marriage to Kitty, he continued, in weakening health, to take his campaign to the people. When he died in 1891, as many as one hundred and fifty thousand people accompanied his sealed coffin to

Glasnevin cemetery, led by the radical Fenians who had supported him at the end. In a revulsion of popular feeling, Parnell gained a kind of mythic status even among those who had attacked him, and as it became clear that Irish nationalism was in disarray, he became the "dead king" who alone could have led Ireland to independence. Following Parnell's death, the nine-year-old Joyce wrote a bitter broadside poem against his betrayers entitled "Et tu Healy," which John Joyce had printed. Joyce came to see Parnell as a martyr, betrayed by his own people, in the mold of earlier nationalist heroes who had led aborted insurrections, such as Wolfe Tone and Robert Emmet. Like Joyce, Stephen Dedalus views himself as their potential successor, an artist-hero who may save his country not only from its enemies but from itself.

When he came to write *A Portrait of the Artist as a Young Man,* Joyce relied heavily on autobiography; in outline and in many details, the novel follows his own life from birth up to the age of twenty. His family and acquaintances often appear recognizably, with only a change of name, while schools, streets, businesses, hotels, and public figures generally appear under their real names—an unusual practice at the time and one that Joyce also followed in his book of short stories, *Dubliners,* causing him endless trouble when he tried to publish the book. But as Joyce's biographer Richard Ellmann (1982) clearly established, there are important differences between James Joyce and Stephen Dedalus. The timing of Stephen's attendance at Clongowes is altered so that Parnell's death occurs earlier. Although Joyce briefly attended a Christian Brothers' school after Clongowes, Stephen does not. Stephen avoids sports of all sorts, whereas Joyce was quite proud of winning a schoolboy race. Joyce in youth was called "Sunny Jim" by his family because of his cheerful disposition, while Stephen is more or less withdrawn and sullen. Joyce's relationship with his father appeared friendly to others, but Stephen's is increasingly bitter and tense. At parties Stephen is aloof; Joyce, who could indeed be distant in manner, was also known for his songs (he had a voice of professional quality), his impersonations, and his occasional manic, spidery dances.

Joyce's family fortunes continued to worsen, in part because his father had been a paid canvasser for Parnell. Joyce began attending the Jesuit Belvedere College in Dublin in 1893. The following year, in a nationwide examination, he won one of the top prizes, or "exhibitions," worth twenty pounds. That year or the next, he began to patronize local prostitutes. Meanwhile, he was chosen prefect of the sodality of the Blessed Virgin Mary at school, an honor meant to recognize both his academic achievements and his moral character, and one that might well indicate that the boy was thought to have a vocation for the priesthood. A retreat sermon delivered by a priest from Clongowes in 1896 had a strong effect on Joyce, who was struggling with sexual guilt and self-hatred at the time; but during the following several years, his precocious reading of Byron and "dangerous" modern authors like Meredith, Hardy, Ibsen, and his countryman Yeats had an even more powerful cumulative effect. From these he began to acquire a critical attitude toward social institutions of bourgeois Ireland, including the Church itself, and from Yeats in particular he learned to see the world of art as an autonomous sphere removed from the pragmatic world of everyday experience and to see the figure of the artist as part prophet, part priest—the potential savior of his race. By the time he entered the Royal University in Dublin, also known as University College, he was permanently disaffected from Catholicism, much to the distress of his mother.

The critic Patrick Parrinder (1984, 17–40) stresses the importance of Joyce's university experience in forming his character and public image. University College had been founded by the famous convert John Henry Newman in 1854 to offer a liberal Catholic education alternative to the predominantly secular Trinity College, where the sons of the Protestant Ascendancy were educated. But Newman had failed to win independence from the bishops in making his appointments, and by the time Joyce entered it in 1898, the school, controlled by the Jesuits, offered a conservative and intellectually undemanding curriculum. Modern thought and modern art were condemned or ignored. When Joyce began to speak enthusiastically about the playwright Ibsen, who had been praised by the London intelligentsia for years, he gained a great deal of local notoriety as a dangerously radical thinker.

But if the instructors were relatively backward, the student body at University College was sensitive to the political and social turmoil of the time. Parnell's cause had not died with him, but after the apparent failure of parliamentary activism, more radical Nationalists came to the fore. A local branch of the Gaelic League, which encouraged the study of the Irish language and the playing of native Irish sports, was established by Joyce's friend George Clancy (Davin in *Portrait*). Somewhat less publicly, it organized military training for Nationalists who hoped for a popular insurrection (such as the one that indeed occurred in 1916); Davin in *A Portrait* is said to be practicing military drill. But from Joyce's perspective, the most significant movement of the time was probably what later became known as the Irish Literary Revival or Irish Renaissance.

This movement, which was responsible for a period of immense literary productivity, lasted from roughly 1890 into the 1920s. It was spearheaded by William Butler Yeats, perhaps the greatest poet writing in English at that time. Yeats, seventeen years Joyce's senior, formed the notion of a national literature that would take its inspiration from Irish myth and folktale. Under the influence of his friend George Russell (who wrote under the mystic name "AE") he imbued his work with a strong element of spiritualism, while under the influence of the Fenian John O'Leary and of Maud Gonne, the woman he loved, he also linked it to nationalist aspirations. The political and aesthetic dimensions of his work did not always coexist easily, however. In 1899 Yeats helped found the Irish Literary Theatre, where he presented his play *Countess Cathleen*. Although his later play *Kathleen Ni Houlihan* was enormously successful with Nationalists, *Countess Cathleen*, relying on an aristocratic figure who sells her soul to the devil in exchange for food for her starving people, caused riots protesting "a libel on Irish womanhood." In *Portrait* Stephen is portrayed as one of the few students at University College who refuse to sign a petition against the play, and in so doing he appears to choose art over politics. Later, he recites a verse from the play. These details are in fact autobiographical. Joyce knew many of Yeats's poems by heart, and he may have been drawn to specialize in prose because he feared he could not compete as a poet.

By the time he left University College, Joyce had met a number of figures prominent in the Revival, including Yeats, George Russell, and Yeats's patron and collaborator, Lady Augusta Gregory. On the strength of a few essays and verses he had begun to make a name for himself. But despite his enthusiasm for Yeats's work, Joyce from the beginning had serious reservations about the direction of Yeats's movement. For one thing, all the major figures were of the Protestant landholding class, and Yeats especially had an almost feudal respect for the "great families" like Lady Gregory's who were his models of aristocracy. For another thing, Yeats also romanticized the unlettered peasantry, whom he saw as a repository of folk wisdom and mystic insight. Joyce, a member of the urban poor with a very different notion of aristocracy, had little patience with this aspect of the Revival. And while he disliked British imperialism as strongly as Yeats's generation of writers, he was reluctant to join a movement such as the Gaelic League, which he saw as bigoted, backward-looking, and Church-dominated. With his friend George Clancy he briefly took Irish lessons from Padraic Pearse, a poet who was later executed after the 1916 insurrection, but objected to Pearse's disparagement of the English language. Also, like Stephen, he feared to commit himself wholly to a political movement in search of martyrs.

In his second year at university, Joyce distinguished himself by presenting a paper entitled "Drama and Life" at the school's Literary and Historical Society, over the objections of school authorities (Mason and Ellmann 38–46). In it he enthusiastically defended modern drama, as exemplified by Ibsen, against its attackers; art has a responsibility to represent life as it is actually lived rather than as convention dictates, he argued. Indeed, art has its own laws and logic as an expression of the artist that is nearly beyond judgment. More impressively, Joyce expanded upon his defense of Ibsen in an article that was published in the influential British *Fortnightly Review.* Ibsen himself responded with an appreciative note that his translator William Archer forwarded to Joyce, and Joyce set himself to learning Dano-Norwegian so as to read the Scandinavian master in the original.

From youth, Joyce had shown a talent for languages. The Jesuits had immediately set him to reading Latin, and at University College he studied Italian, German, and French. Yeats's enthusiasm for the native culture failed to win Joyce; he argued that "a nation which never advanced so far as a miracle play affords no literary model to the artist, and he must look abroad" (Mason and Ellmann 70). Gradually he was becoming convinced that he would have to escape Ireland. Europe he saw as a freer, more cosmopolitan world, and his languages would enable him to survive there. As it turned out, Joyce spent nearly the whole of his mature life in Europe, and his children were raised speaking Italian and French as easily as they did English.

Joyce, of course, was not the only artist or rebel at University College. His friend Francis Skeffington was a committed feminist and pacifist who argued that women should be admitted to Ireland's universities. Joyce and Skeffington, who appears rather unflatteringly as McCann in *Portrait,* published at their own expense a pamphlet containing an essay by Joyce attacking philistines entitled "The Day of the Rabblement" along with a feminist essay by his friend. Skeffington later married a friend of Joyce's and changed his name to Sheehy-Skeffington in her honor. He was murdered by a British officer during the 1916 insurrection after trying to stop British troops from looting. This outrage caused consternation both among the British officer's family, which included the future Anglo-Irish novelist Elizabeth Bowen, and among Skeffington's British relatives, who changed their name in shame at his "treason" (Parrinder 20).

Other friends included John Francis Byrne, who appears as "Cranly" and who later published a book protesting Joyce's version of their relationship, and Vincent Cosgrave ("Lynch"), who caused Joyce pain several years later by falsely claiming to have slept with Joyce's lover, Nora. Cosgrave was to commit suicide, while Thomas Kettle, a talented scholar and writer, died in the Battle of the Somme, and George Clancy, who became mayor of Limerick, was shot by disguised Protestant irregulars in 1921. Joyce was often thought paranoid in later life because he refused to return to Ireland, but surprisingly few of his friends from college who remained in Ireland died a natural death.

Another acquaintance of this period who was to figure importantly in Joyce's writing was Oliver St. John Gogarty, son of a wealthy Anglo-Irish family. Gogarty was attending Trinity and, like many of Joyce's school friends, preparing for a career in medicine. He was a prolifically talented young man who became a protégé of Yeats, writing poems that appeared in several of Yeats's poetry anthologies. In later life he was a successful physician, Irish senator, and a well-known public figure in Dublin. An athlete, scholar, writer, and general carouser, Gogarty "adopted" Joyce for a period, lending him clothing and money. For a week in 1904 the two shared quarters in a Martello tower south of Dublin. This period is immortalized in Joyce's *Ulysses,* where Gogarty appears as Stephen's companion, rival, and—for reasons that remain somewhat obscure—his betrayer, Buck Mulligan. Like several of Joyce's school friends, Gogarty was aware that Joyce was making notes on him, preparing to use him in a literary work. In *Ulysses* Stephen muses, "He fears the lancet of my art." Indeed, in later life Gogarty found himself protesting that he was *not* Buck Mulligan, but a real human being. Like Byrne, he published his own very different version of his relationship with Joyce. Like Joyce's brother Stanislaus, Gogarty appeared in an early version of *Portrait* (part of which has been published as *Stephen Hero*) but was cut from the final draft to give more prominence to Stephen.

For all their differences, Stephen and Joyce in this period shared what Joyce termed an "enigma of a manner" (Scholes and Kain 61), a rather formal and aloof persona with which to confront rival students, and a sometimes showy and pedantic way of speaking. Coupled with a certain reputation for debauchery—Stephen "confesses" some of his experiences with prostitutes to Davin—this manner helped establish his reputation as a young man to be reckoned with. His friend Eugene Sheehy observed that "Joyce, the schoolboy, was as icy, aloof, and imperturbable as . . . Joyce the man." Another friend described him delivering a paper before a debating society: "Joyce, thin and pale, stood erect, scarcely moving, cold and undisturbed by interruptions (and he had many), and seemed in passionless tones to wither the opposition by his air of indifferent disdain" (Scholes and Kain 141, 152). He might have been Yeats facing down the rioters at the Abbey Theatre ("You have disgraced yourselves again!"), or Parnell campaigning in his last years. Following the debate on Joyce's paper and his demolition of each of his critics, a student slapped his back and exclaimed, "Joyce, that was magnificent, but you're raving mad!" (Ellmann 73).

It should be noted that University College students of the time were a more rigorously selected group than those at the average American university today; also, typically they would have had training since childhood in Latin, perhaps Greek, and the classics. Competitiveness was instilled by nationwide examinations and cash prizes. Their primary and secondary education stressed memorization of passages and the preparation of essays modeled on those of the great rhetoricians, so that when Stephen attacks Lynch with his "dagger definitions," for instance, he is merely practicing the art for which he had been trained. The young Joyce's intellectual style was striking mainly because he chose to cite obscure ancients and embattled moderns rather than the accepted greats, and continental rather than English writers. Also, of course, he wrote very well. Still, Joyce's portrait gives Stephen more rigor and sophistication than he himself probably possessed at the time. Although Stephen considers himself a student of Aquinas and Aristotle—and garners intellectual status from this distinction—it appears from his notebooks that Joyce himself studied Aristotle intensely only after leaving the university.

Although Stephen has fixed his romantic yearnings since childhood upon the insubstantial "E—C—," or "Emma," Joyce seems to have had no such abiding passion. His brother Stanislaus has suggested that he may have been infatuated for a time with a girl named Mary Sheehy, and certainly she, along with her bright and talented sisters, served in part as a model for E—C—. In *Stephen Hero* she appears more vigorously as Emma Clery, with whom Stephen is cautiously involved, and in that manuscript argues with him over the right of women to the same education as men receive. Stephen imperiously disagrees and later suggests that the two of them spend a single night of wild passion, then part, never to see each other again. Not surprisingly, this generous offer fails to tempt her. A friend of Stephen's observes that he could marry her, but Stephen thinks that price too high; and like Joyce, he feels that the institution of marriage is an unwarranted intrusion of state and

Church into private relationships. Like the Church, family, and nation, marriage is another "net" thrown up to catch the artist's fledgling soul.

In 1902 Joyce graduated from University College with an undistinguished B.A., briefly enrolled as a medical student, and in December left Dublin for Paris, armed with introductions from Yeats and others and the possibility of supporting himself meagerly by writing book reviews for newspapers. He left with George Russell a group of his unpublished verses. He also left with Russell what he called "epiphanies" or "epicleti," short prose sketches that vary in character from lyrical, dreamlike effusions to literal reportage of overheard vulgar conversations. Joyce struggled in Paris, returned home for money, then returned to Paris, where he stopped attending medical lectures and began studying in the National Library. He met Yeats's protégé, the playwright John Millington Synge, whom he accused of being insufficiently Aristotelian.

Then in April 1903, he was recalled home by a telegram announcing his mother's fatal illness. Her request that he pray with her brought on another religious crisis, and during this time and following her death, he drank heavily, especially with Gogarty. This behavior disgusted Stanislaus, his highly intelligent and more conventional younger brother, whom he bullied, confided in, and depended upon for much of his life. At the beginning of 1904, Joyce taught briefly in a school in a Dublin suburb. Then, sometime around June 16, he met and, in the Irish phrase, "walked out with" Nora Barnacle, a country girl from Galway who worked as a hotel chambermaid. She was to be in many ways the central figure during the remainder of his life.

Joyce began writing in earnest now. He began with a lyrical, revolutionary, and rather obscure essay that Stanislaus entitled "A Portrait of the Artist," which was to be the earliest version of the autobiographical novel his friends had feared he was writing. He published a story entitled "The Sisters," which Russell had commissioned for his magazine *The Irish Homestead,* under the pseudonym "Stephen Daedalus." Russell took two more stories and several of his poems. Joyce sent a collection of his poems entitled *Chamber Music* to the English publisher Grant Richards. Then, in November 1904, he left Dublin with Nora, without benefit of marriage, planning to teach English in a Berlitz school in Zurich. Except for brief visits, he would never return to Ireland. Joyce wound up teaching in Trieste, Italy, and in 1905 completed nine more of the short stories that were to form the book *Dubliners.* He sent the whole collection to Richards, thus beginning a painful eight-year effort to publish the volume.

Stanislaus joined him in Trieste, and a son, George, or "Giorgio," was born to him and Nora. Two years later, his daughter, Lucia Anna, was born. During this period Joyce was under considerable strain: although he had avoided the legal title of husband, he soon discovered that in practical terms he was both husband and father. Like his father he was generally improvident and given to bouts of drinking from which his constitution was never really strong enough to recover easily. At times, he doubted whether he should be with Nora. The responsibility of a family weighed upon him, especially as he never doubted that his primary responsibility should be to his art. Stanislaus often rescued the Joyces and tried to play the role of his brother's good conscience, a kindness that Joyce of course resented. After Joyce's death, Stanislaus wrote a book on James entitled *My Brother's Keeper* (1969).

By 1907 Joyce had added several stories to the *Dubliners* collection, including his masterpiece, "The Dead," and he had conceived the idea of a story involving a Dublin Jew that some fifteen years later was to become the monumental novel *Ulysses*. *Chamber Music* had been published. He was writing newspaper articles and delivering public lectures to the Trieste cultural community. Slowly he began to reshape the long, rambling, rather conventional autobiographical novel on which he had been working into a tight, elliptical, formally experimental work, although this process bore its greatest fruit only after 1913, when Ezra Pound began to encourage him.

Meanwhile, the effort to publish *Dubliners* was a continual frustration. Grant Richards, who had originally accepted the collection in 1906, demanded more and more changes. Joyce agreed to a few, refused others, and Richards finally rejected the book. After four other publishers had rejected it, Maunsel and Company accepted it in 1909. Under British law a printer as well as a publisher could be sued if a book were found libelous or obscene, and Maunsel's printer was timid. Finally, the galley sheets for the book were destroyed in 1912. Enraged, Joyce wrote a scurrilous and funny broadside poem about the publisher and printer entitled "Gas from a Burner" and had it distributed in Dublin. After more rejections by other publishers, Grant Richards reconsidered *Dubliners* in 1913 and printed it in the following year. No one sued or even objected publicly. Meanwhile, in an unsuccessful and uncharacteristic foray into business, in 1909 Joyce had helped establish the first cinema in Ireland.

Ezra Pound was probably as responsible as anyone other than Joyce for the appearance of *A Portrait of the Artist as a Young Man*. The American poet was not only a significant modernist writer in his own right, he was also an indefatigable discoverer and promoter of other artists.

Yeats had sent him a lyric of Joyce's that he decided to include in his anthology *Des Imagistes,* and in response to his letter to Joyce, Pound received a revised first chapter of *Portrait* as well as a copy of *Dubliners.* Pound convinced a literary and philosophical journal called *The Egoist,* which was originally founded as a feminist organ, to serialize the novel. Meanwhile, war had broken out and Joyce had begun work on his only play, an Ibsenesque drama entitled *Exiles.* Generally considered his least interesting work, the play concerns an Irish writer who returns home after living in Europe with his common-law wife and son; he renews acquaintance with a popular journalist and sensualist who attempts to seduce the woman. The writer has insisted that his relationship with his wife should be free and open, and in a sort of experiment asks her to encourage the other man's advances. After much suffering all around, the play ends ambiguously, with both writer and audience unsure whether his wife has been faithful to him, or even what faithfulness might mean. Joyce, always tormented but fascinated by his jealousy of Nora, was to use marital fidelity as an important theme in his later works.

Installments of *Portrait* began to appear in *The Egoist.* Perhaps more important, Harriet Shaw Weaver, the American who had taken over as editor, settled a trust on Joyce in 1919 that freed him from serious financial worries. Her personal as well as financial support was crucial during the remainder of his life. Meanwhile, after some unsuccessful attempts to publish the book in England, *Portrait* was published in New York by B. W. Huebsch in 1916, and Weaver's Egoist Press used the same plates for a British edition the following year. In 1917 Joyce had a serious attack of glaucoma, the beginning of the problems with his eyesight that were to grow increasingly acute until, in the last decade of his life, he was virtually blind. But his major interest during the war years was work on the book that was to become *Ulysses,* parts of which were serialized in the *Little Review* starting in 1918.

In some ways *Ulysses* begins where *Portrait* leaves off. It opens on June 16, 1904, with Stephen Dedalus sharing rooms in a Martello tower on the east coast of Ireland, south of Dublin, with Buck Mulligan and a visiting Englishman named Haines who is studying Irish culture. Stephen has returned from Paris, where he has had experiences much like Joyce's, and he is recovering from the death of his mother. But in the fourth chapter of the book we are introduced to a new character, a Jewish advertising canvasser named Leopold Bloom whose wife, Molly, is planning to commit adultery with a man named "Blazes" Boylan that afternoon. Bloom knows Stephen's father but has no obvious connection to the boy; nevertheless, the meeting of the two is as much of a dramatic climax as the book admits. The entirety of *Ulysses'* seven-hundred-odd pages takes place on the same day, during which we go deeply into the minds of both main characters and, finally, into the mind of Molly as well—and we meet a bewildering variety of subsidiary characters.

Perhaps the book's most striking feature is its narrative innovations. Starting around the ninth chapter, the narration, which had begun in a mode something like the last chapter of *Portrait* (although with more internal monologue), begins to vary wildly. There are interpolated episodes in play form, a chapter narrated by an unnamed barfly, one that is told as if it were a poorly written domestic romance, one told in ludicrously abstract question-and-answer form, and so forth. Perhaps the most noticeable shift in tone from *Portrait* is due to the humor of the book: it is crammed with jokes, from high intellectual verbal play to the most vulgar slapstick. On several occasions Joyce remarked that he wished reviewers, instead of worrying about the book's obscenity, would at least notice that it was funny.

While writing *Ulysses,* Joyce had returned to Trieste, and then in 1920 at the urging of Pound, the Joyces had gone to Paris for a week's excursion. They wound up staying twenty years. With the enthusiastic support of Pound, T. S. Eliot, and a Parisian bookstore owner named Sylvia Beach, Joyce soon gathered around him an admiring circle of friends, French literary luminaries, and aspiring young writers from England and America. When the *Little Review* editors were prosecuted for obscenity because of an episode of *Ulysses* that appeared in the magazine, the incident only added to Joyce's international fame. By the time Beach's bookstore, Shakespeare and Company, published the first edition of the complete book in 1922, Joyce was already the literary toast of Paris and had been acclaimed by many as the greatest modern writer of English prose.

Meanwhile, Joyce circulated among friends a chart showing in detail what the book's title had not made entirely clear: despite its surface naturalism, his novel contained an elaborate series of correspondences to Homer's *Odyssey.* Indeed, in 1930, after considerable help and occasional direction from Joyce, Stuart Gilbert published a book on *Ulysses* exploring these correspondences and many other subtle features of the novel. Critics now conventionally refer to the chapters of the book by the titles of the parallel episodes in the Odyssey, such as "Lestrygonians" or "Aeolus." Gilbert also helped with the French translation of *Ulysses,* which—again with Joyce's advice and encouragement—appeared in 1929, and had substantial impact upon French literature.

Despite the fact that it was banned from publication in the United States, *Ulysses* was frequently smuggled into the country, becoming one of the best-known banned books of all time. Still, it was not until 1934 that Random House, under the leadership of Bennett Cerf, won a landmark court battle and the right to publish *Ulysses* in the United States; two years later it was published in England as well. But in the meantime, starting in 1923, Joyce had begun work on his most radical and ambitious work of prose, parts of which were published as *Work in Progress* (among other provisional titles) but which finally emerged as the book *Finnegans Wake.* From its first fragment, published in Ford Madox Ford's *transatlantic review* in 1924, the *Wake* caused trouble for Joyce. Many of his friends and supporters were dismayed. Pound confessed himself baffled, and even Harriet Weaver expressed disappointment, which hurt Joyce deeply. The book is written in a "night-language" far removed from ordinary English, jammed with portmanteau words and multilingual puns. When a friend objected that some of the puns in the *Wake* were trivial, Joyce replied that some were indeed trivial, and some quadrivial. Worse, there are no fixed characters or events in the book—or, alternatively, there are too many for comfort.

Far more elaborately planned and embellished even than *Ulysses, Finnegans Wake* on one level concerns a publican in the Dublin suburb of Chapelizod named Humphrey Chimpden Earwicker, his wife, two sons, and daughter. But characters, time, and place seldom remain fixed for more than a sentence in this work; the ultimate male character appears in a wide variety of guises signaled by the initials "HCE," such as "Haveth Childers Everywhere" or "Here Comes Everybody," and in a great number of less easily identifiable ones as well, such as Adam, Humpty Dumpty, Parnell, or King Mark of the Tristan and Isolde legend. This figure merges into that of Tim Finnegan, hero of an Irish comic song about a man who arises at his own wake to share the drink, and with the mythic Irish hero Finn, who is also a mountain. The main female figure, usually called Anna Livia Plurabelle, or ALP, is most frequently identified with rivers, although she too has a variety of mythic and historical guises. The two embattled sons, Shem and Shaun, represent respectively the artistic personality—withdrawn, exiled, obsessed with sex and with excrement, a universal scapegoat—and the successful public personality—alternately postman, policeman, politician, and empire builder. The daughter, Issy, merges into virtually any young woman or splinters into groups of them.

But even this vague summary is far too explicitly literal: Joyce indicated his "characters" by "sigla," geometric symbols that seem to represent functions rather than anything we would ordinarily call "characters." In its own strange fashion the book reprises the history of Ireland, the author's life, and a selection of major myths from European culture. But more than any narrative line, the *Wake*'s structure depends upon a conception by the eighteenth-century Italian philosopher Giambattista Vico, the idea that history progresses in a three-part cycle followed by a fourth part, the "ricorso" or return, that returns us to an initial stage after passing through theocratic, aristocratic, democratic, and chaotic phases. The book's three major chapters, followed by a briefer one, mirror this structure.

As with *Ulysses,* Joyce tried to orchestrate the reception of the *Wake.* He encouraged twelve of his friends, including Stuart Gilbert and Samuel Beckett (who had informally apprenticed himself to Joyce), to produce a volume treating the book. This was published as *Our Exagmination round His Factification for Incamination of "Work in Progress"* in 1929. But events conspired against him. By the time the book was finally published, in 1939, the world was on the brink of war once again.

Joyce's own health and eyesight were failing during his last decade. Most painfully, his children, whom he had grown to cherish passionately, were in trouble. By 1929 it was becoming clear that his daughter, Lucia, a bright and talented girl, was mentally unstable. Joyce fought the realization as long as possible, arranging projects in which she could express her artistic impulses and encouraging her in everything. By 1932, however, when she conceived a hopeless passion for Samuel Beckett, even he had to seek treatment and finally institutionalization for her. Joyce's son, Giorgio, was unable to undertake a successful career, and his marriage was failing; in 1939 his wife had a breakdown and the two separated. In 1931, for various reasons including the wish to make a reconciliation with his dying father, Joyce took Nora to a London registry office to legalize their marriage. Perhaps the brightest spot in this period was the birth of Joyce's grandson, Stephen James Joyce, in 1932, less than two months after Joyce's father's death. "Ecce Puer" ("Behold the Child"), perhaps Joyce's most moving poem, commemorates these two events with stunning simplicity.

In 1940 the Joyces were forced to leave Paris for Vichy, where they stayed with a family friend while Joyce carried on protracted negotiations to be allowed to enter Switzerland. Meanwhile, he was assisting a number of Jewish friends to escape to neutral territory. He left only a few scattered comments about his ideas for his next book: that it would be a book of reawakening (after the dream world of the *Wake*) and that it would be short and simple. In December 1940 the Joyces entered Switzerland and soon returned to Zurich. Less than a month later, Joyce was taken to the hospital with severe stomach cramps and was diagnosed as suffering from a perforated duodenal ulcer. Although an operation was apparently successful, he soon weakened, passed into a coma, and died on January 13, just before his fifty-ninth birthday. He was buried in the Fluntern cemetery above Zurich. Nora, out of respect for her husband's lifelong rebellion, refused the offer of Catholic rites.

R. B. Kershner

WORKS CITED

Brown, Malcolm. *The Politics of Irish Literature*. Seattle: U of Washington P, 1972.

Curran, Constantine P. *James Joyce Remembered*. New York: Oxford UP, 1968.

Ellmann, Richard. *James Joyce*. Rev. ed. New York: Oxford UP, 1982. The standard biography of Joyce.

Epstein, Edmund. "James Augustine Aloysius Joyce." *A Companion to Joyce Studies*. Ed. Zack Bowen and James F. Carens. Westport: Greenwood, 1984. 3–38.

Joyce, Stanislaus. *My Brother's Keeper: James Joyce's Early Years*. Ed. Richard Ellmann. New York: Viking, 1969.

Kearney, Colbert. "The Joycead." *Coping with Joyce: Essays from the Copenhagen Symposium*. Ed. Morris Beja and Shari Benstock. Columbus: Ohio State UP, 1989. 55–72.

Lyons, F. S. L. *Ireland Since the Famine*. London: Collins, 1973.

Mason, Ellsworth, and Richard Ellmann, eds. *James Joyce: The Critical Writings*. New York: Viking, 1964.

Parrinder, Patrick. *James Joyce*. Cambridge: Cambridge UP, 1984.

Scholes, Robert and Richard M. Kain, eds. *The Workshop of Daedalus: James Joyce and the Raw Materials for "A Portrait of the Artist as a Young Man."* Evanston: Northwestern UP, 1965.

A Portrait of the Artist as a Young Man

Et ignotas animum dimittit in artes.°
– OVID, *Metamorphoses,* VIII, 188

I

Once upon a time and a very good time it was there was a moocow coming down along the road and this moocow that was coming down along the road met a nicens little boy named baby tuckoo. . . .

His father told him that story: his father looked at him through a glass:° he had a hairy face.

He was baby tuckoo. The moocow came down the road where Betty Byrne lived: she sold lemon platt.

O, the wild rose blossoms
On the little green place.

He sang that song. That was his song.

O, the geen wothe botheth.

When you wet the bed first it is warm then it gets cold. His mother put on the oilsheet. That had the queer smell.

His mother had a nicer smell than his father. She played on the piano the sailor's hornpipe for him to dance. He danced:

Et ignotas animum dimittit in artes: Latin, "And he applies his mind to unknown arts" [the line continues, "and changes the laws of nature"]. Description of Daedalus in Ovid's *Metamorphoses,* VIII:188. [All notes are the volume editor's.] **a glass:** A monocle.

Tralala lala
Tralala tralaladdy
Tralala lala
Tralala lala.

Uncle Charles and Dante clapped. They were older than his father and mother but uncle Charles was older than Dante.

Dante had two brushes in her press.° The brush with the maroon velvet back was for Michael Davitt and the brush with the green velvet back was for Parnell. Dante gave him a cachou° every time he brought her a piece of tissue paper.

The Vances lived in number seven. They had a different father and mother. They were Eileen's father and mother. When they were grown up he was going to marry Eileen. He hid under the table. His mother said:

—O, Stephen will apologise.

Dante said:

—O, if not, the eagles will come and pull out his eyes.

Pull out his eyes,
Apologise,
Apologise,
Pull out his eyes.

Apologise,
Pull out his eyes,
Pull out his eyes,
Apologise.

*

* *

The wide playgrounds were swarming with boys. All were shouting and the prefects° urged them on with strong cries. The evening air was pale and chilly and after every charge and thud of the footballers the greasy leather orb flew like a heavy bird through the grey light. He kept on the fringe of his line, out of sight of his prefect, out of the reach of the rude feet, feigning to run now and then. He felt his body small and weak amid the throng of players and his eyes were weak and watery. Rody Kickham was not like that: he would be captain of the third line° all the fellows said.

Rody Kickham was a decent fellow but Nasty Roche was a stink.

press: Closet. **cachou:** A candy and breath freshener. **prefects:** Teachers who work as housemasters and supervise outside activities. **the third line:** Clongowes boys under thirteen.

Rody Kickham had greaves in his number and a hamper in the refectory.° Nasty Roche had big hands. He called the Friday pudding dog-in-the-blanket. And one day he had asked:

—What is your name?

Stephen had answered:

—Stephen Dedalus.

Then Nasty Roche had said:

—What kind of a name is that?

And when Stephen had not been able to answer Nasty Roche had asked:

—What is your father?

Stephen had answered:

—A gentleman.

Then Nasty Roche had asked:

—Is he a magistrate?

He crept about from point to point on the fringe of his line, making little runs now and then. But his hands were bluish with cold. He kept his hands in the sidepockets of his belted grey suit. That was a belt round his pocket. And belt was also to give a fellow a belt. One day a fellow had said to Cantwell:

—I'd give you such a belt in a second.

Cantwell had answered:

—Go and fight your match. Give Cecil Thunder a belt. I'd like to see you. He'd give you a toe in the rump for yourself.

That was not a nice expression. His mother had told him not to speak with the rough boys in the college. Nice mother! The first day in the hall of the castle when she had said goodbye she had put up her veil double to her nose to kiss him: and her nose and eyes were red. But he had pretended not to see that she was going to cry. She was a nice mother but she was not so nice when she cried. And his father had given him two fiveshilling pieces for pocket money. And his father had told him if he wanted anything to write home to him and, whatever he did, never to peach on° a fellow. Then at the door of the castle the rector° had shaken hands with his father and mother, his soutane° fluttering in the breeze, and the car had driven off with his father and mother on it. They had cried to him from the car, waving their hands:

—Goodbye, Stephen, goodbye!

greaves in his number and a hamper in the refectory: Shinguards in his locker and a private supply of treats in the dining hall. **peach on:** "Tell on." **rector:** Administrative head of the college. **soutane:** Black gown with sleeves.

—Goodbye, Stephen, goodbye!

He was caught in the whirl of a scrimmage and, fearful of the flashing eyes and muddy boots, bent down to look through the legs. The fellows were struggling and groaning and their legs were rubbing and kicking and stamping. Then Jack Lawton's yellow boots dodged out the ball and all the other boots and legs ran after. He ran after them a little way and then stopped. It was useless to run on. Soon they would be going home for the holidays. After supper in the studyhall he would change the number pasted up inside his desk from seventyseven to seventysix.

It would be better to be in the studyhall than out there in the cold. The sky was pale and cold but there were lights in the castle. He wondered from which window Hamilton Rowan had thrown his hat on the haha° and had there been flowerbeds at that time under the windows. One day when he had been called to the castle the butler had shown him the marks of the soldiers' slugs in the wood of the door and had given him a piece of shortbread that the community ate. It was nice and warm to see the lights in the castle. It was like something in a book. Perhaps Leicester Abbey was like that. And there were nice sentences in Doctor Cornwell's Spelling Book. They were like poetry but they were only sentences to learn the spelling from.

Wolsey died in Leicester Abbey
Where the abbots buried him.
Canker is a disease of plants,
Cancer one of animals.

It would be nice to lie on the hearthrug before the fire, leaning his head upon his hands, and think on those sentences. He shivered as if he had cold slimy water next his skin. That was mean of Wells to shoulder him into the square ditch because he would not swop his little snuffbox for Wells's seasoned hacking chestnut,° the conqueror of forty. How cold and slimy the water had been! A fellow had once seen a big rat jump plop into the scum. He shivered and longed to cry. It would be so nice to be at home. Mother was sitting at the fire with Dante waiting for Brigid to bring in the tea. She had her feet on the fender and her jewelly slippers were so hot and they had such a lovely warm smell! Dante knew a lot of things. She had taught him where the Mo-

Hamilton Rowan . . . haha: Patriot and friend of Wolfe Tone, who in 1794 supposedly took refuge from soldiers in the castle and threw his hat on a bank or dry moat as a decoy. **hacking chestnut:** Dried chestnuts attached to strings and swung sharply against one another, the one that does not break being the winner.

zambique Channel was and what was the longest river in America and what was the name of the highest mountain in the moon. Father Arnall knew more than Dante because he was a priest but both his father and uncle Charles said that Dante was a clever woman and a wellread woman. And when Dante made that noise after dinner and then put up her hand to her mouth: that was heartburn.

A voice cried far out on the playground:

—All in!

Then other voices cried from the lower and third lines:°

—All in! All in!

The players closed around, flushed and muddy, and he went among them, glad to go in. Rody Kickham held the ball by its greasy lace. A fellow asked him to give it one last: but he walked on without even answering the fellow. Simon Moonan told him not to because the prefect was looking. The fellow turned to Simon Moonan and said:

—We all know why you speak. You are McGlade's suck.°

Suck was a queer word. The fellow called Simon Moonan that name because Simon Moonan used to tie the prefect's false sleeves behind his back and the prefect used to let on to be angry. But the sound was ugly. Once he had washed his hands in the lavatory of the Wicklow Hotel and his father pulled the stopper up by the chain after and the dirty water went down through the hole in the basin. And when it had all gone down slowly the hole in the basin had made a sound like that: suck. Only louder.

To remember that and the white look of the lavatory made him feel cold and then hot. There were two cocks that you turned and water came out: cold and hot. He felt cold and then a little hot: and he could see the names printed on the cocks. That was a very queer thing.

And the air in the corridor chilled him too. It was queer and wettish. But soon the gas would be lit and in burning it made a light noise like a little song. Always the same: and when the fellows stopped talking in the playroom you could hear it.

It was the hour for sums. Father Arnall wrote a hard sum on the board and then he said:

—Now then, who will win? Go ahead, York! Go ahead, Lancaster!°

Stephen tried his best but the sum was too hard and he felt confused. The little silk badge with the white rose on it that was pinned

lower . . . lines: See p. 20; boys from thirteen to fifteen. **suck:** A sycophant, a boy who "sucks up" to a teacher. **York . . . Lancaster:** The two English houses opposed in the War of the Roses.

on the breast of his jacket began to flutter. He was no good at sums but he tried his best so that York might not lose. Father Arnall's face looked very black but he was not in a wax:° he was laughing. Then Jack Lawton cracked his fingers and Father Arnall looked at his copybook and said:

—Right. Bravo Lancaster! The red rose wins. Come on now, York! Forge ahead!

Jack Lawton looked over from his side. The little silk badge with the red rose on it looked very rich because he had a blue sailor top on. Stephen felt his own face red too, thinking of all the bets about who would get first place in elements,° Jack Lawton or he. Some weeks Jack Lawton got the card for first and some weeks he got the card for first. His white silk badge fluttered and fluttered as he worked at the next sum and heard Father Arnall's voice. Then all his eagerness passed away and he felt his face quite cool. He thought his face must be white because it felt so cool. He could not get out the answer for the sum but it did not matter. White roses and red roses: those were beautiful colours to think of. And the cards for first place and second place and third place were beautiful colours too: pink and cream and lavender. Lavender and cream and pink roses were beautiful to think of. Perhaps a wild rose might be like those colours and he remembered the song about the wild rose blossoms on the little green place. But you could not have a green rose. But perhaps somewhere in the world you could.

The bell rang and then the classes began to file out of the rooms and along the corridors towards the refectory. He sat looking at the two prints of butter on his plate but could not eat the damp bread. The tablecloth was damp and limp. But he drank off the hot weak tea which the clumsy scullion, girt with a white apron, poured into his cup. He wondered whether the scullion's apron was damp too or whether all white things were cold and damp. Nasty Roche and Saurin drank cocoa that their people sent them in tins. They said they could not drink the tea; that it was hogwash. Their fathers were magistrates, the fellows said.

All the boys seemed to him very strange. They had all fathers and mothers and different clothes and voices. He longed to be at home and lay his head on his mother's lap. But he could not: and so he longed for the play and study and prayers to be over and to be in bed.

He drank another cup of hot tea and Fleming said:

a wax: A rage. **elements:** English, math, geography, history, Latin.

—What's up? Have you a pain or what's up with you?

—I don't know, Stephen said.

—Sick in your breadbasket, Fleming said, because your face looks white. It will go away.

—O yes, Stephen said.

But he was not sick there. He thought that he was sick in his heart if you could be sick in that place. Fleming was very decent to ask him. He wanted to cry. He leaned his elbows on the table and shut and opened the flaps of his ears. Then he heard the noise of the refectory every time he opened the flaps of his ears. It made a roar like a train at night. And when he closed the flaps the roar was shut off like a train going into a tunnel. That night at Dalkey the train had roared like that and then, when it went into the tunnel, the roar stopped. He closed his eyes and the train went on, roaring and then stopping; roaring again, stopping. It was nice to hear it roar and stop and then roar out of the tunnel again and then stop.

Then the higher line° fellows began to come down along the matting in the middle of the refectory, Paddy Rath and Jimmy Magee and the Spaniard who was allowed to smoke cigars and the little Portuguese who wore the woolly cap. And then the lower line tables and the tables of the third line. And every single fellow had a different way of walking.

He sat in a corner of the playroom pretending to watch a game of dominos and once or twice he was able to hear for an instant the little song of the gas. The prefect was at the door with some boys and Simon Moonan was knotting his false sleeves. He was telling them something about Tullabeg.

Then he went away from the door and Wells came over to Stephen and said:

—Tell us, Dedalus, do you kiss your mother every night before you go to bed?

Stephen answered:

—I do.

Wells turned to the other fellows and said:

—O, I say, here's a fellow says he kisses his mother every night before he goes to bed.

The other fellows stopped their game and turned round, laughing. Stephen blushed under their eyes and said:

—I do not.

higher line: Boys from fifteen to eighteen.

Wells said:

—O, I say, here's a fellow says he doesn't kiss his mother before he goes to bed.

They all laughed again. Stephen tried to laugh with them. He felt his whole body hot and confused in a moment. What was the right answer to the question? He had given two and still Wells laughed. But Wells must know the right answer for he was in third of grammar. He tried to think of Wells's mother but he did not dare to raise his eyes to Wells's face. He did not like Wells's face. It was Wells who had shouldered him into the square ditch the day before because he would not swop his little snuffbox for Wells's seasoned hacking chestnut, the conqueror of forty. It was a mean thing to do; all the fellows said it was. And how cold and slimy the water had been! And a fellow had once seen a big rat jump plop into the scum.

The cold slime of the ditch covered his whole body; and, when the bell rang for study and the lines filed out of the playrooms, he felt the cold air of the corridor and staircase inside his clothes. He still tried to think what was the right answer. Was it right to kiss his mother or wrong to kiss his mother? What did that mean, to kiss? You put your face up like that to say goodnight and then his mother put her face down. That was to kiss. His mother put her lips on his cheek; her lips were soft and they wetted his cheek; and they made a tiny little noise: kiss. Why did people do that with their two faces?

Sitting in the studyhall he opened the lid of his desk and changed the number pasted up inside from seventyseven to seventysix. But the Christmas vacation was very far away: but one time it would come because the earth moved round always.

There was a picture of the earth on the first page of his geography: a big ball in the middle of clouds. Fleming had a box of crayons and one night during free study he had coloured the earth green and the clouds maroon. That was like the two brushes in Dante's press, the brush with the green velvet back for Parnell and the brush with the maroon velvet back for Michael Davitt. But he had not told Fleming to colour them those colours. Fleming had done it himself.

He opened the geography to study the lesson; but he could not learn the names of places in America. Still they were all different places that had those different names. They were all in different countries and the countries were in continents and the continents were in the world and the world was in the universe.

He turned to the flyleaf of the geography and read what he had written there: himself, his name and where he was.

Stephen Dedalus
Class of Elements
Clongowes Wood College
Sallins
County Kildare
Ireland
Europe
The World
The Universe

That was in his writing: and Fleming one night for a cod° had written on the opposite page:

Stephen Dedalus is my name,
Ireland is my nation.
Clongowes is my dwellingplace
And heaven my expectation.

He read the verses backwards but then they were not poetry. Then he read the flyleaf from the bottom to the top till he came to his own name. That was he: and he read down the page again. What was after the universe? Nothing. But was there anything round the universe to show where it stopped before the nothing place began? It could not be a wall but there could be a thin thin line there all round everything. It was very big to think about everything and everywhere. Only God could do that. He tried to think what a big thought that must be but he could think only of God. God was God's name just as his name was Stephen. *Dieu* was the French for God and that was God's name too; and when anyone prayed to God and said *Dieu* then God knew at once that it was a French person that was praying. But though there were different names for God in all the different languages in the world and God understood what all the people who prayed said in their different languages still God remained always the same God and God's real name was God.

It made him very tired to think that way. It made him feel his head very big. He turned over the flyleaf and looked wearily at the green round earth in the middle of the maroon clouds. He wondered which was right, to be for the green or for the maroon, because Dante had ripped the green velvet back off the brush that was for Parnell one day with her scissors and had told him that Parnell was a bad man. He wondered if they were arguing at home about that. That was called politics. There were two sides in it: Dante was on one side and his father

a cod: A joke or prank.

and Mr Casey were on the other side but his mother and uncle Charles were on no side. Every day there was something in the paper about it.

It pained him that he did not know well what politics meant and that he did not know where the universe ended. He felt small and weak. When would he be like the fellows in poetry and rhetoric? They had big voices and big boots and they studied trigonometry. That was very far away. First came the vacation and then the next term and then vacation again and then again another term and then again the vacation. It was like a train going in and out of tunnels and that was like the noise of the boys eating in the refectory when you opened and closed the flaps of the ears. Term, vacation; tunnel, out; noise, stop. How far away it was! It was better to go to bed to sleep. Only prayers in the chapel and then bed. He shivered and yawned. It would be lovely in bed after the sheets got a bit hot. First they were so cold to get into. He shivered to think how cold they were first. But then they got hot and then he could sleep. It was lovely to be tired. He yawned again. Night prayers and then bed: he shivered and wanted to yawn. It would be lovely in a few minutes. He felt a warm glow creeping up from the cold shivering sheets, warmer and warmer till he felt warm all over, ever so warm; ever so warm and yet he shivered a little and still wanted to yawn.

The bell rang for night prayers and he filed out of the studyhall after the others and down the staircase and along the corridors to the chapel. The corridors were darkly lit and the chapel was darkly lit. Soon all would be dark and sleeping. There was cold night air in the chapel and the marbles were the colour the sea was at night. The sea was cold day and night: but it was colder at night. It was cold and dark under the seawall beside his father's house. But the kettle would be on the hob° to make punch.

The prefect of the chapel prayed above his head and his memory knew the responses:

O Lord, open our lips
And our mouth shall announce Thy praise.
Incline unto our aid, O God!
O Lord, make haste to help us!

There was a cold night smell in the chapel. But it was a holy smell. It was not like the smell of the old peasants who knelt at the back of the chapel at Sunday mass. That was a smell of air and rain and turf and

hob: Shelf at back or side of a fireplace.

corduroy. But they were very holy peasants. They breathed behind him on his neck and sighed as they prayed. They lived in Clane, a fellow said: there were little cottages there and he had seen a woman standing at the halfdoor of a cottage with a child in her arms, as the cars had come past from Sallins. It would be lovely to sleep for one night in that cottage before the fire of smoking turf, in the dark lit by the fire, in the warm dark, breathing the smell of the peasants, air and rain and turf and corduroy. But, O, the road there between the trees was dark! You would be lost in the dark. It made him afraid to think of how it was.

He heard the voice of the prefect of the chapel saying the last prayer. He prayed it too against the dark outside under the trees.

Visit, we beseech Thee, O Lord, this habitation and drive away from it all the snares of the enemy. May Thy holy angels dwell herein to preserve us in peace and may Thy blessing be always upon us through Christ, Our Lord. Amen.

His fingers trembled as he undressed himself in the dormitory. He told his fingers to hurry up. He had to undress and then kneel and say his own prayers and be in bed before the gas was lowered so that he might not go to hell when he died. He rolled his stockings off and put on his nightshirt quickly and knelt trembling at his bedside and repeated his prayers quickly quickly fearing that the gas would go down. He felt his shoulders shaking as he murmured:

God bless my father and my mother and spare them to me!
God bless my little brothers and sisters and spare them to me!
God bless Dante and uncle Charles and spare them to me!

He blessed himself and climbed quickly into bed and, tucking the end of the nightshirt under his feet, curled himself together under the cold white sheets, shaking and trembling. But he would not go to hell when he died; and the shaking would stop. A voice bade the boys in the dormitory goodnight. He peered out for an instant over the coverlet and saw the yellow curtains round and before his bed that shut him off on all sides. The light was lowered quietly.

The prefect's shoes went away. Where? Down the staircase and along the corridors or to his room at the end? He saw the dark. Was it true about the black dog that walked there at night with eyes as big as carriagelamps? They said it was the ghost of a murderer. A long shiver of fear flowed over his body. He saw the dark entrance hall of the castle. Old servants in old dress were in the ironingroom° above the staircase.

ironingroom: Room where armor was formerly stored.

It was long ago. The old servants were quiet. There was a fire there but the hall was still dark. A figure came up the staircase from the hall. He wore the white cloak of a marshal; his face was pale and strange; he held his hand pressed to his side. He looked out of strange eyes at the old servants. They looked at him and saw their master's face and cloak and knew that he had received his deathwound. But only the dark was where they looked: only dark silent air. Their master had received his deathwound on the battlefield of Prague far away over the sea. He was standing on the field; his hand was pressed to his side; his face was pale and strange and he wore the white cloak of a marshal.

O how cold and strange it was to think of that! All the dark was cold and strange. There were pale strange faces there, great eyes like carriagelamps. They were the ghosts of murderers, the figures of marshals who had received their deathwound on battlefields far away over the sea. What did they wish to say that their faces were so strange?

Visit, we beseech Thee, O Lord, this habitation and drive away from it all . . .

Going home for the holidays! That would be lovely: the fellows had told him. Getting up on the cars° in the early wintry morning outside the door of the castle. The cars were rolling on the gravel. Cheers for the rector!

Hurray! Hurray! Hurray!

The cars drove past the chapel and all caps were raised. They drove merrily along the country roads. The drivers pointed with their whips to Bodenstown. The fellows cheered. They passed the farmhouse of the Jolly Farmer. Cheer after cheer after cheer. Through Clane they drove, cheering and cheered. The peasant women stood at the halfdoors, the men stood here and there. The lovely smell there was in the wintry air: the smell of Clane: rain and wintry air and turf smouldering and corduroy.

The train was full of fellows: a long long chocolate train with cream facings. The guards went to and fro opening, closing, locking, unlocking the doors. They were men in dark blue and silver; they had silvery whistles and their keys made a quick music: click, click: click, click.

And the train raced on over the flat lands and past the Hill of Allen. The telegraphpoles were passing, passing. The train went on and on. It knew. There were coloured lanterns in the hall of his father's house and ropes of green branches. There were holly and ivy round the pierglass

cars: Horse-drawn vehicles.

and holly and ivy, green and red, twined round the chandeliers. There were red holly and green ivy round the old portraits on the walls. Holly and ivy for him and for Christmas.

Lovely . . .

All the people. Welcome home, Stephen! Noises of welcome. His mother kissed him. Was that right? His father was a marshal now: higher than a magistrate. Welcome home, Stephen!

Noises . . .

There was a noise of curtainrings running back along the rods, of water being splashed in the basins. There was a noise of rising and dressing and washing in the dormitory: a noise of clapping of hands as the prefect went up and down telling the fellows to look sharp. A pale sunlight showed the yellow curtains drawn back, the tossed beds. His bed was very hot and his face and body were very hot.

He got up and sat on the side of his bed. He was weak. He tried to pull on his stocking. It had a horrid rough feel. The sunlight was queer and cold.

Fleming said:

—Are you not well?

He did not know; and Fleming said:

—Get back into bed. I'll tell McGlade you're not well.

—He's sick.

—Who is?

—Tell McGlade.

—Get back into bed.

—Is he sick?

A fellow held his arms while he loosened the stocking clinging to his foot and climbed back into the hot bed.

He crouched down between the sheets, glad of their tepid glow. He heard the fellows talk among themselves about him as they dressed for mass. It was a mean thing to do, to shoulder him into the square ditch, they were saying.

Then their voices ceased; they had gone. A voice at his bed said:

—Dedalus, don't spy on us, sure you won't?

Wells's face was there. He looked at it and saw that Wells was afraid.

—I didn't mean to. Sure you won't?

His father had told him, whatever he did, never to peach on a fellow. He shook his head and answered no and felt glad. Wells said:

—I didn't mean to, honour bright. It was only for cod. I'm sorry.

The face and the voice went away. Sorry because he was afraid. Afraid that it was some disease. Canker was a disease of plants and cancer one of animals: or another different. That was a long time ago then out on the playgrounds in the evening light, creeping from point to point on the fringe of his line, a heavy bird flying low through the grey light. Leicester Abbey lit up. Wolsey died there. The abbots buried him themselves.

It was not Wells's face, it was the prefect's. He was not foxing. No, no: he was sick really. He was not foxing. And he felt the prefect's hand on his forehead; and he felt his forehead warm and damp against the prefect's cold damp hand. That was the way a rat felt, slimy and damp and cold. Every rat had two eyes to look out of. Sleek shiny coats, little little feet tucked up to jump, black shiny eyes to look out of. They could understand how to jump. But the minds of rats could not understand trigonometry. When they were dead they lay on their sides. Their coats dried then. They were only dead things.

The prefect was there again and it was his voice that was saying that he was to get up, that Father Minister had said he was to get up and dress and go to the infirmary. And while he was dressing himself as quickly as he could the prefect said:

—We must pack off to Brother Michael° because we have the collywobbles! Terrible thing to have the collywobbles! How we wobble when we have the collywobbles!

He was very decent to say that. That was all to make him laugh. But he could not laugh because his cheeks and lips were all shivery: and then the prefect had to laugh by himself.

The prefect cried:

—Quick march! Hayfoot! Strawfoot!

They went together down the staircase and along the corridor and past the bath. As he passed the door he remembered with a vague fear the warm turfcoloured bogwater, the warm moist air, the noise of plunges, the smell of the towels, like medicine.

Brother Michael was standing at the door of the infirmary and from the door of the dark cabinet on his right came a smell like medicine. That came from the bottles on the shelves. The prefect spoke to Brother Michael and Brother Michael answered and called the prefect sir. He had reddish hair mixed with grey and a queer look. It was queer that he would always be a brother. It was queer too that you could not call him sir because he was a brother and had a different kind of look. Was he not holy enough or why could he not catch up on the others?

Brother Michael: A man bound to the Jesuit order by vows but not educated as a priest would be; usually assigned housekeeping duties.

There were two beds in the room and in one bed there was a fellow: and when they went in he called out:

—Hello! It's young Dedalus! What's up?

—The sky is up, Brother Michael said.

He was a fellow out of third of grammar and, while Stephen was undressing, he asked Brother Michael to bring him a round of buttered toast.

—Ah, do! he said.

—Butter you up! said Brother Michael. You'll get your walking papers in the morning when the doctor comes.

—Will I? the fellow said. I'm not well yet.

Brother Michael repeated:

—You'll get your walking papers, I tell you.

He bent down to rake the fire. He had a long back like the long back of a tramhorse. He shook the poker gravely and nodded his head at the fellow out of third of grammar.

Then Brother Michael went away and after a while the fellow out of third of grammar turned in towards the wall and fell asleep.

That was the infirmary. He was sick then. Had they written home to tell his mother and father? But it would be quicker for one of the priests to go himself to tell them. Or he would write a letter for the priest to bring.

Dear Mother

I am sick. I want to go home. Please come and take me home. I am in the infirmary.

Your fond son,
Stephen

How far away they were! There was cold sunlight outside the window. He wondered if he would die. You could die just the same on a sunny day. He might die before his mother came. Then he would have a dead mass in the chapel like the way the fellows had told him it was when Little had died. All the fellows would be at the mass, dressed in black, all with sad faces. Wells too would be there but no fellow would look at him. The rector would be there in a cope of black and gold° and there would be tall yellow candles on the altar and round the catafalque. And they would carry the coffin out of the chapel slowly and he would be buried in the little graveyard of the community off the

cope of black and gold: A long vestment in the colors appropriate for a funeral mass.

main avenue of limes. And Wells would be sorry then for what he had done. And the bell would toll slowly.

He could hear the tolling. He said over to himself the song that Brigid had taught him.

Dingdong! The castle bell!
Farewell, my mother!
Bury me in the old churchyard
Beside my eldest brother.
My coffin shall be black,
Six angels at my back,
Two to sing and two to pray
And two to carry my soul away.

How beautiful and sad that was! How beautiful the words were where they said *Bury me in the old churchyard!* A tremor passed over his body. How sad and how beautiful! He wanted to cry quietly but not for himself: for the words, so beautiful and sad, like music. The bell! The bell! Farewell! O farewell!

The cold sunlight was weaker and Brother Michael was standing at his bedside with a bowl of beeftea. He was glad for his mouth was hot and dry. He could hear them playing on the playgrounds. It was after lunchtime. And the day was going on in the college just as if he were there.

Then Brother Michael was going away and the fellow out of third of grammar told him to be sure and come back and tell him all the news in the paper. He told Stephen that his name was Athy and that his father kept a lot of racehorses that were spiffing jumpers and that his father would give a good tip to Brother Michael any time he wanted it because Brother Michael was very decent and always told him the news out of the paper they got every day up in the castle. There was every kind of news in the paper: accidents, shipwrecks, sports and politics.

—Now it is all about politics in the paper, he said. Do your people talk about that too?

—Yes, Stephen said.

—Mine too, he said.

Then he thought for a moment and said:

—You have a queer name, Dedalus, and I have a queer name too, Athy. My name is the name of a town. Your name is like Latin.

Then he asked:

—Are you good at riddles?

Stephen answered:

—Not very good.

Then he said:

—Can you answer me this one? Why is the county Kildare like the leg of a fellow's breeches?

Stephen thought what could be the answer and then said:

—I give it up.

—Because there is a thigh in it, he said. Do you see the joke? Athy is the town in the county Kildare and a thigh is the other thigh.

—O, I see, Stephen said.

—That's an old riddle, he said.

After a moment he said:

—I say!

—What? asked Stephen.

—You know, he said, you can ask that riddle another way?

—Can you? said Stephen.

—The same riddle, he said. Do you know the other way to ask it?

—No, said Stephen.

—Can you not think of the other way? he said.

He looked at Stephen over the bedclothes as he spoke. Then he lay back on the pillow and said:

—There is another way but I won't tell you what it is.

Why did he not tell it? His father, who kept the racehorses, must be a magistrate too like Saurin's father and Nasty Roche's father. He thought of his own father, of how he sang songs while his mother played and of how he always gave him a shilling when he asked for sixpence and he felt sorry for him that he was not a magistrate like the other boys' fathers. Then why was he sent to that place with them? But his father had told him that he would be no stranger there because his granduncle had presented an address to the liberator there fifty years before. You could know the people of that time by their old dress. It seemed to him a solemn time: and he wondered if that was the time when the fellows in Clongowes wore blue coats with brass buttons and yellow waistcoats and caps of rabbitskin and drank beer like grownup people and kept greyhounds of their own to course the hares with.

He looked at the window and saw that the daylight had grown weaker. There would be cloudy grey light over the playgrounds. There was no noise on the playgrounds. The class must be doing the themes or perhaps Father Arnall was reading a legend out of the book.

It was queer that they had not given him any medicine. Perhaps Brother Michael would bring it back when he came. They said you got stinking stuff to drink when you were in the infirmary. But he felt better now than before. It would be nice getting better slowly. You could get a book then. There was a book in the library about Holland. There were lovely foreign names in it and pictures of strangelooking cities and ships. It made you feel so happy.

How pale the light was at the window! But that was nice. The fire rose and fell on the wall. It was like waves. Someone had put coal on and he heard voices. They were talking. It was the noise of the waves. Or the waves were talking among themselves as they rose and fell.

He saw the sea of waves, long dark waves rising and falling, dark under the moonless night. A tiny light twinkled at the pierhead where the ship was entering: and he saw a multitude of people gathered by the waters' edge to see the ship that was entering their harbour. A tall man stood on the deck, looking out towards the flat dark land: and by the light at the pierhead he saw his face, the sorrowful face of Brother Michael.

He saw him lift his hand towards the people and heard him say in a loud voice of sorrow over the waters:

—He is dead. We saw him lying upon the catafalque.

A wail of sorrow went up from the people.

—Parnell! Parnell! He is dead!

They fell upon their knees, moaning in sorrow.

And he saw Dante in a maroon velvet dress and with a green velvet mantle hanging from her shoulders walking proudly and silently past the people who knelt by the waters' edge.

*

* *

A great fire, banked high and red, flamed in the grate and under the ivytwined branches of the chandelier the Christmas table was spread. They had come home a little late and still dinner was not ready: but it would be ready in a jiffy, his mother had said. They were waiting for the door to open and for the servants to come in, holding the big dishes covered with their heavy metal covers.

All were waiting: uncle Charles, who sat far away in the shadow of the window, Dante and Mr Casey, who sat in the easychairs at either side of the hearth, Stephen, seated on a chair between them, his feet resting on the toasted boss.° Mr Dedalus looked at himself in the pierglass above the mantelpiece, waxed out his moustache-ends and then, parting his coattails, stood with his back to the glowing fire: and still, from time to time, he withdrew a hand from his coattail to wax out

boss: A sort of hassock or footrest.

one of his moustache-ends. Mr Casey leaned his head to one side and, smiling, tapped the gland of his neck with his fingers. And Stephen smiled too for he knew now that it was not true that Mr Casey had a purse of silver in his throat. He smiled to think how the silvery noise which Mr Casey used to make had deceived him. And when he had tried to open Mr Casey's hand to see if the purse of silver was hidden there he had seen that the fingers could not be straightened out: and Mr Casey had told him that he had got those three cramped fingers making a birthday present for Queen Victoria.°

Mr Casey tapped the gland of his neck and smiled at Stephen with sleepy eyes: and Mr Dedalus said to him:

—Yes. Well now, that's all right. O, we had a good walk, hadn't we, John? Yes . . . I wonder if there's any likelihood of dinner this evening. Yes. . . . O, well now, we got a good breath of ozone round the Head today. Ay, bedad.

He turned to Dante and said:

—You didn't stir out at all, Mrs Riordan?

Dante frowned and said shortly:

—No.

Mr Dedalus dropped his coattails and went over to the sideboard. He brought forth a great stone jar of whisky from the locker and filled the decanter slowly, bending now and then to see how much he had poured in. Then replacing the jar in the locker he poured out a little of the whisky into two glasses, added a little water and came back with them to the fireplace.

—A thimbleful, John, he said, just to whet your appetite.

Mr Casey took the glass, drank, and placed it near him on the mantelpiece. Then he said:

—Well, I can't help thinking of our friend Christopher manufacturing . . .

He broke into a fit of laughter and coughing and added:

— . . . manufacturing that champagne for those fellows.

Mr Dedalus laughed loudly.

—Is it Christy? he said. There's more cunning in one of those warts on his bald head than in a pack of jack foxes.°

He inclined his head, closed his eyes, and, licking his lips profusely, began to speak with the voice of the hotelkeeper.

—And he has such a soft mouth when he's speaking to you, don't

a birthday present for Queen Victoria: Probably the result of picking oakum as hard labor in prison for political activities. **jack foxes:** Male foxes.

you know. He's very moist and watery about the dewlaps, God bless him.

Mr Casey was still struggling through his fit of coughing and laughter. Stephen, seeing and hearing the hotelkeeper through his father's face and voice, laughed.

Mr Dedalus put up his eyeglass and, staring down at him, said quietly and kindly:

—What are you laughing at, you little puppy, you?

The servants entered and placed the dishes on the table. Mrs Dedalus followed and the places were arranged.

—Sit over, she said.

Mr Dedalus went to the end of the table and said:

—Now, Mrs Riordan, sit over. John, sit you down, my hearty.

He looked round to where uncle Charles sat and said:

—Now then, sir, there's a bird here waiting for you.

When all had taken their seats he laid his hand on the cover and then said quickly, withdrawing it:

—Now, Stephen.

Stephen stood up in his place to say the grace before meals:

Bless us, O Lord, and these Thy gifts which through Thy bounty we are about to receive through Christ Our Lord. Amen.

All blessed themselves and Mr Dedalus with a sigh of pleasure lifted from the dish the heavy cover pearled around the edge with glistening drops.

Stephen looked at the plump turkey which had lain, trussed and skewered, on the kitchen table. He knew that his father had paid a guinea for it in Dunn's of D'Olier Street and that the man had prodded it often at the breastbone to show how good it was: and he remembered the man's voice when he had said:

—Take that one, sir. That's the real Ally Daly.°

Why did Mr Barrett in Clongowes call his pandybat° a turkey? But Clongowes was far away: and the warm heavy smell of turkey and ham and celery rose from the plates and dishes and the great fire was banked high and red in the grate and the green ivy and red holly made you feel so happy and when dinner was ended the big plumpudding would be carried in, studded with peeled almonds and sprigs of holly, with bluish fire running around it and a little green flag flying from the top.

It was his first Christmas dinner and he thought of his little brothers

Ally Daly: The best. **pandybat:** A stiff, reinforced leather strap.

and sisters who were waiting in the nursery, as he had often waited, till the pudding came. The deep low collar and the Eton jacket made him feel queer and oldish: and that morning when his mother had brought him down to the parlour, dressed for mass, his father had cried. That was because he was thinking of his own father. And uncle Charles had said so too.

Mr Dedalus covered the dish and began to eat hungrily. Then he said:

—Poor old Christy, he's nearly lopsided now with roguery.

—Simon, said Mrs Dedalus, you haven't given Mrs Riordan any sauce.

Mr Dedalus seized the sauceboat.

—Haven't I? he cried. Mrs Riordan, pity the poor blind.

Dante covered her plate with her hands and said:

—No, thanks.

Mr Dedalus turned to uncle Charles.

—How are you off, sir?

—Right as the mail, Simon.

—You, John?

—I'm all right. Go on yourself.

—Mary? Here, Stephen, here's something to make your hair curl.

He poured sauce freely over Stephen's plate and set the boat again on the table. Then he asked uncle Charles was it tender. Uncle Charles could not speak because his mouth was full but he nodded that it was.

—That was a good answer our friend made to the canon. What? said Mr Dedalus.

—I didn't think he had that much in him, said Mr Casey.

—I'll pay you your dues, father, when you cease turning the house of God into a pollingbooth.

—A nice answer, said Dante, for any man calling himself a catholic to give to his priest.

—They have only themselves to blame, said Mr Dedalus suavely. If they took a fool's advice they would confine their attention to religion.

—It is religion, Dante said. They are doing their duty in warning the people.

—We go to the house of God, Mr Casey said, in all humility to pray to our Maker and not to hear election addresses.

—It is religion, Dante said again. They are right. They must direct their flocks.

—And preach politics from the altar, is it? asked Mr Dedalus.

—Certainly, said Dante. It is a question of public morality. A priest would not be a priest if he did not tell his flock what is right and what is wrong.

Mrs Dedalus laid down her knife and fork, saying:

—For pity's sake and for pity sake let us have no political discussion on this day of all days in the year.

—Quite right, ma'am, said uncle Charles. Now, Simon, that's quite enough now. Not another word now.

—Yes, yes, said Mr Dedalus quickly.

He uncovered the dish boldly and said:

—Now then, who's for more turkey?

Nobody answered. Dante said:

—Nice language for any catholic to use!

—Mrs Riordan, I appeal to you, said Mrs Dedalus, to let the matter drop now.

Dante turned on her and said:

—And am I to sit here and listen to the pastors of my church being flouted?

—Nobody is saying a word against them, said Mr Dedalus, so long as they don't meddle in politics.

—The bishops and priests of Ireland have spoken, said Dante, and they must be obeyed.

—Let them leave politics alone, said Mr Casey, or the people may leave their church alone.

—You hear? said Dante turning to Mrs Dedalus.

—Mr Casey! Simon! said Mrs Dedalus. Let it end now.

—Too bad! Too bad! said uncle Charles.

—What? cried Mr Dedalus. Were we to desert him at the bidding of the English people?

—He was no longer worthy to lead, said Dante. He was a public sinner.

—We are all sinners and black sinners, said Mr Casey coldly.

—*Woe be to the man by whom the scandal cometh!* said Mrs Riordan. *It would be better for him that a millstone were tied about his neck and that he were cast into the depths of the sea rather than that he should scandalise one of these, my least little ones.* That is the language of the Holy Ghost.

—And very bad language if you ask me, said Mr Dedalus coolly.

—Simon! Simon! said uncle Charles. The boy.

—Yes, yes, said Mr Dedalus. I meant about the . . . I was thinking about the bad language of that railway porter. Well now, that's all right. Here, Stephen, show me your plate, old chap. Eat away now. Here.

He heaped up the food on Stephen's plate and served uncle Charles and Mr Casey to large pieces of turkey and splashes of sauce. Mrs Dedalus was eating little and Dante sat with her hands in her lap. She was red in the face. Mr Dedalus rooted with the carvers at the end of the dish and said:

—There's a tasty bit here we call the pope's nose.° If any lady or gentleman . . .

He held a piece of fowl up on the prong of the carvingfork. Nobody spoke. He put it on his own plate, saying:

—Well, you can't say but you were asked. I think I had better eat it myself because I'm not well in my health lately.

He winked at Stephen and, replacing the dishcover, began to eat again.

There was a silence while he ate. Then he said:

—Well now, the day kept up fine after all. There were plenty of strangers down too.

Nobody spoke. He said again:

—I think there were more strangers down than last Christmas.

He looked round at the others whose faces were bent towards their plates and, receiving no reply, waited for a moment and said bitterly:

—Well, my Christmas dinner has been spoiled anyhow.

—There could be neither luck nor grace, Dante said, in a house where there is no respect for the pastors of the church.

Mr Dedalus threw his knife and fork noisily on his plate.

—Respect! he said. Is it for Billy with the lip or for the tub of guts up in Armagh? Respect!

—Princes of the church, said Mr Casey with slow scorn.

—Lord Leitrim's coachman, yes, said Mr Dedalus.

—They are the Lord's anointed, Dante said. They are an honour to their country.

—Tub of guts, said Mr Dedalus coarsely. He has a handsome face, mind you, in repose. You should see that fellow lapping up his bacon and cabbage of a cold winter's day. O Johnny!

He twisted his features into a grimace of heavy bestiality and made a lapping noise with his lips.

—Really, Simon, said Mrs Dedalus, you should not speak that way before Stephen. It's not right.

—O, he'll remember all this when he grows up, said Dante hotly—the language he heard against God and religion and priests in his own home.

pope's nose: Part of the turkey's rump.

—Let him remember too, cried Mr Casey to her from across the table, the language with which the priests and the priests' pawns broke Parnell's heart and hounded him into his grave. Let him remember that too when he grows up.

—Sons of bitches! cried Mr Dedalus. When he was down they turned on him to betray him and rend him like rats in a sewer. Lowlived dogs! And they look it! By Christ, they look it!

—They behaved rightly, cried Dante. They obeyed their bishops and their priests. Honour to them!

—Well, it is perfectly dreadful to say that not even for one day of the year, said Mrs Dedalus, can we be free from these dreadful disputes!

Uncle Charles raised his hands mildly and said:

—Come now, come now, come now! Can we not have our opinions whatever they are without this bad temper and this bad language? It is too bad surely.

Mrs Dedalus spoke to Dante in a low voice but Dante said loudly:

—I will not say nothing. I will defend my church and my religion when it is insulted and spit on by renegade catholics.

Mr Casey pushed his plate rudely into the middle of the table and, resting his elbows before him, said in a harsh voice to his host:

—Tell me, did I tell you that story about a very famous spit?

—You did not, John, said Mr Dedalus.

—Why then, said Mr Casey, it is a most instructive story. It happened not long ago in the county Wicklow where we are now.

He broke off and, turning towards Dante, said with quiet indignation:

—And I may tell you, ma'am, that I, if you mean me, am no renegade catholic. I am a catholic as my father was and his father before him and his father before him again when we gave up our lives rather than sell our faith.

—The more shame to you now, Dante said, to speak as you do.

—The story, John, said Mr Dedalus smiling. Let us have the story anyhow.

—Catholic indeed! repeated Dante ironically. The blackest protestant in the land would not speak the language I have heard this evening.

Mr Dedalus began to sway his head to and fro, crooning like a country singer.

—I am no protestant, I tell you again, said Mr Casey flushing.

Mr Dedalus, still crooning and swaying his head, began to sing in a grunting nasal tone:

O, come all you Roman catholics
That never went to mass.

He took up his knife and fork again in good humour and set to eating, saying to Mr Casey:

—Let us have the story, John. It will help us to digest.

Stephen looked with affection at Mr Casey's face which stared across the table over his joined hands. He liked to sit near him at the fire, looking up at his dark fierce face. But his dark eyes were never fierce and his slow voice was good to listen to. But why was he then against the priests? Because Dante must be right then. But he had heard his father say that she was a spoiled nun and that she had come out of the convent in the Alleghanies when her brother had got the money from the savages for the trinkets and the chainies. Perhaps that made her severe against Parnell. And she did not like him to play with Eileen because Eileen was a protestant and when she was young she knew children that used to play with protestants and the protestants used to make fun of the litany of the Blessed Virgin. *Tower of Ivory,* they used to say, *House of Gold!*° How could a woman be a tower of ivory or a house of gold? Who was right then? And he remembered the evening in the infirmary in Clongowes, the dark waters, the light at the pierhead and the moan of sorrow from the people when they had heard.

Eileen had long white hands. One evening when playing tig° she had put her hands over his eyes: long and white and thin and cold and soft. That was ivory: a cold white thing. That was the meaning of *Tower of Ivory.*

—The story is very short and sweet, Mr Casey said. It was one day down in Arklow, a cold bitter day, not long before the chief died. May God have mercy on him!

He closed his eyes wearily and paused. Mr Dedalus took a bone from his plate and tore some meat from it with his teeth, saying:

—Before he was killed, you mean.

Mr Casey opened his eyes, sighed and went on:

—It was down in Arklow one day. We were down there at a meeting and after the meeting was over we had to make our way to the railway station through the crowd. Such booing and baaing, man, you never heard. They called us all the names in the world. Well there was one old lady, and a drunken old harridan she was surely, that paid all her

Tower of Ivory . . . House of Gold: Epithets for the Blessed Virgin Mary from the Roman Catholic Litany of Our Lady. **tig:** A game like hide-and-seek.

attention to me. She kept dancing along beside me in the mud bawling and screaming into my face: *Priesthunter! The Paris Funds! Mr Fox! Kitty O'Shea!*

—And what did you do, John? asked Mr Dedalus.

—I let her bawl away, said Mr Casey. It was a cold day and to keep up my heart I had (saving your presence, ma'am) a quid of Tullamore in my mouth and sure I couldn't say a word in any case because my mouth was full of tobacco juice.

—Well, John?

—Well. I let her bawl away, to her heart's content, *Kitty O'Shea* and the rest of it till at last she called that lady a name that I won't sully this Christmas board nor your ears, ma'am, nor my own lips by repeating.

He paused. Mr Dedalus, lifting his head from the bone, asked:

—And what did you do, John?

—Do! said Mr Casey. She stuck her ugly old face up at me when she said it and I had my mouth full of the tobacco juice. I bent down to her and *Phth!* says I to her like that.

He turned aside and made the act of spitting.

—*Phth!* says I to her like that, right into her eye.

He clapped a hand to his eye and gave a hoarse scream of pain.

—*O Jesus, Mary and Joseph!* says she. *I'm blinded! I'm blinded and drownded!*

He stopped in a fit of coughing and laughter, repeating:

—*I'm blinded entirely.*

Mr Dedalus laughed loudly and lay back in his chair while uncle Charles swayed his head to and fro.

Dante looked terribly angry and repeated while they laughed:

—Very nice! Ha! Very nice!

It was not nice about the spit in the woman's eye. But what was the name the woman had called Kitty O'Shea that Mr Casey would not repeat? He thought of Mr Casey walking through the crowds of people and making speeches from a wagonette. That was what he had been in prison for and he remembered that one night Sergeant O'Neill had come to the house and had stood in the hall, talking in a low voice with his father and chewing nervously at the chinstrap of his cap. And that night Mr Casey had not gone to Dublin by train but a car had come to the door and he had heard his father say something about the Cabinteely road.

He was for Ireland and Parnell and so was his father: and so was Dante too for one night at the band on the esplanade she had hit a gentleman on the head with her umbrella because he had taken off his hat when the band played *God save the Queen* at the end.

Mr Dedalus gave a snort of contempt.

—Ah, John, he said. It is true for them. We are an unfortunate priestridden race and always were and always will be till the end of the chapter.

Uncle Charles shook his head, saying:

—A bad business! A bad business!

Mr Dedalus repeated:

—A priestridden Godforsaken race!

He pointed to the portrait of his grandfather on the wall to his right.

—Do you see that old chap up there, John? he said. He was a good Irishman when there was no money in the job. He was condemned to death as a whiteboy.° But he had a saying about our clerical friends, that he would never let one of them put his two feet under his mahogany.

Dante broke in angrily:

—If we are a priestridden race we ought to be proud of it! They are the apple of God's eye. *Touch them not,* says Christ, *for they are the apple of My eye.*

—And can we not love our country then? asked Mr Casey. Are we not to follow the man that was born to lead us?

—A traitor to his country! replied Dante. A traitor, an adulterer! The priests were right to abandon him. The priests were always the true friends of Ireland.

—Were they, faith? said Mr Casey.

He threw his fist on the table and, frowning angrily, protruded one finger after another.

—Didn't the bishops of Ireland betray us in the time of the union when bishop Lanigan presented an address of loyalty to the Marquess Cornwallis? Didn't the bishops and priests sell the aspirations of this country in 1829 in return for catholic emancipation? Didn't they denounce the fenian movement from the pulpit and in the confessionbox? And didn't they dishonour the ashes of Terence Bellew MacManus?

His face was glowing with anger and Stephen felt the glow rise to his own cheek as the spoken words thrilled him. Mr Dedalus uttered a guffaw of coarse scorn.

whiteboy: Member of a group working for land and tax reform, sometimes using terrorist means.

—O, by God, he cried, I forgot little old Paul Cullen! Another apple of God's eye!

Dante bent across the table and cried to Mr Casey:

—Right! Right! They were always right! God and morality and religion come first.

Mrs Dedalus, seeing her excitement, said to her:

—Mrs Riordan, don't excite yourself answering them.

—God and religion before everything! Dante cried. God and religion before the world!

Mr Casey raised his clenched fist and brought it down on the table with a crash.

—Very well, then, he shouted hoarsely, if it comes to that, no God for Ireland!

—John! John! cried Mr Dedalus, seizing his guest by the coatsleeve.

Dante stared across the table, her cheeks shaking. Mr Casey struggled up from his chair and bent across the table towards her, scraping the air from before his eyes with one hand as though he were tearing aside a cobweb.

—No God for Ireland! he cried. We have had too much God in Ireland. Away with God!

—Blasphemer! Devil! screamed Dante, starting to her feet and almost spitting in his face.

Uncle Charles and Mr Dedalus pulled Mr Casey back into his chair again, talking to him from both sides reasonably. He stared before him out of his dark flaming eyes, repeating:

—Away with God, I say!

Dante shoved her chair violently aside and left the table, upsetting her napkinring which rolled slowly along the carpet and came to rest against the foot of an easychair. Mrs Dedalus rose quickly and followed her towards the door. At the door Dante turned round violently and shouted down the room, her cheeks flushed and quivering with rage:

—Devil out of hell! We won! We crushed him to death! Fiend!

The door slammed behind her.

Mr Casey, freeing his arms from his holders, suddenly bowed his head on his hands with a sob of pain.

—Poor Parnell! he cried loudly. My dead king!

He sobbed loudly and bitterly.

Stephen, raising his terrorstricken face, saw that his father's eyes were full of tears.

*

* *

The fellows talked together in little groups.

One fellow said:

—They were caught near the Hill of Lyons.

—Who caught them?

—Mr Gleeson and the minister. They were on a car.

The same fellow added:

—A fellow in the higher line told me.

Fleming asked:

—But why did they run away, tell us?

—I know why, Cecil Thunder said. Because they had fecked° cash out of the rector's room.

—Who fecked it?

—Kickham's brother. And they all went shares in it.

But that was stealing. How could they have done that?

—A fat lot you know about it, Thunder! Wells said. I know why they scut.°

—Tell us why.

—I was told not to, Wells said.

—O, go on, Wells, all said. You might tell us. We won't let it out.

Stephen bent forward his head to hear. Wells looked round to see if anyone was coming. Then he said secretly:

—You know the altar wine they keep in the press in the sacristy?

—Yes.

—Well, they drank that and it was found out who did it by the smell. And that's why they ran away, if you want to know.

And the fellow who had spoken first said:

—Yes, that's what I heard too from the fellow in the higher line.

The fellows were all silent. Stephen stood among them, afraid to speak, listening. A faint sickness of awe made him feel weak. How could they have done that? He thought of the dark silent sacristy. There were dark wooden presses there where the crimped surplices lay quietly folded. It was not the chapel but still you had to speak under your breath. It was a holy place. He remembered the summer evening he had been there to be dressed as boatbearer,° the evening of the procession to the little altar in the wood. A strange and holy place. The boy that held the censer° had swung it gently to and fro near the door with the silvery cap lifted by the middle chain to keep the coals lighting. That was called charcoal: and it had burned quietly as the fellow had swung

fecked: Stolen. **scut:** Literally, tail of a rabbit; here, "turned tail and ran." **boatbearer:** One who carries the container of incense before it is lighted. **censer:** Vessel in which incense is burned.

it gently and had given off a weak sour smell. And then when all were vested he had stood holding out the boat to the rector and the rector had put a spoonful of incense in and it had hissed on the red coals.

The fellows were talking together in little groups here and there on the playground. The fellows seemed to him to have grown smaller: that was because a sprinter° had knocked him down the day before, a fellow out of second of grammar. He had been thrown by the fellow's machine lightly on the cinderpath and his spectacles had been broken in three pieces and some of the grit of the cinders had gone into his mouth.

That was why the fellows seemed to him smaller and farther away and the goalposts so thin and far and the soft grey sky so high up. But there was no play on the football grounds for cricket was coming: and some said that Barnes would be the prof° and some said it would be Flowers. And all over the playgrounds they were playing rounders° and bowling twisters and lobs. And from here and from there came the sounds of the cricketbats through the soft grey air. They said: pick, pack, pock, puck: like drops of water in a fountain slowly falling in the brimming bowl.

Athy, who had been silent, said quietly:

—You are all wrong.

All turned towards him eagerly.

—Why?

—Do you know?

—Who told you?

—Tell us, Athy.

Athy pointed across the playground to where Simon Moonan was walking by himself kicking a stone before him.

—Ask him, he said.

The fellows looked there and then said:

—Why him?

—Is he in it?

—Tell us, Athy. Go on. You might if you know.

Athy lowered his voice and said:

—Do you know why those fellows scut? I will tell you but you must not let on you know.

He paused for a moment and then said mysteriously:

—They were caught with Simon Moonan and Tusker Boyle in the square° one night.

The fellows looked at him and asked:

sprinter: Someone training in short-distance bicycle racing. **prof:** Captain of cricket team. **rounders:** British ball game. **square:** The school latrine or urinal.

—Caught?
—What doing?
Athy said:
—Smugging.°
All the fellows were silent: and Athy said:
—And that's why.

Stephen looked at the faces of the fellows but they were all looking across the playground. He wanted to ask somebody about it. What did that mean about the smugging in the square? Why did the five fellows out of the higher line run away for that? It was a joke, he thought. Simon Moonan had nice clothes and one night he had shown him a ball of creamy sweets that the fellows of the football fifteen had rolled down to him along the carpet in the middle of the refectory when he was at the door. It was the night of the match against the Bective Rangers and the ball was made just like a red and green apple only it opened and it was full of the creamy sweets. And one day Boyle had said that an elephant had two tuskers instead of two tusks and that was why he was called Tusker Boyle but some fellows called him Lady Boyle because he was always at his nails, paring them.

Eileen had long thin cool white hands too because she was a girl. They were like ivory; only soft. That was the meaning of *Tower of Ivory* but protestants could not understand it and made fun of it. One day he had stood beside her looking into the hotel grounds. A waiter was running up a trail of bunting on the flagstaff and a fox terrier was scampering to and fro on the sunny lawn. She had put her hand into his pocket where his hand was and he had felt how cool and thin and soft her hand was. She had said that pockets were funny things to have: and then all of a sudden she had broken away and had run laughing down the sloping curve of the path. Her fair hair had streamed out behind her like gold in the sun. *Tower of Ivory. House of Gold.* By thinking about things you could understand them.

But why in the square? You went there when you wanted to do something. It was all thick slabs of slate and water trickled all day out of tiny pinholes and there was a queer smell of stale water there. And behind the door of one of the closets there was a drawing in red pencil of a bearded man in a Roman dress with a brick in each hand and underneath was the name of the drawing:

Balbus was building a wall.

Some fellows had drawn it there for a cod. It had a funny face but

Smugging: Probably a mild sort of homosexual play.

it was very like a man with a beard. And on the wall of another closet there was written in backhand in beautiful writing:

Julius Caesar wrote The Calico Belly. °

Perhaps that was why they were there because it was a place where some fellows wrote things for cod. But all the same it was queer what Athy said and the way he said it. It was not a cod because they had run away. He looked with the others in silence across the playground and began to feel afraid.

At last Fleming said:

—And we are all to be punished for what other fellows did?

—I won't come back, see if I do, Cecil Thunder said. Three days' silence in the refectory and sending us up for six and eight° every minute.

—Yes, said Wells. And old Barrett has a new way of twisting the note so that you can't open it and fold it again to see how many ferulæ° you are to get. I won't come back too.

—Yes, said Cecil Thunder, and the prefect of studies° was in second of grammar this morning.

—Let us get up a rebellion, Fleming said. Will we?

All the fellows were silent. The air was very silent and you could hear the cricketbats but more slowly than before: pick, pock.

Wells asked:

—What is going to be done to them?

—Simon Moonan and Tusker are going to be flogged, Athy said, and the fellows in the higher line got their choice of flogging or being expelled.

—And which are they taking? asked the fellow who had spoken first.

—All are taking expulsion except Corrigan, Athy answered. He's going to be flogged by Mr Gleeson.

—Is it Corrigan that big fellow? said Fleming. Why, he'd be able for two of Gleeson!

—I know why, Cecil Thunder said. He is right and the other fellows are wrong because a flogging wears off after a bit but a fellow that has been expelled from college is known all his life on account of it. Besides Gleeson won't flog him hard.

—It's best of his play not to, Fleming said.

—I wouldn't like to be Simon Moonan and Tusker, Cecil Thunder

The Calico Belly: Joke on Caesar's *Commentarii de Bello Gallico* (Commentaries on the Gallic War). **six and eight:** Number of blows with the strap given as punishment. **ferulæ:** Strokes. **prefect of studies:** Assistant to the rector in charge of academics.

said. But I don't believe they will be flogged. Perhaps they will be sent up for twice nine.

—No, no, said Athy. They'll both get it on the vital spot.

Wells rubbed himself and said in a crying voice:

—Please, sir, let me off!

Athy grinned and turned up the sleeves of his jacket, saying:

It can't be helped;
It must be done.
So down with your breeches
And out with your bum.

The fellows laughed; but he felt that they were a little afraid. In the silence of the soft grey air he heard the cricketbats from here and from there: pock. That was a sound to hear but if you were hit then you would feel a pain. The pandybat made a sound too but not like that. The fellows said it was made of whalebone and leather with lead inside: and he wondered what was the pain like. There were different kinds of pains for all the different kinds of sounds. A long thin cane would have a high whistling sound and he wondered what was that pain like. It made him shivery to think of it and cold: and what Athy said too. But what was there to laugh at in it? It made him shivery: but that was because you always felt like a shiver when you let down your trousers. It was the same in the bath when you undressed yourself. He wondered who had to let them down, the master or the boy himself. O how could they laugh about it that way?

He looked at Athy's rolledup sleeves and knuckly inky hands. He had rolled up his sleeves to show how Mr Gleeson would roll up his sleeves. But Mr Gleeson had round shiny cuffs and clean white wrists and fattish white hands and the nails of them were long and pointed. Perhaps he pared them too like Lady Boyle. But they were terribly long and pointed nails. So long and cruel they were though the white fattish hands were not cruel but gentle. And though he trembled with cold and fright to think of the cruel long nails and of the high whistling sound of the cane and of the chill you felt at the end of your shirt when you undressed yourself yet he felt a feeling of queer quiet pleasure inside him to think of the white fattish hands, clean and strong and gentle. And he thought of what Cecil Thunder had said; that Mr Gleeson would not flog Corrigan hard. And Fleming had said he would not because it was best of his play not to. But that was not why.

A voice from far out on the playgrounds cried:

—All in!

And other voices cried:

—All in! All in!

During the writing lesson he sat with his arms folded, listening to the slow scraping of the pens. Mr Harford went to and fro making little signs in red pencil and sometimes sitting beside the boy to show him how to hold the pen. He had tried to spell out the headline for himself though he knew already what it was for it was the last of the book. *Zeal without prudence is like a ship adrift.* But the lines of the letters were like fine invisible threads and it was only by closing his right eye tight tight and staring out of the left eye that he could make out the full curves of the capital.

But Mr Harford was very decent and never got into a wax. All the other masters got into dreadful waxes. But why were they to suffer for what fellows in the higher line did? Wells had said that they had drunk some of the altar wine out of the press in the sacristy and that it had been found out who had done it by the smell. Perhaps they had stolen a monstrance° to run away with it and sell it somewhere. That must have been a terrible sin, to go in there quietly at night, to open the dark press and steal the flashing gold thing into which God was put on the altar in the middle of flowers and candles at benediction while the incense went up in clouds at both sides as the fellow swung the censer and Dominic Kelly sang the first part by himself in the choir. But God was not in it of course when they stole it. But still it was a strange and a great sin even to touch it. He thought of it with deep awe; a terrible and strange sin: it thrilled him to think of it in the silence when the pens scraped lightly. But to drink the altar wine out of the press and be found out by the smell was a sin too: but it was not terrible and strange. It only made you feel a little sickish on account of the smell of the wine. Because on the day when he had made his first holy communion in the chapel he had shut his eyes and opened his mouth and put out his tongue a little: and when the rector had stooped down to give him the holy communion he had smelt a faint winy smell off the rector's breath after the wine of the mass. The word was beautiful: wine. It made you think of dark purple because the grapes were dark purple that grew in Greece outside houses like white temples. But the faint smell off the rector's breath had made him feel a sick feeling on the morning of his first communion. The day of your first communion was the happiest day of your life. And once a lot of generals had asked Napoleon what

monstrance: Vessel of precious metal in which the host is displayed.

was the happiest day of his life. They thought he would say the day he won some great battle or the day he was made an emperor. But he said:

—Gentlemen, the happiest day of my life was the day on which I made my first holy communion.

Father Arnall came in and the Latin lesson began and he remained still, leaning on the desk with his arms folded. Father Arnall gave out the themebooks and he said that they were scandalous and that they were all to be written out again with the corrections at once. But the worst of all was Fleming's theme because the pages were stuck together by a blot: and Father Arnall held it up by a corner and said it was an insult to any master to send him up such a theme. Then he asked Jack Lawton to decline the noun *mare* and Jack Lawton stopped at the ablative singular and could not go on with the plural.

—You should be ashamed of yourself, said Father Arnall sternly. You, the leader of the class!

Then he asked the next boy and the next and the next. Nobody knew. Father Arnall became very quiet, more and more quiet as each boy tried to answer and could not. But his face was blacklooking and his eyes were staring though his voice was so quiet. Then he asked Fleming and Fleming said that that word had no plural. Father Arnall suddenly shut the book and shouted at him:

—Kneel out there in the middle of the class. You are one of the idlest boys I ever met. Copy out your themes again the rest of you.

Fleming moved heavily out of his place and knelt between the two last benches. The other boys bent over their themebooks and began to write. A silence filled the classroom and Stephen, glancing timidly at Father Arnall's dark face, saw that it was a little red from the wax he was in.

Was that a sin for Father Arnall to be in a wax or was he allowed to get into a wax when the boys were idle because that made them study better or was he only letting on to be in a wax? It was because he was allowed because a priest would know what a sin was and would not do it. But if he did it one time by mistake what would he do to go to confession? Perhaps he would go to confession to the minister. And if the minister did it he would go to the rector: and the rector to the provincial: and the provincial to the general° of the jesuits. That was called the order: and he had heard his father say that they were all clever men. They could all have become highup people in the world if they

provincial . . . general: Highest Jesuit authority in Ireland; ultimate Jesuit authority, in Rome.

had not become jesuits. And he wondered what Father Arnall and Paddy Barrett would have become and what Mr McGlade and Mr Gleeson would have become if they had not become jesuits. It was hard to think what because you would have to think of them in a different way with different coloured coats and trousers and with beards and moustaches and different kinds of hats.

The door opened quietly and closed. A quick whisper ran through the class: the prefect of studies. There was an instant of dead silence and then the loud crack of a pandybat on the last desk. Stephen's heart leapt up in fear.

—Any boys want flogging here, Father Arnall? cried the prefect of studies. Any lazy idle loafers that want flogging in this class?

He came to the middle of the class and saw Fleming on his knees.

—Hoho! he cried. Who is this boy? Why is he on his knees? What is your name, boy?

—Fleming, sir.

—Hoho, Fleming! An idler of course. I can see it in your eye. Why is he on his knees, Father Arnall?

—He wrote a bad Latin theme, Father Arnall said, and he missed all the questions in grammar.

—Of course he did! cried the prefect of studies. Of course he did! A born idler! I can see it in the corner of his eye.

He banged his pandybat down on the desk and cried:

—Up, Fleming! Up, my boy!

Fleming stood up slowly.

—Hold out! cried the prefect of studies.

Fleming held out his hand. The pandybat came down on it with a loud smacking sound: one, two, three, four, five, six.

—Other hand!

The pandybat came down again in six loud quick smacks.

—Kneel down! cried the prefect of studies.

Fleming knelt down squeezing his hands under his armpits, his face contorted with pain, but Stephen knew how hard his hands were because Fleming was always rubbing rosin into them. But perhaps he was in great pain for the noise of the pandies was terrible. Stephen's heart was beating and fluttering.

—At your work, all of you! shouted the prefect of studies. We want no lazy idle loafers here, lazy idle little schemers. At your work, I tell you. Father Dolan will be in to see you every day. Father Dolan will be in tomorrow.

He poked one of the boys in the side with the pandybat, saying:

—You, boy! When will Father Dolan be in again?

—Tomorrow, sir, said Tom Furlong's voice.

—Tomorrow and tomorrow and tomorrow, said the prefect of studies. Make up your minds for that. Every day Father Dolan. Write away. You, boy, who are you?

Stephen's heart jumped suddenly.

—Dedalus, sir.

—Why are you not writing like the others?

—I . . . my . . .

He could not speak with fright.

—Why is he not writing, Father Arnall?

—He broke his glasses, said Father Arnall, and I exempted him from work.

—Broke? What is this I hear? What is this your name is? said the prefect of studies.

—Dedalus, sir.

—Out here, Dedalus. Lazy little schemer. I see schemer in your face. Where did you break your glasses?

Stephen stumbled into the middle of the class, blinded by fear and haste.

—Where did you break your glasses? repeated the prefect of studies.

—The cinderpath, sir.

—Hoho! The cinderpath! cried the prefect of studies. I know that trick.

Stephen lifted his eyes in wonder and saw for a moment Father Dolan's whitegrey not young face, his baldy whitegrey head with fluff at the sides of it, the steel rims of his spectacles and his nocoloured eyes looking through the glasses. Why did he say that he knew that trick?

—Lazy idle little loafer! cried the prefect of studies. Broke my glasses! An old schoolboy trick! Out with your hand this moment!

Stephen closed his eyes and held out in the air his trembling hand with the palm upwards. He felt the prefect of studies touch it for a moment at the fingers to straighten it and then the swish of the sleeve of the soutane as the pandybat was lifted to strike. A hot burning stinging tingling blow like the loud crack of a broken stick made his trembling hand crumple together like a leaf in the fire: and at the sound and the pain scalding tears were driven into his eyes. His whole body was shaking with fright, his arm was shaking and his crumpled burning livid hand shook like a loose leaf in the air. A cry sprang to his lips, a prayer to be let off. But though the tears scalded his eyes and his limbs quivered with pain and fright he held back the hot tears and the cry that scalded his throat.

—Other hand! shouted the prefect of studies.

Stephen drew back his maimed and quivering right arm and held out his left hand. The soutane sleeve swished again as the pandybat was lifted and a loud crashing sound and a fierce maddening tingling burning pain made his hand shrink together with the palms and fingers in a livid quivering mass. The scalding water burst forth from his eyes and, burning with shame and agony and fear, he drew back his shaking arm in terror and burst out into a whine of pain. His body shook with a palsy of fright and in shame and rage he felt the scalding cry come from his throat and the scalding tears falling out of his eyes and down his flaming cheeks.

—Kneel down! cried the prefect of studies.

Stephen knelt down quickly pressing his beaten hands to his sides. To think of them beaten and swollen with pain all in a moment made him feel so sorry for them as if they were not his hands but someone else's that he felt so sorry for. And as he knelt, calming the last sobs in his throat and feeling the burning tingling pain pressed in to his sides, he thought of the hands which he had held out in the air with the palms up and of the firm touch of the prefect of studies when he had steadied the shaking fingers and of the beaten swollen reddened mass of palm and fingers that shook helplessly in the air.

—Get at your work, all of you, cried the prefect of studies from the door. Father Dolan will be in every day to see if any boy, any lazy idle little loafer wants flogging. Every day. Every day.

The door closed behind him.

The hushed class continued to copy out the themes. Father Arnall rose from his seat and went among them, helping the boys with gentle words and telling them the mistakes they had made. His voice was very gentle and soft. Then he returned to his seat and said to Fleming and Stephen:

—You may return to your places, you two.

Fleming and Stephen rose and, walking to their seats, sat down. Stephen, scarlet with shame, opened a book quickly with one weak hand and bent down upon it, his face close to the page.

It was unfair and cruel because the doctor had told him not to read without glasses and he had written home to his father that morning to send him a new pair. And Father Arnall had said that he need not study till the new glasses came. Then to be called a schemer before the class and to be pandied when he always got the card for first or second and was the leader of the Yorkists! How could the prefect of studies know that it was a trick? He felt the touch of the prefect's fingers as they had steadied his hand and at first he had thought that he was going to shake hands with him because the fingers were soft and firm: but then in an instant he had heard the swish of the soutane sleeve and the crash. It was cruel and unfair to make him kneel in the middle of the class then: and Father Arnall had told them both that they might return to their places without making any difference between them. He listened to Father Arnall's low and gentle voice as he corrected the themes. Perhaps he was sorry now and wanted to be decent. But it was unfair and cruel. The prefect of studies was a priest but that was cruel and unfair. And his whitegrey face and the nocoloured eyes behind the steelrimmed spectacles were cruel looking because he had steadied the hand first with his firm soft fingers and that was to hit it better and louder.

—It's a stinking mean thing, that's what it is, said Fleming in the corridor as the classes were passing out in file to the refectory, to pandy a fellow for what is not his fault.

—You really broke your glasses by accident, didn't you? Nasty Roche asked.

Stephen felt his heart filled by Fleming's words and did not answer.

—Of course he did! said Fleming. I wouldn't stand it. I'd go up and tell the rector on him.

—Yes, said Cecil Thunder eagerly, and I saw him lift the pandybat over his shoulder and he's not allowed to do that.

—Did they hurt much? Nasty Roche asked.

—Very much, Stephen said.

—I wouldn't stand it, Fleming repeated, from Baldyhead or any other Baldyhead. It's a stinking mean low trick, that's what it is. I'd go straight up to the rector and tell him about it after dinner.

—Yes, do. Yes, do, said Cecil Thunder.

—Yes, do. Yes, go up and tell the rector on him, Dedalus, said Nasty Roche, because he said that he'd come in tomorrow again to pandy you.

—Yes, yes. Tell the rector, all said.

And there were some fellows out of second of grammar listening and one of them said:

—The senate and the Roman people declared that Dedalus had been wrongly punished.

It was wrong; it was unfair and cruel: and, as he sat in the refectory, he suffered time after time in memory the same humiliation until he began to wonder whether it might not really be that there was something in his face which made him look like a schemer and he wished he had a little mirror to see. But there could not be; and it was unjust and cruel and unfair.

He could not eat the blackish fish fritters they got on Wednesdays in Lent and one of his potatoes had the mark of the spade in it. Yes, he would do what the fellows had told him. He would go up and tell the rector that he had been wrongly punished. A thing like that had been done before by somebody in history, by some great person whose head was in the books of history. And the rector would declare that he had been wrongly punished because the senate and the Roman people always declared that the men who did that had been wrongly punished. Those were the great men whose names were in Richmal Magnall's Questions. History was all about those men and what they did and that was what Peter Parley's Tales about Greece and Rome were all about. Peter Parley himself was on the first page in a picture. There was a road over a heath with grass at the side and little bushes: and Peter Parley had a broad hat like a protestant minister and a big stick and he was walking fast along the road to Greece and Rome.

It was easy what he had to do. All he had to do was when the dinner was over and he came out in his turn to go on walking but not out to the corridor but up the staircase on the right that led to the castle. He had nothing to do but that: to turn to the right and walk fast up the staircase and in half a minute he would be in the low dark narrow corridor that led through the castle to the rector's room. And every fellow had said that it was unfair, even the fellow out of second of grammar who had said that about the senate and the Roman people.

What would happen? He heard the fellows of the higher line stand up at the top of the refectory and heard their steps as they came down the matting: Paddy Rath and Jimmy Magee and the Spaniard and the Portuguese and the fifth was big Corrigan who was going to be flogged by Mr Gleeson. That was why the prefect of studies had called him a schemer and pandied him for nothing: and, straining his weak eyes, tired with the tears, he watched big Corrigan's broad shoulders and big hanging black head passing in the file. But he had done something and besides Mr Gleeson would not flog him hard: and he remembered how big Corrigan looked in the bath. He had skin the same colour as the turfcoloured bogwater in the shallow end of the bath and when he walked along the side his feet slapped loudly on the wet tiles and at every slap his thighs shook a little because he was fat.

The refectory was half empty and the fellows were still passing out in file. He could go up the staircase because there was never a priest or a prefect outside the refectory door. But he could not go. The rector would side with the prefect of studies and think it was a schoolboy trick and then the prefect of studies would come in every day the same only it would be worse because he would be dreadfully waxy at any fellow going up to the rector about him. The fellows had told him to go but they would not go themselves. They had forgotten all about it. No, it was best to forget all about it and perhaps the prefect of studies had only said he would come in. No, it was best to hide out of the way because when you were small and young you could often escape that way.

The fellows at his table stood up. He stood up and passed out among them in the file. He had to decide. He was coming near the door. If he went on with the fellows he could never go up to the rector because he could not leave the playground for that. And if he went and was pandied all the same all the fellows would make fun and talk about young Dedalus going up to the rector to tell on the prefect of studies.

He was walking down along the matting and he saw the door before him. It was impossible: he could not. He thought of the baldy head of the prefect of studies with the cruel nocoloured eyes looking at him and he heard the voice of the prefect of studies asking him twice what his name was. Why could he not remember the name when he was told the first time? Was he not listening the first time or was it to make fun out of the name? The great men in the history had names like that and nobody made fun of them. It was his own name that he should have made fun of if he wanted to make fun. Dolan: it was like the name of a woman that washed clothes.

He had reached the door and, turning quickly to the right, walked up the stairs and, before he could make up his mind to come back, he had entered the low dark narrow corridor that led to the castle. And as he crossed the threshold of the door of the corridor he saw, without turning his head to look, that all the fellows were looking after him as they went filing by.

He passed along the narrow dark corridor, passing little doors that were the doors of the rooms of the community. He peered in front of him and right and left through the gloom and thought that those must be portraits. It was dark and silent and his eyes were weak and tired with tears so that he could not see. But he thought they were the portraits of the saints and great men of the order who were looking down on him silently as he passed: saint Ignatius Loyola° holding an open book and

saint Ignatius Loyola: (1491–1556) Founder of Society of Jesus (Jesuit order).

pointing to the words *Ad Majorem Dei Gloriam*° in it, saint Francis Xavier pointing to his chest, Lorenzo Ricci with his berretta on his head like one of the prefects of the lines, the three patrons of holy youth, saint Stanislaus Kostka, saint Aloysius Gonzaga and blessed John Berchmans, all with young faces because they died when they were young, and Father Peter Kenny sitting in a chair wrapped in a big cloak.

He came out on the landing above the entrance hall and looked about him. That was where Hamilton Rowan had passed and the marks of the soldiers' slugs were there. And it was there that the old servants had seen the ghost in the white cloak of a marshal.

An old servant was sweeping at the end of the landing. He asked him where was the rector's room and the old servant pointed to the door at the far end and looked after him as he went on to it and knocked.

There was no answer. He knocked again more loudly and his heart jumped when he heard a muffled voice say:

—Come in!

He turned the handle and opened the door and fumbled for the handle of the green baize door inside. He found it and pushed it open and went in.

He saw the rector sitting at a desk writing. There was a skull on the desk and a strange solemn smell in the room like the old leather of chairs.

His heart was beating fast on account of the solemn place he was in and the silence of the room: and he looked at the skull and at the rector's kindlooking face.

—Well, my little man, said the rector, what is it?

Stephen swallowed down the thing in his throat and said:

—I broke my glasses, sir.

The rector opened his mouth and said:

—O!

Then he smiled and said:

—Well, if we broke our glasses we must write home for a new pair.

—I wrote home, sir, said Stephen, and Father Arnall said I am not to study till they come.

—Quite right! said the rector.

Stephen swallowed down the thing again and tried to keep his legs and his voice from shaking.

Ad Majorem Dei Gloriam: For the Greater Glory of God, the Jesuit motto, which students in a Jesuit school might abbreviate to "A.M.D.G." and attach to their compositions.

—But, sir . . .

—Yes?

—Father Dolan came in today and pandied me because I was not writing my theme.

The rector looked at him in silence and he could feel the blood rising to his face and the tears about to rise to his eyes.

The rector said:

—Your name is Dedalus, isn't it?

—Yes, sir.

—And where did you break your glasses?

—On the cinderpath, sir. A fellow was coming out of the bicycle house and I fell and they got broken. I don't know the fellow's name.

The rector looked at him again in silence. Then he smiled and said:

—O, well, it was a mistake. I am sure Father Dolan did not know.

—But I told him I broke them, sir, and he pandied me.

—Did you tell him that you had written home for a new pair? the rector asked.

—No, sir.

—O well then, said the rector, Father Dolan did not understand. You can say that I excuse you from your lessons for a few days.

Stephen said quickly for fear his trembling would prevent him:

—Yes, sir, but Father Dolan said he will come in tomorrow to pandy me again for it.

—Very well, the rector said, it is a mistake and I shall speak to Father Dolan myself. Will that do now?

Stephen felt the tears wetting his eyes and murmured:

—O yes, sir, thanks.

The rector held his hand across the side of the desk where the skull was and Stephen, placing his hand in it for a moment, felt a cool moist palm.

—Good day now, said the rector, withdrawing his hand and bowing.

—Good day, sir, said Stephen.

He bowed and walked quietly out of the room, closing the doors carefully and slowly.

But when he had passed the old servant on the landing and was again in the low narrow dark corridor he began to walk faster and faster. Faster and faster he hurried on through the gloom, excitedly. He bumped his elbow against the door at the end and, hurrying down the staircase, walked quickly through the two corridors and out into the air.

He could hear the cries of the fellows on the playgrounds. He broke into a run and, running quicker and quicker, ran across the cinderpath and reached the third line playground, panting.

The fellows had seen him running. They closed round him in a ring, pushing one against another to hear.

—Tell us! Tell us!

—What did he say?

—Did you go in?

—What did he say?

—Tell us! Tell us!

He told them what he had said and what the rector had said and, when he had told them, all the fellows flung their caps spinning up into the air and cried:

—Hurroo!

They caught their caps and sent them up again spinning skyhigh and cried again:

—Hurroo! Hurroo!

They made a cradle of their locked hands and hoisted him up among them and carried him along till he struggled to get free. And when he had escaped from them they broke away in all directions, flinging their caps again into the air and whistling as they went spinning up and crying:

—Hurroo!

And they gave three groans for Baldyhead Dolan and three cheers for Conmee and they said he was the decentest rector that was ever in Clongowes.

The cheers died away in the soft grey air. He was alone. He was happy and free: but he would not be anyway proud with Father Dolan. He would be very quiet and obedient: and he wished that he could do something kind for him to show him that he was not proud.

The air was soft and grey and mild and evening was coming. There was the smell of evening in the air, the smell of the fields in the country where they digged up turnips to peel them and eat them when they went out for a walk to Major Barton's, the smell there was in the little wood beyond the pavilion where the gallnuts° were.

The fellows were practising long shies° and bowling lobs and slow twisters. In the soft grey silence he could hear the bump of the balls: and from here and from there through the quiet air the sound of the cricketbats: pick, pack, pock, puck: like drops of water in a fountain falling softly in the brimming bowl.

gallnuts: Rounded growths on trees caused by insects. **long shies:** Long hits by the batsman in cricket.

II

Uncle Charles smoked such black twist° that at last his outspoken nephew suggested to him to enjoy his morning smoke in a little outhouse at the end of the garden.

—Very good, Simon. All serene, Simon, said the old man tranquilly. Anywhere you like. The outhouse will do me nicely: it will be more salubrious.

—Damn me, said Mr Dedalus frankly, if I know how you can smoke such villainous awful tobacco. It's like gunpowder, by God.

—It's very nice, Simon, replied the old man. Very cool and mollifying.

Every morning, therefore, uncle Charles repaired to his outhouse but not before he had creased and brushed scrupulously his back hair and brushed and put on his tall hat. While he smoked the brim of his tall hat and the bowl of his pipe were just visible beyond the jambs of the outhouse door. His arbour, as he called the reeking outhouse which he shared with the cat and the garden tools, served him also as a soundingbox: and every morning he hummed contentedly one of his favourite songs: *O, twine me a bower* or *Blue eyes and golden hair* or *The Groves of Blarney* while the grey and blue coils of smoke rose slowly from his pipe and vanished in the pure air.

During the first part of the summer in Blackrock uncle Charles was Stephen's constant companion. Uncle Charles was a hale old man with a welltanned skin, rugged features and white side whiskers. On week days he did messages between the house in Carysfort Avenue and those shops in the main street of the town with which the family dealt. Stephen was glad to go with him on these errands for uncle Charles helped him very liberally to handfuls of whatever was exposed in open boxes and barrels outside the counter. He would seize a handful of grapes and sawdust or three or four American apples and thrust them generously into his grandnephew's hand while the shopman smiled uneasily; and, on Stephen's feigning reluctance to take them, he would frown and say:

—Take them, sir. Do you hear me, sir? They're good for your bowels.

When the order list had been booked the two would go on to the park where an old friend of Stephen's father, Mike Flynn, would be found seated on a bench, waiting for them. Then would begin Steph-

black twist: Strong tobacco twisted into a rope.

en's run round the park. Mike Flynn would stand at the gate near the railway station, watch in hand, while Stephen ran round the track in the style Mike Flynn favoured, his head high lifted, his knees well lifted and his hands held straight down by his sides. When the morning practice was over the trainer would make his comments and sometimes illustrate them by shuffling along for a yard or so comically in an old pair of blue canvas shoes. A small ring of wonderstruck children and nursemaids would gather to watch him and linger even when he and uncle Charles had sat down again and were talking athletics and politics. Though he had heard his father say that Mike Flynn had put some of the best runners of modern times through his hands Stephen often glanced with mistrust at his trainer's flabby stubblecovered face, as it bent over the long stained fingers through which he rolled his cigarette, and with pity at the mild lustreless blue eyes which would look up suddenly from the task and gaze vaguely into the bluer distance while the long swollen fingers ceased their rolling and grains and fibres of tobacco fell back into the pouch.

On the way home uncle Charles would often pay a visit to the chapel and, as the font was above Stephen's reach, the old man would dip his hand and then sprinkle the water briskly about Stephen's clothes and on the floor of the porch. While he prayed he knelt on his red handkerchief and read above his breath from a thumbblackened prayerbook wherein catchwords were printed at the foot of every page. Stephen knelt at his side respecting, though he did not share, his piety. He often wondered what his granduncle prayed for so seriously. Perhaps he prayed for the souls in purgatory or for the grace of a happy death or perhaps he prayed that God might send him back a part of the big fortune he had squandered in Cork.

On Sundays Stephen with his father and his granduncle took their constitutional. The old man was a nimble walker in spite of his corns and often ten or twelve miles of the road were covered. The little village of Stillorgan was the parting of the ways. Either they went to the left towards the Dublin mountains or along the Goatstown road and thence into Dundrum, coming home by Sandyford. Trudging along the road or standing in some grimy wayside publichouse his elders spoke constantly of the subjects nearest their hearts, of Irish politics, of Munster and of the legends of their own family, to all of which Stephen lent an avid ear. Words which he did not understand he said over and over to himself till he had learned them by heart: and through them he had glimpses of the real world about him. The hour when he too would take his part in the life of that world seemed drawing near and in secret he began to make ready for the great part which he felt awaited him the nature of which he only dimly apprehended.

His evenings were his own; and he pored over a ragged translation of *The Count of Monte Cristo*. The figure of that dark avenger stood forth in his mind for whatever he had heard or divined in childhood of the strange and terrible. At night he built up on the parlour table an image of the wonderful island cave out of transfers and paper flowers and coloured tissue paper and strips of the silver and golden paper in which chocolate is wrapped. When he had broken up this scenery, weary of its tinsel, there would come to his mind the bright picture of Marseilles, of sunny trellisses and of Mercedes. Outside Blackrock, on the road that led to the mountains, stood a small whitewashed house in the garden of which grew many rosebushes: and in this house, he told himself, another Mercedes lived. Both on the outward and on the homeward journey he measured distance by this landmark: and in his imagination he lived through a long train of adventures, marvellous as those in the book itself, towards the close of which there appeared an image of himself, grown older and sadder, standing in a moonlit garden with Mercedes who had so many years before slighted his love, and with a sadly proud gesture of refusal, saying:

—Madam, I never eat muscatel grapes.

He became the ally of a boy named Aubrey Mills and founded with him a gang of adventurers in the avenue. Aubrey carried a whistle dangling from his buttonhole and a bicycle lamp attached to his belt while the others had short sticks thrust daggerwise through theirs. Stephen, who had read of Napoleon's plain style of dress, chose to remain unadorned and thereby heightened for himself the pleasure of taking counsel with his lieutenant before giving orders. The gang made forays into the gardens of old maids or went down to the castle and fought a battle on the shaggy weedgrown rocks, coming home after it weary stragglers with the stale odours of the foreshore in their nostrils and the rank oils of the seawrack upon their hands and in their hair.

Aubrey and Stephen had a common milkman and often they drove out in the milkcar to Carrickmines where the cows were at grass. While the men were milking the boys would take turns in riding the tractable mare round the field. But when autumn came the cows were driven home from the grass: and the first sight of the filthy cowyard at Stradbrook with its foul green puddles and clots of liquid dung and steaming brantroughs sickened Stephen's heart. The cattle which had seemed so beautiful in the country on sunny days revolted him and he could not even look at the milk they yielded.

The coming of September did not trouble him this year for he knew he was not to be sent back to Clongowes. The practice in the park came to an end when Mike Flynn went into hospital. Aubrey was at school and had only an hour or two free in the evening. The gang fell asunder and there were no more nightly forays or battles on the rocks. Stephen sometimes went round with the car which delivered the evening milk: and these chilly drives blew away his memory of the filth of the cowyard and he felt no repugnance at seeing the cowhairs and hayseeds on the milkman's coat. Whenever the car drew up before a house he waited to catch a glimpse of a wellscrubbed kitchen or of a softlighted hall and to see how the servant would hold the jug and how she would close the door. He thought it should be a pleasant life enough, driving along the roads every evening to deliver milk, if he had warm gloves and a fat bag of gingernuts in his pocket to eat from. But the same foreknowledge which had sickened his heart and made his limbs sag suddenly as he raced round the park, the same intuition which had made him glance with mistrust at his trainer's flabby stubblecovered face as it bent heavily over his long stained fingers, dissipated any vision of the future. In a vague way he understood that his father was in trouble and that this was the reason why he himself had not been sent back to Clongowes. For some time he had felt the slight changes in his house; and these changes in what he had deemed unchangeable were so many slight shocks to his boyish conception of the world. The ambition which he felt astir at times in the darkness of his soul sought no outlet. A dusk like that of the outer world obscured his mind as he heard the mare's hoofs clattering along the tramtrack on the Rock Road and the great can swaying and rattling behind him.

He returned to Mercedes and, as he brooded upon her image, a strange unrest crept into his blood. Sometimes a fever gathered within him and led him to rove alone in the evening along the quiet avenue. The peace of the gardens and the kindly lights in the windows poured a tender influence into his restless heart. The noise of children at play annoyed him and their silly voices made him feel, even more keenly than he had felt at Clongowes, that he was different from others. He did not want to play. He wanted to meet in the real world the unsubstantial image which his soul so constantly beheld. He did not know where to seek it or how: but a premonition which led him on told him that this image would, without any overt act of his, encounter him. They would meet quietly as if they had known each other and had made their tryst, perhaps at one of the gates or in some more secret place. They would be alone, surrounded by darkness and silence: and in that moment of supreme tenderness he would be transfigured. He would fade into something impalpable under her eyes and then, in a moment, he would be transfigured. Weakness and timidity and inexperience would fall from him in that magic moment.

*

* *

Two great yellow caravans° had halted one morning before the door and men had come tramping into the house to dismantle it. The furniture had been hustled out through the front garden which was strewn with wisps of straw and rope ends and into the huge vans at the gate. When all had been safely stowed the vans had set off noisily down the avenue: and from the window of the railway carriage, in which he had sat with his redeyed mother, Stephen had seen them lumbering heavily along the Merrion Road.

The parlour fire would not draw that evening and Mr Dedalus rested the poker against the bars of the grate to attract the flame. Uncle Charles dozed in a corner of the half furnished uncarpeted room and near him the family portraits leaned against the wall. The lamp on the table shed a weak light over the boarded floor, muddied by the feet of the vanmen. Stephen sat on a footstool beside his father listening to a long and incoherent monologue. He understood little or nothing of it at first but he became slowly aware that his father had enemies and that some fight was going to take place. He felt too that he was being enlisted for the fight, that some duty was being laid upon his shoulders. The sudden flight from the comfort and revery of Blackrock, the passage through the gloomy foggy city, the thought of the bare cheerless house in which they were now to live made his heart heavy: and again an intuition or foreknowledge of the future came to him. He understood also why the servants had often whispered together in the hall and why his father had often stood on the hearthrug, with his back to the fire, talking loudly to uncle Charles who urged him to sit down and eat his dinner.

—There's a crack of the whip left in me yet, Stephen, old chap, said Mr Dedalus, poking at the dull fire with fierce energy. We're not dead yet, sonny. No, by the Lord Jesus (God forgive me) nor half dead.

Dublin was a new and complex sensation. Uncle Charles had grown so witless that he could no longer be sent out on errands and the disorder in settling in the new house left Stephen freer than he had been in Blackrock. In the beginning he contented himself with circling timidly

caravans: Horse-drawn, covered carts or wagons.

round the neighbouring square or, at most, going half way down one of the side streets: but when he had made a skeleton map of the city in his mind he followed boldly one of its central lines until he reached the customhouse. He passed unchallenged among the docks and along the quays wondering at the multitude of corks that lay bobbing on the surface of the water in a thick yellow scum, at the crowds of quay porters and the rumbling carts and the illdressed bearded policeman. The vastness and strangeness of the life suggested to him by the bales of merchandise stacked along the walls or swung aloft out of the holds of steamers wakened again in him the unrest which had sent him wandering in the evening from garden to garden in search of Mercedes. And amid this new bustling life he might have fancied himself in another Marseilles but that he missed the bright sky and the sunwarmed trellisses of the wineshops. A vague dissatisfaction grew up within him as he looked on the quays and on the river and on the lowering skies and yet he continued to wander up and down day after day as if he really sought someone that eluded him.

He went once or twice with his mother to visit their relatives: and, though they passed a jovial array of shops lit up and adorned for Christmas, his mood of embittered silence did not leave him. The causes of his embitterment were many, remote and near. He was angry with himself for being young and the prey of restless foolish impulses, angry also with the change of fortune which was reshaping the world about him into a vision of squalor and insincerity. Yet his anger lent nothing to the vision. He chronicled with patience what he saw, detaching himself from it and tasting its mortifying flavour in secret.

He was sitting on the backless chair in his aunt's kitchen. A lamp with a reflector hung on the japanned wall of the fireplace and by its light his aunt was reading the evening paper that lay on her knees. She looked a long time at a smiling picture that was set in it and said musingly:

—The beautiful Mabel Hunter!

A ringletted girl stood on tiptoe to peer at the picture and said softly:

—What is she in, mud?

—In the pantomime,° love.

The child leaned her ringletted head against her mother's sleeve, gazing on the picture, and murmured as if fascinated:

—The beautiful Mabel Hunter!

pantomime: Popular show with song, dance, a loose story line, and local references.

As if fascinated, her eyes rested long upon those demurely taunting eyes and she murmured again devotedly:

—Isn't she an exquisite creature?

And the boy who came in from the street, stamping crookedly under his stone° of coal, heard her words. He dropped his load promptly on the floor and hurried to her side to see. But she did not raise her easeful head to let him see. He mauled the edges of the paper with his reddened and blackened hands, shouldering her aside and complaining that he could not see.

He was sitting in the narrow breakfast room high up in the old darkwindowed house. The firelight flickered on the wall and beyond the window a spectral dusk was gathering upon the river. Before the fire an old woman was busy making tea and, as she bustled at her task, she told in a low voice of what the priest and the doctor had said. She told too of certain changes that she had seen in her of late and of her odd ways and sayings. He sat listening to the words and following the ways of adventure that lay open in the coals, arches and vaults and winding galleries and jagged caverns.

Suddenly he became aware of something in the doorway. A skull appeared suspended in the gloom of the doorway. A feeble creature like a monkey was there, drawn thither by the sound of voices at the fire. A whining voice came from the door, asking:

—Is that Josephine?

The old bustling woman answered cheerily from the fireplace:

—No, Ellen. It's Stephen.

—O . . . O, good evening, Stephen.

He answered the greeting and saw a silly smile break out over the face in the doorway.

—Do you want anything, Ellen? asked the old woman at the fire.

But she did not answer the question and said:

—I thought it was Josephine. I thought you were Josephine, Stephen.

And, repeating this several times, she fell to laughing feebly.

He was sitting in the midst of a children's party at Harold's Cross. His silent watchful manner had grown upon him and he took little part in the games. The children, wearing the spoils of their crackers,° danced and romped noisily and, though he tried to share their merriment, he felt himself a gloomy figure amid the gay cocked hats and sunbonnets.

stone: Fourteen pounds. **crackers:** Decorated noisemakers, often with small gifts inside.

But when he had sung his song and withdrawn into a snug corner of the room he began to taste the joy of his loneliness. The mirth, which in the beginning of the evening had seemed to him false and trivial, was like a soothing air to him, passing gaily by his senses, hiding from other eyes the feverish agitation of his blood while through the circling of the dancers and amid the music and laughter her glances travelled to his corner, flattering, taunting, searching, exciting his heart.

In the hall the children who had stayed latest were putting on their things: the party was over. She had thrown a shawl about her and, as they went together towards the tram,° sprays of her fresh warm breath flew gaily above her cowled head and her shoes tapped blithely on the glassy road.

It was the last tram. The lank brown horses knew it and shook their bells to the clear night in admonition. The conductor talked with the driver, both nodding often in the green light of the lamp. On the empty seats of the tram were scattered a few coloured tickets. No sound of footsteps came up or down the road. No sound broke the peace of the night save when the lank brown horses rubbed their noses together and shook their bells.

They seemed to listen, he on the upper step and she on the lower. She came up to his step many times and went down to hers again between their phrases and once or twice stood close beside him for some moments on the upper step, forgetting to go down, and then went down. His heart danced upon her movements like a cork upon a tide. He heard what her eyes said to him from beneath their cowl and knew that in some dim past, whether in life or in revery, he had heard their tale before. He saw her urge her vanities, her fine dress and sash and long black stockings, and knew that he had yielded to them a thousand times. Yet a voice within him spoke above the noise of his dancing heart, asking him would he take her gift to which he had only to stretch out his hand. And he remembered the day when he and Eileen had stood looking into the hotel grounds, watching the waiters running up a trail of bunting on the flagstaff and the fox terrier scampering to and fro on the sunny lawn, and how, all of a sudden, she had broken out into a peal of laughter and had run down the sloping curve of the path. Now, as then, he stood listlessly in his place, seemingly a tranquil watcher of the scene before him.

—She too wants me to catch hold of her, he thought. That's why she

tram: Means of public transport, during this period changing from horse-drawn vehicle to electric-powered streetcar.

came with me to the tram. I could easily catch hold of her when she comes up to my step: nobody is looking. I could hold her and kiss her.

But he did neither: and, when he was sitting alone in the deserted tram, he tore his ticket into shreds and stared gloomily at the corrugated footboard.

The next day he sat at his table in the bare upper room for many hours. Before him lay a new pen, a new bottle of ink and a new emerald exercise.° From force of habit he had written at the top of the first page the initial letters of the jesuit motto: A.M.D.G. On the first line of the page appeared the title of the verses he was trying to write: To E—— C——. He knew it was right to begin so for he had seen similar titles in the collected poems of Lord Byron. When he had written this title and drawn an ornamental line underneath he fell into a daydream and began to draw diagrams on the cover of the book. He saw himself sitting at his table in Bray the morning after the discussion at the Christmas dinnertable, trying to write a poem about Parnell on the back of one of his father's second moiety notices.° But his brain had then refused to grapple with the theme and, desisting, he had covered the page with the names and addresses of certain of his classmates:

Roderick Kickham
John Lawton
Anthony MacSwiney
Simon Moonan

Now it seemed as if he would fail again but, by dint of brooding on the incident, he thought himself into confidence. During this process all those elements which he deemed common and insignificant fell out of the scene. There remained no trace of the tram itself nor of the tram-men nor of the horses: nor did he and she appear vividly. The verses told only of the night and the balmy breeze and the maiden lustre of the moon. Some undefined sorrow was hidden in the hearts of the protagonists as they stood in silence beneath the leafless trees and when the moment of farewell had come the kiss, which had been withheld by one, was given by both. After this the letters L.D.S.° were written at the foot of the page and, having hidden the book, he went into his mother's bedroom and gazed at his face for a long time in the mirror of her dressingtable.

emerald exercise: Patriotic green notebook for student work. **second moiety notices:** Legal notices involving bankruptcy. **L.D.S.:** *Laus Deo Semper* (Praise to the Lord Always), a Jesuit motto that might be appended to student work.

But his long spell of leisure and liberty was drawing to its end. One evening his father came home full of news which kept his tongue busy all through dinner. Stephen had been awaiting his father's return for there had been mutton hash that day and he knew that his father would make him dip his bread in the gravy. But he did not relish the hash for the mention of Clongowes had coated his palate with a scum of disgust.

—I walked bang into him, said Mr Dedalus for the fourth time, just at the corner of the square.

—Then I suppose, said Mrs Dedalus, he will be able to arrange it. I mean about Belvedere.

—Of course he will, said Mr Dedalus. Don't I tell you he's provincial of the order now?

—I never liked the idea of sending him to the christian brothers° myself, said Mrs Dedalus.

—Christian brothers be damned! said Mr Dedalus. Is it with Paddy Stink and Mickey Mud? No, let him stick to the jesuits in God's name since he began with them. They'll be of service to him in after years. Those are the fellows that can get you a position.

—And they're a very rich order, aren't they, Simon?

—Rather. They live well, I tell you. You saw their table at Clongowes. Fed up, by God, like gamecocks.

Mr Dedalus pushed his plate over to Stephen and bade him finish what was on it.

—Now then, Stephen, he said, you must put your shoulder to the wheel, old chap. You've had a fine long holiday.

—O, I'm sure he'll work very hard now, said Mrs Dedalus, especially when he has Maurice with him.

—O, Holy Paul, I forgot about Maurice, said Mr Dedalus. Here, Maurice! Come here, you thickheaded ruffian! Do you know I'm going to send you to a college where they'll teach you to spell c.a.t.: cat. And I'll buy you a nice little penny handkerchief to keep your nose dry. Won't that be grand fun.

Maurice grinned at his father and then at his brother. Mr Dedalus screwed his glass into his eye and stared hard at both his sons. Stephen mumbled his bread without answering his father's gaze.

—By the bye, said Mr Dedalus at length, the rector, or provincial, rather, was telling me that story about you and Father Dolan. You're an impudent thief, he said.

—O, he didn't, Simon!

christian brothers: Another order like the Jesuits, thought to be less prestigious.

—Not he! said Mr Dedalus. But he gave me a great account of the whole affair. We were chatting, you know, and one word borrowed another. And, by the way, who do you think he told me will get that job in the corporation?° But I'll tell you that after. Well, as I was saying, we were chatting away quite friendly and he asked me did our friend here wear glasses still and then he told me the whole story.

—And was he annoyed, Simon?

—Annoyed! Not he! *Manly little chap!* he said.

Mr Dedalus imitated the mincing nasal tone of the provincial.

—Father Dolan and I, when I told them all at dinner about it, Father Dolan and I had a great laugh over it. *You better mind yourself, Father Dolan,* said I, *or young Dedalus will send you up for twice nine.* We had a famous laugh together over it. Ha! Ha! Ha!

Mr Dedalus turned to his wife and interjected in his natural voice:

—Shows you the spirit in which they take the boys there. O, a jesuit for your life, for diplomacy!

He reassumed the provincial's voice and repeated:

—I told them all at dinner about it and Father Dolan and I and all of us we had a hearty laugh together over it. Ha! Ha! Ha!

*

* *

The night of the Whitsuntide° play had come and Stephen from the window of the dressingroom looked out on the small grassplot across which lines of Chinese lanterns were stretched. He watched the visitors come down the steps from the house and pass into the theatre. Stewards° in evening dress, old Belvedereans, loitered in groups about the entrance to the theatre and ushered in the visitors with ceremony. Under the sudden glow of a lantern he could recognise the smiling face of a priest.

The Blessed Sacrament had been removed from the tabernacle and the first benches had been driven back so as to leave the dais of the altar and the space before it free. Against the walls stood companies of barbells and Indian clubs; the dumbbells were piled in one corner: and in the midst of countless hillocks of gymnasium shoes and sweaters and singlets in untidy brown parcels there stood the stout leatherjacketed vaulting horse waiting its turn to be carried up onto the stage. A large bronze shield, tipped with silver, leaned against the panel of the altar

the corporation: The Dublin Corporation, the city's administrative and legislative body. **Whitsuntide:** Week beginning with Pentecost, the seventh Sunday after Easter. **Stewards:** Ushers.

also waiting its turn to be carried up onto the stage and set in the middle of the winning team at the end of the gymnastic display.

Stephen, though in deference to his reputation for essay-writing he had been elected secretary to the gymnasium, had no part in the first section of the programme but in the play which formed the second section he had the chief part, that of a farcical pedagogue. He had been cast for it on account of his stature and grave manners for he was now at the end of his second year at Belvedere and in number two.

A score of the younger boys in white knickers and singlets came pattering down from the stage, through the vestry and into the chapel. The vestry and chapel were peopled with eager masters and boys. The plump bald sergeantmajor was testing with his foot the springboard of the vaulting horse. The lean young man in a long overcoat, who was to give a special display of intricate club swinging, stood near watching with interest, his silvercoated clubs peeping out of his deep sidepockets. The hollow rattle of the wooden dumbbells was heard as another team made ready to go up on the stage: and in another moment the excited prefect was hustling the boys through the vestry like a flock of geese, flapping the wings of his soutane nervously and crying to the laggards to make haste. A little troop of Neapolitan peasants were practising their steps at the end of the chapel, some circling their arms above their heads, some swaying their baskets of paper violets and curtseying. In a dark corner of the chapel at the gospel side of the altar a stout old lady knelt amid her copious black skirts. When she stood up a pinkdressed figure, wearing a curly golden wig and an oldfashioned straw sunbonnet, with black pencilled eyebrows and cheeks delicately rouged and powdered, was discovered. A low murmur of curiosity ran round the chapel at the discovery of this girlish figure. One of the prefects, smiling and nodding his head, approached the dark corner and, having bowed to the stout old lady, said pleasantly:

—Is this a beautiful young lady or a doll that you have here, Mrs Tallon?

Then, bending down to peer at the smiling painted face under the leaf of the bonnet, he exclaimed:

—No! Upon my word I believe it's little Bertie Tallon after all!

Stephen at his post by the window heard the old lady and the priest laugh together and heard the boys' murmur of admiration behind him as they pressed forward to see the little boy who had to dance the sunbonnet dance by himself. A movement of impatience escaped him. He let the edge of the blind fall and, stepping down from the bench on which he had been standing, walked out of the chapel.

He passed out of the schoolhouse and halted under the shed that flanked the garden. From the theatre opposite came the muffled noise of the audience and sudden brazen clashes of the soldiers' band. The light spread upwards from the glass roof making the theatre seem a festive ark, anchored amid the hulks of houses, her frail cables of lanterns looping her to her moorings. A sidedoor of the theatre opened suddenly and a shaft of light flew across the grassplots. A sudden burst of music issued from the ark, the prelude of a waltz: and when the sidedoor closed again the listener could hear the faint rhythm of the music. The sentiment of the opening bars, their languor and supple movement, evoked the incommunicable emotion which had been the cause of all his day's unrest and of his impatient movement of a moment before. His unrest issued from him like a wave of sound: and on the tide of flowing music the ark was journeying, trailing her cables of lanterns in her wake. Then a noise like dwarf artillery broke the movement. It was the clapping that greeted the entry of the dumbbell team on the stage.

At the far end of the shed near the street a speck of pink light showed in the darkness and as he walked towards it he became aware of a faint aromatic odour. Two boys were standing in the shelter of a doorway, smoking, and before he reached them he had recognised Heron by his voice.

—Here comes the noble Dedalus! cried a high throaty voice. Welcome to our trusty friend!

This welcome ended in a soft peal of mirthless laughter as Heron salaamed and then began to poke the ground with his cane.

—Here I am, said Stephen, halting and glancing from Heron to his friend.

The latter was a stranger to him but in the darkness, by the aid of the glowing cigarettetips, he could make out a pale dandyish face, over which a smile was travelling slowly, a tall overcoated figure and a hard hat. Heron did not trouble himself about an introduction but said instead:

—I was just telling my friend Wallis what a lark it would be tonight if you took off the rector in the part of the schoolmaster. It would be a ripping good joke.

Heron made a poor attempt to imitate for his friend Wallis the rector's pedantic bass and then, laughing at his failure, asked Stephen to do it.

—Go on, Dedalus, he urged, you can take him off rippingly. *He that will not hear the churcha let him be to theea as the heathena and the publicana.*

The imitation was prevented by a mild expression of anger from

Wallis in whose mouthpiece the cigarette had become too tightly wedged.

—Damn this blankety blank holder, he said, taking it from his mouth and smiling and frowning upon it tolerantly. It's always getting stuck like that. Do you use a holder?

—I don't smoke, answered Stephen.

—No, said Heron, Dedalus is a model youth. He doesn't smoke and he doesn't go to bazaars and he doesn't flirt and he doesn't damn anything or damn all.

Stephen shook his head and smiled in his rival's flushed and mobile face, beaked like a bird's. He had often thought it strange that Vincent Heron had a bird's face as well as a bird's name. A shock of pale hair lay on the forehead like a ruffled crest: the forehead was narrow and bony and a thin hooked nose stood out between the closeset prominent eyes which were light and inexpressive. The rivals were school friends. They sat together in class, knelt together in the chapel, talked together after beads° over their lunches. As the fellows in number one were undistinguished dullards Stephen and Heron had been during the year the virtual heads of the school. It was they who went up to the rector together to ask for a free day or to get a fellow off.

—O by the way, said Heron suddenly, I saw your governor going in.

The smile waned on Stephen's face. Any allusion made to his father by a fellow or by a master put his calm to rout in a moment. He waited in timorous silence to hear what Heron might say next. Heron, however, nudged him expressively with his elbow and said:

—You're a sly dog, Dedalus!

—Why so? said Stephen.

—You'd think butter wouldn't melt in your mouth, said Heron. But I'm afraid you're a sly dog.

—Might I ask you what you are talking about? said Stephen urbanely.

—Indeed you might, answered Heron. We saw her, Wallis, didn't we? And deucedly pretty she is too. And so inquisitive! *And what part does Stephen take, Mr Dedalus? And will Stephen not sing, Mr Dedalus?* Your governor was staring at her through that eyeglass of his for all he was worth so that I think the old man has found you out too. I wouldn't care a bit, by Jove. She's ripping, isn't she, Wallis?

—Not half bad, answered Wallis quietly as he placed his holder once more in a corner of his mouth.

beads: Saying of the rosary.

A shaft of momentary anger flew through Stephen's mind at these indelicate allusions in the hearing of a stranger. For him there was nothing amusing in a girl's interest and regard. All day he had thought of nothing but their leavetaking on the steps of the tram at Harold's Cross, the stream of moody emotions it had made to course through him, and the poem he had written about it. All day he had imagined a new meeting with her for he knew that she was to come to the play. The old restless moodiness had again filled his breast as it had done on the night of the party but had not found an outlet in verse. The growth and knowledge of two years of boyhood stood between then and now, forbidding such an outlet: and all day the stream of gloomy tenderness within him had started forth and returned upon itself in dark courses and eddies, wearying him in the end until the pleasantry of the prefect and the painted little boy had drawn from him a movement of impatience.

—So you may as well admit, Heron went on, that we've fairly found you out this time. You can't play the saint on me any more, that's one sure five.

A soft peal of mirthless laughter escaped from his lips and, bending down as before, he struck Stephen lightly across the calf of the leg with his cane, as if in jesting reproof.

Stephen's movement of anger had already passed. He was neither flattered nor confused but simply wished the banter to end. He scarcely resented what had seemed to him at first a silly indelicateness for he knew that the adventure in his mind stood in no danger from their words: and his face mirrored his rival's false smile.

—Admit! repeated Heron, striking him again with his cane across the calf of the leg.

The stroke was playful but not so lightly given as the first one had been. Stephen felt the skin tingle and glow slightly and almost painlessly; and bowing submissively, as if to meet his companion's jesting mood, began to recite the *Confiteor.*° The episode ended well for both Heron and Wallis laughed indulgently at the irreverence.

The confession came only from Stephen's lips and while they spoke the words, a sudden memory had carried him to another scene called up, as if by magic, at the moment when he had noted the faint cruel dimples at the corners of Heron's smiling lips and had felt the familiar stroke of the cane against his calf and heard the familiar word of admonition:

Confiteor: Prayer in preparation for confession.

—Admit!

It was towards the close of his first term in the college when he was in number six. His sensitive nature was still smarting under the lashes of an undivined and squalid way of life. His soul was still disquieted and cast down by the dull phenomenon of Dublin. He had emerged from a two years' spell of revery to find himself in the midst of a new scene, every event and figure of which affected him intimately, disheartened him or allured him and, whether alluring or disheartening, filled him always with unrest and bitter thoughts. All the leisure that his school life left him was passed in the company of subversive writers whose gibes and violence of speech set up a ferment in his brain before they passed out of it into his crude writings.

The essay was for him the chief labour of his week and every Tuesday, as he marched from home to the school, he read his fate in the incidents of the way, pitting himself against some figure ahead of him and quickening his pace to outstrip it before a certain goal was reached or planting his steps scrupulously in the spaces of the patchwork of the footpath and telling himself that he would be first and not first in the weekly essay.

On a certain Tuesday the course of his triumphs was rudely broken. Mr Tate, the English master, pointed his finger at him and said bluntly:

—This fellow has heresy in his essay.

A hush fell on the class. Mr Tate did not break it but dug with his hand between his crossed thighs while his heavily starched linen creaked about his neck and wrists. Stephen did not look up. It was a raw spring morning and his eyes were still smarting and weak. He was conscious of failure and of detection, of the squalor of his own mind and home, and felt against his neck the raw edge of his turned and jagged collar.

A short loud laugh from Mr Tate set the class more at ease.

—Perhaps you didn't know that, he said.

—Where? asked Stephen.

Mr Tate withdrew his delving hand and spread out the essay.

—Here. It's about the Creator and the soul. Rrm . . . rrm . . . rrm. . . . Ah! *without a possibility of ever approaching nearer*. That's heresy.

Stephen murmured:

—I meant *without a possibility of ever reaching*.

It was a submission and Mr Tate, appeased, folded up the essay and passed it across to him, saying:

—O . . . Ah! *ever reaching*. That's another story.

But the class was not so soon appeased. Though nobody spoke to him of the affair after class he could feel about him a vague general malignant joy.

A few nights after this public chiding he was walking with a letter along the Drumcondra Road when he heard a voice cry:

—Halt!

He turned and saw three boys of his own class coming towards him in the dusk. It was Heron who had called out and, as he marched forward between his two attendants, he cleft the air before him with a thin cane, in time to their steps. Boland, his friend, marched beside him, a large grin on his face, while Nash came on a few steps behind, blowing from the pace and wagging his great red head.

As soon as the boys had turned into Clonliffe Road together they began to speak about books and writers, saying what books they were reading and how many books there were in their fathers' bookcases at home. Stephen listened to them in some wonderment for Boland was the dunce and Nash the idler of the class. In fact after some talk about their favourite writers Nash declared for Captain Marryat who, he said, was the greatest writer.

—Fudge! said Heron. Ask Dedalus. Who is the greatest writer, Dedalus?

Stephen noted the mockery in the question and said:

—Of prose, do you mean?

—Yes.

—Newman, I think.

—Is it Cardinal Newman? asked Boland.

—Yes, answered Stephen.

The grin broadened on Nash's freckled face as he turned to Stephen and said:

—And do you like Cardinal Newman, Dedalus?

—O many say that Newman has the best prose style, Heron said to the other two in explanation. Of course, he's not a poet.

—And who is the best poet, Heron? asked Boland.

—Lord Tennyson, of course, answered Heron.

—O, yes, Lord Tennyson, said Nash. We have all his poetry at home in a book.

At this Stephen forgot the silent vows he had been making and burst out:

—Tennyson a poet! Why, he's only a rhymester!

—O, get out! said Heron. Everyone knows that Tennyson is the greatest poet.

—And who do you think is the greatest poet? asked Boland, nudging his neighbour.

—Byron, of course, answered Stephen.

Heron gave the lead and all three joined in a scornful laugh.

—What are you laughing at? asked Stephen.

—You, said Heron. Byron the greatest poet! He's only a poet for uneducated people.

—He must be a fine poet! said Boland.

—You may keep your mouth shut, said Stephen, turning on him boldly. All you know about poetry is what you wrote up on the slates in the yard° and were going to be sent to the loft° for.

Boland, in fact, was said to have written on the slates in the yard a couplet about a classmate of his who often rode home from the college on a pony:

As Tyson was riding into Jerusalem
He fell and hurt his Alec Kafoozelum.

This thrust put the two lieutenants to silence but Heron went on:

—In any case Byron was a heretic and immoral too.

—I don't care what he was, cried Stephen hotly.

—You don't care whether he was a heretic or not? said Nash.

—What do you know about it? shouted Stephen. You never read a line of anything in your life except a trans or Boland either.

—I know that Byron was a bad man, said Boland.

—Here, catch hold of this heretic, Heron called out.

In a moment Stephen was a prisoner.

—Tate made you buck up the other day, Heron went on, about the heresy in your essay.

—I'll tell him tomorrow, said Boland.

—Will you? said Stephen. You'd be afraid to open your lips.

—Afraid?

—Ay. Afraid of your life.

—Behave yourself! cried Heron, cutting at Stephen's legs with his cane.

It was the signal for their onset. Nash pinioned his arms behind while Boland seized a long cabbage stump which was lying in the gutter. Struggling and kicking under the cuts of the cane and the blows of the knotty stump Stephen was borne back against a barbed wire fence.

slates in the yard: On the walls of the urinal. **the loft:** Place for punishment at Clongowes.

—Admit that Byron was no good.

—No.

—Admit.

—No.

—Admit.

—No. No.

At last after a fury of plunges he wrenched himself free. His tormentors set off towards Jones's Road, laughing and jeering at him, while he, torn and flushed and panting, stumbled after them half blinded with tears, clenching his fists madly and sobbing.

While he was still repeating the *Confiteor* amid the indulgent laughter of his hearers and while the scenes of that malignant episode were still passing sharply and swiftly before his mind he wondered why he bore no malice now to those who had tormented him. He had not forgotten a whit of their cowardice and cruelty but the memory of it called forth no anger from him. All the descriptions of fierce love and hatred which he had met in books had seemed to him therefore unreal. Even that night as he stumbled homewards along Jones's Road he had felt that some power was divesting him of that suddenwoven anger as easily as a fruit is divested of its soft ripe peel.

He remained standing with his two companions at the end of the shed, listening idly to their talk or to the bursts of applause in the theatre. She was sitting there among the others perhaps waiting for him to appear. He tried to recall her appearance but could not. He could remember only that she had worn a shawl about her head like a cowl and that her dark eyes had invited and unnerved him. He wondered had he been in her thoughts as she had been in his. Then in the dark and unseen by the other two he rested the tips of the fingers of one hand upon the palm of the other hand, scarcely touching it and yet pressing upon it lightly. But the pressure of her fingers had been lighter and steadier: and suddenly the memory of their touch traversed his brain and body like an invisible warm wave.

A boy came towards them, running along under the shed. He was excited and breathless.

—O, Dedalus, he cried, Doyle is in a great bake° about you. You're to go in at once and get dressed for the play. Hurry up, you better.

—He's coming now, said Heron to the messenger with a haughty drawl, when he wants to.

The boy turned to Heron and repeated:

in a great bake: Angry or agitated.

—But Doyle is in an awful bake.

—Will you tell Doyle with my best compliments that I damned his eyes? answered Heron.

—Well, I must go now, said Stephen, who cared little for such points of honour.

—I wouldn't, said Heron, damn me if I would. That's no way to send for one of the senior boys. In a bake, indeed! I think it's quite enough that you're taking a part in his bally old play.

This spirit of quarrelsome comradeship which he had observed lately in his rival had not seduced Stephen from his habits of quiet obedience. He mistrusted the turbulence and doubted the sincerity of such comradeship which seemed to him a sorry anticipation of manhood. The question of honour here raised was, like all such questions, trivial to him. While his mind had been pursuing its intangible phantoms and turning back in irresoluteness from such pursuit he had heard about him the constant voices of his father and of his masters, urging him to be a gentleman above all things and urging him to be a good catholic above all things. These voices had now come to be hollowsounding in his ears. When the gymnasium had been opened he had heard another voice urging him to be strong and manly and healthy and when the movement towards national revival had begun to be felt in the college yet another voice had bidden him be true to his country and help to raise up her fallen language and tradition. In the profane world, as he foresaw, a worldly voice would bid him raise up his father's fallen state by his labours and, meanwhile, the voice of his schoolcomrades urged him to be a decent fellow, to shield others from blame or to beg them off and to do his best to get free days for the school. And it was the din of all these hollowsounding voices that made him halt irresolutely in the pursuit of phantoms. He gave them ear only for a time but he was happy only when he was far from them, beyond their call, alone or in the company of phantasmal comrades.

In the vestry a plump freshfaced jesuit and an elderly man, in shabby blue clothes, were dabbling in a case of paints and chalks. The boys who had been painted walked about or stood still awkwardly, touching their faces in a gingerly fashion with their furtive fingertips. In the middle of the vestry a young jesuit, who was then on a visit to the college, stood rocking himself rhythmically from the tips of his toes to his heels and back again, his hands thrust well forward into his two sidepockets. His small head set off with glossy red curls and his newly shaven face agreed well with the spotless decency of his soutane and with his spotless shoes.

As he watched this swaying form and tried to read for himself the legend of the priest's mocking smile there came into Stephen's memory a saying which he had heard from his father before he had been sent to Clongowes, that you could always tell a jesuit by the style of his clothes. At the same moment he thought he saw a likeness between his father's mind and that of this smiling welldressed priest: and he was aware of some desecration of the priest's office or of the vestry itself, whose silence was now routed by loud talk and joking and its air pungent with the smells of the gasjets and the grease.

While his forehead was being wrinkled and his jaws painted black and blue by the elderly man he listened distractedly to the voice of the plump young jesuit which bade him speak up and make his points clearly. He could hear the band playing *The Lily of Killarney* and knew that in a few moments the curtain would go up. He felt no stage fright but the thought of the part he had to play humiliated him. A remembrance of some of his lines made a sudden flush rise to his painted cheeks. He saw her serious alluring eyes watching him from among the audience and their image at once swept away his scruples, leaving his will compact. Another nature seemed to have been lent him: the infection of the excitement and youth about him entered into and transformed his moody mistrustfulness. For one rare moment he seemed to be clothed in the real apparel of boyhood: and, as he stood in the wings among the other players, he shared the common mirth amid which the drop scene was hauled upwards by two ablebodied priests with violent jerks and all awry.

A few moments after he found himself on the stage amid the garish gas and the dim scenery, acting before the innumerable faces of the void. It surprised him to see that the play which he had known at rehearsals for a disjointed lifeless thing had suddenly assumed a life of its own. It seemed now to play itself, he and his fellow actors aiding it with their parts. When the curtain fell on the last scene he heard the void filled with applause and, through a rift in the side scene, saw the simple body before which he had acted magically deformed, the void of faces breaking at all points and falling asunder into busy groups.

He left the stage quickly and rid himself of his mummery and passed out through the chapel into the college garden. Now that the play was over his nerves cried for some further adventure. He hurried onwards as if to overtake it. The doors of the theatre were all open and the audience had emptied out. On the lines which he had fancied the moorings of an ark a few lanterns swung in the night breeze, flickering cheerlessly. He mounted the steps from the garden in haste, eager that some prey should not elude him, and forced his way through the crowd in the hall and past the two jesuits who stood watching the exodus and bowing and shaking hands with the visitors. He pushed onward nervously, feigning a still greater haste and faintly conscious of the smiles and stares and nudges which his powdered head left in its wake.

When he came out on the steps he saw his family waiting for him at the first lamp. In a glance he noted that every figure of the group was familiar and ran down the steps angrily.

—I have to leave a message down in George's Street, he said to his father quickly. I'll be home after you.

Without waiting for his father's questions he ran across the road and began to walk at breakneck speed down the hill. He hardly knew where he was walking. Pride and hope and desire like crushed herbs in his heart sent up vapours of maddening incense before the eyes of his mind. He strode down the hill amid the tumult of suddenrisen vapours of wounded pride and fallen hope and baffled desire. They streamed upwards before his anguished eyes in dense and maddening fumes and passed away above him till at last the air was clear and cold again.

A film still veiled his eyes but they burned no longer. A power, akin to that which had often made anger or resentment fall from him, brought his steps to rest. He stood still and gazed up at the sombre porch of the morgue and from that to the dark cobbled laneway at its side. He saw the word *Lotts* on the wall of the lane and breathed slowly the rank heavy air.

—That is horse piss and rotted straw, he thought. It is a good odour to breathe. It will calm my heart. My heart is quite calm now. I will go back.

*

* *

Stephen was once again seated beside his father in the corner of a railway carriage at Kingsbridge. He was travelling with his father by the night mail to Cork. As the train steamed out of the station he recalled his childish wonder of years before and every event of his first day at Clongowes. But he felt no wonder now. He saw the darkening lands slipping past him, the silent telegraphpoles passing his window swiftly every four seconds, the little glimmering stations, manned by a few silent sentries, flung by the mail behind her and twinkling for a moment in the darkness like fiery grains flung backwards by a runner.

He listened without sympathy to his father's evocation of Cork and of scenes of his youth, a tale broken by sighs or draughts from his pocketflask whenever the image of some dead friend appeared in it or whenever the evoker remembered suddenly the purpose of his actual visit. Stephen heard but could feel no pity. The images of the dead were all strange to him save that of uncle Charles, an image which had lately been fading out of memory. He knew, however, that his father's property was going to be sold by auction and in the manner of his own dispossession he felt the world give the lie rudely to his phantasy.

At Maryborough he fell asleep. When he awoke the train had passed out of Mallow and his father was stretched asleep on the other seat. The cold light of the dawn lay over the country, over the unpeopled fields and the closed cottages. The terror of sleep fascinated his mind as he watched the silent country or heard from time to time his father's deep breath or sudden sleepy movement. The neighbourhood of unseen sleepers filled him with strange dread as though they could harm him; and he prayed that the day might come quickly. His prayer, addressed neither to God nor saint, began with a shiver, as the chilly morning breeze crept through the chink of the carriage door to his feet, and ended in a trail of foolish words which he made to fit the insistent rhythm of the train: and silently, at intervals of four seconds, the telegraphpoles held the galloping notes of the music between punctual bars. This furious music allayed his dread and, leaning against the windowledge, he let his eyelids close again.

They drove in a jingle° across Cork while it was still early morning and Stephen finished his sleep in a bedroom of the Victoria Hotel. The bright warm sunlight was streaming through the window and he could hear the din of traffic. His father was standing before the dressingtable, examining his hair and face and moustache with great care, craning his neck across the waterjug and drawing it back sideways to see the better. While he did so he sang softly to himself with quaint accent and phrasing:

'Tis youth and folly
Makes young men marry,
So here, my love, I'll
   No longer stay.
What can't be cured, sure,
Must be injured, sure,
   So I'll go
   To Amerikay.

My love she's handsome,
My love she's bonny:

jingle: A horse-drawn car.

She's like good whisky
When it is new;
But when 'tis old
And growing cold
It fades and dies like
The mountain dew.

The consciousness of the warm sunny city outside his window and the tender tremors with which his father's voice festooned the strange sadhappy air drove off all the mists of the night's illhumour from Stephen's brain. He got up quickly to dress and, when the song had ended, said:

—That's much prettier than any of your other *come-all-yous.*°

—Do you think so? asked Mr Dedalus.

—I like it, said Stephen.

—It's a pretty old air, said Mr Dedalus, twirling the points of his moustache. Ah, but you should have heard Mick Lacy sing it! Poor Mick Lacy! He had little turns for it, gracenotes he used to put in that I haven't got. That was the boy could sing a *come-all-you,* if you like.

Mr Dedalus had ordered drisheens° for breakfast and during the meal he crossexamined the waiter for local news. For the most part they spoke at crosspurposes when a name was mentioned, the waiter having in mind the present holder and Mr Dedalus his father or perhaps his grandfather.

—Well, I hope they haven't moved the Queen's College anyhow, said Mr Dedalus, for I want to show it to this youngster of mine.

Along the Mardyke the trees were in bloom. They entered the grounds of the college and were led by the garrulous porter across the quadrangle. But their progress across the gravel was brought to a halt after every dozen or so paces by some reply of the porter's.

—Ah, do you tell me so? And is poor Pottlebelly dead?

—Yes, sir. Dead, sir.

During these halts Stephen stood awkwardly behind the two men, weary of the subject and waiting restlessly for the slow march to begin again. By the time they had crossed the quadrangle his restlessness had risen to fever. He wondered how his father, whom he knew for a shrewd suspicious man, could be duped by the servile manners of the porter: and the lively southern speech which had entertained him all the morning now irritated his ears.

come-all-yous: Street ballads. **drisheens:** A sort of sweetbread, made with sheep's intestines.

They passed into the anatomy theatre where Mr Dedalus, the porter aiding him, searched the desks for his initials. Stephen remained in the background, depressed more than ever by the darkness and silence of the theatre and by the air it wore of jaded and formal study. On the desk before him he read the word *Fœtus* cut several times in the dark stained wood. The sudden legend startled his blood: he seemed to feel the absent students of the college about him and to shrink from their company. A vision of their life, which his father's words had been powerless to evoke, sprang up before him out of the word cut in the desk. A broadshouldered student with a moustache was cutting in the letters with a jackknife, seriously. Other students stood or sat near him laughing at his handiwork. One jogged his elbow. The big student turned on him, frowning. He was dressed in loose grey clothes and had tan boots.

Stephen's name was called. He hurried down the steps of the theatre so as to be as far away from the vision as he could be and, peering closely at his father's initials, hid his flushed face.

But the word and the vision capered before his eyes as he walked back across the quadrangle and towards the college gate. It shocked him to find in the outer world a trace of what he had deemed till then a brutish and individual malady of his own mind. His recent monstrous reveries came thronging into his memory. They too had sprung up before him, suddenly and furiously, out of mere words. He had soon given in to them and allowed them to sweep across and abase his intellect, wondering always where they came from, from what den of monstrous images, and always weak and humble towards others, restless and sickened of himself when they had swept over him.

—Ay, bedad! And there's the Groceries sure enough! cried Mr Dedalus. You often heard me speak of the Groceries, didn't you, Stephen. Many's the time we went down there when our names had been marked, a crowd of us, Harry Peard and little Jack Mountain and Bob Dyas and Maurice Moriarty, the Frenchman, and Tom O'Grady and Mick Lacy that I told you of this morning and Joe Corbet and poor little goodhearted Johnny Keevers of the Tantiles.

The leaves of the trees along the Mardyke were astir and whispering in the sunlight. A team of cricketers passed, agile young men in flannels and blazers, one of them carrying the long green wicketbag. In a quiet bystreet a German band of five players in faded uniforms and with battered brass instruments was playing to an audience of street arabs° and leisurely messenger boys. A maid in a white cap and apron was watering

street arabs: Poor or Gypsy children.

a box of plants on a sill which shone like a slab of limestone in the warm glare. From another window open to the air came the sound of a piano, scale after scale rising into the treble.

Stephen walked on at his father's side, listening to stories he had heard before, hearing again the names of the scattered and dead revellers who had been the companions of his father's youth. And a faint sickness sighed in his heart. He recalled his own equivocal position in Belvedere, a free boy,° a leader afraid of his own authority, proud and sensitive and suspicious, battling against the squalor of his life and against the riot of his mind. The letters cut in the stained wood of the desk stared upon him, mocking his bodily weakness and futile enthusiasms and making him loathe himself for his own mad and filthy orgies. The spittle in his throat grew bitter and foul to swallow and the faint sickness climbed to his brain so that for a moment he closed his eyes and walked on in darkness.

He could still hear his father's voice.

—When you kick out for yourself, Stephen—as I daresay you will one of those days—remember, whatever you do, to mix with gentlemen. When I was a young fellow I tell you I enjoyed myself. I mixed with fine decent fellows. Everyone of us could do something. One fellow had a good voice, another fellow was a good actor, another could sing a good comic song, another was a good oarsman or a good racket-player, another could tell a good story and so on. We kept the ball rolling anyhow and enjoyed ourselves and saw a bit of life and we were none the worse of it either. But we were all gentlemen, Stephen—at least I hope we were—and bloody good honest Irishmen too. That's the kind of fellows I want you to associate with, fellows of the right kidney. I'm talking to you as a friend, Stephen. I don't believe in playing the stern father. I don't believe a son should be afraid of his father. No, I treat you as your grandfather treated me when I was a young chap. We were more like brothers than father and son. I'll never forget the first day he caught me smoking. I was standing at the end of the South Terrace one day with some maneens° like myself and sure we thought we were grand fellows because we had pipes stuck in the corners of our mouths. Suddenly the governor passed. He didn't say a word or stop even. But the next day, Sunday, we were out for a walk together and when we were coming home he took out his cigar case and said: *By the bye, Simon, I didn't know you smoked:* or something like that. Of course I tried to carry it off as best I could. *If you want a good*

free boy: Boy on a scholarship. **maneens:** Insulting term (little men).

smoke, he said, *try one of these cigars. An American captain made me a present of them last night in Queenstown.*

Stephen heard his father's voice break into a laugh which was almost a sob.

—He was the handsomest man in Cork at that time, by God he was! The women used to stand to look after him in the street.

He heard the sob passing loudly down his father's throat and opened his eyes with a nervous impulse. The sunlight breaking suddenly on his sight turned the sky and clouds into a fantastic world of sombre masses with lakelike spaces of dark rosy light. His very brain was sick and powerless. He could scarcely interpret the letters of the signboards of the shops. By his monstrous way of life he seemed to have put himself beyond the limits of reality. Nothing moved him or spoke to him from the real world unless he heard in it an echo of the infuriated cries within him. He could respond to no earthly or human appeal, dumb and insensible to the call of summer and gladness and companionship, wearied and dejected by his father's voice. He could scarcely recognise as his his own thoughts: and repeated slowly to himself:

—I am Stephen Dedalus. I am walking beside my father whose name is Simon Dedalus. We are in Cork, in Ireland. Cork is a city. Our room is in the Victoria Hotel. Victoria and Stephen and Simon. Simon and Stephen and Victoria. Names. labels

The memory of his childhood suddenly grew dim. He tried to call forth some of its vivid moments but could not. He recalled only names: Dante, Parnell, Clane, Clongowes. A little boy had been taught geography by an old woman who kept two brushes in her wardrobe. Then he had been sent away from home to a college. In the college he had made his first communion and eaten slim jim° out of his cricketcap and watched the firelight leaping and dancing on the wall of a little bedroom in the infirmary and dreamed of being dead, of mass being said for him by the rector in a black and gold cope, of being buried then in the little graveyard of the community off the main avenue of limes. But he had not died then. Parnell had died. There had been no mass for the dead in the chapel and no procession. He had not died but he had faded out like a film in the sun. He had been lost or had wandered out of existence for he no longer existed. How strange to think of him passing out of existence in such a way, not by death but by fading out in the sun or by being lost and forgotten somewhere in the universe! It was strange to see his small body appear again for a moment: a little boy in a grey

slim jim: A long jelly candy.

belted suit. His hands were in his sidepockets and his trousers were tucked in at the knees by elastic bands.

On the evening of the day on which the property was sold Stephen followed his father meekly about the city from bar to bar. To the sellers in the market, to the barmen and barmaids, to the beggars who importuned him for a lob° Mr Dedalus told the same tale, that he was an old Corkonian, that he had been trying for thirty years to get rid of his Cork accent up in Dublin and that Peter Pickackafax beside him was his eldest son but that he was only a Dublin jackeen.°

They had set out early in the morning from Newcombe's coffeehouse where Mr Dedalus' cup had rattled noisily against its saucer and Stephen had tried to cover that shameful sign of his father's drinking-bout of the night before by moving his chair and coughing. One humiliation had succeeded another: the false smiles of the market sellers, the curvettings and oglings of the barmaids with whom his father flirted, the compliments and encouraging words of his father's friends. They had told him that he had a great look of his grandfather and Mr Dedalus had agreed that he was an ugly likeness. They had unearthed traces of a Cork accent in his speech and made him admit that the Lee was a much finer river than the Liffey. One of them in order to put his Latin to the proof had made him translate short passages from Dilectus and asked him whether it was correct to say: *Tempora mutantur nos et mutamur in illis* or *Tempora mutantur et nos mutamur in illis.*° Another, a brisk old man, whom Mr Dedalus called Johnny Cashman, had covered him with confusion by asking him to say which were prettier, the Dublin girls or the Cork girls.

—He's not that way built, said Mr Dedalus. Leave him alone. He's a levelheaded thinking boy who doesn't bother his head about that kind of nonsense.

—Then he's not his father's son, said the little old man.

—I don't know, I'm sure, said Mr Dedalus, smiling complacently.

—Your father, said the little old man to Stephen, was the boldest flirt in the city of Cork in his day. Do you know that?

Stephen looked down and studied the tiled floor of the bar into which they had drifted.

—Now don't be putting ideas into his head, said Mr Dedalus. Leave him to his Maker.

lob: Some amount of money. **jackeen:** Arrogant, lower-class person. ***Tempora mutantur nos . . . illis:*** Circumstances change and we change in them (in the second version, "with them"); both are grammatically correct, the second metrically correct.

—Yerra, sure I wouldn't put any ideas into his head. I'm old enough to be his grandfather. And I am a grandfather, said the little old man to Stephen. Do you know that?

—Are you? asked Stephen.

—Bedad I am, said the little old man. I have two bouncing grandchildren out at Sunday's Well. Now then! What age do you think I am? And I remember seeing your grandfather in his red coat riding out to hounds. That was before you were born.

—Ay or thought of, said Mr Dedalus.

—Bedad I did! repeated the little old man. And more than that, I can remember even your greatgrandfather, old John Stephen Dedalus, and a fierce old fireeater he was. Now then! There's a memory for you!

—That's three generations—four generations, said another of the company. Why, Johnny Cashman, you must be nearing the century.

—Well, I'll tell you the truth, said the little old man. I'm just twenty-seven years of age.

—We're as old as we feel, Johnny, said Mr Dedalus. And just finish what you have there and we'll have another. Here, Tim or Tom or whatever your name is, give us the same again here. By God, I don't feel more than eighteen myself. There's that son of mine there not half my age and I'm a better man than he is any day of the week.

—Draw it mild now, Dedalus. I think it's time for you to take a back seat, said the gentleman who had spoken before.

—No, by God! asserted Mr Dedalus. I'll sing a tenor song against him or I'll vault a fivebarred gate against him or I'll run with him after the hounds across the country as I did thirty years ago along with the Kerry Boy and the best man for it.

—But he'll beat you here, said the little old man, tapping his forehead and raising his glass to drain it.

—Well, I hope he'll be as good a man as his father. That's all I can say, said Mr Dedalus.

—If he is, he'll do, said the little old man.

—And thanks be to God, Johnny, said Mr Dedalus, that we lived so long and did so little harm.

—But did so much good, Simon, said the little old man gravely. Thanks be to God we lived so long and did so much good.

Stephen watched the three glasses being raised from the counter as his father and his two cronies drank to the memory of their past. An abyss of fortune or of temperament sundered him from them. His mind seemed older than theirs: it shone coldly on their strifes and happiness and regrets like a moon upon a younger earth. No life or youth stirred in him as it had stirred in them. He had known neither the pleasure of companionship with others nor the vigour of rude male health nor filial piety. Nothing stirred within his soul but a cold and cruel and loveless lust. His childhood was dead or lost and with it his soul capable of simple joys: and he was drifting amid life like the barren shell of the moon.

Art thou pale for weariness
Of climbing heaven and gazing on the earth,
Wandering companionless . . . ?

He repeated to himself the lines of Shelley's fragment. Its alternation of sad human ineffectualness with vast inhuman cycles of activity chilled him: and he forgot his own human and ineffectual grieving.

*

* *

Stephen's mother and his brother and one of his cousins waited at the corner of quiet Foster Place while he and his father went up the steps and along the colonnade where the highland sentry was parading. When they had passed into the great hall and stood at the counter Stephen drew forth his orders on the governor of the bank of Ireland for thirty and three pounds; and these sums, the moneys of his exhibition° and essay prize, were paid over to him rapidly by the teller in notes and in coin respectively. He bestowed them in his pockets with feigned composure and suffered the friendly teller, to whom his father chatted, to take his hand across the broad counter and wish him a brilliant career in after life. He was impatient of their voices and could not keep his feet at rest. But the teller still deferred the serving of others to say that he was living in changed times and that there was nothing like giving a boy the best education that money could buy. Mr Dedalus lingered in the hall gazing about him and up at the roof and telling Stephen, who urged him to come out, that they were standing in the house of commons of the old Irish parliament.

God help us! he said piously, to think of the men of those times, Stephen, Hely Hutchinson and Flood and Henry Grattan and Charles Kendal Bushe, and the noblemen we have now, leaders of the Irish people at home and abroad. Why, by God, they wouldn't be seen dead in a tenacre field with them. No, Stephen, old chap, I'm sorry to say

exhibition: Outstanding performance in one of the annual national academic examinations.

that they are only as I roved out one fine May morning in the merry month of sweet July.

A keen October wind was blowing round the bank. The three figures standing at the edge of the muddy path had pinched cheeks and watery eyes. Stephen looked at his thinly clad mother and remembered that a few days before he had seen a mantle priced at twenty guineas in the window of Barnardo's.

—Well that's done, said Mr Dedalus.

—We had better go to dinner, said Stephen. Where?

—Dinner? said Mr Dedalus. Well, I suppose we had better, what?

—Some place that's not too dear, said Mrs Dedalus.

—Underdone's?

—Yes. Some quiet place.

—Come along, said Stephen quickly. It doesn't matter about the dearness.

He walked on before them with short nervous steps, smiling. They tried to keep up with him, smiling also at his eagerness.

—Take it easy like a good young fellow, said his father. We're not out for the half mile, are we?

For a swift season of merrymaking the money of his prizes ran through Stephen's fingers. Great parcels of groceries and delicacies and dried fruits arrived from the city. Every day he drew up a bill of fare for the family and every night led a party of three or four to the theatre to see *Ingomar* or *The Lady of Lyons*. In his coat pockets he carried squares of Vienna chocolate for his guests while his trousers' pockets bulged with masses of silver and copper coins. He bought presents for everyone, overhauled his room, wrote out resolutions, marshalled his books up and down their shelves, pored upon all kinds of price lists, drew up a form of commonwealth for the household by which every member of it held some office, opened a loan bank for his family and pressed loans on willing borrowers so that he might have the pleasure of making out receipts and reckoning the interests on the sums lent. When he could do no more he drove up and down the city in trams. Then the season of pleasure came to an end. The pot of pink enamel paint gave out and the wainscot of his bedroom remained with its unfinished and illplastered coat.

His household returned to its usual way of life. His mother had no further occasion to upbraid him for squandering his money. He too returned to his old life at school and all his novel enterprises fell to pieces. The commonwealth fell, the loan bank closed its coffers and its books on a sensible loss, the rules of life which he had drawn about himself fell into desuetude.

How foolish his aim had been! He had tried to build a breakwater of order and elegance against the sordid tide of life without him and to dam up, by rules of conduct and active interests and new filial relations, the powerful recurrence of the tides within him. Useless. From without as from within the water had flowed over his barriers: their tides began once more to jostle fiercely above the crumbled mole.

He saw clearly too his own futile isolation. He had not gone one step nearer the lives he had sought to approach nor bridged the restless shame and rancour that divided him from father and mother and brother and sister. He felt that he was hardly of the one blood with them but stood to them rather in the mystical kinship of fosterage, fosterchild and fosterbrother.

He burned to appease the fierce longings of his heart before which everything else was idle and alien. He cared little that he was in mortal sin, that his life had grown to be a tissue of subterfuges and falsehood. Beside the savage desire within him to realise the enormities which he brooded on nothing was sacred. He bore cynically with the shameful details of his secret riots in which he exulted to defile with patience whatever image had attracted his eyes. By day and by night he moved among distorted images of the outer world. A figure that had seemed to him by day demure and innocent came towards him by night through the winding darkness of sleep, her face transfigured by a lecherous cunning, her eyes bright with brutish joy. Only the morning pained him with its dim memory of dark orgiastic riot, its keen and humiliating sense of transgression.

He returned to his wanderings. The veiled autumnal evenings led him from street to street as they had led him years before along the quiet avenues of Blackrock. But no vision of trim front gardens or of kindly lights in the windows poured a tender influence upon him now. Only at times, in the pauses of his desire, when the luxury that was wasting him gave room to a softer languor, the image of Mercedes traversed the background of his memory. He saw again the small white house and the garden of rosebushes on the road that led to the mountains and he remembered the sadly proud gesture of refusal which he was to make there, standing with her in her moonlit garden after years of estrangement and adventure. At those moments the soft speeches of Claude Melnotte rose to his lips and eased his unrest. A tender premonition touched him of the tryst he had then looked forward to and, in spite of the horrible reality which lay between his hope of then and now, of the holy encounter he had then imagined at which weakness and timidity and inexperience were to fall from him.

Such moments passed and the wasting fires of lust sprang up again. The verses passed from his lips and the inarticulate cries and the unspoken brutal words rushed forth from his brain to force a passage. His blood was in revolt. He wandered up and down the dark slimy streets peering into the gloom of lanes and doorways, listening eagerly for any sound. He moaned to himself like some baffled prowling beast. He wanted to sin with another of his kind, to force another being to sin with him and to exult with her in sin. He felt some dark presence moving irresistibly upon him from the darkness, a presence subtle and murmurous as a flood filling him wholly with itself. Its murmur besieged his ears like the murmur of some multitude in sleep; its subtle streams penetrated his being. His hands clenched convulsively and his teeth set together as he suffered the agony of its penetration. He stretched out his arms in the street to hold fast the frail swooning form that eluded him and incited him: and the cry that he had strangled for so long in his throat issued from his lips. It broke from him like a wail of despair from a hell of sufferers and died in a wail of furious entreaty, a cry for an iniquitous abandonment, a cry which was but the echo of an obscene scrawl which he had read on the oozing wall of a urinal.

He had wandered into a maze of narrow and dirty streets. From the foul laneways he heard bursts of hoarse riot and wrangling and the drawling of drunken singers. He walked onward, undismayed, wondering whether he had strayed into the quarter of the jews. Women and girls dressed in long vivid gowns traversed the street from house to house. They were leisurely and perfumed. A trembling seized him and his eyes grew dim. The yellow gasflames arose before his troubled vision against the vapoury sky, burning as if before an altar. Before the doors and in the lighted halls groups were gathered arrayed as for some rite. He was in another world: he had awakened from a slumber of centuries.

He stood still in the middle of the roadway, his heart clamouring against his bosom in a tumult. A young woman dressed in a long pink gown laid her hand on his arm to detain him and gazed into his face. She said gaily:

—Good night, Willie dear!

Her room was warm and lightsome. A huge doll sat with her legs apart in the copious easychair beside the bed. He tried to bid his tongue speak that he might seem at ease, watching her as she undid her gown, noting the proud conscious movements of her perfumed head.

As he stood silent in the middle of the room she came over to him and embraced him gaily and gravely. Her round arms held him firmly to her and he, seeing her face lifted to him in serious calm and feeling the warm calm rise and fall of her breast, all but burst into hysterical weeping. Tears of joy and of relief shone in his delighted eyes and his lips parted though they would not speak.

She passed her tinkling hand through his hair, calling him a little rascal.

—Give me a kiss, she said.

His lips would not bend to kiss her. He wanted to be held firmly in her arms, to be caressed slowly, slowly, slowly. In her arms he felt that he had suddenly become strong and fearless and sure of himself. But his lips would not bend to kiss her.

With a sudden movement she bowed his head and joined her lips to his and he read the meaning of her movements in her frank uplifted eyes. It was too much for him. He closed his eyes, surrendering himself to her, body and mind, conscious of nothing in the world but the dark pressure of her softly parting lips. They pressed upon his brain as upon his lips as though they were the vehicle of a vague speech; and between them he felt an unknown and timid pressure, darker than the swoon of sin, softer than sound or odour.

III

The swift December dusk had come tumbling clownishly after its dull day and, as he stared through the dull square of the window of the schoolroom, he felt his belly crave for its food. He hoped there would be stew for dinner, turnips and carrots and bruised potatoes and fat mutton pieces to be ladled out in thick peppered flourfattened sauce. Stuff it into you, his belly counselled him.

It would be a gloomy secret night. After early nightfall the yellow lamps would light up, here and there, the squalid quarter of the brothels. He would follow a devious course up and down the streets, circling always nearer and nearer in a tremor of fear and joy, until his feet led him suddenly round a dark corner. The whores would be just coming out of their houses making ready for the night, yawning lazily after their sleep and settling the hairpins in their clusters of hair. He would pass by them calmly waiting for a sudden movement of his own will or a sudden call to his sinloving soul from their soft perfumed flesh. Yet as he prowled in quest of that call, his senses, stultified only by his desire, would note keenly all that wounded or shamed them; his eyes, a ring of porter froth on a clothless table or a photograph of two soldiers standing to attention or a gaudy playbill; his ears, the drawling jargon of greeting:

—Hello, Bertie, any good in your mind?

—Is that you, pigeon?

—Number ten. Fresh Nelly is waiting on you.

—Goodnight, husband! Coming in to have a short time?

The equation on the page of his scribbler began to spread out a widening tail, eyed and starred like a peacock's: and when the eyes and stars of its indices had been eliminated, began slowly to fold itself together again. The indices appearing and disappearing were eyes opening and closing; the eyes opening and closing were stars being born and being quenched. The vast cycle of starry life bore his weary mind outward to its verge and inward to its centre, a distant music accompanying him outward and inward. What music? The music came nearer and he recalled the words, the words of Shelley's fragment upon the moon wandering companionless, pale for weariness. The stars began to crumble and a cloud of fine stardust fell through space.

The dull light fell more faintly upon the page whereon another equation began to unfold itself slowly and to spread abroad its widening tail. It was his own soul going forth to experience, unfolding itself sin by sin, spreading abroad the balefire° of its burning stars and folding back upon itself, fading slowly, quenching its own lights and fires. They were quenched: and the cold darkness filled chaos.

A cold lucid indifference reigned in his soul. At his first violent sin he had felt a wave of vitality pass out of him and had feared to find his body or his soul maimed by the excess. Instead the vital wave had carried him on its bosom out of himself and back again when it receded: and no part of body or soul had been maimed but a dark peace had been established between them. The chaos in which his ardour extinguished itself was a cold indifferent knowledge of himself. He had sinned mortally not once but many times and he knew that, while he stood in danger of eternal damnation for the first sin alone, by every succeeding sin he multiplied his guilt and his punishment. His days and works and thoughts could make no atonement for him, the fountains of sanctifying grace having ceased to refresh his soul. At most by an alms given to a beggar, whose blessing he fled from, he might hope wearily to win for himself some measure of actual grace. Devotion had

balefire: Large fire in the open air.

gone by the board. What did it avail to pray when he knew that his soul lusted after its own destruction? A certain pride, a certain awe, withheld him from offering to God even one prayer at night though he knew it was in God's power to take away his life while he slept and hurl his soul hellward ere he could beg for mercy. His pride in his own sin, his loveless awe of God, told him that his offence was too grievous to be atoned for in whole or in part by a false homage to the Allseeing and Allknowing.

—Well now, Ennis, I declare you have a head and so has my stick! Do you mean to say that you are not able to tell me what a surd is?

The blundering answer stirred the embers of his contempt of his fellows. Towards others he felt neither shame nor fear. On Sunday mornings as he passed the churchdoor he glanced coldly at the worshippers who stood bareheaded, four deep, outside the church, morally present at the mass which they could neither see nor hear. Their dull piety and the sickly smell of the cheap hairoil with which they had anointed their heads repelled him from the altar they prayed at. He stooped to the evil of hypocrisy with others, sceptical of their innocence which he could cajole so easily.

On the wall of his bedroom hung an illuminated scroll, the certificate of his prefecture in the college of the sodality° of the Blessed Virgin Mary. On Saturday mornings when the sodality met in the chapel to recite the little office his place was a cushioned kneelingdesk at the right of the altar from which he led his wing of boys through the responses. The falsehood of his position did not pain him. If at moments he felt an impulse to rise from his post of honour and, confessing before them all his unworthiness, to leave the chapel, a glance at their faces restrained him. The imagery of the psalms of prophecy soothed his barren pride. The glories of Mary held his soul captive: spikenard and myrrh and frankincense, symbolising the preciousness of God's gifts to her soul, rich garments, symbolising her royal lineage, her emblems, the lateflowering plant and lateblossoming tree, symbolising the agelong gradual growth of her cultus among men. When it fell to him to read the lesson towards the close of the office he read it in a veiled voice, lulling his conscience to its music.

Quasi cedrus exaltata sum in Libanon et quasi cupressus in monte Sion. Quasi palma exaltata sum in Gades et quasi plantatio rosae in Jericho. Quasi uliva speciosa in campis et quasi platanus exaltata sum juxta aquam in plateis.

prefecture . . . of the sodality: Leadership of an honorific student association.

Sicut cinnamomum et balsamum aromatizans odorem dedi et quasi myrrha electa dedi suavitatem odoris.°

His sin, which had covered him from the sight of God, had led him nearer to the refuge of sinners. Her eyes seemed to regard him with mild pity; her holiness, a strange light glowing faintly upon her frail flesh, did not humiliate the sinner who approached her. If ever he was impelled to cast sin from him and to repent the impulse that moved him was the wish to be her knight. If ever his soul, reentering her dwelling shyly after the frenzy of his body's lust had spent itself, was turned towards her whose emblem is the morning star, *bright and musical, telling of heaven and infusing peace,* it was when her names were murmured softly by lips whereon there still lingered foul and shameful words, the savour itself of a lewd kiss.

That was strange. He tried to think how it could be but the dusk, deepening in the schoolroom, covered over his thoughts. The bell rang. The master marked the sums and cuts° to be done for the next lesson and went out. Heron, beside Stephen, began to hum tunelessly.

My excellent friend Bombados.

Ennis, who had gone to the yard, came back, saying:

—The boy from the house is coming up for the rector.

A tall boy behind Stephen rubbed his hands and said:

—That's game ball.° We can scut the whole hour. He won't be in till after half two. Then you can ask him questions on the catechism, Dedalus.

Stephen, leaning back and drawing idly on his scribbler, listened to the talk about him which Heron checked from time to time by saying:

—Shut up, will you. Don't make such a bally racket!

It was strange too that he found an arid pleasure in following up to the end the rigid lines of the doctrines of the church and penetrating into obscure silences only to hear and feel the more deeply his own condemnation. The sentence of saint James which says that he who offends against one commandment becomes guilty of all had seemed to him first a swollen phrase until he had begun to grope in the darkness

Quasi cedrus . . . odoris: I was exalted like a cedar in Libanus [Lebanon], and as a cypress tree in Mount Sion. I was exalted like a palm tree in Cades and as a rose plant in Jericho. As a fair olive tree in the plains, and as a plane tree by the water in the streets was I exalted. I gave forth a sweet smell like cinnamon and aromatic balm; I gave forth a sweet odor like the best myrrh. . . . ; from Ecclesiasticus 24, 13–15, a book of the Catholic Bible, corresponding to what Protestants call the Apocrypha. **sums and cuts:** Math problems, generally based on Euclid. **game ball:** Good luck.

of his own state. From the evil seed of lust all other deadly sins had sprung forth: pride in himself and contempt of others, covetousness in using money for the purchase of unlawful pleasure, envy of those whose vices he could not reach to and calumnious murmuring against the pious, gluttonous enjoyment of food, the dull glowering anger amid which he brooded upon his longing, the swamp of spiritual and bodily sloth in which his whole being had sunk.

As he sat in his bench gazing calmly at the rector's shrewd harsh face his mind wound itself in and out of the curious questions proposed to it. If a man had stolen a pound in his youth and had used that pound to amass a huge fortune how much was he obliged to give back, the pound he had stolen only or the pound together with the compound interest accruing upon it or all his huge fortune? If a layman in giving baptism pour the water before saying the words is the child baptised? Is baptism with a mineral water valid? How comes it that while the first beatitude promises the kingdom of heaven to the poor of heart the second beatitude° promises also to the meek that they shall possess the land? Why was the sacrament of the eucharist instituted under the two species of bread and wine if Jesus Christ be present body and blood, soul and divinity, in the bread alone and in the wine alone? Does a tiny particle of the consecrated bread contain all the body and blood of Jesus Christ or a part only of the body and blood? If the wine change into vinegar and the host crumble into corruption after they have been consecrated is Jesus Christ still present under their species as God and as man?

—Here he is! Here he is!

A boy from his post at the window had seen the rector come from the house. All the catechisms were opened and all heads bent upon them silently. The rector entered and took his seat on the dais. A gentle kick from the tall boy in the bench behind urged Stephen to ask a difficult question.

The rector did not ask for a catechism to hear the lesson from. He clasped his hands on the desk and said:

—The retreat will begin on Wednesday afternoon in honour of saint Francis Xavier whose feast day is Saturday. The retreat will go on from Wednesday to Friday. On Friday confessions will be heard all the afternoon after beads. If any boys have special confessors° perhaps it will be

first beatitude . . . second beatitude: Being "poor in spirit" and "meek"; from the Sermon on the Mount in the Douay (Catholic) Bible version, Matthew 5. **special confessors:** Priests to whom a penitent goes regularly.

better for them not to change. Mass will be on Saturday morning at nine o'clock and general communion for the whole college. Saturday will be a free day. Sunday of course. But Saturday and Sunday being free days some boys might be inclined to think that Monday is a free day also. Beware of making that mistake. I think you, Lawless, are likely to make that mistake.

—I, sir? Why, sir?

A little wave of quiet mirth broke forth over the class of boys from the rector's grim smile. Stephen's heart began slowly to fold and fade with fear like a withering flower.

The rector went on gravely:

—You are all familiar with the story of the life of saint Francis Xavier, I suppose, the patron of your college. He came of an old and illustrious Spanish family and you remember that he was one of the first followers of saint Ignatius. They met in Paris where Francis Xavier was professor of philosophy at the university. This young and brilliant nobleman and man of letters entered heart and soul into the ideas of our glorious founder and you know that he, at his own desire, was sent by saint Ignatius to preach to the Indians. He is called, as you know, the apostle of the Indies. He went from country to country in the east, from Africa to India, from India to Japan, baptising the people. He is said to have baptised as many as ten thousand idolaters in one month. It is said that his right arm had grown powerless from having been raised so often over the heads of those whom he baptised. He wished then to go to China to win still more souls for God but he died of fever on the island of Sancian. A great saint, saint Francis Xavier! A great soldier of God!

The rector paused and then, shaking his clasped hands before him, went on:

—He had the faith in him that moves mountains. Ten thousand souls won for God in a single month! That is a true conqueror, true to the motto of our order: *ad majorem Dei gloriam!* A saint who has great power in heaven, remember: power to intercede for us in our grief, power to obtain whatever we pray for if it be for the good of our souls, power above all to obtain for us the grace to repent if we be in sin. A great saint, saint Francis Xavier! A great fisher of souls!

He ceased to shake his clasped hands and, resting them against his forehead, looked right and left of them keenly at his listeners out of his dark stern eyes.

In the silence their dark fire kindled the dusk into a tawny glow. Stephen's heart had withered up like a flower of the desert that feels the simoom° coming from afar.

simoom: A hot wind, seasonal in some deserts.

*

* *

—*Remember only thy last things and thou shalt not sin for ever*—words taken, my dear little brothers in Christ, from the book of Ecclesiastes, seventh chapter, fortieth verse. In the name of the Father and of the Son and of the Holy Ghost. Amen.

Stephen sat in the front bench of the chapel. Father Arnall sat at a table to the left of the altar. He wore about his shoulders a heavy cloak; his pale face was drawn and his voice broken with rheum. The figure of his old master, so strangely rearisen, brought back to Stephen's mind his life at Clongowes: the wide playgrounds, swarming with boys, the square ditch, the little cemetery off the main avenue of limes where he had dreamed of being buried, the firelight on the wall of the infirmary where he lay sick, the sorrowful face of Brother Michael. His soul, as these memories came back to him, became again a child's soul.

—We are assembled here today, my dear little brothers in Christ, for one brief moment far away from the busy bustle of the outer world to celebrate and to honour one of the greatest of saints, the apostle of the Indies, the patron saint also of your college, saint Francis Xavier. Year after year for much longer than any of you, my dear little boys, can remember or than I can remember the boys of this college have met in this very chapel to make their annual retreat before the feast day of their patron saint. Time has gone on and brought with it its changes. Even in the last few years what changes can most of you not remember? Many of the boys who sat in those front benches a few short years ago are perhaps now in distant lands, in the burning tropics or immersed in professional duties or in seminaries or voyaging over the vast expanse of the deep or, it may be, already called by the great God to another life and to the rendering up of their stewardship. And still as the years roll by, bringing with them changes for good and bad, the memory of the great saint is honoured by the boys of his college who make every year their annual retreat on the days preceding the feast day set apart by our holy mother the church to transmit to all the ages the name and fame of one of the greatest sons of catholic Spain.

—Now what is the meaning of this word *retreat* and why is it allowed on all hands to be a most salutary practice for all who desire to lead before God and in the eyes of men a truly christian life? A retreat, my dear boys, signifies a withdrawal for a while from the cares of our life, the cares of this workaday world, in order to examine the state of our conscience, to reflect on the mysteries of holy religion and to understand better why we are here in this world. During these few days I intend to put before you some thoughts concerning the four last things. They are, as you know from your catechism, death, judgment, hell and heaven. We shall try to understand them fully during these few days so that we may derive from the understanding of them a lasting benefit to our souls. And remember, my dear boys, that we have been sent into this world for one thing and for one thing alone: to do God's holy will and to save our immortal souls. All else is worthless. One thing alone is needful, the salvation of one's soul. What doth it profit a man to gain the whole world if he suffer the loss of his immortal soul? Ah, my dear boys, believe me there is nothing in this wretched world that can make up for such a loss.

—I will ask you therefore, my dear boys, to put away from your minds during these few days all worldly thoughts, whether of study or pleasure or ambition, and to give all your attention to the state of your souls. I need hardly remind you that during the days of the retreat all boys are expected to preserve a quiet and pious demeanour and to shun all loud unseemly pleasure. The elder boys, of course, will see that this custom is not infringed and I look especially to the prefects and officers of the sodality of Our Blessed Lady and of the sodality of the holy angels to set a good example to their fellowstudents.

—Let us try therefore to make this retreat in honour of saint Francis with our whole heart and our whole mind. God's blessing will then be upon all your year's studies. But, above and beyond all, let this retreat be one to which you can look back in after years when maybe you are far from this college and among very different surroundings, to which you can look back with joy and thankfulness and give thanks to God for having granted you this occasion of laying the first foundation of a pious honourable zealous christian life. And if, as may so happen, there be at this moment in these benches any poor soul which has had the unutterable misfortune to lose God's holy grace and to fall into grievous sin I fervently trust and pray that this retreat may be the turningpoint in the life of that soul. I pray to God through the merits of its zealous servant Francis Xavier that such a soul may be led to sincere repentance and that the holy communion on saint Francis' day of this year may be a lasting covenant between God and that soul. For just and unjust, for saint and sinner alike, may this retreat be a memorable one.

—Help me, my dear little brothers in Christ. Help me by your pious attention, by your own devotion, by your outward demeanour. Banish from your minds all worldly thoughts and think only of the last things, death, judgment, hell and heaven. He who remembers these things, says Ecclesiastes, shall not sin for ever. He who remembers the last things will act and think with them always before his eyes. He will live a good life and die a good death, believing and knowing that, if he has sacrificed much in this earthly life, it will be given to him a hundredfold and a thousandfold more in the life to come, in the kingdom without end—a blessing, my dear boys, which I wish you from my heart, one and all, in the name of the Father and of the Son and of the Holy Ghost. Amen.

As he walked home with silent companions a thick fog seemed to compass his mind. He waited in stupor of mind till it should lift and reveal what it had hidden. He ate his dinner with surly appetite and, when the meal was over and the greasestrewn plates lay abandoned on the table, he rose and went to the window, clearing the thick scum from his mouth with his tongue and licking it from his lips. So he had sunk to the state of a beast that licks his chaps after meat. This was the end: and a faint glimmer of fear began to pierce the fog of his mind. He pressed his face against the pane of the window and gazed out into the darkening street. Forms passed this way and that way through the dull light. And that was life. The letters of the name of Dublin lay heavily upon his mind, pushing one another surlily hither and thither with slow boorish insistence. His soul was fattening and congealing into a gross grease, plunging ever deeper in its dull fear into a sombre threatening dusk, while the body that was his stood, listless and dishonoured, gazing out of darkened eyes, helpless, perturbed and human for a bovine god to stare upon.

The next day brought death and judgment, stirring his soul slowly from its listless despair. The faint glimmer of fear became a terror of spirit as the hoarse voice of the preacher blew death into his soul. He suffered its agony. He felt the deathchill touch the extremities and creep onward towards the heart, the film of death veiling the eyes, the bright centres of the brain extinguished one by one like lamps, the last sweat oozing upon the skin, the powerlessness of the dying limbs, the speech thickening and wandering and failing, the heart throbbing faintly and more faintly, all but vanquished, the breath, the poor timid breath, the poor helpless human spirit, sobbing and sighing, gurgling and rattling in the throat. No help! No help! He, he himself, his body to which he had yielded was dying. Into the grave with it! Nail it down into a wooden box, the corpse. Carry it out of the house on the shoulders of hirelings. Thrust it out of men's sight into a long hole in the ground, into the grave, to rot, to feed the mass of its creeping worms and to be devoured by scuttling plumpbellied rats.

And while the friends were still standing in tears by the bedside the soul of the sinner was judged. At the last moment of consciousness the whole earthly life passed before the vision of the soul and, ere it had time to reflect, the body had died and the soul stood terrified before the judgmentseat. God, who had long been merciful, would then be just. He had long been patient, pleading with the sinful soul, giving it time to repent, sparing it yet awhile. But that time had gone. Time was to sin and to enjoy, time was to scoff at God and at the warnings of His holy church, time was to defy His majesty, to disobey His commands, to hoodwink one's fellow men, to commit sin after sin and sin after sin and to hide one's corruption from the sight of men. But that time was over. Now it was God's turn: and He was not to be hoodwinked or deceived. Every sin would then come forth from its lurkingplace, the most rebellious against the divine will and the most degrading to our poor corrupt nature, the tiniest imperfection and the most heinous atrocity. What did it avail then to have been a great emperor, a great general, a marvellous inventor, the most learned of the learned? All were as one before the judgmentseat of God. He would reward the good and punish the wicked. One single instant was enough for the trial of a man's soul. One single instant after the body's death, the soul had been weighed in the balance. The particular judgment was over and the soul had passed to the abode of bliss or to the prison of purgatory or had been hurled howling into hell.

Nor was that all. God's justice had still to be vindicated before men: after the particular there still remained the general judgment. The last day had come. Doomsday was at hand. The stars of heaven were falling upon the earth like the figs cast by the figtree which the wind has shaken. The sun, the great luminary of the universe, had become as sackcloth of hair. The moon was bloodred. The firmament was as a scroll rolled away. The archangel Michael, the prince of the heavenly host, appeared glorious and terrible against the sky. With one foot on the sea and one foot on the land he blew from the archangelical trumpet the brazen death of time. The three blasts of the angel filled all the universe. Time is, time was but time shall be no more. At the last blast the souls of universal humanity throng towards the valley of Jehoshaphat, rich and poor, gentle and simple, wise and foolish, good and wicked. The soul of every human being that has ever existed, the souls of all those who shall yet be born, all the sons and daughters of Adam, all are assembled on that supreme day. And lo the supreme judge is coming! No longer the lowly Lamb of God, no longer the meek Jesus of Nazareth, no longer the Man of Sorrows, no longer the Good Shepherd, He is seen now coming upon the clouds, in great power and majesty, attended by nine choirs of angels, angels and archangels, principalities, powers and virtues, thrones and dominations, cherubim and seraphim, God Omnipotent, God Everlasting. He speaks: and His voice is heard even at the farthest limits of space, even in the bottomless abyss. Supreme Judge, from His sentence there will be and can be no appeal. He calls the just to His side, bidding them enter into the kingdom, the eternity of bliss, prepared for them. The unjust He casts from Him, crying in His offended majesty: *Depart from me, ye cursed, into everlasting fire which was prepared for the devil and his angels.* O what agony then for the miserable sinners! Friend is torn apart from friend, children are torn from their parents, husbands from their wives. The poor sinner holds out his arms to those who were dear and near to him in this earthly world, to those whose simple piety perhaps he made a mock of, to those who counselled him and tried to lead him on the right path, to a kind brother, to a loving sister, to the mother and father who loved him so dearly. But it is too late: the just turn away from the wretched damned souls which now appear before the eyes of all in their hideous and evil character. O you hypocrites, O you whited sepulchres, O you who present a smooth smiling face to the world while your soul within is a foul swamp of sin, how will it fare with you in that terrible day?

And this day will come, shall come, must come; the day of death and the day of judgment. It is appointed unto man to die and after death the judgment. Death is certain. The time and manner are uncertain, whether from long disease or from some unexpected accident: the Son of God cometh at an hour when you little expect Him. Be therefore ready every moment, seeing that you may die at any moment. Death is the end of us all. Death and judgment, brought into the world by the sin of our first parents, are the dark portals that close our earthly existence, the portals that open into the unknown and the unseen, portals through which every soul must pass, alone, unaided save by its good works, without friend or brother or parent or master to help it, alone and trembling. Let that thought be ever before our minds and then we cannot sin. Death, a cause of terror to the sinner, is a blessed moment for him who has walked in the right path, fulfilling the duties of his station in life, attending to his morning and evening prayers, approaching the holy sacrament frequently and performing good and merciful works. For the pious and believing catholic, for the just man, death is no cause of terror. Was it not Addison, the great English writer, who, when on his deathbed, sent for the wicked young earl of Warwick to let him see how a christian can meet his end. He it is and he alone, the pious and believing christian, who can say in his heart:

O grave, where is thy victory?
O death, where is thy sting?

Every word of it was for him. Against his sin, foul and secret, the whole wrath of God was aimed. The preacher's knife had probed deeply into his diseased conscience and he felt now that his soul was festering in sin. Yes, the preacher was right. God's turn had come. Like a beast in its lair his soul had lain down in its own filth but the blasts of the angel's trumpet had driven him forth from the darkness of sin into the light. The words of doom cried by the angel shattered in an instant his presumptuous peace. The wind of the last day blew through his mind; his sins, the jeweleyed harlots of his imagination, fled before the hurricane, squeaking like mice in their terror and huddled under a mane of hair.

As he crossed the square, walking homeward, the light laughter of a girl reached his burning ears. The frail gay sound smote his heart more strongly than a trumpetblast, and, not daring to lift his eyes, he turned aside and gazed, as he walked, into the shadows of the tangled shrubs. Shame rose from his smitten heart and flooded his whole being. The image of Emma appeared before him and, under her eyes, the flood of shame rushed forth anew from his heart. If she knew to what his mind had subjected her or how his brutelike lust had torn and trampled upon her innocence! Was that boyish love? Was that chivalry? Was that poetry? The sordid details of his orgies stank under his very nostrils: the sootcoated packet of pictures which he had hidden in the flue of the fireplace and in the presence of whose shameless or bashful wantonness he lay for hours sinning in thought and deed: his monstrous dreams, peopled by apelike creatures and by harlots with gleaming jewel eyes: the foul long letters he had written in the joy of guilty confession and carried secretly for days and days only to throw them under cover of night among the grass in the corner of a field or beneath some hingeless door or in some niche in the hedges where a girl might come upon them as she walked by and read them secretly. Mad! Mad! Was it possible he had done these things? A cold sweat broke out upon his forehead as the foul memories condensed within his brain.

When the agony of shame had passed from him he tried to raise his soul from its abject powerlessness. God and the Blessed Virgin were too far from him: God was too great and stern and the Blessed Virgin too pure and holy. But he imagined that he stood near Emma in a wide land and, humbly and in tears, bent and kissed the elbow of her sleeve.

In a wide land under a tender lucid evening sky, a cloud drifting westward amid a pale green sea of heaven, they stood together, children that had erred. Their error had offended deeply God's majesty though it was the error of two children, but it had not offended her whose beauty *is not like earthly beauty, dangerous to look upon, but like the morning star which is its emblem, bright and musical.* The eyes were not offended which she turned upon them nor reproachful. She placed their hands together, hand in hand, and said, speaking to their hearts:

—Take hands, Stephen and Emma. It is a beautiful evening now in heaven. You have erred but you are always my children. It is one heart that loves another heart. Take hands together, my dear children, and you will be happy together and your hearts will love each other.

The chapel was flooded by the dull scarlet light that filtered through the lowered blinds; and through the fissure between the last blind and the sash a shaft of wan light entered like a spear and touched the embossed brasses of the candlesticks upon the altar that gleamed like the battleworn mail armour of angels.

Rain was falling on the chapel, on the garden, on the college. It would rain for ever, noiselessly. The water would rise inch by inch, covering the grass and shrubs, covering the trees and houses, covering the monuments and the mountain tops. All life would be choked off, noiselessly: birds, men, elephants, pigs, children: noiselessly floating corpses amid the litter of the wreckage of the world. Forty days and forty nights the rain would fall till the waters had covered the face of the earth.

It might be. Why not?

—*Hell has enlarged its soul and opened its mouth without any limits*—words taken, my dear little brothers in Christ Jesus, from the book of Isaias, fifth chapter, fourteenth verse. In the name of the Father and of the Son and of the Holy Ghost. Amen.

The preacher took a chainless watch from a pocket within his soutane and, having considered its dial for a moment in silence, placed it silently before him on the table.

He began to speak in a quiet tone.

—Adam and Eve, my dear boys, were, as you know, our first parents and you will remember that they were created by God in order that the seats in heaven left vacant by the fall of Lucifer and his rebellious angels might be filled again. Lucifer, we are told, was a son of the morning, a radiant and mighty angel; yet he fell: he fell and there fell with him a third part of the host of heaven: he fell and was hurled with his rebellious angels into hell. What his sin was we cannot say. Theologians consider that it was the sin of pride, the sinful thought conceived in an instant: *non serviam:*° *I will not serve*. That instant was his ruin. He offended the majesty of God by the sinful thought of one instant and God cast him out of heaven into hell for ever.

—Adam and Eve were then created by God and placed in Eden, in the plain of Damascus, that lovely garden resplendent with sunlight and colour, teeming with luxuriant vegetation. The fruitful earth gave them her bounty: beasts and birds were their willing servants: they knew not the ills our flesh is heir to, disease and poverty and death: all that a great and generous God could do for them was done. But there was one condition imposed on them by God: obedience to His word. They were not to eat of the fruit of the forbidden tree.

—Alas, my dear little boys, they too fell. The devil, once a shining angel, a son of the morning, now a foul fiend, came to them in the shape of a serpent, the subtlest of all the beasts of the field. He envied them. He, the fallen great one, could not bear to think that man, a being of clay, should possess the inheritance which he by his sin had forfeited for ever. He came to the woman, the weaker vessel, and poured the poison of his eloquence into her ear, promising her—O, the blasphemy of that promise!—that if she and Adam ate of the forbidden fruit they would become as gods, nay as God Himself. Eve yielded to the wiles of the archtempter. She ate the apple and gave it also to Adam who had not the moral courage to resist her. The poison tongue of Satan had done its work. They fell.

—And then the voice of God was heard in that garden, calling His creature man to account: and Michael, prince of the heavenly host, with a sword of flame in his hand appeared before the guilty pair and drove them forth from Eden into the world, the world of sickness and striving, of cruelty and disappointment, of labour and hardship, to earn their bread in the sweat of their brow. But even then how merciful was God! He took pity on our poor degraded first parents and promised that in the fulness of time He would send down from heaven One who would redeem them, make them once more children of God and heirs to the kingdom of heaven: and that One, that Redeemer of fallen man, was to be God's onlybegotten Son, the Second Person of the Most Blessed Trinity, the Eternal Word.

non serviam: Satan's defiant statement.

—He came. He was born of a virgin pure, Mary the virgin mother. He was born in a poor cowhouse in Judea and lived as a humble carpenter for thirty years until the hour of His mission had come. And then, filled with love for men, He went forth and called to men to hear the new gospel.

—Did they listen? Yes, they listened but would not hear. He was seized and bound like a common criminal, mocked at as a fool, set aside to give place to a public robber, scourged with five thousand lashes, crowned with a crown of thorns, hustled through the streets by the jewish rabble and the Roman soldiery, stripped of His garments and hanged upon a gibbet and His side was pierced with a lance and from the wounded body of Our Lord water and blood issued continually.

—Yet even then, in that hour of supreme agony, Our Merciful Redeemer had pity for mankind. Yet even there, on the hill of Calvary, He founded the holy catholic church against which, it is promised, the gates of hell shall not prevail. He founded it upon the rock of ages and endowed it with His grace, with sacraments and sacrifice, and promised that if men would obey the word of His church they would still enter into eternal life but if, after all that had been done for them, they still persisted in their wickedness there remained for them an eternity of torment: hell.

The preacher's voice sank. He paused, joined his palms for an instant, parted them. Then he resumed:

—Now let us try for a moment to realise, as far as we can, the nature of that abode of the damned which the justice of an offended God has called into existence for the eternal punishment of sinners. Hell is a strait and dark and foulsmelling prison, an abode of demons and lost souls, filled with fire and smoke. The straitness of this prisonhouse is expressly designed by God to punish those who refused to be bound by His laws. In earthly prisons the poor captive has at least some liberty of movement, were it only within the four walls of his cell or in the gloomy yard of his prison. Not so in hell. There, by reason of the great number of the damned, the prisoners are heaped together in their awful prison, the walls of which are said to be four thousand miles thick: and the damned are so utterly bound and helpless that, as a blessed saint, saint Anselm, writes in his book on similitudes, they are not even able to remove from the eye a worm that gnaws it.

—They lie in exterior darkness. For, remember, the fire of hell gives forth no light. As, at the command of God, the fire of the Babylonian furnace lost its heat but not its light so, at the command of God, the fire of hell, while retaining the intensity of its heat, burns eternally in darkness. It is a neverending storm of darkness, dark flames and dark smoke of burning brimstone, amid which the bodies are heaped one upon another without even a glimpse of air. Of all the plagues with which the land of the Pharaohs was smitten one plague alone, that of darkness, was called horrible. What name, then, shall we give to the darkness of hell which is to last not for three days alone but for all eternity?

—The horror of this strait and dark prison is increased by its awful stench. All the filth of the world, all the offal and scum of the world, we are told, shall run there as to a vast reeking sewer when the terrible conflagration of the last day has purged the world. The brimstone too which burns there in such prodigious quantity fills all hell with its intolerable stench; and the bodies of the damned themselves exhale such a pestilential odour that as saint Bonaventure says, one of them alone would suffice to infect the whole world. The very air of this world, that pure element, becomes foul and unbreathable when it has been long enclosed. Consider then what must be the foulness of the air of hell. Imagine some foul and putrid corpse that has lain rotting and decomposing in the grave, a jellylike mass of liquid corruption. Imagine such a corpse a prey to flames, devoured by the fire of burning brimstone and giving off dense choking fumes of nauseous loathsome decomposition. And then imagine this sickening stench multiplied a millionfold and a millionfold again from the millions upon millions of fetid carcasses massed together in the reeking darkness, a huge and rotting human fungus. Imagine all this and you will have some idea of the horror of the stench of hell.

—But this stench is not, horrible though it is, the greatest physical torment to which the damned are subjected. The torment of fire is the greatest torment to which the tyrant has ever subjected his fellowcreatures. Place your finger for a moment in the flame of a candle and you will feel the pain of fire. But our earthly fire was created by God for the benefit of man, to maintain in him the spark of life and to help him in the useful arts whereas the fire of hell is of another quality and was created by God to torture and punish the unrepentant sinner. Our earthly fire also consumes more or less rapidly according as the object which it attacks is more or less combustible so that human ingenuity has even succeeded in inventing chemical preparations to check or frustrate its action. But the sulphurous brimstone which burns in hell is a substance which is specially designed to burn for ever and for ever with unspeakable fury. Moreover our earthly fire destroys at the same time as it burns so that the more intense it is the shorter is its duration: but the fire of hell has this property that it preserves that which it burns and though it rages with incredible intensity it rages for ever.

—Our earthly fire again, no matter how fierce or widespread it may be, is always of a limited extent: but the lake of fire in hell is boundless, shoreless and bottomless. It is on record that the devil himself, when asked the question by a certain soldier, was obliged to confess that if a whole mountain were thrown into the burning ocean of hell it would be burned up in an instant like a piece of wax. And this terrible fire will not afflict the bodies of the damned only from without but each lost soul will be a hell unto itself, the boundless fire raging in its very vitals. O, how terrible is the lot of those wretched beings! The blood seethes and boils in the veins, the brains are boiling in the skull, the heart in the breast glowing and bursting, the bowels a redhot mass of burning pulp, the tender eyes flaming like molten balls.

—And yet what I have said as to the strength and quality and boundlessness of this fire is as nothing when compared to its intensity, an intensity which it has as being the instrument chosen by divine design for the punishment of soul and body alike. It is a fire which proceeds directly from the ire of God, working not of its own activity but as an instrument of divine vengeance. As the waters of baptism cleanse the soul with the body so do the fires of punishment torture the spirit with the flesh. Every sense of the flesh is tortured and every faculty of the soul therewith: the eyes with impenetrable utter darkness, the nose with noisome odours, the ears with yells and howls and execrations, the taste with foul matter, leprous corruption, nameless suffocating filth, the touch with redhot goads and spikes, with cruel tongues of flame. And through the several torments of the senses the immortal soul is tortured eternally in its very essence amid the leagues upon leagues of glowing fires kindled in the abyss by the offended majesty of the Omnipotent God and fanned into everlasting and ever increasing fury by the breath of the anger of the Godhead.

—Consider finally that the torment of this infernal prison is increased by the company of the damned themselves. Evil company on earth is so noxious that even the plants, as if by instinct, withdraw from the company of whatsoever is deadly or hurtful to them. In hell all laws are overturned: there is no thought of family or country, of ties or relationships. The damned howl and scream at one another, their torture and rage intensified by the presence of beings tortured and raging like themselves. All sense of humanity is forgotten. The yells of the suffering sinners fill the remotest corners of the vast abyss. The mouths of the damned are full of blasphemies against God and of hatred for their fellowsufferers and of curses against those souls which were their accomplices in sin. In olden times it was the custom to punish the parricide, the man who had raised his murderous hand against his father, by casting him into the depths of the sea in a sack in which were placed a cock, a monkey and a serpent. The intention of those lawgivers who framed such a law, which seems cruel in our times, was to punish the criminal by the company of hateful and hurtful beasts. But what is the fury of those dumb beasts compared with the fury of execration which bursts from the parched lips and aching throats of the damned in hell when they behold in their companions in misery those who aided and abetted them in sin, those whose words sowed the first seeds of evil thinking and evil living in their minds, those whose immodest suggestions led them on to sin, those whose eyes tempted and allured them from the path of virtue. They turn upon those accomplices and upbraid them and curse them. But they are helpless and hopeless: it is too late now for repentance.

—Last of all consider the frightful torment to those damned souls, tempters and tempted alike, of the company of the devils. These devils will afflict the damned in two ways, by their presence and by their reproaches. We can have no idea of how horrible these devils are. Saint Catherine of Siena once saw a devil and she has written that, rather than look again for one single instant on such a frightful monster, she would prefer to walk until the end of her life along a track of red coals. These devils, who were once beautiful angels, have become as hideous and ugly as they once were beautiful. They mock and jeer at the lost souls whom they dragged down to ruin. It is they, the foul demons, who are made in hell the voices of conscience. Why did you sin? Why did you lend an ear to the temptings of fiends? Why did you turn aside from your pious practices and good works? Why did you not shun the occasions of sin? Why did you not leave that evil companion? Why did you not give up that lewd habit, that impure habit? Why did you not listen to the counsels of your confessor? Why did you not, even after you had fallen the first or the second or the third or the fourth or the hundredth time, repent of your evil ways and turn to God who only waited for your repentance to absolve you of your sins? Now the time for repentance has gone by. Time is, time was but time shall be no more! Time was to sin in secrecy, to indulge in that sloth and pride, to covet the unlawful, to yield to the promptings of your lower nature, to live like the beasts of the field, nay worse than the beasts of the field for they, at least, are but brutes and have not reason to guide them: time was but time shall be no more. God spoke to you by so many voices but you would not hear. You would not crush out that pride and anger in your heart, you would not restore those illgotten goods, you would not obey the precepts of your holy church nor attend to your religious duties, you would not abandon those wicked companions, you would not avoid those dangerous temptations. Such is the language of those fiendish tormentors, words of taunting and of reproach, of hatred and of disgust. Of disgust, yes! For even they, the very devils, when they sinned sinned by such a sin as alone was compatible with such angelical natures, a rebellion of the intellect: and they, even they, the foul devils must turn away, revolted and disgusted, from the contemplation of those unspeakable sins by which degraded man outrages and defiles the temple of the Holy Ghost, defiles and pollutes himself.

—O, my dear little brothers in Christ, may it never be our lot to hear that language! May it never be our lot, I say! In the last day of terrible reckoning I pray fervently to God that not a single soul of those who are in this chapel today may be found among those miserable beings whom the Great Judge shall command to depart for ever from His sight, that not one of us may ever hear ringing in his ears the awful sentence of rejection: *Depart from me, ye cursed, into everlasting fire which was prepared for the devil and his angels!*

He came down the aisle of the chapel, his legs shaking and the scalp of his head trembling as though it had been touched by ghostly fingers. He passed up the staircase and into the corridor along the walls of which the overcoats and waterproofs hung like gibbeted malefactors, headless and dripping and shapeless. And at every step he feared that he had already died, that his soul had been wrenched forth of the sheath of his body, that he was plunging headlong through space.

He could not grip the floor with his feet and sat heavily at his desk, opening one of his books at random and poring over it. Every word for him! It was true. God was almighty. God could call him now, call him as he sat at his desk, before he had time to be conscious of the summons. God had called him. Yes? What? Yes? His flesh shrank together as it felt the approach of the ravenous tongues of flames, dried up as it felt about it the swirl of stifling air. He had died. Yes. He was judged. A wave of fire swept through his body: the first. Again a wave. His brain began to glow. Another. His brain was simmering and bubbling within the cracking tenement of the skull. Flames burst forth from his skull like a corolla, shrieking like voices:

—Hell! Hell! Hell! Hell! Hell!

Voices spoke near him:

—On hell.

—I suppose he rubbed it into you well.

—You bet he did. He put us all into a blue funk.°

—That's what you fellows want: and plenty of it to make you work.

He leaned back weakly in his desk. He had not died. God had spared him still. He was still in the familiar world of the school. Mr Tate and Vincent Heron stood at the window, talking, jesting, gazing out at the bleak rain, moving their heads.

—I wish it would clear up. I had arranged to go for a spin on the bike with some fellows out by Malahide. But the roads must be kneedeep.

—It might clear up, sir.

The voices that he knew so well, the common words, the quiet of the classroom when the voices paused and the silence was filled by the sound of softly browsing cattle as the other boys munched their lunches tranquilly, lulled his aching soul.

There was still time. O Mary, refuge of sinners, intercede for him! O Virgin Undefiled, save him from the gulf of death!

The English lesson began with the hearing of the history. Royal persons, favourites, intriguers, bishops passed like mute phantoms behind their veil of names. All had died: all had been judged. What did it profit a man to gain the whole world if he lost his soul? At last he had understood: and human life lay around him, a plain of peace whereon antlike men laboured in brotherhood, their dead sleeping under quiet mounds. The elbow of his companion touched him and his heart was touched: and when he spoke to answer a question of his master he heard his own voice full of the quietude of humility and contrition.

His soul sank back deeper into depths of contrite peace, no longer able to suffer the pain of dread, and sending forth, as she sank, a faint prayer. Ah yes, he would still be spared; he would repent in his heart and be forgiven: and then those above, those in heaven, would see what he would do to make up for the past: a whole life, every hour of life. Only wait.

—All, God! All, all!

A messenger came to the door to say that confessions were being heard in the chapel. Four boys left the room; and he heard others passing down the corridor. A tremulous chill blew round his heart, no stronger than a little wind, and yet, listening and suffering silently, he seemed to have laid an ear against the muscle of his own heart, feeling it close and quail, listening to the flutter of its ventricles.

blue funk: Extreme depression and fear.

No escape. He had to confess, to speak out in words what he had done and thought, sin after sin. How? How?

—Father, I . . .

The thought slid like a cold shining rapier into his tender flesh: confession. But not there in the chapel of the college. He would confess all, every sin of deed and thought, sincerely: but not there among his school companions. Far away from there in some dark place he would murmur out his own shame: and he besought God humbly not to be offended with him if he did not dare to confess in the college chapel: and in utter abjection of spirit he craved forgiveness mutely of the boyish hearts about him.

Time passed.

He sat again in the front bench of the chapel. The daylight without was already failing and, as it fell slowly through the dull red blinds, it seemed that the sun of the last day was going down and that all souls were being gathered for the judgment.

—*I am cast away from the sight of Thine eyes:* words taken, my dear little brothers in Christ, from the Book of Psalms, thirtieth chapter, twentythird verse. In the name of the Father and of the Son and of the Holy Ghost. Amen.

The preacher began to speak in a quiet friendly tone. His face was kind and he joined gently the fingers of each hand, forming a frail cage by the union of their tips.

—This morning we endeavoured, in our reflection upon hell, to make what our holy founder calls in his book of spiritual exercises, the composition of place. We endeavoured, that is, to imagine with the senses of the mind, in our imagination, the material character of that awful place and of the physical torments which all who are in hell endure. This evening we shall consider for a few moments the nature of the spiritual torments of hell.

—Sin, remember, is a twofold enormity. It is a base consent to the promptings of our corrupt nature to the lower instincts, to that which is gross and beastlike; and it is also a turning away from the counsel of our higher nature, from all that is pure and holy, from the Holy God Himself. For this reason mortal sin is punished in hell by two different forms of punishment, physical and spiritual.

—Now of all these spiritual pains by far the greatest is the pain of loss, so great, in fact, that in itself it is a torment greater than all the others. Saint Thomas, the greatest doctor of the church, the angelic doctor, as he is called, says that the worst damnation consists in this that the understanding of man is totally deprived of divine light and his affection obstinately turned away from the goodness of God. God, remember, is a being infinitely good and therefore the loss of such a being must be a loss infinitely painful. In this life we have not a very clear idea of what such a loss must be but the damned in hell, for their greater torment, have a full understanding of that which they have lost and understand that they have lost it through their own sins and have lost it for ever. At the very instant of death the bonds of the flesh are broken asunder and the soul at once flies towards God. The soul tends towards God as towards the centre of her existence. Remember, my dear little boys, our souls long to be with God. We come from God, we live by God, we belong to God: we are His, inalienably His. God loves with a divine love every human soul and every human soul lives in that love. How could it be otherwise? Every breath that we draw, every thought of our brain, every instant of life proceed from God's inexhaustible goodness. And if it be pain for a mother to be parted from her child, for a man to be exiled from hearth and home, for friend to be sundered from friend, O think what pain, what anguish, it must be for the poor soul to be spurned from the presence of the supremely good and loving Creator Who has called that soul into existence from nothingness and sustained it in life and loved it with an immeasurable love. This, then, to be separated for ever from its greatest good, from God, and to feel the anguish of that separation, knowing full well that it is unchangeable, this is the greatest torment which the created soul is capable of bearing, *pœna damni,*° the pain of loss.

—The second pain which will afflict the souls of the damned in hell is the pain of conscience. Just as in dead bodies worms are engendered by putrefaction so in the souls of the lost there arises a perpetual remorse from the putrefaction of sin, the sting of conscience, the worm, as Pope Innocent the Third calls it, of the triple sting. The first sting inflicted by this cruel worm will be the memory of past pleasures. O what a dreadful memory will that be! In the lake of alldevouring flame the proud king will remember the pomps of his court, the wise but wicked man his libraries and instruments of research, the lover of artistic pleasures his marbles and pictures and other art treasures, he who delighted in the pleasures of the table his gorgeous feasts, his dishes prepared with such delicacy, his choice wines; the miser will remember his hoard of gold, the robber his illgotten wealth, the angry and revengeful and merciless murderers their deeds of blood and violence in which they revelled, the impure and adulterous the unspeakable and filthy pleasures

pœna damni: Torment of the damned (removal from God's sight).

in which they delighted. They will remember all this and loathe themselves and their sins. For how miserable will all those pleasures seem to the soul condemned to suffer in hellfire for ages and ages. How they will rage and fume to think that they have lost the bliss of heaven for the dross of earth, for a few pieces of metal, for vain honours, for bodily comforts, for a tingling of the nerves. They will repent indeed: and this is the second sting of the worm of conscience, a late and fruitless sorrow for sins committed. Divine justice insists that the understanding of those miserable wretches be fixed continually on the sins of which they were guilty and, moreover, as saint Augustine points out, God will impart to them His own knowledge of sin so that sin will appear to them in all its hideous malice as it appears to the eyes of God Himself. They will behold their sins in all their foulness and repent but it will be too late and then they will bewail the good occasions which they neglected. This is the last and deepest and most cruel sting of the worm of conscience. The conscience will say: You had time and opportunity to repent and would not. You were brought up religiously by your parents. You had the sacraments and graces and indulgences of the church to aid you. You had the minister of God to preach to you, to call you back when you had strayed, to forgive you your sins, no matter how many, how abominable, if only you had confessed and repented. No. You would not. You flouted the ministers of holy religion, you turned your back on the confessional, you wallowed deeper and deeper in the mire of sin. God appealed to you, threatened you, entreated you to return to Him. O what shame, what misery! The Ruler of the universe entreated you, a creature of clay, to love Him Who made you and to keep His law. No. You would not. And now, though you were to flood all hell with your tears if you could still weep, all that sea of repentance would not gain for you what a single tear of true repentance shed during your mortal life would have gained for you. You implore now a moment of earthly life wherein to repent: in vain. That time is gone: gone for ever.

—Such is the threefold sting of conscience, the viper which gnaws the very heart's core of the wretches in hell so that filled with hellish fury they curse themselves for their folly and curse the evil companions who have brought them to such ruin and curse the devils who tempted them in life and now mock them and torture them in eternity and even revile and curse the Supreme Being Whose goodness and patience they scorned and slighted but Whose justice and power they cannot evade.

—The next spiritual pain to which the damned are subjected is the pain of extension. Man, in this earthly life, though he be capable of many evils, is not capable of them all at once inasmuch as one evil corrects and counteracts another just as one poison frequently corrects another. In hell on the contrary one torment, instead of counteracting another, lends it still greater force: and moreover as the internal faculties are more perfect than the external senses so are they more capable of suffering. Just as every sense is afflicted with a fitting torment so is every spiritual faculty; the fancy with horrible images, the sensitive faculty with alternate longing and rage, the mind and understanding with an interior darkness more terrible even than the exterior darkness which reigns in that dreadful prison. The malice, impotent though it be, which possesses these demon souls is an evil of boundless extension, of limitless duration, a frightful state of wickedness which we can scarcely realise unless we bear in mind the enormity of sin and the hatred God bears to it.

—Opposed to this pain of extension and yet coexistent with it we have the pain of intensity. Hell is the centre of evils and, as you know, things are more intense at their centres than at their remotest points. There are no contraries or admixtures of any kind to temper or soften in the least the pains of hell. Nay, things which are good in themselves become evil in hell. Company, elsewhere a source of comfort to the afflicted, will be there a continual torment: knowledge, so much longed for as the chief good of the intellect, will there be hatred worse than ignorance: light, so much coveted by all creatures from the lord of creation down to the humblest plant in the forest, will be loathed intensely. In this life our sorrows are either not very long or not very great because nature either overcomes them by habits or puts an end to them by sinking under their weight. But in hell the torments cannot be overcome by habit. For while they are of terrible intensity they are at the same time of continual variety, each pain, so to speak, taking fire from another and reendowing that which has enkindled it with a still fiercer flame. Nor can nature escape from these intense and various tortures by succumbing to them for the soul in hell is sustained and maintained in evil so that its suffering may be the greater. Boundless extension of torment, incredible intensity of suffering, unceasing variety of torture—this is what the divine majesty, so outraged by sinners, demands, this is what the holiness of heaven, slighted and set aside for the lustful and low pleasures of the corrupt flesh, requires, this is what the blood of the innocent Lamb of God, shed for the redemption of sinners, trampled upon by the vilest of the vile, insists upon.

—Last and crowning torture of all the tortures of that awful place is the eternity of hell. Eternity! O, dread and dire word. Eternity! What mind of man can understand it? And, remember, it is an eternity of pain. Even though the pains of hell were not so terrible as they are yet they would become infinite as they are destined to last for ever. But while they are everlasting they are at the same time, as you know, intolerably intense, unbearably extensive. To bear even the sting of an insect for all eternity would be a dreadful torment. What must it be, then, to bear the manifold tortures of hell for ever! For ever! For all eternity! Not for a year or for an age but for ever. Try to imagine the awful meaning of this. You have often seen the sand on the seashore. How fine are its tiny grains! And how many of those tiny little grains go to make up the small handful which a child grasps in its play. Now imagine a mountain of that sand, a million miles high, reaching from the earth to the farthest heavens, and a million miles broad, extending to remotest space, and a million miles in thickness: and imagine such an enormous mass of countless particles of sand multiplied as often as there are leaves in the forest, drops of water in the mighty ocean, feathers on birds, scales on fish, hairs on animals, atoms in the vast expanse of the air: and imagine that at the end of every million years a little bird came to that mountain and carried away in its beak a tiny grain of that sand. How many millions upon millions of centuries would pass before that bird had carried away even a square foot of that mountain, how many eons upon eons of ages before it had carried away all. Yet at the end of that immense stretch of time not even one instant of eternity could be said to have ended. At the end of all those billions and trillions of years eternity would have scarcely begun. And if that mountain rose again after it had been all carried away and if the bird came again and carried it all away again grain by grain: and if it so rose and sank as many times as there are stars in the sky, atoms in the air, drops of water in the sea, leaves on the trees, feathers upon birds, scales upon fish, hairs upon animals, at the end of all those innumerable risings and sinkings of that immeasurably vast mountain not one single instant of eternity could be said to have ended: even then, at the end of such a period, after that eon of time the mere thought of which makes our very brain reel dizzily, eternity would have scarcely begun.

—A holy saint (one of our own fathers I believe it was) was once vouchsafed a vision of hell. It seemed to him that he stood in the midst of a great hall, dark and silent save for the ticking of a great clock. The ticking went on unceasingly; and it seemed to this saint that the sound of the ticking was the ceaseless repetition of the words: ever, never: ever, never. Ever to be in hell, never to be in heaven; ever to be shut off from the presence of God, never to enjoy the beatific vision; ever to be eaten with flames, gnawed by vermin, goaded with burning spikes, never to be free from those pains; ever to have the conscience upbraid one, the memory enrage, the mind filled with darkness and despair, never to escape; ever to curse and revile the foul demons who gloat fiendishly over the misery of their dupes, never to behold the shining raiment of the blessed spirits; ever to cry out of the abyss of fire to God for an instant, a single instant, of respite from such awful agony, never to receive, even for an instant, God's pardon; ever to suffer, never to enjoy; ever to be damned, never to be saved; ever, never; ever, never. O what a dreadful punishment! An eternity of endless agony, of endless bodily and spiritual torment, without one ray of hope, without one moment of cessation, of agony limitless in extent, limitless in intensity, of torment infinitely lasting, infinitely varied, of torture that sustains eternally that which it eternally devours, of anguish that everlastingly preys upon the spirit while it racks the flesh, an eternity, every instant of which is itself an eternity, and that eternity an eternity of woe. Such is the terrible punishment decreed for those who die in mortal sin by an almighty and a just God.

—Yes, a just God! Men, reasoning always as men, are astonished that God should mete out an everlasting and infinite punishment in the fires of hell for a single grievous sin. They reason thus because, blinded by the gross illusion of the flesh and the darkness of human understanding, they are unable to comprehend the hideous malice of mortal sin. They reason thus because they are unable to comprehend that even venial sin is of such a foul and hideous nature that even if the omnipotent Creator could end all the evil and misery in the world, the wars, the diseases, the robberies, the crimes, the deaths, the murders, on condition that He allowed a single venial sin to pass unpunished, a single venial sin, a lie, an angry look, a moment of wilful sloth, He, the great omnipotent God, could not do so because sin, be it in thought or deed, is a transgression of His law and God would not be God if He did not punish the transgressor.

—A sin, an instant of rebellious pride of the intellect, made Lucifer and a third part of the cohorts of angels fall from their glory. A sin, an instant of folly and weakness, drove Adam and Eve out of Eden and brought death and suffering into the world. To retrieve the consequences of that sin the onlybegotten Son of God came down to earth, lived and suffered and died a most painful death, hanging for three hours on the cross.

—O, my dear little brethren in Christ Jesus, will we then offend that good Redeemer and provoke His anger? Will we trample again upon that torn and mangled corpse? Will we spit upon that face so full of sorrow and love? Will we too, like the cruel jews and the brutal soldiers, mock that gentle and compassionate Saviour Who trod alone for our sake the awful winepress of sorrow? Every word of sin is a wound in His tender side. Every sinful act is a thorn piercing His head. Every impure thought, deliberately yielded to, is a keen lance transfixing that sacred and loving heart. No, no. It is impossible for any human being to do that which offends so deeply the divine majesty, that which is punished by an eternity of agony, that which crucifies again the Son of God and makes a mockery of Him.

—I pray to God that my poor words may have availed today to confirm in holiness those who are in a state of grace, to strengthen the wavering, to lead back to the state of grace the poor soul that has strayed if any such be among you. I pray to God, and do you pray with me, that we may repent of our sins. I will ask you now, all of you, to repeat after me the act of contrition,° kneeling here in this humble chapel in the presence of God. He is there in the tabernacle, burning with love for mankind, ready to comfort the afflicted. Be not afraid. No matter how many or how foul the sins if only you repent of them they will be forgiven you. Let no worldly shame hold you back. God is still the merciful Lord Who wishes not the eternal death of the sinner but rather that he be converted and live.

—He calls you to Him. You are His. He made you out of nothing. He loved you as only a God can love. His arms are open to receive you even though you have sinned against Him. Come to Him, poor sinner, poor vain and erring sinner. Now is the acceptable time. Now is the hour.

The priest rose and, turning towards the altar, knelt upon the step before the tabernacle in the fallen gloom. He waited till all in the chapel had knelt and every least noise was still. Then, raising his head, he repeated the act of contrition, phrase by phrase, with fervour. The boys answered him phrase by phrase. Stephen, his tongue cleaving to his palate, bowed his head, praying with his heart.

—O my God!—
—O my God!—
—I am heartily sorry—
—I am heartily sorry—
—for having offended Thee—
—for having offended Thee—

act of contrition: Formal prayer expressing remorse.

—and I detest my sins—
—and I detest my sins—
—above every other evil—
—above every other evil—
—because they displease Thee, my God—
—because they displease Thee, my God—
—Who art so deserving—
—Who art so deserving—
—of all my love—
—of all my love—
—and I firmly purpose—
—and I firmly purpose—
—by Thy holy grace—
—by Thy holy grace—
—never more to offend Thee—
—never more to offend Thee—
—and to amend my life—
—and to amend my life—

*

* *

He went up to his room after dinner in order to be alone with his soul: and at every step his soul seemed to sigh: at every step his soul mounted with his feet, sighing in the ascent, through a region of viscid gloom.

He halted on the landing before the door and then, grasping the porcelain knob, opened the door quickly. He waited in fear, his soul pining within him, praying silently that death might not touch his brow as he passed over the threshold, that the fiends that inhabit darkness might not be given power over him. He waited still at the threshold as at the entrance to some dark cave. Faces were there; eyes: they waited and watched.

—We knew perfectly well of course that although it was bound to come to the light he would find considerable difficulty in endeavouring to try to induce himself to try to endeavour to ascertain the spiritual plenipotentiary and so we knew of course perfectly well—

Murmuring faces waited and watched; murmurous voices filled the dark shell of the cave. He feared intensely in spirit and in flesh but, raising his head bravely, he strode into the room firmly. A doorway, a room, the same room, same window. He told himself calmly that those words had absolutely no sense which had seemed to rise murmurously from the dark. He told himself that it was simply his room with the door open.

He closed the door and, walking swiftly to the bed, knelt beside it and covered his face with his hands. His hands were cold and damp and his limbs ached with chill. Bodily unrest and chill and weariness beset him, routing his thoughts. Why was he kneeling there like a child saying his evening prayers? To be alone with his soul, to examine his conscience, to meet his sins face to face, to recall their times and manners and circumstances, to weep over them. He could not weep. He could not summon them to his memory. He felt only an ache of soul and body, his whole being, memory, will, understanding, flesh, benumbed and weary.

That was the work of devils, to scatter his thoughts and overcloud his conscience, assailing him at the gates of the cowardly and sincorrupted flesh: and, praying God timidly to forgive him his weakness, he crawled up on to the bed and, wrapping the blankets closely about him, covered his face again with his hands. He had sinned. He had sinned so deeply against heaven and before God that he was not worthy to be called God's child.

Could it be that he, Stephen Dedalus, had done those things? His conscience sighed in answer. Yes, he had done them, secretly, filthily, time after time, and, hardened in sinful impenitence, he had dared to wear the mask of holiness before the tabernacle itself while his soul within was a living mass of corruption. How came it that God had not struck him dead? The leprous company of his sins closed about him, breathing upon him, bending over him from all sides. He strove to forget them in an act of prayer, huddling his limbs closer together and binding down his eyelids: but the senses of his soul would not be bound and, though his eyes were shut fast, he saw the places where he had sinned and, though his ears were tightly covered, he heard. He desired with all his will not to hear or see. He desired till his frame shook under the strain of his desire and until the senses of his soul closed. They closed for an instant and then opened. He saw.

A field of stiff weeds and thistles and tufted nettlebunches. Thick among the tufts of rank stiff growth lay battered canisters and clots and coils of solid excrement. A faint marshlight struggled upwards from all the ordure through the bristling greygreen weeds. An evil smell, faint and foul as the light, curled upwards sluggishly out of the canisters and from the stale crusted dung.

Creatures were in the field; one, three, six: creatures were moving in the field, hither and thither. Goatish creatures with human faces, hornybrowed, lightly bearded and grey as indiarubber. The malice of evil glittered in their hard eyes, as they moved hither and thither, trailing their long tails behind them. A rictus of cruel malignity lit up greyly their old bony faces. One was clasping about his ribs a torn flannel waistcoat, another complained monotonously as his beard stuck in the tufted weeds. Soft language issued from their spittleless lips as they swished in slow circles round and round the field, winding hither and thither through the weeds, dragging their long tails amid the rattling canisters. They moved in slow circles, circling closer and closer to enclose, to enclose, soft language issuing from their lips, their long swishing tails besmeared with stale shite, thrusting upwards their terrific faces . . .

Help!

He flung the blankets from him madly to free his face and neck. That was his hell. God had allowed him to see the hell reserved for his sins: stinking, bestial, malignant, a hell of lecherous goatish fiends. For him! For him!

He sprang from the bed, the reeking odour pouring down his throat, clogging and revolting his entrails. Air! The air of heaven! He stumbled towards the window, groaning and almost fainting with sickness. At the washstand a convulsion seized him within: and, clasping his cold forehead wildly, he vomited profusely in agony.

When the fit had spent itself he walked weakly to the window and, lifting the sash, sat in a corner of the embrasure and leaned his elbow upon the sill. The rain had drawn off; and amid the moving vapours from point to point of light the city was spinning about herself a soft cocoon of yellowish haze. Heaven was still and faintly luminous and the air sweet to breathe, as in a thicket drenched with showers: and amid peace and shimmering lights and quiet fragrances he made a covenant with his heart.

He prayed:

—He once had meant to come on earth in heavenly glory but we sinned: and then He could not safely visit us but with a shrouded majesty and a bedimmed radiance for He was God. So He came Himself in weakness not in power and He sent thee, a creature in His stead, with a creature's comeliness and lustre suited to our state. And now thy very face and form, dear mother, speak to us of the Eternal; not like earthly beauty, dangerous to look upon, but like the morning star which is thy emblem, bright and musical, breathing purity, telling of heaven and infusing peace. O harbinger of day! O light of the pilgrim! Lead us still as thou hast led. In the dark night, across the bleak wilderness guide us on to our Lord Jesus, guide us home.

His eyes were dimmed with tears and, looking humbly up to heaven, he wept for the innocence he had lost.

When evening had fallen he left the house and the first touch of the damp dark air and the noise of the door as it closed behind him made ache again his conscience, lulled by prayer and tears. Confess! Confess! It was not enough to lull the conscience with a tear and a prayer. He had to kneel before the minister of the Holy Ghost and tell over his hidden sins truly and repentantly. Before he heard again the footboard of the housedoor trail over the threshold as it opened to let him in, before he saw again the table in the kitchen set for supper he would have knelt and confessed. It was quite simple.

The ache of conscience ceased and he walked onward swiftly through the dark streets. There were so many flagstones on the footpath of that street and so many streets in that city and so many cities in the world. Yet eternity had no end. He was in mortal sin. Even once was a mortal sin. It could happen in an instant. But how so quickly? By seeing or by thinking of seeing. The eyes see the thing, without having wished first to see. Then in an instant it happens. But does that part of the body understand or what? The serpent, the most subtle beast of the field. It must understand when it desires in one instant and then prolongs its own desire instant after instant, sinfully. It feels and understands and desires. What a horrible thing! Who made it to be like that, a bestial part of the body able to understand bestially and desire bestially? Was that then he or an inhuman thing moved by a lower soul than his soul? His soul sickened at the thought of a torpid snaky life feeding itself out of the tender marrow of his life and fattening upon the slime of lust. O why was that so? O why?

He cowered in the shadow of the thought, abasing himself in the awe of God Who had made all things and all men. Madness. Who could think such a thought? And, cowering in darkness and abject, he prayed mutely to his angel guardian to drive away with his sword the demon that was whispering to his brain.

The whisper ceased and he knew then clearly that his own soul had sinned in thought and word and deed wilfully through his own body. Confess! He had to confess every sin. How could he utter in words to the priest what he had done? Must, must. Or how could he explain without dying of shame? Or how could he have done such things without shame? A madman, a loathsome madman! Confess! O he would indeed to be free and sinless again! Perhaps the priest would know. O dear God!

He walked on and on through illlit streets, fearing to stand still for a moment lest it might seem that he held back from what awaited him, fearing to arrive at that towards which he still turned with longing. How beautiful must be a soul in the state of grace when God looked upon it with love!

Frowsy girls sat along the curbstones before their baskets of herrings. Their dank hair hung trailed over their brows. They were not beautiful to see as they crouched in the mire. But their souls were seen by God; and if their souls were in a state of grace they were radiant to see: and God loved them, seeing them.

A wasting breath of humiliation blew bleakly over his soul to think of how he had fallen, to feel that those souls were dearer to God than his. The wind blew over him and passed on to the myriads and myriads of other souls on whom God's favour shone now more and now less, stars now brighter and now dimmer, sustained and failing. And the glimmering souls passed away, sustained and failing, merged in a moving breath. One soul was lost; a tiny soul: his. It flickered once and went out, forgotten, lost. The end: black cold void waste.

Consciousness of place came ebbing back to him slowly over a vast tract of time, unlit, unfelt, unlived. The squalid scene composed itself around him; the common accents, the burning gasjets in the shops, odours of fish and spirits and wet sawdust, moving men and women. An old woman was about to cross the street, an oilcan in her hand. He bent down and asked her was there a chapel near.

—A chapel, sir? Yes, sir. Church Street chapel.

—Church?

She shifted the can to her other hand and directed him: and, as she held out her reeking withered right hand under its fringe of shawl, he bent lower towards her, saddened and soothed by her voice.

—Thank you.

—You are quite welcome, sir.

The candles on the high altar had been extinguished but the fragrance of incense still floated down the dim nave. Bearded workmen with pious faces were guiding a canopy out through a sidedoor, the sacristan aiding them with quiet gestures and words. A few of the faithful still lingered, praying before one of the sidealtars or kneeling in the benches near the confessionals. He approached timidly and knelt at the last bench in the body, thankful for the peace and silence and fragrant shadow of the church. The board on which he knelt was narrow and worn and those who knelt near him were humble followers of Jesus. Jesus too had been born in poverty and had worked in the shop of a carpenter, cutting boards and planing them, and had first spoken of the kingdom of God to poor fishermen, teaching all men to be meek and humble of heart.

He bowed his head upon his hands, bidding his heart be meek and humble that he might be like those who knelt beside him and his prayer as acceptable as theirs. He prayed beside them but it was hard. His soul was foul with sin and he dared not ask forgiveness with the simple trust of those whom Jesus, in the mysterious ways of God, had called first to His side, the carpenters, the fishermen, poor and simple people following a lowly trade, handling and shaping the wood of trees, mending their nets with patience.

A tall figure came down the aisle and the penitents stirred: and at the last moment, glancing up swiftly, he saw a long grey beard and the brown habit of a capuchin.° The priest entered the box and was hidden. Two penitents rose and entered the confessional at either side. The wooden slide was drawn back and the faint murmur of a voice troubled the silence.

His blood began to murmur in his veins, murmuring like a sinful city summoned from its sleep to hear its doom. Little flakes of fire fell and powdery ashes fell softly, alighting on the houses of men. They stirred, waking from sleep, troubled by the heated air.

The slide was shot back. The penitent emerged from the side of the box. The farther slide was drawn. A woman entered quietly and deftly where the first penitent had knelt. The faint murmur began again.

He could still leave the chapel. He could stand up, put one foot before the other and walk out softly and then run, run, run swiftly through the dark streets. He could still escape from the shame. O what shame! His face was burning with shame. Had it been any terrible crime but that one sin! Had it been murder! Little fiery flakes fell and touched him at all points, shameful thoughts, shameful words, shameful acts. Shame covered him wholly like fine glowing ashes falling continually. To say it in words! His soul, stifling and helpless, would cease to be.

The slide was shot back. A penitent emerged from the farther side of the box. The near slide was drawn. A penitent entered where the other penitent had come out. A soft whispering noise floated in vaporous cloudlets out of the box. It was the woman: soft whispering cloudlets, soft whispering vapour, whispering and vanishing.

He beat his breast with his fist humbly, secretly under cover of the wooden armrest. He would be at one with others and with God. He

brown habit of a capuchin: Belted robe worn by Capuchins, a branch of the Franciscan order of friars.

would love his neighbour. He would love God Who had made and loved him. He would kneel and pray with others and be happy. God would look down on him and on them and would love them all.

It was easy to be good. God's yoke was sweet and light. It was better never to have sinned, to have remained always a child, for God loved little children and suffered them to come to Him. It was a terrible and a sad thing to sin. But God was merciful to poor sinners who were truly sorry. How true that was! That was indeed goodness.

The slide was shot to suddenly. The penitent came out. He was next. He stood up in terror and walked blindly into the box.

At last it had come. He knelt in the silent gloom and raised his eyes to the white crucifix suspended above him. God could see that he was sorry. He would tell all his sins. His confession would be long, long. Everybody in the chapel would know then what a sinner he had been. Let them know. It was true. But God had promised to forgive him if he was sorry. He was sorry. He clasped his hands and raised them towards the white form, praying with his darkened eyes, praying with all his trembling body, swaying his head to and fro like a lost creature, praying with whimpering lips.

—Sorry! Sorry! O sorry!

The slide clicked back and his heart bounded in his breast. The face of an old priest was at the grating, averted from him, leaning upon a hand. He made the sign of the cross and prayed of the priest to bless him for he had sinned. Then, bowing his head, he repeated the *Confiteor* in fright. At the words *my most grievous fault* he ceased, breathless.

—How long is it since your last confession, my child?

—A long time, father.

—A month, my child?

—Longer, father.

—Three months, my child?

—Longer, father.

—Six months?

—Eight months, father.

He had begun. The priest asked:

—And what do you remember since that time?

He began to confess his sins: masses missed, prayers not said, lies.

—Anything else, my child?

Sins of anger, envy of others, gluttony, vanity, disobedience.

—Anything else, my child?

—Sloth.

—Anything else, my child?

There was no help. He murmured:

—I . . . committed sins of impurity, father.

The priest did not turn his head.

—With yourself, my child?

—And . . . with others.

—With women, my child?

—Yes, father.

—Were they married women, my child?

He did not know. His sins trickled from his lips, one by one, trickled in shameful drops from his soul festering and oozing like a sore, a squalid stream of vice. The last sins oozed forth, sluggish, filthy. There was no more to tell. He bowed his head, overcome.

The priest was silent. Then he asked:

—How old are you, my child?

—Sixteen, father.

The priest passed his hand several times over his face. Then, resting his forehead against his hand, he leaned towards the grating and, with eyes still averted, spoke slowly. His voice was weary and old.

—You are very young, my child, he said, and let me implore of you to give up that sin. It is a terrible sin. It kills the body and it kills the soul. It is the cause of many crimes and misfortunes. Give it up, my child, for God's sake. It is dishonourable and unmanly. You cannot know where that wretched habit will lead you or where it will come against you. As long as you commit that sin, my poor child, you will never be worth one farthing to God. Pray to our mother Mary to help you. She will help you, my child. Pray to Our Blessed Lady when that sin comes into your mind. I am sure you will do that, will you not? You repent of all those sins. I am sure you do. And you will promise God now that by His holy grace you will never offend Him any more by that wicked sin. You will make that solemn promise to God, will you not?

—Yes, father.

The old and weary voice fell like sweet rain upon his quaking parching heart. How sweet and sad!

—Do so, my poor child. The devil has led you astray. Drive him back to hell when he tempts you to dishonour your body in that way—the foul spirit who hates Our Lord. Promise God now that you will give up that sin, that wretched wretched sin.

Blinded by his tears and by the light of God's mercifulness he bent his head and heard the grave words of absolution spoken and saw the priest's hand raised above him in token of forgiveness.

—God bless you, my child. Pray for me.

He knelt to say his penance, praying in a corner of the dark nave: and his prayers ascended to heaven from his purified heart like perfume streaming upwards from a heart of white rose.

The muddy streets were gay. He strode homeward, conscious of an invisible grace pervading and making light his limbs. In spite of all he had done it. He had confessed and God had pardoned him. His soul was made fair and holy once more, holy and happy.

It would be beautiful to die if God so willed. It was beautiful to live if God so willed, to live in grace a life of peace and virtue and forbearance with others.

He sat by the fire in the kitchen, not daring to speak for happiness. Till that moment he had not known how beautiful and peaceful life could be. The green square of paper pinned round the lamp cast down a tender shade. On the dresser was a plate of sausages and white pudding and on the shelf there were eggs. They would be for the breakfast in the morning after the communion in the college chapel. White pudding and eggs and sausages and cups of tea. How simple and beautiful was life after all! And life lay all before him.

In a dream he fell asleep. In a dream he rose and saw that it was morning. In a waking dream he went through the quiet morning towards the college.

The boys were all there, kneeling in their places. He knelt among them, happy and shy. The altar was heaped with fragrant masses of white flowers: and in the morning light the pale flames of the candles among the white flowers were clear and silent as his own soul.

He knelt before the altar with his classmates, holding the altarcloth with them over a living rail of hands. His hands were trembling: and his soul trembled as he heard the priest pass with the ciborium° from communicant to communicant.

—*Corpus Domini nostri.*°

Could it be? He knelt there sinless and timid: and he would hold upon his tongue the host and God would enter his purified body.

—*In vitam eternam.*° *Amen.*

Another life! A life of grace and virtue and happiness! It was true. It was not a dream from which he would wake. The past was past.

—*Corpus Domini nostri.*

The ciborium had come to him.

ciborium: Vessel that holds the host during communion. ***Corpus Domini nostri:*** The Body of Our Lord. ***In vitam eternam:*** Unto everlasting life.

IV

Sunday was dedicated to the mystery of the Holy Trinity, Monday to the Holy Ghost, Tuesday to the Guardian Angels, Wednesday to Saint Joseph, Thursday to the Most Blessed Sacrament of the Altar, Friday to the Suffering Jesus, Saturday to the Blessed Virgin Mary.

Every morning he hallowed himself anew in the presence of some holy image or mystery. His day began with an heroic offering of its every moment of thought or action for the intentions of the sovereign pontiff and with an early mass. The raw morning air whetted his resolute piety; and often as he knelt among the few worshippers at the sidealtar, following with his interleaved prayerbook the murmur of the priest, he glanced up for an instant towards the vested figure standing in the gloom between the two candles which were the old and the new testaments and imagined that he was kneeling at mass in the catacombs.

His daily life was laid out in devotional areas. By means of ejaculations° and prayers he stored up ungrudgingly for the souls in purgatory centuries of days and quarantines and years; yet the spiritual triumph which he felt in achieving with ease so many fabulous ages of canonical penances did not wholly reward his zeal of prayer since he could never know how much temporal punishment he had remitted by way of suffrage for the agonising souls: and, fearful lest in the midst of the purgatorial fire, which differed from the infernal only in that it was not everlasting, his penance might avail no more than a drop of moisture, he drove his soul daily through an increasing circle of works of supererogation.°

Every part of his day, divided by what he regarded now as the duties of his station in life, circled about its own centre of spiritual energy. His life seemed to have drawn near to eternity; every thought, word and deed, every instant of consciousness could be made to revibrate radiantly in heaven: and at times his sense of such immediate repercussion was so lively that he seemed to feel his soul in devotion pressing like fingers the keyboard of a great cashregister and to see the amount of his purchase start forth immediately in heaven, not as a number but as a frail column of incense or as a slender flower.

The rosaries too which he said constantly—for he carried his beads loose in his trousers' pockets that he might tell them as he walked the streets— transformed themselves into coronals of flowers of such vague

ejaculations: Brief outcries or prayers. **supererogation:** Acts beyond the requirements of duty to establish a "reservoir of merit."

unearthly texture that they seemed to him as hueless and odourless as they were nameless. He offered up each of his three daily chaplets° that his soul might grow strong in each of the three theological virtues, in faith in the Father, in hope in the Son, in charity in the Holy Ghost, and as daily offerings of thanksgiving to the Father Who had created him, to the Son Who had redeemed him and to the Holy Ghost Who had sanctified him: and this thrice triple prayer he offered to the Three Persons through Mary in the name of her joyful and sorrowful and glorious mysteries.

On each of the seven days of the week he further prayed that one of the seven gifts of the Holy Ghost might descend upon his soul and drive out of it day by day the seven deadly sins which had defiled it in the past: and he prayed for each gift on its appointed day, confident that it would descend upon him, though it seemed to him strange at times that wisdom and understanding and knowledge were so distinct in their nature that each should be prayed for apart from the others. Yet he believed that at some future stage of his spiritual progress this difficulty would be removed when his sinful soul had been raised up from its weakness and enlightened by the Third Person of the Most Blessed Trinity. He believed this all the more and with trepidation because of the divine gloom and silence wherein dwelt the unseen Paraclete,° Whose symbols were a dove and a mighty wind, to sin against Whom was a sin beyond forgiveness, the eternal, mysterious, secret Being to Whom, as God, the priests offered up mass once a year, robed in the scarlet of the tongues of fire.

The imagery through which the nature and kinship of the Three Persons of the Trinity were darkly shadowed forth in the books of devotion which he read— the Father contemplating from all eternity as in a mirror His Divine Perfections and thereby begetting eternally the Eternal Son and the Holy Spirit proceeding out of Father and Son from all eternity—were easier of acceptance by his mind by reason of their august incomprehensibility than was the simple fact that God had loved his soul from all eternity, for ages before he had been born into the world, for ages before the world itself had existed. He had heard the names of the passions of love and hate pronounced solemnly on the stage and in the pulpit, had found them set forth solemnly in books, and had wondered why his soul was unable to harbour them for any time or to force his lips to utter their names with conviction. A brief anger had often

chaplets: The three divisions of the cycle of prayers called a rosary, each of which is subdivided into decades. **Paraclete:** Term for the Holy Ghost.

invested him but he had never been able to make it an abiding passion and had always felt himself passing out of it as if his very body were being divested with ease of some outer skin or peel. He had felt a subtle, dark and murmurous presence penetrate his being and fire him with a brief iniquitous lust: it too had slipped beyond his grasp leaving his mind lucid and indifferent. This, it seemed, was the only love and that the only hate his soul would harbour.

But he could no longer disbelieve in the reality of love since God Himself had loved his individual soul with divine love from all eternity. Gradually, as his soul was enriched with spiritual knowledge, he saw the whole world forming one vast symmetrical expression of God's power and love. Life became a divine gift for every moment and sensation of which, were it even the sight of a single leaf hanging on the twig of a tree, his soul should praise and thank the Giver. The world for all its solid substance and complexity no longer existed for his soul save as a theorem of divine power and love and universality. So entire and unquestionable was this sense of the divine meaning in all nature granted to his soul that he could scarcely understand why it was in any way necessary that he should continue to live. Yet that also was part of the divine purpose and he dared not question its use, he above all others who had sinned so deeply and so foully against the divine purpose. Meek and abased by this consciousness of the one eternal omnipresent perfect reality his soul took up again her burden of pieties, masses and prayers and sacraments and mortifications, and only then for the first time since he had brooded on the great mystery of love did he feel within him a warm movement like that of some newly born life or virtue of the soul itself. The attitude of rapture in sacred art, the raised and parted hands, the parted lips and eyes as of one about to swoon, became for him an image of the soul in prayer, humiliated and faint before her Creator.

But he had been forewarned of the dangers of spiritual exaltation and did not allow himself to desist from even the least or lowliest devotion, striving also by constant mortification to undo the sinful past rather than to achieve a saintliness fraught with peril. Each of his senses was brought under a rigorous discipline. In order to mortify the sense of sight he made it his rule to walk in the street with downcast eyes, glancing neither to right nor left and never behind him. His eyes shunned every encounter with the eyes of women. From time to time also he balked them by a sudden effort of the will, as by lifting them suddenly in the middle of an unfinished sentence and closing the book. To mortify his hearing he exerted no control over his voice which was then breaking, neither sang nor whistled and made no attempt to flee from noises which caused him painful nervous irritation such as the sharpening of knives on the knifeboard, the gathering of cinders on the fireshovel and the twigging° of the carpet. To mortify his smell was more difficult as he found in himself no instinctive repugnance to bad odours, whether they were the odours of the outdoor world such as those of dung and tar or the odours of his own person among which he had made many curious comparisons and experiments. He found in the end that the only odour against which his sense of smell revolted was a certain stale fishy stink like that of longstanding urine: and whenever it was possible he subjected himself to this unpleasant odour. To mortify the taste he practised strict habits at table, observed to the letter all the fasts of the church and sought by distraction to divert his mind from the savours of different foods. But it was to the mortification of touch that he brought the most assiduous ingenuity of inventiveness. He never consciously changed his position in bed, sat in the most uncomfortable positions, suffered patiently every itch and pain, kept away from the fire, remained on his knees all through the mass except at the gospels, left parts of his neck and face undried so that the air might sting them and, whenever he was not saying his beads, carried his arms stiffly at his sides like a runner and never in his pockets or clasped behind him.

He had no temptations to sin mortally. It surprised him however to find that at the end of his course of intricate piety and selfrestraint he was so easily at the mercy of childish and unworthy imperfections. His prayers and fasts availed him little for the suppression of anger at hearing his mother sneeze or at being disturbed in his devotions. It needed an immense effort of his will to master the impulse which urged him to give outlet to such irritation. Images of the outbursts of trivial anger which he had often noted among his masters, their twitching mouths, closeshut lips and flushed cheeks, recurred to his memory, discouraging him, for all his practice of humility, by the comparison. To merge his life in the common tide of other lives was harder for him than any fasting or prayer, and it was his constant failure to do this to his own satisfaction which caused in his soul at last a sensation of spiritual dryness together with a growth of doubts and scruples. His soul traversed a period of desolation in which the sacraments themselves seemed to have turned into dried up sources. His confession became a channel for the escape of scrupulous and unrepented imperfections. His actual reception of the eucharist did not bring him the same dissolving

twigging: Brushing with a short broom.

moments of virginal selfsurrender as did those spiritual communions made by him sometimes at the close of some visit to the Blessed Sacrament. The book which he used for these visits was an old neglected book written by saint Alphonsus Liguori, with fading characters and sere foxpapered° leaves. A faded world of fervent love and virginal responses seemed to be evoked for his soul by the reading of its pages in which the imagery of the canticles° was interwoven with the communicant's prayers. An inaudible voice seemed to caress the soul, telling her names and glories, bidding her arise as for espousal and come away, bidding her look forth, a spouse, from Amana and from the mountains of the leopards; and the soul seemed to answer with the same inaudible voice, surrendering herself:

Inter ubera mea commorabitur. °

This idea of surrender had a perilous attraction for his mind now that he felt his soul beset once again by the insistent voices of the flesh which began to murmur to him again during his prayers and meditations. It gave him an intense sense of power to know that he could, by a single act of consent, in a moment of thought, undo all that he had done. He seemed to feel a flood slowly advancing towards his naked feet and to be waiting for the first faint timid noiseless wavelet to touch his fevered skin. Then, almost at the instant of that touch, almost at the verge of sinful consent, he found himself standing far away from the flood upon a dry shore, saved by a sudden act of the will or a sudden ejaculation: and, seeing the silver line of the flood far away and beginning again its slow advance towards his feet, a new thrill of power and satisfaction shook his soul to know that he had not yielded nor undone all.

When he had eluded the flood of temptation many times in this way he grew troubled and wondered whether the grace which he had refused to lose was not being filched from him little by little. The clear certitude of his own immunity grew dim and to it succeeded a vague fear that his soul had really fallen unawares. It was with difficulty that he won back his old consciousness of his state of grace by telling himself that he had prayed to God at every temptation and that the grace which he had prayed for must have been given to him inasmuch as God was obliged to give it. The very frequency and violence of temptations showed him at last the truth of what he had heard about the trials of the

foxpapered: Having pages that are "foxed," or discolored. **canticles:** The Song of Songs or Song of Solomon in the Protestant Bible. ***Inter ubera mea commorabitur:*** He shall lie between my breasts; from the Song of Solomon.

saints. Frequent and violent temptations were a proof that the citadel of the soul had not fallen and that the devil raged to make it fall.

Often when he had confessed his doubts and scruples, some momentary inattention at prayer, a movement of trivial anger in his soul or a subtle wilfulness in speech or act, he was bidden by his confessor to name some sin of his past life before absolution was given him. He named it with humility and shame and repented of it once more. It humiliated and shamed him to think that he would never be freed from it wholly, however holily he might live or whatever virtues or perfections he might attain. A restless feeling of guilt would always be present with him: he would confess and repent and be absolved, confess and repent again and be absolved again, fruitlessly. Perhaps that first hasty confession wrung from him by the fear of hell had not been good? Perhaps, concerned only for his imminent doom, he had not had sincere sorrow for his sin? But the surest sign that his confession had been good and that he had had sincere sorrow for his sin was, he knew, the amendment of his life.

—I have amended my life, have I not? he asked himself.

*

* *

The director stood in the embrasure of the window, his back to the light, leaning an elbow on the brown crossblind and, as he spoke and smiled, slowly dangling and looping the cord of the other blind. Stephen stood before him, following for a moment with his eyes the waning of the long summer daylight above the roofs or the slow deft movements of the priestly fingers. The priest's face was in total shadow but the waning daylight from behind him touched the deeply grooved temples and the curves of the skull. Stephen followed also with his ears the accents and intervals of the priest's voice as he spoke gravely and cordially of indifferent themes, the vacation which had just ended, the colleges of the order abroad, the transference of masters. The grave and cordial voice went on easily with its tale and in the pauses Stephen felt bound to set it on again with respectful questions. He knew that the tale was a prelude and his mind waited for the sequel. Ever since the message of summons had come for him from the director his mind had struggled to find the meaning of the message; and during the long restless time he had sat in the college parlour waiting for the director to come in his eyes had wandered from one sober picture to another around the walls and his mind had wandered from one guess to another until the meaning of the summons had almost become clear. Then, just as he was wishing that some unforeseen cause might prevent the director from coming, he had heard the handle of the door turning and the swish of a soutane.

The director had begun to speak of the dominican° and franciscan° orders and of the friendship between saint Thomas and saint Bonaventure. The capuchin dress, he thought, was rather too . . .

Stephen's face gave back the priest's indulgent smile and, not being anxious to give an opinion, he made a slight dubitative movement with his lips.

—I believe, continued the director, that there is some talk now among the capuchins themselves of doing away with it and following the example of the other franciscans.

—I suppose they would retain it in the cloister, said Stephen.

—O, certainly, said the director. For the cloister it is all right but for the street I really think it would be better to do away with it, don't you?

—It must be troublesome, I imagine.

—Of course it is: of course. Just imagine, when I was in Belgium I used to see them out cycling in all kinds of weather with this thing up about their knees! It was really ridiculous. *Les jupes,*° they call them in Belgium.

The vowel was so modified as to be indistinct.

—What do they call them?

—*Les jupes.*

—O.

Stephen smiled again in answer to the smile which he could not see on the priest's shadowed face, its image or spectre only passing rapidly across his mind as the low discreet accent fell upon his ear. He gazed calmly before him at the waning sky, glad of the cool of the evening and of the faint yellow glow which hid the tiny flame kindling upon his cheek.

The names of articles of dress worn by women or of certain soft and delicate stuffs used in their making brought always to his mind a delicate and sinful perfume. As a boy he had imagined the reins by which horses are driven as slender silken bands and it shocked him to feel at Stradbrook the greasy leather of harness. It had shocked him too when he had felt for the first time beneath his tremulous fingers the brittle texture of a woman's stocking for, retaining nothing of all he read save that which seemed to him an echo or a prophecy of his own state, it was

dominican: Order founded by St. Dominic. **franciscan:** Order founded by St. Francis of Assisi. ***Les jupes:*** Skirts (French).

only amid softworded phrases or within rosesoft stuffs that he dared to conceive of the soul or body of a woman moving with tender life.

But the phrase on the priest's lips was disingenuous for he knew that a priest should not speak lightly on that theme. The phrase had been spoken lightly with design and he felt that his face was being searched by the eyes in the shadow. Whatever he had heard or read of the craft of jesuits he had put aside frankly as not borne out by his own experience. His masters, even when they had not attracted him, had seemed to him always intelligent and serious priests, athletic and high-spirited prefects. He thought of them as men who washed their bodies briskly with cold water and wore clean cold linen. During all the years he had lived among them in Clongowes and in Belvedere he had received only two pandies and, though these had been dealt him in the wrong, he knew that he had often escaped punishment. During all those years he had never heard from any of his masters a flippant word: it was they who had taught him christian doctrine and urged him to live a good life and, when he had fallen into grievous sin, it was they who had led him back to grace. Their presence had made him diffident of himself when he was a muff° in Clongowes and it had made him diffident of himself also while he had held his equivocal position in Belvedere. A constant sense of this had remained with him up to the last year of his school life. He had never once disobeyed or allowed turbulent companions to seduce him from his habit of quiet obedience: and, even when he doubted some statement of a master, he had never presumed to doubt openly. Lately some of their judgments had sounded a little childish in his ears and had made him feel a regret and pity as though he were slowly passing out of an accustomed world and were hearing its language for the last time. One day when some boys had gathered round a priest under the shed near the chapel, he had heard the priest say:

—I believe that Lord Macaulay was a man who probably never committed a mortal sin in his life, that is to say, a deliberate mortal sin.

Some of the boys had then asked the priest if Victor Hugo were not the greatest French writer. The priest had answered that Victor Hugo had never written half so well when he had turned against the church as he had written when he was a catholic.

—But there are many eminent French critics, said the priest, who consider that even Victor Hugo, great as he certainly was, had not so pure a French style as Louis Veuillot.

muff: A bungler, novice, or outsider.

The tiny flame which the priest's allusion had kindled upon Stephen's cheek had sunk down again and his eyes were still fixed calmly on the colorless sky. But an unresting doubt flew hither and thither before his mind. Masked memories passed quickly before him: he recognised scenes and persons yet he was conscious that he had failed to perceive some vital circumstance in them. He saw himself walking about the grounds watching the sports in Clongowes and eating slim jim out of his cricketcap. Some jesuits were walking round the cycletrack in the company of ladies. The echoes of certain expressions used in Clongowes sounded in remote caves of his mind.

His ears were listening to these distant echoes amid the silence of the parlour when he became aware that the priest was addressing him in a different voice.

—I sent for you today, Stephen, because I wished to speak to you on a very important subject.

—Yes, sir.

—Have you ever felt that you had a vocation?°

Stephen parted his lips to answer yes and then withheld the word suddenly. The priest waited for the answer and added:

—I mean have you ever felt within yourself, in your soul, a desire to join the order. Think.

—I have sometimes thought of it, said Stephen.

The priest let the blindcord fall to one side and, uniting his hands, leaned his chin gravely upon them, communing with himself.

—In a college like this, he said at length, there is one boy or perhaps two or three boys whom God calls to the religious life. Such a boy is marked off from his companions by his piety, by the good example he shows to others. He is looked up to by them; he is chosen perhaps as prefect by his fellow sodalists. And you, Stephen, have been such a boy in this college, prefect of Our Blessed Lady's sodality. Perhaps you are the boy in this college whom God designs to call to Himself.

A strong note of pride reinforcing the gravity of the priest's voice made Stephen's heart quicken in response.

—To receive that call, Stephen, said the priest, is the greatest honour that the Almighty God can bestow upon a man. No king or emperor on this earth has the power of the priest of God. No angel or archangel in heaven, no saint, not even the Blessed Virgin herself has the power of a priest of God: the power of the keys, the power to bind and to loose from sin, the power of exorcism, the power to cast out from the

a vocation: A "calling" for the priesthood.

creatures of God the evil spirits that have power over them, the power, the authority, to make the great God of Heaven come down upon the altar and take the form of bread and wine. What an awful power, Stephen!

A flame began to flutter again on Stephen's cheek as he heard in this proud address an echo of his own proud musings. How often had he seen himself as a priest wielding calmly and humbly the awful power of which angels and saints stood in reverence! His soul had loved to muse in secret on this desire. He had seen himself, a young and silent-mannered priest, entering a confessional swiftly, ascending the altar-steps, incensing, genuflecting, accomplishing the vague acts of the priesthood which pleased him by reason of their semblance of reality and of their distance from it. In that dim life which he had lived through in his musings he had assumed the voices and gestures which he had noted with various priests. He had bent his knee sideways like such a one, he had shaken the thurible° only slightly like such a one, his chasuble° had swung open like that of such another as he had turned to the altar again after having blessed the people. And above all it had pleased him to fill the second place in those dim scenes of his imagining. He shrank from the dignity of celebrant because it displeased him to imagine that all the vague pomp should end in his own person or that the ritual should assign to him so clear and final an office. He longed for the minor sacred offices, to be vested with the tunicle of subdeacon° at high mass, to stand aloof from the altar, forgotten by the people, his shoulders covered with a humeral veil,° holding the paten° within its folds, or, when the sacrifice had been accomplished, to stand as deacon in a dalmatic° of cloth of gold on the step below the celebrant, his hands joined and his face towards the people, and sing the chant *Ite, missa est.*° If ever he had seen himself celebrant it was as in the pictures of the mass in his child's massbook, in a church without worshippers, save for the angel of the sacrifice, at a bare altar and served by an acolyte scarcely more boyish than himself. In vague sacrificial or sacramental acts alone his will seemed drawn to go forth to encounter reality: and it was partly the absence of an appointed rite which had always con-

thurible: Censer, in which incense is burned. **chasuble:** Long outer vestment worn by a priest celebrating the mass. **tunicle of subdeacon:** Wide-sleeved vestment worn by the person who prepares the sacred vessels during the celebration of the Mass. **humeral veil:** Veil covering the shoulders. **paten:** Plate on which the eucharistic bread is placed. **dalmatic:** Wide-sleeved vestment worn during celebration of High Mass by the deacon, the person ranked second to the celebrant himself. ***Ite, missa est:*** Go, the Mass is completed.

strained him to inaction whether he had allowed silence to cover his anger or pride or had suffered only an embrace he longed to give.

He listened in reverent silence now to the priest's appeal and through the words he heard even more distinctly a voice bidding him approach, offering him secret knowledge and secret power. He would know then what was the sin of Simon Magus and what the sin against the Holy Ghost for which there was no forgiveness. He would know obscure things, hidden from others, from those who were conceived and born children of wrath. He would know the sins, the sinful longings and sinful thoughts and sinful acts, of others, hearing them murmured into his ear in the confessional under the shame of a darkened chapel by the lips of women and of girls: but rendered immune mysteriously at his ordination by the imposition of hands his soul would pass again uncontaminated to the white peace of the altar. No touch of sin would linger upon the hands with which he would elevate and break the host; no touch of sin would linger on his lips in prayer to make him eat and drink damnation to himself, not discerning the body of the Lord. He would hold his secret knowledge and secret power, being as sinless as the innocent: and he would be a priest for ever according to the order of Melchisedec.

—I will offer up my mass tomorrow morning, said the director, that Almighty God may reveal to you His holy will. And let you, Stephen, make a novena° to your holy patron saint, the first martyr, who is very powerful with God, that God may enlighten your mind. But you must be quite sure, Stephen, that you have a vocation because it would be terrible if you found afterwards that you had none. Once a priest always a priest, remember. Your catechism tells you that the sacrament of Holy Orders is one of those which can be received only once because it imprints on the soul an indelible spiritual mark which can never be effaced. It is before you must weigh well, not after. It is a solemn question, Stephen, because on it may depend the salvation of your eternal soul. But we will pray to God together.

He held open the heavy halldoor and gave his hand as if already to a companion in the spiritual life. Stephen passed out on to the wide platform above the steps and was conscious of the caress of mild evening air. Towards Findlater's Church a quartet of young men were striding along with linked arms, swaying their heads and stepping to the agile melody of their leader's concertina. The music passed in an instant, as the first bars of sudden music always did, over the fantastic fabrics of

novena: A series of spiritual exercises lasting nine days.

his mind, dissolving them painlessly and noiselessly as a sudden wave dissolves the sandbuilt turrets of children. Smiling at the trivial air he raised his eyes to the priest's face and, seeing in it a mirthless reflection of the sunken day, detached his hand slowly which had acquiesced faintly in that companionship.

As he descended the steps the impression which effaced his troubled selfcommunion was that of a mirthless mask reflecting a sunken day from the threshold of the college. The shadow, then, of the life of the college passed gravely over his consciousness. It was a grave and ordered and passionless life that awaited him, a life without material cares. He wondered how he would pass the first night in the novitiate° and with what dismay he would wake the first morning in the dormitory. The troubling odour of the long corridors of Clongowes came back to him and he heard the discreet murmur of the burning gasflames. At once from every part of his being unrest began to irradiate. A feverish quickening of his pulses followed and a din of meaningless words drove his reasoned thoughts hither and thither confusedly. His lungs dilated and sank as if he were inhaling a warm moist unsustaining air and he smelt again the warm moist air which hung in the bath in Clongowes above the sluggish turfcoloured water.

Some instinct, waking at these memories, stronger than education or piety, quickened within him at every near approach to that life, an instinct subtle and hostile, and armed him against acquiescence. The chill and order of the life repelled him. He saw himself rising in the cold of the morning and filing down with the others to early mass and trying vainly to struggle with his prayers against the fainting sickness of his stomach. He saw himself sitting at dinner with the community of a college. What, then, had become of that deeprooted shyness of his which had made him loth to eat or drink under a strange roof? What had come of the pride of his spirit which had always made him conceive himself as a being apart in every order?

The Reverend Stephen Dedalus, S.J.°

His name in that new life leaped into characters before his eyes and to it there followed a mental sensation of an undefined face or colour of a face. The colour faded and became strong like a changing glow of pallid brick red. Was it the raw reddish glow he had so often seen on wintry mornings on the shaven gills of the priests? The face was eyeless and sourfavoured and devout, shot with pink tinges of suffocated anger.

novitiate: Time of probation for aspiring priests. **S.J.:** Society of Jesus (the Jesuit order).

Was it not a mental spectre of the face of one of the jesuits whom some of the boys called Lantern Jaws and others Foxy Campbell?

He was passing at that moment before the jesuit house in Gardiner Street and wondered vaguely which window would be his if he ever joined the order. Then he wondered at the vagueness of his wonder, at the remoteness of his soul from what he had hitherto imagined her sanctuary, at the frail hold which so many years of order and obedience had of him when once a definite and irrevocable act of his threatened to end for ever, in time and in eternity, his freedom. The voice of the director urging upon him the proud claims of the church and the mystery and power of the priestly office repeated itself idly in his memory. His soul was not there to hear and greet it and he knew now that the exhortation he had listened to had already fallen into an idle formal tale. He would never swing the thurible before the tabernacle as priest. His destiny was to be elusive of social or religious orders. The wisdom of the priest's appeal did not touch him to the quick. He was destined to learn his own wisdom apart from others or to learn the wisdom of others himself wandering among the snares of the world.

The snares of the world were its ways of sin. He would fall. He had not yet fallen but he would fall silently, in an instant. Not to fall was too hard, too hard: and he felt the silent lapse of his soul, as it would be at some instant to come, falling, falling but not yet fallen, still unfallen but about to fall.

He crossed the bridge over the stream of the Tolka and turned his eyes coldly for an instant towards the faded blue shrine of the Blessed Virgin which stood fowlwise on a pole in the middle of a hamshaped encampment of poor cottages. Then, bending to the left, he followed the lane which led up to his house. The faint sour stink of rotted cabbages came towards him from the kitchengardens on the rising ground above the river. He smiled to think that it was this disorder, the misrule and confusion of his father's house and the stagnation of vegetable life, which was to win the day in his soul. Then a short laugh broke from his lips as he thought of that solitary farmhand in the kitchengardens behind their house whom they had nicknamed the man with the hat. A second laugh, taking rise from the first after a pause, broke from him involuntarily as he thought of how the man with the hat worked, considering in turn the four points of the sky and then regretfully plunging his spade in the earth.

He pushed open the latchless door of the porch and passed through the naked hallway into the kitchen. A group of his brothers and sisters was sitting round the table. Tea was nearly over and only the last of the second watered tea remained in the bottoms of the small glassjars and jampots which did service for teacups. Discarded crusts and lumps of sugared bread, turned brown by the tea which had been poured over them, lay scattered on the table. Little wells of tea lay here and there on the board and a knife with a broken ivory handle was stuck through the pith of a ravaged turnover.

The sad quiet greyblue glow of the dying day came through the window and the open door, covering over and allaying quietly a sudden instinct of remorse in Stephen's heart. All that had been denied them had been freely given to him, the eldest: but the quiet glow of evening showed him in their faces no sign of rancour.

He sat near them at the table and asked where his father and mother were. One answered:

—Goneboro toboro lookboro atboro aboro houseboro.

Still another removal! A boy named Fallon in Belevedere had often asked him with a silly laugh why they moved so often. A frown of scorn darkened quickly his forehead as he heard again the silly laugh of the questioner.

He asked:

—Why are we on the move again, if it's a fair question?

The same sister answered:

—Becauseboro theboro landboro lordboro willboro putboro usboro outboro.

The voice of his youngest brother from the farther side of the fireplace began to sing the air *Oft in the Stilly Night*. One by one the others took up the air until a full choir of voices was singing. They would sing so for hours, melody after melody, glee after glee, till the last pale light died down on the horizon, till the first dark nightclouds came forth and night fell.

He waited for some moments, listening, before he too took up the air with them. He was listening with pain of spirit to the overtone of weariness behind their frail fresh innocent voices. Even before they set out on life's journey they seemed weary already of the way.

He heard the choir of voices in the kitchen echoed and multiplied through an endless reverberation of the choirs of endless generations of children: and heard in all the echoes an echo also of the recurring note of weariness and pain. All seemed weary of life even before entering upon it. And he remembered that Newman had heard this note also in the broken lines of Virgil *giving utterance, like the voice of Nature herself, to that pain and weariness yet hope of better things which has been the experience of her children in every time.*

*

* *

He could wait no longer.

From the door of Byron's publichouse to the gate of Clontarf Chapel, from the gate of Clontarf Chapel to the door of Byron's publichouse and then back again to the chapel and then back again to the publichouse he had paced slowly at first, planting his steps scrupulously in the spaces of the patchwork of the footpath, then timing their fall to the fall of verses. A full hour had passed since his father had gone in with Dan Crosby, the tutor, to find out for him something about the university. For a full hour he had paced up and down, waiting: but he could wait no longer.

He set off abruptly for the Bull, walking rapidly lest his father's shrill whistle might call him back; and in a few moments he had rounded the curve at the police barrack and was safe.

Yes, his mother was hostile to the idea, as he had read from her listless silence. Yet her mistrust pricked him more keenly than his father's pride and he thought coldly how he had watched the faith which was fading down in his soul aging and strengthening in her eyes. A dim antagonism gathered force within him and darkened his mind as a cloud against her disloyalty: and when it passed, cloudlike, leaving his mind serene and dutiful towards her again, he was made aware dimly and without regret of a first noiseless sundering of their lives.

The university! So he had passed beyond the challenge of the sentries who had stood as guardians of his boyhood and had sought to keep him among them that he might be subject to them and serve their ends. Pride after satisfaction uplifted him like long slow waves. The end he had been born to serve yet did not see had led him to escape by an unseen path: and now it beckoned to him once more and a new adventure was about to be opened to him. It seemed to him that he heard notes of fitful music leaping upwards a tone and downwards a diminished fourth, upwards a tone and downwards a major third, like triple-branching flames leaping fitfully, flame after flame, out of a midnight wood. It was an elfin prelude, endless and formless: and, as it grew wilder and faster, the flames leaping out of time, he seemed to hear from under the boughs and grasses wild creatures racing, their feet pattering like rain upon the leaves. Their feet passed in pattering tumult over his mind, the feet of hares and rabbits, the feet of hinds and harts and antelopes, until he heard them no more and remembered only a proud cadence from Newman: *Whose feet are as the feet of harts and underneath the everlasting arms.*

The pride of that dim image brought back to his mind the dignity of the office he had refused. All through his boyhood he had mused upon that which he had so often thought to be his destiny and when the moment had come for him to obey the call he had turned aside, obeying a wayward instinct. Now time lay between: the oils of ordination would never anoint his body. He had refused. Why?

He turned seaward from the road at Dollymount and as he passed on to the thin wooden bridge he felt the planks shaking with the tramp of heavily shod feet. A squad of christian brothers was on its way back from the Bull and had begun to pass, two by two, across the bridge. Soon the whole bridge was trembling and resounding. The uncouth faces passed him two by two, stained yellow or red or livid by the sea, and, as he strove to look at them with ease and indifference, a faint stain of personal shame and commiseration rose to his own face. Angry with himself he tried to hide his face from their eyes by gazing down sideways into the shallow swirling water under the bridge but he still saw a reflection therein of their topheavy silk hats and humble tapelike collars and loosely hanging clerical clothes.

—Brother Hickey.

Brother Quaid.

Brother MacArdle.

Brother Keogh.

Their piety would be like their names, like their faces, like their clothes: and it was idle for him to tell himself that their humble and contrite hearts, it might be, paid a far richer tribute of devotion than his had ever been, a gift tenfold more acceptable than his elaborate adoration. It was idle for him to move himself to be generous towards them, to tell himself that if he ever came to their gates, stripped of his pride, beaten and in beggar's weeds, that they would be generous towards him, loving him as themselves. Idle and embittering, finally, to argue, against his own dispassionate certitude, that the commandment of love bade us not to love our neighbour as ourselves with the same amount and intensity of love but to love him as ourselves with the same kind of love.

He drew forth a phrase from his treasure and spoke it softly to himself:

—A day of dappled seaborne clouds.

The phrase and the day and the scene harmonised in a chord. Words. Was it their colours? He allowed them to glow and fade, hue after hue: sunrise gold, the russet and green of apple orchards, azure of waves, the greyfringed fleece of clouds. No, it was not their colours: it was the poise and balance of the period itself. Did he then love the rhythmic rise and fall of words better than their associations of legend and colour? Or was it that, being as weak of sight as he was shy of mind, he drew less pleasure from the reflection of the glowing sensible world through the prism of a language manycoloured and richly storied than from the contemplation of an inner world of individual emotions mirrored perfectly in a lucid supple periodic prose?

He passed from the trembling bridge on to firm land again. At that instant, as it seemed to him, the air was chilled and looking askance towards the water he saw a flying squall darkening and crisping suddenly the tide. A faint click at his heart, a faint throb in his throat told him once more of how his flesh dreaded the cold infrahuman odour of the sea: yet he did not strike across the downs on his left but held straight on along the spine of rocks that pointed against the river's mouth.

A veiled sunlight lit up faintly the grey sheet of water where the river was embayed. In the distance along the course of the slowflowing Liffey slender masts flecked the sky and, more distant still, the dim fabric of the city lay prone in haze. Like a scene on some vague arras, old as man's weariness, the image of the seventh city of christendom was visible to him across the timeless air, no older nor more weary nor less patient of subjection than in the days of the thingmote.°

Disheartened, he raised his eyes towards the slowdrifting clouds, dappled and seaborne. They were voyaging across the deserts of the sky, a host of nomads on the march, voyaging high over Ireland, westward bound. The Europe they had come from lay out there beyond the Irish Sea, Europe of strange tongues and valleyed and woodbegirt and citadelled and of entrenched and marshalled races. He heard a confused music within him as of memories and names which he was almost conscious of but could not capture even for an instant; then the music seemed to recede, to recede, to recede: and from each receding trail of nebulous music there fell always one longdrawn calling note, piercing like a star the dusk of silence. Again! Again! Again! Again! A voice from beyond the world was calling.

—Hello, Stephanos!°

—Here comes The Dedalus!

—Ao! . . . Eh, give it over, Dwyer, I'm telling you or I'll give you a stuff in the kisser for yourself. . . . Ao!

—Good man, Towser! Duck him!

thingmote: Place where Danes held council of law when they ruled Dublin in medieval times. **Stephanos:** Greek for crown, wreath, or garland.

—Come along, Dedalus! Bous Stephanoumenos! Bous Stephaneforos!°

—Duck him! Guzzle him now, Towser!

—Help! Help! . . . Ao!

He recognised their speech collectively before he distinguished their faces. The mere sight of that medley of wet nakedness chilled him to the bone. Their bodies, corpsewhite or suffused with a pallid golden light or rawly tanned by the suns, gleamed with the wet of the sea. Their divingstone, poised on its rude supports and rocking under their plunges, and the roughhewn stones of the sloping breakwater over which they scrambled in their horseplay gleamed with cold wet lustre. The towels with which they smacked their bodies were heavy with cold seawater: and drenched with cold brine was their matted hair.

He stood still in deference to their calls and parried their banter with easy words. How characterless they looked: Shuley without his deep unbuttoned collar, Ennis without his scarlet belt with the snaky clasp and Connolly without his Norfolk coat with the flapless sidepockets! It was a pain to see them and a swordlike pain to see the signs of adolescence that made repellent their pitiable nakedness. Perhaps they had taken refuge in number and noise from the secret dread in their souls. But he, apart from them and in silence, remembered in what dread he stood of the mystery of his own body.

—Stephanos Dedalos! Bous Stephanoumenos! Bous Stephaneforos!

Their banter was not new to him and now, as always, it flattered his mild proud sovereignty. Now, as never before, his strange name seemed to him a prophecy. So timeless seemed the grey warm air, so fluid and impersonal his own mood, that all ages were as one to him. A moment before the ghost of the ancient kingdom of the Danes had looked forth through the vesture of the hazewrapped city. Now, at the name of the fabulous artificer,° he seemed to hear the noise of dim waves and to see a winged form flying above the waves and slowly climbing the air. What did it mean? Was it a quaint device opening a page of some medieval book of prophecies and symbols, a hawklike man flying sunward above the sea, a prophecy of the end he had been born to serve and had been following through the mists of childhood and boyhood, a symbol of the artist forging anew in his workshop out of the sluggish matter of the earth a new soaring impalpable imperishable being?

His heart trembled; his breath came faster and a wild spirit passed

Bous Stephanoumenos! Bous Stephaneforos!: Greek variants for "ox bearing wreaths" (i.e., being led for sacrifice). **artificer:** Inventor or craftsman (i.e., Daedalus).

over his limbs as though he were soaring sunward. His heart trembled in an ecstasy of fear and his soul was in flight. His soul was soaring in an air beyond the world and the body he knew was purified in a breath and delivered of incertitude and made radiant and commingled with the element of the spirit. An ecstasy of flight made radiant his eyes and wild his breath and tremulous and wild and radiant his windswept limbs.

—One! Two! . . . Look out!

—O, cripes, I'm drownded!

—One! Two! Three and away!

—Me next! Me next!

—One! . . . Uk!

—Stephaneforos!

His throat ached with a desire to cry aloud, the cry of a hawk or eagle on high, to cry piercingly of his deliverance to the winds. This was the call of life to his soul not the dull gross voice of the world of duties and despair, not the inhuman voice that had called him to the pale service of the altar. An instant of wild flight had delivered him and the cry of triumph which his lips withheld cleft his brain.

—Stephaneforos!

What were they now but the cerements shaken from the body of death—the fear he had walked in night and day, the incertitude that had ringed him round, the shame that had abased him within and without—cerements,° the linens of the grave?

His soul had arisen from the grave of boyhood, spurning her graveclothes. Yes! Yes! Yes! He would create proudly out of the freedom and power of his soul, as the great artificer whose name he bore, a living thing, new and soaring and beautiful, impalpable, imperishable.

He started up nervously from the stoneblock° for he could no longer quench the flame in his blood. He felt his cheeks aflame and his throat throbbing with song. There was a lust of wandering in his feet that burned to set out for the ends of the earth. On! On! his heart seemed to cry. Evening would deepen above the sea, night fall upon the plains, dawn glimmer before the wanderer and show him strange fields and hills and faces. Where?

He looked northward towards Howth. The sea had fallen below the line of seawrack on the shallow side of the breakwater and already the tide was running out fast along the foreshore. Already one long oval bank of sand lay warm and dry amid the wavelets. Here and there warm

the stoneblock: Term for a group of rocks on the side of Bull Wall suitable for diving.
cerements: Burial clothes.

isles of sand gleamed above the shallow tide: and about the isles and around the long bank and amid the shallow currents of the beach were lightclad gayclad figures, wading and delving.

In a few moments he was barefoot, his stockings folded in his pockets and his canvas shoes dangling by their knotted laces over his shoulders: and, picking a pointed salteaten stick out of the jetsam among the rocks, he clambered down the slope of the breakwater.

There was a long rivulet in the strand: and, as he waded slowly up its course, he wondered at the endless drift of seaweed. Emerald and black and russet and olive, it moved beneath the current, swaying and turning. The water of the rivulet was dark with endless drift and mirrored the highdrifting clouds. The clouds were drifting above him silently and silently the seatangle was drifting below him; and the grey warm air was still: and a new wild life was singing in his veins.

Where was his boyhood now? Where was the soul that had hung back from her destiny, to brood alone upon the shame of her wounds and in her house of squalor and subterfuge to queen it in faded cerements and in wreaths that withered at the touch? Or where was he?

He was alone. He was unheeded, happy and near to the wild heart of life. He was alone and young and wilful and wildhearted, alone amid a waste of wild air and brackish waters and the seaharvest of shells and tangle and veiled grey sunlight and gayclad lightclad figures, of children and girls and voices childish and girlish in the air.

A girl stood before him in midstream: alone and still, gazing out to sea. She seemed like one whom magic had changed into the likeness of a strange and beautiful seabird. Her long slender bare legs were delicate as a crane's and pure save where an emerald trail of seaweed had fashioned itself as a sign upon the flesh. Her thighs, fuller and softhued as ivory, were bared almost to the hips where the white fringes of her drawers were like featherings of soft white down. Her slateblue skirts were kilted boldly about her waist and dovetailed behind her. Her bosom was as a bird's, soft and slight; slight and soft as the breast of some darkplumaged dove. But her long fair hair was girlish; and girlish and touched with the wonder of mortal beauty, her face.

She was alone and still, gazing out to sea; and when she felt his presence and the worship of his eyes her eyes turned to him in quiet sufferance of his gaze, without shame or wantonness. Long, long she suffered his gaze and then quietly withdrew her eyes from his and bent them towards the stream, gently stirring the water with her foot hither and thither. The first faint noise of gently moving water broke the silence, low and faint and whispering, faint as the bells of sleep; hither and thither, hither and thither: and a faint flame trembled on her cheek.

—Heavenly God! cried Stephen's soul, in an outburst of profane joy.

He turned away from her suddenly and set off across the strand. His cheeks were aflame; his body was aglow; his limbs were trembling. On and on and on and on he strode, far out over the sands, singing wildly to the sea, crying to greet the advent of the life that had cried to him.

Her image had passed into his soul for ever and no word had broken the holy silence of his ecstasy. Her eyes had called him and his soul had leaped at the call. To live, to err, to fall, to triumph, to recreate life out of life! A wild angel had appeared to him, the angel of mortal youth and beauty, an envoy from the fair courts of life, to throw open before him in an instant of ecstasy the gates of all the ways of error and glory. On and on and on and on!

He halted suddenly and heard his heart in the silence. How far had he walked? What hour was it?

There was no human figure near him nor any sound borne to him over the air. But the tide was near the turn and already the day was on the wane. He turned landward and ran towards the shore and, running up the sloping beach, reckless of the sharp shingle, found a sandy nook amid a ring of tufted sandknolls and lay down there that the peace and silence of the evening might still the riot of his blood.

He felt above him the vast indifferent dome and the calm processes of the heavenly bodies: and the earth beneath him, the earth that had borne him, had taken him to her breast.

He closed his eyes in the languor of sleep. His eyelids trembled as if they felt the vast cyclic movement of the earth and her watchers, trembled as if they felt the strange light of some new world. His soul was swooning into some new world, fantastic, dim, uncertain as under sea, traversed by cloudy shapes and beings. A world, a glimmer or a flower? Glimmering and trembling, trembling and unfolding, a breaking light, an opening flower, it spread in endless succession to itself, breaking in full crimson and unfolding and fading to palest rose, leaf by leaf and wave of light by wave of light, flooding all the heavens with its soft flushes, every flush deeper than other.

Evening had fallen when he woke and the sand and arid grasses of his bed glowed no longer. He rose slowly and, recalling the rapture of his sleep, sighed at its joy.

He climbed to the crest of the sandhill and gazed about him. Evening had fallen. A rim of the young moon cleft the pale waste of sky like the rim of a silver hoop embedded in grey sand: and the tide was flowing in fast to the land with a low whisper of her waves, islanding a few last figures in distant pools.

V

He drained his third cup of watery tea to the dregs and set to chewing the crusts of fried bread that were scattered near him, staring into the dark pool of the jar. The yellow dripping had been scooped out like a boghole and the pool under it brought back to his memory the dark turfcoloured water of the bath in Clongowes. The box of pawntickets at his elbow had just been rifled and he took up idly one after another in his greasy fingers the blue and white dockets, scrawled and sanded and creased and bearing the name of the pledger as Daly or MacEvoy.

1 Pair Buskins.

1 D. Coat

3 Articles and White.

1 Man's Pants.

Then he put them aside and gazed thoughtfully at the lid of the box, speckled with lousemarks, and asked vaguely:

—How much is the clock fast now?

His mother straightened the battered alarmclock that was lying on its side in the middle of the kitchen mantelpiece until its dial showed a quarter to twelve and then laid it once more on its side.

—An hour and twentyfive minutes, she said. The right time now is twenty past ten. The dear knows you might try to be in time for your lectures.

—Fill out the place for me to wash, said Stephen.

—Katey, fill out the place for Stephen to wash.

—Boody, fill out the place for Stephen to wash.

—I can't, I'm going for blue.° Fill it out, you, Maggie.

When the enamelled basin had been fitted into the well of the sink and the old washingglove flung on the side of it he allowed his mother to scrub his neck and root into the folds of his ears and into the interstices at the wings of his nose.

—Well, it's a poor case, she said, when a university student is so dirty that his mother has to wash him.

—But it gives you pleasure, said Stephen calmly.

going for blue: Working as hard as possible (alternatively, "bluing" is used in washing clothes).

An earsplitting whistle was heard from upstairs and his mother thrust a damp overall into his hands, saying:

—Dry yourself and hurry out for the love of goodness.

A second shrill whistle, prolonged angrily, brought one of the girls to the foot of the staircase.

—Yes, father?

—Is your lazy bitch of a brother gone out yet?

—Yes, father.

—Sure?

—Yes, father.

—Hm!

The girl came back making signs to him to be quick and go out quietly by the back. Stephen laughed and said:

—He has a curious idea of genders if he thinks a bitch is masculine.

—Ah, it's a scandalous shame for you, Stephen, said his mother, and you'll live to rue the day you set your foot in that place. I know how it has changed you.

—Good morning, everybody, said Stephen, smiling and kissing the tips of his fingers in adieu.

The lane behind the terrace was waterlogged and as he went down it slowly, choosing his steps amid heaps of wet rubbish, he heard a mad nun screeching in the nuns' madhouse beyond the wall.

—Jesus! O Jesus! Jesus!

He shook the sound out of his ears by an angry toss of his head and hurried on, stumbling through the mouldering offal, his heart already bitten by an ache of loathing and bitterness. His father's whistle, his mother's mutterings, the screech of an unseen maniac were to him now so many voices offending and threatening to humble the pride of his youth. He drove their echoes even out of his heart with an execration: but, as he walked down the avenue and felt the grey morning light falling about him through the dripping trees and smelt the strange wild smell of the wet leaves and bark, his soul was loosed of her miseries.

The rainladen trees of the avenue evoked in him, as always, memories of the girls and women in the plays of Gerhart Hauptmann: and the memory of their pale sorrows and the fragrance falling from the wet branches mingled in a mood of quiet joy. His morning walk across the city had begun: and he foreknew that as he passed the sloblands° of Fairview he would think of the cloistral silverveined prose of Newman, that as he walked along the North Strand Road, glancing idly at the

sloblands: Local term for a particular trashy area of tidal flatland.

windows of the provision shops, he would recall the dark humour of Guido Cavalcanti and smile, that as he went by Baird's stonecutting works in Talbot Place the spirit of Ibsen would blow through him like a keen wind, a spirit of wayward boyish beauty, and that passing a grimy marinedealer's shop beyond the Liffey he would repeat the song by Ben Jonson which begins:

I was not wearier where I lay.

His mind, when wearied of its search for the essence of beauty amid the spectral words of Aristotle or Aquinas, turned often for its pleasure to the dainty songs of the Elizabethans. His mind, in the vesture of a doubting monk, stood often in shadow under the windows of that age, to hear the grave and mocking music of the lutenists or the frank laughter of waistcoateers° until a laugh too low, a phrase, tarnished by time, of chambering° and false honour, stung his monkish pride and drove him on from his lurkingplace.

The lore which he was believed to pass his days brooding upon so that it had rapt him from the companionships of youth was only a garner of slender sentences from Aristotle's poetics and psychology and a *Synopsis Philosophiæ Scholasticæ ad mentem divi Thomæ.*° His thinking was a dusk of doubt and selfmistrust lit up at moments by the lightnings of intuition, but lightnings of so clear a splendour that in those moments the world perished about his feet as if it had been fireconsumed: and thereafter his tongue grew heavy and he met the eyes of others with unanswering eyes for he felt that the spirit of beauty had folded him round like a mantle and that in revery at least he had been acquainted with nobility. But, when this brief pride of silence upheld him no longer, he was glad to find himself still in the midst of common lives, passing on his way amid the squalor and noise and sloth of the city fearlessly and with a light heart.

Near the hoardings° on the canal he met the consumptive man with the doll's face and the brimless hat coming towards him down the slope of the bridge with little steps, tightly buttoned into his chocolate overcoat and holding his furled umbrella a span or two from him like a diviningrod. It must be eleven, he thought, and peered into a dairy to see the time. The clock in the dairy told him that it was five minutes to five but, as he turned away, he heard a clock somewhere near him

waistcoateers: Prostitutes (Elizabethan term). **chambering:** Wanton sexual indulgence (Elizabethan term). ***Synopsis Philosophiæ . . . : A Synopsis of Scholastic Philosophy for the Understanding of St. Thomas*** (Aquinas). **hoardings:** Billboards.

but unseen beating eleven strokes in swift precision. He laughed as he heard it for it made him think of MacCann, and he saw him a squat figure in a shooting jacket and breeches and with a fair goatee, standing in the wind at Hopkins' corner, and heard him say:

—Dedalus, you're an antisocial being, wrapped up in yourself. I'm not. I'm a democrat: and I'll work and act for social liberty and equality among all classes and sexes in the United States of the Europe of the future.

Eleven! Then he was late for that lecture too. What day of the week was it? He stopped at a newsagent's to read the headline of a placard. Thursday. Ten to eleven, English; eleven to twelve, French; twelve to one, physics. He fancied to himself the English lecture and felt, even at that distance, restless and helpless. He saw the heads of his classmates meekly bent as they wrote in their notebooks the points they were bidden to note, nominal definitions, essential definitions and examples or dates of birth or death, chief works, a favourable and an unfavourable criticism side by side. His own head was unbent for his thoughts wandered abroad and whether he looked around the little class of students or out of the window across the desolate gardens of the green an odour assailed him of cheerless cellardamp and decay. Another head than his, right before him in the first benches, was poised squarely above its bending fellows like the head of a priest appealing without humility to the tabernacle for the humble worshippers about him. Why was it that when he thought of Cranly he could never raise before his mind the entire image of his body but only the image of the head and face? Even now against the grey curtain of the morning he saw it before him like the phantom of a dream, the face of a severed head or deathmask, crowned on the brows by its stiff black upright hair as by an iron crown. It was a priestlike face, priestlike in its pallor, in the widewinged nose, in the shadowings below the eyes and along the jaws, priestlike in the lips that were long and bloodless and faintly smiling: and Stephen, remembering swiftly how he had told Cranly of all the tumults and unrest and longings in his soul, day after day and night by night, only to be answered by his friend's listening silence, would have told himself that it was the face of a guilty priest who heard confessions of those whom he had not power to absolve but that he felt again in memory the gaze of its dark womanish eyes.

Through this image he had a glimpse of a strange dark cavern of speculation but at once turned away from it, feeling that it was not yet the hour to enter it. But the nightshade of his friend's listlessness seemed to be diffusing in the air around him a tenuous and deadly exhalation and he found himself glancing from one casual word to another on his right or left in stolid wonder that they had been so silently emptied of instantaneous sense until every mean shop legend bound his mind like the words of a spell and his soul shrivelled up, sighing with age as he walked on in a lane among heaps of dead language. His own consciousness of language was ebbing from his brain and trickling into the very words themselves which set to band and disband themselves in wayward rhythms:

The ivy whines upon the wall
And whines and twines upon the wall
The ivy whines upon the wall
The yellow ivy on the wall
Ivy, ivy up the wall.

Did any one ever hear such drivel? Lord Almighty! Who ever heard of ivy whining on a wall? Yellow ivy: that was all right. Yellow ivory also. And what about ivory ivy?

The word now shone in his brain, clearer and brighter than any ivory sawn from the mottled tusks of elephants. *Ivory, ivoire, avorio, ebur.*° One of the first examples that he had learnt in Latin had run: *India mittit ebur;*° and he recalled the shrewd northern face of the rector who had taught him to construe the Metamorphoses of Ovid in a courtly English, made whimsical by the mention of porkers and potsherds and chines of bacon. He had learnt what little he knew of the laws of Latin verse from a ragged book written by a Portuguese priest.

Contrahit orator, variant in carmine vates.°

The crises and victories and secessions in Roman history were handed on to him in the trite words *in tanto discrimine*° and he had tried to peer into the social life of the city of cities through the words *implere ollam denariorum*° which the rector had rendered sonorously as the filling of a pot with denaries. The pages of his timeworn Horace never felt cold to the touch even when his own fingers were cold: they were human pages: and fifty years before they had been turned by the human fingers of John Duncan Inverarity and by his brother William Malcolm Inverarity. Yes, those were noble names on the dusky flyleaf and, even for so poor a Latinist as he, the dusky verses were as fragrant as though they

Ivory, ivoire, avorio, ebur: The same word in English, French, Italian, and Latin. ***India mittit ebur:*** India sends (or produces) ivory. ***Contrahit orator . . . vates:*** The orator summarizes; the poet (or prophet) amplifies (or transforms). ***in tanto discrimine:*** In such a crisis. ***implere ollam denariorum:*** To fill the jar with denarii (Roman silver coins).

had lain all those years in myrtle and lavender and vervain: but yet it wounded him to think that he would never be but a shy guest at the feast of the world's culture and that the monkish learning, in terms of which he was striving to forge out an esthetic philosophy, was held no higher by the age he lived in than the subtle and curious jargons of heraldry and falconry.

The grey block of Trinity on his left, set heavily in the city's ignorance like a great dull stone set in a cumbrous ring, pulled his mind downward: and while he was striving this way and that to free his feet from the fetters of the reformed conscience he came upon the droll statue of the national poet of Ireland.

He looked at it without anger: for, though sloth of the body and of the soul crept over it like unseen vermin, over the shuffling feet and up the folds of the cloak and around the servile head, it seemed humbly conscious of its indignity. It was a Firbolg in the borrowed cloak of a Milesian; and he thought of his friend Davin, the peasant student. It was a jesting name between them but the young peasant bore with it lightly saying:

—Go on, Stevie. I have a hard head, you tell me. Call me what you will.

The homely version of his christian name on the lips of his friend had touched Stephen pleasantly when first heard for he was as formal in speech with others as they were with him. Often, as he sat in Davin's rooms in Grantham Street, wondering at his friend's wellmade boots that flanked the wall pair by pair and repeating for his friend's simple ear the verses and cadences of others which were the veils of his own longing and dejection, the rude Firbolg mind of his listener had drawn his mind towards it and flung it back again, drawing it by a quiet inbred courtesy of attention or by a quaint turn of old English speech or by the force of its delight in rude bodily skill—for Davin had sat at the feet of Michael Cusack, the Gael°— repelling swiftly and suddenly by a grossness of intelligence or by a bluntness of feeling or by a dull stare of terror in the eyes, the terror of soul of a starving Irish village in which the curfew was still a nightly fear.

Side by side with his memory of the deeds of prowess of his uncle Mat Davin, the athlete, the young peasant worshipped the sorrowful legend of Ireland. The gossip of his fellowstudents which strove to render the flat life of the college significant at any cost loved to think of him as a young fenian. His nurse had taught him Irish and shaped his

Gael: Irishman or Celt.

rude imagination by the broken lights of Irish myth. He stood towards this myth upon which no individual mind had ever drawn out a line of beauty and to its unwieldy tales that divided against themselves as they moved down the cycles° in the same attitude as towards the Roman catholic religion, the attitude of a dullwitted loyal serf. Whatsoever of thought or of feeling came to him from England or by way of English culture his mind stood armed against in obedience to a password: and of the world that lay beyond England he knew only the foreign legion of France in which he spoke of serving.

Coupling this ambition with the young man's diffident humour Stephen had often called him one of the tame geese:° and there was even a point of irritation in the name pointed against that very reluctance of speech and deed in his friend which seemed so often to stand between Stephen's mind, eager of speculation, and the hidden ways of Irish life.

One night the young peasant, his spirit stung by the violent or luxurious language in which Stephen escaped from the cold silence of intellectual revolt, had called up before Stephen's mind a strange vision. The two were walking slowly towards Davin's room through the dark narrow streets of the poorer jews.

—A thing happened to myself, Stevie, last autumn, coming on winter, and I never told it to a living soul and you are the first person now I ever told it to. I disremember if it was October or November. It was October because it was before I came up here to join the matriculation class.

Stephen had turned his smiling eyes towards his friend's face, flattered by his confidence and won over to sympathy by the speaker's simple accent.

—I was away all that day from my own place over in Buttevant—I don't know if you know where that is—at a hurling match° between the Croke's Own Boys and the Fearless Thurles and by God, Stevie, that was the hard fight. My first cousin, Fonsy Davin, was stripped to his buff° that day minding cool° for the Limericks but he was up with the forwards half the time and shouting like mad. I never will forget that day. One of the Crokes made a woeful wipe° at him one time with his camaun° and I declare to God he was within an aim's ace° of getting

cycles: Related groups of Irish myths and legends. **tame geese:** Joke on "the wild geese," a term for Irish who went into exile. **hurling match:** Irish game, a sort of field hockey. **buff:** Skin. **minding cool:** Playing safety defender. **woeful wipe:** Huge blow to the ball. **camaun:** Curved stick used in hurling. **aim's ace:** Very small amount or distance.

it at the side of the temple. O, honest to God, if the crook of it caught him that time he was done for.

—I am glad he escaped, Stephen had said with a laugh, but surely that's not the strange thing that happened to you?

—Well, I suppose that doesn't interest you but leastways there was such noise after the match that I missed the train home and I couldn't get any kind of a yoke° to give me a lift for, as luck would have it, there was a mass meeting that same day over in Castletownroche and all the cars in the country were there. So there was nothing for it only to stay the night or to foot it out. Well, I started to walk and on I went and it was coming on night when I got into the Ballyhoura hills; that's better than ten miles from Kilmallock and there's a long lonely road after that. You wouldn't see the sign of a christian house along the road or hear a sound. It was pitch dark almost. Once or twice I stopped by the way under a bush to redden my pipe and only for the dew was thick I'd have stretched out there and slept. At last, after a bend of the road, I spied a little cottage with a light in the window. I went up and knocked at the door. A voice asked who was there and I answered I was over at the match in Buttevant and was walking back and that I'd be thankful for a glass of water. After a while a young woman opened the door and brought me out a big mug of milk. She was half undressed as if she was going to bed when I knocked and she had her hair hanging: and I thought by her figure and by something in the look of her eyes that she must be carrying a child. She kept me in talk a long while at the door and I thought it strange because her breast and her shoulders were bare. She asked me was I tired and would I like to stop the night there. She said she was all alone in the house and that her husband had gone that morning to Queenstown with his sister to see her off. And all the time she was talking, Stevie, she had her eyes fixed on my face and she stood so close to me I could hear her breathing. When I handed her back the mug at last she took my hand to draw me in over the threshold and said: *Come in and stay the night here. You've no call to be frightened. There's no-one in it but ourselves.* . . . I didn't go in, Stevie. I thanked her and went on my way again, all in a fever. At the first bend of the road I looked back and she was standing in the door.

The last words of Davin's story sang in his memory and the figure of the woman in the story stood forth reflected in other figures of the peasant women whom he had seen standing in the doorways at Clane as the college cars drove by, as a type of her race and his own, a batlike

yoke: Idiomatic Irish expression for "thing" (any artifact).

soul waking to the consciousness of itself in darkness and secrecy and loneliness and, through the eyes and voice and gesture of a woman without guile, calling the stranger to her bed.

A hand was laid on his arm and a young voice cried:

—Ah, gentleman, your own girl, sir! The first handsel° today, gentleman. Buy that lovely bunch. Will you, gentleman?

The blue flowers which she lifted towards him and her young blue eyes seemed to him at that instant images of guilelessness: and he halted till the image had vanished and he saw only her ragged dress and damp coarse hair and hoydenish face.

—Do, gentleman! Don't forget your own girl, sir!

—I have no money, said Stephen.

—Buy them lovely ones, will you, sir? Only a penny.

—Did you hear what I said? asked Stephen, bending towards her. I told you I had no money. I tell you again now.

—Well, sure, you will some day, sir, please God, the girl answered after an instant.

—Possibly, said Stephen, but I don't think it likely.

He left her quickly fearing that her intimacy might turn to gibing and wishing to be out of the way before she offered her ware to another, a tourist from England or a student of Trinity. Grafton Street along which he walked prolonged that moment of discouraged poverty. In the roadway at the head of the street a slab was set to the memory of Wolfe Tone and he remembered having been present with his father at its laying. He remembered with bitterness that scene of tawdry tribute. There were four French delegates in a brake° and one, a plump smiling young man, held, wedged on a stick, a card on which were printed the words: *Vive l'Irlande!*

But the trees in Stephen's Green were fragrant of rain and the rain-sodden earth gave forth its mortal odour, a faint incense rising upward through the mould from many hearts. The soul of the gallant venal city which his elders had told him of had shrunk with time to a faint mortal odour rising from the earth and he knew that in a moment when he entered the sombre college he would be conscious of a corruption other than that of Buck Egan and Burnchapel Whaley.

It was too late to go upstairs to the French class. He crossed the hall and took the corridor to the left which led to the physics theatre. The corridor was dark and silent but not unwatchful. Why did he feel that it was not unwatchful? Was it because he had heard that in Buck

handsel: Good-luck omen or gift; also money, as in a tip. **brake:** Scaffold.

Whaley's time there was a secret staircase there? Or was the jesuit house extraterritorial and was he walking among aliens? The Ireland of Tone and of Parnell seemed to have receded in space.

He opened the door of the theatre and halted in the chilly grey light that struggled through the dusty windows. A figure was crouching before the large grate and by its leanness and greyness he knew that it was the dean of studies lighting the fire. Stephen closed the door quietly and approached the fireplace.

—Good morning, sir! Can I help you?

The priest looked up quickly and said:

—One moment now, Mr Dedalus, and you will see. There is an art in lighting a fire. We have the liberal arts and we have the useful arts. This is one of the useful arts.

—I will try to learn it, said Stephen.

—Not too much coal, said the dean, working briskly at his task, that is one of the secrets.

He produced four candlebutts from the sidepockets of his soutane and placed them deftly among the coals and twisted papers. Stephen watched him in silence. Kneeling thus on the flagstone to kindle the fire and busied with the disposition of his wisps of paper and candlebutts he seemed more than ever a humble server making ready the place of sacrifice in an empty temple, a levite° of the Lord. Like a levite's robe of plain linen the faded worn soutane draped the kneeling figure of one whom the canonicals° or the bellbordered ephod° would irk and trouble. His very body had waxed old in lowly service of the Lord—in tending the fire upon the altar, in bearing tidings secretly, in waiting upon worldlings, in striking swiftly when bidden—and yet had remained ungraced by aught of saintly or of prelatic beauty. Nay, his very soul had waxed old in that service without growing towards light and beauty or spreading abroad a sweet odour of her sanctity—a mortified will no more responsive to the thrill of its obedience than was to the thrill of love or combat his aging body, spare and sinewy, greyed with a silverpointed down.

The dean rested back on his hunkers and watched the sticks catch. Stephen, to fill the silence, said:

—I am sure I could not light a fire.

—You are an artist, are you not, Mr Dedalus, said the dean, glancing up and blinking his pale eyes. The object of the artist is the creation of the beautiful. What the beautiful is is another question.

levite: Subordinate priest. **canonicals:** Prescribed vestments. **ephod:** Old Testament religious garment.

He rubbed his hands slowly and drily over the difficulty.

—Can you solve that question now? he asked.

—Aquinas, answered Stephen, says *Pulcra sunt quæ visa placent.*°

—This fire before us, said the dean, will be pleasing to the eye. Will it therefore be beautiful?

—In so far as it is apprehended by the sight, which I suppose means here esthetic intellection, it will be beautiful. But Aquinas also says *Bonum est in quod tendit appetitus.*° In so far as it satisfies the animal craving for warmth fire is a good. In hell however it is an evil.

—Quite so, said the dean, you have certainly hit the nail on the head.

He rose nimbly and went towards the door, set it ajar and said:

—A draught is said to be a help in these matters.

As he came back to the hearth, limping slightly but with a brisk step, Stephen saw the silent soul of a jesuit look out at him from the pale loveless eyes. Like Ignatius he was lame but in his eyes burned no spark of Ignatius' enthusiasm. Even the legendary craft of the company, a craft subtler and more secret than its fabled books of secret subtle wisdom, had not fired his soul with the energy of apostleship. It seemed as if he used the shifts and lore and cunning of the world, as bidden to do, for the greater glory of God, without joy in their handling or hatred of that in them which was evil but turning them, with a firm gesture of obedience, back upon themselves: and for all this silent service it seemed as if he loved not at all the master and little, if at all, the ends he served. *Similiter atque senis baculus,*° he was, as the founder would have had him, like a staff in an old man's hand, to be left in a corner, to be leaned on in the road at nightfall or in stress of weather, to lie with a lady's nosegay on a garden seat, to be raised in menace.

The dean returned to the hearth and began to stroke his chin.

—When may we expect to have something from you on the esthetic question? he asked.

—From me! said Stephen in astonishment. I stumble on an idea once a fortnight if I am lucky.

—These questions are very profound, Mr Dedalus, said the dean. It is like looking down from the cliffs of Moher into the depths. Many go down into the depths and never come up. Only the trained diver can go down into those depths and explore them and come to the surface again.

Pulcra sunt quæ visa placent: That is beautiful which gives pleasure to the eye. ***Bonum est in quod tendit appetitus:*** That is good toward which the appetite is moved (or which is desired). ***Similiter atque senis baculus:*** Like an old man's walking stick.

—If you mean speculation, sir, said Stephen, I also am sure that there is no such thing as free thinking inasmuch as all thinking must be bound by its own laws.

—Ha!

—For my purpose I can work on at present by the light of one or two ideas of Aristotle and Aquinas.

—I see. I quite see your point.

—I need them only for my own use and guidance until I have done something for myself by their light. If the lamp smokes or smells I shall try to trim it. If it does not give light enough I shall sell it and buy or borrow another.

—Epictetus also had a lamp, said the dean, which was sold for a fancy price after his death. It was the lamp he wrote his philosophical dissertations by. You know Epictetus?

—An old gentleman, said Stephen coarsely, who said that the soul is very like a bucketful of water.

—He tells us in his homely way, the dean went on, that he put an iron lamp before a statue of one of the gods and that a thief stole the lamp. What did the philosopher do? He reflected that it was the character of a thief to steal and determined to buy an earthen lamp next day instead of the iron lamp.

A smell of molten tallow came up from the dean's candlebutts and fused itself in Stephen's consciousness with the jingle of the words, bucket and lamp and lamp and bucket. The priest's voice too had a hard jingling tone. Stephen's mind halted by instinct, checked by the strange tone and the imagery and by the priest's face which seemed like an unlit lamp or a reflector hung in a false focus. What lay behind it or within it? A dull torpor of the soul or the dullness of the thundercloud, charged with intellection and capable of the gloom of God?

—I meant a different kind of lamp, sir, said Stephen.

—Undoubtedly, said the dean.

—One difficulty, said Stephen, in esthetic discussion is to know whether words are being used according to the literary tradition or according to the tradition of the marketplace. I remember a sentence of Newman's in which he says of the Blessed Virgin that she was detained in the full company of the saints. The use of the word in the marketplace is quite different. *I hope I am not detaining you.*

—Not in the least, said the dean politely.

—No, no, said Stephen, smiling, I mean . . .

—Yes, yes: I see, said the dean quickly, I quite catch the point: *detain.*

He thrust forward his under jaw and uttered a dry short cough.

—To return to the lamp, he said, the feeding of it is also a nice problem. You must choose the pure oil and you must be careful when you pour it in not to overflow it, not to pour in more than the funnel can hold.

—What funnel? asked Stephen.

—The funnel through which you pour the oil into your lamp.

—That? said Stephen. Is that called a funnel? Is it not a tundish?

—What is a tundish?

—That. The . . . the funnel.

—Is that called a tundish in Ireland? asked the dean. I never heard the word in my life.

—It is called a tundish in Lower Drumcondra, said Stephen laughing, where they speak the best English.

—A tundish, said the dean reflectively. That is a most interesting word. I must look that word up. Upon my word I must.

His courtesy of manner rang a little false and Stephen looked at the English convert with the same eyes as the elder brother in the parable may have turned on the prodigal. A humble follower in the wake of clamorous conversions, a poor Englishman in Ireland, he seemed to have entered on the stage of jesuit history when that strange play of intrigue and suffering and envy and struggle and indignity had been all but given through—a latecomer, a tardy spirit. From what had he set out? Perhaps he had been born and bred among serious dissenters, seeing salvation in Jesus only and abhorring the vain pomps of the establishment. Had he felt the need of an implicit faith amid the welter of sectarianism and the jargon of its turbulent schisms, six principle men, peculiar people, seed and snake baptists, supralapsarian dogmatists? Had he found the true church all of a sudden in winding up to the end like a reel of cotton some finespun line of reasoning upon insufflation° or the imposition of hands or the procession of the Holy Ghost? Or had Lord Christ touched him and bidden him follow, like that disciple who had sat at the receipt of custom, as he sat by the door of some zinc-roofed chapel, yawning and telling over his church pence?

The dean repeated the word yet again.

—Tundish! Well now, that is interesting!

—The question you asked me a moment ago seems to me more interesting. What is that beauty which the artist struggles to express from lumps of earth, said Stephen coldly.

insufflation: Breathing on someone or something to symbolize the coming of the Holy Ghost and the banishing of evil spirits.

The little word seemed to have turned a rapier point of his sensitiveness against this courteous and vigilant foe. He felt with a smart of dejection that the man to whom he was speaking was a countryman of Ben Jonson. He thought:

—The language in which we are speaking is his before it is mine. How different are the words *home, Christ, ale, master* on his lips and on mine! I cannot speak or write these words without unrest of spirit. His language, so familiar and so foreign, will always be for me an acquired speech. I have not made or accepted its words. My voice holds them at bay. My soul frets in the shadow of his language.

—And to distinguish between the beautiful and the sublime, the dean added. To distinguish between moral beauty and material beauty. And to inquire what kind of beauty is proper to each of the various arts. These are some interesting points we might take up.

Stephen, disheartened suddenly by the dean's firm dry tone, was silent. The dean also was silent: and through the silence a distant noise of many boots and confused voices came up the staircase.

—In pursuing these speculations, said the dean conclusively, there is however the danger of perishing of inanition. First you must take your degree. Set that before you as your first aim. Then, little by little, you will see your way. I mean in every sense, your way in life and in thinking. It may be uphill pedalling at first. Take Mr Moonan. He was a long time before he got to the top. But he got there.

—I may not have his talent, said Stephen quietly.

—You never know, said the dean brightly. We never can say what is in us. I most certainly should not be despondent. *Per aspera ad astra.* °

He left the hearth quickly and went towards the landing to oversee the arrival of the first arts' class.

Leaning against the fireplace Stephen heard him greet briskly and impartially every student of the class and could almost see the frank smiles of the coarser students. A desolating pity began to fall like a dew upon his easily embittered heart for this faithful servingman of the knightly Loyola, for this halfbrother of the clergy, more venal than they in speech, more steadfast of soul than they, one whom he would never call his ghostly father: and he thought how this man and his companions had earned the name of worldlings at the hands not of the unworldly only but of the worldly also for having pleaded, during all their history, at the bar of God's justice for the souls of the lax and the lukewarm and the prudent.

Per aspera ad astra: By rough ways to the stars (a cliché).

The entry of the professor was signalled by a few rounds of Kentish fire° from the heavy boots of those students who sat on the highest tier of the gloomy theatre under the grey cobwebbed windows. The calling of the roll began and the responses to the names were given out in all tones until the name of Peter Byrne was reached.

—Here!

A deep bass note in response came from the upper tier, followed by coughs of protest along the other benches.

The professor paused in his reading and called the next name:

—Cranly!

No answer.

—Mr Cranly!

A smile flew across Stephen's face as he thought of his friend's studies.

—Try Leopardstown! said a voice from the bench behind.

Stephen glanced up quickly but Moynihan's snoutish face outlined on the grey light was impassive. A formula was given out. Amid the rustling of the notebooks Stephen turned back again and said:

—Give me some paper for God's sake.

—Are you as bad as that? asked Moynihan with a broad grin.

He tore a sheet from his scribbler and passed it down, whispering:

—In case of necessity any layman or woman can do it.

The formula which he wrote obediently on the sheet of paper, the coiling and uncoiling calculations of the professor, the spectrelike symbols of force and velocity fascinated and jaded Stephen's mind. He had heard some say that the old professor was an atheist freemason. O the grey dull day! It seemed a limbo of painless patient consciousness through which souls of mathematicians might wander, projecting long slender fabrics from plane to plane of ever rarer and paler twilight, radiating swift eddies to the last verges of a universe ever vaster, farther and more impalpable.

—So we must distinguish between elliptical and ellipsoidal. Perhaps some of you gentlemen may be familiar with the works of Mr W. S. Gilbert. In one of his songs he speaks of the billiard sharp who is condemned to play:

On a cloth untrue
With a twisted cue
And elliptical billiard balls.

He means a ball having the form of the ellipsoid of the principal axes of which I spoke a moment ago.

Kentish fire: Prolonged stamping or clapping to show impatience or disapproval.

Moynihan leaned down towards Stephen's ear and murmured:

—What price ellipsoidal balls! Chase me, ladies, I'm in the cavalry!

His fellowstudent's rude humour ran like a gust through the cloister of Stephen's mind, shaking into gay life limp priestly vestments that hung upon the walls, setting them to sway and caper in a sabbath of misrule. The forms of the community emerged from the gustblown vestments, the dean of studies, the portly florid bursar with his cap of grey hair, the president, the little priest with feathery hair who wrote devout verses, the squat peasant form of the professor of economics, the tall form of the young professor of mental science discussing on the landing a case of conscience with his class like a giraffe cropping high leafage among a herd of antelopes, the grave troubled prefect of the sodality, the plump roundheaded professor of Italian with his rogue's eyes. They came ambling and stumbling, tumbling and capering, kilting their gowns for leap frog, holding one another back, shaken with deep false laughter, smacking one another behind and laughing at their rude malice, calling to one another by familiar nicknames, protesting with sudden dignity at some rough usage, whispering two and two behind their hands.

The professor had gone to the glass cases on the sidewall from a shelf of which he took down a set of coils, blew away the dust from many points and, bearing it carefully to the table, held a finger on it while he proceeded with his lecture. He explained that the wires in modern coils were of a compound called platinoid lately discovered by F. W. Martino.

He spoke clearly the initials and surname of the discoverer. Moynihan whispered from behind:

—Good old Fresh Water Martin!

—Ask him, Stephen whispered back with weary humour, if he wants a subject for electrocution. He can have me.

Moynihan, seeing the professor bend over the coils, rose in his bench and, clacking noiselessly the fingers of his right hand, began to call with the voice of a slobbering urchin:

—Please, teacher! Please, teacher! This boy is after saying a bad word, teacher.

—Platinoid, the professor said solemnly, is preferred to German silver because it has a lower coefficient of resistance variation by changes of temperature. The platinoid wire is insulated and the covering of silk that insulates it is wound double on the ebonite bobbins just where my finger is. If it were wound single an extra current would be induced in the coils. The bobbins are saturated in hot paraffin wax . . .

A sharp Ulster voice said from the bench below Stephen:

—Are we likely to be asked questions on applied science?

The professor began to juggle gravely with the terms pure science and applied science. A heavybuilt student wearing gold spectacles stared with some wonder at the questioner. Moynihan murmured from behind in his natural voice:

—Isn't MacAlister a devil for his pound of flesh?

Stephen looked down coldly on the oblong skull beneath him overgrown with tangled twinecoloured hair. The voice, the accent, the mind of the questioner offended him and he allowed the offence to carry him towards wilful unkindness, bidding his mind think that the student's father would have done better had he sent his son to Belfast to study and have saved something on the trainfare by so doing.

The oblong skull beneath did not turn to meet this shaft of thought and yet the shaft came back to its bowstring: for he saw in a moment the student's wheypale face.

—That thought is not mine, he said to himself quickly. It came from the comic Irishman in the bench behind. Patience. Can you say with certitude by whom the soul of your race was bartered and its elect betrayed—by the questioner or by the mocker? Patience. Remember Epictetus. It is probably in his character to ask such a question at such a moment in such a tone and to pronounce the word *science* as a monosyllable.

The droning voice of the professor continued to wind itself slowly round and round the coils it spoke of, doubling, trebling, quadrupling its somnolent energy as the coil multiplied its ohms of resistance.

Moynihan's voice called from behind in echo to a distant bell:

—Closing time, gents!°

The entrance hall was crowded and loud with talk. On a table near the door were two photographs in frames and between them a long roll of paper bearing an irregular tail of signatures. MacCann went briskly to and fro among the students, talking rapidly, answering rebuffs and leading one after another to the table. In the inner hall the dean of studies stood talking to a young professor, stroking his chin gravely and nodding his head.

Stephen, checked by the crowd at the door, halted irresolutely. From under the wide falling leaf of a soft hat Cranly's dark eyes were watching him.

—Have you signed? Stephen asked.

Closing time, gents!: How the end of legal drinking hours might be announced at a pub.

Cranly closed his long thinlipped mouth, communed with himself an instant and answered:

—*Ego habeo.*°

—What is it for?

—*Quod?*°

—What is it for?

Cranly turned his pale face to Stephen and said blandly and bitterly:

—*Per pax universalis.*°

Stephen pointed to the Czar's photograph and said:

—He has the face of a besotted Christ.

The scorn and anger in his voice brought Cranly's eyes back from a calm survey of the walls of the hall.

—Are you annoyed? he asked.

—No, answered Stephen.

—Are you in bad humour?

—No.

—*Credo ut vos sanguinarius mendax estis,* said Cranly, *quia facies vostra monstrat ut vos in damno malo humore estis.*°

Moynihan, on his way to the table, said in Stephen's ear:

—MacCann is in tiptop form. Ready to shed the last drop. Brand-new world. No stimulants and votes for the bitches.

Stephen smiled at the manner of this confidence and, when Moynihan had passed, turned again to meet Cranly's eyes.

—Perhaps you can tell me, he said, why he pours his soul so freely into my ear. Can you?

A dull scowl appeared on Cranly's forehead. He stared at the table where Moynihan had bent to write his name on the roll, and then said flatly:

—A sugar!

—*Quis est in malo humore,* said Stephen, *ego aut vos?*°

Cranly did not take up the taunt. He brooded sourly on his judgment and repeated with the same flat force:

—A flaming bloody sugar, that's what he is!

It was his epitaph for all dead friendships and Stephen wondered whether it would ever be spoken in the same tone over his memory. The heavy lumpish phrase sank slowly out of hearing like a stone

Ego habeo: I have, in "dog Latin," a humorous schoolboy imitation of Latin that translates English words literally and is scattered throughout the following conversations. ***Quod?:*** What? ***Per pax universalis:*** For universal peace. ***Credo ut vos . . . estis:*** I think you are a bloody liar, because your face shows you are in a damned bad humor. ***Quis est . . . vos?:*** Who is in a bad humor, you or I?

through a quagmire. Stephen saw it sink as he had seen many an other, feeling its heaviness depress his heart. Cranly's speech, unlike that of Davin, had neither rare phrases of Elizabethan English nor quaintly turned versions of Irish idioms. Its drawl was an echo of the quays of Dublin given back by a bleak decaying seaport, its energy an echo of the sacred eloquence of Dublin given back flatly by a Wicklow pulpit.

The heavy scowl faded from Cranly's face as MacCann marched briskly towards them from the other side of the hall.

—Here you are! said MacCann cheerily.

—Here I am! said Stephen.

—Late as usual. Can you not combine the progressive tendency with a respect for punctuality?

—That question is out of order, said Stephen. Next business.

His smiling eyes were fixed on a silverwrapped tablet of milk chocolate which peeped out of the propagandist's breastpocket. A little ring of listeners closed round to hear the war of wits. A lean student with olive skin and lank black hair thrust his face between the two, glancing from one to the other at each phrase and seeming to try to catch each flying phrase in his open moist mouth. Cranly took a small grey handball from his pocket and began to examine it closely, turning it over and over.

—Next business? said MacCann. Hom!

He gave a loud cough of laughter, smiled broadly and tugged twice at the strawcoloured goatee which hung from his blunt chin.

—The next business is to sign the testimonial.

—Will you pay me anything if I sign? asked Stephen.

—I thought you were an idealist, said MacCann.

The gipsylike student looked about him and addressed the onlookers in an indistinct bleating voice.

—By hell, that's a queer notion. I consider that notion to be a mercenary notion.

His voice faded into silence. No heed was paid to his words. He turned his olive face, equine in expression, towards Stephen, inviting him to speak again.

MacCann began to speak with fluent energy of the Czar's rescript,° of Stead, of general disarmament, arbitration in cases of international disputes, of the signs of the times, of the new humanity and the new gospel of life which would make it the business of the community to

rescript: Originally, an epistle issued by the pope regarding some question referred to him.

secure as cheaply as possible the greatest possible happiness of the greatest possible number.

The gipsy student responded to the close of the period by crying:

—Three cheers for universal brotherhood!

—Go on, Temple, said a stout ruddy student near him. I'll stand you a pint after.

—I'm a believer in universal brotherhood, said Temple, glancing about him out of his dark, oval eyes. Marx is only a bloody cod.°

Cranly gripped his arm tightly to check his tongue, smiling uneasily, and repeated:

—Easy, easy, easy!

Temple struggled to free his arm but continued, his mouth flecked by a thin foam:

—Socialism was founded by an Irishman and the first man in Europe who preached the freedom of thought was Collins. Two hundred years ago. He denounced priestcraft, the philosopher of Middlesex. Three cheers for John Anthony Collins!

A thin voice from the verge of the ring replied:

—Pip! pip!

Moynihan murmured beside Stephen's ear:

—And what about John Anthony's poor little sister:

Lottie Collins lost her drawers;
Won't you kindly lend her yours?

Stephen laughed and Moynihan, pleased with the result, murmured again:

—We'll have five bob each way on John Anthony Collins.

—I am waiting for your answer, said MacCann briefly.

—The affair doesn't interest me in the least, said Stephen wearily. You know that well. Why do you make a scene about it?

—Good! said MacCann, smacking his lips. You are a reactionary then?

—Do you think you impress me, Stephen asked, when you flourish your wooden sword?

—Metaphors! said MacCann bluntly. Come to facts.

Stephen blushed and turned aside. MacCann stood his ground and said with hostile humour:

—Minor poets, I suppose, are above such trivial questions as the question of universal peace.

cod: A joker or fool.

Cranly raised his head and held the handball between the two students by way of a peaceoffering, saying:

—*Pax super totum sanguinarium globum.*°

Stephen, moving away the bystanders, jerked his shoulder angrily in the direction of the Czar's image, saying:

—Keep your icon. If we must have a Jesus, let us have a legitimate Jesus.

—By hell, that's a good one! said the gipsy student to those about him. That's a fine expression. I like that expression immensely.

He gulped down the spittle in his throat as if he were gulping down the phrase and, fumbling at the peak of his tweed cap, turned to Stephen, saying:

—Excuse me, sir, what do you mean by that expression you uttered just now?

Feeling himself jostled by the students near him, he said to them:

—I am curious to know now what he meant by that expression.

He turned again to Stephen and said in a whisper:

—Do you believe in Jesus? I believe in man. Of course, I don't know if you believe in man. I admire you, sir. I admire the mind of man independent of all religions. Is that your opinion about the mind of Jesus?

—Go on, Temple, said the stout ruddy student, returning, as was his wont, to his first idea, that pint is waiting for you.

—He thinks I'm an imbecile, Temple explained to Stephen, because I'm a believer in the power of mind.

Cranly linked his arms into those of Stephen and his admirer and said:

—*Nos ad manum ballum jocabimus.*°

Stephen, in the act of being led away, caught sight of MacCann's flushed bluntfeatured face.

—My signature is of no account, he said politely. You are right to go your way. Leave me to go mine.

—Dedalus, said MacCann crisply, I believe you're a good fellow but you have yet to learn the dignity of altruism and the responsibility of the human individual.

A voice said:

—Intellectual crankery is better out of this movement than in it.

Stephen, recognising the harsh tone of MacAlister's voice, did not

Pax super . . . globum: Peace over the whole bloody world. ***Nos ad . . . jocabimus:*** Let's go play handball.

turn in the direction of the voice. Cranly pushed solemnly through the throng of students, linking Stephen and Temple like a celebrant attended by his ministers on his way to the altar.

Temple bent eagerly across Cranly's breast and said:

—Did you hear MacAlister what he said? That youth is jealous of you. Did you see that? I bet Cranly didn't see that. By hell, I saw that at once.

As they crossed the inner hall the dean of studies was in the act of escaping from the student with whom he had been conversing. He stood at the foot of the staircase, a foot on the lowest step, his threadbare soutane gathered about him for the ascent with womanish care, nodding his head often and repeating:

—Not a doubt of it, Mr Hackett! Very fine! Not a doubt of it!

In the middle of the hall the prefect of the college sodality was speaking earnestly, in a soft querulous voice, with a boarder. As he spoke he wrinkled a little his freckled brow and bit, between his phrases, at a tiny bone pencil.

—I hope the matric men will all come. The first arts men are pretty sure. Second arts° too. We must make sure of the newcomers.

Temple bent again across Cranly, as they were passing through the doorway, and said in a swift whisper:

—Do you know that he is a married man? He was a married man before they converted him. He has a wife and children somewhere. By hell, I think that's the queerest notion I ever heard! Eh?

His whisper trailed off into sly cackling laughter. The moment they were through the doorway Cranly seized him rudely by the neck and shook him, saying:

—You flaming floundering fool! I'll take my dying bible there isn't a bigger bloody ape, do you know, than you in the whole flaming bloody world!

Temple wriggled in his grip, laughing still with sly content, while Cranly repeated flatly at every rude shake:

—A flaming flaring bloody idiot!

They crossed the weedy garden together. The president, wrapped in a heavy loose cloak, was coming towards them along one of the walks, reading his office. At the end of the walk he halted before turning and raised his eyes. The students saluted, Temple fumbling as before at the peak of his cap. They walked forward in silence. As they neared the

matric men . . . Second arts: Referring to a set of four examinations to be passed before a degree is granted.

alley Stephen could hear the thuds of the players' hands and the wet smacks of the ball and Davin's voice crying out excitedly at each stroke.

The three students halted round the box on which Davin sat to follow the game. Temple, after a few moments, sidled across to Stephen and said:

—Excuse me, I wanted to ask you do you believe that Jean Jacques Rousseau was a sincere man.

Stephen laughed outright. Cranly, picking up the broken stave of a cask from the grass at his foot, turned swiftly and said sternly:

—Temple, I declare to the living God if you say another word, do you know, to anybody on any subject I'll kill you *super spottum.*°

—He was like you, I fancy, said Stephen, an emotional man.

—Blast him, curse him! said Cranly broadly. Don't talk to him at all. Sure, you might as well be talking, do you know, to a flaming chamberpot as talking to Temple. Go home, Temple. For God's sake, go home.

—I don't care a damn about you, Cranly, answered Temple, moving out of reach of the uplifted stave and pointing at Stephen. He's the only man I see in this institution that has an individual mind.

—Institution! Individual! cried Cranly. Go home, blast you, for you're a hopeless bloody man.

—I'm an emotional man, said Temple. That's quite rightly expressed. And I'm proud that I'm an emotionalist.

He sidled out of the alley, smiling slily. Cranly watched him with a blank expressionless face.

—Look at him! he said. Did you ever see such a go-by-the-wall?

His phrase was greeted by a strange laugh from a student who lounged against the wall, his peaked cap down on his eyes. The laugh, pitched in a high key and coming from a so muscular frame, seemed like the whinny of an elephant. The student's body shook all over and, to ease his mirth, he rubbed both his hands delightedly, over his groins.

—Lynch is awake, said Cranly.

Lynch, for answer, straightened himself and thrust forward his chest.

—Lynch puts out his chest, said Stephen, as a criticism of life.

Lynch smote himself sonorously on the chest and said:

—Who has anything to say about my girth?

Cranly took him at the word and the two began to tussle. When their faces had flushed with the struggle they drew apart, panting.

super spottum: On the spot.

Stephen bent down towards Davin who, intent on the game, had paid no heed to the talk of the others.

—And how is my little tame goose? he asked. Did he sign too?

Davin nodded and said:

—And you, Stevie?

Stephen shook his head.

—You're a terrible man, Stevie, said Davin, taking the short pipe from his mouth. Always alone.

—Now that you have signed the petition for universal peace, said Stephen, I suppose you will burn that little copybook I saw in your room.

As Davin did not answer Stephen began to quote:

—Long pace, fianna!° Right incline, fianna! Fianna, by numbers, salute, one, two!

—That's a different question, said Davin. I'm an Irish nationalist, first and foremost. But that's you all out. You're a born sneerer, Stevie.

—When you make the next rebellion with hurleysticks, said Stephen, and want the indispensable informer tell me. I can find you a few in this college.

—I can't understand you, said Davin. One time I hear you talk against English literature. Now you talk against the Irish informers. What with your name and your ideas . . . Are you Irish at all?

—Come with me now to the office of arms and I will show you the tree of my family, said Stephen.

—Then be one of us, said Davin. Why don't you learn Irish? Why did you drop out of the league class° after the first lesson?

—You know one reason why, answered Stephen.

Davin tossed his head and laughed.

—O, come now, he said. Is it on account of that certain young lady and Father Moran? But that's all in your own mind, Stevie. They were only talking and laughing.

Stephen paused and laid a friendly hand upon Davin's shoulder.

—Do you remember, he said, when we knew each other first? The first morning we met you asked me to show you the way to the matriculation class, putting a very strong stress on the first syllable. You remember? Then you used to address the jesuits as father. You remember? I ask myself about you: *Is he as innocent as his speech?*

fianna: Irish (Gaelic) for Fenians. **league class:** Class in Irish language sponsored by the Gaelic League.

—I'm a simple person, said Davin. You know that. When you told me that night in Harcourt Street those things about your private life, honest to God, Stevie, I was not able to eat my dinner. I was quite bad. I was awake a long time that night. Why did you tell me those things?

—Thanks, said Stephen. You mean I am a monster.

—No, said Davin, but I wish you had not told me.

A tide began to surge beneath the calm surface of Stephen's friendliness.

—This race and this country and this life produced me, he said. I shall express myself as I am.

—Try to be one of us, repeated Davin. In your heart you are an Irishman but your pride is too powerful.

—My ancestors threw off their language and took on another, Stephen said. They allowed a handful of foreigners to subject them. Do you fancy I am going to pay in my own life and person debts they made? What for?

—For our freedom, said Davin.

—No honourable and sincere man, said Stephen, has given up to you his life and his youth and his affections from the days of Tone to those of Parnell but you sold him to the enemy or failed him in need or reviled him and left him for another. And you invite me to be one of you. I'd see you damned first.

—They died for their ideals, Stevie, said Davin. Our day will come yet, believe me.

Stephen, following his own thought, was silent for an instant.

—The soul is born, he said vaguely, first in those moments I told you of. It has a slow and dark birth, more mysterious than the birth of the body. When the soul of a man is born in this country there are nets flung at it to hold it back from flight. You talk to me of nationality, language, religion. I shall try to fly by those nets.

Davin knocked the ashes from his pipe.

—Too deep for me, Stevie, he said. But a man's country comes first. Ireland first, Stevie. You can be a poet or a mystic after.

—Do you know what Ireland is? asked Stephen with cold violence. Ireland is the old sow that eats her farrow.

Davin rose from his box and went towards the players, shaking his head sadly. But in a moment his sadness left him and he was hotly disputing with Cranly and the two players who had finished their game. A match of four was arranged, Cranly insisting, however, that his ball should be used. He let it rebound twice or thrice to his hand and struck it strongly and swiftly towards the base of the alley, exclaiming in answer to its thud:

—Your soul!

Stephen stood with Lynch till the score began to rise. Then he plucked him by the sleeve to come away. Lynch obeyed, saying:

—Let us eke° go, as Cranly has it.

Stephen smiled at this sidethrust. They passed back through the garden and out through the hall where the doddering porter was pinning up a notice in the frame. At the foot of the steps they halted and Stephen took a packet of cigarettes from his pocket and offered it to his companion.

—I know you are poor, he said.

—Damn your yellow insolence, answered Lynch.

This second proof of Lynch's culture made Stephen smile again.

—It was a great day for European culture, he said, when you made up your mind to swear in yellow.

They lit their cigarettes and turned to the right. After a pause Stephen began:

—Aristotle has not defined pity and terror. I have. I say . . .

Lynch halted and said bluntly:

—Stop! I won't listen! I am sick. I was out last night on a yellow drunk with Horan and Goggins.

Stephen went on:

—Pity is the feeling which arrests the mind in the presence of whatsoever is grave and constant in human sufferings and unites it with the human sufferer. Terror is the feeling which arrests the mind in the presence of whatsoever is grave and constant in human sufferings and unites it with the secret cause. →selfishness Terror felt 4 self Pity for another → tragedy

—Repeat, said Lynch.

Stephen repeated the definitions slowly.

—A girl got into a hansom a few days ago, he went on, in London. She was on her way to meet her mother whom she had not seen for many years. At the corner of a street the shaft of a lorry shivered the window of the hansom in the shape of a star. A long fine needle of the shivered glass pierced her heart. She died on the instant. The reporter called it a tragic death. It is not. It is remote from terror and pity according to the terms of my definitions.

—The tragic emotion, in fact, is a face looking two ways, towards

eke: Archaic for "also" (Cranly probably means to say "e'en").

terror and towards pity, both of which are phases of it. You see I use the word *arrest*. I mean that the tragic emotion is static. Or rather the dramatic emotion is. The feelings excited by improper art are kinetic, desire or loathing. Desire urges us to possess, to go to something; loathing urges us to abandon, to go from something. These are kinetic emotions. The arts which excite them, pornographical or didactic, are therefore improper arts. The esthetic emotion (I use the general term) is therefore static. The mind is arrested and raised above desire and loathing.

—You say that art must not excite desire, said Lynch. I told you that one day I wrote my name in pencil on the backside of the Venus of Praxiteles in the Museum. Was that not desire?

—I speak of normal natures, said Stephen. You also told me that when you were a boy in that charming carmelite° school you ate pieces of dried cowdung.

Lynch broke again into a whinny of laughter and again rubbed both his hands over his groins but without taking them from his pockets.

—O I did! I did! he cried.

Stephen turned towards his companion and looked at him for a moment boldly in the eyes. Lynch, recovering from his laughter, answered his look from his humbled eyes. The long slender flattened skull beneath the long pointed cap brought before Stephen's mind the image of a hooded reptile. The eyes, too, were reptilelike in glint and gaze. Yet at that instant, humbled and alert in their look, they were lit by one tiny human point, the window of a shrivelled soul, poignant and selfembittered.

—As for that, Stephen said in polite parenthesis, we are all animals. I also am an animal.

—You are, said Lynch.

—But we are just now in a mental world, Stephen continued. The desire and loathing excited by improper esthetic means are really unesthetic emotions not only because they are kinetic in character but also because they are not more than physical. Our flesh shrinks from what it dreads and responds to the stimulus of what it desires by a purely reflex action of the nervous system. Our eyelid closes before we are aware that the fly is about to enter our eye.

—Not always, said Lynch critically.

—In the same way, said Stephen, your flesh responded to the stimulus of a naked statue but it was, I say, simply a reflex action of the

carmelite: Order of nuns.

nerves. Beauty expressed by the artist cannot awaken in us an emotion which is kinetic or a sensation which is purely physical. It awakens, or ought to awaken, or induces, or ought to induce, an esthetic stasis, an ideal pity or an ideal terror, a stasis called forth, prolonged and at last dissolved by what I call the rhythm of beauty.

—What is that exactly? asked Lynch.

—Rhythm, said Stephen, is the first formal esthetic relation of part to part in any esthetic whole or of an esthetic whole to its part or parts or of any part to the esthetic whole of which it is a part.

—If that is rhythm, said Lynch, let me hear what you call beauty: and, please remember, though I did eat a cake of cowdung once, that I admire only beauty.

Stephen raised his cap as if in greeting. Then, blushing slightly, he laid his hand on Lynch's thick tweed sleeve.

—We are right, he said, and the others are wrong. To speak of these things and to try to understand their nature and, having understood it, to try slowly and humbly and constantly to express, to press out again, from the gross earth or what it brings forth, from sound and shape and colour which are the prison gates of our soul, an image of the beauty we have come to understand—that is art.

They had reached the canal bridge and, turning from their course, went on by the trees. A crude grey light, mirrored in the sluggish water, and a smell of wet branches over their heads seemed to war against the course of Stephen's thought.

—But you have not answered my question, said Lynch. What is art? What is the beauty it expresses?

—That was the first definition I gave you, you sleepyheaded wretch, said Stephen, when I began to try to think out the matter for myself. Do you remember the night? Cranly lost his temper and began to talk about Wicklow bacon.

—I remember, said Lynch. He told us about them flaming fat devils of pigs.

—Art, said Stephen, is the human disposition of sensible or intelligible matter for an esthetic end. You remember the pigs and forget that. You are a distressing pair, you and Cranly.

Lynch made a grimace at the raw grey sky and said:

—If I am to listen to your esthetic philosophy give me at least another cigarette. I don't care about it. I don't even care about women. Damn you and damn everything. I want a job of five hundred a year. You can't get me one.

Stephen handed him the packet of cigarettes. Lynch took the last one that remained, saying simply:

—Proceed!

—Aquinas, said Stephen, says that is beautiful the apprehension of which pleases.

Lynch nodded.

—I remember that, he said. *Pulcra sunt quæ visa placent.*°

—He uses the word *visa,* said Stephen, to cover esthetic apprehension of all kinds, whether through sight or hearing or through any other avenue of apprehension. This word, though it is vague, is clear enough to keep away good and evil which excite desire and loathing. It means certainly a stasis and not a kinesis. How about the true? It produces also a stasis of the mind. You would not write your name in pencil across the hypothenuse of a rightangled triangle.

—No, said Lynch, give me the hypothenuse of the Venus of Praxiteles.

—Static therefore, said Stephen. Plato, I believe, said that beauty is the splendour of truth. I don't think that it has a meaning but the true and the beautiful are akin. Truth is beheld by the intellect which is appeased by the most satisfying relations of the intelligible: beauty is beheld by the imagination which is appeased by the most satisfying relations of the sensible. The first step in the direction of truth is to understand the frame and scope of the intellect itself, to comprehend the act itself of intellection. Aristotle's entire system of philosophy rests upon his book of psychology and that, I think, rests on his statement that the same attribute cannot at the same time and in the same connection belong to and not belong to the same subject. The first step in the direction of beauty is to understand the frame and scope of the imagination, to comprehend the act itself of esthetic apprehension. Is that clear?

—But what is beauty? asked Lynch impatiently. Out with another definition. Something we see and like! Is that the best you and Aquinas can do?

—Let us take woman, said Stephen.

—Let us take her! said Lynch fervently.

—The Greek, the Turk, the Chinese, the Copt, the Hottentot, said Stephen, all admire a different type of female beauty. That seems to be a maze out of which we cannot escape. I see however two ways out. One is this hypothesis: that every physical quality admired by men in

Pulcra sunt . . . placent: See p. 163.

women is in direct connection with the manifold functions of women for the propagation of the species. It may be so. The world, it seems, is drearier than even you, Lynch, imagined. For my part I dislike that way out. It leads to eugenics rather than to esthetic. It leads you out of the maze into a new gaudy lectureroom where MacCann, with one hand on *The Origin of Species* and the other hand on the new testament, tells you that you admired the great flanks of Venus because you felt that she would bear you burly offspring and admired her great breasts because you felt that she would give good milk to her children and yours.

—Then MacCann is a sulphuryellow liar, said Lynch energetically.

—There remains another way out, said Stephen, laughing.

—To wit? said Lynch.

—This hypothesis, Stephen began.

A long dray laden with old iron came round the corner of sir Patrick Dun's hospital covering the end of Stephen's speech with the harsh roar of jangled and rattling metal. Lynch closed his ears and gave out oath after oath till the dray had passed. Then he turned on his heel rudely. Stephen turned also and waited for a few moments till his companion's illhumour had had its vent.

—This hypothesis, Stephen repeated, is the other way out: that, though the same object may not seem beautiful to all people, all people who admire a beautiful object find in it certain relations which satisfy and coincide with the stages themselves of all esthetic apprehension. These relations of the sensible, visible to you through one form and to me through another, must be therefore the necessary qualities of beauty. Now, we can return to our old friend saint Thomas for another pennyworth of wisdom.

Lynch laughed.

—It amuses me vastly, he said, to hear you quoting him time after time like a jolly round friar. Are you laughing in your sleeve?

—MacAlister, answered Stephen, would call my esthetic theory applied Aquinas. So far as this side of esthetic philosophy extends Aquinas will carry me all along the line. When we come to the phenomena of artistic conception, artistic gestation and artistic reproduction I require a new terminology and a new personal experience.

—Of course, said Lynch. After all Aquinas, in spite of his intellect, was exactly a good round friar. But you will tell me about the new personal experience and new terminology some other day. Hurry up and finish the first part.

—Who knows? said Stephen, smiling. Perhaps Aquinas would understand me better than you. He was a poet himself. He wrote a hymn for Maundy Thursday. It begins with the words *Pange lingua gloriosi.*° They say it is the highest glory of the hymnal. It is an intricate and soothing hymn. I like it: but there is no hymn that can be put beside that mournful and majestic processional song, the *Vexilla Regis*° of Venantius Fortunatus.

Lynch began to sing softly and solemnly in a deep bass voice:

Impleta sunt quæ concinit
David fideli carmine
Dicendo nationibus
Regnavit a ligno Deus.°

—That's great! he said, well pleased. Great music!

They turned into Lower Mount Street. A few steps from the corner a fat young man, wearing a silk neckcloth, saluted them and stopped.

—Did you hear the results of the exams? he asked. Griffin was plucked.° Halpin and O'Flynn are through the home civil. Moonan got fifth place in the Indian. O'Shaughnessy got fourteenth. The Irish fellows in Clarke's gave them a feed last night. They all ate curry.

His pallid bloated face expressed benevolent malice and, as he had advanced through his tidings of success, his small fatencircled eyes vanished out of sight and his weak wheezing voice out of hearing.

In reply to a question of Stephen's his eyes and his voice came forth again from their lurkingplaces.

—Yes, MacCullagh and I, he said. He's taking pure mathematics and I'm taking constitutional history. There are twenty subjects. I'm taking botany too. You know I'm a member of the field club.

He drew back from the other two in a stately fashion and placed a plump woollengloved hand on his breast from which muttered wheezing laughter at once broke forth.

—Bring us a few turnips and onions the next time you go out, said Stephen drily, to make a stew.

The fat student laughed indulgently and said:

—We are all highly respectable people in the field club. Last Saturday we went out to Glenmalure, seven of us.

—With women, Donovan? said Lynch.

Pange lingua gloriosi: Tell, my tongue, in glorious . . . ; part of the opening line of a hymn by Aquinas. ***Vexilla Regis:*** From "Vexilla Regis Prodeunt," "The Banners of the King Advance." ***Impleta sunt . . . Deus:*** Fulfilled is all that David told / In true prophetic song of old: / Amidst the nations, God, saith he, / Hath reigned and triumphed from the Tree. **was plucked:** Flunked.

Donovan again laid his hand on his chest and said:

—Our end is the acquisition of knowledge.

Then he said quickly:

—I hear you are writing some essay about esthetics.

Stephen made a vague gesture of denial.

—Goethe and Lessing, said Donovan, have written a lot on that subject, the classical school and the romantic school and all that. The *Laocoon* interested me very much when I read it. Of course it is idealistic, German, ultraprofound.

Neither of the others spoke. Donovan took leave of them urbanely.

—I must go, he said softly and benevolently. I have a strong suspicion, amounting almost to a conviction, that my sister intended to make pancakes today for the dinner of the Donovan family.

—Goodbye, Stephen said in his wake. Don't forget the turnips for me and my mate.

Lynch gazed after him, his lip curling in slow scorn till his face resembled a devil's mask:

—To think that that yellow pancakeeating excrement can get a good job, he said at length, and I have to smoke cheap cigarettes!

They turned their faces towards Merrion Square and went on for a little in silence.

—To finish what I was saying about beauty, said Stephen, the most satisfying relations of the sensible must therefore correspond to the necessary phases of artistic apprehension. Find these and you find the qualities of universal beauty. Aquinas says: *ad pulcritudinem tria requiruntur, integritas, consonantia, claritas*. I translate it so: *Three things are needed for beauty, wholeness, harmony and radiance*. Do these correspond to the phases of apprehension? Are you following?

—Of course, I am, said Lynch. If you think I have an excrementitious intelligence run after Donovan and ask him to listen to you.

Stephen pointed to a basket which a butcher's boy had slung inverted on his head.

—Look at that basket, he said.

—I see it, said Lynch.

—In order to see that basket, said Stephen, your mind first of all separates the basket from the rest of the visible universe which is not the basket. The first phase of apprehension is a bounding line drawn about the object to be apprehended. An esthetic image is presented to us either in space or in time. What is audible is presented in time, what is visible is presented in space. But, temporal or spatial, the esthetic image is first luminously apprehended as selfbounded and selfcontained upon the immeasurable background of space or time which is not it. You apprehend it as *one* thing. You see it as one whole. You apprehend its wholeness. That is *integritas*.

—Bull's eye! said Lynch, laughing. Go on.

—Then, said Stephen, you pass from point to point, led by its formal lines; you apprehend it as balanced part against part within its limits; you feel the rhythm of its structure. In other words the synthesis of immediate perception is followed by the analysis of apprehension. Having first felt that it is *one* thing you feel now that it is *a thing*. You apprehend it as complex, multiple, divisible, separable, made up of its parts, the result of its parts and their sum, harmonious. That is *consonantia*.

—Bull's eye again! said Lynch wittily. Tell me now what is *claritas* and you win the cigar.

—The connotation of the word, Stephen said, is rather vague. Aquinas uses a term which seems to be inexact. It baffled me for a long time. It would lead you to believe that he had in mind symbolism or idealism, the supreme quality of beauty being a light from some other world, the idea of which the matter is but the shadow, the reality of which it is but the symbol. I thought he might mean that *claritas* is the artistic discovery and representation of the divine purpose in anything or a force of generalisation which would make the esthetic image a universal one, make it outshine its proper conditions. But that is literary talk. I understand it so. When you have apprehended that basket as one thing and have then analysed it according to its form and apprehended it as a thing you make the only synthesis which is logically and esthetically permissible. You see that it is that thing which it is and no other thing. The radiance of which he speaks is the scholastic *quidditas*, the *whatness* of a thing. This supreme quality is felt by the artist when the esthetic image is first conceived in his imagination. The mind in that mysterious instant Shelley likened beautifully to a fading coal. The instant wherein that supreme quality of beauty, the clear radiance of the esthetic image, is apprehended luminously by the mind which has been arrested by its wholeness and fascinated by its harmony is the luminous silent stasis of esthetic pleasure, a spiritual state very like to that cardiac condition which the Italian physiologist Luigi Galvani, using a phrase almost as beautiful as Shelley's, called the enchantment of the heart.

Stephen paused and, though his companion did not speak, felt that his words had called up around them a thoughtenchanted silence.

—What I have said, he began again, refers to beauty in the wider sense of the word, in the sense which the word has in the literary tradition. In the marketplace it has another sense. When we speak of beauty in the second sense of the term our judgment is influenced in the first place by the art itself and by the form of that art. The image, it is clear, must be set between the mind or senses of the artist himself and the mind or senses of others. If you bear this in memory you will see that art necessarily divides itself into three forms progressing from one to the next. These forms are: the lyrical form, the form wherein the artist presents his image in immediate relation to himself; the epical form, the form wherein he presents his image in mediate relation to himself and to others; the dramatic form, the form wherein he presents his image in immediate relation to others.

—That you told me a few nights ago, said Lynch, and we began the famous discussion.

—I have a book at home, said Stephen, in which I have written down questions which are more amusing than yours were. In finding the answers to them I found the theory of esthetic which I am trying to explain. Here are some questions I set myself: *Is a chair finely made tragic or comic? Is the portrait of Mona Lisa good if I desire to see it? Is the bust of Sir Philip Crampton lyrical, epical or dramatic? Can excrement or a child or a louse be a work of art? If not, why not?*

—Why not, indeed? said Lynch, laughing.

—*If a man hacking in fury at a block of wood,* Stephen continued, *make there an image of a cow is that image a work of art? If not, why not?*

—That's a lovely one, said Lynch, laughing again. That has the true scholastic stink.

—Lessing, said Stephen, should not have taken a group of statues to write of. The art, being inferior, does not present the forms I spoke of distinguished clearly one from another. Even in literature, the highest and most spiritual art, the forms are often confused. The lyrical form is in fact the simplest verbal vesture of an instant of emotion, a rhythmical cry such as ages ago cheered on the man who pulled at the oar or dragged stones up a slope. He who utters it is more conscious of the instant of emotion than of himself as feeling emotion. The simplest epical form is seen emerging out of lyrical literature when the artist prolongs and broods upon himself as the centre of an epical event and this form progresses till the centre of emotional gravity is equidistant from the artist himself and from others. The narrative is no longer purely personal. The personality of the artist passes into the narration itself, flowing round and round the persons and the action like a vital sea. This progress you will see easily in that old English ballad *Turpin Hero* which begins in the first person and ends in the third person. The dramatic form is reached when the vitality which has flowed and eddied round each person fills every person with such vital force that he or she assumes a proper and intangible esthetic life. The personality of the artist, at first a cry or a cadence or a mood and then a fluid and lambent narrative, finally refines itself out of existence, impersonalises itself, so to speak. The esthetic image in the dramatic form is life purified in and reprojected from the human imagination. The mystery of esthetic like that of material creation is accomplished. The artist, like the God of the creation, remains within or behind or beyond or above his handiwork, invisible, refined out of existence, indifferent, paring his fingernails.

—Trying to refine them also out of existence, said Lynch.

A fine rain began to fall from the high veiled sky and they turned into the duke's lawn, to reach the national library before the shower came.

—What do you mean, Lynch asked surlily, by prating about beauty and the imagination in this miserable Godforsaken island? No wonder the artist retired within or behind his handiwork after having perpetrated this country.

The rain fell faster. When they passed through the passage beside the royal Irish academy they found many students sheltering under the arcade of the library. Cranly, leaning against a pillar, was picking his teeth with a sharpened match, listening to some companions. Some girls stood near the entrance door. Lynch whispered to Stephen:

—Your beloved is here.

Stephen took his place silently on the step below the group of students, heedless of the rain which fell fast, turning his eyes towards her from time to time. She too stood silently among her companions. She has no priest to flirt with, he thought with conscious bitterness, remembering how he had seen her last. Lynch was right. His mind, emptied of theory and courage, lapsed back into a listless peace.

He heard the students talking among themselves. They spoke of two friends who had passed the final medical examination, of the chances of getting places on ocean liners, of poor and rich practices.

—That's all a bubble. An Irish country practice is better.

—Hynes was two years in Liverpool and he says the same. A frightful hole he said it was. Nothing but midwifery cases. Half a crown cases.

—Do you mean to say it is better to have a job here in the country than in a rich city like that? I know a fellow . . .

—Hynes has no brains. He got through by stewing,° pure stewing.

stewing: Unintelligent, grinding study.

—Don't mind him. There's plenty of money to be made in a big commercial city.

—Depends on the practice.

—*Ego credo ut vita pauperum est simpliciter atrox, simpliciter sanguinarius atrox, in Liverpoolio.*°

Their voices reached his ears as if from a distance in interrupted pulsation. She was preparing to go away with her companions.

The quick light shower had drawn off, tarrying in clusters of diamonds among the shrubs of the quadrangle where an exhalation was breathed forth by the blackened earth. Their trim boots prattled as they stood on the steps of the colonnade talking quietly and gaily, glancing at the clouds, holding their umbrellas at cunning angles against the few last raindrops, closing them again, holding their skirts demurely.

And if he had judged her harshly? If her life were a simple rosary of hours, her life simple and strange as a bird's life, gay in the morning, restless all day, tired at sundown? Her heart simple and wilful as a bird's heart?

*

*   *

Towards dawn he awoke. O what sweet music! His soul was all dewy wet. Over his limbs in sleep pale cool waves of light had passed. He lay still, as if his soul lay amid cool waters, conscious of faint sweet music. His mind was waking slowly to a tremulous morning knowledge, a morning inspiration. A spirit filled him, pure as the purest water, sweet as dew, moving as music. But how faintly it was inbreathed, how passionlessly, as if the seraphim° themselves were breathing upon him! His soul was waking slowly, fearing to awake wholly. It was that windless hour of dawn when madness wakes and strange plants open to the light and the moth flies forth silently.

An enchantment of the heart! The night had been enchanted. In dream or vision he had known the ecstasy of seraphic life. Was it an instant of enchantment only or long hours and days and years and ages?

The instant of inspiration seemed now to be reflected from all sides at once from a multitude of cloudy circumstance of what had happened or of what might have happened. The instant flashed forth like a point of light and now from cloud on cloud of vague circumstance confused form was veiling softly its afterglow. O! In the virgin womb of the imagination the word was made flesh. Gabriel the seraph had come to the virgin's chamber. An afterglow deepened within his spirit, whence the

Ego credo . . . Liverpoolio: I believe that the life of the poor is simply awful, simply bloody awful, in Liverpool (dog Latin). **seraphim:** The highest order of angels.

white flame had passed, deepening to a rose and ardent light. That rose and ardent light was her strange wilful heart, strange that no man had known or would know, wilful from before the beginning of the world: and lured by that ardent roselike glow the choirs of the seraphim were falling from heaven.

Are you not weary of ardent ways,
Lure of the fallen seraphim?
Tell no more of enchanted days.

The verses passed from his mind to his lips and, murmuring them over, he felt the rhythmic movement of a villanelle° pass through them. The roselike glow sent forth its rays of rhyme; ways, days, blaze, praise, raise. Its rays burned up the world, consumed the hearts of men and angels: the rays from the rose that was her wilful heart.

Your eyes have set man's heart ablaze
And you have had your will of him.
Are you not weary of ardent ways?

And then? The rhythm died away, ceased, began again to move and beat. And then? Smoke, incense ascending from the altar of the world.

Above the flame the smoke of praise
Goes up from ocean rim to rim.
Tell no more of enchanted days.

Smoke went up from the whole earth, from the vapoury oceans, smoke of her praise. The earth was like a swinging swaying smoking censer, a ball of incense, an ellipsoidal ball. The rhythm died out at once; the cry of his heart was broken. His lips began to murmur the first verses over and over; then went on stumbling through half verses, stammering and baffled; then stopped. The heart's cry was broken.

The veiled windless hour had passed and behind the panes of the naked window the morning light was gathering. A bell beat faintly very far away. A bird twittered; two birds, three. The bell and the bird ceased: and the dull white light spread itself east and west, covering the world, covering the roselight in his heart.

Fearing to lose all he raised himself suddenly on his elbow to look for paper and pencil. There was neither on the table; only the soupplate he had eaten the rice from for supper and the candlestick with its ten-

villanelle: Nineteen-line poem using only two rhymes, with rhymes and lines repeated according to a set pattern.

drils of tallow and its paper socket, singed by the last flame. He stretched his arm wearily towards the foot of the bed, groping with his hand in the pockets of the coat that hung there. His fingers found a pencil and then a cigarette packet. He lay back and, tearing open the packet, placed the last cigarette on the windowledge and began to write out the stanzas of the villanelle in small neat letters on the rough cardboard surface.

Having written them out he lay back on the lumpy pillow, murmuring them again. The lumps of knotted flock under his head reminded him of the lumps of knotted horsehair in the sofa of her parlour on which he used to sit, smiling or serious, asking himself why he had come, displeased with her and with himself, confounded by the print of the Sacred Heart above the untenanted sideboard. He saw her approach him in a lull of the talk and beg him to sing one of his curious songs. Then he saw himself sitting at the old piano, striking chords softly from its speckled keys and singing, amid the talk which had risen again in the room, to her who leaned beside the mantelpiece a dainty song of the Elizabethans, a sad and sweet loth to depart, the victory chant of Agincourt, the happy air of Greensleeves. While he sang and she listened, or feigned to listen, his heart was at rest but when the quaint old songs had ended and he heard again the voices in the room he remembered his own sarcasm: the house where young men are called by their christian names a little too soon.

At certain instants her eyes seemed about to trust him but he had waited in vain. She passed now dancing lightly across his memory as she had been that night at the carnival ball, her white dress a little lifted, a white spray nodding in her hair. She danced lightly in the round. She was dancing towards him and, as she came, her eyes were a little averted and a faint glow was on her cheek. At the pause in the chain of hands her hand had lain in his an instant, a soft merchandise.

—You are a great stranger now.

—Yes. I was born to be a monk.

—I am afraid you are a heretic.

—Are you much afraid?

For answer she had danced away from him along the chain of hands, dancing lightly and discreetly, giving herself to none. The white spray nodded to her dancing and when she was in shadow the glow was deeper on her cheek.

A monk! His own image started forth a profaner of the cloister, a heretic franciscan, willing and willing not to serve, spinning like Gherardino da Borgo San Donnino a lithe web of sophistry and whispering in her ear.

No, it was not his image. It was the image of the young priest in whose company he had seen her last, looking at him out of dove's eyes, toying with the pages of her Irish phrasebook.

—Yes, yes, the ladies are coming round to us. I can see it every day. The ladies are with us. The best helpers the language has.

—And the church, Father Moran?

—The church too. Coming round too. The work is going ahead there too. Don't fret about the church.

Bah! he had done well to leave the room in disdain. He had done well not to salute her on the steps of the library. He had done well to leave her to flirt with her priest, to toy with a church which was the scullerymaid of christendom.

Rude brutal anger routed the last lingering instant of ecstasy from his soul. It broke up violently her fair image and flung the fragments on all sides. On all sides distorted reflections of her image started from his memory: the flowergirl in the ragged dress with damp coarse hair and a hoyden's face who had called herself his own girl and begged his handsel, the kitchengirl in the next house who sang over the clatter of her plates with the drawl of a country singer the first bars of *By Killarney's Lakes and Fells,* a girl who had laughed gaily to see him stumble when the iron grating in the footpath near Cork Hill had caught the broken sole of his shoe, a girl he had glanced at, attracted by her small ripe mouth as she passed out of Jacob's biscuit factory, who had cried to him over her shoulder:

—Do you like what you seen of me, straight hair and curly eyebrows?

And yet he felt that, however he might revile and mock her image, his anger was also a form of homage. He had left the classroom in disdain that was not wholly sincere, feeling that perhaps the secret of her race lay behind those dark eyes upon which her long lashes flung a quick shadow. He had told himself bitterly as he walked through the streets that she was a figure of the womanhood of her country, a batlike soul waking to the consciousness of itself in darkness and secrecy and loneliness, tarrying awhile, loveless and sinless, with her mild lover and leaving him to whisper of innocent transgressions in the latticed ear of a priest. His anger against her found vent in coarse railing at her paramour, whose name and voice and features offended his baffled pride: a priested peasant, with a brother a policeman in Dublin and a brother a potboy° in Moycullen. To him she would unveil her soul's shy nakedness, to one who was but schooled in the discharging of a formal rite rather than to him, a priest of the eternal imagination, transmuting the daily bread of experience into the radiant body of everliving life.

The radiant image of the eucharist united again in an instant his bitter and despairing thoughts, their cries arising unbroken in a hymn of thanksgiving.

Our broken cries and mournful lays
Rise in one eucharistic hymn.
Are you not weary of ardent ways?

While sacrificing hands upraise
The chalice flowing to the brim,
Tell no more of enchanted days.

He spoke the verses aloud from the first lines till the music and rhythm suffused his mind, turning it to quiet indulgence; then copied them painfully to feel them the better by seeing them; then lay back on his bolster.

The full morning light had come. No sound was to be heard: but he knew that all around him life was about to awaken in common noises, hoarse voices, sleepy prayers. Shrinking from that life he turned towards the wall, making a cowl of the blanket and staring at the great overblown scarlet flowers of the tattered wallpaper. He tried to warm his perishing joy in their scarlet glow, imagining a roseway from where he lay upwards to heaven, all strewn with scarlet flowers. Weary! Weary! He too was weary of ardent ways.

A gradual warmth, a languorous weariness passed over him, descending along his spine from his closely cowled head. He felt it descend and, seeing himself as he lay, smiled. Soon he would sleep.

He had written verses for her again after ten years. Ten years before she had worn her shawl cowlwise about her head, sending sprays of her warm breath into the night air, tapping her foot upon the glassy road. It was the last tram; the lank brown horses knew it and shook their bells to the clear night in admonition. The conductor talked with the driver, both nodding often in the green light of the lamp. They stood on the steps of the tram, he on the upper, she on the lower. She came up to his step many times between their phrases and went down again and once or twice remained beside him forgetting to go down and then went down. Let be! Let be!

potboy: Waiter who serves beer or ale.

Ten years from that wisdom of children to his folly. If he sent her the verses? They would be read out at breakfast amid the tapping of eggshells. Folly indeed! The brothers would laugh and try to wrest the page from each other with their strong hard fingers. The suave priest, her uncle, seated in his armchair, would hold the page at arm's length, read it smiling and approve of the literary form.

No, no: that was folly. Even if he sent her the verses she would not show them to others. No, no: she could not.

He began to feel that he had wronged her. A sense of her innocence moved him almost to pity her, an innocence he had never understood till he had come to the knowledge of it through sin, an innocence which she too had not understood while she was innocent or before the strange humiliation of her nature had first come upon her. Then first her soul had begun to live as his soul had when he had first sinned: and a tender compassion filled his heart as he remembered her frail pallor and her eyes, humbled and saddened by the dark shame of womanhood.

While his soul had passed from ecstasy to languor where had she been? Might it be, in the mysterious ways of spiritual life, that her soul at those same moments had been conscious of his homage? It might be.

A glow of desire kindled again his soul and fired and fulfilled all his body. Conscious of his desire she was waking from odorous sleep, the temptress of his villanelle. Her eyes, dark and with a look of languor, were opening to his eyes. Her nakedness yielded to him, radiant, warm, odorous and lavishlimbed, enfolded him like a shining cloud, enfolded him like water with a liquid life: and like a cloud of vapour or like waters circumfluent in space the liquid letters of speech, symbols of the element of mystery, flowed forth over his brain.

Are you not weary of ardent ways,
Lure of the fallen seraphim?
Tell no more of enchanted days.

Your eyes have set man's heart ablaze
And you have had your will of him.
Are you not weary of ardent ways?

Above the flame the smoke of praise
Goes up from ocean rim to rim.
Tell no more of enchanted days.

Our broken cries and mournful lays
Rise in one eucharistic hymn.

Are you not weary of ardent ways?

While sacrificing hands upraise
The chalice flowing to the brim,
Tell no more of enchanted days.

And still you hold our longing gaze
With languorous look and lavish limb!
Are you not weary of ardent ways?
Tell no more of enchanted days.

*

* *

What birds were they? He stood on the steps of the library to look at them, leaning wearily on his ashplant.° They flew round and round the jutting shoulder of a house in Molesworth Street. The air of the late March evening made clear their flight, their dark darting quivering bodies flying clearly against the sky as against a limphung cloth of smoky tenuous blue.

He watched their flight: bird after bird: a dark flash, a swerve, a flash again, a dart aside, a curve, a flutter of wings. He tried to count them before all their darting quivering bodies passed: six, ten, eleven: and wondered were they odd or even in number. Twelve, thirteen: for two came wheeling down from the upper sky. They were flying high and low but ever round and round in straight and curving lines and ever flying from left to right, circling about a temple of air.

He listened to the cries: like the squeak of mice behind the wainscot: a shrill twofold note. But the notes were long and shrill and whirring, unlike the cry of vermin, falling a third or a fourth and trilled as the flying beaks clove the air. Their cry was shrill and clear and fine and falling like threads of silken light unwound from whirring spools.

The inhuman clamour soothed his ears in which his mother's sobs and reproaches murmured insistently and the dark frail quivering bodies wheeling and fluttering and swerving round an airy temple of the tenuous sky soothed his eyes which still saw the image of his mother's face.

Why was he gazing upwards from the steps of the porch, hearing their shrill twofold cry, watching their flight? For an augury of good or evil? A phrase of Cornelius Agrippa flew through his mind and then there flew hither and thither shapeless thoughts from Swedenborg on the correspondence of birds to things of the intellect and of how the creatures of the air have their knowledge and know their times and sea-

ashplant: Joyce's term for a staff made of ash.

sons because they, unlike man, are in the order of their life and have not perverted that order by reason.

And for ages men had gazed upward as he was gazing at birds in flight. The colonnade above him made him think vaguely of an ancient temple and the ashplant on which he leaned wearily of the curved stick of an augur.° A sense of fear of the unknown moved in the heart of his weariness, a fear of symbols and portents, of the hawklike man whose name he bore soaring out of his captivity on osierwoven wings, of Thoth, the god of writers, writing with a reed upon a tablet and bearing on his narrow ibis head the cusped moon.

He smiled as he thought of the god's image for it made him think of a bottlenosed judge in a wig, putting commas into a document which he held at arm's length and he knew that he would not have remembered the god's name but that it was like an Irish oath. It was folly. But was it for this folly that he was about to leave for ever the house of prayer and prudence into which he had been born and the order of life out of which he had come?

They came back with shrill cries over the jutting shoulder of the house, flying darkly against the fading air. What birds were they? He thought that they must be swallows who had come back from the south. Then he was to go away for they were birds ever going and coming, building ever an unlasting home under the eaves of men's houses and ever leaving the homes they had built to wander.

Bend down your faces, Oona and Aleel.
I gaze upon them as the swallow gazes
Upon the nest under the eave before
He wander the loud waters.

A soft liquid joy like the noise of many waters flowed over his memory and he felt in his heart the soft peace of silent spaces of fading tenuous sky above the waters, of oceanic silence, of swallows flying through the seadusk over the flowing waters.

A soft liquid joy flowed through the words where the soft long vowels hurtled noiselessly and fell away, lapping and flowing back and ever shaking the white bells of their waves in mute chime and mute peal and soft low swooning cry: and he felt that the augury he had sought in the wheeling darting birds and in the pale space of sky above him had come forth from his heart like a bird from a turret quietly and swiftly.

augur: Roman professional prophet.

Symbol of departure or of loneliness? The verses crooned in the ear of his memory composed slowly before his remembering eyes the scene of the hall on the night of the opening of the national theatre. He was alone at the side of the balcony, looking out of jaded eyes at the culture of Dublin in the stalls and at the tawdry scenecloths and human dolls framed by the garish lamps of the stage. A burly policeman sweated behind him and seemed at every moment about to act. The catcalls and hisses and mocking cries ran in rude gusts round the hall from his scattered fellowstudents.

—A libel on Ireland!

—Made in Germany!

—Blasphemy!

—We never sold our faith!

—No Irish woman ever did it!

—We want no amateur atheists.

—We want no budding buddhists.

A sudden swift hiss fell from the windows above him and he knew that the electric lamps had been switched on in the reader's room. He turned into the pillared hall, now calmly lit, went up the staircase and passed in through the clicking turnstile.

Cranly was sitting over near the dictionaries. A thick book, opened at the frontispiece, lay before him on the wooden rest. He leaned back in his chair, inclining his ear like that of a confessor to the face of the medical student who was reading to him a problem from the chess page of a journal. Stephen sat down at his right and the priest at the other side of the table closed his copy of *The Tablet* with an angry snap and stood up.

Cranly gazed after him blandly and vaguely. The medical student went on in a softer voice:

—Pawn to king's fourth.

—We had better go, Dixon, said Stephen in warning. He has gone to complain.

Dixon folded the journal and rose with dignity, saying:

—Our men retired in good order.

—With guns and cattle, added Stephen, pointing to the titlepage of Cranly's book on which was printed *Diseases of the Ox*.

As they passed through a lane of the tables Stephen said:

—Cranly, I want to speak to you.

Cranly did not answer or turn. He laid his book on the counter and passed out, his wellshod feet sounding flatly on the floor. On the staircase he paused and gazing absently at Dixon repeated:

—Pawn to king's bloody fourth.

—Put it that way if you like, Dixon said.

He had a quiet toneless voice and urbane manners and on a finger of his plump clean hand he displayed at moments a signet ring.

As they crossed the hall a man of dwarfish stature came towards them. Under the dome of his tiny hat his unshaven face began to smile with pleasure and he was heard to murmur. The eyes were melancholy as those of a monkey.

—Good evening, captain, said Cranly, halting.

—Good evening, gentlemen, said the stubblegrown monkeyish face.

—Warm weather for March, said Cranly. They have the windows open upstairs.

Dixon smiled and turned his ring. The blackish monkey-puckered face pursed its human mouth with gentle pleasure: and its voice purred:

—Delightful weather for March. Simply delightful.

—There are two nice young ladies upstairs, captain, tired of waiting, Dixon said.

Cranly smiled and said kindly:

—The captain has only one love: sir Walter Scott. Isn't that so, captain?

—What are you reading now, captain? Dixon asked. *The Bride of Lammermoor?*

—I love old Scott, the flexible lips said. I think he writes something lovely. There is no writer can touch sir Walter Scott.

He moved a thin shrunken brown hand gently in the air in time to his praise and his thin quick eyelids beat often over his sad eyes.

Sadder to Stephen's ear was his speech: a genteel accent, low and moist, marred by errors: and listening to it he wondered was the story true and was the thin blood that flowed in his shrunken frame noble and come of an incestuous love.

The park trees were heavy with rain and rain fell still and ever in the lake, lying grey like a shield. A game of swans flew there and the water and the shore beneath were fouled with their greenwhite slime. They embraced softly, impelled by the grey rainy light, the wet silent trees, the shieldlike witnessing lake, the swans. They embraced without joy or passion, his arm about his sister's neck. A grey woolen cloak was wrapped athwart her from her shoulder to her waist: and her fair head was bent in willing shame. He had loose redbrown hair and tender shapely strong freckled hands. Face. There was no face seen. The brother's face was bent upon her fair rainfragrant hair. The hand freckled and strong and shapely and caressing was Davin's hand.

He frowned angrily upon his thought and on the shrivelled mannikin who had called it forth. His father's gibes at the Bantry gang leaped out of his memory. He held them at a distance and brooded uneasily on his own thought again. Why were they not Cranly's hands? Had Davin's simplicity and innocence stung him more secretly?

He walked on across the hall with Dixon, leaving Cranly to take leave elaborately of the dwarf.

Under the colonnade Temple was standing in the midst of a little group of students. One of them cried:

—Dixon, come over till you hear. Temple is in grand form.

Temple turned on him his dark gipsy eyes.

—You're a hypocrite, O'Keeffe, he said, and Dixon's a smiler. By hell, I think that's a good literary expression.

He laughed slily, looking in Stephen's face, repeating:

—By hell, I'm delighted with that name. A smiler.

A stout student who stood below them on the steps said:

—Come back to the mistress, Temple. We want to hear about that.

—He had, faith, Temple said. And he was a married man too. And all the priests used to be dining there. By hell, I think they all had a touch.°

—We shall call it riding a hack to spare the hunter,° said Dixon.

—Tell us, Temple, O'Keeffe said, how many quarts of porter have you in you?

—All your intellectual soul is in that phrase, O'Keeffe, said Temple with open scorn.

He moved with a shambling gait round the group and spoke to Stephen.

—Did you know that the Forsters are the kings of Belgium? he asked.

Cranly came out through the door of the entrance hall, his hat thrust back on the nape of his neck and picking his teeth with care.

—And here's the wiseacre, said Temple. Do you know that about the Forsters?

He paused for an answer. Cranly dislodged a figseed from his teeth on the point of his rude toothpick and gazed at it intently.

—The Forster family, Temple said, is descended from Baldwin the First, king of Flanders. He was called the Forester. Forester and Forster are the same name. A descendant of Baldwin the First, captain Francis Forster, settled in Ireland and married the daughter of the last chieftain

a touch: Sexual play or intercourse. **hack . . . hunter:** Ordinary horse . . . prize horse.

of Clanbrassil. Then there are the Blake Forsters. That's a different branch.

—From Baldhead, king of Flanders, Cranly repeated, rooting again deliberately at his gleaming uncovered teeth.

—Where did you pick up all that history? O'Keeffe asked.

—I know all the history of your family too, Temple said, turning to Stephen. Do you know what Giraldus Cambrensis says about your family?

—Is he descended from Baldwin too? asked a tall consumptive student with dark eyes.

—Baldhead, Cranly repeated, sucking at a crevice in his teeth.

—*Pernobilis et pervetusta familia,*° Temple said to Stephen.

The stout student who stood below them on the steps farted briefly. Dixon turned towards him saying in a soft voice:

—Did an angel speak?

Cranly turned also and said vehemently but without anger:

—Goggins, you're the flamingest dirty devil I ever met, do you know.

—I had it on my mind to say that, Goggins answered firmly. It did no-one any harm, did it?

—We hope, Dixon said suavely, that it was not of the kind known to science as a *paulo post futurum.*°

—Didn't I tell you he was a smiler? said Temple, turning right and left. Didn't I give him that name?

—You did. We're not deaf, said the tall consumptive.

Cranly still frowned at the stout student below him. Then, with a snort of disgust, he shoved him violently down the steps.

—Go away from here, he said rudely. Go away, you stinkpot. And you are a stinkpot.

Goggins skipped down on to the gravel and at once returned to his place with good humour. Temple turned back to Stephen and asked:

—Do you believe in the law of heredity?

—Are you drunk or what are you or what are you trying to say? asked Cranly, facing round on him with an expression of wonder.

—The most profound sentence ever written, Temple said with enthusiasm, is the sentence at the end of the zoology. Reproduction is the beginning of death.

He touched Stephen timidly at the elbow and said eagerly:

Pernobilis et pervetusta familia: Of a noble and venerable family. ***paulo post futurum:*** Grammatical term referring to the verb form used for an event about to happen.

—Do you feel how profound that is because you are a poet?

Cranly pointed his long forefinger.

—Look at him! he said with scorn to the others. Look at Ireland's hope!

They laughed at his words and gesture. Temple turned on him bravely, saying:

—Cranly, you're always sneering at me. I can see that. But I am as good as you are any day. Do you know what I think about you now as compared with myself?

—My dear man, said Cranly urbanely, you are incapable, do you know, absolutely incapable of thinking.

—But do you know, Temple went on, what I think of you and of myself compared together?

—Out with it, Temple! the stout student cried from the steps. Get it out in bits!

Temple turned right and left, making sudden feeble gestures as he spoke.

—I'm a ballocks,° he said, shaking his head in despair. I am. And I know I am. And I admit it that I am.

Dixon patted him lightly on the shoulder and said mildly:

—And it does you every credit, Temple.

—But he, Temple said, pointing to Cranly. He is a ballocks too like me. Only he doesn't know it. And that's the only difference I see.

A burst of laughter covered his words. But he turned again to Stephen and said with a sudden eagerness:

—That word is a most interesting word. That's the only English dual number.° Did you know?

—Is it? Stephen said vaguely.

He was watching Cranly's firmfeatured suffering face, lit up now by a smile of false patience. The gross name had passed over it like foul water poured over an old stone image, patient of injuries: and, as he watched him, he saw him raise his hat in salute and uncover the black hair that stood up stiffly from his forehead like an iron crown.

She passed out from the porch of the library and bowed across Stephen in reply to Cranly's greeting. He also? Was there not a slight flush on Cranly's cheek? Or had it come forth at Temple's words? The light had waned. He could not see.

Did that explain his friend's listless silence, his harsh comments, the

ballocks: Set of testicles (figuratively, a clumsy oaf or a mess). **dual number:** Obsolete grammatical form for nouns indicating a pair.

sudden intrusions of rude speech with which he had shattered so often Stephen's ardent wayward confessions? Stephen had forgiven freely for he had found this rudeness also in himself towards himself. And he remembered an evening when he had dismounted from a borrowed creaking bicycle to pray to God in a wood near Malahide. He had lifted up his arms and spoken in ecstasy to the sombre nave of the trees, knowing that he stood on holy ground and in a holy hour. And when two constabularymen had come into sight round a bend in the gloomy road he had broken off his prayer to whistle loudly an air from the last pantomime.

He began to beat the frayed end of his ashplant against the base of a pillar. Had Cranly not heard him? Yet he could wait. The talk about him ceased for a moment: and a soft hiss fell again from a window above. But no other sound was in the air and the swallows whose flight he had followed with idle eyes were sleeping.

She had passed through the dusk. And therefore the air was silent save for one soft hiss that fell. And therefore the tongues about him had ceased their babble. Darkness was falling.

Darkness falls from the air.

A trembling joy, lambent as a faint light, played like a fairy host around him. But why? Her passage through the darkening air or the verse with its black vowels and its opening sound, rich and lutelike?

He walked away slowly towards the deeper shadows at the end of the colonnade, beating the stone softly with his stick to hide his revery from the students whom he had left: and allowed his mind to summon back to itself the age of Dowland and Byrd and Nash.

Eyes, opening from the darkness of desire, eyes that dimmed the breaking east. What was their languid grace but the softness of chambering? And what was their shimmer but the shimmer of the scum that mantled the cesspool of the court of a slobbering Stuart. And he tasted in the language of memory ambered wines, dying fallings of sweet airs, the proud pavan:° and saw with the eyes of memory kind gentlewomen in Covent Garden wooing from their balconies with sucking mouths and the poxfouled wenches of the taverns and young wives that, gaily yielding to their ravishers, clipped° and clipped again.

The images he had summoned gave him no pleasure. They were secret and enflaming but her image was not entangled by them. That was not the way to think of her. It was not even the way in which he

pavan: A formal kind of Elizabethan dance. **clipped:** Embraced.

thought of her. Could his mind then not trust itself? Old phrases, sweet only with a disinterred sweetness like the figseeds Cranly rooted out of his gleaming teeth.

It was not thought nor vision though he knew vaguely that her figure was passing homeward through the city. Vaguely first and then more sharply he smelt her body. A conscious unrest seethed in his blood. Yes, it was her body that he smelt: a wild and languid smell: the tepid limbs over which his music had flowed desirously and the secret soft linen upon which her flesh distilled odour and a dew.

A louse crawled over the nape of his neck and, putting his thumb and forefinger deftly beneath his loose collar, he caught it. He rolled its body, tender yet brittle as a grain of rice, between thumb and finger for an instant before he let it fall from him and wondered would it live or die. There came to his mind a curious phrase from Cornelius a Lapide which said that the lice born of human sweat were not created by God with the other animals on the sixth day. But the tickling of the skin of his neck made his mind raw and red. The life of his body, illclad, illfed, louseeaten, made him close his eyelids in a sudden spasm of despair: and in the darkness he saw the brittle bright bodies of lice falling from the air and turning often as they fell. Yes: and it was not darkness that fell from the air. It was brightness.

Brightness falls from the air.

He had not even remembered rightly Nash's line. All the images it had awakened were false. His mind bred vermin. His thoughts were lice born of the sweat of sloth.

He came back quickly along the colonnade towards the group of students. Well then let her go and be damned to her. She could love some clean athlete who washed himself every morning to the waist and had black hair on his chest. Let her.

Cranly had taken another dried fig from the supply in his pocket and was eating it slowly and noisily. Temple sat on the pediment of a pillar, leaning back, his cap pulled down on his sleepy eyes. A squat young man came out of the porch, a leather portfolio tucked under his armpit. He marched towards the group, striking the flags with the heels of his boots and with the ferule of his heavy umbrella. Then, raising the umbrella in salute, he said to all:

—Good evening, sirs.

He struck the flags again and tittered while his head trembled with a slight nervous movement. The tall consumptive student and Dixon and O'Keeffe were speaking in Irish and did not answer him. Then, turning to Cranly, he said:

—Good evening, particularly to you.

He moved the umbrella in indication and tittered again. Cranly, who was still chewing the fig, answered with loud movements of his jaws.

—Good? Yes. It is a good evening.

The squat student looked at him seriously and shook his umbrella gently and reprovingly.

—I can see, he said, that you are about to make obvious remarks.

—Um, Cranly answered, holding out what remained of the half-chewed fig and jerking it towards the squat student's mouth in sign that he should eat.

The squat student did not eat it but, indulging his special humour, said gravely, still tittering and prodding his phrase with his umbrella:

—Do you intend that . . .

He broke off, pointed bluntly to the munched pulp of the fig and said loudly:

—I allude to that.

—Um, Cranly said as before.

—Do you intend that now, the squat student said, as *ipso facto* or, let us say, as so to speak?

Dixon turned aside from his group, saying:

—Goggins was waiting for you, Glynn. He has gone round to the Adelphi to look for you and Moynihan. What have you there? he asked, tapping the portfolio under Glynn's arm.

—Examination papers, Glynn answered. I give them monthly examinations to see that they are profiting by my tuition.

He also tapped the portfolio and coughed gently and smiled.

—Tuition! said Cranly rudely. I suppose you mean the barefooted children that are taught by a bloody ape like you. God help them!

He bit off the rest of the fig and flung away the butt.

—I suffer little children to come unto me, Glynn said amiably.

—A bloody ape, Cranly repeated with emphasis, and a blasphemous bloody ape!

Temple stood up and, pushing past Cranly, addressed Glynn:

—That phrase you said now, he said, is from the new testament about suffer the children to come to me.

—Go to sleep again, Temple, said O'Keeffe.

—Very well, then, Temple continued, still addressing Glynn, and if

Jesus suffered the children to come why does the church send them all to hell if they die unbaptised? Why is that?

—Were you baptised yourself, Temple? the consumptive student asked.

—But why are they sent to hell if Jesus said they were all to come? Temple said, his eyes searching in Glynn's eyes.

Glynn coughed and said gently, holding back with difficulty the nervous titter in his voice and moving his umbrella at every word:

—And, as you remark, if it is thus I ask emphatically whence comes this thusness.

—Because the church is cruel like all old sinners, Temple said.

—Are you quite orthodox on that point, Temple? Dixon said suavely.

—Saint Augustine says that about unbaptised children going to hell, Temple answered, because he was a cruel old sinner too.

—I bow to you, Dixon said, but I had the impression that limbo existed for such cases.

—Don't argue with him, Dixon, Cranly said brutally. Don't talk to him or look at him. Lead him home with a sugan° the way you'd lead a bleating goat.

—Limbo! Temple cried. That's a fine invention too. Like hell.

—But with the unpleasantness left out, Dixon said.

He turned smiling to the others and said:

—I think I am voicing the opinions of all present in saying so much.

—You are, Glynn said in a firm tone. On that point Ireland is united.

He struck the ferule of his umbrella on the stone floor of the colonnade.

—Hell, Temple said. I can respect that invention of the grey spouse of Satan. Hell is Roman, like the walls of the Romans, strong and ugly. But what is limbo?

—Put him back into the perambulator, Cranly, O'Keeffe called out.

Cranly made a swift step towards Temple, halted, stamping his foot and crying as if to a fowl:

—Hoosh!

Temple moved away nimbly.

—Do you know what limbo is? he cried. Do you know what we call a notion like that in Roscommon?

—Hoosh! Blast you! Cranly cried, clapping his hands.

sugan: Rope made of straw (Irish).

—Neither my arse nor my elbow! Temple cried out scornfully. And that's what I call limbo.

—Give us that stick here, Cranly said.

He snatched the ashplant roughly from Stephen's hand and sprang down the steps: but Temple, hearing him move in pursuit, fled through the dusk like a wild creature, nimble and fleetfooted. Cranly's heavy boots were heard loudly charging across the quadrangle and then returning heavily, foiled and spurning the gravel at each step.

His step was angry and with an angry abrupt gesture he thrust the stick back into Stephen's hand. Stephen felt that his anger had another cause but, feigning patience, touched his arm slightly and said quietly:

—Cranly, I told you I wanted to speak to you. Come away.

Cranly looked at him for a few moments and asked:

—Now?

—Yes, now, Stephen said. We can't speak here. Come away.

They crossed the quadrangle together without speaking. The birdcall from *Siegfried* whistled softly followed them from the steps of the porch. Cranly turned: and Dixon, who had whistled, called out:

—Where are you fellows off to? What about that game, Cranly?

They parleyed in shouts across the still air about a game of billiards to be played in the Adelphi hotel. Stephen walked on alone and out into the quiet of Kildare Street. Opposite Maple's hotel he stood to wait, patient again. The name of the hotel, a colourless polished wood, and its colourless quiet front stung him like a glance of polite disdain. He stared angrily back at the softly lit drawingroom of the hotel in which he imagined the sleek lives of the patricians of Ireland housed in calm. They thought of army commissions and land agents: peasants greeted them along the roads in the country: they knew the names of certain French dishes and gave orders to jarvies° in highpitched provincial voices which pierced through their skintight accents.

How could he hit their conscience or how cast his shadow over the imaginations of their daughters, before their squires begat upon them, that they might breed a race less ignoble than their own? And under the deepened dusk he felt the thoughts and desires of the race to which he belonged flitting like bats across the dark country lanes, under trees by the edges of streams and near the poolmottled bogs. A woman had waited in the doorway as Davin had passed by at night and, offering him a cup of milk, had all but wooed him to her bed: for Davin had

jarvies: Horse-cab drivers.

the mild eyes of one who could be secret. But him no woman's eyes had wooed.

His arm was taken in a strong grip and Cranly's voice said:

—Let us eke go.

They walked southward in silence. Then Cranly said:

—That blithering idiot Temple! I swear to Moses, do you know, that I'll be the death of that fellow one time.

But his voice was no longer angry and Stephen wondered was he thinking of her greeting to him under the porch.

They turned to the left and walked on as before. When they had gone on so for some time Stephen said:

—Cranly, I had an unpleasant quarrel this evening.

—With your people? Cranly asked.

—With my mother.

—About religion?

—Yes, Stephen answered.

After a pause Cranly asked:

—What age is your mother?

—Not old, Stephen said. She wishes me to make my easter duty.°

—And will you?

—I will not, Stephen said.

—Why not? Cranly said.

—I will not serve, answered Stephen.

—That remark was made before, Cranly said calmly.

—It is made behind now, said Stephen hotly.

Cranly pressed Stephen's arm, saying:

—Go easy, my dear man. You're an excitable bloody man, do you know.

He laughed nervously as he spoke and, looking up into Stephen's face with moved and friendly eyes, said:

—Do you know that you are an excitable man?

—I daresay I am, said Stephen, laughing also.

Their minds, lately estranged, seemed suddenly to have been drawn closer, one to the other.

—Do you believe in the eucharist? Cranly asked.

—I do not, Stephen said.

—Do you disbelieve then?

—I neither believe in it nor disbelieve in it, Stephen answered.

—Many persons have doubts, even religious persons, yet they over-

easter duty: Going to communion service on Easter.

come them or put them aside, Cranly said. Are your doubts on that point too strong?

—I do not wish to overcome them, Stephen answered.

Cranly, embarrassed for a moment, took another fig from his pocket and was about to eat it when Stephen said:

—Don't, please. You cannot discuss this question with your mouth full of chewed fig.

Cranly examined the fig by the light of a lamp under which he halted. Then he smelt it with both nostrils, bit a tiny piece, spat it out and threw the fig rudely into the gutter. Addressing it as it lay, he said:

—Depart from me, ye cursed, into everlasting fire!

Taking Stephen's arm, he went on again and said:

—Do you not fear that those words may be spoken to you on the day of judgment?

—What is offered me on the other hand? Stephen asked. An eternity of bliss in the company of the dean of studies?

—Remember, Cranly said, that he would be glorified.

—Ay, Stephen said somewhat bitterly, bright, agile, impassible and, above all, subtle.

—It is a curious thing, do you know, Cranly said dispassionately, how your mind is supersaturated with the religion in which you say you disbelieve. Did you believe in it when you were at school? I bet you did.

—I did, Stephen answered.

—And were you happier then? Cranly asked softly. Happier than you are now, for instance?

—Often happy, Stephen said, and often unhappy. I was someone else then.

—How someone else? What do you mean by that statement?

—I mean, said Stephen, that I was not myself as I am now, as I had to become.

—Not as you are now, not as you had to become, Cranly repeated. Let me ask you a question. Do you love your mother?

Stephen shook his head slowly.

—I don't know what your words mean, he said simply.

—Have you never loved anyone? Cranly asked.

—Do you mean women?

—I am not speaking of that, Cranly said in a colder tone. I ask you if you ever felt love towards anyone or anything.

Stephen walked on beside his friend, staring gloomily at the footpath.

—I tried to love God, he said at length. It seems now I failed. It is very difficult. I tried to unite my will with the will of God instant by instant. In that I did not always fail. I could perhaps do that still . . .

Cranly cut him short by asking:

—Has your mother had a happy life?

—How do I know? Stephen said.

—How many children had she?

—Nine or ten, Stephen answered. Some died.

—Was your father. . . . Cranly interrupted himself for an instant: and then said: I don't want to pry into your family affairs. But was your father what is called well-to-do? I mean when you were growing up?

—Yes, Stephen said.

—What was he? Cranly asked after a pause.

Stephen began to enumerate glibly his father's attributes.

—A medical student, an oarsman, a tenor, an amateur actor, a shouting politician, a small landlord, a small investor, a drinker, a good fellow, a storyteller, somebody's secretary, something in a distillery, a taxgatherer, a bankrupt and at present a praiser of his own past.

Cranly laughed, tightening his grip on Stephen's arm, and said:

—The distillery is damn good.

—Is there anything else you want to know? Stephen asked.

—Are you in good circumstances at present?

—Do I look it? Stephen asked bluntly.

—So then, Cranly went on musingly, you were born in the lap of luxury.

He used the phrase broadly and loudly as he often used technical expressions as if he wished his hearer to understand that they were used by him without conviction.

—Your mother must have gone through a good deal of suffering, he said then. Would you not try to save her from suffering more even if . . . or would you?

—If I could, Stephen said. That would cost me very little.

—Then do so, Cranly said. Do as she wishes you to do. What is it for you? You disbelieve in it. It is a form: nothing else. And you will set her mind at rest.

He ceased and, as Stephen did not reply, remained silent. Then, as if giving utterance to the process of his own thought, he said:

—Whatever else is unsure in this stinking dunghill of a world a mother's love is not. Your mother brings you into the world, carries you first in her body. What do we know about what she feels? But whatever she feels, it, at least, must be real. It must be. What are our ideas or ambitions? Play. Ideas! Why, that bloody bleating goat Temple has ideas. MacCann has ideas too. Every jackass going the roads thinks he has ideas.

Stephen, who had been listening to the unspoken speech behind the words, said with assumed carelessness:

—Pascal, if I remember rightly, would not suffer his mother to kiss him as he feared the contact of her sex.

—Pascal was a pig, said Cranly.

—Aloysius Gonzaga, I think, was of the same mind, Stephen said.

—And he was another pig then, said Cranly.

—The church calls him a saint, Stephen objected.

—I don't care a flaming damn what anyone calls him, Cranly said rudely and flatly. I call him a pig.

Stephen, preparing the words neatly in his mind, continued:

—Jesus too seems to have treated his mother with scant courtesy in public but Suarez, a jesuit theologian and Spanish gentleman, has apologised for him.

—Did the idea ever occur to you, Cranly asked, that Jesus was not what he pretended to be?

—The first person to whom that idea occurred, Stephen answered, was Jesus himself.

—I mean, Cranly said, hardening in his speech, did the idea ever occur to you that he was himself a conscious hypocrite, what he called the jews of his time, a whited sepulchre? Or, to put it more plainly, that he was a blackguard?

—That idea never occurred to me, Stephen answered. But I am curious to know are you trying to make a convert of me or a pervert of yourself?

He turned towards his friend's face and saw there a raw smile which some force of will strove to make finely significant.

Cranly asked suddenly in a plain sensible tone:

—Tell me the truth. Were you at all shocked by what I said?

—Somewhat, Stephen said.

—And why were you shocked, Cranly pressed on in the same tone, if you feel sure that our religion is false and that Jesus was not the son of God?

—I am not at all sure of it, Stephen said. He is more like a son of God than a son of Mary.

—And is that why you will not communicate, Cranly asked, because you are not sure of that too, because you feel that the host too may be the body and blood of the son of God and not a wafer of bread? And because you fear that it may be?

—Yes, Stephen said quietly. I feel that and I also fear it.

—I see, Cranly said.

Stephen, struck by his tone of closure, reopened the discussion at once by saying:

—I fear many things: dogs, horses, firearms, the sea, thunderstorms, machinery, the country roads at night.

—But why do you fear a bit of bread?

—I imagine, Stephen said, that there is a malevolent reality behind those things I say I fear.

—Do you fear then, Cranly asked, that the God of the Roman catholics would strike you dead and damn you if you made a sacrilegious communion?

—The God of the Roman catholics could do that now, Stephen said. I fear more than that the chemical action which would be set up in my soul by a false homage to a symbol behind which are massed twenty centuries of authority and veneration.

—Would you, Cranly asked, in extreme danger commit that particular sacrilege? For instance, if you lived in the penal days?°

—I cannot answer for the past, Stephen replied. Possibly not.

—Then, said Cranly, you do not intend to become a protestant?

—I said that I had lost the faith, Stephen answered, but not that I had lost selfrespect. What kind of liberation would that be to forsake an absurdity which is logical and coherent and to embrace one which is illogical and incoherent?

They had walked on towards the township of Pembroke and now, as they went on slowly along the avenues, the trees and the scattered lights in the villas soothed their minds. The air of wealth and repose diffused about them seemed to comfort their neediness. Behind a hedge of laurel a light glimmered in the window of a kitchen and the voice of a servant was heard singing as she sharpened knives. She sang, in short broken bars, *Rosie O'Grady.*

Cranly stopped to listen, saying:

—*Mulier cantat.*°

The soft beauty of the Latin word touched with an enchanting touch the dark of the evening, with a touch fainter and more persuading

penal days: Period (mostly in the eighteenth century) when especially repressive "penal laws" against Irish Catholics were enforced. ***Mulier cantat:*** The [or a] woman sings.

than the touch of music or of a woman's hand. The strife of their minds was quelled. The figure of woman as she appears in the liturgy of the church passed silently through the darkness: a whiterobed figure, small and slender as a boy and with a falling girdle. Her voice, frail and high as a boy's, was heard intoning from a distant choir the first words of a woman which pierce the gloom and clamour of the first chanting of the passion:

—*Et tu cum Jesu Galilæo eras.*°

And all hearts were touched and turned to her voice, shining like a young star, shining clearer as the voice intoned the proparoxyton° and more faintly as the cadence died.

The singing ceased. They went on together, Cranly repeating in strongly stressed rhythm the end of the refrain:

And when we are married,
O, how happy we'll be
For I love sweet Rosie O'Grady
And Rosie O'Grady loves me.

—There's real poetry for you, he said. There's real love.

He glanced sideways at Stephen with a strange smile and said:

—Do you consider that poetry? Or do you know what the words mean?

—I want to see Rosie first, said Stephen.

—She's easy to find, Cranly said.

His hat had come down on his forehead. He shoved it back: and in the shadow of the trees Stephen saw his pale face, framed by the dark, and his large dark eyes. Yes. His face was handsome: and his body was strong and hard. He had spoken of a mother's love. He felt then the sufferings of women, the weaknesses of their bodies and souls: and would shield them with a strong and resolute arm and bow his mind to them.

Away then: it is time to go. A voice spoke softly to Stephen's lonely heart, bidding him go and telling him that his friendship was coming to an end. Yes, he would go. He could not strive against another. He knew his part.

—Probably I shall go away, he said.

—Where? Cranly asked.

—Where I can, Stephen said.

Et tu cum Jesu Galilæo eras: And you were with Jesus of Galilee. **proparoxyton:** Rhetorical term for a (Latin) word having the acute accent on the next to last syllable.

—Yes, Cranly said. It might be difficult for you to live here now. But is it that that makes you go?

—I have to go, Stephen answered.

—Because, Cranly continued, you need not look upon yourself as driven away if you do not wish to go or as a heretic or an outlaw. There are many good believers who think as you do. Would that surprise you? The church is not the stone building nor even the clergy and their dogmas. It is the whole mass of those born into it. I don't know what you wish to do in life. Is it what you told me the night we were standing outside Harcourt Street station?

—Yes, Stephen said, smiling in spite of himself at Cranly's way of remembering thoughts in connection with places. The night you spent half an hour wrangling with Doherty about the shortest way from Sallygap to Larras.

—Pothead! Cranly said with calm contempt. What does he know about the way from Sallygap to Larras? Or what does he know about anything for that matter? And the big slobbering washingpot head of him!

He broke out into a loud long laugh.

—Well? Stephen said. Do you remember the rest?

—What you said, is it? Cranly asked. Yes, I remember it. To discover the mode of life or of art whereby your spirit could express itself in unfettered freedom.

Stephen raised his hat in acknowledgment.

—Freedom! Cranly repeated. But you are not free enough yet to commit a sacrilege. Tell me, would you rob?

—I would beg first, Stephen said.

—And if you got nothing, would you rob?

—You wish me to say, Stephen answered, that the rights of property are provisional and that in certain circumstances it is not unlawful to rob. Everyone would act in that belief. So I will not make you that answer. Apply to the jesuit theologian Juan Mariana de Talavera who will also explain to you in what circumstances you may lawfully kill your king and whether you had better hand him his poison in a goblet or smear it for him upon his robe or his saddlebow. Ask me rather would I suffer others to rob me or, if they did, would I call down upon them what I believe is called the chastisement of the secular arm?

—And would you?

—I think, Stephen said, it would pain me as much to do so as to be robbed.

—I see, Cranly said.

He produced his match and began to clean the crevice between two teeth. Then he said carelessly:

—Tell me, for example, would you deflower a virgin?

—Excuse me, Stephen said politely, is that not the ambition of most young gentlemen?

—What then is your point of view? Cranly asked.

His last phrase, soursmelling as the smoke of charcoal and disheartening, excited Stephen's brain, over which its fumes seemed to brood.

—Look here, Cranly, he said. You have asked me what I would do and what I would not do. I will tell you what I will do and what I will not do. I will not serve that in which I no longer believe whether it call itself my home, my fatherland or my church: and I will try to express myself in some mode of life or art as freely as I can and as wholly as I can, using for my defence the only arms I allow myself to use, silence, exile, and cunning.

Cranly seized his arm and steered him round so as to head back towards Leeson Park. He laughed almost slily and pressed Stephen's arm with an elder's affection.

—Cunning indeed! he said. Is it you? You poor poet, you!

—And you made me confess to you, Stephen said, thrilled by his touch, as I have confessed to you so many other things, have I not?

—Yes, my child, Cranly said, still gaily.

—You made me confess the fears that I have. But I will tell you also what I do not fear. I do not fear to be alone or to be spurned for another or to leave whatever I have to leave. And I am not afraid to make a mistake, even a great mistake, a lifelong mistake and perhaps as long as eternity too.

Cranly, now grave again, slowed his pace and said:

—Alone, quite alone. You have no fear of that. And you know what that word means? Not only to be separate from all others but to have not even one friend.

—I will take the risk, said Stephen.

—And not to have any one person, Cranly said, who would be more than a friend, more even than the noblest and truest friend a man ever had.

His words seemed to have struck some deep chord in his own nature. Had he spoken of himself, of himself as he was or wished to be? Stephen watched his face for some moments in silence. A cold sadness was there. He had spoken of himself, of his own loneliness which he feared.

—Of whom are you speaking? Stephen asked at length.

Cranly did not answer.

*

* *

20 *March:* Long talk with Cranly on the subject of my revolt. He had his grand manner on. I supple and suave. Attacked me on the score of love for one's mother. Tried to imagine his mother: cannot. Told me once, in a moment of thoughtlessness, his father was sixtyone when he was born. Can see him. Strong farmer type. Pepper and salt suit. Square feet. Unkempt grizzled beard. Probably attends coursing-matches. Pays his dues regularly but not plentifully to Father Dwyer of Larras. Sometimes talks to girls after nightfall. But his mother? Very young or very old? Hardly the first. If so, Cranly would not have spoken as he did. Old then. Probably, and neglected. Hence Cranly's despair of soul: the child of exhausted loins.

21 *March, morning:* Thought this in bed last night but was too lazy and free to add it. Free, yes. The exhausted loins are those of Elisabeth and Zachary. Then is he the precursor. Item:° he eats chiefly belly bacon and dried figs. Read locusts and wild honey. Also, when thinking of him, saw always a stern severed head or deathmask as if outlined on a grey curtain or veronica.° Decollation they call it in the fold. Puzzled for the moment by saint John at the Latin gate. What do I see? A decollated° precursor trying to pick the lock.

21 *March, night:* Free. Soulfree and fancyfree. Let the dead bury the dead. Ay. And let the dead marry the dead.

22 *March:* In company with Lynch followed a sizable hospital nurse. Lynch's idea. Dislike it. Two lean hungry greyhounds walking after a heifer.

23 *March:* Have not seen her since that night. Unwell? Sits at the fire perhaps with mamma's shawl on her shoulders. But not peevish. A nice bowl of gruel? Won't you now?

24 *March:* Began with a discussion with my mother. Subject: B.V.M.° Handicapped by my sex and youth. To escape held up relations between Jesus and Papa against those between Mary and her Son. Said religion was not a lying-in hospital. Mother indulgent. Said I have a queer mind and have read too much. Not true. Have read little and understood less. Then she said I would come back to faith because I had a restless mind. This means to leave church by backdoor of sin and

Item: Term used in wills in enumerating bequests. **veronica:** A cloth bearing the image of Jesus' face. **decollated:** Beheaded. **B.V.M.:** Blessed Virgin Mary.

reenter through the skylight of repentance. Cannot repent. Told her so and asked for sixpence. Got threepence.

Then went to college. Other wrangle with little roundhead rogue's-eye Ghezzi. This time about Bruno the Nolan. Began in Italian and ended in pidgin English. He said Bruno was a terrible heretic. I said he was terribly burned. He agreed to this with some sorrow. Then gave me recipe for what he calls *risotto alla bergamasca.*° When he pronounces a soft *o* he protrudes his full carnal lips as if he kissed the vowel. Has he? And could he repent? Yes, he could: and cry two round rogue's tears, one from each eye.

Crossing Stephen's, that is, my green, remembered that his countrymen and not mine had invented what Cranly the other night called our religion. A quartet of them, soldiers of the ninetyseventh infantry regiment, sat at the foot of the cross and tossed up dice for the overcoat of the crucified.

Went to library. Tried to read three reviews. Useless. She is not out yet. Am I alarmed? About what? That she will never be out again.

Blake wrote:

I wonder if William Bond will die
For assuredly he is very ill.

Alas, poor William!

I was once at a diorama in Rotunda. At the end were pictures of big nobs. Among them William Ewart Gladstone, just then dead. Orchestra played *O, Willie, we have missed you.*

A race of clodhoppers!

25 *March, morning:* A troubled night of dreams. Want to get them off my chest.

A long curving gallery. From the floor ascend pillars of dark vapours. It is peopled by the images of fabulous kings, set in stone. Their hands are folded upon their knees in token of weariness and their eyes are darkened for the errors of men go up before them for ever as dark vapours.

Strange figures advance from a cave. They are not as tall as men. One does not seem to stand quite apart from another. Their faces are phosphorescent, with darker streaks. They peer at me and their eyes seem to ask me something. They do not speak.

30 *March:* This evening Cranly was in the porch of the library, proposing a problem to Dixon and her brother. A mother let her child fall

risotto alla bergamasca: A rice dish made as in Bergamo (Italy).

into the Nile. Still harping on the mother. A crocodile seized the child. Mother asked it back. Crocodile said all right if she told him what he was going to do with the child, eat it or not eat it.

This mentality, Lepidus would say, is indeed bred out of your mud by the operation of your sun.

And mine? Is it not too? Then into Nilemud with it!

1 *April:* Disapprove of this last phrase.

2 *April:* Saw her drinking tea and eating cakes in Johnston, Mooney and O'Brien's. Rather, lynxeyed Lynch saw her as we passed. He tells me Cranly was invited there by brother. Did he bring his crocodile? Is he the shining light now? Well, I discovered him. I protest I did. Shining quietly behind a bushel of Wicklow bran.

3 *April:* Met Davin at the cigar shop opposite Findlater's church. He was in a black sweater and had a hurleystick. Asked me was it true I was going away and why. Told him the shortest way to Tara was *via* Holyhead.° Just then my father came up. Introduction. Father, polite and observant. Asked Davin if he might offer him some refreshment. Davin could not, was going to a meeting. When we came away father told me he had a good honest eye. Asked me why I did not join a rowingclub. I pretended to think it over. Told me then how he broke Pennyfeather's heart. Wants me to read law. Says I was cut out for that. More mud, more crocodiles.

5 *April:* Wild spring. Scudding clouds. O life! Dark stream of swirling bogwater on which appletrees have cast down their delicate flowers. Eyes of girls among the leaves. Girls demure and romping. All fair or auburn: no dark ones. They blush better. Houp-la!

6 *April:* Certainly she remembers the past. Lynch says all women do. Then she remembers the time of her childhood—and mine if I was ever a child. The past is consumed in the present and the present is living only because it brings forth the future. Statues of women, if Lynch be right, should always be fully draped, one hand of the woman feeling regretfully her own hinder parts.

6 *April, later:* Michael Robartes remembers forgotten beauty and, when his arms wrap her round, he presses in his arms the loveliness which has long faded from the world. Not this. Not at all. I desire to press in my arms the loveliness which has not yet come into the world.

10 *April:* Faintly, under the heavy night, through the silence of the city which has turned from dreams to dreamless sleep as a weary lover

Tara . . . Holyhead: Tara is the traditional Irish seat of kings, Holyhead a Welsh port commonly used by Irish leaving the country.

whom no caresses move, the sound of hoofs upon the road. Not so faintly now as they come near the bridge: and in a moment as they pass the darkened windows the silence is cloven by alarm as by an arrow. They are heard now far away, hoofs that shine amid the heavy night as gems, hurrying beyond the sleeping fields to what journey's end—what heart?—bearing what tidings?

11 *April:* Read what I wrote last night. Vague words for a vague emotion. Would she like it? I think so. Then I should have to like it also.

13 *April:* That tundish has been on my mind for a long time. I looked it up and find it is English and good old blunt English too. Damn the dean of studies and his funnel! What did he come here for to teach us his own language or to learn it from us? Damn him one way or the other!

14 *April:* John Alphonsus Mulrennan has just returned from the west of Ireland. (European and Asiatic papers please copy.) He told us he met an old man there in a mountain cabin. Old man had red eyes and short pipe. Old man spoke Irish. Mulrennan spoke Irish. Then old man and Mulrennan spoke English. Mulrennan spoke to him about universe and stars. Old man sat, listened, smoked, spat. Then said:

—Ah, there must be terrible queer creatures at the latter end of the world.

I fear him. I fear his redrimmed horny eyes. It is with him I must struggle all through this night till day come, till he or I lie dead, gripping him by the sinewy throat till . . . Till what? Till he yield to me? No. I mean him no harm.

15 *April:* Met her today pointblank in Grafton Street. The crowd brought us together. We both stopped. She asked me why I never came, said she had heard all sorts of stories about me. This was only to gain time. Asked me was I writing poems? About whom? I asked her. This confused her more and I felt sorry and mean. Turned off that valve at once and opened the spiritual-heroic refrigerating apparatus, invented and patented in all countries by Dante Alighieri. Talked rapidly of myself and my plans. In the midst of it unluckily I made a sudden gesture of a revolutionary nature. I must have looked like a fellow throwing a handful of peas up into the air. People began to look at us. She shook hands a moment after and, in going away, said she hoped I would do what I said.

Now I call that friendly, don't you?

Yes, I liked her today. A little or much? Don't know. I liked her and it seems a new feeling to me. Then, in that case, all the rest, all that I thought I thought and all that I felt I felt, all the rest before now, in fact . . . O, give it up, old chap! Sleep it off!

16 *April:* Away! Away!

The spell of arms and voices: the white arms of roads, their promise of close embraces and the black arms of tall ships that stand against the moon, their tale of distant nations. They are held out to say: We are alone. Come. And the voices say with them: We are your kinsmen. And the air is thick with their company as they call to me, their kinsman, making ready to go, shaking the wings of their exultant and terrible youth.

26 *April:* Mother is putting my new secondhand clothes in order. She prays now, she says, that I may learn in my own life and away from home and friends what the heart is and what it feels. Amen. So be it. Welcome, O life! I go to encounter for the millionth time the reality of experience and to forge in the smithy of my soul the uncreated conscience of my race.

27 *April:* Old father, old artificer, stand me now and ever in good stead.

Dublin 1904
Trieste 1914

PART TWO

A Portrait of the Artist as a Young Man: A Case Study in Contemporary Criticism

A Critical History of *A Portrait of the Artist as a Young Man*

Joyce is arguably the most influential modern writer in the Western world. His influence on the fictional technique of twentieth-century writers, from traditional realists to the most wildly experimental postmodernists, has been decisive. Although Joyce's *Ulysses* has evoked a far greater amount of critical discussion, there is no doubt that *A Portrait of the Artist as a Young Man* is Joyce's most widely read work. *Portrait* is among the most frequently taught novels in modern university curricula, but it is also a novel undergraduates often discover on their own. Despite its surface difficulties, young people still respond to the book's eerily convincing portrayal of a sensitive youth who is harrowed by religious and sexual guilt and transfigured by an idea of beauty. Stephen's remarkable self-involvement and his frustration under the authority of Church, state, and parents rings especially true for undergraduate readers today, however different the specifics of circumstance.

So well established is *Portrait* as a modern classic that it is difficult to imagine the situation of the book's early reviewers, faced with writing of a sort they had not encountered before. Spotting literary greatness on its first appearance is an almost impossible task; Ezra Pound did it with Joyce, and so did T. S. Eliot, but even as perceptive a reader as Edward Garnett, who had encouraged Joseph Conrad, Ford Madox Ford, and D. H. Lawrence, balked at Joyce. In a reader's report for the publisher Duckworth and Company, collected with many other early reviews in Robert Deming's two-volume *James Joyce: The Critical Heritage,* Garnett admitted that the book was "ably written" but suggested that it needed revision because it was too "discursive, formless, unrestrained, and ugly things, ugly words, are too prominent." The novel was too "unconventional," Garnett asserted, and "unless the author will use restraint and proportion he will not gain readers" (Deming 81). Given this sort of misjudgment by a usually sensitive reader, it is all the more surprising that so many of the initial reviews of *Portrait* hailed it as a major achievement, even a work of "genius."

Ezra Pound's review in *The Egoist,* where the book had appeared in installments, stressed that it was well written—and tried to suggest just how rare that was among novels in English. Indeed, "Joyce produces the nearest thing to Flaubertian prose that we now have in English." Aside from that, "I doubt if a comparison of Mr. Joyce to other English writers or Irish writers would help much to define him." Pound stressed Joyce's realism and the book's value as "diagnosis," but otherwise said virtually nothing about the novel's content (83). Others were more struck by what they saw as the book's unpleasantness. A review in *Everyman* entitled "A Study in Garbage" called it "an astonishingly powerful and extraordinary dirty study of the upbringing of a young man by Jesuits" and suggested that at the end of the book Stephen goes mad (85). Similarly, H. G. Wells, in a rather awestruck essay comparing Joyce with Swift, Sterne, and Conrad, nevertheless complained about Joyce's "cloacal obsession" (86–88). The *Times* protested the "occasional improprieties"; the *Literary World* complained of "the brutal probing of the depths of uncleanness," and the *Manchester Guardian* of the novel's "astounding bad manners" (89,92,93).

Like other reviewers, the *Guardian's* essayist found in Stephen "a passion for foul-smelling things" (93), confusing Joyce's unusual technique of documenting odors and textures with his protagonist's tastes. Irish reviewers were, if anything, more offended than British ones. The *Freeman's Journal* claimed that "Mr. Joyce plunges and drags his readers after him into the slime of foul sewers" (98). These critics' stress on *Portrait's* unpleasantness is likely to be somewhat baffling to modern readers until we realize that the "impropriety" found on the book's "very first page" (89) can only be the reference to bed-wetting; at this point we understand what a large part of human existence in 1916 was held to be inappropriate for mention in literature. One theme not picked up in later criticism is the concern over whether Stephen and his companions are representative of Irish youth in their ideas. Wells noted that "every human being" in the book "accepts as a matter of course

. . . that the English are to be hated,'' and adds that he thinks that picture is ''only too true'' (88). The *Freeman's Journal,* on the other hand, protested that ''English critics, with a complacency that makes one despair of their intelligence, are already hailing the author as a typical Irishman, and his book as a faithful picture of Irish life.'' It would be just as accurate to see De Quincy's *Confessions of an English Opium-Eater* as a typical picture of British youth, the reviewer asserted (99).

Still, Joyce's technique was so convincing that the reviewers had to admit that something beyond conventional realism was at work. A. Clutton-Brock said that ''[Joyce] can make anything happen that he chooses'' in his writing, and that ''no living writer is better at conversations'' (89). J. C. Squire agreed that the dialogue ''is as close to the dialogue of life as anything I have ever come across'' (101). Virtually all reviewers praised the writing, and some were swept away despite themselves, protesting all the while. The *Guardian*'s writer began, ''When one recognizes genius in a book one can perhaps best leave criticism alone,'' and then went on to give his reservations. Interestingly, he continued, ''Not for its apparent formlessness should the book be condemned. A subtle sense of art has worked amidst the chaos, making this hither-and-thither record of a young mind and soul . . . a complete and ordered thing'' (92). In noting this he is unusual, for nearly all the early reviewers complained of the book's formlessness, its abrupt transitions, its lack of plot, and its unusual demands upon the reader. Just as the term ''naturalism'' was used to evoke the ''gutter realism'' of the notorious Emile Zola, the term ''impressionism'' occurred frequently to suggest an aesthetic combination of shapelessness and sensitivity in both protagonist and book.

But reaction to the novel did not develop in a vacuum, because within two years installments of Joyce's even more challenging *Ulysses* began to appear in *The Little Review.* In a now-famous essay entitled ''Modern Novels'' that appeared in 1919, Virginia Woolf hailed Joyce's writing as an example of a revolutionary sort of fiction that does away with outmoded conventions. ''Let us record the atoms as they fall upon the mind in the order in which they fall, let us trace the pattern, however disconnected and incoherent in appearance, which each sight or incident scores upon the consciousness,'' she urged. In doing this—in shifting the focus inward, toward momentary perceptions and a ''spiritual'' dimension of consciousness—Woolf felt the artist would produce something closer to ''life itself'' (125–26). Gradually it began to be realized that a group of writers —including Eliot, Pound, Joyce, and (somewhat later) Woolf herself—was engaged in similar challenges to literary conventions, and that the art of such writers demanded evaluation on its own terms rather than censure for departing from the norms of Victorian prose and verse. This development had two effects: first, published commentary on writers like Joyce tended to become either exclusively laudatory or exclusively derogatory, depending on which position the reviewer took in the politics of art. And further, as comments by Joyce's increasing circle of admirers appeared, those critics who took him seriously began to devote their energies to explicating his work rather than evaluating it.

The advent of *Ulysses* in 1922 helped draw the battle lines more clearly than *Portrait* had done. Stuart Gilbert's 1930 book, *James Joyce's "Ulysses,"* written with the help of Joyce, revealed to an uninformed public the complexity of Joyce's mythic structure in that book, as well as the richness and variety of his stylistic and narrative effects. One implication was that *Portrait* and even the earlier story collection *Dubliners* might well have formal complexities of their own that—as with *Ulysses*—had gone unnoticed. Gilbert also put some stress on Joyce's use of symbolism, a characteristic of his prose that his early reviewers, obsessed by his use of naturalistic detail, had slighted. This cut little ice with reviewers on the political left who, especially during the reign of "socialist realism" in the 1930s, dismissed Joyce as obscure, bourgeois, and apolitical. A Russian essay translated in *New Masses* (1933) saw the stream-of-consciousness method of *Ulysses* as "too closely connected with the ultrasubjectivism of the parasitic, rentier bourgeoisie, and entirely unadaptable to the art of one who is building socialist society." The naturalism of *Portrait* might at first seem more promising, since it exposes the material evils of capitalism, but it has its roots in "a morbid, defeatist delight in the ugly and repulsive" and in "an aesthetico-proprietary desire for the possession of 'things' " (Deming 591–92). As for the portions of *Work in Progress* (the temporary title of *Finnegans Wake*) that had so far appeared in journals, the Marxist reviewer (like mainstream reviewers throughout Europe and America) dismissed them as nonsense.

Meanwhile, another artistic trend was on Joyce's side. Increasingly during the twentieth century, Anglophone writers became aware of the Continental literary tradition; indeed, in the 1920s both British and American writers migrated to Paris, often to sit at the feet of Joyce or Gertrude Stein, the great expatriates. Since Joyce's literary models were generally European rather than British or Irish, his work was more intelligible and less frighteningly original when seen in this context. Indeed,

Ulysses was probably the first important work of English literature to be explicated and celebrated first by French critics. During the 1930s and 1940s a generation of American critics who were conversant with European literature naturally named Joyce among the great contemporary writers. Most notably, Edmund Wilson in his 1931 book, *Axel's Castle: A Study in the Imaginative Literature of 1870–1930,* placed Joyce in the literary tradition of the French Symbolist poets of 1870–90.

The first serious study of Joyce's writing as a whole, apart from early biographical studies and the writing of Joyce's friends, was Harry Levin's pioneering *James Joyce: A Critical Introduction* (1941). This remarkable book, much of it written when only portions of *Finnegans Wake* had appeared, is still one of the better introductions to Joyce's work. Levin treats *Portrait* as autobiography and sees little irony in Joyce's treatment of Stephen. Levin presents *Portrait* as a late example of the *Bildungsroman,* or "novel of development," such as Stendhal's *The Red and the Black* or Flaubert's *A Sentimental Education.* He briefly discusses Stephen's aesthetic theory, and suggests that the progression from "lyric" to "epic" to "dramatic" forms characterizes Joyce's work as a whole. Levin presents Joyce as heir to the two apparently opposed late nineteenth-century strains of naturalism and symbolism, and he argues that in Joyce, as in Flaubert, the two "come to terms" (Levin 4). In a rather general way he discusses the structural balance of *Portrait*'s five chapters. Although most of his discussion in the book concerns *Ulysses* and the *Wake,* Levin does point out the dominant symbolic motif of flight and the role of the mythical Daedalus, the "fabulous artificer," in *Portrait.*

A number of other introductory works on Joyce were published during the 1940s, none of Levin's quality. One general study from the 1950s that is still useful is Richard Kain and Marvin Magalaner's *Joyce: The Man, the Work, the Reputation* (1956). Surveying both the early reviews and the serious criticism available up to then, Kain and Magalaner intelligently discuss the problem of Joyce's biography, quoting from then-unpublished letters. Their treatment of *Portrait* is particularly interesting. They compare *Portrait* with its first-draft version, published as *Stephen Hero* (1955), stress the revision's condensation, abrupt transitions, and impressionist technique, and explore some of the references to obscure or popular works such as Bulwer-Lytton's play *The Lady of Lyons* and Dumas's *The Count of Monte Cristo.* Most of their discussion centers on motifs such as apology, names, and blindness, and upon the idea of the epiphany and its function in the book. Kain and Magalaner also highlight for discussion the single most influential essay on *Portrait* of the time, Hugh Kenner's "The *Portrait* in Perspective," first published in 1948 and revised in his book *Dublin's Joyce* (1956).

Kenner's essay reads *Portrait* in the light of *Ulysses* and the *Wake* and finds in the earlier book similar complexities of implication. Where "the two major works strive toward an inclusive mythopoeic vision embracing in an archetypal pattern of fall, struggle, and redemption every mode of human activity," *Portrait* does this only on the level of individual human action, suggesting "other possible levels of analogy" by implication (1948, 142). By pursuing these implications, Kenner shows how the book's first two pages "enact the entire action in microcosm" (137). He pursues the "verbal leitmotif" linking whiteness, cold, and damp as a repellent complex and shows how words with their tricky meanings and associations illustrate stages in Stephen's development. Kenner argues that Stephen's "epiphanies," which arrest and embody artistic meaning in a single moment, are not Joyce's method; instead, in each chapter of the book Joyce repeats the same pattern of showing Stephen embracing a dream in contempt of reality and then seeing the dream destroyed. "The movement of the book is dialectical; each chapter closes with a synthesis of triumph which in turn feeds the sausage-machine set up in the next chapter" (169). Most important, Kenner argues that "Stephen's flight into adolescent 'freedom' is not meant to be the 'message' of the book" (153). Stephen, in Kenner's view an "indigestibly Byronic" figure, is regarded ironically throughout. His rather Neoplatonic aesthetic is not Joyce's; his Romanticism is scorned by the more classically minded Joyce; and instead of becoming the author of *Portrait* and *Ulysses,* Stephen will become a "parlor esthete" (157), priggish, horrified by the sensual world, and egotistically self-involved.

Although Kenner qualified his argument in later books and articles, his essay sets the terms for the arguments of other critics. The question is that of Joyce's ironic distance from his protagonist, and since the narrative voice itself changes greatly in the course of *Portrait,* the answer is not easy to determine. In his critical edition of *Portrait* (1968), Chester G. Anderson summarizes the debate (446–54) and includes relevant essays by Wayne C. Booth and Robert Scholes. Booth's essay, which originally appeared in his *Rhetoric of Fiction,* contends that the degree of Joyce's irony—his "authorial distance"—cannot be established with any certainty because Joyce at times clearly admires Stephen and at times clearly satirizes him. As Booth points out, the problem is epitomized by Stephen's poem, the "Villanelle of the Temptress"; it is unclear to many readers whether we are to take the poem as a success or as a failure. For Booth the problem is that Joyce was never certain of his own attitude toward his protagonist, although when Stephen appears in *Ulysses* with his wings clipped, it seems likely that we are to assume that the boy was self-deluded in his more grandiose moments. The problem, according to Booth, is a flaw in *Portrait* itself. In response, Robert Scholes points out that the villanelle was written by Joyce long before the novel and argues that it is "a far richer poem" than may first appear (472). Similarly, Scholes implies, Stephen is far more of an artist than Kenner allows or than Booth will admit. This argument is by no means settled, and echoes down to the present day in the debate over whether Stephen's misogyny is also Joyce's or is being ironically displayed by a Joyce sympathetic to feminism.

Meanwhile, many critics were less concerned with Joyce's moral stance toward his hero than with the internal complexities of his work. William York Tindall wrote three influential studies during the 1950s—*James Joyce: His Way of Interpreting the Modern World* (1950), *A Reader's Guide to James Joyce* (1959), and *The Joyce Country* (1960)—all of which mingle Tindall's flair for close, "New Critical" textual explication with his interest in literary symbolism and in Freud. In his *Reader's Guide* Tindall begins by asserting that Stephen may not be Joyce but that he is indeed the artist-hero-rebel. True to the formalist assumptions of the New Critics, Tindall looks at the four sections of chapters one, two, and five and the three sections of chapters three and four, and asserts that while he is unsure of the function of each part, "I am sure from what I know of Joyce that no part could be omitted or placed elsewhere without injuring the great design" (62). True to the New Critical valuation of irony,. Tindall catalogues some of the ironic juxtapositions and echoes in the novel.

Like other formalists, Tindall is passionately interested in symbolism as well as structure. He therefore spends a number of pages on the wings and labyrinth built by the mythical Daedalus—echoed by Stephen's imaginative "flights" and the maze of Dublin streets—not to mention the sexual contrivance he made for Queen Pasiphaë and the "robot" Talos he fashioned to protect Crete, neither of which, unfortunately, Tindall finds present in *Portrait.* Tindall explores Stephen's less sweeping identifications with Jesus Christ—with Cranly playing John the Baptist, the "precursor"—and with Napoleon, Parnell, the Count of Monte Cristo, Dante, and St. Stephen (the first Christian martyr) before lingering awhile on Lucifer ("bearer of light"), who like Stephen declares "I will not serve" and like Prometheus brings mankind the forbidden fire of knowledge.

Less significant than symbols but also helping to unify the work, motifs greatly interest Tindall. He finds on the opening pages *road, cow, water, woman, flower,* and *bird,* all of which will recur meaningfully and musically (86). *Dogs, darkness,* and *light,* and the related *blindness* and *sight,* work similarly. Tindall "unpacks" a few of these images, showing how birds can be threatening (Heron, the eagles), images of escape (the birds above the library), or images of beauty (the wading "bird-girl" of Stephen's epiphany in chapter four). Birds also, of course, relate to the Daedalus myth. Similarly, the flower, a Neoplatonic symbol for the woman who exemplifies transcendent beauty and thus the poet's path to the divine world, is complicated by Stephen's invocation of an artificial "green rose." The green rose relates also to the red-green opposition throughout the book: green suggests the imagination, fertility, Ireland, while red suggests British authority, the Church, hellfire, and so forth.

Not all of these insights are unique to Tindall, of course, but aside from his own contributions he conveniently and wittily synthesizes the work of many scholars for a generation of readers. Among other studies exploring aspects of the book on which Tindall touches, Chester Anderson's "The Sacrificial Butter" (Connolly 124–36) specifically discusses images that Joyce draws from Roman Catholic iconography; David Hayman's "Daedalian Imagery in *A Portrait*" (1964) further explores Joyce's use of that myth; and Bernard Benstock's "A Light from Some Other World" (Staley and Benstock 185–212) shows how many image patterns contribute to the book's meaning. Studies of the novel's structure include Lee T. Lemon's "*Portrait of the Artist as a Young Man:* Motif as Motivation and Structure" (1966), an analysis inspired by the Russian formalists, and Sidney Feshbach's "A Slow and Dark Birth: A Study of the Organization of *A Portrait*" (1967), which is more psychological in orientation. Meanwhile, Tindall's student Chester Anderson produced in *James Joyce and His World* (1968) one of the more widely read and frequently translated introductions to Joyce's work. Other essays representative of work produced in the 1950s and 1960s can be found in the collections of essays on *Portrait* edited by Connolly (1962), Morris and Nault (1962), Anderson (1968), and Schutte (1968).

But New Critical studies of the book as a self-contained structure unified by symbols and motifs were not the only work done during this period, nor even, in some respects, the most important work. The natural course of Joycean criticism was altered forever by the publication in 1959 of Richard Ellmann's magisterial biography, *James Joyce*. Trained as a New Critic, Ellmann nonetheless "read" Joyce's life as if it were a literary text. Given a writer whose life and work were as intimately intertwined as they were in the case of Joyce, this approach proved to be extremely convincing, especially as Ellmann skillfully interwove literary interpretation with biography throughout. Stuart Gilbert edited a collection of Joyce's letters in 1957; in 1966 Ellmann reedited that volume and produced two additional volumes. Ellmann's publishing so many personal letters was a controversial act; his volumes included letters in which Joyce pleaded with friends and acquaintances for money or support and also letters addressed to Nora that were clearly erotic. Even more controversy arose when, in the 1975 *Selected Letters*, Ellmann included additional letters to Nora whose erotic explicitness rivalled anything in Joyce's published work. Perhaps surprisingly, Joyce's literary reputation does not seem to have suffered since publication of the letters, although it can be argued that Joyce's private life has become inappropriately involved in evaluations of his work.

The New Critics, in their concern for the purity of the work of art, insistently warned readers against what they termed the "biographical fallacy"—the assumption that an author's life and opinions would necessarily illuminate the work. But now the sheer mass of information about Joyce, some of it quite intimate, was enough to make some critics forget the dangers of invoking this knowledge too freely. Meanwhile, Robert Scholes and Richard Kain's *The Workshop of Daedalus* (1965) made available Joyce's unpublished "epiphanies," along with various working notebooks, manuscript fragments, and a considerable amount of biographical information. All of these spurred interest in Joyce's composition process and his artistic development generally. For instance, the most influential essay to explore Joyce's actual composition process in writing *Portrait* is Hans Walter Gabler's "The Seven Lost Years of *A Portrait*" (Staley and Benstock 25–60).

The 1970s saw the impact on American and British criticism of a variety of Continental critical approaches, most of which had been strenuously resisted during the previous decades. The so-called phenomenological criticism of the Geneva School, whose best American practitioner was the early J. Hillis Miller, is reflected in Suzette Henke's *Joyce's Moraculous Sindbook* (1978), which deals with *Ulysses*, and by R. B. Kershner's "Time and Language in Joyce's *Portrait*" (1976), a study of the interiority of Stephen's time-sense and the ways in which subjectivity and objectivity are unified in his experience. *The Exile of James Joyce* (1972) by Hélène

Cixous, who was to become best known as a major French feminist, combines a psychological approach to Joyce's whole work with themes such as absence and silence or art as transgression, which were of particular interest to structuralists and poststructuralists.

A renewed interest in Marxist criticism, especially as adapted by the Frankfurt School, and in socially and politically based criticism in general, led to a new critical distance from the society of which both Stephen and Joyce were a part; issues like Joyce's sexual tastes now seemed less important in themselves and more significant as markers of social development at a given historical moment. James Naremore's "Consciousness and Society in *A Portrait*" (1976) discusses "some of the ways that Stephen Dedalus's ideas, language, and art have been affected by his economic status and his Catholic upbringing" (114) and also reveals Joyce's fictional technique as a variety of realism that betrays the author's defensive reaction against his own "excremental vision." The Godlike impersonality that Stephen claimed for the artist, and that New Critics claimed for Joyce, was wearing thin. While Naremore asserts that Joyce was a more politically aware writer than most earlier critics thought, Richard Ellmann's *The Consciousness of Joyce* (1977) provides evidence for the writer's interest in politics from Joyce's own library. Joyce had early termed himself a socialist and had referred to the change in the relationship between men and women as the most important social change of his time; Ellmann demonstrates that Joyce's political awareness was not simply a fashion of his youth. Dominic Manganiello's full-scale study, *Joyce's Politics* (1980), broadens the argument, presenting Joyce—in contrast to other major modernists such as Yeats, Eliot, or Pound—as a social progressive.

During the 1970s and 1980s, different varieties of historically responsive criticism evolved, and with them a broad spectrum of interests that might once have seemed peripheral to Joyce's art. Richard Brown's *James Joyce and Sexuality* (1985) shows how the sexual rebelliousness, oddity, or experimentation of Joyce's characters occurred within a political context in which, for instance, assenting to a conventional marriage could be seen as ceding control of one's sexuality to the state. Cheryl Herr's groundbreaking *Joyce's Anatomy of Culture* (1986) sets Joyce's work within the context of the popular press, the popular theater, and the tradition of popular religious oratory, arguing that Joyce's use of these materials produced a powerful social critique. And R. B. Kershner's *Joyce, Bakhtin, and Popular Literature* (1989), which treats Joyce's early writing, makes a similar argument from an analysis of Joyce's sources in popular writing of the late nineteenth century, and includes an extended discussion of *Portrait*.

Meanwhile, structuralism, deconstruction, and poststructuralism began to have a major impact on Joycean studies. Relatively few of the Continental critics and their followers address *Portrait* directly though, preferring to use *Ulysses* and especially the *Wake* to exemplify the ways in which language itself forms complex structures independent of signification or, alternatively, undermines itself. Starting in the 1970s, essays on Joyce by Roland Barthes and Jacques Derrida began appearing in Joyce conference volumes, and books and articles devoted to Joyce took on a new theoretical rigor. Following Barthes's announcement of the "death of the author" in modern literature, the new work paid increased attention to style and structure in Joyce's work—especially to their linguistic and philosophical implications—and once again shunned the biographical. Derrida's critique of structuralism in many ways exaggerates these tendencies.

The book that best exemplifies these trends and applies them to *Portrait* as well is Colin MacCabe's poststructuralist *James Joyce and the Revolution of the Word* (1979). Summarizing a book such as this is difficult, especially as MacCabe refuses to "interpret" Joyce in any conventional sense: "Instead of constructing a meaning, Joyce's texts concern themselves with the position of the subject in language" (4). While MacCabe also refuses to "psychologize" Joyce in any ordinary way, he does rely heavily on the work of Jacques Lacan, a revisionist Freudian who redirected attention to language as the primary material of the psychoanalytic method. Further, MacCabe insists that his reading of Joyce is radically political because Joyce's revolutionary politics are inherent in his *language* and its new relationship to representation rather than residing in any particular statements in his texts.

MacCabe sees in the movement from *Stephen Hero* to *Portrait* a change from the ordered world of the "classic realist text," in which meaning is guaranteed by a "Father" and resolution is implied by the very narrative, to a new world in which all meanings are provisory, in which third and first person blend, and in which sound carries more weight than sense. Although the language of the artist threatens to establish a "meta-language" (66) that will enable us to evaluate the other languages represented in the book, even this possibility is frustrated by the book's discontinuities. The technical problems that, for critics like Booth, had marked flaws in *Portrait* are precisely those MacCabe celebrates as liberating us from the epistemology of bourgeois humanism.

The general trend of criticism in the past two decades has been away from the New Critical presumption of organic unity in Joyce's works, away from symbolic interpretation, and in some ways away from biography; the stress has been upon close analysis of style, a reexamination of the social and political context of Joyce's work, an intense theoretical examination of the implications of Joyce's writing project, and a questioning of previous interpretations of the entire modernist movement. A good article that exemplifies at least some of these points is Michael Levenson's "Stephen's Diary in Joyce's *Portrait*—the Shape of Life" (1985). Important works on *Ulysses* and, especially, *Finnegans Wake* have appeared under the stimulus of Continental approaches, and the fact that both Derrida and Lacan have championed Joyce has encouraged a great deal of work in deconstructive and other poststructuralist modes. Both the collection of politically oriented contemporary critical approaches loosely grouped together as "cultural critique" and the allied approach known as "New Historicism" have had an impact. The most important intellectual event of the past twenty years, the rise of feminist criticism, has been reflected in a wide variety of feminist approaches to Joyce as well. Most of these developments are discussed and exemplified in the essays and introductions that follow. For a more extensive discussion and summary of numerous critical studies, the student may want to consult Alan Roughley's *James Joyce and Critical Theory: An Introduction* (1991). Roughley includes chapters on structuralism, semiotics, feminism, psychoanalytic theory, Marxist criticism, and poststructuralism.

R. B. Kershner

WORKS CITED

Anderson, Chester G., ed. *A Portrait of the Artist as a Young Man: Text, Criticism, and Notes*. New York: Viking, 1968.

———. *James Joyce and His World*. New York: Viking, 1968.

———. "The Sacrificial Butter." Connolly 124–36.

Booth, Wayne C. "The Problem of Distance in *A Portrait*." *The Rhetoric of Fiction*. Chicago: U of Chicago P, 1961. 323–36.

Brown, Richard. *James Joyce and Sexuality*. Cambridge: Cambridge UP, 1985.

Benstock, Bernard. "A Light from Some Other World." Staley and Benstock 185–212.

Connolly, Thomas, ed. *Joyce's "Portrait": Criticisms and Critiques*. New York: Appleton-Century-Crofts, 1962.

Deming, Robert H., ed. *James Joyce: The Critical Heritage.* 2 vols. London: Routledge, 1970. Contains all the early reviews quoted in the preceding essay.

Ellmann, Richard. *The Consciousness of Joyce.* New York: Oxford UP, 1977.

———. *James Joyce.* New York: Oxford UP, 1959. Rev. ed. 1982.

Feshbach, Sidney. "A Slow and Dark Birth: A Study of the Organization of *A Portrait of the Artist as a Young Man.*" *James Joyce Quarterly* 4 (Summer 1967), 289–300.

Gabler, Hans Walter. "The Seven Lost Years of *A Portrait of the Artist as a Young Man.*" Staley and Benstock 25–60.

Hayman, David. "Daedalian Imagery in *A Portrait.*" *Hereditas: Seven Essays on the Modern Experience of the Classical.* Ed. Frederick Will. Austin: U of Texas P, 1964. 31–54.

Herr, Cheryl. *Joyce's Anatomy of Culture.* Urbana: U of Illinois P, 1986.

Kain, Richard M. and Marvin Magalaner. *James Joyce: The Man, the Work, the Reputation.* New York: New York UP, 1956.

Kenner, Hugh. "The *Portrait* in Perspective." *James Joyce: Two Decades of Criticism.* Ed. Seon Givens. New York: Vanguard, 1948. 132–74.

———. *Dublin's Joyce.* Bloomington: Indiana UP, 1956.

Kershner, R. B. *Joyce, Bakhtin and Popular Literature.* Chapel Hill: U of North Carolina P, 1989.

———. "Time and Language in Joyce's *Portrait of the Artist.*" *ELH* 43 (1976), 604–19.

Lemon, Lee T. "*Portrait of the Artist as a Young Man:* Motif as Motivation and Structure." *Modern Fiction Studies* 12 (Winter 1966/67): 430–50.

Levenson, Michael. "Stephen's Diary in Joyce's *Portrait*—The Shape of Life." *ELH* 52 (1985): 1017–35.

Levin, Harry. *James Joyce: A Critical Introduction.* New York: New Directions, 1941. Rev. ed. 1960.

MacCabe, Colin. *James Joyce and the Revolution of the Word.* New York: Barnes, 1979.

Manganiello, Dominic. *Joyce's Politics.* London: Routledge, 1980.

Morris, William, and Clifford Nault, eds. *Portraits of an Artist: A Casebook for James Joyce's "A Portrait."* New York: Odyssey Press, 1962.

Naremore, James. "Consciousness and Society in *A Portrait.*" Staley and Benstock 113–34.

Roughley, Alan. *James Joyce and Critical Theory: An Introduction.* New York: Harvester, 1991.

Scholes, Robert, and Richard M. Kain, eds. *The Workshop of Daedalus: James Joyce and the Raw Materials for "A Portrait of the Artist as a Young Man."* Evanston, IL: Northwestern UP, 1965.

Schutte, William, ed. *Twentieth-Century Interpretations of "A Portrait of the Artist as a Young Man."* Englewood Cliffs: Prentice, 1968.

Staley, Thomas F., and Bernard Benstock, eds. *Approaches to Joyce's "Portrait": Ten Essays.* Pittsburgh: U of Pittsburgh P, 1976.

Tindall, William York. *A Reader's Guide to James Joyce.* New York: Noonday P, 1959.

Psychoanalytic Criticism and *A Portrait of the Artist as a Young Man*

WHAT IS PSYCHOANALYTIC CRITICISM?

It seems natural to think about novels in terms of dreams. Like dreams, novels are fictions, inventions of the mind that, although based on reality, are by definition not literally true. Like a novel, a dream may have some truth to tell, but, like a novel, it may need to be interpreted before that truth can be grasped. Many novels, Joyce's *Portrait* included, contain dreams and reveal important aspects of character through dreams.

There are other reasons why it seems natural to make an analogy between dreams and novels. We can live vicariously through romantic fictions, much as we can through daydreams. Terrifying novels and nightmares affect us in much the same way, plunging us into an atmosphere that continues to cling, even after the last chapter has been read—or the alarm clock has sounded. Thus it is not surprising to hear someone say in class that Mary Shelley's *Frankenstein* is a nightmarish tale. Nor are we likely to be surprised by the claim of Frederick Karl, Joseph Conrad's biographer, that *Heart of Darkness* is characterized by the same kind of distortion, condensation, and displacement that Sigmund Freud described in his *Interpretation of Dreams* (1900).

Karl, who invokes Conrad's text and psychoanalytic theory in the same breath, is a Freudian literary critic. But what about the reader who simply compares *Frankenstein* to a nightmare, or Emily Brontë's

Wuthering Heights to a dream? Is such a reader a Freudian as well? Is he or she, too, a psychoanalytic critic?

To some extent the answer to both questions has to be yes. We are all Freudians, really, whether or not we have read a single work by the famous Austrian psychoanalyst. At one time or another, most of us have referred to ego, libido, complexes, unconscious desires, and sexual repression. The premises of Freud's thought have changed the way the Western world thinks about itself. Psychoanalytic criticism has influenced the teachers our teachers studied with, the works of scholarship and criticism they read, and the critical and creative writers *we* read as well.

What Freud did was develop a language that described, a model that explained, a theory that encompassed human psychology. Many of the elements of psychology he sought to describe and explain are present in the literary works of various ages and cultures, from Sophocles' *Oedipus Rex* to Shakespeare's *Hamlet* to works being written in our own day. When the great novel of the twenty-first century is written, many of these same elements of psychology will probably inform its discourse as well. If, by understanding human psychology according to Freud, we can appreciate literature on a new level, then we should acquaint ourselves with his insights.

Freud's theories are either directly or indirectly concerned with the nature of the unconscious mind. Freud didn't invent the notion of the unconscious; others before him had suggested that even the supposedly "sane" human mind was conscious and rational only at times, and even then at possibly only one level. But Freud went further, suggesting that the powers motivating men and women are *mainly* and *normally* unconscious.

Freud, then, powerfully developed an old idea: that the human mind is essentially dual in nature. He called the predominantly passional, irrational, unknown, and unconscious part of the psyche the *id*, or "it." The *ego*, or "I," was his term for the predominantly rational, logical, orderly, conscious part. Another aspect of the psyche, which he called the *superego*, is really a projection of the ego. The superego almost seems to be outside of the self, making moral judgments, telling us to make sacrifices for good causes even though self-sacrifice may not be quite logical or rational. And, in a sense, the superego *is* "outside," since much of what it tells us to do or think we have learned from our parents, our schools, or our religious institutions.

What the ego and superego tell us *not* to do or think is repressed, forced into the unconscious mind. One of Freud's most important contributions to the study of the psyche, the theory of repression, goes something like this: much of what lies in the unconscious mind has been put there by consciousness, which acts as a censor, driving underground unconscious or conscious thoughts or instincts that it deems unacceptable. Censored materials often involve infantile sexual desires, Freud postulated. Repressed to an unconscious state, they emerge only in disguised forms: in dreams, in language (so-called Freudian slips), in creative activity that may produce art (including literature), and in neurotic behavior.

According to Freud, all of us have repressed wishes and fears; we all have dreams in which repressed feelings and memories emerge disguised, and thus we are all potential candidates for dream analysis. One of the unconscious desires most commonly repressed is the childhood wish to displace the parent of our own sex and take his or her place in the affections of the parent of the opposite sex. This desire really involves a number of different but related wishes and fears. (A boy—and it should be remarked in passing that Freud here concerns himself mainly with the male—may fear that his father will castrate him, and he may wish that his mother would return to nursing him.) Freud referred to the whole complex of feelings by the word "oedipal," naming the complex after the Greek tragic hero Oedipus, who unwittingly killed his father and married his mother.

Why are oedipal wishes and fears repressed by the conscious side of the mind? And what happens to them after they have been censored? As Roy P. Basler puts it in *Sex, Symbolism, and Psychology in Literature* (1975), "from the beginning of recorded history such wishes have been restrained by the most powerful religious and social taboos, and as a result have come to be regarded as 'unnatural,'" even though "Freud found that such wishes are more or less characteristic of normal human development":

> In dreams, particularly, Freud found ample evidence that such wishes persisted. . . . Hence he conceived that natural urges, when identified as "wrong," may be repressed but not obliterated. . . . In the unconscious, these urges take on symbolic garb, regarded as nonsense by the waking mind that does not recognize their significance. (14)

Freud's belief in the significance of dreams, of course, was no more original than his belief that there is an unconscious side to the psyche. Again, it was the extent to which he developed a theory of how dreams work—and the extent to which that theory helped him, by analogy, to understand far more than just dreams—that made him unusual, important, and influential beyond the perimeters of medical schools and psychiatrists' offices.

The psychoanalytic approach to literature not only rests on the theories of Freud; it may even be said to have *begun* with Freud, who was interested in writers, especially those who relied heavily on symbols. Such writers regularly cloak or mystify ideas in figures that make sense only when interpreted, much as the unconscious mind of a neurotic disguises secret thoughts in dream stories or bizarre actions that need to be interpreted by an analyst. Freud's interest in literary artists led him to make some unfortunate generalizations about creativity; for example, in the twenty-third lecture in *Introductory Lectures on Psycho-Analysis* (1922), he defined the artist as "one urged on by instinctive needs that are too clamorous" (314). But it also led him to write creative literary criticism of his own, including an influential essay on "The Relation of a Poet to Daydreaming" (1908) and "The Uncanny" (1919), a provocative psychoanalytic reading of E. T. A. Hoffmann's supernatural tale "The Sandman."

Freud's application of psychoanalytic theory to literature quickly caught on. In 1909, only a year after Freud had published "The Relation of a Poet to Daydreaming," the psychoanalyst Otto Rank published *The Myth of the Birth of the Hero.* In that work, Rank subscribes to the notion that the artist turns a powerful, secret wish into a literary fantasy, and he uses Freud's notion about the "oedipal" complex to explain why the popular stories of so many heroes in literature are so similar. A year after Rank had published his psychoanalytic account of heroic texts, Ernest Jones, Freud's student and eventual biographer, turned his attention to a tragic text: Shakespeare's *Hamlet.* In an essay first published in the *American Journal of Psychology,* Jones, like Rank, makes use of the oedipal concept: he suggests that Hamlet is a victim of strong feelings toward his mother, the queen.

Between 1909 and 1949 numerous other critics decided that psychological and psychoanalytic theory could assist in the understanding of literature. I. A. Richards, Kenneth Burke, and Edmund Wilson were among the most influential to become interested in the new approach. Not all of the early critics were committed to the approach; neither were all of them Freudians. Some followed Alfred Adler, who believed that writers wrote out of inferiority complexes, and others applied the ideas of Carl Gustav Jung, who had broken with Freud over Freud's emphasis on sex and who had developed a theory of the *collective* unconscious. According to Jungian theory, a great work of literature is not a disguised expression of its author's personal, repressed wishes; rather, it is a manifestation of desires once held by the whole human race but now repressed because of the advent of civilization.

It is important to point out that among those who relied on Freud's models were a number of critics who were poets and novelists as well. Conrad Aiken wrote a Freudian study of American literature, and poets such as Robert Graves and W. H. Auden applied Freudian insights when writing critical prose. William Faulkner, Henry James, James Joyce, D. H. Lawrence, Marcel Proust, and Toni Morrison are only a few of the novelists who have either written criticism influenced by Freud or who have written novels that conceive of character, conflict, and creative writing itself in Freudian terms. The poet H. D. (Hilda Doolittle) was actually a patient of Freud's and provided an account of her analysis in her book *Tribute to Freud*. By giving Freudian theory credibility among students of literature that only they could bestow, such writers helped to endow psychoanalytic criticism with the largely Freudian orientation that, one could argue, it still exhibits today.

The willingness, even eagerness, of writers to use Freudian models in producing literature and criticism of their own consummated a relationship that, to Freud and other pioneering psychoanalytic theorists, had seemed fated from the beginning; after all, therapy involves the close analysis of language. René Wellek and Austin Warren included "psychological" criticism as one of the five "extrinsic" approaches to literature described in their influential book, *Theory of Literature* (1942). Psychological criticism, they suggest, typically attempts to do at least one of the following: provide a psychological study of an individual writer; explore the nature of the creative process; generalize about "types and laws present within works of literature"; or theorize about the psychological "effects of literature upon its readers" (81). Entire books on psychoanalytic criticism even began to appear, such as Frederick J. Hoffman's *Freudianism and the Literary Mind* (1945).

Probably because of Freud's characterization of the creative mind as "clamorous" if not ill, psychoanalytic criticism written before 1950 tended to psychoanalyze the individual author. Poems were read as fantasies that allowed authors to indulge repressed wishes, to protect themselves from deep-seated anxieties, or both. A perfect example of author analysis would be Marie Bonaparte's 1933 study of Edgar Allan Poe. Bonaparte found Poe to be so fixated on his mother that his repressed longing emerges in his stories in images such as the white spot on a black cat's breast, said to represent mother's milk.

A later generation of psychoanalytic critics often paused to analyze the characters in novels and plays before proceeding to their authors. But not for long, since characters, both evil and good, tended to be seen by these critics as the author's potential selves, or projections of various repressed aspects of his or her psyche. For instance, in *A Psychoanalytic Study of the Double in Literature* (1970), Robert Rogers begins with the view that human beings are double or multiple in nature. Using this assumption, along with the psychoanalytic concept of "dissociation" (best known by its result, the dual or multiple personality), Rogers concludes that writers reveal instinctual or repressed selves in their books, often without realizing that they have done so.

In the view of critics attempting to arrive at more psychological insights into an author than biographical materials can provide, a work of literature is a fantasy or a dream—or at least so analogous to daydream or dream that Freudian analysis can help explain the nature of the mind that produced it. The author's purpose in writing is to gratify secretly some forbidden wish, in particular an infantile wish or desire that has been repressed into the unconscious mind. To discover what the wish is, the psychoanalytic critic employs many of the terms and procedures developed by Freud to analyze dreams.

The literal surface of a work is sometimes spoken of as its "manifest content" and treated as a "manifest dream" or "dream story" would be treated by a Freudian analyst. Just as the analyst tries to figure out the "dream thought" behind the dream story—that is, the latent or hidden content of the manifest dream—so the psychoanalytic literary critic tries to expose the latent, underlying content of a work. Freud used the words *condensation* and *displacement* to explain two of the mental processes whereby the mind disguises its wishes and fears in dream stories. In condensation several thoughts or persons may be condensed into a single manifestation or image in a dream story; in displacement, an anxiety, a wish, or a person may be displaced onto the image of another, with which or whom it is loosely connected through a string of associations that only an analyst can untangle. Psychoanalytic critics treat metaphors as if they were dream condensations; they treat metonyms—figures of speech based on extremely loose, arbitrary associations—as if they were dream displacements. Thus figurative literary language in general is treated as something that evolves as the writer's conscious mind resists what the unconscious tells it to picture or describe. A symbol is, in Daniel Weiss's words, "a meaningful concealment of truth as the truth promises to emerge as some frightening or forbidden idea'' (20).

In a 1970 article entitled ''The 'Unconscious' of Literature,'' Norman Holland, a literary critic trained in psychoanalysis, succinctly sums up the attitudes held by critics who would psychoanalyze authors, but without quite saying that it is the *author* that is being analyzed by the psychoanalytic critic. ''When one looks at a poem psychoanalytically,'' he writes, ''one considers it as though it were a dream or as though some ideal patient [were speaking] from the couch in iambic pentameter.'' One ''looks for the general level or levels of fantasy associated with the language. By level I mean the familiar stages of childhood development—oral [when desires for nourishment and infantile sexual desires overlap], anal [when infants receive their primary pleasure from defecation], urethral [when urinary functions are the locus of sexual pleasure], phallic [when the penis or, in girls, some penis substitute is of primary interest], oedipal.'' Holland continues by analyzing not Robert Frost but Frost's poem ''Mending Wall'' as a specifically oral fantasy that is not unique to its author. ''Mending Wall'' is ''about breaking down the wall which marks the separated or individuated self so as to return to a state of closeness to some Other''—including and perhaps essentially the nursing mother (''Unconscious'' 136, 139).

While not denying the idea that the unconscious plays a role in creativity, psychoanalytic critics such as Holland began to focus more on the ways in which authors create works that appeal to *our* repressed wishes and fancies. Consequently, they shifted their focus away from the psyche of the author and toward the psychology of the reader and the text. Holland's theories, which have concerned themselves more with the reader than with the text, have helped to establish another school of critical theory: reader-response criticism. Elizabeth Wright explains Holland's brand of modern psychoanalytic criticism in this way: ''What draws us as readers to a text is the secret expression of what we desire to hear, much as we protest we do not. The disguise must be good enough to fool the censor into thinking that the text is respectable, but bad enough to allow the unconscious to glimpse the unrespectable'' (117).

Whereas Holland came increasingly to focus on the reader rather than on the work being read, others who turned away from character and author diagnosis preferred to concentrate on texts; they remained skeptical that readers regularly fulfill wishes by reading. Following the theories of D. W. Winnicott, a psychoanalytic theorist who has argued that even babies have relationships as well as raw wishes, these textually oriented psychoanalytic critics contend that the relationship between reader and text depends greatly on the text. To be sure, some works fulfill the reader's secret wishes, but others—maybe most—do not. The texts created by some authors effectively resist the reader's involvement.

In determining the nature of the text, such critics may regard the text in terms of a dream. But no longer do they assume that dreams are meaningful in the way that works of literature are. Rather, they assume something more complex. "If we move outward" from one "scene to others in the [same] novel," Meredith Skura writes, "as Freud moves from the dream to its associations, we find that the paths of movement are really quite similar" (181). Dreams are viewed more as a language than as symptoms of repression. In fact, the French structuralist psychoanalyst Jacques Lacan treats the unconscious *as* a language, a form of discourse. Thus we may study dreams psychoanalytically in order to learn about literature, even as we may study literature in order to learn more about the unconscious. In Lacan's seminar on Poe's "The Purloined Letter," a pattern of repetition like that used by psychoanalysts in their analyses is used to arrive at a reading of the story. According to Wright, "the new psychoanalytic structural approach to literature" employs "analogies from psychoanalysis . . . to explain the workings of the text as distinct from the workings of a particular author's, character's, or even reader's mind" (125).

Lacan, however, did far more than extend Freud's theory of dreams, literature, and the interpretation of both. More significantly, he took Freud's whole theory of psyche and gender and added to it a crucial third term—that of language. In the process, he used but adapted Freud's ideas about the oedipal complex and oedipal stage, both of which Freud saw as crucial to the development of the child, and especially of male children.

Lacan points out that the pre-oedipal stage, in which the child at first does not even recognize its independence from its mother, is also a pre*verbal* stage, one in which the child communicates without the medium of language, or—if we insist upon calling the child's communications a language—in a language that can only be called *literal.* ("Coos," certainly, cannot be said to be figurative or symbolic!) Then, while still in the pre-oedipal stage, the child enters the *mirror* stage.

During the mirror period, the child comes to see itself and its mother, later other people as well, *as* independent selves. This is the stage in which the child is first able to fear the aggressions of another, desire what is recognizably beyond the self (initially the mother), and, finally, to want to compete with another for the same, desired object. This is also the stage at which the child first becomes able to feel sympathy with another being who is being hurt by a third—to cry, in other words, when another cries. All of these developments, of course, involve projecting beyond the self and, by extension, being able to envision one's own self (or "ego" or "I") as others view one—that is, as *another.* For these reasons, Lacan refers to the mirror stage as the *Imaginary* stage.

The Imaginary stage, however, is usually superseded. It normally ends with the onset of the oedipal stage, which it makes possible. (The Imaginary stage makes possible the oedipal stage insofar as it makes possible not only desire and fear of another but also the sense of another as a rival.)

The oedipal stage, as in Freud, begins when the child, having recognized the self *as* self and the father and mother as *separate* selves, recognizes gender and gender differences between its parents and between itself and one of its parents. For a boy, that recognition involves another, more powerful recognition, because the recognition of the phallus as the mark of difference from the mother involves, at the same time, the recognition that his older and more powerful father is also his rival. That realization, in turn, leads to the understanding that what once seemed wholly his and even undistinguishable from himself is in fact someone else's: something properly to be desired only at a greater distance and in the form of socially acceptable *substitutes.* (The old song "I Want a Girl Just Like the Girl Who Married Dear Old Dad" is a clear and straightforward restatement of the psychoanalytic theory that men's lives are searches for adequate and sufficient substitutes for the lost mother.)

The fact that the oedipal stage roughly coincides with the entry of the child into language is extremely important, even critical, for Lacan. For the linguistic order is essentially a figurative or "Symbolic order"; words are not the things they stand for but are, rather, stand-ins—substitutions—for those things. Hence boys, who in the most critical period of their development have had to submit to what Lacan calls the "Law of the Father"—a law that prohibits direct desire for and communicative intimacy with what has been the boy's whole world—enter more easily into the realm of language and the Symbolic order than do girls, who have never really had to renounce that which once seemed continuous with the self: the mother. The gap that has been opened up for boys, which includes the gap between signs and what they substitute for—the gap marked by the phallus and encoded with the boy's sense of his maleness—has not opened up for girls, or has not opened up in the same way, to the same degree.

Lacan, moreover, takes Freud a step further in the process of making Freud's gender-based psychoanalytic theory a theory of language as well. He suggests that the father does not even have to be present to trigger the oedipal crisis; nor, then, does his phallus have to be seen to catalyze the boy's (easier) transition into the Symbolic order. Rather, he argues, a child's recognition of his or her gender, gender that may be the same as or different from that of the now separate-seeming mother, is intricately tied up with a growing recognition of the system of names and naming. A child has little doubt about who its mother is, but who is its father—and how would one know? The father's claim rests on the mother's *word* that he is in fact the father; the father's relationship to the child is thus established through language and a system of marriage and kinship—names—that in turn is basic to rules of everything from property to law. Thus gender, for Lacan, is intimately connected in the mind of the developing child with names and language. Or, rather, the *male* gender is tied to that world in an association analogously as intimate as is the mother's early, physical (including umbilical) connection with the infant.

Lacan's development of Freud has had several important results. First, his sexist-seeming association of maleness with the Symbolic order, together with his claim that women cannot therefore enter easily into the order, has prompted feminists not to reject his theory out of hand but, rather, to look more closely at the relation between language and gender, language and women's inequality. Some feminists have gone so far as to suggest that the social and political relationships between male and female will not be fundamentally altered until language itself has been radically changed. (That change might begin dialectically, with the development of some kind of "feminine language" grounded in the presymbolic—the literal-to-imaginary—communication between mother and child.)

Second, Lacan's theory has proved of interest to deconstructors and other poststructuralists, in part because it holds that the ego (which in Freud's view is as necessary as it is natural) is a product or construct. The ego-artifact, produced during the mirror stage, *seems* at once unified, consistent, and organized around a determinate center. But the unified self, or ego, is a fiction, according to Lacan. The yoking together of fragments and destructively dissimilar elements takes its psychic toll, and it is the job of the Lancanian psychoanalyst to "deconstruct," as it were, the ego, to show its continuities to be contradictions as well.

In the pages that follow, Sheldon Brivic focuses on Stephen Dedalus's gradual alienation from family, Church, and nation. He grounds the process of self-isolation in early, unconscious fantasies and fears.

Specifically, Brivic traces Stephen's adolescent and adult behavior patterns back to an oedipal desire for the mother, arguing that the romantic fantasies and feelings of guilt attendant upon the oedipal complex explain everything from Stephen's "minor relationship with Eileen" to his fears of castration, violence, and homosexuality. Brivic finds evidence of the oedipal complex in Stephen's longings (to lay his head on his mother's lap, for instance) and dreams, the latter of which are populated by dead, wounded, or wounding father figures.

As the discussion of Stephen's dreams reminds us, the oedipal complex involves fear of the father (and of threatening males in general) as fully as it involves desire for the mother (and for inferior, inadequate mother substitutes). Brivic focuses consideration on Stephen's preoccupation with threats of male violence, discussing the pandying scene and the consequent scene in the rector's office in terms of oedipal fear and resistance. The church fathers, in other words, come to be replacements for the biological father in the novel's oedipal drama.

Brivic focuses on the novel's substitutes as well as on its patriarchal representations. He discusses Emma Clery, whom Stephen "spiritualizes," the prostitute Stephen turns to in desperation, and the "sheltering arms" of the Virgin in terms of oedipal desire and guilt. Finally, and most significantly, he views the girl on the beach, Stephen's imaginative reconfiguration of her, and the subsequent pursuit of transcendental art in terms of a mother transfigured and a typical oedipal longing for phallic sexuality, power, control.

Building on other critics' observations about the parallel form of *Portrait*—an Irish muse replaces the Virgin who replaces the prostitute who replaces E— C— who replaces the mother as Feminine Ideal—Brivic sees these repetitions in terms of compulsive behavior, in which people become locked in cyclical patterns of frustration and failure. Stephen's feeling that he is destined to become an artist is viewed as just another myth "generated by" his "neurotic need" to alienate himself again and again from that which he feels he cannot have. It is little wonder, Brivic comments, that "his parental attachments and anxieties return in the fifth chapter."

Brivic's essay functions on at least three levels. At the most obvious, it tells us that "Joyce knew about Freud" and illustrated Freud's theories novelistically in the process of writing *Portrait*. At another level, Brivic provides a psychoanalytic analysis of a literary character, Stephen, and shows that the goals and struggles of his life are grounded in unconscious complexes and motivations. At its deepest level, however, the subject of Brivic's analysis is not Stephen but *Portrait* itself, a "structure" whose "motivation" is said to be "unconscious," an artifact that contains and describes dreams and at the same time functions something *like* a dream, revealing what its author (and reader) might not otherwise speak (or hear) of.

Ross C Murfin

PSYCHOANALYTIC CRITICISM: A SELECTED BIBLIOGRAPHY

Some Short Introductions to Psychological and Psychoanalytic Criticism

Holland, Norman. "The 'Unconscious' of Literature." *Contemporary Criticism*. Ed. Norman Bradbury and David Palmer. Stratford-upon-Avon Series 12. New York: St. Martin's, 1970. 131–54.

Natoli, Joseph, and Frederik L. Rusch, comps. *Psychocriticism: An Annotated Bibliography.* Westport: Greenwood, 1984.

Scott, Wilbur. *Five Approaches to Literary Criticism*. London: Collier-Macmillan, 1962. See the essays by Burke and Gorer as well as Scott's introduction to the section "The Psychological Approach: Literature in the Light of Psychological Theory."

Wellek, René, and Austin Warren. *Theory of Literature*. New York: Harcourt, 1942. See the chapter "Literature and Psychology" in pt. 3, "The Extrinsic Approach to the Study of Literature."

Wright, Elizabeth. "Modern Psychoanalytic Criticism." *Modern Literary Theory: A Comparative Introduction*. Ed. Ann Jefferson and David Robey. Totowa: Barnes, 1982. 113–33.

Freud, Lacan, and Their Influence

Basler, Roy P. *Sex, Symbolism, and Psychology in Literature*. New York: Octagon, 1975. See especially 13–19.

Clément, Catherine. *The Lives and Legends of Jacques Lacan*. Trans. Arthur Goldhammer. New York: Columbia UP, 1983.

Freud, Sigmund. *Introductory Lectures on Psycho-Analysis*. Trans. Joan Riviere. London: Allen, 1922.

Gallop, Jane. *Reading Lacan*. Ithaca: Cornell UP, 1985.

Hoffman, Frederick J. *Freudianism and the Literary Mind.* Baton Rouge: Louisiana State UP, 1945.

Kazin, Alfred. "Freud and His Consequences." *Contemporaries.* Boston: Little, 1962. 351–93.

Lacan, Jacques. *Écrits: A Selection.* Trans. Alan Sheridan. New York: Norton, 1977.

———. *Feminine Sexuality: Lacan and the école freudienne.* Ed. Juliet Mitchell and Jacqueline Rose. Trans. Rose. New York: Norton, 1982.

———. *The Four Fundamental Concepts of Psychoanalysis.* Trans. Alan Sheridan. London: Penguin, 1980.

Meisel, Perry, ed. *Freud: A Collection of Critical Essays.* Englewood Cliffs: Prentice, 1981.

Muller, John P., and William J. Richardson. *Lacan and Language: A Reader's Guide to "Écrits."* New York: International UP, 1982.

Porter, Laurence M. *"The Interpretation of Dreams": Freud's Theories Revisited.* Twayne's Masterwork Studies Series. Boston: G. K. Hall, 1986.

Ragland-Sullivan, Ellie. *Jacques Lacan and the Philosophy of Psychoanalysis.* U of Illinois P, 1986.

Reppen, Joseph, and Maurice Charney. *The Psychoanalytic Study of Literature.* Hillsdale: Analytic, 1985.

Schneiderman, Stuart. *Jacques Lacan: The Death of an Intellectual Hero.* Cambridge: Harvard UP, 1983.

Selden, Raman. *A Reader's Guide to Contemporary Literary Theory.* 2nd ed. Lexington: U of Kentucky P, 1989. See "Jacques Lacan: Language and the Unconscious."

Trilling, Lionel. "Art and Neurosis." *The Liberal Imagination.* New York: Scribner's, 1950. 160–80.

Wilden, Anthony. "Lacan and the Discourse of the Other." In Lacan, *Speech and Language in Psychoanalysis.* Trans. Wilden. Baltimore: Johns Hopkins UP, 1981. (Published as *The Language of the Self* in 1968.) 159–311.

Psychoanalysis, Feminism, and Literature

Chodorow, Nancy. *The Reproduction of Mothering: Psychoanalysis and the Sociology of Gender.* Berkeley: U of California P, 1978.

Gallop, Jane. *The Daughter's Seduction: Feminism and Psychoanalysis.* Ithaca: Cornell UP, 1982.

Garner, Shirley Nelson, Claire Kahane, and Madelon Sprengnether.

The (M)other Tongue: Essays in Feminist Psychoanalytic Interpretation. Ithaca: Cornell UP, 1985.

Irigaray, Luce. *This Sex Which Is Not One.* Trans. Catherine Porter. Ithaca: Cornell UP, 1985.

———. *The Speculum of the Other Woman.* Trans. Gillian C. Gill. Ithaca: Cornell UP, 1985.

Jacobus, Mary. "Is There a Woman in This Text?" *New Literary History* 14 (1982): 117–41.

Kristeva, Julia. *The Kristeva Reader.* Ed. Toril Moi. New York: Columbia UP, 1986. See especially the selection from *Revolution in Poetic Language,* 89–136.

Mitchell, Juliet. *Psychoanalysis and Feminism.* New York: Random House, 1974.

Mitchell, Juliet, and Jacqueline Rose, "Introduction I" and "Introduction II." Lacan, *Feminine Sexuality: Jacques Lacan and the école freudienne.* 1–26, 27–57.

Sprengnether, Madelon. *The Spectral Mother: Freud, Feminism, and Psychoanalysis.* Ithaca: Cornell UP, 1990.

Psychological and Psychoanalytic Studies of Literature

Bettelheim, Bruno. *The Uses of Enchantment: The Meaning and Importance of Fairy Tales.* New York: Knopf, 1976. Although this book is about fairy tales instead of literary works written for publication, it offers model Freudian readings of well-known stories.

Crews, Frederick C. *Out of My System: Psychoanalysis, Ideology, and Critical Method.* New York: Oxford UP, 1975.

———. *Relations of Literary Study.* New York: MLA, 1967. See the chapter "Literature and Psychology."

Diehl, Joanne Feit. "Re-Reading *The Letter*: Hawthorne, the Fetish, and the (Family) Romance." *Nathaniel Hawthorne, The Scarlet Letter.* Ed. Ross C Murfin. Case Studies in Contemporary Criticism Series. Ed. Ross C Murfin. Boston: Bedford–St. Martin's, 1991. 235–51.

Hallman, Ralph. *Psychology of Literature: A Study of Alienation and Tragedy.* New York: Philosophical Library, 1961.

Hartman, Geoffrey, ed. *Psychoanalysis and the Question of the Text.* Baltimore: Johns Hopkins UP, 1978. See especially the essays by Hartman, Johnson, Nelson, and Schwartz.

Hertz, Neil. *The End of the Line: Essays on Psychoanalysis and the Sublime.* New York: Columbia UP, 1985.

Holland, Norman N. *Dynamics of Literary Response*. New York: Oxford UP, 1968.

———. *Poems in Persons: An Introduction to the Psychoanalysis of Literature*. New York: Norton, 1973.

Kris, Ernest. *Psychoanalytic Explorations in Art*. New York: International, 1952.

Lucas, F. L. *Literature and Psychology*. London: Cassell, 1951.

Natoli, Joseph, ed. *Psychological Perspectives on Literature: Freudian Dissidents and Non-Freudians: A Casebook*. Hamden: Archon Books–Shoe String, 1984.

Phillips, William, ed. *Art and Psychoanalysis*. New York: Columbia UP, 1977.

Rogers, Robert. *A Psychoanalytic Study of the Double in Literature*. Detroit: Wayne State UP, 1970.

Skura, Meredith. *The Literary Use of the Psychoanalytic Process*. New Haven: Yale UP, 1981.

Strelka, Joseph P. *Literary Criticism and Psychology*. University Park: Pennsylvania State UP, 1976. See especially the essays by Lerner and Peckham.

Weiss, Daniel. *The Critic Agonistes: Psychology, Myth, and the Art of Fiction*. Ed. Eric Solomon and Stephen Arkin. Seattle: U of Washington P, 1985.

Lacanian Psychoanalytic Studies of Literature

Collings, David. "The Monster and the Imaginary Mother: A Lacanian Reading of *Frankenstein*." *Mary Shelley, Frankenstein*. Ed. Johanna M. Smith. Case Studies in Contemporary Criticism Series. Ed. Ross C Murfin. Boston: Bedford–St. Martin's, 1992. 245–58.

Davis, Robert Con, ed. *The Fictional Father: Lacanian Readings of the Text*. Amherst: U of Massachusetts P, 1981.

———, ed. "Lacan and Narration." *Modern Language Notes* 5 (1983): 843–1063.

Felman, Shoshana, ed. *Literature and Psychoanalysis: The Question of Reading: Otherwise*. Baltimore: Johns Hopkins UP, 1982.

Froula, Christine. "When Eve Reads Milton: Undoing the Canonical Economy." *Canons*. Ed. Robert von Hallberg. Chicago: U of Chicago P, 1984. 149–75.

Homans, Margaret. *Bearing the Word: Language and Female Experience in Nineteenth-Century Women's Writing*. Chicago: U of Chicago P, 1986.

Muller, John P., and William J. Richardson, eds. *The Purloined Poe: Lacan, Derrida, and Psychoanalytic Reading*. Baltimore: Johns Hopkins UP, 1988. Includes Lacan's seminar on Poe's "The Purloined Letter."

Psychoanalytic Approaches to Joyce

Anderson, Chester G. "Baby Tuckoo: Joyce's 'Features of Infancy,'" *Approaches to Joyce's "Portrait": Ten Essays*. Ed. Thomas F. Staley and Bernard Benstock. Pittsburgh: U of Pittsburgh P, 1976. 135–169.

Boheemen, Christine van. *The Novel as Family Romance: Language, Gender, and Authority from Fielding to Joyce*. Ithaca: Cornell UP, 1987, passim.

Brivic, Sheldon. *Joyce the Creator*. Madison and London: U of Wisconsin P, 1985.

———. *Joyce Between Freud and Jung*. Port Washington, NY, and London: Kennikat P, 1980.

———. *The Veil of Signs: Joyce, Lacan, and Perception*. Champaign: U of Illinois P, 1991.

Fenichel, Robert. "A Portrait of the Artist as a Young Orphan." *Literature and Psychology* 9 (Spring 1959): 19–22.

Henke, Suzette. *James Joyce and the Politics of Desire*. New York: Routledge, 1990.

Hoffman, Frederick C. "Infroyce." *Freudianism and the Literary Mind*. Baton Rouge: Louisiana State UP, 1945.

James Joyce Quarterly 13 (Spring 1976). "Joyce and Modern Psychology" issue.

James Joyce Quarterly 29 (Fall 1991). "Joyce Between Genders: Lacanian Views" issue.

Kimball, Jean. "Freud, Leonardo, and Joyce: The Dimensions of a Childhood Memory." *The Seventh of Joyce*. Ed. Bernard Benstock. Bloomington: Indiana UP, 1982. 57–73.

Leonard, Garry. "Joyce and Lacan: 'The Woman' as a Symptom of 'Masculinity' in 'The Dead.'" *James Joyce Quarterly* 28 (Winter 1991): 451–72.

O'Brien, Darcy. "Some Psychological Determinants of Joyce's View of Love and Sex." *New Light on Joyce from the Dublin Symposium*. Ed. Fritz Senn. Bloomington: Indiana UP, 1970. 137–55.

Rea, Joanne E. "Joyce's 'Beastly' Bitch Motif: Sadic Castration Threat and Separation Anxiety." *Journal of Evolutionary Psychology* 7 (Mar. 1986): 28–33.

Shechner, Mark. *Joyce in Nighttown: A Psychoanalytic Inquiry into "Ulysses."* Berkeley: U of California P, 1974.

Wasson, Richard. "Stephen Dedalus and the Imagery of Sight: A Psychological Approach." *Literature and Psychology* 15 (Fall 1965): 195–209.

A PSYCHOANALYTIC PERSPECTIVE

use p266 mayfield to prove/disprove thesis show intentions of Joyce

SHELDON BRIVIC

The Disjunctive Structure of Joyce's *Portrait*[1]

Psychoanalysis shows how the images that weave through *Portrait* are linked by unconscious motivation to form a dynamic structure. Within this structure Stephen Dedalus develops his thinking around a central principle of connecting with the world through alienation. And the conflicts and transformations in the structure enact opposing views by which Joyce both supports and condemns Stephen. Joyce knew about Freud during the last years of his work on *Portrait*,[2] so many patterns I will trace may have been consciously designed. But most of the novel's motivation was unconscious and sprang from Joyce's personal vision of his youthful development: he usually stuck close to the facts, only occasionally altering them for artistic purposes. According to the theory that the subject is made up of opposing agencies, an idea of Freud's that was expanded by Lacan (*Écrits* 292–305), the different sides of Stephen in *Portrait* express different intentions of Joyce's. The interaction of these opposed intentions makes up the rhythm of Stephen's mental life. thesis

The action of *Portrait* consists of Stephen's sundering of himself

[1]This essay is a condensation of a more detailed Freudian reading of *Portrait* in my *Joyce Between Freud and Jung* (15–83).

[2]Richard Ellmann (54) reports that Joyce bought three psychoanalytic works by Freud, Ernest Jones, and C. G. Jung around the time they were published in 1909–1911. Hans Walter Gabler (34) believes that Joyce revised the first three chapters of *Portrait* extensively after 1911.

from his society, his parents, his church, his beloved E— C—, and his nation. The book justifies these alienations by its critical portrayal of institutions and its presentation of ideas about freedom, personal development, and aesthetics. These ideas have great validity, but the root of Stephen's alienation, while it is shaped by social systems, is already planted in his unconscious before he can criticize society.

Stephen's first six years are represented in the section that takes up the first page and a half of *Portrait,* introducing many key images, including his looming, hairy father and the "nicer smell" (p. 19) of mother. The conclusion of this section, based on an early incident in Joyce's life recorded in his *Epiphanies* (Anderson 267–68), poses a threat that echoes through *Portrait:*

> When they were grown up he was going to marry Eileen. He hid under the table. His mother said:
>
> —O, Stephen will apologise.
>
> Dante said:
>
> —O, if not, the eagles will come and pull out his eyes.
>
> *Pull out his eyes,*
> *Apologise,*
> *Apologise,*
> *Pull out his eyes.* (p. 20)

The loss of eyes is an image of castration, having been established by Oedipus himself. Freud says that the idea of castration starts to be important for children during the phallic or oedipal stage, around ages four and five, which seems to be the time of Stephen's "Eagle" epiphany. The child at this stage develops a strong desire for genital contact with the parent of the opposite gender, desire that is forced out of consciousness by the fear of castration, bringing on years of latency (Freud 19: 174–76). In this scene from *Portrait* the oedipal content is naturally disguised, but Stephen is being punished for wanting to play the role of the father: "When they were grown up he was going to marry Eileen." That the minor relationship with Eileen serves as a screen for a deeper love for mother is suggested by its importance in establishing basic patterns for the novel. As Hélène Cixous points out, Stephen already practices here the silence, exile, and cunning that he will advocate later (278). He deals with his threat by turning it into poetry, focusing on the formal qualities of language, the common rhythm of "pull out his eyes" and "apologise."

Images of inadequacy pervade the following football scene: ". . .

the greasy leather orb flew like a heavy bird . . . He kept . . . out of the reach of the rude feet . . . felt his body small and weak amid the throng . . . and his eyes were weak and watery" (p. 20). The inability to rise and the sense of smallness or weakness define a feeling of bodily negation that is based on genital negation. As the game goes on, Stephen remains "fearful of the [other boys'] flashing eyes and muddy boots" (p. 22). His dread of being unmanned or reduced to femininity makes him sensitive to suggestions of violence or homosexuality. Such a suggestion propels him into a mental flight along paths of association that lead to the main source of his comfort and object of his desire. One of Joyce's key innovations is to follow these paths by reproducing the movement of the mind beneath its superstructure of logic. The Joycean stream of consciousness often parallels Freud's free association:

> Cantwell had answered [to another boy]:
>
> . . . Give Cecil Thunder a belt. I'd like to see you. He'd give you a toe in the rump for yourself.
>
> That was not a nice expression. His mother had told him not to speak with the rough boys in the college. Nice mother! . . . when she had said goodbye she had put up her veil double to her nose to kiss him: and her nose and eyes were red. (p. 21)

The emotionally charged memory of the parting kiss, with its overtones of moist, pink exposure, is soon followed by escape into a revery of mother that expands and clarifies a prevailing contrast between a cold paternal threat and a warm maternal haven, using a hearth as womb:

> It would be nice to lie on the hearthrug before the fire . . . and think on those sentences. He shivered as if he had cold slimy water next his skin. That was mean of Wells to shoulder him into the square ditch. . . . Mother was sitting at the fire. . . . She had her feet on the fender and her jewelly slippers were so hot and they had such a lovely warm smell! (p. 22)

The bully Wells embodies the threat visited on Stephen for thoughts of the "hearth" and so is called to mind by them. Wells initiates a series of father figures who knock Stephen down by degrading or dispossessing him in each chapter. The presentation of the mother in terms of feet and jewelly slippers is fetishistic. Freud says that the child's discovery that his mother does not have a penis is shocking because it suggests his own castration. This shock may lead to fetishism, in which a woman must bear a phallic symbol in order to be attractive (21: 152–57). Fetishism prevails in Joyce and defines gender roles as ambivalent by showing how woman wields phallic power.

A few pages later the masculine competition of Clongowes again forces Stephen to yearn for the womb: "He longed to . . . lay his head on his mother's lap" (p. 24). Stephen is separated from the other boys by a sense of guilt that makes him feel threatened by them, and the source of this guilt is touched when Wells asks, "Tell us, Dedalus, do you kiss your mother every night before you go to bed?" (p. 25). Whether Stephen answers yes or no, Wells mocks him and the other boys laugh: "Stephen blushed under their eyes . . ." (p. 25). As Richard Wasson first pointed out, eyes, male or female, have phallic value throughout the novel, generally being either aggressive and piercing or defeated and downcast. The idea of kissing mother is given great weight here and seems to stand for more than kissing. Reminded of his guilt, Stephen is reduced to impotence and does "not dare to raise his eyes" (p. 26). He now punishes himself by reviewing the square ditch incident in detail, but then turns again from these unpleasant images to meditate on "motherkiss" in an abstract way that represses the feelings involved: "Was it right to kiss his mother or wrong to kiss his mother? . . . Why did people do that with their two faces?" (p. 26).

When the characteristic combination of longing for the mother and the resultant fear of castration next recurs, the womb again appears as a hearth, and the vagina is a half-door:

> . . . he had seen a woman standing at the halfdoor of a cottage with a child in her arms. . . . It would be lovely to sleep for one night in that cottage before the fire of smoking turf, in the dark lit by the fire, in the warm dark. . . . But, O, the road there between the trees was dark! You would be lost in the dark. It made him afraid to think of how it was. (p. 29)

Stephen's fear of the dark is related to repressed patricidal impulses. He is preoccupied by the ghost of a mortally wounded marshal who is said to have haunted Clongowes. Stephen fears this image but is fascinated by it. Its appeal as an image of wounded, mature, male authority is confirmed by the long dream he has immediately after brooding on the marshal. This is the dream's climax: "Welcome home, Stephen! . . . His mother kissed him. Was that right? His father was a marshal now: higher than a magistrate" (p. 31). Evert Sprinchorn points out that while Stephen seems to be doing his father a favor by making him a marshal, the latent content involves killing him because the marshal is associated with death (Sprinchorn 17–18). This is the oedipal combination of loving mother and killing father, and Stephen's dream of a ship bearing Parnell's body may also evoke patricide (p. 36). But more prominent in Stephen's experience is a pattern in which attacking the father is transformed by guilt into fear of being injured by him.

Stephen's anxiety may be reflected in the illness he develops in this part of the novel, for he feels that he is "sick in his heart" (p. 25). The prospect of the infirmary appeals to Stephen because there he can be safely alone with a book (p. 36). Because his mind generates the paternal threat whenever it approaches the maternal goal, Stephen cannot sustain the active male role. Such an emphasis on the inseparability of satisfaction from guilt is linked by Freud to compulsion neurosis. Compulsives tend to forgo action in favor of controlling and rationalizing their feelings. They focus on language as a controllable substitute for reality; and they regress from the genital to the anal stage, which is bisexual or ambivalent (Freud 20: 113–23). The pattern is illustrated in *Portrait* by a math competition in which Stephen stops competing when he hears the voice of the father: ". . . he worked at the next sum and heard Father Arnall's voice. Then all his eagerness passed away and he felt his face quite cool" (p. 24). Stephen gives up the real rose of victory and starts theorizing about imaginary roses in aesthetic colors. The roots of his art and intellectual life lie in defenses against conflict.

The compulsive seesaw brings out sexual ambivalence, and indeed Stephen enacts Freud's idea that all people contain both genders. His anxiety about homosexuality is strongly developed as he meditates on the word *suck,* which is linked here to the terms *cock* and *queer,* and to the ambivalence of "cold and hot": all of these terms get repeated within a page (p. 23). An indication of why Stephen has difficulty claiming manhood appears in the Christmas dinner scene, where he sees his father's manhood broken: "Stephen, raising his terrorstricken face, saw that his father's eyes were full of tears" (p. 46). The destruction of the father here is a product of colonialism and religion, which emasculate Simon Dedalus by cutting off his great leader, Parnell.

Following this breaking of the father, Stephen is intensely preoccupied with threats of male violence. We return to Stephen at school to find that a "sprinter" has knocked him down and broken his glasses, putting his eyes out of commission (p. 48). Now his mind dwells on a mysterious crime he hears called "smugging," and although he doesn't seem to realize the fact, the term refers to homosexual petting. Smugging leads to thoughts of flogging:

> And though he trembled with cold and fright to think of [Mr. Gleeson's] cruel long nails and of the high whistling sound of the cane and of the chill you felt at the end of your shirt when you

> undressed yourself yet he felt a feeling of queer quiet pleasure inside him to think of the white fattish hands, clean and strong and gentle. (p. 51)

Stephen's mind swarms with unconsciously perverse fantasies for a time, but when he is finally beaten by Father Dolan, he experiences the pandying as a terrifyingly direct breakage: "A hot burning stinging tingling blow like the loud crack of a broken stick made his trembling hand crumple together like a leaf in the fire . . ." (p. 55). The acuteness of the sense of castration involved in the actual experience negates the pleasurable aspect of the fantasies and causes a reaction against the idea of submission. The pandying aggravates anxieties instead of placating them.

Stephen now affirms his manhood by striking out from his peers and going to the rector. In doing so, he uses literary sources (making reference, for instance, to heroes of antiquity [pp. 59–60]) to overcome a system that Joyce saw as designed to break his manhood by abusing him within an all-male environment. His trip to the rector's office, as an assertion of masculinity, is described repeatedly as an entrance into the female: ". . . he would be in the low dark narrow corridor that led . . . to the rector's room . . . had entered the low dark narrow corridor . . . passed along the narrow dark corridor . . ." (pp. 58–59). After this channel, Stephen passes through a pair of doors to be hailed by the rector as "my little man" (p. 60). The chapter ends in victory for his masculinity, but he is disillusioned when he finds at the beginning of the second chapter that his father and the rector were amused by his protest (p. 73). His compulsive alternation of submission and assertion will continue.

The first chapter establishes a fundamental model for all of *Portrait* and, with modification, for *Ulysses*. The desire for mother is clear here and the paternal threat is physical. Later, these elements grow sublimated and disguised as the original sources of Stephen's attitudes are denied and isolated from feeling. Yet a longing for a distant mother and a causally related fear of a father remain as the ground plan for all of Stephen's experience.

When the threat of the church fathers grew intolerable in chapter one, Stephen diverged in a new direction. In the second chapter the masculine threat is represented paradoxically by the collapse of Stephen's actual father, whose failure and aging are emphasized throughout: "There's a crack of the whip left in me yet, Stephen, old chap, said Mr Dedalus, poking at the dull fire with fierce energy. We're not dead yet

. . ." (p. 67). This paternal defeat stirs guilt and anxiety in Stephen. He now wanders around Blackrock, repeating the divergence of the first chapter:

> . . . he was different from others. He did not want to play. He wanted to meet in the real world the unsubstantial image which his soul so constantly beheld. He did not know where to seek it or how: but a premonition . . . told him that this image would, without any overt act of his, encounter him. They would meet quietly as if they had known each other and had made their tryst, perhaps at one of the gates or in some more secret place. They would be alone, surrounded by darkness and silence: and in that moment of supreme tenderness he would be transfigured. . . . Weakness and timidity and inexperience would fall from him in that magic moment. (pp. 66–67)

He does "not know where to seek" this "unsubstantial image," and on the next page, when he has moved to Dublin, "a vague dissatisfaction" has grown in him and he continues "to wander up and down day after day as if he really sought someone that eluded him" (p. 68). If this does not seem odd, it may be because all adolescents are subject to such vague longings; but it is absurd to yearn for something without knowing what one yearns for. Psychoanalysis explains that the object of such desire is repressed. But if Stephen does not know what he seeks, he indicates by details the nature of this object. He will meet it "perhaps at one of the gates or in some more secret place . . . surrounded by darkness." This associates his image with the womb, and he associates it too with tenderness and security. He also says, "They would meet quietly as if they had known each other . . . ," and later, when he feels tempted by E—— C——, he thinks, "He heard what her eyes said to him . . . and knew that in some dim past, whether in life or in revery, he had heard their tale before" (p. 70). Freud's theory shows us why Stephen projects his complex onto the girl. Both in his vague state of "unsubstantial" desire and in the later stage in which he focuses on E—— C——, he senses that the object of desire is one with which he has somehow been familiar for a long time, one he knew in the "dim past." It is his mother. But the idea of mother has now been sublimated into a spiritual ideal associated with transfiguration. Stephen soon finds that his mind wants to pursue "intangible phantoms," but the voices of his father, his masters, and his (male) peers interrupt this pursuit to urge him to accept responsibility (p. 82). Mother fixation has now become intellectual opposition to the norms of society and the expected roles of son and man.

Stephen's interest in Emma Clery is a more concrete aspect of his now-splintered pursuit of his mother. He is first drawn to Emma immediately after an epiphany in which he is mistaken for a woman (p. 69), showing that he asserts his masculinity primarily in order to deny his femininity. His scene with Emma on the tram emphasizes his sense of having known her before: seeing her temptations, he "knew that he had yielded to them a thousand times" (p. 70). He wants to "catch hold" of her and believes she wants him to, yet he stands "listlessly in his place, seemingly a tranquil watcher of the scene before him" (p. 70). His unexplained passivity suggests not only the artist's stance, but the relation of son to mother, with its powerful inhibition. Nothing of E— C— is described but her clothing and her eyes; these details represent her fetishistically, but they also serve another function. By reducing Emma to eyes and apparel, just as he also abstracts her name, Stephen eliminates her body and thus spiritualizes her. Though he regards her as a calculating temptress, he cannot touch her; and when he writes a poem about her, it is set between Jesuit mottoes and colored by "the maiden lustre of the moon" (p. 71). The poem concludes with a parting kiss—a prominent image in chapter one—and after writing it, Stephen gazes at his face in the mirror of his mother's dressing table.

The two aspects of woman as temptress and virgin, a commonplace of Joycean criticism, are evident here. We can understand this Joycean dichotomy through Freud's essay "On the Universal Tendency to Debasement in the Sphere of Love" (11: 177–90). Here Freud describes how many boys cultivate ideal, desexualized visions of their mothers. A boy reaches adolescence hearing that sex is nasty and refusing to admit that his mother engages in it. As a man, he separates women into two types, one of which is idealized and loved but cannot be defiled by sex, while the other is sexually approachable but can never be respected. Stephen sees both sides in Emma, but the idealizing tendency is clearly dominant, for it dictates his actions to her, while the temptress finds expression only in his fantasies.

In chapter two, as the Dedaluses move to poorer quarters and adolescence advances, Stephen repeatedly feels disturbed by a conjunction of tides of filth inside and outside him (p. 65, p. 68, p. 88). Unconsciously blaming the external disorder on his dirty thoughts, he strives to control "the squalor of his own mind and home" (p. 78). But the compulsive "breakwater of order" that he has erected "against the sordid tide" (p. 94) is finally overwhelmed, and he is driven to seek release in vice. Joyce emphasizes Stephen's feminine relation to paternal power by imaging the desire that drives him to lose his virginity as an incubus that penetrates his body (p. 96).

At the end of the second chapter Stephen finds his transfiguration in the maternal arms of a prostitute. He wants to be "held firmly" and "caressed slowly": "In her arms he felt that he had suddenly become strong and fearless and sure of himself" (p. 96). But as he achieves contact with the mother through prostitution in the third chapter, the paternal threat arises, and soon Stephen feels himself pierced by the phallic force of the words of Father Arnall: "The preacher's knife had probed deeply into his diseased conscience . . ." (p. 107); "The thought slid like a cold shining rapier into his tender flesh: confession" (p. 116). As he wandered then in search of a prostitute, Stephen now wanders in search of a confessional, and he seeks the sheltering arms of the Virgin whose name is that of his mother. But in his religious life in chapter four, he comes to feel threatened because the submissive attitude he adopts toward God the Father is felt as a reduction to femininity. This threat is indicated by repeated references to Stephen's soul (*anima*) as female: "His soul sank . . . into depths of contrite peace . . . sending forth, as she sank, a faint prayer" (p. 115); ". . . his soul took up again her burden of pieties . . . humiliated and faint before her Creator" (p. 134).

Freud described parallels between the rituals practiced by compulsives and those of religion (9: 115–28); and during his religious phase, Stephen focuses on ascetic rituals that help to control his feelings. He is having difficulty maintaining this retentive control when his interview with the Jesuit director brings matters to a head. The looped cord of the blind that the director dangles before Stephen represents hanging and also castration. *Les jupes,* the skirts worn by Capuchins that the director mentions to test Stephen (p. 138), suggest that the priestly role offered to Stephen here is feminine.

Having left the church, Stephen wanders once more, once more uncertain about what he seeks: "He had refused. Why? He turned seaward . . ." (p. 147). What he is looking for is indicated by the value he places on words: "He drew forth a phrase from his treasure . . ." (p. 147). What is this value?

> . . . was it that, being as weak of sight as he was shy of mind, he drew less pleasure from the reflection of the glowing sensible world through the prism of a language manycoloured and richly storied than from the contemplation of an inner world of individual emotions mirrored perfectly in a lucid supple periodic prose? (p. 148)

He indicates here that his use of words is subjective, that he writes primarily to mirror the inner world; but the statement is expressed in language that is circuitous and distorted. The subordination of the important but vague "shy of mind" to the less important "weak of sight," the fancy, indistinct adjectives, and the general emphasis on sound over sense tend to obscure the meaning of the words. This language is typical of the beach scene and of what is called the "purple prose" of *Portrait.* This sort of writing represents strong ideas and emotions so ornately that they are submerged by virtuosity, and in the following chapter Stephen constructs an aesthetic theory that, among other things, serves to deny that he uses art to express his emotions.

The "treasure" image shows that Stephen is now compulsively accumulating words, as he accumulated penances at the start of this chapter, or money for vice at the start of the previous one. His words express desire and aggression without exposing him to action. In chapter two, when Simon boasts that he is stronger and more of a man than Stephen, a friend of Simon's, "tapping his forehead," says, "But he'll beat you here" (p. 91). Soon after this, Stephen uses money he wins by his writing to temporarily take over his family, dumbfounding his father (p. 93). Words are Stephen's major weapon, and he frequently uses the "rapier point of his sensitiveness" (p. 166) to thrust and parry in the dialogues of the final chapter.

On the beach, Stephen's sense of the power of art inspires a vision of Daedalus aflight. Freud says in his study of da Vinci, which Joyce bought around the time it came out in 1910 (Ellmann 54), that the common dream image of flying usually represents erection and phallic sexuality. Here the image is spiritualized and dissociated from its physical basis: "His soul was soaring in an air beyond the world and the body he knew was purified in a breath and delivered of incertitude and made radiant and commingled with the element of the spirit" (p. 150). This description parallels Stephen's earlier adolescent sexual longings: "He would fade into something impalpable under her eyes and then, in a moment, he would be transfigured. Weakness and timidity and inexperience would fall from him . . ." (p. 67). This passage is echoed when Stephen meets the prostitute (pp. 95–96), and at his conversion, when his soul is raised and "made fair and holy" (p. 165). These recurrent transfigurations are all based on a lost original dream of union with mother.

Stephen pursues his phantom of transcendence through many fields: schoolwork, rebellion, debauchery, religion, and now words. Whenever he settles in an area close to some maternal surrogate, senses of dissatisfaction and emasculation arise linked to a father figure in league with established authority. This threat forces him to wander off, expanding his horizons, in search of a new goal. Each chapter ends with a triumphant sense of uplift as he finds his goal, which is portrayed with an image of nurture, either maternal or oral. But soon this new goal begins to disappoint and to evoke the paternal threat in the following chapter. Parallel form in the chapters of *Portrait* was first pointed out by Hugh Kenner (129), but psychoanalysis allows us to diagram this structure in greater causal detail (Table 1).

There is more than one way to read the table, and I will sketch an opposition between two of its main aspects. In the Freudian terms on which I have based it, the diagram emphasizes how the pattern of Stephen's experience repeats. Otto Fenichel says of compulsives, "The patients enter an ever-growing cycle: remorse, penitence, new transgressions, new remorse" (294). Stephen can develop significantly insofar as he recognizes and accepts this cycle, and doing so is a sort of self-analysis. But there is another element in his development, which is indicated on the beach when he thinks, "The end he had been born to serve yet did not see had led him to escape by an unseen path . . ." (p. 146). Once Stephen assumes that he is destined to be an artist, all of his alienation and conflict turn out to serve a positive purpose. This destiny is not a fact, but a myth generated by Stephen's neurotic need. His belief in it, however, is powerfully productive, and this is why Jung's theories of the spiritual power of the unconscious have a place. In mythic terms, each chapter involves a ritual sacrifice, and from each death Stephen is reborn stronger, with a more ambitious aim, and freed from his compulsions.[3]

On the beach, Stephen tells himself that he has risen from the repressive "grave of boyhood" and that he will create out of freedom (p. 150). He uses the birdlike girl he sees to project his new freedom of seeing reality without idealizing or condemning it, for he claims that her beauty is "without shame or wantonness" (p. 151). Nevertheless, details of her appearance suggest that in fact she is *not* without shame, for "a faint flame trembled on her cheek," and she can hardly be "without wantonness" if at the turn of the century her "skirts were kilted boldly about her waist" (pp. 151–52).[4] Stephen's myth of transcen-

[3]For a Lacanian reading of this diagram, see my *Veil of Signs* 37–60.

[4]Thomas Flanagan has suggested in conversation that the girl's position and the "noise of gently moving water" that issues from her probably indicate that she is urinating. The stream of her urine could constitute a phallic symbol and so add to the fetishism of the scene.

Table 1. Cyclical Structure of *A Portrait*

	Chapter I	*Chapter II*	*Chapter III*	*Chapter IV*	*Chapter V*
New world	School	Family homes	Nighttown	Church	College
Maternal goal	Mother (and alma mater)	E——C—— as ideal	Prostitutes	Virgin	Irish Muse
Paternal threat	Wells and Dolan	Heron and father's collapse	Arnall's sermon	Director's offer	Cranly (as conventional Ireland)
Wandering	To rector	To whore	To confession	To beach	To Europe
Triumph	Lifted by boys	Kiss	Eucharist	Vocation	Flight
Nursing image	"the brimming bowl" (p. 62)	Kiss	Taking wafer	"The earth that had borne him . . . to her breast" (p. 152)	"The white arms of roads, their promise of close embraces" (p. 218)

dence is not an escape from his neurosis but a product of it, and his parental attachments and anxieties return in the fifth chapter. His fantasies of transcendence are contained in a framework that shows them to be illusions, but without them Stephen could not build his vision. The presence of both opposing vectors in the diagram, repetition and transcendence, is what allows the structure to embody the vitality of Stephen's mind.

Inspired by his vision on the beach, Stephen devotes himself to art and begins to formulate his system of aesthetics. These theories fashion art into a means of protection and a means of escape from entrapment by the past and by crippling fixations. Stephen is anxious to prove that art can be isolated from intense personal feelings. To this compulsive end he seizes on Aquinas's statement that art satisfies the mind, not the body, and expands it into his idea of stasis. The statement that in art "the mind is arrested and raised above desire and loathing" (p. 179) has some truth, although as Lynch suggests there may be exceptions. But Stephen's explanation of this stasis is false. He claims that art operates on an entirely different level from kinetic emotions:

> Our flesh shrinks from what it dreads and responds to . . . what it desires by a purely reflex action of the nervous system. . . . [But] Beauty expressed by the artist cannot awaken in us an emotion which is kinetic or a sensation which is purely physical. It awakens . . . an esthetic stasis, an ideal pity or an ideal terror, a stasis called forth, prolonged and at last dissolved by what I call the rhythm of beauty. (p. 179)

It is not true that desire and loathing are purely physical reflexes. Stephen is trying to divide mental activity, which mixes reason with feeling, into two exclusive levels. Even as he does so, however, his ideas are dictated by his desires, for he is trying to build an intellectual edifice to shelter him from neurotic anxiety, an art to fulfill a maternal function.

Nor is it true that art "cannot awaken . . . an emotion which is kinetic": there is no such thing as nonkinetic emotion, only emotion whose kinesis is relatively weak or indirect. Art is built on the same drives, conscious and unconscious, that operate in life. But in art these drives are so manipulated by sublimation, construction, and disguise that the reader who participates in the feelings involved controls tension and achieves gratification (Lesser 59–144). The peace of stasis is arrived at by balancing opposed psychic forces in a pleasing way. If this balance is not achieved and drives obtrude in such a way that they violate truth, morality, or some other function of psychic balance, the work is dismissed as pornographic or didactic, cheap or prohibitive, untrue or unhealthy. *Portrait* appeals to people partly by enacting the conflicts of youth, and the stasis it achieves is suspended in a balance between desire of mother and fear of father, between ideal and reality—a stasis of conflict between opposing values.

Stephen senses the dynamic nature of this stasis when he speaks of "the rhythm of beauty." And although his explanation of beauty in terms of three stages of perception—wholeness, harmony, and radiance—elevates formal considerations at the expense of content, it does focus on a process of interaction with the object. Formalistic as it is, Stephen's aesthetics still contains hints that for him art is fundamentally a sexual activity. The object he uses as his main example in discussion with Lynch is a beautiful woman; and the final stage of apprehension—*claritas*, or radiance—is described as a luminous state of mind like a fading coal (p. 185). This description suggests orgasm, which Joyce represents through fading fireworks in the "Nausicaa" episode of *Ulysses*. The phases following this aesthetic consummation are described as "artistic conception, artistic gestation and artistic reproduction" (p. 182). I surmise that on an important level the sexual union involved in Stephen's idea of art is union with mother. The villanelle he composes in the following section is addressed to a female figure who seems to be E—— C——. But she combines elements of the Blessed Virgin with the idea of the temptress, and her heart is "wilful from before the beginning of the world" (p. 189). She was there before he was, and these are signs of Stephen's maternal fixation.

While Stephen is preparing to strive for union through art with an idealization of the mother, in the last third of the novel he is renouncing his real mother and her surrogates in life. In chapter four he begins to have a growing feeling that his mother is betraying him by her devotion to the Church: "A dim antagonism . . . darkened his mind as a cloud against her disloyalty: and when it passed . . . he was made aware dimly and without regret of a first noiseless sundering of their lives" (p. 146). Stephen's "dim" feeling that his mother has betrayed him follows what Freud sees as a universal tendency of adolescents to blame their mothers for infidelity because their mothers have given themselves to their fathers (11: 165–75).

Stephen's vision of a defiled, treacherous mother expands in the last chapter to include all of Ireland. He thinks of his country as a "venal" woman who has given herself over to domination by England and Rome. He sees images of decay and corruption all about him as he walks the streets "amid heaps of wet rubbish . . . stumbling through the mouldering offal" (p. 154). Whether he looks at his class or out the window, "an odour assailed him of cheerless cellardamp and decay" (p. 156). A lane is filled with "heaps of dead language" (p. 157), and "sloth of the body and of the soul" creeps over a statue of Thomas Moore "like unseen vermin" (p. 158). In Stephen's nostrils the soul of Dublin "had shrunk with time to a faint mortal odour rising from the earth and he knew that in a moment when he entered the sombre college he would be conscious of a corruption . . ." (p. 161).

Likewise he dwells on thoughts of morally questionable women, such as a flower girl whom he sees as selling not only her blue flowers but her blue eyes (p. 161) and a factory girl who calls to him (p. 191). Stephen sees the peasant woman who offered herself to his friend Davin as "a type of her race and his own, a batlike soul waking to the consciousness of itself in darkness and secrecy . . . a woman without guile, calling the stranger to her bed" (pp. 160–61). Irish womanhood gives itself away because the Irish "allowed a handful of foreigners to subject them" (p. 177).

Stephen's obsession with the idea of the unfaithful mother assimilates E— C—, whom he links to two father figures, Father Moran and Cranly. When Cranly is angry, Stephen sees his anger as a sign that he is thinking of Emma (pp. 200–01), and when Cranly's anger goes away, Stephen again believes he is thinking of her (p. 200). No matter what the evidence, Stephen will put the woman he loves in the position of his mother by finding her attached to another man. Cranly's recommendation that Stephen compromise is quite reasonable and considerate, which is why it represents the ultimate threat that would cut Stephen off from development by keeping him from disaster. Cranly's very attractiveness and considerateness make Stephen see him as bound to take Emma away (p. 211), thus confirming his own decision to leave.

With friendship as with love, Stephen cannot approach satisfaction without feeling a threat. The compulsive link between gratification and anxiety makes Stephen a wanderer endlessly compelled to shift toward new goals. This pattern is powerful in Joyce's work, in which each book not only differs in form from every other one but also changes its nature and increases in complexity between its inception and its conclusion. Stephen's neurosis here feeds his creativity, as it does through his compulsive preoccupation with words. At each stage of the structure of *Portrait,* Stephen could not make progress if he did not entrap himself.

In chapter five Stephen blames or projects his problems onto Irish society. One must be alienated to attack one's own world, and Stephen could not criticize his society so strongly if he did not have a transcendent aim and a psychosexual motivation. Joyce insists on the transcendent and sexual elements in the book's structure because he believes that the idea that one can criticize society objectively is the most dangerous delusion.

Those who dismiss Stephen for having the wrong ideology overlook his irony about himself and his involvement in change (as well as the deadness of a character with correct ideology). Far from validating his own views, Stephen, who denies his own Shakespeare theory in *Ulysses,* sees his thinking as "a dusk of doubt and selfmistrust" (*Portrait* p. 155) and recognizes that "his mind bred vermin" (p. 202). He repeatedly retracts his condemnation of E— C— for her conventionality (p. 193, pp. 201–02, pp. 217–18), having a strong realization within a page of the end that he has been all wrong about her.

Stephen's commitment "to live, to err, to fall, to triumph, to recreate life out of life!" (p. 152) makes him aware that any position he takes is only a stage in a process of reversals. From the 1904 sketch "A Portrait of the Artist," Joyce conceived of his portrait as "the development of an entity of which our actual present is a phase only . . . individuating rhythm . . . not an identificative paper but rather the curve of an emotion" (Anderson 257–58). This rhythmic curve, reflected in my diagram, indicates that Stephen's personality consists of ongoing opposition. He senses the cycle of his life well enough to suspect that his triumph at the end, as he sets out to encounter reality "for the millionth time" (p. 218), must be followed by a fall; and having passed through childhood, vice, and religion before art, he knows his views must change radically. It is by seeing how he repeats that he prepares for change.

Stephen has a powerful relationship to history. Although he is a socialist, he knows that joining a contemporary Irish leftist movement will endanger his life while yet leaving him under the dominance of the Church. He correctly realizes that by far the most valuable historical role he can play is "to forge in the smithy of my soul the uncreated conscience of my race" (p. 218). He aims to re-form human consciousness by bringing a new awareness of the mind through self-exploration. He succeeds to the extent that *Portrait*—together with Lawrence's *The Rainbow* (chapter 11), also written in 1915—vividly establishes the idea that every person is entitled to define his or her self apart from Church, state, and family (p. 177). Once this idea has spread, with *Portrait* inspiring writers as diverse as Ralph Ellison and Yukio Mishima, human freedom has advanced in a way that may be critical and lasting.

WORKS CITED

Anderson, Chester G., ed. *James Joyce, "A Portrait of the Artist as a Young Man": Text, Criticism, and Notes.* New York: Viking, 1968.

Brivic, Sheldon R. *Joyce between Freud and Jung.* Port Washington: Kennikat, 1980.

———. *The Veil of Signs: Joyce, Lacan, and Perception.* Urbana: U. of Illinois P, 1991.

Cixous, Hélène. *The Exile of James Joyce.* Trans. Sally A. J. Purcell. New York: David Lewis, 1972.

Ellmann, Richard. *The Consciousness of Joyce.* New York: Oxford UP, 1977.

Fenichel, Otto. *The Psychoanalytic Theory of Neurosis.* New York: Norton, 1945.

Freud, Sigmund. *The Standard Edition of the Complete Psychological Works of Sigmund Freud.* Ed. James Strachey. 24 vols. London: Hogarth, 1953–74.

Gabler, Hans Walter. "The Seven Lost Years of *A Portrait* . . ." *Approaches to Joyce's "Portrait": Ten Essays.* Ed. Thomas F. Staley and Bernard Benstock. Pittsburgh: U of Pittsburgh P, 1976.

Kenner, Hugh. *Dublin's Joyce.* Boston: Beacon, 1962.

Lacan, Jacques. *Écrits: A Selection.* Trans. Alan Sheridan. New York: Norton, 1977.

Lesser, Simon O. *Fiction and the Unconscious.* New York: Vintage, 1962.

Sprinchorn, Evert. "A Portrait of the Artist as Achilles." *Approaches to the Twentieth-Century Novel.* Ed. John E. Unterecker. New York: Thomas Y. Crowell, 1965.

Wasson, Richard. "Stephen Dedalus and the Imagery of Sight: A Psychological Approach." *Literature and Psychology* 15 (1965): 195–209.

Reader-Response Criticism and *A Portrait of the Artist as a Young Man*

WHAT IS READER-RESPONSE CRITICISM?

Students are routinely asked in English courses for their reactions to texts they are reading. Sometimes there are so many different reactions that we may wonder whether everyone has read the same text. And some students respond so idiosyncratically to what they read that we say their responses are "totally off the wall."

Reader-response critics are interested in the variety of our responses. Reader-response criticism raises theoretical questions about whether our responses to a work are the same as its meanings, whether a work can have as many meanings as we have responses to it, and whether some responses are more valid than, or superior to, others. It asks us to pose the following questions: What have we internalized that helps us determine what is and what isn't "off the wall"? In other words, what is the wall, and what standards help us to define it?

Reader-response criticism also provides models that are useful in answering such questions. Adena Rosmarin has suggested that a work can be likened to an incomplete work of sculpture: to see it fully, we *must* complete it imaginatively, taking care to do so in a way that responsibly takes into account what is there. An introduction to several other models of reader-response theory will allow you to understand better the reader-oriented essay that follows as well as to see a variety of ways in which, as a reader-response critic, you might respond to literary works.

Reader-response criticism, which emerged during the 1970s, focuses on what texts do to, or in, the mind of the reader, rather than regarding a text as something with properties exclusively its own. A poem, Louise M. Rosenblatt wrote as early as 1969, "is what the reader lives through under the guidance of the text and experiences as relevant to the text." Rosenblatt knew her definition would be difficult for many to accept: "The idea that a *poem* presupposes a *reader* actively involved with a *text,*" she wrote, "is particularly shocking to those seeking to emphasize the objectivity of their interpretations" (127).

Rosenblatt is implicitly referring to the formalists, the old "New Critics," when she speaks of supposedly objective interpreters shocked by the notion that readers help make poems. Formalists preferred to discuss "the poem itself," the "concrete work of art," the "real poem." And they refused to describe what a work of literature makes a reader "live through." In fact, in *The Verbal Icon* (1954), William K. Wimsatt and Monroe C. Beardsley defined as fallacious the very notion that a reader's response is part of the meaning of a literary work:

> The Affective Fallacy is a confusion between the poem and its *results* (what it *is* and what it *does*). . . . It begins by trying to derive the standards of criticism from the psychological effects of a poem and ends in impressionism and relativism. The outcome . . . is that the poem itself, as an object of specifically critical judgment, tends to disappear. (21)

Reader-response critics take issue with their formalist predecessors. Stanley Fish, author of a highly influential article entitled "Literature in the Reader: Affective Stylistics" (1970), argues that any school of criticism that would see a work of literature as an object, that would claim to describe what it *is* and never what it *does,* is guilty of misconstruing what literature and reading really are. Literature exists when it is read, Fish suggests, and its force is an affective force. Furthermore, reading is a temporal process. Formalists assume it is a spatial one as they step back and survey the literary work as if it were an object spread out before them. They may find elegant patterns in the texts they examine and reexamine, but they fail to take into account that the work is quite different to a reader who is turning the pages and being moved, or affected, by lines that appear and disappear as the reader reads.

In a discussion of the effect that a sentence penned by the seventeenth-century physician Thomas Browne has on a reader reading, Fish pauses to say this about his analysis and also, by extension, about the overall critical strategy he has largely developed: "Whatever is persuasive and illuminating about [it] . . . is the result of my substituting for one question – what does this sentence mean? – another, more operational question – what does this sentence do?" He then quotes a line from John Milton's *Paradise Lost,* a line that refers to Satan and the other fallen angels: "Nor did they not perceive their evil plight." Whereas more traditional critics might say that the "meaning" of the line is "They did perceive their evil plight," Fish relates the uncertain movement of the reader's mind *to* that half-satisfying interpretation. Furthermore, he declares that "the reader's inability to tell whether or not 'they' do perceive and his involuntary question . . . are part of the line's *meaning,* even though they take place in the mind, not on the page" (*Text* 26).

This stress on what pages *do* to minds pervades the writings of most, if not all, reader-response critics. Wolfgang Iser, author of *The Implied Reader* (1974) and *The Act of Reading: A Theory of Aesthetic Response* (1976), finds texts to be full of "gaps," and these gaps, or "blanks," as he sometimes calls them, powerfully affect the reader. The reader is forced to explain them, to connect what the gaps separate, literally to create in his or her mind a poem or novel or play that isn't *in* the text but that the text incites. Stephen Booth, who greatly influenced Fish, equally emphasizes what words, sentences, and passages "do." He stresses in his analyses the "reading experience that results" from a "multiplicity of organizations" in, say, a Shakespeare sonnet (*Essay* ix). Sometimes these organizations don't make complete sense, and sometimes they even seem curiously contradictory. But that is precisely what interests reader-response critics, who, unlike formalists, are at least as interested in fragmentary, inconclusive, and even unfinished texts as in polished, unified works. For it is the reader's struggle to *make sense* of a challenging work that reader-response critics seek to describe.

In *Self-Consuming Artifacts: The Experience of Seventeenth-Century Literature* (1972), Fish reveals his preference for literature that makes readers work at making meaning. He contrasts two kinds of literary presentation. By the phrase "rhetorical presentation," he describes literature that reflects and reinforces opinions that readers already hold; by "dialectical presentation," he refers to works that prod and provoke. A dialectical text, rather than presenting an opinion as if it were truth, challenges readers to discover truths on their own. Such a text may not even have the kind of symmetry that formalist critics seek. Instead of offering a "single, sustained argument," a dialectical text, or self-consuming artifact, may be "so arranged that to enter into the spirit and assumptions of any one of [its] . . . units is implicitly to reject the spirit and assumptions of the unit immediately preceding" (*Artifacts* 9). Such a text needs a reader-response critic to elucidate its workings. Another kind of critic is likely to try to explain why the units are unified and coherent, not why such units are contradicting and "consuming" their predecessors. The reader-response critic proceeds by describing the reader's way of dealing with the sudden twists and turns that characterize the dialectical text, making the reader return to earlier passages and see them in an entirely new light.

"The value of such a procedure," Fish has written, "is predicated on the idea of meaning as *an event,*" not as something "located (presumed to be embedded) *in* the utterance" or "verbal object as a thing in itself" (*Text* 28). By redefining meaning as an event, the reader-response critic once again locates meaning in time: the reader's time. A text exists and signifies while it is being read, and what it signifies or means will depend, to no small extent, on *when* it is read. (*Paradise Lost* had some meanings for a seventeenth-century Puritan that it would not have for a twentieth-century atheist.)

With the redefinition of literature as something that only exists meaningfully in the mind of the reader, with the redefinition of the literary work as a catalyst of mental events, comes a concurrent redefinition of the reader. No longer is the reader the passive recipient of those ideas that an author has planted in a text. "The reader is *active,*" Rosenblatt insists (123). Fish begins "Literature in the Reader" with a similar observation: "If at this moment someone were to ask, 'what are you doing,' you might reply, 'I am reading,' and thereby acknowledge that reading is . . . something *you do*" (*Text* 22). In "How to Recognize a Poem When You See One," he is even more provocative: "Interpreters do not decode poems: they make them" (*Text* 327). Iser, in focusing critical interest on the gaps in texts, on what is not expressed, similarly redefines the reader as an active maker. In an essay entitled "Interaction between Text and Reader," he argues that what is missing from a narrative causes the reader to fill in the blanks creatively.

Iser's title implies a cooperation between reader and text that is also implied by Rosenblatt's definition of a poem as "what the reader lives through under the guidance of the text." Indeed, Rosenblatt borrowed the term "transactional" to describe the dynamics of the reading process, which in her view involves interdependent texts and readers interacting. The view that texts and readers make poems together, though, is not shared by *all* interpreters generally thought of as reader-response critics. Steven Mailloux has divided reader-response critics into several categories, one of which he labels "subjective." Subjective critics, like David Bleich (or Norman Holland after his conversion by Bleich), assume what Mailloux calls the "absolute priority of individual selves as creators of texts" (*Conventions* 31). In other words, these critics do not see the reader's response as one "guided" by the text but rather as one motivated by deep-seated, personal, psychological needs. What they find in texts is, in Holland's phrase, their own "identity theme." Holland has argued that as readers we use "the literary work to symbolize and finally to replicate ourselves. We work out through the text our own characteristic patterns of desire" ("UNITY" 816).

Subjective critics, as you may already have guessed, often find themselves confronted with the following question: If all interpretation is a function of private, psychological identity, then why have so many readers interpreted, say, Shakespeare's *Hamlet* in the same way? Different subjective critics have answered the question differently. Holland simply has said that common identity themes exist, such as that involving an oedipal fantasy. Fish, who went through a subjectivist stage, has provided a different answer. In "Interpreting the *Variorum,*" he argues that the "stability of interpretation among readers" is a function of shared "interpretive strategies." These strategies, which "exist prior to the act of reading and therefore determine the shape of what is read," are held in common by "interpretive communities" such as the one comprised by American college students reading a novel as a class assignment (*Text* 167, 171).

As I have suggested in the paragraph above, reader-response criticism is not a monolithic school of thought, as is assumed by some detractors who like to talk about the "School of Fish." Several of the critics mentioned thus far have, over time, adopted different versions of reader-response criticism. I have hinted at Holland's growing subjectivism as well as the evolution of Fish's own thought. Fish, having at first viewed meaning as the cooperative production of readers and texts, went on to become a subjectivist, and very nearly a "deconstructor" ready to suggest that all criticism is imaginative creation, fiction about literature, or *metafiction.* In developing the notion of interpretive communities, however, Fish has become more of a social, structuralist, reader-response critic; currently, he is engaged in studying reading communities and their interpretive conventions in order to understand the conditions that give rise to a work's intelligibility.

In spite of the gaps between reader-response critics and even between the assumptions that they have held at various stages of their respective careers, all try to answer similar questions and to use similar strategies to describe the reader's response to a given text. One question these critics are commonly asked has already been discussed: Why do individual readers come up with such similar interpretations if meaning is not embedded *in* the work itself? Other recurring, troubling questions include the following interrelated ones: Just who *is* the reader? (or, to place the emphasis differently, Just who is *the* reader?) Aren't you reader-response critics just talking about your own idiosyncratic responses when you describe what a line from *Paradise Lost* "does" in and to "the reader's" mind? What about my responses? What if they're different? Will you be willing to say that all responses are equally valid?

Fish defines "the reader" in this way: "*the* reader is the *informed* reader." The informed reader is someone who is "sufficiently experienced as a reader to have internalized the properties of literary discourses, including everything from the most local of devices (figures of speech, etc.) to whole genres." And, of course, the informed reader is in full possession of the "semantic knowledge" (knowledge of idioms, for instance) assumed by the text (*Artifacts* 406).

Other reader-response critics use terms besides "the *informed* reader" to define "*the* reader," and these other terms mean slightly different things. Wayne Booth uses the phrase "the implied reader" to mean the reader "created by the work." (Only "by agreeing to play the role of this created audience," Susan Suleiman explains, "can an actual reader correctly understand and appreciate the work" [8].) Gerard Genette and Gerald Prince prefer to speak of "the narratee, . . . the necessary counterpart of a given narrator, that is, the person or figure who receives a narrative" (Suleiman 13). Like Booth, Iser employs the term "the implied reader," but he also uses "the educated reader" when he refers to what Fish calls the "informed" or "intended" reader. Thus, with different terms, each critic denies the claim that reader-response criticism might lead people to think that there are as many correct interpretations of a work as there are readers to read it.

As Mailloux has shown, reader-response critics share not only questions, answers, concepts, and terms for those concepts but also strategies of reading. Two of the basic "moves," as he calls them, are to show that a work gives readers something to do, and to describe what the reader does by way of response. And there are more complex moves as well. For instance, a reader-response critic might typically (1) cite direct references to reading in the text, in order to justify the focus on reading and show that the inside of the text is continuous with what the reader is doing; (2) show how other nonreading situations in the text nonetheless mirror the situation the reader is in ("Fish shows how in *Paradise Lost* Michael's teaching of Adam in Book XI resembles Milton's teaching of the reader throughout the poem"); and (3) show, therefore, that the reader's response is, or is perfectly analogous to, the topic of the story. For Stephen Booth, *Hamlet* is the tragic story of "an audience that cannot make up its mind." In the view of Roger Easson, Blake's *Jerusalem* "may be read as a poem about the experience of reading *Jerusalem*" (Mailloux, "Learning" 103).

Norman N. Holland begins the essay on *Portrait* that follows with two words: "*non serviam.*" Taken directly from Joyce's text, the phrase is the one with which Stephen declares his unwillingness to serve home, fatherland, and Church.

In good reader-response fashion, however, Holland quickly proceeds to turn that textual fragment into an occasion for speaking of his own *reaction* to *Portrait.* And that reaction, he tells us, has in the past been a rather troubled one, for "this is not only a novel about rebellion but also a novel I rebel against." Holland admits to having long resisted the language of both Stephen and Joyce. He has resented having to watch the novel's terrible preacher "carving religion into the minds of the young." As a "freethinking sexual being," he has cringed at the way the text polarizes "woman into virgin or whore."

A funny thing happens, though, in the process of writing about the novel, and it is that something that Holland's essay implicitly demonstrates. A personal "experience" is "achieved"; a "new relation" is consequently formed. Indeed, the very act of critically "resisting" both the book and "the forces the book describes" leads Holland to new insights. He comes to view some characters within the world of the text as being *analogous to* the resisting reader, and he comes to see other characters (Stephen, for example) as being like the writer using words to control. Moreover, he comes to see the desire to achieve control in terms of his own desire to master, not serve, the text. Joyce's novel as read by Holland is, finally, a book *about* words and their "power"—their power to "mark," "imprison," and "control" but also to "free us."

Holland, who in the past has been associated with the more subjectivist strains of reader-response criticism, nonetheless shows in this essay an implicit understanding of the degree to which individual readings will overlap insofar as readers share the same reading communities. He recognizes, for instance, that he writes as one who spent "childhood hours" in "church and Sunday school," as one who *didn't* go to a college in which young men quipped in "dog Latin" or "quoted from the church fathers." He admits that he is "a male writing as a male" and that he can contrast his own reading with "a female reader's" response before proceeding to identify points of tangency.

Holland's subjectivist background, however, is still apparent, for again and again he represents the process of reading and writing about a text as a highly individual experience. We may, to be sure, grow similarly as we submit to and struggle against the power of a given writer's words, as we struggle to "make" the author's text "our own making." But the growth of the reader is finally and fundamentally, in Holland's view, the growth of the individual. That fact comes through in the last paragraph of his essay, which in spite of its thickly sprinkled references to "you and I" and "our task as readers" and "every one of us" and "each of us" makes clear that, in the last analysis, "we make our own sense of what we read," and the sense we make is what sets us free.

Ross C Murfin

READER-RESPONSE CRITICISM: A SELECTED BIBLIOGRAPHY

Some Introductions to Reader-Response Criticism

Fish, Stanley E. "Literature in the Reader: Affective Stylistics." *New Literary History* 2 (1970): 123–61. Rpt. in Fish 21–67 and in Primeau 154–79.

Freund, Elizabeth. *The Return of the Reader: Reader-Response Criticism.* London: Methuen, 1987.

Holland, Norman N. "UNITY IDENTITY TEXT SELF." *PMLA* 90 (1975): 813–22.

Holub, Robert C. *Reception Theory: A Critical Introduction.* New York: Methuen, 1984.

Mailloux, Steven. "Learning to Read: Interpretation and Reader-Response Criticism." *Studies in the Literary Imagination* 12 (1979): 93–108.

———. "Reader-Response Criticism?" *Genre* 10 (1977): 413–31.

Rosenblatt, Louise M. "Towards a Transactional Theory of Reading." *Journal of Reading Behavior* 1 (1969): 31–47. Rpt. in Primeau 121–46.

Suleiman, Susan R. "Introduction: Varieties of Audience-Oriented Criticism." Suleiman and Crosman 3–45.

Tompkins, Jane P. "An Introduction to Reader-Response Criticism." Tompkins ix–xxiv.

Reader-Response Criticism in Anthologies and Collections

Fish, Stanley Eugene. *Is There a Text in This Class? The Authority of Interpretive Communities.* Cambridge: Harvard UP, 1980. In this volume are collected most of Fish's most influential essays, including "Literature in the Reader: Affective Stylistics," "What It's Like to Read *L'Allegro* and *Il Penseroso,*" "Interpreting the *Variorum,*" "Is There a Text in This Class?" "How to Recognize a Poem When You See One," and "What Makes an Interpretation Acceptable?"

Garvin, Harry R., ed. *Theories of Reading, Looking, and Listening.* Lewisburg: Bucknell UP, 1981. See the essays by Cain and Rosenblatt.

Leitch, Vincent B. *American Literary Criticism from the Thirties to the Eighties.* New York: Columbia UP, 1988.

Primeau, Ronald, ed. *Influx: Essays on Literary Influence.* Port Washington: Kennikat, 1977. See the essays by Fish, Holland, and Rosenblatt.

Suleiman, Susan R., and Inge Crosman, eds. *The Reader in the Text: Essays on Audience and Interpretation.* Princeton: Princeton UP, 1980. See especially the essays by Culler, Iser, and Todorov.

Tompkins, Jane P., ed. *Reader-Response Criticism: From Formalism to Post-Structuralism.* Baltimore: Johns Hopkins UP, 1980. See especially the essays by Bleich, Fish, Holland, Prince, and Tompkins.

Reader-Response Criticism: Some Major Works

Bleich, David. *Subjective Criticism.* Baltimore: Johns Hopkins UP, 1978.

Booth, Stephen. *An Essay on Shakespeare's Sonnets.* New Haven: Yale UP, 1969.

Eco, Umberto. *The Role of the Reader.* Bloomington: Indiana UP, 1979.

Fish, Stanley Eugene. *Self-Consuming Artifacts: The Experience of Seventeenth-Century Literature.* Berkeley: U of California P, 1972.

———. *Surprised by Sin: The Reader in Paradise Lost.* 2nd ed. Berkeley: U of California P, 1971.

Holland, Norman N. *5 Readers Reading.* New Haven: Yale UP, 1975.

Iser, Wolfgang. *The Act of Reading: A Theory of Aesthetic Response.* Baltimore: Johns Hopkins UP, 1978.

———. *The Implied Reader: Patterns of Communication in Prose Fiction from Bunyan to Beckett.* Baltimore: Johns Hopkins UP, 1974.

Jauss, Hans Robert. *Toward an Aesthetic of Reception.* Trans. Timothy Bahti. Intro. Paul de Man. Brighton, Eng.: Harvester, 1982.

Mailloux, Steven. *Interpretive Conventions: The Reader in the Study of American Fiction.* Ithaca: Cornell UP, 1982.

Messent, Peter. *New Readings of the American Novel: Narrative Theory and Its Application.* New York: Macmillan, 1991.

Prince, Gerald. *Narratology.* New York: Mouton, 1982.

Rabinowitz, Peter. *Before Reading: Narrative Conventions and the Politics of Interpretation.* Ithaca: Cornell UP, 1987.

Steig, Michael. *Stories of Reading: Subjectivity and Literary Understanding.* Baltimore: Johns Hopkins UP, 1989.

Exemplary Short Readings of Major Texts

Anderson, Howard. "*Tristram Shandy* and the Reader's Imagination." *PMLA* 86 (1971): 966–73.

Berger, Carole. "The Rake and the Reader in Jane Austen's Novels." *Studies in English Literature, 1500–1900* 15 (1975): 531–44.

Booth, Stephen. "On the Value of *Hamlet.*" *Reinterpretations of English Drama: Selected Papers from the English Institute.* Ed. Norman Rabkin. New York: Columbia UP, 1969. 137–76.

Easson, Robert R. "William Blake and His Reader in *Jerusalem.*" *Blake's Sublime Allegory.* Ed. Stuart Curran and Joseph A. Wittreich. Madison: U of Wisconsin P, 1973. 309–28.

Kirk, Carey H. "*Moby-Dick:* The Challenge of Response." *Papers on Language and Literature* 13 (1977): 383–90.

Leverenz, David. "Mrs. Hawthorne's Headache: Reading *The Scarlet Letter.*" *The Scarlet Letter: A Case Study in Contemporary Criticism.* Ed. Ross C Murfin. Boston: Bedford–St. Martin's, 1991. 263–74.

Lowe-Evans, Mary. "Reading with a 'Nicer Eye': Responding to *Frankenstein.*" *Mary Shelley, Frankenstein.* Ed. Johanna M. Smith. Case Studies in Contemporary Criticism Series. Ed. Ross C Murfin. Boston: Bedford–St. Martin's, 1992. 215–29.

Rosmarin, Adena. "Darkening the Reader: Reader-Response Criticism and *Heart of Darkness.*" *Heart of Darkness: A Case Study in Con-*

temporary Criticism. Ed. Ross C Murfin. Boston: Bedford–St. Martin's, 1989. 148–69.

Reader-Response Approaches to Joyce

Bleich, David. "The Conception and Documentation of the Author." *Subjective Criticism*. Baltimore: Johns Hopkins UP, 1978. On *Portrait*.

Iser, Wolfgang. *The Act of Reading: A Theory of Aesthetic Response*. Baltimore: Johns Hopkins UP, 1978; London: Routledge, 1979.

———. *The Implied Reader*. Ch. 7, "Doing Things in Style: An Interpretation of 'The Oxen of the Sun' in James Joyce's *Ulysses*." Baltimore: Johns Hopkins UP, 1974. 179–95.

———. "Patterns of Communication in Joyce's *Ulysses*." *New Perspectives in German Literary Criticism*. Ed. Richard E. Armacher & Victor Lange. Princeton: Princeton UP, 1979. 320–56.

James Joyce Quarterly 16 (Fall 1978/Winter 1979). "Structuralist/Reader-Response" issue.

Ruthrof, Horst. *The Reader's Construction of Narrative*. London and Boston: Routledge, 1981.

Thomas, Brook. *James Joyce's "Ulysses": A Book of Many Happy Returns*. Baton Rouge: Louisiana State UP, 1982.

Other Work Referred to in "What Is Reader-Response Criticism?"

Wimsatt, William K., and Monroe C. Beardsley. *The Verbal Icon*. Lexington: U of Kentucky P, 1954. See especially the discussion of "The Affective Fallacy," with which reader-response critics have so sharply disagreed.

A READER-RESPONSE PERSPECTIVE

NORMAN N. HOLLAND

A Portrait as Rebellion

Non serviam. That, to me, is the finest moment, the core of this novel, the point at which I engage it. "I will not serve that in which I no longer believe whether it call itself my home, my fatherland or my church" is the way Stephen finally puts it (p. 213).

For me, though, this is not only a novel about rebellion but also a novel that I rebel against. Lucifer's proud boast is my own, for I resist not only the forces the book describes but the book itself.

Were I writing in a modernist—by which I mean a formalist or "New Critical"—mode, I would not mention such negative feelings. I would be looking instead at the novel as a thing-in-itself. I would be doing "close reading," based on the assumption that the novel has its own internal logic, structure, and unity, all quite independent of me, simply waiting there to be discovered.

I might, for example (as in John Kelleher's classically New Critical exercise of 1958) trace the images of red and green, red for Michael Davitt, green for the martyred Parnell. Red for holly and hellfire, green for ivy and Ireland. Stephen transcends them as he moves toward white, the white crucifix (p. 129), white starlight, the white moon, "the white arms of roads, their promise of close embraces" (p. 218). This is the way we are expected to read Joyce, so as to achieve for ourselves his "symbolist" method (see Kelleher or O'Faolain 1954).

If so, I would be valuing Joyce's novel to the extent that it embodies enduring themes in complex forms. I would judge it according to whether it transcends the limitations of its particular time and place, turn-of-the-century Dublin, and achieves some universal meaning. But is there such a thing? Some meaning that holds true for believer and nonbeliever, feminist and masculinist, teenager and old-timer? I doubt it.

Writing as a postmodernist—and reader-response is a postmodern mode of criticism—I consider instead my relationship to *Portrait.* I achieve an experience of the novel in my act of writing about it. Indeed, from a psychological point of view, *Portrait* only comes into being as one or another of us experiences it. We can never know the novel except through some human mode of perceiving it.

It might then, following a suggestion of Jane Tompkins, value the novel in terms of my experience of it. What does it do for me? More properly, in reading it, what do I do for myself? This is a stance that reader-response criticism and feminist criticism share: Works of art offer strategies for dealing with personal, historical, and cultural issues, issues that matter to me and, I assume, to you. Reading *Portrait* in that way means exploring my own feelings and experience as I read, even though they might seem at first quite irrelevant.

I never much liked *Portrait* (until I started writing this essay and began to form a new relationship to it). I have trouble with its very first words. I find "baby tuckoo" unconvincing as baby talk. Who ever heard of "baby tuckoo"? It may be, as Chester G. Anderson suggests (142), that it echoes *tuck,* slang for food. Maybe baby Stephen is being told he is good or cute enough to eat, but that does not seem to me to improve the sound of it. As Anderson says, adults making baby talk do not substitute *t-* sounds for *k*-sounds. More likely, I think, Joyce is echoing here the cuckoo, famed for laying eggs in other birds' nests and hence an emblem for the cuckolding that so endlessly fascinated him. His mother plays the hornpipe, we might note.

The baby talk sounds unconvincing to me. So does his schoolboys' and his collegians' banter. I have to admit that my friends and I in school and college were by no means as clever. Danny and Burky and Hutch and I didn't go around dropping quips in dog Latin or making jokes about saints or quotations from the church fathers as do Dedalus and Lynch and Cranly and the rest. How fancy, how precious, how learned but how aimlessly learned are Joyce's Irish collegians.

Because of *Portrait*'s peculiar combination of novel and autobiography, I feel called upon to see Joyce's schoolfellows in two ways at once. They are characters in a novel, bigger than life, and they are real people like me and my school and college pals. Joyce insists that we take Stephen as seriously as we would take James Joyce himself, but surely no schoolboy has a right to demand that. Frankly, I end up feeling competitive with Cranly and Lynch and Quaid and Davin, no matter how deficient Joyce makes them out to be.

I have the most trouble of all with the last paragraphs. There at the finale, when Joyce should be most convincing, Stephen seems to me simply gassy. I find the final apostrophe insufferably pompous and pretentious, like a teenager with a walking-stick (as indeed Stephen is. The essayist Richard Steele remarked somewhere, "A cane is part of the dress of a prig." If that was true in the eighteenth century, how much more so was it in Stephen's day.) Stephen with his ashplant looks the dandy, no matter what its symbolic value as phallus, tree of life, ashes, the curved stick of an augur, and so on.

It's like Stephen's prose in that final apostrophe. That, too, I find inflated, foppish, Romantic with a capital *R*: "Welcome, O life! I go to encounter for the millionth time the reality of experience and to forge in the smithy of my soul the uncreated conscience of my race" (p. 218). How can one take this seriously? "Welcome, O life!" Give me a break! I'll let you in on something. Life is already here. "The reality of experience"? Don't I face that every time I drink my morning coffee? "The smithy of my soul." For a late twentieth-century freethinker like me, it is hard to hear the word "soul" as other than Romantic maundering. It reminds me of the gray-bearded poets of my high school textbooks. Joyce echoes clichés like Longfellow's thumpity-thump trochaic tetrameters:

> Life is real! Life is earnest!
> And the grave is not its goal;
> Dust thou art, to dust returnest,
> Was not spoken of the soul.

Indeed, Joyce's sentence is uncomfortably close to Browning's consummately Victorian ejaculation, "I go to prove my soul!" "The hyperbolic resonance of Stephen's invocation leads us to suspect that his fate will prove Icarian rather than Daedalian," writes Suzette Henke in a wily academic joke (p. 324). "The artist's talents are woefully incommensurate with his idealistic conceptions," she comments, referring to the villanelle that Stephen so contemns. Yet the villanelle is far better than this.

"The uncreated conscience of my race." Surely one of the problems of the Irish as Joyce describes them is that they have altogether too much conscience. Stephen treats himself much too seriously here. Has he no sense of humor? He needs rather to take himself *cum grano sanguinarii salis,* (with a grain of bloody salt), as Cranly might say.

Joyce baffles me here. How could he, with his incredible ear for the voices of others, choose such phrasings at such a crucial point in his novel? That is, for me, the mystery of mysteries in *Portrait.* It is a mystery to many other critics too, to judge from James Sosnoski's earlier reader-response essay on *Portrait* or Hugh Kenner's disappointment: "The dark intensity of the first four chapters is moving enough, but our impulse on being confronted with the final edition of Stephen Dedalus is to laugh" (Kenner 132).

"Old father, old artificer, stand me now and ever in good stead."

Now that's better. Stephen's invocation of Daedalus and the spirit of the artist-scientist using his genius to soar free from the tyrant Minos—that is the true *non serviam*. That speaks to me as a skeptic, a freethinker, unbeliever, atheist. I can share Joyce/Stephen's resistance to the theocracy of his Ireland.

As an irreligious, even antireligious man, I resent the trip being run on these young men. I read *Portrait* as the terrible wrong of carving religion into the minds of the young. As I imagine Stephen and his classmates sitting in rows listening to "the preacher," I think of the image from Kafka's *In the Penal Colony* of a horrible punishment machine scratching into the skin of its nameless victim the name of his sin. The education of Stephen and his pals creates a gap in their minds that will ever after have to be filled. Ever after, there will be that longing for the soothing illusion that something supernatural exists that will somehow nurture or punish or reward you. Even if you rebel, the subject can never be neutral for you. The gap is always there, the wish for, and the absence of, a benevolent all-soul.

And it's all pinned to sex. I read Joyce's autobiographical novel as the memoirs of a Christian adolescence, not unlike my own, probably like a lot of people's. Joyce documents the time-honored conflict between adolescent glands swelling with desire against our ancient Judeo-Christian prudery. God is Who watches you masturbate. Joyce used to complain that readers would leave out the last four words of his title. This is a portrait of the artist *as a young man*, as a sexually driven creature, awash in testosterone.

As a freethinking sexual being, I have a morbid curiosity about those three sermons. For me, they form the centerpiece of the novel. Reflecting, I suppose, my own childhood hours spent in church and Sunday school, as well as my present unbelief, they sound utterly convincing to me. I've heard these priestly words before, enforcing ideas of sin, guilt, and fear.

The first sermon (pp. 102–04) sets the stage for the others. We are to hear of "the four last things. . . . death, judgment, hell, and heaven" (p. 103). Joyce uses direct quotation. The preacher speaks in his own voice to the "dear little brothers in Christ." "The next day brought death and judgment" (p. 104). Stephen/Joyce writes as though the words were the things themselves.

I find this second sermon an astonishing narrative achievement. I hear it as though I am inside Stephen's head, as in his mind he makes the preacher's words and images his own. Those words and images are like a thing. "The preacher's knife had probed deeply into his diseased conscience" (p. 107). Words—he remembers writing obscene letters and leaving them for girls to find. Now he fantasizes himself and Emma united like loving, erring children, but as he imagines the red-lit chapel of their wedding it becomes the chapel of the third sermon (pp. 108–14).

This one deals with hell, and we hear it in the preacher's words directly, as he urges his listeners into various acts of imagination to make the torments of hell the more real. "Remember the fire of hell gives forth no light." "Imagine some foul and putrid corpse. . . ." "Place your finger for a moment in the flame of a candle. . . ." Imagination in the service of guilt. Outside the rain pours down in what seems like the biblical flood of forty days and forty nights. (But in one of Joyce's vitalist touches, a boy says, "It might clear up, sir" [p. 115]).

"Time passed," and Stephen goes to the fourth sermon. (I had expected a sermon on heaven, but we will not get it from this gifted but life-denying orator. All his eloquence goes to death and torture.) Again, the preacher impresses the very faculty of imagination into the service of torment for guilt.

> This morning we endeavoured . . . to imagine with the senses of the mind, in our imagination, the material character of that awful place and of the physical torments which all who are in hell endure. This evening we shall consider for a few moments the nature of the spiritual torments of hell. (p. 116)

He begins with loss, goes on to the "threefold sting of conscience," to extension, to intensity, and then to the tour de force: eternity.

The preacher asks us to imagine a mountain of sand and a bird coming once every million years to carry one grain away—that would not be even one instant of eternity. Skeptic though I may be, I cannot help being swept up in this astonishing act of imagination. Never before have I come even close to imagining eternity. Yet my more rational self drily says, "If you will believe that you will believe anything."

Stephen, of course, does believe it. "The thought slid like a cold shining rapier into his tender flesh" (p. 116). He imagines his own particular excremental hell, prays for forgiveness, and confesses. But here is another of Joyce's vitalist touches. He does not confess at the school, but at a church and to a priest where he is not known. Stephen repents but does not seek the fullest punishment or shame he could inflict on himself. Bravo.

He may have hedged his bets, but nevertheless he can go to mass. "The ciborium had come to him" (from the Greek *kiborion*, the seed vessel of the lotus). "God would enter his purified body." The word made flesh would enter his body, the word which is the seed. The novel is all about words, in a way, and their power apparently to imprison us, to mark us, to free us, but most of all to control us, particularly our sexuality.

Look, for example, at what this drilled-in sexual inhibition does to Stephen's attitudes toward women. A woman cannot simply be a human being. Stephen is living out Freud's classic oedipal paradigm. "God was too great and stern and the Blessed Virgin too pure and holy" (p. 108). Because of the severity of the resulting repression of sexuality, woman becomes either a figure of supernatural goodness, a blessed virgin, a madonna, or, if she allows sex at all, a whore. (It is surely no coincidence that the most commercially successful female entertainer of the 1980s, and the most ingeniously and profitably sexual, should choose to be known by the name Madonna.) "The glories of Mary held his soul captive" (p. 98). "If ever he was impelled to cast sin from him and to repent the impulse that moved him was the wish to be her knight" (p. 99). I sense here not only Joyce's thoughts on Stephen's problems with women but also Joyce's own tormented jealousy of Nora, his hankering after her underwear, his fantastic love letters to her. He can pray to her as the spirit of eternal beauty and tenderness in one sentence and in the next create a catalogue of positions and orifices that would exhaust the imagination of the most ingenious or sadistic eroticist. Then he retracts, claiming that what he has written is only a moment of brutish madness (Shechner 90–91).

I agree with Suzette Henke's claim that before Stephen can become a priest of the imagination (as the finale bombastically proposes), he needs to shed the adolescent—and Christian—combination of fear, idealization, and contempt of woman. I do not think he does, nor did Joyce himself. Joyce's letters show the mature husband still polarized in the classic Freudian manner between woman as virginal ideal and woman as whore. And it interfered with his writing. Joyce the novelist was never able fully to realize a woman character. Even the magnificent Molly Bloom, Mark Shechner points out (205), lacks the inner conflicts of a realistic human being (unlike Bloom or Stephen).

Less classically Freudian than Joyce's polarization of woman into virgin or whore is his feeling that woman is also the punisher (at least as I read *Portrait*). It derives from woman's being not simply a human being but a mystical figure endowed with vast powers for good or evil. I sense it first with Stephen's mother's power on the first page: "She played . . . the sailor's hornpipe for him to dance" (p. 19). It goes on to Dante. She threatens that eagles will pull out the boy's eyes for his amorous fantasies. She rages at the adulterous Parnell. "God and religion before everything! Dante cried. God and religion before the world!" "We won! We crushed him to death!" (p. 46).

Woman as punisher grows into the punishing priests in their skirts (*les jupes*). The swish of the soutane. The swish of the cane and the pandybat. The swish of a skirt. *Frou-frou.* Part of what drives Stephen to prostitutes and guilty promiscuity is sheer physical need to assert his masculinity against his passive, priest-ridden countrymen, his "dear little brothers in Christ."

If woman was the occasion for Stephen's guilt, I think it fitting, then, if not entirely healthy, that Stephen finds his freedom from guilt through a vision of woman. Woman as virgin? Woman as object of desire? Woman as muse? The crane-girl, anyway. He turns to the sea, symbol of the ancient mother, rebirth, the unconscious:

> A girl stood before him in midstream: alone and still, gazing out to sea. She seemed like one whom magic had changed into the likeness of a strange and beautiful seabird. Her long slender bare legs were delicate as a crane's. . . . Her thighs, fuller and soft-hued as ivory, were bared almost to the hips where the white fringes of her drawers were like featherings of soft white down. (p. 151)

What an extraordinary comparison! I can't help wondering if Joyce knew the various meanings people have given the crane. (Knowing Joyce, I think it likely he did.) Robert Graves noted that in India the crane is associated with the mother-goddess Kali, the destroyer (Graves 538). The cranes also make letters as they fly—in their *V*-formations (242, 507). Hence, in ancient Ireland, the crane was associated with literary secrets (249). Hence, too, the crane is sacred to Delian Apollo, god of learning, and to Thoth, whose symbol was a cranelike white ibis, who invented writing and reformed the calendar (241). Thoth and Apollo are, of course, two of Stephen's tutelary deities, literary ideals that substitute for the punitive God of the priests.

According to various classical legends, Graves reports, the alphabet was brought to Greece by Mercury, carried in a bag made of the skin of a crane (248). The bag itself was protected with a Gorgon head (248), which, if we follow Freud (1940), symbolizes the female genitals. In a very literal way, the downy drawers of the crane-girl contain both the creative secret of woman and the secret of writing. She is both the punishing mother (Dante) and the desired woman who holds the secret of creativity, at least if I read her according to goddess-obsessed Graves; and *se non é vero, é ben trovato* (even if it isn't true, it's a clever invention).

The ivory in her coloring echoes Solomon's Song of Songs: "Thy neck is as a tower of ivory" (7:4). Joyce mentions the passage before, attributing it to the Virgin Mary, as is traditional in Roman Catholic readings of the Song of Songs. But here it is the woman's thighs that are ivory. The ivory tower is also the traditional retreat of poets, making Stephen's, like Hamlet's, "a fair thought to lie between maid's legs."

No wonder, then, that Stephen takes his redemptive vision of the crane-girl as both a spiritual and a bodily experience. "Heavenly God! cried Stephen's soul, in an outburst of profane joy." *Profane* is *pro* + *fana,* before or outside the temple, hence not sacred, as this sentence is outside the phrase preceding, "the bells of sleep." But to me the temple and bell here are the church of her body with its green seaweed and crimson secret.

I am, however, a male writing as a male. Fortunately, we can contrast a female reader's response. Florence Howe responds to "Stephen's inability to relate humanly to a young girl" in this way:

> Why, I asked myself, should a young Catholic Irishman look at a young girl on a beach and think not of loving or marrying her (or of other things) but rather of flying away—of rising as a "hawklike man" and evading family, church, nation? I had never asked the question before, nor [as a student] had it been asked of me.
>
> Why does the youthful male artist have to see a *girl,* not a bird or a young man in order to make his decision, to know that he must split from his family, church, nation? to feel "the riot of his blood?"
>
> "The riot of his blood" sends him flying—away from the girl. He even takes the measure of maleness against the girl's biological potential as a woman. . . . Stephen, too, will be able "to recreate life out of life." Not as a biological woman, but as an artist, an image-maker.
>
> But to see the scene and the novel with this point of view is also to make specific the maleness of Joyce's view—rather than its alleged universality. (Howe 261–63)

I agree with Howe. Joyce's polarized view of women reveals deep limits to his vision.

Nevertheless, if I may be male and abstract, I think Joyce is reaching for universality around an issue different from gender: the word. "Her image had passed into his soul for ever, and no word had broken the holy silence of his ecstasy." This is a call but a kind of call far different from the preacher's call to avoid sin that led to guilt and words entering his body like a knife. This is image, not word, indeed no word at all. This is a call "to live, to err, to fall, to triumph, to recreate life out of life!" Stephen has seen "an envoy from the fair courts of life . . . throw open before him in an instant of ecstasy the gates of all the ways of error and glory" (p. 152), all the joy and triumph of being the imperfect, natural beings we are. The colors that *Portrait* has associated with the Virgin—white, gold, blue, and ivory—come together in the figure of the crane-girl and with them, red and green again, the seaweed on her leg "and a faint flame . . . on her cheek" (p. 152), and, although he does not mention it, her crimson lips within the downy white drawers.

At that moment, Stephen feels above him "the vast indifferent dome" and below him "the earth that had borne him, had taken him to her breast." He is freed of the father-god, now indifferent, and he lies down in a "nook" of mother earth.

Half-asleep, he has a vision of a rose. I feel sure Joyce intends here to echo the vision of the Celestial Rose with the Virgin Mary at its center that climaxes the *Paradiso* and *The Divine Comedy.* Here he sees it: "an opening flower, it spread in endless succession to itself, breaking in full crimson and unfolding and fading to palest rose, leaf by leaf and . . . every flush deeper than other" (p. 152). Red and green again, but this is a far different Dante and a far different red and green from Dante's hairbrushes.

This, for me, is the moment at which Stephen achieves freedom from the sin-and-punishment religion, the "squalor and insincerity" (p. 68) of Dublin, the "squalor and subterfuge" (p. 151) of his own boyhood and body. But Joyce is wiser than I. It will take more.

Chapter four ends with the vision. Chapter five plunges Stephen back into the dirty kitchen of the Dedalus household, the lousemarked box of pawn tickets, the incoherent clocks, his mother's anti-intellectualism, his father's drunken profanity, his own lackadaisical career at the university, and the limitations of his fellow students. It will take more than a vision to free Stephen Dedalus. It will take words.

"Ivory," however, is now just a word emptied of sense. The ivy, we might note, is sacred to Osiris and Dionysus, symbolizing rebirth because it grows in a spiral (Graves 190), *"twines upon the wall"* (p. 157). But in Stephen's ear, "Ivory ivy." "Did any one ever hear such drivel?" As for drawers,

> *Lottie Collins lost her drawers;*
> *Won't you kindly lend her yours?* (p. 172)

The vision of the crane-girl allows Stephen only a momentary escape from the squalor of Dublin, the letters of whose name are, in his mind, "pushing one another surlily hither and thither with slow boorish insistence" (p. 104). B-l-i-n-d, b-u-i-l-d, d-u-b-l, b-l-u-i-n, u-n-b-i-d, b-i-n-d, n-i-l, n-u-l, d-u-n. Stephen has gone back to where words instead of the sexual image enter his mind and body.

That is the way words work in *Portrait*. They enter you and you enter them. Either way the word is made flesh, your flesh. In the opening sentences of the novel, his father told him that story. He *was* baby tuckoo. "Baby tuckoo" literally exists only *in* his father's story. Words surround and control him then, at the beginning, and throughout the rest of the novel until the final apostrophe.

As a psychological critic, I have to protest. This is not the way the human mind makes meaning from language. This is a nineteenth-century idea of language, invented before there was such a thing as psycholinguistics (Holland). Now, post-Chomsky, this idea of language is outmoded and disproven. Yet I grant Joyce a psychological truth. It *feels* as though this is the way language works. It *feels* as though the preacher's words could enter a conscience like a knife.

We began with Joyce in his father's story. As we end he invokes his father again, but now the mythic Daedalus, neither Irish father nor priestly "Father." Had Stephen become a priest he would have been a "Father," but in a purely verbal way—not an actual father.

At the same time Stephen is the son. He is the sacrificial victim who gives himself up to forge the conscience of his race. Throughout the novel there are recurring fantasies of rebirth, but of a spiritual, not a sexual kind (although there is that word, *Fœtus,* carved in the medical students' desk).

We can read *Portrait* as a battle of wills and a battle of words, a *logomachia*. What Stephen needs to free himself from is guilt over sex, and it is a sexual vision that frees him. So with words. They are both the instrument of his imprisonment and the key to his freedom. On the one side there are the words that seek to overpower Stephen and unsex him. On the other, as we have seen, are the wordless sexual images and, now, the words he mounts as his defense against the "squalor."

Words do more than just defend. They counterattack. That is, words are Stephen's way of entering the minds and bodies of others. He finds their being by imitating their language. He gets into the minds of his father or the preacher or his schoolfellows by finding and creating their voices. He has to read them, trying to understand the mysteries, in the same way as he reads the birds in Molesworth Street as augurs. He gets into girls' minds by leaving obscene letters for them to find.

As with those letters, when Stephen/Joyce counterattacks, he tries to use words to control others. That is another reason I find this book so hard to like. Joyce controls me so, or tries to. He even tells me, in the aesthetics lecture Stephen delivers to Lynch, how to read his book. I feel I have to follow his prescription if I am fully to experience his novel.

Stephen addresses (like a reader-response critic!) the question of how we respond to art, "the necessary phases of artistic apprehension" (p. 184). Drawing on Aquinas's logic he "proves" the "qualities of universal beauty." They are, of course, three, in this Thomistic world, where triune syllogisms march down the classroom aisle as the triforia and the tricostate arches march down the aisles of a gothic cathedral. *Integritas,* "a bounding line drawn about the object to be apprehended" (p. 184). Then *consonantia:* "you apprehend it as balanced part against part within its limits; you feel the rhythm of its structure" (p. 185). Finally, *claritas.* This is the most elusive. Stephen describes it in terms of light, "radiance." The mind is in "the luminous silent stasis of esthetic pleasure" (p. 185).

As I read him, Joyce is trying to articulate the novel, the character Stephen within the novel and himself outside it, as Aquinas articulated the beautiful. Stephen's ethical program follows Aquinas's aesthetic formula.

At this point in the novel, Stephen's lecture on the apprehension of beauty, we are halfway through chapter five. So far, we have seen Stephen's own development approximate the theory. At first he must be, simply, Stephen, separated from his parents and his schoolmates, a separation he achieves by his sexual and spiritual promiscuity. Second, in the middle of the novel, we get *consonantia,* "complex, multiple, divisible, separable, made up of its parts, the result of its parts and their sum, harmonious." We get, in fact, the conflict within Stephen between his sexual and his spiritual natures, uneasily harmonized in chapter four. (For a different, but appealing, reading of the structure, see Sheldon Brivic's 1976 essay and his chart reproduced here on p. 262.)

The final apostrophe, is that the wished-for *claritas?* Far from it, I think. *Claritas* Stephen describes as the essential "*whatness* of a thing," "that thing which it is and no other thing" (p. 185). But this is precisely what Stephen does not have: a sense of who or what he is. From his theory of beauty we proceed to his liquid morning composition of the doubtful villanelle ("in the virgin womb of the imagination the word was made flesh''), to his trying to read the birds, to the music hall and the raucous banter of his fellow students. No whatness there.

What I see instead in the last half of chapter five is Stephen's return to the beginning of his Thomistic aesthetics, to *integritas*. By his final rebellion and exile, he isolates himself. "Not only to be separate from all others but to have not even one friend," says Cranly. "I will take the risk, said Stephen."

From that passage (p. 213), he goes on to the final series of journal entries, and in *Portrait* the last paragraphs show no sign of Thomistic harmony. The tundish and the secondhand clothes and the superstitious old peasant jostle the romantic dreams about hoofs that shine like gems and the arms of roads and the voices of ships calling to him their "exultant and terrible youth" (p. 218). The final pages of the novel, both in form and content, give us the analysis of Stephen/Joyce into his conflicted parts, culminating in the final apostrophe.

The elusive *claritas?* I don't see it. Stephen's final values, "the reality of experience" and "the uncreated conscience of my race" seem to me altogether un-Thomistic. Rather, they are full of earthy complexity and spiritual rebellion. He will make his own conscience and that of his people, not take it from the Angelic Doctor.

Joyce tells us how to read his novel. Joyce is trying to free us all, but paradoxically he tries to control us to do it. He is rather like the priests in that. He would control us as he was controlled. But in the ending, he abandons the harmonies of St. Thomas, and he gives up his effort to control us. In that sense, Joyce tries to free us as he tries to free himself.

In the final paragraphs, he finds agreement with his mother's plea that he learn what the heart is. "Amen. So be it. Welcome, O life!" At this moment, Joyce seems to me to come close to one of the two fantasies of the novel. I must immerse myself in what is feminizing, dangerous, even filthy in order to transmute it to art and beauty. It goes back to the earliest pages: the warm smell of his mother's slippers and of the oilcloth she put on his bed-wetting. Stephen accepts the need to embrace what is earthy, low, dirty, foul, or simply trivial—and yes, Howe is right, Joyce thinks of that as feminine—before he will turn it into beauty.

To do the transforming, he calls on his father, who is both the scheming, drunken Simon who eludes landlords and the Greek artificer who eludes a tyrant-king. As the craftsman, as Thoth or Daedalus, he makes words as a defense against the words that seek to overpower him. That is the second fantasy. He will make words inside his own body, words that are not the words of others entering him, words that are not dirt, but beauty and life. Stephen will become Daedalus, "the artist forging anew in his workshop out of the sluggish matter of the earth a new soaring impalpable imperishable being" (p. 149). "Yes! he would create proudly out of the freedom and power of his soul, as the great artificer whose name he bore, a living thing, new and soaring and beautiful, impalpable, imperishable" (p. 150). He will give birth.

There is an unquoted part of the line from Ovid's *Metamorphoses* (VIII, 188) that Joyce chose as his epigraph. It is about Daedalus: *Et ignotas animum dimittit in artes* (He turned his thinking toward strange arts). But people don't quote—Joyce himself didn't quote—the rest of the sentence: *naturam novatque* (and he changed the order of nature).

"I go to forge in the smithy of my soul." There, in his dark, sooty, fiery innards, reminiscent of the preacher's smelly hell, but hardly "the virgin womb of the imagination" where he made the mushy villanelle, there he will forge (form, but also counterfeit) words.

These words will be the conscience of his race. The word, like the epigraph, is artfully chosen. *Com* + *scire* in Latin means to know with others, but *com* is also an intensive, so the combination means to know well, intensely, like conscience. *Scire* is to know, as in *science* or *conscious* or *prescient,* but these noble Roman words rest on the Indo-European root *skei-*, to cut or split, as in *schism* or *schizo-* but also, laughably, from the root's fundamental meaning (separation) to *shit.*

So, too, the last word of the novel, *stead,* a place (customarily occupied by another). It is both related to the Latin *stare* and stems from the Indo-European root, *sta-*, to stand. From it come all kinds of masculine words: *steed, stallion, stud, stalwart,* but also *stool* (hence an altogether suitable word on which to end—no pun intended).

I am saying that we could talk about Stephen's fantasies of making things from his insides as anality, but let me leave that to my psychoanalytic colleague, Sheldon Brivic. It is enough for me to say that I find the deepest element of my response to the novel is control. Will words enter my body, or will I make my own? Who will control this making of words? Not the priests, not the collegians, not the parents—Stephen himself.

I understand the final pages as Stephen's way of dealing with the question of control in his terms. Partly, he accepts being controlled. He accepts his mother's plea and with it the joy and triumph implicit in our messy human imperfection. But partly he asserts his own control, when he accepts his father (as "old artificer") and his own inner making with the proud claim that he *will* transcend the imperfection he has just accepted. Together, these last invocations make a resolution of sorts. They echo the first page's invocation of a narrator-father, a protomuse (Betty Byrne of the lemon platt), and his desired (but controlling), smelly mother.

In these last pages, I feel Joyce is asking me—us—to recognize the artist even if he is not there yet. He asks me to recognize as he does, not just his "new secondhand clothes" but his new secondhand prose, and to accept it. He asks me to have faith that it is out of that raw material that he will make the amazing art of *Ulysses* and the *Wake*. He is not that fabulous artificer yet. He asks me to have faith that Joyce is more than Stephen, and, of course, I know he will be, although he did not yet know it. This is a portrait of the artist *as a young man,* before he has succeeded in becoming the artist. Joyce asks me to have his faith in himself as an artist, a faith very different from the priests' faith.

I can recover Stephen's florid prose, then (as, for example, Hugh Kenner does) by recognizing that it is not Joyce's but Stephen's. Joyce is using Stephen's very pretentiousness to create a larger context and a greater art. It is for that high aim that Stephen is to become the fabulous artificer. In these last paragraphs he is not yet.

In effect, I am to swap with Joyce. I am to accept Stephen's overdone prose as I would accept any of the other idioms in the book, as part of life. If I accept the failure of the ending, then I accept this secondhand world as Joyce says I should, and so I accept the novel as a whole.

I do so because I long to possess this novel, to enjoy it. I long as Stephen longs to possess his muse, the crane-girl, the Virgin Mother, the ideal beauty. I long to sense and have the wholeness of Joyce's creation, to put the red and green together. To do that, I need to unbend. I need to relax my rebellion. If I can accept the prose, I can enjoy the novel.

At the same time, I feel competitive with Joyce. I wish that I could write— could have written—such funny and lifelike dialogue as his collegians' banter. I feel controlled by Joyce's imagination, even as he feels controlled by the eloquence of "the preacher" and the other clergy who try to shape his life for him. I resent his efforts to control me, while at the same time I feel sympathy for his efforts to escape the rhetoric that surrounds him and threatens to sink him in the paralysis of Dublin. I hear in his situation echoes of my own adolescence, my parents' plan for me—I was to be a lawyer —and my straining against them, trying to free myself to be a writer and critic. Stephen/Joyce's struggle is mine. But I still feel competitive with Joyce.

I have been rambling, as reader-response critics are entitled to do. At least as important as Joyce's issues of control, then, are my own. What have I been writing here? If you were to read this essay as you read *Portrait,* what themes would you find? I have said, first of all and last of all, *non serviam.* He asks me, in those final paragraphs, to have faith, and I have refused. I resist Joyce's control.

I resist his baby talk, the students' banter, and the final romantic shout. Instead, I choose what to admire, and I choose the sermons, knowing I can and do limit them. I'm in control. I can admire his vision of the crane-girl, and I can share it, but I can also attack Joyce for his failure to see women whole and for his masculinist bias. I share his *logomachia:* Will society's words control me, or will I and my words escape? I infer Joyce's unconscious fantasies about his mother and father and, at the deepest level, his fantasy that he can accept into himself the imperfections of the world and, inside his body, turn them into eternal beauty, just as a woman makes a baby inside her body. Reading the novel that way, putting my psychoanalytic, mythological, and philological talents to work, I can make it into an occasion for my own act of creation. Then, and only then, do I submit to it. Only then do I accept Joyce's final pages.

What am I submitting to? I think it is the power of the artist over me, the power that is so immense in Joyce. It feels dangerous to me. I do not like the idea of another man controlling me. (Is that why I am a reader-response critic? Devoutly insisting that authors do not have that power? But I am right. I am, I am.) And am I not dealing with the same thing that Joyce—as I read him—fears and escapes and transcends? Am I not trying to do exactly what Stephen, my version of Stephen, does? To come to terms with what I fear and idolize, to be able to work it as a smith works metal at his forge and so make it my own making? To have a faith that I have, in other contexts, refused?

It is in this sense that, as critics like to say nowadays, we read the text, but the text reads us. When I ask whether I am controlling the novel or being controlled by it, I am showing my own concern with control as much as Joyce's. The question for you is, do you share that concern? I suspect that you may.

You and I may not be freeing ourselves from Ireland or Catholicism or aestheticism, but we *are* freeing ourselves. The very act of reading, whatever the actual psychology of it, requires that we agree to *feel* as though Joyce's words enter and control our minds. Our task as readers, though, is also to make ourselves new from his words, to free ourselves from them. In that sense *Portrait* is a portrait, not just of the artist, but of every one of us. It lets us see ourselves as we make our own sense of what we read. When we do, Joyce makes into an artist not only himself, but every one of us.

WORKS CITED

Anderson, Chester G. "Baby Tuckoo: Joyce's 'Features of Infancy.'" *Approaches to Joyce's "Portrait": Ten Essays.* Ed. Thomas F. Staley and Bernard Benstock. Pittsburgh: U of Pittsburgh P, 1976. 135–69.

Brivic, Sheldon. "Joyce in Progress: A Freudian View." *James Joyce Quarterly* 13 (1976): 306–27.

Freud, Sigmund. "Medusa's Head" (1940). *Standard Edition* 18: 273–74.

Graves, Robert. *The White Goddess: A Historical Grammar of Poetic Myth.* Amended and enlarged ed. New York: Vintage, 1960.

Henke, Suzette. "Stephen Dedalus and Women: A Portrait of the Artist as a Young Misogynist." *Women in Joyce.* Ed. Suzette Henke and Elaine Unkeless. Urbana: U of Illinois P, 1982.

Holland, Norman N. *The Critical I.* New York: Columbia UP, 1991.

Howe, Florence. "Feminism and Literature." *Images of Women in Fiction: Feminist Perspectives.* Ed. Susan Koppelman Cornillon. Bowling Green: Bowling Green U Popular P, 1972. 253–77.

Joyce, James. *A Portrait of the Artist as a Young Man: Text, Criticism, and Notes.* Ed. Chester G. Anderson. New York: Viking/Penguin, 1968.

Kelleher, John V. "The Perceptions of James Joyce." *Atlantic Monthly* 201.3 (1958): 82–90.

Kenner, Hugh. "The *Portrait* in Perspective." *Dublin's Joyce* (1956). Boston: Beacon, 1962. 109–133.

O'Faolain, Sean. "Commentary." *A Portrait of the Artist as a Young Man.* By James Joyce. New York: Signet Books/New American Library, 1954. i–iv; 200–02.

Ovid. *Metamorphoses. Ovid in Six Volumes.* Trans. Frank Justus Miller. 2nd ed. Rev. G. P. Goold. The Loeb Classical Library. Cambridge: Harvard UP, 1974.

Shechner, Mark. *Joyce in Nighttown.* Berkeley: U of California P, 1974.

Sosnoski, James J. "Reading Acts and Reading Warrants: Some Implications for Readers Responding to Joyce's Portrait of Stephen." *James Joyce Quarterly* (Fall 1978/Winter 1979), 43–63.

Tompkins, Jane. *Sensational Designs: The Cultural Work of American Fiction, 1790–1860.* New York: Oxford UP, 1985.

Feminist Criticism and *A Portrait of the Artist as a Young Man*

WHAT IS FEMINIST CRITICISM?

From the title page on, *A Portrait of the Artist as a Young Man* seems to focus mainly on men and the masculine experience. Where women appear in its pages, they seem to be either virgins or whores, mothers or muses. Can such a novel survive, let alone be enriched by, feminist analysis? What would feminist criticism have to gain from an analysis of *Portrait*? Joyce's novel seems too easy a target; a novel by Emily Brontë or Mary Shelley, even Nathaniel Hawthorne or Thomas Hardy, would seem to offer better rewards all around—to the author, to the text, to the reader, and to the feminist project.

In fact, though, there *is* value in looking at *Portrait* from a feminist perspective. For one thing, feminist criticism comes in many forms, and feminist critics have a variety of goals. One group of feminist critics, for instance, revisits books by male authors and looks at them from a woman's point of view to see how they reflect attitudes that have held women back. Furthermore, books by male authors may contain within them not only the chauvinistic prejudices of their times but also the seeds of a more enlightened perspective.

The following survey of several feminist approaches and goals indicates why a feminist critic might want to write about Joyce's *Portrait*. And the essay that follows this introduction will suggest ways in which Joyce's novel advances the cause of women *and* men by revealing sexist attitudes stifling the very creativity by which the young artist would live.

Since the early 1970s three strains of feminist criticism have emerged, strains that can be categorized as French, American, and British. These categories should not be allowed to obscure either the global implications of the women's movement or the fact that interests and ideas have been shared by feminists from France, Great Britain, and the United States. British and American feminists have examined similar problems while writing about many of the same writers and works, and American feminists have recently become more receptive to French theories about femininity and writing. Historically speaking, however, French, American, and British feminists have examined similar problems from somewhat different perspectives.

French feminists have tended to focus their attention on language, analyzing the ways in which meaning is produced. They have concluded that language as we commonly think of it is a decidedly male realm. Drawing on the ideas of the psychoanalytic philosopher Jacques Lacan, French feminists remind us that language is a realm of public discourse. A child enters the linguistic realm just as it comes to grasp its separateness from its mother, just about the time that boys identify with their father, the family representative of culture. The language learned reflects a binary logic that opposes such terms as active/passive, masculine/feminine, sun/moon, father/mother, head/heart, son/daughter, intelligent/sensitive, brother/sister, form/matter, phallus/vagina, reason/emotion. Because this logic tends to group with masculinity such qualities as light, thought, and activity, French feminists have said that the structure of language is phallocentric: it privileges the phallus and, more generally, masculinity by associating them with things and values more appreciated by the (masculine-dominated) culture. Moreover, French feminists believe, "masculine desire dominates speech and posits woman as an idealized fantasy-fulfillment for the incurable emotional lack caused by separation from the mother" (Jones 83).

In the view of French feminists, language is associated with separation from the mother. Its distinctions represent the world from the male point of view, and it systematically forces women to choose: either they can imagine and represent themselves as men imagine and represent them (in which case they may speak, but will speak as men) or they can choose "silence," becoming in the process "the invisible and unheard sex" (Jones 83).

But some influential French feminists have argued that language only *seems* to give women such a narrow range of choices. There is another possibility, namely that women can develop a *feminine* language. In various ways, early French feminists such as Annie Leclerc, Xavière Gauthier, and Marguerite Duras have suggested that there is something that may be called *l'écriture féminine:* women's writing. Recently, Julia Kristeva has said that feminine language is "semiotic," not "symbolic." Rather than rigidly opposing and ranking elements of reality, rather than symbolizing one thing but not another in terms of a third, feminine language is rhythmic and unifying. If from the male perspective it seems fluid to the point of being chaotic, that is a fault of the male perspective.

According to Kristeva, feminine language is derived from the preoedipal period of fusion between mother and child. Associated with the maternal, feminine language is not only threatening to culture, which is patriarchal, but also a medium through which women may be creative in new ways. But Kristeva has paired her central, liberating claim – that truly feminist innovation in all fields requires an understanding of the relation between maternity and feminine creation – with a warning. A feminist language that refuses to participate in "masculine" discourse, that places its future entirely in a feminine, semiotic discourse, risks being politically marginalized by men. That is to say, it risks being relegated to the outskirts (pun intended) of what is considered socially and politically significant.

Kristeva, who associates feminine writing with the female body, is joined in her views by other leading French feminists. Hélène Cixous, for instance, also posits an essential connection between the woman's body, whose sexual pleasure has been repressed and denied expression, and women's writing. "Write your self. Your body must be heard," Cixous urges; once they learn to write their bodies, women will not only realize their sexuality but enter history and move toward a future based on a "feminine" economy of giving rather than the "masculine" economy of hoarding (Cixous 250). For Luce Irigaray, women's sexual pleasure (*jouissance*) cannot be expressed by the dominant, ordered, "logical," masculine language. She explores the connection between women's sexuality and women's language through the following analogy: as women's *jouissance* is more multiple than men's unitary, phallic pleasure ("woman has sex organs just about everywhere"), so "feminine" language is more diffusive than its "masculine" counterpart. ("That is undoubtedly the reason . . . her language . . . goes off in all directions and . . . he is unable to discern the coherence," Irigaray writes [101–03].)

Cixous's and Irigaray's emphasis on feminine writing as an expression of the female body has drawn criticism from other French feminists. Many argue that an emphasis on the body either reduces "the feminine" to a biological essence or elevates it in a way that shifts the valuation of masculine and feminine but retains the binary categories. For Christine Fauré, Irigaray's celebration of women's difference fails to address the issue of masculine dominance, and a Marxist-feminist, Catherine Clément, has warned that "poetic" descriptions of what constitutes the feminine will not challenge that dominance in the realm of production. The boys will still make the toys and decide who gets to use them. In her effort to redefine women as political rather than as sexual beings, Monique Wittig has called for the abolition of sexual categories that Cixous and Irigaray retain and revalue as they celebrate women's writing.

American feminist critics have shared with French critics both an interest in and a cautious distrust of the concept of feminine writing. Annette Kolodny, for instance, has worried that the "richness and variety of women's writing" will be missed if we see in it only its "feminine mode" or "style" ("Some Notes" 78). And yet Kolodny herself proceeds, in the same essay, to point out that women *have* had their own style, which includes reflexive constructions ("she found herself crying") and particular, recurring themes (clothing and self-fashioning are two that Kolodny mentions; other American feminists have focused on madness, disease, and the demonic).

Interested as they have become in the "French" subject of feminine style, American feminist critics began by analyzing literary texts rather than philosophizing abstractly about language. Many reviewed the great works by male writers, embarking on a revisionist rereading of literary tradition. These critics examined the portrayals of women characters, exposing the patriarchal ideology implicit in such works and showing how clearly this tradition of systematic masculine dominance is inscribed in our literary tradition. Kate Millett, Carolyn Heilbrun, and Judith Fetterley, among many others, created this model for American feminist criticism, a model that Elaine Showalter came to call "the feminist critique" of "male-constructed literary history" ("Poetics" 25).

Meanwhile another group of critics including Sandra Gilbert, Susan Gubar, Patricia Meyer Spacks, and Showalter herself created a somewhat different model. Whereas feminists writing "feminist critique" have analyzed works by men, practitioners of what Showalter used to refer to as "gynocriticism" have studied the writings of those women who, against all odds, produced what she calls "a literature of their own." In *The Female Imagination* (1975), Spacks examines the female literary tradition to find out how great women writers across the ages have felt, perceived themselves, and imagined reality. Gilbert and Gubar, in *The Madwoman in the Attic* (1979), concern themselves with well-known women writers of the nineteenth century, but they too find that general concerns, images, and themes recur, because the authors that they treat wrote "in a culture whose fundamental definitions of literary authority are both overtly and covertly patriarchal" (45).

If one of the purposes of gynocriticism is to (re)study well-known women authors, another is to rediscover women's history and culture, particularly women's communities that have nurtured female creativity. Still another related purpose is to discover neglected or forgotten women writers and thus to forge an alternative literary tradition, a canon that better represents the female perspective by better representing the literary works that have been written by women. Showalter, in *A Literature of Their Own* (1977), admirably began to fulfill this purpose, providing a remarkably comprehensive overview of women's writing through three of its phases. She defines these as the "Feminine, Feminist, and Female" phases, phases during which women first imitated a masculine tradition (1840–80), then protested against its standards and values (1880–1920), and finally advocated their own autonomous, female perspective (1920 to the present).

With the recovery of a body of women's texts, attention has returned to a question raised a decade ago by Lillian Robinson: Doesn't American feminist criticism need to formulate a theory of its own practice? Won't reliance on theoretical assumptions, categories, and strategies developed by men and associated with nonfeminist schools of thought prevent feminism from being accepted as equivalent to these other critical discourses? Not all American feminists believe that a special or unifying theory of feminist practice is urgently needed; Showalter's historical approach to women's culture allows a feminist critic to use theories based on nonfeminist disciplines. Kolodny has advocated a "playful pluralism" that encompasses a variety of critical schools and methods. But Jane Marcus and others have responded that if feminists adopt too wide a range of approaches, they may relax the tensions between feminists and the educational establishment necessary for political activism.

The question of whether feminism weakens or fortifies itself by emphasizing its separateness — and by developing unity through separateness — is one of several areas of debate within American feminism.

Another area of disagreement touched on earlier, between feminists who stress universal feminine attributes (the feminine imagination, feminine writing) and those who focus on the political conditions experienced by certain groups of women at certain times in history, parallels a larger distinction between American feminist critics and their British counterparts.

While it has been customary to refer to an Anglo-American tradition of feminist criticism, British feminists tend to distinguish themselves from what they see as an American overemphasis on texts linking women across boundaries and decades and an underemphasis on popular art and culture. They regard their own critical practice as more political than that of American feminists, whom they have often faulted for being uninterested in historical detail. They would join such American critics as Myra Jehlen to suggest that a continuing preoccupation with women writers might create the danger of placing women's texts outside the history that conditions them.

In the view of British feminists, the American opposition to male stereotypes that denigrate women has often led to counterstereotypes of feminine virtue that ignore real differences of race, class, and culture among women. In addition, they argue that American celebrations of individual heroines falsely suggest that powerful individuals may be immune to repressive conditions and may even imply that *any* individual can go through life unconditioned by the culture and ideology in which she or he lives.

Similarly, the American endeavor to recover women's history — for example, by emphasizing that women developed their own strategies to gain power within their sphere — is seen by British feminists like Judith Newton and Deborah Rosenfelt as an endeavor that "mystifies" male oppression, disguising it as something that has created for women a special world of opportunities. More important from the British standpoint, the universalizing and "essentializing" tendencies in both American practice and French theory disguise women's oppression by highlighting sexual difference, suggesting that a dominant system is impervious to political change. By contrast, British feminist theory emphasizes an engagement with historical process in order to promote social change.

Suzette Henke begins the feminist encounter with *Portrait* that follows this introduction by examining the images of women in Stephen Dedalus's consciousness. She points out that Stephen's conception of women exists within a framework of dichotomies (flesh and spirit, politics and religion, Davitt and Parnell). In general, women are aligned in Stephen's mind with the realm of the physical, toward which Stephen is deeply ambivalent. Grounding her argument in the psychoanalytic theories of Freud and Lacan, Henke suggests that Stephen's divided attitude toward the world of the senses is rooted in what Freud referred to as the Oedipus complex. (A boy's passion for his mother generates feelings of desire and pleasure but also of guilt and fear.)

Having suggested that Stephen's consciousness generally connects women with physicality, Henke goes on to show that, within that general association, more destructive dichotomies exist. The realm of the physical, after all, includes the warmth of a protective mother's slippers as well as the very different warmth of a prostitute's embrace. Stephen's all too typical, nineteenth-century tendency to see women as one or the other—as virgins or whores—is as limited and limiting as his tendency to seem them in terms of the physical. Henke relates Stephen's conception of women not only to an earlier, psychological complex but also to the voices and images of his education; the novels he reads, as well as popular entertainments of his culture, project the same images of women, with few variations.

The poetry Stephen writes is, in Henke's view, an attempted compensation for the relationships with women that he cannot achieve. Like his experience with the prostitute, it only seems to promise release and relief from frustration and failure. Stephen's response to these repeated cycles of frustration, hope, and failure is, according to Henke, "a panicky retreat into the security of Catholic law and patriarchal protection." In the Church — and in the Church alone, it seems to Stephen — is to be found a safe and satisfactory image of women: that of a Virgin who is also a mother, that of a female at once physical and sinless. Although he eventually rejects the calling of the priesthood for an artistic vocation, he does so in an epiphanic moment in which he imaginatively transfigures a girl on a beach into a "profane virgin," another masculine version of woman at once "mortal and angelic, sensuous and sane."

The novel ends with Stephen "once again accosted by ubiquitous reminders of Mother Church and Mother Ireland." But Stephen repudiates both and repudiates his mother as well, refusing to take communion at Easter. "Unlike his companion Cranly, who glorifies mother love, Stephen resolves to detach himself from 'the sufferings of women, the weaknesses of their bodies and souls.' In casting off the yoke of matriarchy, Stephen asserts his manhood in fraternal collusion with his classical mentor, Daedalus."

Henke's view of Stephen, finally, is of one who "has relentlessly attempted to achieve mastery over the outer world by adopting a male model of creation." Henke sees *Portrait* as an ironic novel, calling it "Joyce's satirical rendering of Stephen's logocentric paradigm." The "conclusion of Joyce's text," she writes, "seems to imply that the developing artist's notorious misogyny will prove to be still another dimension (and limitation) of his youthful priggishness." In taking this tack, Henke proves to be neither the kind of feminist whose project is to expose the chauvinism of phallocentric male writers nor the kind who would eschew such authors in favor of women writers whose visions offer a feminist critique of patriarchal ideology and masculine-dominated culture. Rather, with the help of psychoanalytic theories from Jung and Freud to Lacan, she finds vestiges of a feminist critique in a male writer's fiction, arguing that "Joyce makes clear to his audience that Stephen's fear of women and his contempt for sensuous life are among the many inhibitions that stifle his budding creativity."

Ross C Murfin

FEMINIST CRITICISM: A SELECTED BIBLIOGRAPHY

French Feminist Theories

Beauvoir, Simone de. *The Second Sex*. 1953. Trans. and ed. H. M. Parshley. New York: Bantam, 1961.

Cixous, Hélène. "The Laugh of the Medusa." Trans. Keith Cohen and Paula Cohen. *Signs* 1 (1976): 875–94.

Cixous, Hélène, and Catherine Clément. *The Newly Born Woman*. Trans. Betsy Wing. Minneapolis: U of Minnesota P, 1986.

French Feminist Theory. Special issue, *Signs* 7.1 (1981).

Irigaray, Luce. *This Sex Which Is Not One*. Trans. Catherine Porter. Ithaca: Cornell UP, 1985.

Jones, Ann Rosalind. "Writing the Body: Toward an Understanding of *L'Écriture féminine*." Showalter, *New Feminist Criticism* 361–77.

Kristeva, Julia. *Desire in Language: A Semiotic Approach to Literature and Art*. Ed. Leon S. Roudiez. Trans. Thomas Gora, Alice Jardine, and Roudiez. New York: Columbia UP, 1980.

Marks, Elaine, and Isabelle de Courtivron, eds. *New French Feminisms: An Anthology.* Amherst: U of Massachusetts P, 1980.

Moi, Toril, ed. *French Feminist Thought: A Reader.* Oxford: Basil Blackwell, 1987.

British and American Feminist Theories

Belsey, Catherine, and Jane Moore, eds. *The Feminist Reader: Essays in Gender and the Politics of Literary Criticism.* New York: Basil Blackwell, 1989.

Benhabib, Seyla, and Drucilla Cornell, eds. *Feminism as Critique: On the Politics of Gender.* Minneapolis: U of Minnesota P, 1987.

Collins, Patricia Hill. *Black Feminist Thought: Knowledge, Consciousness, and the Politics of Empowerment.* Boston: Unwin Hyman, 1990.

de Lauretis, Teresa, ed. *Feminist Studies/Critical Studies.* Bloomington: Indiana UP, 1986.

Feminist Readings: French Texts/American Contexts. Special issue, *Yale French Studies* 62 (1982). Essays by Jardine and Spivak.

hooks, bell. *Ain't I a Woman?: Black Women and Feminism.* Boston: South End, 1981.

Keohane, Nannerl O., Michelle Z. Rosaldo, and Barbara C. Gelpi, eds. *Feminist Theory: A Critique of Ideology.* Chicago: U of Chicago P, 1982.

Kolodny, Annette. "Dancing Through the Minefield: Some Observations on the Theory, Practice, and Politics of a Feminist Literary Criticism." Showalter, *New Feminist Criticism* 144–67.

The Lesbian Issue. Special issue, *Signs* 9 (Summer 1984).

Malson, Micheline, et al., eds. *Feminist Theory in Practice and Process.* Chicago: U of Chicago P, 1986.

Rich, Adrienne. *On Lies, Secrets, and Silence: Selected Prose, 1966–1979.* New York: Norton, 1979.

Showalter, Elaine. "Toward a Feminist Poetics." Showalter, *New Feminist Criticism* 125–43.

———, ed. *The New Feminist Criticism: Essays on Women, Literature, and Theory.* New York: Pantheon, 1985.

The Feminist Critique

Fetterley, Judith. *The Resisting Reader: A Feminist Approach to American Fiction.* Bloomington: Indiana UP, 1978.

Greer, Germaine. *The Female Eunuch.* New York: McGraw, 1971.

Millett, Kate. *Sexual Politics*. Garden City: Doubleday, 1970.

Robinson, Lillian S. *Sex, Class, and Culture*. 1978. New York: Methuen, 1986.

Wittig, Monique. *Les Guérillères*. 1969. Trans. David Le Vay. New York: Avon, 1973.

Woolf, Virginia. *A Room of One's Own*. New York: Harcourt, 1929.

Women's Writing and Creativity

Abel, Elizabeth, ed. *Writing and Sexual Difference*. Chicago: U of Chicago P, 1982.

Abel, Elizabeth, Marianne Hirsch, and Elizabeth Langland, eds. *The Voyage In: Fictions of Female Development*. Hanover: UP of New England, 1983.

Auerbach, Nina. *Communities of Women: An Idea in Fiction*. Cambridge: Harvard UP, 1978.

Christian, Barbara. *Black Feminist Criticism: Perspectives on Black Women Writers*. New York: Pergamon, 1985.

Gilbert, Sandra M., and Susan Gubar. *The Madwoman in the Attic: The Woman Writer and the Nineteenth-Century Literary Imagination*. New Haven: Yale UP, 1979.

Jacobus, Mary, ed. *Women Writing and Writing about Women*. New York: Barnes, 1979.

Miller, Nancy K., ed. *The Poetics of Gender*. New York: Columbia UP, 1986.

Newton, Judith Lowder. *Women, Power and Subversion: Social Strategies in British Fiction, 1778–1860*. Athens: U of Georgia P, 1981.

Poovey, Mary. *The Proper Lady and the Woman Writer: Ideology as Style in the Works of Mary Wollstonecraft, Mary Shelley, and Jane Austen*. Chicago: U of Chicago P, 1984.

Showalter, Elaine. *A Literature of Their Own: British Women Novelists from Brontë to Lessing*. Princeton: Princeton UP, 1977.

Marxist and Class Analysis

Barrett, Michèle. *Women's Oppression Today: Problems in Marxist Feminist Analysis*. London: Verso, 1980.

Delphy, Christine. *Close to Home: A Materialist Analysis of Women's Oppression*. Trans. and ed. Diana Leonard. Amherst: U of Massachusetts P, 1984.

Hartsock, Nancy C. M. *Money, Sex, and Power: Toward a Feminist Historical Materialism*. Boston: Northeastern UP, 1985.

Kaplan, Cora. *Sea Changes: Culture and Feminism*. London: Verso, 1986.

Mitchell, Juliet. *Woman's Estate*. New York: Pantheon, 1971.

Newton, Judith, and Deborah Rosenfelt, eds. *Feminist Criticism and Social Change: Sex, Class and Race in Literature and Culture*. New York: Methuen, 1985.

Sargent, Lydia, ed. *Women and Revolution: A Discussion of the Unhappy Marriage of Marxism and Feminism*. Montreal: Black Rose, 1981.

Women's History / Women's Studies

Bridenthal, Renate, and Claudia Koonz, eds. *Becoming Visible: Women in European History*. Boston: Houghton, 1977.

Farnham, Christie, ed. *The Impact of Feminist Research in the Academy*. Bloomington: Indiana UP, 1987.

Kelly, Joan. *Women, History and Theory*. Chicago: U of Chicago P, 1984.

McConnell-Ginet, Sally, et al., eds. *Woman and Language in Literature and Society*. New York: Praeger, 1980.

Mitchell, Juliet, and Ann Oakley, eds. *The Rights and Wrongs of Women*. London: Penguin, 1976.

Newton, Judith L., et al., eds. *Sex and Class in Women's History*. London: Routledge, 1983.

Riley, Denise. *"Am I That Name?": Feminism and the Category of "Women" in History*. Minneapolis: U of Minnesota P, 1988.

Rowbotham, Sheila. *Woman's Consciousness, Man's World*. Harmondsworth: Penguin, 1973.

Schipper, Mineke, ed. *Unheard Words: Women and Literature in Africa, the Arab World, Asia, the Caribbean, and Latin America*. London: Allison, 1985.

Scott, Joan Wallach. *Gender and the Politics of History*. New York: Columbia UP, 1988.

Smith-Rosenberg, Carroll. *Disorderly Conduct: Visions of Gender in Victorian America*. New York: Knopf, 1985.

Feminism and Other Critical Approaches

Armstrong, Nancy, ed. *Literature as Women's History I*. A special issue of *Genre* 19–20 (1986–87).

Diamond, Irene, and Lee Quinby, eds. *Feminism and Foucault: Reflections on Resistance*. Boston: Northeastern UP, 1988.

Feminist Studies 14 (1988). Special issue on feminism and deconstruction.

Gallop, Jane. *The Daughter's Seduction: Feminism and Psychoanalysis.* Ithaca: Cornell UP, 1982.

Keller, Evelyn Fox. *Reflections on Gender and Science.* New Haven: Yale UP, 1985.

Meese, Elizabeth, and Alice Parker, eds. *The Difference Within: Feminism and Critical Theory.* Amsterdam/Philadelphia: John Benjamins, 1989.

Penley, Constance, ed. *Feminism and Film Theory.* New York: Routledge, 1988.

Feminist Approaches to Joyce

Benstock, Shari. "City Spaces and Women's Places in Joyce's Dublin." *James Joyce: The Augmented Ninth.* Ed. Bernard Benstock. Syracuse: Syracuse UP, 1988. 293–307.

———. *Women of the Left Bank.* Austin: U of Texas P, 1986.

Church, Margaret. "The Adolescent Point of View Toward Women in Joyce's *Portrait.*" *Irish Renaissance Annual* 2 (1981). 158–65.

Cixous, Hélène. "Joyce: The (r)use of writing." *Post-Structuralist Joyce.* Ed. Derek Attridge and Daniel Ferrer. Cambridge: Cambridge UP, 1984. 15–30.

Devlin, Kimberly J. "The Female Eye: Joyce's Voyeuristic Narcissists." *New Alliances in Joyce Studies.* Ed. Bonnie Kime Scott. Newark: U of Delaware P, 1988. 135–43.

French, Marilyn. *The Book as World.* Cambridge: Harvard UP, 1975.

———. "Women in Joyce's Dublin." *James Joyce: The Augmented Ninth.* Ed. Bernard Benstock. Syracuse: Syracuse UP, 1988. 267–72.

Henke, Suzette and Elaine Unkeless, eds. *Women in Joyce.* Urbana: U of Illinois P, 1982.

Henke, Suzette. *James Joyce and the Politics of Desire.* New York: Routledge, 1990.

Modern Fiction Studies 35 (Autumn 1989). "Feminist Readings of Joyce" issue.

Norris, Margot. *The Decentered Universe of "Finnegans Wake."* Baltimore: Johns Hopkins UP, 1974.

———. "Portraits of the Artist as a Young Lover." *New Alliances in Joyce Studies.* Ed. Bonnie Kime Scott. Newark: U of Delaware P, 1988. 144–52.

Scott, Bonnie Kime. *James Joyce*. Feminist Readings Series. Brighton, Eng.: Harvester P; Atlantic Highlands: Humanities P Intl., 1987.
———. *Joyce and Feminism*. Bloomington: Indiana UP, 1984.

A FEMINIST PERSPECTIVE

SUZETTE HENKE

Stephen Dedalus and Women: A Feminist Reading of *Portrait*

I. Mother and Child

Female characters are present everywhere and nowhere in *A Portrait of the Artist as a Young Man*. They pervade the novel, yet remain elusive. Their sensuous figures haunt the developing consciousness of Stephen Dedalus and provide a foil against which he defines himself as both man and artist. Like everything else in *A Portrait*, women are portrayed almost exclusively from Stephen's point of view. Seen through his eyes and colored by his fantasies, they often appear as one-dimensional projections of a narcissistic imagination. Demonized by Stephen's childhood sense of abjection, women emerge as powerful emblems of the flesh—frightening reminders of sex, generation, and bodily decay.

At the dawn of infantile consciousness, Stephen interprets the external world in terms of complementary pairs: male and female, father and mother, politics and religion, Davitt and Parnell. Baby Stephen's cosmos is organized in binary structures that set the stage for a dialectic of personal development. He perceives his father as a primordial storyteller who inaugurates the linguistic apprenticeship that inscribes the boy into the symbolic order of patriarchal authority. Simon Dedalus is a bearer of the law and the word, twin instruments of the will that promise psychological mastery over a hostile material environment. The male parent appeals to Stephen's imagination, awakening him to a sense of individual identity at the moment when language necessarily establishes a gap between subjective desire and self-representation: "He was baby tuckoo. . . . He sang that song. That was his song" (p. 19). By virtue of receiving a forename, Stephen is able to enunciate himself as a subject of discourse and to gain access to narrative representation. Inscribed into the linguistic circuit of exchange, he identifies himself in terms of the dominant culture's signifying practices.

At the psychological juncture between pre-oedipal attachment and oedipal separation, Stephen first sees his mother as a powerful and beneficent source of physical pleasure. She ministers to her son's corporal needs, changes the oilsheet, and encourages his artistic expression by playing the piano. This sweet-smelling guardian is more directly responsive to the boy's infantile emotional demands and more closely associated with sensuous comfort and bodily joy. It is the "nice" mother, however, whom Stephen recognizes as one of the women principally responsible for introducing him to a hostile external world and to the repressive strictures of middle-class morality. The first of the many imperatives that thwart his ego, "apologise," is associated in his mind and vivid imagination with matriarchal threats.

Dante and Mrs. Dedalus both represent the inhibitions of an ominous reality principle that begins, at this point, to take precedence over the polymorphously perverse gratifications of infantile narcissism. As Dorothy Dinnerstein explains in *The Mermaid and the Minotaur,* it is usually a woman who serves as

> every infant's first love, first witness and first boss. . . . The initial experience of dependence on a largely uncontrollable outside source of good is focused on a woman, and so is the earliest experience of vulnerability to disappointment and pain. (28)

Nancy Chodorow, in her work on object relations, observes that this pre-oedipal mother,

> simply as a result of her omnipotence and activity, causes a 'narcissistic wound.' . . . Children of both sexes . . . will maintain a fearsome unconscious maternal image as a result of projecting upon it the hostility derived from their own feelings of impotence. (122)

As Simone de Beauvoir explains in *The Second Sex,* the male child, in particular, has a tendency to associate the maternal figure with viscosity and immanence—with a chaotic, uncontrollable world of physicality, process, and unsatisfied desire. He develops a conviction that women are bound by the generative demands of the species, and the presence of his own mother becomes a reminder of contingency, the shame of his animal nature and the threat of personal extinction.

> The uncleanness of birth is reflected upon the mother. . . . And if the little boy remains in early childhood sensually attached to

> the maternal flesh, when he grows older, becomes socialized, and takes note of his individual existence, this same flesh frightens him . . . calls him back to those realms of immanence whence he would fly. (136)

"Reproduction is the beginning of death" (p. 199), argued Hegel, and so argues Stephen's friend Temple. The Manichean dichotomy between flesh and spirit, body and mind, has long been allied in the writings of male philosophers with a fantasized polarity between the sexes and the linguistic construction of sexual difference. Stephen extends the tradition of Nietzsche and Schopenhauer when, in *Stephen Hero,* he proposes a misogynist "theory of dualism which would symbolise the twin eternities of spirit and nature in the twin eternities of male and female" (*Stephen Hero* 210). According to Simone de Beauvoir, man's symbolic association of woman with the flesh reflects an embedded infantile disdain for corporality and anarchic libidinal drives. The male identifies himself as spirit by virtue of his own subjective consciousness; he then perceives the female as "the Other, who limits and denies him" (129).

The sexual antagonism that pervades Irish society is impressed on Stephen at an early age. He loathes his mother's feminine vulnerability and thinks that she is "not nice" when she bursts into tears. Armed with ten shillings and his father's injunction toward a code of masculine loyalty, he enters the competitive joust of life at Clongowes determined to adopt an ethic of manly stoicism: "his father had told him . . . whatever he did, never to peach on a fellow" (p. 21).

In a world of social Darwinism where only the ruthless survive, Stephen defines himself as both literally and figuratively marginal. Small, frail, and feeling very much like an outsider in this thundering herd of pugnacious schoolboys, he mentally takes refuge in artistic evocations of the family hearth protected by beneficent female spirits. As he relives the horror of being shouldered into a rat-infested urinal ditch by the bully Wells, Stephen projects himself beyond the vermin and the scum to an apparently dissociated reverie of his mother sitting by the fire in hot "jewelly slippers" that exude a "lovely warm smell" (p. 22). Alienated from a brutal male environment, Stephen longs to return to this female figure of security and comfort, "to be at home and lay his head on his mother's lap" (p. 24).

As the growing boy moves in the direction of manhood, he feels increasingly compelled to cast off the shackles of female influence. His childhood educator Dante, "a clever woman and a wellread woman" who teaches him geography and lunar lore, is supplanted by male instructors: "Father Arnall knew more than Dante because he was a priest" (p. 23). The Jesuit masters at Clongowes invite Stephen to ponder the mysteries of religion, death, canker, and cancer. They introduce him to a system of male authority and discipline, to a pedagogical regimen that will ensure his correct training and proper socialization. Through examinations that pit red roses against white, Yorks against Lancastrians, they make education an aggressive game of simulated warfare in which students, like soldiers, are depersonalized through institutional surveillance.

By the time Stephen is old enough to join his parents' table at Christmas, his mother can no longer protect him from the world of masculine aggression or the turbulence of Irish politics. At the holiday meal, the impressionable child assimilates the knowledge that rabid women like Dante Riordan support ecclesiastical authority in the name of moral righteousness. Like the Irish sow devouring her farrow, Dante is willing to sacrifice Parnell as a political scapegoat to the prelates of Irish Catholicism. In the face of Mr. Casey's Fenianism and Simon's contemptuous snorting, she labels the Catholic clergy "the apple of God's eye" (p. 45). "*Touch them not,* says Christ, *for they are the apple of My eye*" (p. 45). As Ireland's perverted Eve, Dante defends this ecclesiastical apple against an adulterous Nationalist leader, a scandalous sinner crushed by an irate populace. Her impassioned ravings, bred of puritanical self-righteousness, suggest a formidable alliance between the Catholic church and the ideals of bourgeois morality guarded by a horde of pious women. "God and morality and religion come first," shrieks Dante (p. 46), and Mr. Casey counters with his own incendiary slogan.

In the battle between male and female, Mother Church emerges as a bastion of sexual repression. Dante's own credibility is socially diminished by her age, gender, and involuntary celibacy. Stephen "had heard his father say that she was a spoiled nun and that she had come out of the convent in the Alleghanies when her brother had got the money from the savages for the trinkets and the chainies" (p. 43). Stephen's own role models, Simon Dedalus and John Casey, boldly assert masculine prowess through republican fervor directed against dissenting countrymen rather than their imperial masters. In this mock scenario of political self-assertion, women and children prove fair game. Hence Casey's braggadocio in recounting his triumph over the hag who screamed "whore": "I had my mouth full of the tobacco juice. I bent down to her and *Phth!* says I to her like that . . . right into her eye" (p. 44).

When Stephen returns to Clongowes, he realizes that his peacemaking mother, a mollifying agent of social arbitration, has failed to offer a viable sanctuary from the male-dominated power structure that controls the outer world. He must learn to survive in a society that protects bullies like Wells and sadists like Father Dolan, condones brutality, and takes advantage of the weak and the helpless. The pandybat incident at the end of chapter one symbolically reinforces the rites of objectification characteristic of Jesuit training. Stephen is being socialized into what Philip Slater identifies in *The Glory of Hera* as a culture of male narcissism. According to Slater, single-sex education and the separation of young boys from maternal nurturance promotes misogyny, narcissism, and a residual terror of the female. Little boys suffer from an "unconscious fear of being feminine, which leads to 'protest masculinity,' exaggeration of the difference between men and women" (Slater 416). Once the child is deprived of his mother's affection, he "seeks compensation through self-aggrandizement—renouncing love for admiration. . . . He becomes vain, hypersensitive, invidious, ambitious, . . . boastful, and exhibitionistic" (439).

Stephen's brash appeal to Father Conmee at the end of the episode is motivated not only by optimistic faith in a male-controlled world but by personal vanity and a tendency toward exhibitionism. "The prefect of studies was a priest but that was cruel and unfair," he insists (p. 57). With an absurdly Panglossian view of the world, he feels certain of ethical exoneration from Conmee. Having rebelled against Father Dolan's totalitarian power, Stephen is unanimously acclaimed a revolutionary hero by his jubilant peers. But the child, apparently triumphant, later discovers an ironic sequel to his ostensible victory: Dolan and Conmee, in smug condescension, treat the incident as a riproaring joke. Stephen has unwittingly played the fool at the court of his Jesuit masters and, in a bold attempt to assert his budding manhood, has merely served as an object of wry patriarchal amusement.

II. Virgin and Whore

In chapter five of *Portrait,* Cranly asks Stephen if he would deflower a virgin. His companion replies by posing another half-mocking query: "Excuse me, . . . is that not the ambition of most young gentlemen?" (p. 213). Figuratively, it is Stephen's ambition throughout the novel to deflower the Blessed Virgin of Catholicism and supplant the Italian Madonna with a profane surrogate—a voluptuous Irish muse rooted in sensuous reality.

With the Count of Monte Cristo as his model, Stephen conjures up adolescent fantasies of a beautiful Mercedes whom he stalks in the suburbs of Blackrock. He envisages a scene of beatific transformation in a moonlit garden when the romantic heroine, meeting her erstwhile lover, blesses him with nothing less than the power of refusal. In spiritualizing his life, she paradoxically endows him with sufficient grace to conquer libidinal temptation. When Stephen dreams of himself as Edmond Dantes, he identifies with a man betrayed by his friends and his mistress, unjustly exiled and imprisoned, but eventually able to wreak vengeance on those who failed him. Monte Cristo's adventures culminate in a "sadly proud gesture of refusal": "Madam, I never eat muscatel grapes" (p. 65). As a nascent artist, Stephen admires the self-sufficiency of Dantes, an isolated hero who eventually conquers the woman he loves through a complex process of amorous sublimation.

In a different, more realistic setting, the Dublin family ménage provides an unsalubrious atmosphere for those smiling soubrettes whose delicate features grace the evening papers and capture the attention of Stephen's aunt and cousins. "The beautiful Mabel Hunter" of pantomime fame stares from a newspaper photograph with "demurely taunting eyes" (pp. 68–69). This "exquisite creature" intrudes on the squalor of Irish life to provide a popular though elusive model of seductive femininity. Stephen's ringleted cousin admires the music-hall artiste with a kind of religious devotion. The popular press has constructed an icon of girlish charm, a figure of the female body as a desirable and coyly inaccessible market commodity. The price of such fetishistic commodification of women is reflected in the aggressive behavior of Stephen's unidentified male relative, a boy growing up in an atmosphere of boorish insensitivity. Like a voracious animal, he mauls the edges of the paper and roughly pushes his sister aside to get a glimpse of Mabel's photograph. Greedy and whining, he appropriates this pretty pinup for his own lascivious enjoyment.

Unmoved by such popular representations of feminine charm, Stephen seeks refuge from reality in the priesthood of art: he longs to confront the beauty and mystery of creation while tasting the joy of loneliness. Before the tantalizing face of Emma cowled in nun's veiling, he forces himself to remain calm and controlled, repressing "the feverish agitation of his blood" (p. 70). He characteristically projects his own erotic vulnerability onto the girl he believes to be "flattering, taunting, searching, exciting his heart" (p. 70). Emma appears in the guise of Kathleen Ni Houlihan, a Celtic figure inviting Stephen to romantic initiation in the peaceful stillness of a moonlit evening. Depersonalized and seen through the haze of mythic reverie, she emerges as a shadowy emblem out of the unconscious— Mercedes in Dublin garb, Eve in nun's habit.

> He saw her urge her vanities, her fine dress and sash and long black stockings, and knew that he had yielded to them a thousand times. Yet a voice within him spoke above the noise of his dancing heart, asking him would he take her gift to which he had only to stretch out his hand. (p. 70)

In this self-indulgent exercise, Stephen gains symbolic mastery over Emma's erratic movements by assuming that he can, at will, catch hold of her darting figure. Focusing on fetishes of stockings and dress, he casts her in the incongruous role of Irish temptress and refuses her gift of an adolescent kiss. On the verge of losing emotional composure, Stephen refuses to yield to this purported temptation. Like the Count of Monte Cristo, he turns away from Emma in proud abnegation, determined to possess his mistress wholly through art.

Blurring the figures of himself and his beloved in the womb of his artistic imagination, Stephen is able to give cathartic expression to the pain of loss associated with unacted desire. Byronic verses written to E— C— consummate the memory of romantic intimacy, as Stephen imagines that "the kiss, which had been withheld by one, was given by both" (p. 71). Poetry offers aesthetic compensation for frustrated physical desire, and the stirrings of adolescent sexuality are deftly sublimated through an exercise in lyrical fulfillment. The artist's mind is cold, chaste, and detached, like that of the virginal muse Diana, as his disciplined verses statically embalm the experience of romantic epiphany. The scene has been purged of reality and naturalistic detail, the participants vaguely depersonalized. Emotional mutuality has been restricted to art: Stephen feels fulfilled, but Emma is left to pine in her nunlike cowl. Her desires are safely crystallized in Byronic verses framed by two Jesuit mottoes.

Refusing to communicate his passion, Stephen mediates libidinal desire through the literary language of courtly love and nineteenth-century romantic convention. Taking Daddy Byron as master, he succeeds in mastering the young woman who would otherwise be mistress of his heart. The poem that he pens provides an emotional circuit of substitution that short-circuits libidinal drive and sublimates Eros to the symbolic order of Daedalus/Byron/Stephen/Father/Joyce.

The night of the Whitsuntide play two years later, Stephen remembers the touch of Emma's hand and the sight of dark eyes that "had invited and unnerved him" (p. 81). "All day he had thought of nothing but their leavetaking on the steps of the tram at Harold's Cross" (p. 77). Despite the lapse in time, he continues to feel tormented by the stream of moody emotions that hurt him into poetry, as he imagines a tender reunion and a chance to rewrite the scene with a different ending. Clothing his frustration in a tapestry of lyrical effects, Stephen is able to defuse the seminal eruptions of repressed physicality through psychological strategies of erotic displacement.

Dashing to an alley behind the Dublin morgue, he soberly takes comfort in the "good odour" of "horse piss and rotted straw" (p. 84), mortifying the flesh in a repulsive atmosphere chosen to vent his residual contempt for female physiology. Urine and ordure symbolically cling to the archaic memory of an inaccessible maternal body always lost to the ego's field of insatiable demands. Stephen's morbid sentiments are Thomistic and medieval, reminiscent of religious triptychs that portray a woman first at the height of vanity and sensuous beauty, then aged and wrinkled, and finally as a skeleton draped in richly embroidered grave-clothes. Accosted by the immanence of his carnal connection with the world, Stephen, like the fathers of the Church, rebels against mortality by renouncing the fires of lust. As Saint Augustine wryly noted, *"Inter faeces et urinam nascimur"* (we are born between feces and urine). Joyce's artist is well on his way to developing a similar excremental vision of sex.

Stephen no longer seeks to emulate the Count of Monte Cristo when the transfiguration he once sought through Mercedes is consummated in the embrace of a Dublin whore. He finds himself stalking a prostitute as if she were an animal in a dark, foreboding jungle. "His blood was in revolt. . . . He moaned to himself like some baffled prowling beast" (p. 95). His search is motivated by a perverse desire for temporary communion, as he seeks release from his own imprisoned ego: "He wanted to sin with another of his kind, to force another being to sin with him and to exult with her in sin" (p. 95). The sexual imagery at the end of chapter two is ironically inverted. As Stephen feels the shadow of a streetwalker "moving irresistibly upon him" in penumbrous alleyways, he figuratively suffers the "agony of its penetration" and surrenders to a murmurous flood of physical excitation (p. 95). The fusion of erotic and romantic imagery degenerates into a vague rite of sexual initiation that reverses traditional symbolism. Stephen envisages himself in the role of deflowered virgin, raped by a phallic figure and flooded with seminal streams. His "cry for an iniquitous abandonment" again evokes an excremental vision of sex, as his moans reverberate with "the echo of an obscene scrawl which he had read on the oozing wall of a urinal" (p. 95).

When Stephen/Icarus, wandering through a Daedalian maze of narrow and dirty streets, steps before a phantasmal altar illumined by yellow gasflames, he resembles both a sacrificial victim and a child about to burst into hysterical weeping. The perfumed female who takes him in her arms recalls his nice-smelling mother at the same time that she functions as high priestess or Vestal virgin in a contemporary phallic cult. Clothed in a long pink gown, she leads the boy into a womblike chamber, tousles his hair, calls him "little rascal," and embraces him with a vaguely maternal caress. Soothed like a baby or a fetus by the "warm calm rise and fall of her breast," Stephen momentarily retrieves an illusion of infant satiety: "He closed his eyes, surrendering himself to her, body and mind, conscious of nothing in the world but the dark pressure of her softly parting lips" (p. 96).

In this oral-regressive encounter, the prostitute becomes mistress of Stephen's lips and, through a lingual kiss that inaugurates a fantasy of pre-oedipal bliss, temporarily appropriates the highly guarded powers of artistic speech. Inarticulate and swooning, the boy feels reduced to a lavish, infantile dependency that leaves him childlike and passive, penetrated by a foreign tongue, but gloriously centered in the mystified presence of an imaginary figure of wholeness and coherence. Stephen feels that he has at last realized spiritual transfiguration: "He was in another world: he had awakened from a slumber of centuries" into a sybaritic, pagan sanctuary (p. 95).

III. The Catholic Virgin

At the outset of chapter three, Stephen approaches the forbidden pleasures of the Dublin red-light district almost ritualistically, pursuing a devious course among back streets and alleys until surprised by the joy of soft, perfumed flesh. Wallowing in the pleasures of a physicality that has always repelled him, Stephen delights in a riot of sensuality. His defiant sexual practices mesmerize consciousness until, watched by a thousand flickering heavenly eyes, his weary mind is transported into a "vast cycle of starry life" (p. 97).

As prefect of the sodality of the Blessed Virgin, Stephen chants Mary's praises in an act of proud dissimulation. "His sin, which had covered him from the sight of God, had led him nearer to the refuge of sinners" (p. 99). The Catholic Virgin becomes a figure of courtly devotion, whose holiness radiates a hypnotic, translucent glow. Desirous of serving as her knight and courtier, Stephen prostrates himself in sacerdotal obeisance before his vision of the adored female. He worships the flesh of an icon that seems an object of both veneration and desire. A sanctuary of heavenly peace after the fervor of sexual frenzy, the Virgin becomes a postcoital Madonna offering refuge from the turmoil of hormonal agitation. The self-conscious sinner takes perverse satisfaction in befouling her image by reciting the Holy Office with "lips whereon there still lingered foul and shameful words, the savour itself of a lewd kiss" (p. 99). Later in the episode, Stephen will offer a panicked prayer to Mary, whom he invokes in the guise of a beneficent mother. Repentant of his fall from grace, he no longer imagines her as a frail-fleshed virgin but appeals to the powerful *magna mater,* whose beauty is *"not like earthly beauty, dangerous to look upon, but like the morning star"* (p. 125).

As the "jeweleyed harlots" of lascivious transgression dance before the boy's fevered imagination, he feels horrified by the realization that he has besmirched the icon of his beloved Emma by making her the object of masturbatory fantasy: "The image of Emma appeared before him and, under her eyes, the flood of shame rushed forth anew from his heart. If she knew to what his mind had subjected her or how his brutelike lust had torn and trampled upon her innocence!" (p. 107). He feels that he has violated both Emma's honor and his own code of chivalry, not to mention the rigorous ethic of purity enforced by Irish Catholicism.

Without the innocent Emma to serve as a surrogate Beatrice, Stephen feels as "helpless and hopeless" as the souls of the damned in Dante's hell (p. 113) and hallucinates a vision of the libidinous inferno prepared especially for him, "a hell of lecherous goatish fiends" (p. 125). These "goatish creatures with human faces, hornybrowed, lightly bearded and grey as indiarubber" (p. 124) are demonic satyrs who mimic the goat-god Pan but whose dry, spittleless lips are incapable of communicative utterance. They embody the artist's most terrible nightmare: a hell in which language has been deracinated from meaning, articulation is torturous, and spoken sounds echo in waves of vacuous gibberish.

Stephen's Catholic training forces him simultaneously to renounce Satan, the female, and his own genitalia in an act of psychological castration. Haunted by fantasies of sexual alienation, he feels compelled to assert moral superiority over an antagonistic penis that seems to operate with a will of its own: "His soul sickened at the thought of a torpid snaky life feeding itself out of the tender marrow of his life and fattening upon the slime of lust" (p. 126). Like the confused adolescent boy described by Simone de Beauvoir in *The Second Sex,* Stephen feels "possessed by a magic not of himself. . . . That organ by which he thought to assert himself does not obey him; heavy with unsatisfied desires, unexpectedly becoming erect, . . . it manifests a suspicious and capricious vitality" (150–51).

In order to confess his sins against the sixth and ninth commandments, Stephen must self-consciously revert to a state of childhood innocence and amend his life for the sake of at-onement with the Christian community. Echoing the inaugural words of catechismal instruction and droning a litany of religious clichés, he determines to repress budding sexual urges by renouncing the one sin that shames him even more than murder. The temptress has reduced his soul to a syphilitic chancre "festering and oozing like a sore, a squalid stream of vice" (p. 130). Repelled by the lurid imagery of venereal disease, Stephen humbles himself before the old and weary voice of a father-priest-confessor, who counsels a "life of grace and virtue and happiness" (p. 131) and invokes the Virgin Mary as moral guardian of Christian manliness.

As penitential prefect of Our Blessed Lady's sodality, Stephen scrupulously disciplines his senses to the point of masochistic self-abuse. He obsessively attempts to recapture, through puritanical self-mortification, the prepubescent calm of juvenile innocence. Fervently invoking the Virgin to *"guide us home"* (p. 125), he fails to realize the futility of such a project. One cannot go home again to the lost womb of sexual latency.

IV. The Bird-Girl: Aesthetic Muse

In his return to ritualistic devotion, Stephen becomes involved in an aesthetic love affair with his own soul. The *anima,* the feminine aspect of the psyche, has won his passion and holds him enthralled. Like Narcissus, Stephen has fallen in love with his projected self-image clothed in female garb.

> The attitude of rapture in sacred art, the raised and parted hands, the parted lips and eyes as of one about to swoon, became for him an image of the soul in prayer, humiliated and faint before her Creator. (p. 134)

In the glorified female, says Simone de Beauvoir, "man also perceives his mysterious double; man's soul is Psyche, a woman" (166–67). The feminine side of Stephen's identity, personified as the soul, swoons in erotic ecstasy before her Creator, just as the young man earlier swooned in the arms of a Dublin prostitute.

The Catholic priesthood offers Stephen a chance to consummate this narcissistic love affair with his psyche. It bestows on the soul the magical power of transubstantiation, and it promises a rite of passage into male-guarded mysteries that successfully counteract female authority: "No angel or archangel in heaven, no saint, not even the Blessed Virgin herself has the power of a priest of God" (p. 140). A Jesuit vocation would guarantee Stephen ascendancy over the Catholic Madonna. By virtue of the secret knowledge promised by an exclusively masculine fraternity, he would be admitted to the inner sanctum of patriarchal privilege.

The price, however, of this "awful power of which angels and saints stood in reverence" is an irrevocable act that would condemn him to the "grave and ordered and passionless life" of Jesuit conformity (pp. 141–43). Still painting himself in the images of Lord Byron and Edmond Dantes, Stephen passionately embraces the marginal stance of aesthetic outlaw. He chooses the misrule and confusion of his father's house, the messiness and chaos of sensuous experience, over a "mirthless reflection of the sunken day" (p. 143) evinced by his Jesuit counselor's spectral visage. Turning away from this symbolic death's head, Stephen instinctively rejects the blind, eyeless obedience demanded by Catholic orders. He will commit himself, instead, to the pagan priesthood of that fabulous artificer, old Father Daedalus.

Stephen's implicit choice of an artistic vocation seems emotionally confirmed by his climactic encounter with a profane virgin emblematic of earthly beauty—a wading girl "whom magic had changed into the likeness of a strange and beautiful seabird" (p. 151). Her epiphanic figure amalgamates a plethora of images from pagan, Christian, and Celtic iconography. She is at once mortal and angelic, sensuous and serene. Her softhued, ivory thighs recall Eileen's ivory hands as well as the Catholic Virgin, Tower of Ivory. Her avian transformation harks back to the Greek myth of Leda and the swan. And because her bosom, like "the breast of some darkplumaged dove" (p. 151), suggests the Holy Ghost of Catholicism, Stephen, as purveyor of the word, imaginatively begets a surrogate Holy Spirit.

The irony of this romantic moment is subtle but implicit. If Stephen feels sexual arousal in the presence of exposed female thighs, he quickly sublimates erotic agitation beneath effusions of purple prose. Confronted with an attractive nubile form, he immediately detaches himself from participation in the scene. His reaction is self-consciously static, theoretically purged of desire or loathing. Once again, his leap into aesthetic fantasy quenches an initial impulse to approach the girl, to reach out and touch her, or to risk social intercourse.

As the girl rises out of the sea, she is reminiscent of Venus, the goddess of love born of the ocean foam. She is pure and virginal, yet an emerald trail of seaweed functions as a sign of mortality stamped upon her flesh. She belongs to the mundane world of decay and corruption, and the vegetation clinging to her ankle suggests a fetishistic image of emotional entrapment. The woman appears as an "angel of mortal youth and beauty, an envoy from the fair courts of life" (p. 152). But like an Irish Circe, she has the potential to drag Stephen down into the emerald green nets of Dublin paralysis.

In sociological terms this attractive young woman, approached and courted, might well threaten Stephen with the kind of domestic entrapment associated with Catholic marriage. The aspiring poet knows that he may look but not touch, admire but not speak. He glorifies the wading girl as angelic muse but never actually joins her in the teeming ocean waters. Communication has been safely limited to narcissistic projection: "Her image had passed into his soul for ever and no word had broken the holy silence of his ecstasy" (p. 152). Afraid of the "waters circumfluent in space" (p. 193) that symbolize the fluidity of female desire, Stephen is determined to control the world of physiological process by freezing life in the sacrament of art. His "spiritual-heroic refrigerating apparatus" (p. 217) has already begun to implement this psychological flight from woman. His response to the girl is exclusively specular, as he takes refuge in a masculine, visual, sexual economy and sublimates tactile and olfactory drives that would move him toward sensuous contact. The mimesis of romantic passion offers a successfully mediated and comfortably mastered form of sexual gratification.

For Joyce's young man, an exercise in scopophilia (love of looking) masquerades as aesthetic delight. If, as Freud suggests, the specular gaze is anal and obsessive, an unconscious expression of a sadistic will to power, then Stephen's cold, pellucid *regard* penetrates its object through a strategy of phallocentric framing and claims it as a fetishistic trophy to grace the scene of writing. The bird-girl functions as an imaginary symbol of beauty and coherence, of desire playfully, masterfully, and joyously deferred through an endless dissemination of creative pleasure. Woman proves to be the blind spot in Stephen's poetic discourse. She is represented as a fantasized paradigm of psychic cohesion, the Other whose realistic fragmentation would threaten the poet's idealized aesthetic project. Because the girl remains a mute, fetishized, and perpetually mediated object of desire, her difference assures psychological stability to the speaking/seeing subject, the authorial I/eye who frames and appropriates her figure.

At nightfall, the exhausted poet feels his soul "swooning into some new world, fantastic, dim, uncertain as under sea, traversed by cloudy shapes and beings. A world, a glimmer, or a flower?" (p. 152). His spirit seems to embark on an archetypal journey toward the multifoliate rose of Dante's beatific vision. The bird-girl has imaginatively served as Stephen's profane virgin, a Beatrice who ushers him into paradisal experience. The Dantesque underworld may symbolize the artistic unconscious, but the pre-Raphaelite rose imagery casts satirical light on Stephen's romantic reverie. As the young man attempts to "still the riot of his blood," he swoons in languorous ecstasy. He moodily contemplates an opening flower "breaking in full crimson and unfolding and fading to palest rose, . . . flooding all the heavens with its soft flushes" (p. 152). Sublimating the sexual component of his experience, Stephen vividly imagines a metaphorical rose engulfing the heavens, and his language of flowers suggests a psychoanalytic exercise in erotic mimesis. The boy's fantasy re-creates a repressed vision of female genitalia spreading in luxuriant, rose pink petals before his aroused phallic consciousness. His active libido summons veiled images of a woman's body revealing its vulvular mysteries and palpitating with the crimson flush of physical stimulation. Florid prose imitates the orgasmic rhythms of sexual excitement, as tension mounts "leaf by leaf and wave of light by wave of light" until the dream suddenly climaxes in a flood of soft flushes. Stephen may want to believe that he has purified his sensuous encounter by making it into a mimetic replication of spiritual transcendence, but even his Dantesque beatitude is founded on sexual passion thinly disguised by the language of Freudian displacement.

V. Flight from the Mother

Although the gates of salvation open at the end of chapter four, Stephen finds himself, at the beginning of chapter five, exiled from the Garden of Eden. Chewing crusts of fried bread, he remembers the "turfcoloured" water in the bath at Clongowes—a spectral image that resonates with associations of death, drowning, and spiritual claustrophobia. As the nascent artist tries to escape the sordid reality of Dublin by taking shelter in a world of words, he continues to struggle for liberation from the nets of a cloying family life, the demands of Irish nationality, and the stultifying authority of the Catholic church.

Proudly proclaiming that he "will not serve," Stephen nevertheless relies on his mother's service for physical nurturance and psychological support. Mary Dedalus washes her son's face and ears, enjoins him to receive the Eucharist, and packs his secondhand clothes in preparation for his exodus to France. Having magically transmuted the power of the female into a static object of aesthetic contemplation, Stephen is once again accosted by ubiquitous reminders of Mother Church and Mother Ireland. He feels compelled simultaneously to reject all three mothers—biological, ecclesiastical, and political. His refusal to take communion at Easter is as much a gesture of rebellion against a pleading Mary Dedalus as it is a rejection of Catholic authority. The image of woman metonymically absorbs all the paralyzing nets that constrain the potential artist. Unlike his companion Cranly, who glorifies mother love, Stephen resolves to detach himself from "the sufferings of women, the weaknesses of their bodies and souls" (p. 211). In casting off the yoke of matriarchy, he asserts his manhood in filial collusion with Daedalus, his classical mentor.

It is not enough, however, to repudiate the female: the artist must successfully usurp her procreative powers. Stephen seems to consider the aesthetic endeavor a kind of symbolic couvade, a rite of psychological compensation for the male inability to give birth. He describes the act of aesthetic postcreation in metaphors of parturition, explaining to Lynch: "When we come to the phenomena of artistic conception, artistic gestation and artistic reproduction I require a new terminology and a new personal experience" (p. 182).

After awakening from what seems to have been a wet dream, Stephen feels inspired to compose a lyrical aubade to a fantasized temptress. The poet welters in a confused haze of light and beauty, but the instant of inspiration is climactic: "In the virgin womb of the imagination the word was made flesh" (p. 188). The moment of mental conception simulates a sexual process culminating in erotic ecstasy. In a strange instance of mental transsexuality, Stephen envisions his own aesthetic impregnation by the Holy Spirit, an experience modeled on the Virgin Mary's biblical gestation of the word of God. As the artist falls into a vision of rapturous enchantment, he conflates the ingenuous Emma with Mercedes and the bird-girl, then re-creates this female figure in the awesome, uncanny form of eternal temptress—a seductive Lilith luring the seraphim from heaven. His courtly villanelle is inspired by a shudder in the loins that engenders not Leda or a burning Troy, but a handful of precious verses.

The enchantment of the heart that Stephen and Shelley both praise for its radiance now bursts forth into fire and flame. The metaphor of smoky praise issuing from a chivalric heart seems puerile at best, part of an ecclesiastical rite complete with "swaying censer" and ellipsoidal incense balls. With decadent weariness, Stephen gropes for his tablets and finds, instead, an abandoned cigarette packet. The smoke from the censer of the world is recorded on the cardboard remnant of a package of smokes, all smoked but one. Stephen longs to immerse himself in a Dantesque ambiance of secret roses reminiscent of the multifoliate flower of paradise, but he is forced to fashion a phantasmal, rose-strewn path to heaven from the "great overblown scarlet flowers of the tattered wallpaper" that plaster his dingy room in Dublin (p. 192).

Unable to win the young and fickle heart of Emma, Stephen re-creates her in baleful, aesthetic guise. Her figure is kaleidoscopically reflected in memories of lower-class peasant women: a flowergirl, a kitchengirl "with the drawl of a country singer," a girl who mocked him, and a vamp whose "small ripe mouth" made her good enough to eat (p. 191). Seeing Emma on the steps of the National Library, Stephen wonders if her life might be as "simple and strange as a bird's life" and her heart as "simple and wilful as a bird's" (p. 188). But the bird, an emblem of simplicity and trust, quickly melds with the iconography of the inscrutable bat, a creature whose enigmatic flight and dark habitation makes it a symbol of mystery and cunning. "Bat," too, is an Irish slang term for "prostitute," an association implicit in the multiple bat references that pepper the final pages of *Portrait*. Stephen condescends to think of Emma as a younger incarnation of the pregnant woman who tried to seduce Davin in the Ballyhoura Hills and who emerges as a symbol of Mother Ireland, a nurturant and guileless female ingenuously bedding the stranger. Emma, too, becomes "a figure of the womanhood of her country, a batlike soul waking to the consciousness of itself in darkness and secrecy and loneliness" (p. 191).

By purging Emma of naturalistic dross, by abstracting her from an Irish domestic scene of horsehair and flirtation and celebrating her as archetypal temptress, Stephen, "a priest of the eternal imagination, transmuting the daily bread of experience into the radiant body of everliving life" (p. 192), metaphorically consumes her body in the sacramental act of aesthetic communion. Erotic union gives way to a spiritual Eucharist, as the poet raises the sacred chalice of devotion before the altar of the muse. Emma figuratively surrenders herself to the artist who conquers her voluptuous form: "Her nakedness yielded to him, radiant, warm, odorous and lavishlimbed" (p. 193).

Stephen paradoxically composes the villanelle out of the same pornographic urgency that his Thomistic theory earlier censured. The fires of lust inspire his aubade, a poetic explosion that conceals lascivious motives: "A glow of desire kindled again his soul and fired . . . his body" (p. 193). Weary of the ardent ways of frustrated passion, he cools his blazing heart through a masturbatory ritual that explodes in both aesthetic and physical ecstasy. By raising Emma to heights of Circean power that pique her erotic desirability, Stephen magically defuses her flirtatious spell and reduces her to a mystified figure controlled by his priestly imagination.

The formal, highly wrought verses of the villanelle ingeniously subdue the seductress whose *"eyes have set man's heart ablaze"* from the beginning of time. Against overwhelming enchantment, Stephen arrays the forces of aesthetic transformation. As poet-priest, he transubstantiates the eternal feminine into a disembodied muse that, once out of nature, ceases to threaten. Consigned to the realm of Byzantium, the Circean figure can no longer arouse animal lust or sensuous desire.

Throughout the novel, Stephen seeks the evacuation of affect from language and a reinscription of his filial self into the symbolic order and law of the father. By replicating himself in a discursive process of substitutability, he acquires a male aesthetic signature and triumphantly appropriates the female body/text. Inscribing himself into an august company of paternal authority figures (Daedalus, Edmond Dantes, Lord Byron, Father Conmee, Father Arnall, Dante Alighieri, Simon Dedalus, and Cranly), he fabricates an authorial persona purged of unsettling libidinal drives. The eternal temptress he celebrates is a disguised replica of the phallic mother who tantalizes with nurturant pleasure, then obstinately withholds satisfaction. Incestuous attraction to the body of the mother is repressed and displaced onto a radiant icon of female beauty. Emma provides a substitute for the mother (both consubstantial and Catholic Madonna) whose image, in turn, is reproduced in the specular icon of a wading bird-girl, then lyrically transformed into an enchantress idealized out of existence and consigned to the icy realm of Platonic stasis.

Through *Portrait,* Stephen manifests a psychological horror of woman as a figure of immanence, a symbol of unsettling sexual difference, and a perpetual reminder of bodily abjection. At the conclusion of chapter five, he prepares to flee from all the women who have served as catalysts in his own adolescent development. His journey into exile will release him from what he perceives as a cloying matriarchal authority. He must blot from his ears "his mother's sobs and reproaches" and strike from his eyes the insistent "image of his mother's face"

(p. 194). Alone and proud, isolated and free, Stephen proclaims joyful allegiance to the masculine fraternity of Daedalus, his priest and patron: "Welcome, O life! I go to encounter for the millionth time the reality of experience and to forge in the smithy of my soul the uncreated conscience of my race" (p. 218).

The hyperbolic resonance of Stephen's invocation leads us to suspect that his fate will prove Icarian rather than Daedalian. Insofar as women are concerned, he goes to encounter the reality of experience not for the millionth time but for the first. Much of the irony in *Portrait* results from Joyce's satirical rendering of Stephen's logocentric paradigm. The sociopathic hero, pompous and aloof, passionately gathers phrases for his word hoard without infusing his "capful of light odes" (*Ulysses* 14:1119) with the generative spark of human sympathy.

Certainly, the reader may feel baffled or uneasy about the degree of irony implicit in Joyce's portrait of the artist as a young narcissist. Stephen/Icarus has flown from one youthful illusion to another, first trusting the rectitude of his Clongowes masters and emulating the Count of Monte Cristo, then sliding into illicit sexual exultation in an initiation ritual immediately undercut by scenes of debased sensuality and emotional self-hatred. As the body, in turn, is disciplined and mortified, a devotion to the priesthood of art displaces the young man's Catholic asceticism. Embracing his newfound mission with all the exuberance of an aesthetic convert, Stephen is left exhausted and swooning before the sanctified icon of a wading girl transformed in his imagination into a mystical muse. Incapable of sustaining this romantic fantasy in the hostile environment of Dublin, he takes psychological refuge in vaguely erotic verses generated by a wet dream and/or by masturbatory excitation. Toward the end of the novel, Stephen adopts a Wildean pose of triumphant perversity as he proclaims revolutionary freedom and projects a vision of liberating flight "across the kathartic ocean" (*Finnegans Wake* 185.6) to the haunts of bohemian Paris. Emotionally static and incapable of meaningful connection with other human beings, the aspiring poet is poised in a stance of Icarian impotence. His final diary entries suggest imminent emigration, but they delineate neither flight nor failure.

The conclusion of Joyce's text seems to imply that the artist's notorious misogyny will prove to be still another dimension (and limitation) of his youthful priggishness. The pervasive irony that tinges the hero's scrupulous devotions and gives his aesthetic theory that "true scholastic stink" surely informs his relations with women—from his mother and Dante Riordan to Emma and the unnamed bird-girl he transfigures on the beach. In a tone of gentle mockery, Joyce makes clear to his audience that Stephen's fear of women and his contempt for sensuous life are among the many inhibitions that stifle his creativity. Before he can become a true priest of the eternal imagination, Stephen must first divest himself of "the spiritual-heroic refrigerating apparatus" that characterizes the egocentric aesthete. Narcissism and misogyny are adolescent traits he has to outgrow on the path to artistic maturity. Not until the epic *Ulysses* will a new model begin to emerge, one that recognizes the need for the intellectual artist to make peace with the mother/lover of his dreams and to incorporate into his masterful work those mysterious breaks, flows, gaps, and ruptures associated with the repressed and sublimated flow of male-female desire.

WORKS CITED

Beauvoir, Simone de. *The Second Sex*. 1953. Trans. and ed. H. M. Parshley. New York: Bantam, 1961.

Chodorow, Nancy. *The Reproduction of Mothering*. Berkeley: U of California P, 1978.

Dinnerstein, Dorothy. *The Mermaid and the Minotaur: Sexual Arrangements and Human Malaise*. New York: Harper, 1976.

Joyce, James. *Finnegans Wake*. New York: Viking, 1939.

———. *Stephen Hero*. Ed. John J. Slocum and Herbert Cahoon. New York: New Directions, 1963.

———. *Ulysses*. Ed. Hans Walter Gabler, et al. New York: Random House, 1986.

Slater, Philip E. *The Glory of Hera*. 1968. Rpt. Boston: Beacon, 1971.

Deconstruction and *A Portrait of the Artist as a Young Man*

WHAT IS DECONSTRUCTION?

Deconstruction has a reputation for being the most complex and forbidding of contemporary critical approaches to literature, but in fact almost all of us have, at one time, either deconstructed a text or badly wanted to deconstruct one. Sometimes when we hear a lecturer effectively marshal evidence to show that a book means primarily one thing, we long to interrupt and ask what he or she would make of other, conveniently overlooked passages, passages that seem to contradict the lecturer's thesis. Sometimes, after reading a provocative critical article that *almost* convinces us that a familiar work means the opposite of what we assumed it meant, we may wish to make an equally convincing case for our former reading of the text. We may not think that the poem or novel in question better supports our interpretation, but we may recognize that the text can be used to support *both* readings. And sometimes we simply want to make that point: texts can be used to support seemingly irreconcilable positions.

To reach this conclusion is to feel the deconstructive itch. J. Hillis Miller, the preeminent American deconstructor, puts it this way: "Deconstruction is not a dismantling of the structure of a text, but a demonstration that it has already dismantled itself. Its apparently solid ground is no rock but thin air" ("Stevens' Rock" 341). To deconstruct a text isn't to show that all the high old themes aren't there to be found in it. Rather, it is to show that a text — not unlike DNA with its double helix — can have intertwined, opposite "discourses" — strands of narrative, threads of meaning.

Ultimately, of course, deconstruction refers to a larger and more complex enterprise than the practice of demonstrating that a text means contradictory things. The term refers to a way of reading texts practiced by critics who have been influenced by the writings of the French philosopher Jacques Derrida. It is important to gain some understanding of Derrida's project and of the historical backgrounds of his work before reading the deconstruction that follows, let alone attempting to deconstruct a text. But it is important, too, to approach deconstruction with anything but a scholar's sober and almost worshipful respect for knowledge and truth. Deconstruction offers a playful alternative to traditional scholarship, a confidently adversarial alternative, and deserves to be approached in the spirit that animates it.

Derrida, a philosopher of language who coined the term "deconstruction," argues that we tend to think and express our thoughts in terms of opposites. Something is black but not white, masculine and therefore not feminine, a cause rather than an effect, and so forth. These mutually exclusive pairs or dichotomies are too numerous to list but would include beginning/end, conscious/unconscious, presence/absence, speech/writing, and construction/destruction (the last being the opposition that Derrida's word deconstruction tries to contain and subvert). If we think hard about these dichotomies, Derrida suggests, we will realize that they are not simply oppositions; they are also hierarchies in miniature. In other words, they contain one term that our culture views as being superior and one term viewed as negative or inferior. Sometimes the superior term seems only subtly superior (*speech, masculine, cause*), whereas sometimes we know immediately which term is culturally preferable (*presence* and *beginning* and *consciousness* are easy choices). But the hierarchy always exists.

Of particular interest to Derrida, perhaps because it involves the language in which all the other dichotomies are expressed, is the hierarchical opposition speech/writing. Derrida argues that the "privileging" of speech, that is, the tendency to regard speech in positive terms and writing in negative terms, cannot be disentangled from the privileging of presence. (Postcards are written by absent friends; we read Plato because he cannot speak from beyond the grave.) Furthermore, according to Derrida, the tendency to privilege both speech and presence is part of the Western tradition of *logocentrism,* the belief that in some ideal beginning were creative *spoken* words, words such as "Let there be light," spoken by an ideal, *present* God. According to logocentric tradition, these words can now only be represented in unoriginal speech or writing (such as the written phrase in quotation marks above). Derrida doesn't seek to reverse the hierarchized opposition between speech and writing, or presence and absence, or early and late, for to do so would be to fall into a trap of perpetuating the same forms of thought and expression that he seeks to deconstruct. Rather, his goal is to erase the boundary between oppositions such as speech and writing, and to do so in such a way as to throw the order and values implied by the opposition into question.

Returning to the theories of Ferdinand de Saussure, who invented the modern science of linguistics, Derrida reminds us that the association of speech with present, obvious, and ideal meaning and writing with absent, merely pictured, and therefore less reliable meaning is suspect, to say the least. As Saussure demonstrated, words are *not* the things they name and, indeed, they are only arbitrarily associated with those things. Neither spoken nor written words have present, positive, identifiable attributes themselves; they have meaning only by virtue of their difference from other words (*red, read, reed*). In a sense, meanings emerge from the gaps or spaces between them. Take *read* as an example. To know whether it is the present or past tense of the verb—whether it rhymes with *red* or *reed*—we need to see it in relation to some other word (for example, *yesterday*).

Because the meanings of words lie in the differences between them and in the differences between them and the things they name, Derrida suggests that all language is constituted by *différance,* a word he has coined that puns on two French words meaning "to differ" and "to defer": words are the deferred presences of the things they "mean," and their meaning is grounded in difference. Derrida, by the way, changes the *e* in the French word *différence* to an *a* in his neologism *différance*; the change, which can be seen in writing but cannot be heard in spoken French, is itself a playful, witty challenge to the notion that writing is inferior or "fallen" speech.

In *De la grammatologie* [*Of Grammatology*] (1967) and *Dissemination* (1972), Derrida begins to redefine writing by deconstructing some old definitions. In *Dissemination,* he traces logocentrism back to Plato, who in the *Phaedrus* has Socrates condemn writing and who, in all the great dialogues, powerfully postulates that metaphysical longing for origins and ideals that permeates Western thought. "What Derrida does in his reading of Plato," Barbara Johnson points out, "is to unfold dimensions of Plato's *text* that work against the grain of (Plato's own) Platonism" (xxiv). Remember: that is what deconstruction does according to Miller; it shows a text dismantling itself.

In *Of Grammatology,* Derrida turns to the *Confessions* of Jean-Jacques Rousseau and exposes a grain running against the grain. Rousseau, another great Western idealist and believer in innocent, noble origins, on one hand condemned writing as mere representation, a corruption of the more natural, childlike, direct, and therefore undevious speech. On the other hand, Rousseau admitted his own tendency to lose self-presence and blurt out exactly the wrong thing in public. He confesses that, by writing at a distance from his audience, he often expressed himself better: "If I were present, one would never know what I was worth," Rousseau admitted (Derrida, *Of Grammatology* 142). Thus, writing is a *supplement* to speech that is at the same time *necessary.* Barbara Johnson, sounding like Derrida, puts it this way: "Recourse to writing . . . is necessary to recapture a presence whose lack has not been preceded by any fullness" (Derrida, *Dissemination* xii). Thus, Derrida shows that one strand of Rousseau's discourse made writing seem a secondary, even treacherous supplement, while another made it seem necessary to communication.

Have Derrida's deconstructions of *Confessions* and the *Phaedrus* explained these texts, interpreted them, opened them up and shown us what they mean? Not in any traditional sense. Derrida would say that anyone attempting to find a single, correct meaning in a text is simply imprisoned by that structure of thought that would oppose two readings and declare one to be right and not wrong, correct rather than incorrect. In fact, any work of literature that we interpret defies the laws of Western logic, the laws of opposition and noncontradiction. In the views of poststructuralist critics, texts don't say "A and not B." They say "A and not-A," as do texts written by literary critics, who are also involved in producing creative writing.

Miller has written that the purpose of deconstruction is to show "the existence in literature of structures of language which contradict the law of non-contradiction." Why find the grain that runs against the grain? To restore what Miller has called "the strangeness of literature," to reveal the "capacity of each work to surprise the reader," to demonstrate that "literature continually exceeds any formula or theory with which the critic is prepared to encompass it" (Miller, *Fiction* 5).

Although its ultimate aim may be to critique Western idealism and logic, deconstruction began as a response to structuralism and to formalism, another structure-oriented theory of reading. (Deconstruction, which is really only one kind of a poststructuralist criticism, is sometimes referred to as poststructuralist criticism, or even as poststructuralism.)

Structuralism, Robert Scholes tells us, may now be seen as a reaction to modernist alienation and despair (3). Using Saussure's theory as Derrida was to do later, European structuralists attempted to create a *semiology,* or science of signs, that would give humankind at once a scientific and a holistic way of studying the world and its human inhabitants. Roland Barthes, a structuralist who later shifted toward poststructuralism, hoped to recover literary language from the isolation in which it had been studied and to show that the laws that govern it govern all signs, from road signs to articles of clothing. Claude Lévi-Strauss, a structural anthropologist who studied everything from village structure to the structure of myths, found in myths what he called *mythemes,* or building blocks, such as basic plot elements. Recognizing that the same mythemes occur in similar myths from different cultures, he suggested that all myths may be elements of one great myth being written by the collective human mind.

Derrida could not accept the notion that structuralist thought might someday explain the laws governing human signification and thus provide the key to understanding the form and meaning of everything from an African village to a Greek myth to Rousseau's *Confessions*. In his view, the scientific search by structural anthropologists for what unifies humankind amounts to a new version of the old search for the lost ideal, whether that ideal be Plato's bright realm of the Idea or the Paradise of Genesis or Rousseau's unspoiled Nature. As for the structuralist belief that texts have "centers" of meaning, in Derrida's view that derives from the logocentric belief that there is a reading of the text that accords with "the book as seen by God." Jonathan Culler, who thus translates a difficult phrase from Derrida's *L'Écriture et la différence* [*Writing and Difference*] (1967) in his book *Structuralist Poetics* (1975), goes on to explain what Derrida objects to in structuralist literary criticism:

> [When] one speaks of the structure of a literary work, one does so from a certain vantage point: one starts with notions of the meaning or effects of a poem and tries to identify the structures responsible for those effects. Possible configurations or patterns that make no contribution are rejected as irrelevant. That is to say, an intuitive understanding of the poem functions as the "centre" . . . : it is both a starting point and a limiting principle. (244)

For these reasons, Derrida and his poststructuralist followers reject the very notion of "linguistic competence" introduced by Noam Chomsky, a structural linguist. The idea that there is a competent reading "gives a privileged status to a particular set of rules of reading, . . . granting preeminence to certain conventions and excluding from the realm of language all the truly creative and productive violations of those rules" (Culler, *Structuralist Poetics* 241).

Poststructuralism calls into question assumptions made about literature by formalist, as well as by structuralist, critics. Formalism, or the New Criticism as it was once commonly called, assumes a work of literature to be a freestanding, self-contained object, its meanings found in the complex network of relations that constitute its parts (images, sounds, rhythms, allusions, and so on). To be sure, deconstruction is somewhat like formalism in several ways. Both the formalist and the deconstructor focus on the literary text; neither is likely to interpret a poem or a novel by relating it to events in the author's life, letters, historical period, or even culture. And formalists, long before deconstructors, discovered counterpatterns of meaning in the same text. Formalists find ambiguity and irony, deconstructors find contradiction and undecidability.

Here, though, the two groups part ways. Formalists believe a complete understanding of a literary work is possible, an understanding in which even the ambiguities will fulfill a definite, meaningful function. Poststructuralists celebrate the apparently limitless possibilities for the production of meaning that develop when the language of the critic enters the language of the text. Such a view is in direct opposition to the formalist view that a work of literary art has organic unity (therefore, structuralists would say, a "center"), if only we could find it.

Poststructuralists break with formalists, too, over an issue they have debated with structuralists. The issue involves metaphor and metonymy, two terms for different kinds of rhetorical *tropes,* or figures of speech. *Metonymy* refers to a figure that is chosen to stand for something that it is commonly associated with, or with which it happens to be contiguous or juxtaposed. When said to a waitress, "I'll have the cold plate today" is a metonymic figure of speech for "I'll eat the cold food you're serving today." We refer to the food we want as a plate simply because plates are what food happens to be served on and because everyone understands that by *plate* we mean food. A *metaphor,* on the other hand, is a figure of speech that involves a special, intrinsic, nonarbitrary relationship with what it represents. When you say you are blue, if you believe that there is an intrinsic, timeless likeness between that color and melancholy feeling — a likeness that just doesn't exist between sadness and yellow — then you are using the word *blue* metaphorically.

Although both formalists and structuralists make much of the difference between metaphor and metonymy, Derrida, Miller and Paul de Man have contended with the distinction deconstructively. They have questioned not only the distinction but also, and perhaps especially, the privilege we grant to metaphor, which we tend to view as the positive and superior figure of speech. De Man, in *Allegories of Reading* (1979), analyzes a passage from Proust's *Swann's Way,* arguing that it is about the nondistinction between metaphor and metonymy — and that it makes its claim metonymically. In *Fiction and Repetition: Seven English Novels* (1982), Miller connects the belief in metaphorical correspondences with other metaphysical beliefs, such as those in origins, endings, transcendence, and underlying truths. Isn't it likely, deconstructors keep implicitly asking, that every metaphor was once a metonym, but that we have simply forgotten what arbitrary juxtaposition or contiguity gave rise to the association that now seems mysteriously special?

The hypothesis that what we call metaphors are really old metonyms may perhaps be made clearer by the following example. We used the word *Watergate* as a metonym to refer to a political scandal that began in the Watergate building complex. Recently, we have used part of the building's name (*gate*) to refer to more recent scandals (*Irangate*). However, already there are people who use and "understand" these terms who are unaware that Watergate is the name of a building. In the future, isn't it possible that *gate,* which began as part of a simple metonym, will seem like the perfect metaphor for scandal — a word that suggests corruption and wrongdoing with a strange and inexplicable rightness?

This is how deconstruction works: by showing that what was prior and privileged in the old hierarchy (for instance, metaphor and speech) can just as easily seem secondary, the deconstructor causes the formerly privileged term to exchange properties with the formerly devalued one. Causes become effects and (d)evolutions become origins, but the result is neither the destruction of the old order or hierarchy nor the construction of a new one. It is, rather, *deconstruction*. In Robert Scholes's words, "If either cause or effect can occupy the position of an origin, then origin is no longer originary; it loses its metaphorical privilege" (88).

Once deconstructed, literal and figurative can exchange properties, so that the prioritizing between them is erased: all words, even dog and cat, are understood to be figures. It's just that we have used some of them so long that we have forgotten how arbitrary and metonymic they are. And, just as literal and figurative can exchange properties, criticism can exchange properties with literature, in the process coming to be seen not merely as a supplement — the second, negative, and inferior term in the binary opposition creative writing/literary criticism — but rather as an equally creative form of work. Would we write if there were not critics — intelligent readers motivated and able to make sense of what is written? Who, then, depends on whom?

"It is not difficult to see the attractions" of deconstructive reading, Jonathan Culler has commented. "Given that there is no ultimate or absolute justification for any system or for the interpretations from it," the critic is free to value "the activity of interpretation itself, . . . rather than any results which might be obtained" (*Structuralist Poetics* 248). Not everyone, however, has so readily seen the attractions of deconstruction. Two eminent critics, M. H. Abrams and Wayne Booth, have observed that a deconstructive reading "is plainly and simply parasitical" on what Abrams calls "the obvious or univocal meaning" (Abrams 457–58). In other words, there would be no deconstructors if critics did not already exist who can see and show central and definite meanings in texts. Miller responded in an essay entitled "The Critic as Host," in which he not only deconstructed the oppositional hierarchy (host/parasite), but also the two terms themselves, showing that each derives from two definitions meaning nearly opposite things. *Host* means "hospitable welcomer" and "military horde." *Parasite* originally had a positive connotation; in Greek, *parasitos* meant "beside the grain" and referred to a friendly guest. Finally, Miller suggests, the words *parasite* and *host* are inseparable, depending on one another for their meaning in a given work, much as do hosts and parasites, authors and critics, structuralists and poststructuralists.

Like poststructuralist readers from Derrida onward, Cheryl Herr tends to speak of literature in terms of "incongruities" and "nonsymmetries" instead of in terms of recognizable and meaningful patterns. On the first page of the essay that follows, she sets the stage for her deconstructive reading of Joyce's *Portrait* by figuring the text as a labyrinth or maze. However, since classical labyrinths can potentially be figured out, she quickly follows up the comparison with a contrast. *Portrait* is neither like "unicursal" mazes with one path to the center and out again, nor like their more complex, "multicursal" counterparts. It is like neither and both, its paths and patterns being characterized by utterly atypical complexities.

Several pages into her argument, Herr turns from the subject of the text as labyrinth to that of Stephen Dedalus as a person lost in a funhouse, a place in which nothing makes sense because everything contradicts itself—and everything else as well. Focusing on the coldness, aloofness, and indifference that we may assume to be Stephen's innate psychological characteristics, Herr views them as emotional responses to the confusion experienced in a cultural labyrinth. Even his aesthetic theory, Herr argues, "serves principally to support the emotional stance protecting him from the relentless disappointments of the social labyrinth and to bolster the detachment that he carefully cultivates."

One of the reasons Herr's argument about *Portrait* is so wonderfully compelling is that it doesn't just use labyrinths as metaphors to describe Stephen's social—or Joyce's textual—labyrinth. Rather, it points out that the idea of the labyrinth is alluded to by the very text of *Portrait*. Daedalus, after all, was the mythical Greek who built the labyrinth in which the Minotaur was kept. Thus, when Herr relates the choices faced by Stephen ("Should one kiss one's mother? Does God or Ireland come first? Is it better to be flogged for a misdemeanor or to accept expulsion from school?") to the confusions of the labyrinth, she does so in a way that the novel invites.

And what of the reader who, though on another plane, is in a labyrinth every bit as complex as the one in which Stephen finds himself? What Herr suggests is that the "indifferentness" characterizing Stephen's dealings with the cultural labyrinth comes to characterize our dealings with Joyce's textural maze as well; ironic withdrawal is as necessary for us to deal with textual anomalies, inconsistencies, and constrictions as it is for Stephen to deal with the facts of his Irishness, his Roman Catholicism, his education.

But to say these things is to say too little and too much, for Herr's deconstruction of *Portrait* proceeds playfully and in a a way that defies simple synopsis or summary. She makes us realize that there is no "answer" to the puzzle that is Joyce's novel, anymore than there is an answer to the question, "Who was Daedalus?"—a question posed and debated by a number of mythographers who have attempted to explain conflicting versions of mythical accounts and fragments. Herr is speaking of the mythological Daedalus and the Daedalus myth when she makes the following comment:

> His reappearance from story to story becomes unsettling; how

> could Daedalus have done and made all that he is recorded as being involved with? It is clear that each narrative unit, each transfiguring metamorphosis, marks the site of a being that is not unitary and whose presence is never now, always in the future.

But she might as well be speaking about Stephen Dedalus or even about *Portrait* itself, for if there is any one conclusion we can draw from her argument (and as a deconstructor, Herr would doubtless warn against drawing conclusions), it is that all questions concerning what *Portrait* is about—what its patterns are and what they mean—have as answers ones "that [are] not unitary and whose presence is never now, always in the future."

Ross C Murfin

DECONSTRUCTION: A SELECTED BIBLIOGRAPHY

Deconstruction, Poststructuralism, and Structuralism: Introductions, Guides, and Surveys

Arac, Jonathan, Wlad Godzich, and Wallace Martin, eds. *The Yale Critics: Deconstruction in America.* Minneapolis: U of Minnesota P, 1983. See especially the essays by Bové, Godzich, Pease, and Corngold.

Berman, Art. *From the New Criticism to Deconstruction: The Reception of Structuralism and Post-Structuralism.* Urbana: U of Illinois P, 1988.

Cain, William E. "Deconstruction in America: The Recent Literary Criticism of J. Hillis Miller." *College English* 41 (1979): 367–82.

Culler, Jonathan. *On Deconstruction: Theory and Criticism After Structuralism.* Ithaca: Cornell UP, 1982.

———. *Structuralist Poetics: Structuralism, Linguistics and the Study of Literature.* Ithaca: Cornell UP, 1975. See especially ch. 10.

Jefferson, Ann. "Structuralism and Post Structuralism." *Modern Literary Theory: A Comparative Introduction.* Totowa, N.J.: Barnes, 1982. 84–112.

Leitch, Vincent B. *Deconstructive Criticism: An Advanced Introduction and Survey.* New York: Columbia UP, 1983.

Melville, Stephen W. *Philosophy Beside Itself: On Deconstruction and*

Modernism. Theory and History of Literature 27. Minneapolis: U of Minnesota P, 1986.

Norris, Christopher. *Deconstruction and the Interests of Theory*. Oklahoma Project for Discourse and Theory 4. Norman: U of Oklahoma P, 1989.

———. *Deconstruction: Theory and Practice*. London: Methuen, 1982.

Raval, Suresh. *Metacriticism*. Athens: U of Georgia P, 1981.

Scholes, Robert. *Structuralism in Literature: An Introduction*. New Haven: Yale UP, 1974.

Selected Works by Jacques Derrida

Derrida, Jacques. *Dissemination*. 1972. Trans. Barbara Johnson. Chicago: U of Chicago P, 1981. See especially the concise, incisive "Translator's Introduction," which provides a useful point of entry into this work and others by Derrida.

———. *Of Grammatology*. Trans. Gayatri C. Spivak. Baltimore: Johns Hopkins UP, 1976. Trans. of *De la grammatologie*. 1967.

———. *Speech and Phenomena, and Other Essays on Husserl's Theory of Signs*. 1973. Trans. David B. Allison. Evanston: Northwestern UP, 1978.

———. *Writing and Difference*. 1967. Trans. Alan Bass. Chicago: U of Chicago P, 1978.

Poststructuralist Essays on Language and Literature

Barthes, Roland. *S/Z*. Trans. Richard Miller. New York: Hill, 1974. In this influential work, Barthes turns from a structuralist to a poststructuralist approach.

Bloom, Harold, et al., eds. *Deconstruction and Criticism*. New York: Seabury, 1979. Includes Miller's "The Critic as Host." Also see the essays by Bloom, de Man, Derrida, and Hartman.

de Man, Paul. *Allegories of Reading*. New Haven: Yale UP, 1979. See pt. I ("Rhetoric"), especially ch. 1 ("Semiology and Rhetoric").

———. *Blindness and Insight*. New York: Oxford UP, 1971. Minneapolis: U of Minnesota P, 1983. The 1983 edition contains essays not included in the original edition.

Johnson, Barbara. *The Critical Difference: Essays in the Contemporary Rhetoric of Reading*. Baltimore: Johns Hopkins UP, 1980.

Miller, J. Hillis. "Ariadne's Thread: Repetition and the Narrative Line." *Critical Inquiry* 3 (1976): 57–77.

———. Introduction. *Bleak House.* By Charles Dickens. Ed. Norman Page. Harmondsworth: Penguin, 1971. 11–34.

———. *Fiction and Repetition: Seven English Novels.* Cambridge, Mass.: Harvard UP, 1982.

———. "*Heart of Darkness* Revisited." *Joseph Conrad, Heart of Darkness.* Ed. Ross C Murfin. Case Studies in Contemporary Criticism Series. Ed. Ross C Murfin. Boston: Bedford–St. Martin's, 1989. 209–24.

———. "Stevens' Rock and Criticism as Cure." *The Georgia Review* 30 (1976): 5–31, 330–48.

Poststructuralist Approaches to Joyce

Attridge, Derek, and Daniel Ferrer, eds. *Post-Structuralist Joyce: Essays from the French.* Cambridge: Cambridge UP, 1984.

Attridge, Derek. "Criticism's Wake." *James Joyce: The Augmented Ninth.* Ed. Bernard Benstock. Syracuse: Syracuse UP, 1988. 80–87.

Boheemen-Saaf, Christine van. "Deconstruction After Joyce." *New Alliances in Joyce Studies.* Ed. Bonnie Kime Scott. Newark: U of Newark P, 1988. 29–36.

———. "Joyce, Derrida, and the Discourse of 'The Other.'" *James Joyce: The Augmented Ninth.* Ed. Bernard Benstock. Syracuse: Syracuse UP, 1988. 88–102.

Derrida, Jacques. "Ulysses Gramophone: Hear Say Yes in Joyce." *James Joyce: The Augmented Ninth.* Ed. Bernard Benstock. Syracuse: Syracuse UP, 1988. 27–75.

Ellman, Maud. "Disremembering Dedalus: *A Portrait of the Artist as a Young Man.*" *Untying the Text: A Post-Structuralist Reader.* Ed. Robert Young. Boston and London: Routledge, 1981. 189–206.

MacCabe, Colin. *James Joyce and the Revolution of the Word.* London: Macmillan, 1978; New York: Barnes and Noble, 1979.

———, ed. *James Joyce: New Perspectives.* Bloomington: Indiana UP, 1982.

McGee, Patrick. *Paperspace.* Lincoln: U of Nebraska P, 1988.

Rabaté, Jean-Michel. "A Portrait of the Artist as a Bogeyman." *James Joyce: The Augmented Ninth.* Ed. Bernard Benstock. Syracuse: Syracuse UP, 1988. 103–34.

Riquelme, John Paul. "The Preposterous Shape of Portraiture: *Por-*

trait." *James Joyce's "Portrait."* Modern Critical Interpretations. Ed. Harold Bloom. New York: Chelsea, 1988. 87–107.

Other Work Referred to in "What Is Deconstruction?"

Abrams, M. H. "Rationality and the Imagination in Cultural History." *Critical Inquiry* 2 (1976): 447–64.

A DECONSTRUCTIONIST PERSPECTIVE

CHERYL HERR

Deconstructing Dedalus

This essay moves down three paths. Along the first, I invoke certain feelings attendant on wandering, first pleasurably, then painfully, and finally numbly, in any mazelike structure. At the crossroad and along the second byway, I emphasize some of the major beliefs that Stephen Dedalus was asked to accept unquestioningly during his childhood education. Finally, I track the role played in upsetting those beliefs by the myth of Daedalus's labyrinth, even in undoing our sense of Stephen's ritually and repeatedly inscribed identity. Joyce's *Portrait* exploits every register of meaning—from the reader's emotions to Stephen's often surprising lack of them, from the mythic underpinnings of the narrative to the story's stretch into the aspects of human experience not yet linguistically rendered—in order to display the incongruities between philosophic system and lived experience, the nonsymmetries that form the crux of Joyce's epistemologically interrogative art.

I

Let's say that you (I would say "we," but our mutual isolation is part of the point) are walking down a narrow, curving path with walls on both sides high enough to block your view of anything but the sky. The steady swerve of the walkway suggests that just around the next bend you will encounter whatever it is that the pavement leads to. Following the smooth road, you unexpectedly turn into a dead end, unmistakable in that a high wall indistinguishable from those on left and right suddenly faces you. Nothing marks these barriers—no signs, no directives—so that backtracking seems an unattractive alternative to the impossibility of climbing the sheer face in front of you. Looking down at your feet you see, almost indistinguishable in the growing dusk, what appears to be the entrance to a tunnel: you warily lower your body into the apparently empty space; your feet miraculously locate another path; you walk forward in the dim light; you find yourself moving downward and then, oddly enough, what seems to be upward, until you emerge at a new but deeply familiar site. The fact that you now face another impasse with seemingly identical walls to front, left, and right prompts you to go forward, or what seems like forward, along the gently curving walkway. You feel that you may be trapped in a drawing by Escher, with oddly disconnected paths turning back on themselves, with roads emerging not only above but also below in the weirdly distorting half-light. As the day endlessly falters, you become convinced that there is no way out, but then you spot a landmark, a carillon rising above the sheer and uniform walls. Relieved, you try to head for the silent bell tower that you believe to have been near the entrance; you circle, as does the path, turn into yet another blind alley, peer up to orient yourself again, and discover that the carillon has mysteriously veered in front of you. Or is it the same structure? Hours pass; one or more undifferentiable towers appear and disappear in the steady twilight; what was anxiety becomes full-blown panic, then desperation, then an exhausted resignation, a resentful and depressed indifference.

Classicists have long been interested in the labyrinth that King Minos commissioned the cunning artisan Daedalus to build, a structure associated with the story of Pasiphaë's lust for a bull and consequent birthing of the Minotaur, which was eventually restrained by and hidden within the puzzle-as-prison. As social artifacts, labyrinths have also engaged the attention of architects, urban planners, and human geographers, all of whom study how the experience of negotiating a maze makes us feel and what kinds of cognitive processes we go through in producing provisional interpretations of supercomplex spaces. Environmental designer Romedi Passini writes in *Wayfinding in Architecture* (1984) that mazes, which are common to all human cultures and which have existed for at least five thousand years, are of two kinds. The simpler style, called "unicursal," which is what the putatively historical Daedalian structure would have been like, has a

> more or less complex but unique path that, if followed, leads to the center and out again. The challenge in such a design is not to find one's way but to understand the spatial configuration and one's position in it. . . . By contrast, the multicursal type is composed of a number of paths, forking, intersecting, and possibly leading to impasses or dead ends. Here one is not only confronted with the difficulty of identifying one's position in the

> maze but also of finding the way into a destination and, more important, of finding a way out again. (Passini 10)

Presumably unconcerned with these structural distinctions, Joyce does not force us to envision any single form of verbal and spatial labyrinth in *Portrait,* although, as many critics have noticed, the several chapters of the novel appear to function as independent mazes or as individual rings within a total design[1] that draws on visual images (labyrinths are frequently depicted in two-dimensional art) of both historical forms; Joyce's narrative structure echoes the multidimensionality and overall complexity that a cross-structuring of forms would produce.

John Paul Riquelme speaks specifically to this infrastructural feature of Joyce's *Portrait:*

> A kind of feedback is created whereby Stephen's later experiences, which are in some ways repetitions of earlier ones, are not in fact exact repetitions, in part because they occur against the background of what has gone before. The reader has access to this feedback through the increasingly mixed language that leads back to earlier scenes of different kinds. Because the language is complexly layered, the reader comes to every scene with frames of reference derived from earlier elements of the narrative, but each scene in turn results in new retrospective framings of what has gone before and new prospective framings of what is to come, and so on until the various frames overlap or nest within one another. The highly unusual effect, which is difficult to describe in an expository way, mimics the process of Stephen's remembering his complicated, differential past as he encounters each new experience, but it depends on the reader's active recollection of earlier passages. (Riquelme 118)

Riquelme is correct that the effect resists description, precisely because the locus for the effect is not verbal but visual; Joyce conjures architectural structures, allowing unicursal and multicursal forms to coexist. Each term or event is both repeated and interpenetrated by obstructions that block our ready construction of meaning and nudge us constantly toward the conclusions of deconstruction, toward undoing the very solidity of cultural and aesthetic values—values that Stephen wishes to recover as well as to critique by turning to the past. The recursive paths

[1]The most thorough expositor of this idea is Fortuna. Her essay bears comparison with Gutierrez, Hayman, Hodgart, Lord, and Nims. More peripherally, Faris concentrates on labyrinthine structures in *Ulysses,* as do several Joycean critics. I am indebted to my graduate research assistant, Anne Bartlett, for assistance in tracking the extensive scholarship on labyrinths in literature as a whole and in Joyce in particular.

of his thought and desire map the terms of irrecoverable losses, portraying those lacks by using language that already infinitely mourns its inability to become the concrete artifact that it names.

Of course, in the best of circumstances, "the prime characteristic of the labyrinth is to disorient," or so Passini argues:

> The Minoan myth is quite specific on that score. Not even Daedalus could escape without resorting to the bird's way. The labyrinth is the dwelling place of the Minotaur. He alone knows its ways, and he represents its danger. It can be argued that the Minotaur stands for the fear, the anxiety, and even the terror of being lost. (Passini 11)

Falling out of one's place in the structure of things, like suddenly finding oneself stranded in a foreign culture without a passport or knowledge of local mores, provides an acute and painful view of how unstable, how constructed every aspect of our socially programmed lives may well be. This is an experience Stephen absorbs firsthand when he confronts the political turmoil produced by Parnell's death, when his family undergoes economic decline and frequent removal from rented lodging to ever-worse housing, when he must come to terms with the variety and confusion of Dublin after the quiet order of his early suburban childhood. The mazes that every culture in the world has produced, regardless of their occasional entertainment value for members of those cultures, stand in some measure for that frightening recognition of ultimate instability; such spatial puzzles challenge the brave to test the limits of their tolerance for the disorder that always already lurks in the darkness. And so Passini argues that complex spaces remain associated with "unpredictability, the unknown, and the mysterious" (Passini 11)—in fact, with everything that the adult world represents to the young Stephen Dedalus and, ironically, with much to which his church arrogates the right to provide privileged access. Even so, the mazed mysteries that the Jesuits offer Stephen do not encompass the multicursal labyrinths of his own sexual desires and somatic responses. There are disappointments and monsters at every turn, and Stephen lacks even the most minimal diagram for many of the byways that he must navigate.

It is worth mentioning at this point that mazes generally are not meant to be *entirely* unconquerable. As human geographer Yi-Fu Tuan argues, moving in a labyrinth merely taps a larger, fundamental social skill. Tuan asks:

> How do human beings acquire the ability to thread their way through a strange environment, such as unfamiliar city streets?

> Visual cues are of primary importance, but people are less dependent on imagery and on consciously held mental maps than they perhaps realize. . . . They learn a succession of movements rather than a spatial configuration or map. (Tuan 70)

Ambiguous space, marked initially only by an entry point, gives way on successive tries to a set of landmarks and a drafted image (Tuan 71). Quoting from a 1932 essay by experimental psychologist Warner Brown, Tuan adds:

> The integration of space is an incremental process during which the appropriate movements for the entrance and the exit, and for the intermediate localities, continue to expand until they are contiguous. "When the subject is able to tread the maze without error (or with only rare errors) the whole maze becomes *one locality* with appropriate movements." What begins as undifferentiated space ends as a single object-situation or place.

Interestingly, in experimental situations, after having successfully negotiated a maze, most subjects do not reproduce it very well on a blank floor, and do not recall when they turned right and when left. People retain knowledge rather of "a succession of movements appropriate to recognized landmarks" (Tuan 72).

In the case of Stephen Dedalus, appropriate gestures, the too familiar dance of ideologies that routinely fail him, are often precisely what he wants to avoid. Although it is the ideological "fit" that makes space fully "familiar," enables it to "become place," with all of the security and protection that "place" suggests (Tuan 73), Stephen consciously cultivates different paths in the cultural maze; he knows that the more appropriate the turn of phrase or cultural maneuver, the more one is protected—protected not from danger but from the zone that the aspiring artist designates as freedom. This is not to say that Stephen can actually break free of his society. Self-determination is, in Joyce's world, one of the more persistent and deadly fictions propagated by Western culture, and this assertion is very much to the point of *Portrait's* meditation on mazes. However, Joyce's posture toward the mysterious is always optimistic; recall that Joyce chose as his epigraph to *Portrait* a line about Daedalus from Ovid's *Metamorphoses,* Book viii: *"Et ignotas animum dimittit in artes."* A. D. Melville's recent Oxford translation reads, "So then to unimagined arts / He set his mind and altered nature's laws" (Melville 177). The set of the mind, the turn of phrase find meaningful relation in Joyce as the unknown becomes less a limit than a porous frontier, a zone that one can turn toward and then turn within and perhaps even turn behind or beyond. Freedom becomes no more important (and possibly less so) than the search for new moves in old spaces.

While mazes teach us much about how the mind, socially programmed even in regard to space, works, the maze in Joyce is clearly the sign of an unknown quantity that generates feelings first of anxiety and then of a curious indifference that students often puzzle over. Why does the narrative, which follows Stephen's movements so closely, emphasize his coldness? I would say that his emotional responses accurately parallel the negative affects of folks lost in a funhouse, bumping their noses on glass walls and catapulting down chutes that a moment before looked like solid floors. In chapter three, in which Stephen powerfully responds to Father Arnall's retreat sermons—lectures that evoke in every sensory register the horrors of hell—the reader as well as Stephen may be pulled into a tornado funnel (or tundish) of despair and terror, every turned corner leading to even more horrible scenes of putrefaction and anguish. But the more typical emotion associated with Stephen throughout his youth is that of semiresigned indifference, the attitude of one inured to the maze or trying hard to deny that the labyrinth is not only all there is but is so disorienting that it terrifies him. Again and again, words appear like those at the beginning of chapter three, when Stephen, about to be theologically assaulted, is still wandering in the backstreets of nighttown: "A cold lucid indifference reigned in his soul" (p. 97). New readers frequently complain that Stephen is in fact a chilly and unappealing adolescent. Confronted with the yeasty confusion of early modern Dublin, subjected to tremendous shifts in social setting, educated in almost mandarin fashion despite his considerable poverty, a person of immense contradictions, Stephen as often as not seems to respond not with intellectual agility but with unnatural remoteness and disregard: "The noise of children at play annoyed him and their silly voices made him feel, even more keenly than he had felt at Clongowes, that he was different from others. He did not want to play" (pp. 66–67). Indifferent to possible playmates, Stephen clearly irritates them as much as they do him: in the famous battle over whether Byron was "the greatest poet" (p. 80) or "no good" (p. 81), Stephen struggles to defend himself from physical abuse, and yet immediately feels that "all the descriptions of fierce love and hatred which he had met in books had seemed to him . . . unreal" (p. 81). Sometimes he is so fearful of the strength of his own sexual desire that he actually uses Shelley's poetry to achieve a dissociated insensibility (p. 92); on other occasions he employs academic theological questions ("Is baptism with a mineral water valid?'' [p. 100]) to gain this emotional numbness. Repeatedly, his mind becomes "lucid and indifferent" (p. 134), so that he even finds it relatively easy to ignore the narcissistic wound of his mother's preference for her simple faith over her son's intellectual speculations (p. 146).

Stephen, cultivating emotional detachment, gradually adopts universal time as a sort of emblem of labyrinthine space: on the occasion when his playfully swimming friends call him "Stephanos Dedalos," we are told, "Their banter was not new to him. . . . Now, as never before, his strange name seemed to him a prophecy. So timeless seemed the grey warm air, so fluid and impersonal his own mood, that all ages were as one to him" (p. 149). Amid the ironies of Stephen's self-importance and his obvious efforts to keep at bay the painfully deep feelings that threaten to overwhelm him, there stands the characteristic emotional-rhetorical maneuver whereby his indifference enables a mythic dimension to move into place. Although he talks with some precision about pity and terror (p. 178), Stephen relates to them indifferently, as one who does not feel but who seeks only an "esthetic" stance that will mercifully elevate the mind "above desire and loathing" (p. 179). More than anything else, the artist that Stephen aspires to be is "like the God of the creation . . . within or behind or beyond or above his handiwork, invisible, refined out of existence, indifferent, paring his fingernails" (p. 187). The immanence of the artist in the work has tended to draw a great deal of critical attention, as has the comic picture of the artist with manicure mania, but it seems to me that Stephen's aesthetic theory serves principally to support the emotional stance protecting him from the relentless disappointments of the social labyrinth and to bolster the detachment that he carefully cultivates. So it is that when Cranly asks Stephen whether he loves his mother, Stephen merely says, "I don't know what your words mean" (p. 207). In his ability to register any change or assimilate any information, however shocking, without deviating for long from a fairly two-dimensional affective self-image, Stephen aligns entirely with the heroes of Greek myth. He does so especially with Daedalus, who engineers Pasiphaë's copulation with a bull, then builds the labyrinth to hide her offspring, finds himself trapped within the structure of his own making, devises a means of escape, is forced to bury his own son, and moves through numerous other highly charged adventures without sacrificing in any regard his primary identity as cold and cunning artificer. Further, Stephen *insists* on his indifference, agreeing to "take the risk" of losing all human contact in the quest for a fixed and aloof identity (p. 213). Beyond objectivity, he moves into the Nietzschean *Supermensch* zone of the "spiritual-heroic refrigerating apparatus" (p. 217), stubbornly maintaining this pose of isolated self-sufficiency as he wanders through the maze of growing up.

II

Against what, precisely, is Stephen preserving a failing fiction of emotional coherence and self-control? Beyond his individual terror of being lost in the labyrinth of individual identity, it would also appear that indifference is the self-protective stance that he adopts because of the disparity between philosophical tenets propagated by his culture as absolute truths and his own considerably divergent experiences of body, mind, spirit, and nationality. Hence, the maze of differences forces Stephen into a state of *in-difference* that belies its own distantiation from the welter of change. For this reason, no doubt, *Portrait* begins by concentrating on Stephen's education into the rules of discourse and cultural interaction, the familial and religious truths, and the philosophical principles that make up the belief structure of middle-class, early modern Dublin.

How are these beliefs rendered? From the first moment of *Portrait* Joyce insists that readers focus their collective attention on Stephen's education into figures of speech and on his ability to move from one linguistic maneuver or turn to the inevitable next trope. We have no choice but to attend to the laborious construction of meaning as the first infantile and then childish Stephen learns to distinguish between father and mother, between pater and Uncle Charles, and between taste and sight. He learns that "belt" has at least two senses, discovers the onomatopoetic force of "suck," works out what "wine" has to do with "whine," realizes the arbitrariness of designations ("that was heartburn" [p. 23]), learns that certain words like "smugging" tend to remain unexplained, sees that there are manifold differences among the boys whom he knows but notes also, despite his concerted effort to discern a palpable order in his life, that he does not have satisfactorily precise ways of registering for himself the logic of those differences. Different boys, different parents, different sounds for different pains, different names for God impress Stephen. Even more, we know from his belief that he will find justice in the rector's office that he has assimilated the logocentrism associated with Greek and Roman tradition (p. 58). In the Ireland of Joyce's day, classical mythology and history were not merely pleasant reading but the foundation of an educational system predicated on the belief that ancient literature, history, language, mythology, and especially philosophy embodied the truths on which all of Western culture depended. To understand and accept the logic underlying these disciplines was to be able to tell truth from falsehood, authenticity from imposture.

Now in the *Metamorphoses* Ovid wrote a morally puzzling tale about a labyrinth, but Stephen's teachers assumed that the culture that produced the story of Daedalus was lucid and defensible in its principles of right and wrong, of being and substance, of form and idea. That culture was also taken to be eminently logical in its organization, insistent that nothing could be both true and not true at the same time. And it was hierarchical: ideal forms, spiritual truths, and incorporeal substance preceded and superseded the flux of material reality that was nonetheless bound by rules of order and priority. The Christianity that Stephen Dedalus learns and the tenets of Thomas Aquinas that he obliquely honors in his aesthetic theory are both enlightened extensions of the physical and metaphysical concepts of Aristotle and his fellow philosophers. It is fair to say that the Minoan myth represents in Joyce the panoplied classical world that produced it, especially for Aristotle and his pathbreaking rendering of ontological reality.

On Stephen's part, we have abundant evidence that he believes that God's name signifies absolute essence (p. 27) and that all the universe exists in a rigid echelon (p. 26) that gives Stephen himself a specific place in relation to the divine mind. That the Church, which encompasses "twenty centuries of authority and veneration" (p. 210), is known to him through "the order" that educates him (p. 53) neatly aligns with this hierarchical picture. The cognitive map that Stephen's culture provides for him has a site on it for the "self" (whole, determining, purposeful), spots for various centers of meaning (the family, the academy, the Church, the state), and an area allotted to the city of Dublin and the island of Ireland. Father Arnall's eminently orderly sermon explores the depths of physical and mental torture, but in such a way that these horrors do not destabilize for Stephen the absolute legitimacy of the spot that they mark, the correctness of their response to mortal sin.

Correctness is an important issue for Stephen. It is right to apologize, wrong to hide under the table. It is right to have a magistrate for a father, wrong to be educated beyond one's social class. But again and again Stephen must ask himself, "Who was right then?" (p. 43) Should one kiss one's mother? Does God or Ireland come first? Is it better to be flogged for a misdemeanor or to accept expulsion from school? Stephen's uncertainty is understandable, as is his important, repeated, and socially sanctioned gesture to choose between *two* poles.

Again and again, he is left stranded without the ability to choose binarily, and yet so fiercely has his world trained him in binary logic that he insists on seeking *the* answer. Long after he has ceased to worry about ordered morality in the day-to-day sense, Stephen still tries to set up an ethical artistic hierarchy that mirrors his logocentric culture (pp. 184–87). Degrees of beauty occupy him, as do degrees of verbal skill and intellectual excellence. So, of course, does a certain reliance on causality: Stephen believes without question (and virtually no reader questions this point) that he is ill *because* of being pushed into the square ditch. We are led to imagine that his father's political enemies have caused his family's economic decline. And we are also encouraged to accept that Simon Dedalus's golden tongue engineers a spot for Stephen at Belvedere. All such "certainties" come under overt, satiric attack by the time Joyce composes the "Ithaca" episode of *Ulysses,* but *Portrait* still asks the reader to do much of the work of interrogating the knee-jerk logic of causality.

In Stephen's world, either-or logic and cause-effect reasoning join hands with social and intellectual hierarchies to represent what the educated person knows – that is, what was accepted as the truth of experience. What Stephen shows us during the first arc of the novel is how a child acquires the ability to erase his acute perception of infinite differences between received "truths" and his own sensations, how a child negotiates an unavoidable anxiety about the conclusions that escape false-dilemma reasoning. The manifold undecidabilities of sensation and interpretation resound in Stephen's awareness from the first page of the text. Although everything in Stephen's early experience encourages him to organize observed differences in terms of binary relations, right or wrong answers, and the predictabilities of social discourse, he develops strategies of evasion as well as of acquiescence. Numbing his sensibilities to the more distressing urgencies of the labyrinth, he also interrogates language itself as the vehicle of these depressing "certainties" marketed by family, school, and Church. Even in regard to his own lyrical imaginings, he questions: "Words. Was it their colours? . . . No, it was not their colours: it was the poise and balance of the period itself. Did he then love the rhythmic rise and fall of words better than their associations of legend and colour? Or was it that . . . ?" (pp. 147–48). The endless self-inquisition and his own uneasy relationship to a language that he knows to be both imbued with dead philosophic platitudes and untapped in terms of its prismatic possibilities for free play, for the endless transfiguration that he desires in his own life – these developments permanently texture Stephen's understanding of language. Much more interested in questioning words than in arriving at answers, Stephen thereby signifies his profound understanding that meaning is always deferred, that it will always "glow and fade" (p. 147).

Still, social training dies hard if at all, and Stephen may be found much later in the "Scylla and Charybdis" chapter of *Ulysses* reminding himself that "one hat is one hat,"[2] echoing his aesthetic theory's insistence on firm philosophic distinctions and on what he regards as the "necessary phases of artistic apprehension" (p. 184) that stand in for more general processes of seeing and knowing. We watch as Stephen's acuity is expended on a clichéd discourse on perception, on a predictable definition of beauty, and on the relationship of subject and object. As a college student, Stephen invests an inordinate amount of time reinventing, from the perspective of his ever-present concern with the nature of language, the wheel of Western epistemological tradition. Stephen's so-called aesthetic theory, which frequently brings the new reader of Joyce to a dismayed halt, seems gratuitously boring. At the same time it obviously reinvokes the earliest pages of the text and their fragmentary meditation on how we know, on the role of language in knowing, and on the manifold gaps between received social beliefs and the spontaneous cognitive gracenotes of individual perception. Because of Stephen's pomposity and persistence, because his friends are obviously used to his discourses and tolerate them, we as readers try to figure out why the aesthetic theory occupies such a weighty and strategic place in this story of Stephen's maturation. If he is an artist, we reason, he is entitled to an aesthetic theory, and so we tend to accept his thoughts about seeing and naming as somehow inherently necessary to the artistic vocation. Early Joyceans expended much energy on unfolding the implications of these theories, their relationship to the entire narrative, and the clues that they provide to whether Joyce intended us to view Stephen as a budding artist, a pathetic dilettante, or a talented individual crushed by social convention. Measuring the theory against the few shreds of poetic fervor that we are favored with in *Portrait,* critics have generally concluded that Stephen has some talent but is by no means a shoo-in for a future Nobel Prize for literature, despite the fact that three Irish authors have been so honored.

In any event, Stephen expounds one turn in his theory by attending to "a basket which a butcher's boy had slung inverted on his head." He asserts the existence of a "bounding line drawn about the object to

[2]"Aristotle's experiment. One or two? Necessity is that in virtue of which it is impossible that one can be otherwise. Argal, one hat is one hat." (*Ulysses* 192)

be apprehended," a gesture that may remind us less of our own experience of visuality than of Stephen's feverish query at Clongowes: "What was after the universe? . . . It could not be a wall but there could be a thin thin line there all round everything." (p. 27). For the older Stephen, the "esthetic image is first luminously apprehended as selfbounded and selfcontained upon the immeasurable background of space or time which is not it" (pp. 184–85). Proceeding to describe the analysis of "*one* thing" first into its several parts and then in terms of its *"whatness,"* an essence that falls under the sign of "silent stasis," Stephen displays the insidious and ineradicable impact of his culture upon his modes of seeing and feeling. He makes all the appropriate moves, right up to the point where the intellectual turns dead-end. Refusing—resolutely excluding—the literally infinite relationality of basket to butcher boy, Lynch, passing traffic, imaginative inversion and reversion, Stephen displays one reason for his long-cultivated indifference, his emotional stasis. The unpredictability and endlessness of the labyrinth of meaning horrify him; despite his desire to be an artist he spends most of his intellectual currency arresting precisely the play of meaning that would enable his art. From the beginning of the novel, we have witnessed his naive, self-deceptive bridging of the gap between words and things: "Words which he did not understand he said over and over to himself till he had learned them by heart: and through them he had glimpses of the real world about him" (p. 64). When he reasons, "By thinking about things you could understand them" (p. 49), we recognize the counterdeconstructive and socially "appropriate" movement to evade the obvious chasm between word and thing, to will away conflicting sensory information. The fact that the butcher boy's basket might call forth all manner of associations, connections, refigurings, cubist turns into other-space, different viewpoints, does not enter the theory, though this unmanageable multiplicity palpably intrudes on every aspect of Stephen's rather painful life. What we witness is Stephen's endless effort to reinstall some kind of order, right down to his ultimate projection backwards of a cultural "conscience" that he wrongly construes as potentially under his control.

For Stephen, then, understanding can be equated with evading difference, maintaining indifferentness; but that withdrawal ironically provides the reader with the distance necessary to register Stephen's aloofness as an acute state of being *in*-difference. Cannily, Joyce merges Stephen's emotional withdrawal with the novel's own metaphysical revisionism, a turn in the maze that forces the reader to register both affectively and intellectually the unstable but philosophically ineluctable site for Derridean *différance,* for something like a third term of infinite variability and ever-changing import. Given Stephen's insistence throughout all such echoing events that every moment has its own peculiar resonance, *Portrait* may well be the most sustained modernist narrative meditation on *différance* that we possess, every moment not only inevitably but quite self-consciously pregnant with and reliant on some impossible future unfolding of significance.

In contrast to this perspective, earlier Joycean critics concentrated on what they regarded as Joyce's direct appropriation of a realist Aristotelian and Thomistic theory of knowledge. For example, S. L. Goldberg maintains in *The Classical Temper* that even in *Ulysses* Stephen still seeks an art that is both subjective "personal expression" and "objective . . . 'truth'" (Goldberg 69). Goldberg posits that the Stephen we encounter throughout Joyce's writings never achieves the self-knowledge that will enable him to be fully objective, to enjoy artistic freedom as well as emotional self-understanding and integrity (Goldberg 77, 92–93). According to this argument, by the time he propounds his famous Shakespeare theory in *Ulysses,* Stephen shows his desire to understand and to cast off the "burden of his environment, of obsessive ideas, of ruling emotions" so that he can fulfill the basic human task of creating order from experience (Goldberg 82, 91–92). In this postdeconstructive era, however, we would phrase things differently from Goldberg. We would be less impressed by the possibilities of some purely fictive future in which Stephen's emotional maturity enables him to become the artist of the real, telling truly and fully what life is like, and we would be more likely to seek a postbinary, third-term equivalent to the unstable world of in-*différance.*

And in-*différance* clearly sweeps up Stephen's numerous labyrinthine sexual obsessions, passions, and barely controlled emotions. All of these are represented by the "viscid gloom" of Stephen's spiritual distress after Father Arnall's sermon, the mysterious murmuring that he discerns in the darkness, the fact that his own body responds against his conscious will to the calls of female flesh. The passage in which Stephen, horrified beyond measure, tries to reason out the power of desire offers much to the reader interested in the Joycean conception of understanding:

> But how so quickly? By seeing or by thinking of seeing. The eyes see the thing, without having wished first to see. Then in an instant it happens. But does that part of the body understand or what? The serpent, the most subtle beast of the field. It must

> understand when it desires in one instant and then prolongs its own desire instant after instant, sinfully. It feels and understands and desires. What a horrible thing! Who made it to be like that, a bestial part of the body able to understand bestially and desire bestially? Was that then he or an inhuman thing moved by a lower soul than his soul? His soul sickened at the thought of a torpid snaky life feeding itself out of the tender marrow of his life and fattening upon the slime of lust. O why was that so? O why? (p. 126)

Coming to an appreciation of the fact that existing epistemologies did not even address the body, with its multiple independent excesses, represents for Stephen a more profound education than any offered at Clongowes, Belvedere, or University College. In childhood he underwent the usual indoctrination; now the writing by which he is presented to us accedes to Stephen's own half-evaded perception—more acute, more literal, more abject, proto-deconstructive, never fixed or final, neither good nor debased but simply, complexly different. For the attentive reader, it becomes ever clearer that Joyce's writing practice struggles to implicate explicitly all of the forces acting on the here and now, despite Stephen's presumptuous effort to enforce a highly delimiting sense of how the mind and eye work together to create statements: *that* basket is one basket and not any other basket. In the passage quoted above, in which Stephen is confronted with an unruly penis and simultaneously wrestles with the universal signifier, the word "understand" occurs four times, each iteration signaling Stephen's recognition that his previous experience of "understanding" falls far short of the actual excess signified by sensory experience. Where he had trained himself to use words repetitively and specifically to screen out meanings that had not received an establishment imprimatur, now he puzzles over this other form of understanding, a "bestial" pressure that did not and would never yield its destabilizing and proliferative power to ritual invocations, prayers, or the will. Ironically, the penis becomes Stephen's lever for upsetting the power of phallogocentrism. Stephen's constantly replayed struggle to produce a linear and highly ordered theory about seeing, knowing, and naming—a struggle reinitiated in different terms with each chapter—demonstrates how fully the ideological primings of our culture override his intimately registered experience of things that muddy those noetic waters. The clean outlines he seeks are like the thin line he imagines around the universe, the products of antiquated, coercive educational and theological systems. But his own body, his own thoughts, and the language in which they are revealed to us complicate at every turn the kinds of assertions that Stephen wants to make. Seeking similarity, identity, a host of connections that can affirm presence and unity, Stephen instead constantly registers dissonance, fracture, dissimilarity, dissemination, deflection from the expected.

What Joyce sets up narratively is a remarkably adept deconstruction of the received theory of knowledge, a critique that comes about by introducing within, behind, beyond, and above subject and object an utterly provisional third term, or rather the possibility of a third term that eludes definition, a pure differential principle so multiple as to resist the concept of "principle." *Portrait* does not aim merely to refine or remake Western epistemology and does not want merely to turn binary distinctions into some kind of synthesizing dialectic. Rather, the concept of a third term, as always in Joyce's works when "threes" are invoked, falls under the sign of in-*différance;* the category unfolds for us into an aggressively unchartable array of distinctions that render Stephen's childish vocabulary, like the one he must rely on as an adult, comically inadequate. We might argue that the psychological dimensions of Stephen's maturation, which embrace those most intimate moments of growing up and reaching out to life, enforce their purely linguistic nature; they insist that we understand how fully the words available to us and the concepts that they claim to signify fail to bring into meaningful relation to one another the complexity of experience, development, and emotion.

III

To argue thus is not only to participate in what has become a familiar deconstructive legerdemain, in which *différance* and the infinite play of meaning are steadily teased out of any and every textual moment, in which the language of narrative, right down to the spaces between the letters, is foregrounded lest we forget that art is not life and that life isn't either. Rather than approach *Portrait* only from above, as it were, with a full-blown Derridean theory templating my interpretation, I would emphasize the fact that Joyce's close attention to classical texts themselves enabled him to discover much that Derrida would later help us all to understand; indeed, if Derrida is to be believed, Joyce profoundly tutored the theorists of the 1960s and after. I would assert, then, that Joyce's encounters with Ovid's *Metamorphoses* insistently reshaped the epistemological truths that he learned from Aristotle and Aquinas. Already implied in the realist theory of knowledge, with its steady dichotomies and jesuitically sharp distinctions, was an openness to transfiguration in the literal or even overliteral sense, to endless displacements of form and being. For Joyce, metamorphosis, rendered in words, is embodied in the movement from one figure to another, as the linear processes that we know as writing and reading force us to depend on the always-next word to "complete" what has preceded in any given sentence. Each figure marks a metamorphosis of meaning, and Stephen realizes, even as a schoolboy, that his culture conspires to deny this situation. Joyce appears to have come upon the notion of deferral quite literally through the metonymic movement from linguistic turn to linguistic turn, from one path in the maze to another. Ovid's Daedalian maze stands as an equivalent to the narrative structure of *Portrait* and paces the unchartable accretion of meanings in Stephen's story.

What may be surprising, given the inherently puzzling nature of mazes and the way in which Joyce uses them, is the fact that in his day, the culture was so anxious about stability and order that the labyrinth itself was, in a sense, a ground of meaning. By far the most elaborately developed interpretation of the stabilizing role played by the Minoan myth in *Portrait* is a long, well-researched article by Diane Fortuna. This 1972 study provides ample evidence that Joyce's sources for the myth would have exceeded even a schoolboy's considerable knowledge of Ovid. As it happens, the first decade of the twentieth century witnessed an explosion of archaeological and anthropological research guided by the lights of classical mythology: much to the point, in 1900 the London *Times* announced that Arthur Evans had excavated in Crete the sites referred to in the Daedalus myth: Minos's palace and its attendant labyrinth. As the discoverer of this site, Evans was credited not only with being the chief authority on the Minoan story but also with having demonstrated that these tales of initiation, desire, renewal, and revenge were true, were at some level authoritative records of what actually happened. Like the search for Noah's ark, the discovery of the labyrinth and similar structures promised to plant ever more solidly the integrity of the classical tradition and thus the philosophical and social foundations of the Western world. The story overtly dwells on the vagaries of lust (Pasiphaë's unnatural yearning for a bull's love) and the horrors that might be lurking at the heart of order (the Minotaur moving in the center of the maze). But in that the rituals associated with the story of Daedalus involve initiation—the taking of one's place in an ordered adult world—the narrative further insists that we recognize a natural order and respect its ability to survive amidst bloodshed, chaos, fear, and strife. Fortuna's long, detailed essay is required reading for anyone interested in the archaeological background to *Portrait*. She positions the Daedalus story in terms of a prior, authorizing history, a ground of facts of which Joyce was fully aware and which for Fortuna establishes as the meaning of the narrative Stephen's initiation to adulthood.

In taking this tack, Fortuna sails toward the end of a long line of Victorian and early modern writers who were invested in ascertaining the variations on mythic tales among the many classical writers who referenced them, in producing fully detailed and complete linear narratives from these scattered fragments, and in drawing connections between myth and historically verifiable events and rituals. Robert Graves's famous work *The Greek Myths* (1955) speaks to this encyclopedic task of organizing, cataloguing, and historicizing. So it is that Graves, citing Ovid's *Metamorphoses* and Liberalis's *Transformations* among the many sources for the Daedalus story, emphasizes that Pasiphaë's tale is initially spun around ritual icons such as bull masks; in assigning a literal grounding to the Daedalian portion of the story, he asserts that the labyrinth exists not only as a maze but also as a dance pattern marked on a mosaic floor (Graves, I, 297). Graves summarizes several versions of the story, suggesting that far from flying out of the maze, Daedalus leaves Crete in a boat that Pasiphaë gave him, while his son merely falls out and drowns. In this version, what Daedalus invents are sails, not wings (Graves, I, 313).

So significant a difference from the traditional story marks a larger strangeness revealed by compilations such as Graves's; mythic characters like Daedalus, two-dimensional but in narrative terms terrifically agile, feature in an amazing number of crises, discoveries, machinations, extrications, tragedies, close calls. The modern reader is hard pressed to accept Daedalus as one and only one person, so various are his activities and so incongruent the time-planes among which he moves. His reappearance from story to story becomes unsettling; how could Daedalus have done and made all that he is recorded as doing and making? It is clear that each narrative unit, each transfiguring metamorphosis, marks the site of a being that is not unitary and whose presence is never now, but always in the future. Privilege cannot be accorded to Daedalus's identity or even to his role as father, for when Icarus, disregarding paternal advice, follows his solar course and dies, Daedalus is no longer a father,[3] any more than he retains creative control when he becomes incarcerated in his own labyrinth. What entraps him identifies him;

[3]Compare Stephen's Ovidian thoughts about Shakespeare in the "Scylla and Charybdis" episode of *Ulysses* (208): "if the father who has not a son be not a father can the son who has not a father be a son?"

when he escapes from that identifying structure which houses a monster offspring, he thereby leaves behind first an aspect of his makerliness, then his fatherhood. Whether he is constructing jointed dolls (seemingly at the time an almost sacrilegious activity akin to producing clones or cyborgs), building a wooden cow to house Pasiphaë's lust, containing the offspring of her desire in a conundrum, or fashioning wings to escape from his own stifling art, Daedalus lives within a maze of his own making. He overtly constructs his world against the laws of nature, that is, against all that any given society regards as given ("But you could not have a green rose. But perhaps somewhere in the world you could" [p. 24]), and in doing so creates the scene for his particular identity, the terms of his own survival, and the prison that both threatens him and causes the death of his child.

The series of "A and not-A" formulations underlying the Daedalus myth determines the nature of the labyrinth far more than spatial switchbacks and impasses. Both labyrinth and son are unmanageable supplements that clear a space for the Daedalian identity and then partially cancel that projection. It is often noted that *Portrait* is itself a narrative maze but not that the terms of the maze describe the space of deconstruction. The labyrinth is an emblem of how we learn, how we cast information as knowledge, and how we negotiate the relationship between spatial complexity and in-*différance*. Classical mythology, in the "Peter Parley" version known to Stephen or the archaeological story known to Joyce, unfolds linearly and coherently, but Joyce understands that within and around those textbook adaptations stand highly self-critical and incongruent narratives that challenge classicists, historians, and archaeologists to make sense of a past that will not stay put. That each translation of the *Metamorphoses* enforces the transfiguring principle of the work is actually made explicit in *Portrait* when Stephen recalls "the shrewd northern face of the rector who had taught him to construe the Metamorphoses of Ovid in a courtly English, made whimsical by the mention of porkers and potsherds and chines of bacon" (p. 157). There is, however, a distance between imagining that there is an original, inviolate Ovidian text that has engendered numerous translations (*Portrait* among them) and insisting, as *Portrait* does, that the Ovidian narrative can be received only as a plural, decomposing, fractured, and inchoate collection of poetic turns, figures of speech endlessly reconfiguring the relations of self and experience, subject and object.

I would argue that it is this quality of myth that fascinated Joyce: the disjunction and internal contradictions that unfold precisely when the Victorian impulse to collect, catalogue, organize, and historicize is indulged. Joyce ritually unravels myth, history, authority, and initiation, and puts a nonfinite spin on them. Instead of making the myth a center of condensed truths ready to be archaeologically excavated in the manner of Arthur Evans, Joyce implodes the implicit variants, allowing them to decenter his own narrative and to be decentered by the events of his telling and taling. The processes I describe here are, properly speaking, not those that T. S. Eliot assigns to the mythic motive and Joyce's apparent use of it; we are not concerned with rescuing ancient myth in order to reinvent stability in the modern era, nor are we involved in merely tracing the complicated ironies that chart our twentieth-century failures of heroism. Rather, the myth reveals to us its destabilizing role vis-à-vis history, and its peculiarly dissociative uses in contemporary processes of reading and writing. If the Daedalus myth began from ritual icons that became narratives, Joyce's procedure is to resorb the stories into icons again, to reduce them to monstrously pregnant figures like the goatish beasts of Stephen's personal Hades. Thus everything signifies fiercely, compactly, densely, and silently—each icon emitting information at a great rate without that information necessarily bearing linearly on the story at hand. This has always been a Joycean trademark, roughly called "symbolism" by many readers but having a peculiar, ritual resonance and philosophic import that is far in excess of symbolism.

Of course, Joyce's strategy of referring to Greek mythology for narrative patterns, as he does also by invoking *The Odyssey* in *Ulysses,* runs the eternal risk of elevating the prior narrative, however duplicitous its significance. Indeed, classical culture long maintained its hegemony over the Irish mind, and as Derrida observes, hierarchies are inherently violent, one term always controlling its subordinate other. Deconstruction, in overturning, interminably, any given ordered set of terms, participates in that violence, makes clear the omnipresence of force and compulsion in the processes of reading and writing. In that the Daedalus myth appears to pace Stephen's story, it is clear that the myth aggresses against and does violence to the protagonist's self-experience. And yet, Joyce's text stands not secondary to the *Metamorphoses* and not as a translation, not even, as Fortuna argues, as a replica of the myth. Rather, Stephen's experience decenters the myth while he is simultaneously decentered *by* the myth.

This latter point requires a bit of unraveling. We do not need the priming of the narrative to remind us that Stephen—aspiring artist, claimer of silence, cunning, and exile—asks to be measured against and even typecast as the artful Daedalus. In addition, Stephen's own invincible youth, his vexed relationship with his father (Stephen invariably ignores Simon's advice whether he wants to or not), and his willful flight from Ireland, all impel us to see him as the doomed Icarus. Then again, there are many suggestions that Stephen must also be equated with the maze itself; when he encounters the beasts of his imagination in his postsermon hallucinations, we know that his own mind engenders these monsters. Similarly, his dreams are scenes of "dark orgiastic riot" (p. 94), transgressive spaces that relocate reality from external world to inner, recursive, tangled imagination. Even his initial immense satisfaction at attending the university comes to him complete with a cadenced environment of his own making, a world in which "supple periodic prose" (p. 148) creates an encircling, encompassing *mise en scène*.

With Stephen's multiple connections to the myth in mind, we might consider the passage from Ovid in which the labyrinth is described:

> The structure was designed by Daedalus,
> That famous architect. Appearances
> Were all confused; he led the eye astray
> By a mazy multitude of winding ways,
> Just as Maeander plays among the meads
> Of Phrygia and in its puzzling flow
> Glides back and forth and meets itself and sees
> Its waters on their way and winds along
> Facing sometimes its source, sometimes the sea.
> So Daedalus in countless corridors
> Built bafflement, and hardly could himself
> Make his way out, so puzzling was the maze. (Ovid 176)

The poem insists on an almost infinite instability, as puzzling as the "maze of narrow and dirty streets" that Stephen knows as Dublin (p. 95). Although (or possibly because) he does not attend Trinity College, his conception of it is rather dire: "The grey block of Trinity on his left, set heavily in the city's ignorance like a great dull stone set in a cumbrous ring, pulled his mind downward . . ." (p. 158). Real life for Stephen, which very soon finds itself opposed to all that any university represents, is always a maze, and that life, those streets, he moves along, now not only as Maker, Son, and Maze but also as the Minotaur that must be contained by Stephen's own devices: "He wandered up and down the dark slimy streets peering into the gloom of lanes and doorways, listening eagerly for any sound. He moaned to himself like some baffled prowling beast" (p. 95). And the female mate that he longs to "sin with" assimilates at many levels to the ever-present image of Ireland as sow or to the "bovine god" that Stephen imagines in his own bestial state of sin (p. 104). Invoking various cultures' notions of beauty as "a maze out of which we cannot escape," Stephen reclaims the Daedalian or overreaching role by proposing "two ways out," one of which, of course, returns us to his mazelike aesthetic theory (p. 181), itself only a temporary containment strategy ineffectively countering Stephen's endless dissemination of image and idea.

Stephen, then, is the "fabulous artificer," who makes art out of the ordinary stuff of life. He is also Icarus, the always fallen son, the eternal caveat, the comic-tragic figure who exists only *as* figure, his reality only a turn in the story, a cautionary ideological projection into absence. Again, Stephen is the monster of lust, both maternal and bestial, as well as the monstrous offspring of his own fanciful parenting.[4] The myth, then, is decentered and decentering, scattered throughout the text and undoing Stephen's coherence as an individual: we can invoke Derrida's reminder that consciousness or individual identity is merely (or wonderfully) "an economy of differential forces" (Krell 7). Stephen's creations—the villanelle, the aesthetic theory—are less important as signs of intellectual prowess than they are as self-generated artisanal efforts to maze in the beast that exists everywhere but that he perceives first in his own loins and heart. Stephen's in-*différance* remains, given the mores of his culture, a sort of social defect, a perceptual lack that manifests itself as the discovery of excess meaning in all transactions and relations. This excess is marked by the paradox by which Stephen's patronymic—the Name of Father—is part of his multiple status as son, space, and maternal transgression. Whenever the narrative tries to make him fill one and only one mythic role, Stephen "himself" aligns indifferently with "the ages." Joyce's cunning uses of the Daedalus story imply "not only" the symbolic multireferentiality and initiatory ritual critically proclaimed in the past "but rather" an endless disintegration of the conditions for and possibility of personal identity.

In the preface to *Of Grammatology* (1967), Derrida, whom I would call the philosopher of the breakdown between space and place, claims,

[4]Gutierrez agrees that Stephen is both Icarus and Daedalus, and he adds Theseus to the list of identifications (Gutierrez, 18–20). Although his essay is too early to be explicitly deconstructive, Hayman also associates Stephen with the labyrinth of emotions and what Stephen views with horror as the monstrosity of lust.

"The future can only be anticipated in the form of an absolute danger. It is that which breaks absolutely with constituted normality and can only be proclaimed, *presented,* as a sort of monstrosity" (Derrida 5). So it is that although the deconstructive wayfinder orients to landmarks, the landmarks may well shift eternally out of alignment with entrance or center. And no signpost twice seen may be said to be the same. If we admit any of these circumstances as possible, we violate the logic of the maze, however multicursal and cross-structural; and this barbarous transgression redounds in our reading, in our writing, and in whatever indifference we can manage to share with Stephen Dedalus.

WORKS CITED

Derrida, Jacques. *Of Grammatology.* Trans. Gayatri Chakravorty Spivak. Baltimore and London: Johns Hopkins UP, 1976.

Faris, Wendy B. *Labyrinths of Language: Symbolic Landscape and Narrative Design in Modern Fiction.* Baltimore and London: Johns Hopkins UP, 1988.

Fortuna, Diane. "The Labyrinth as Controlling Image in Joyce's *A Portrait of the Artist as a Young Man.*" *Bulletin of the New York Public Library* 76 (1972): 120–81.

Goldberg, S. L. *The Classical Temper: A Study of James Joyce's "Ulysses."* London: Chatto and Windus, 1961.

Graves, Robert. *The Greek Myths.* 2 vols. New York: Penguin, 1960.

Gutierrez, Donald. *The Maze in the Mind and the World: Labyrinths in Modern Literature.* Troy: Whitston Publishing, 1985.

Hayman, David. "Daedalian Imagery in *A Portrait of the Artist as a Young Man.*" *Hereditas: Seven Essays on the Modern Experience of the Classical.* Ed. Frederic Will. Austin: U of Texas, 1964.

Hodgart, Matthew. *James Joyce: A Student's Guide.* London: Routledge, 1978.

Joyce, James. *Ulysses.* New York: Random, 1961.

Krell, David Farrell. "Engorged Philosophy: A Note on Freud, Derrida, and *Differance.*" *Derrida and "Differance."* Ed. David Wood and Robert Bernasconi. Evanston: Northwestern UP, 1988. 7–11.

Lord, George deForest. *Heroic Mockery: Variations on Epic Themes from Homer to Joyce.* Newark: U of Delaware P, 1977.

Nims, John Frederick. "Daedalus in Crete." *Daedalus in Crete: Essays in the Implications of Joyce's "A Portrait of the Artist as a Young Man."* Los Angeles: Immaculate Heart College, 1956.

Ovid. *Metamorphoses.* Trans. A. D. Melville. New York and Oxford: Oxford UP, 1986.

Passini, Romedi. *Wayfinding in Architecture.* [Environmental Design Series.] New York: Van Nostrand Reinhold, 1984.

Riquelme, John Paul. "*Stephen Hero, Dubliners,* and *A Portrait of the Artist as a Young Man:* Styles of Realism and Fantasy." *The Cambridge Companion to James Joyce.* Ed. Derek Attridge. Cambridge: Cambridge UP, 1990. 103–30.

Tuan, Yi-Fu. *Space and Place: The Perspective of Experience.* Minneapolis: U of Minnesota P, 1977.

The New Historicism and *A Portrait of the Artist as a Young Man*

WHAT IS THE NEW HISTORICISM?

The new historicism is, first of all, *new:* one of the most recent developments in contemporary theory, it is still evolving. Enough of its contours have come into focus for us to realize that it exists and deserves a name, but any definition of the new historicism is bound to be somewhat fuzzy, like a partially developed photographic image. Some individual critics that we may label new historicist may also be deconstructors, or feminists, or Marxists. Some would deny that the others are even writing the new kind of historical criticism.

All of them, though, share the conviction that, somewhere along the way, something important was lost from literary studies: historical consciousness. Poems and novels came to be seen in isolation, as urnlike objects of precious beauty. The new historicists, whatever their differences and however defined, want us to see that even the most urnlike poems are caught in a web of historical conditions, relationships, and influences. In an essay on "The Historical Necessity for—and Difficulties with—New Historical Analysis in Introductory Literature Courses" (1987), Brook Thomas suggests that discussions of Keats's "Ode on a Grecian Urn" might begin with questions such as the following: Where would Keats have seen such an urn? How did a Grecian urn end up in a museum in England? Some very important historical and political realities, Thomas suggests, lie behind and inform Keats's definitions of art, truth, beauty, the past, and timelessness. They are realities that psychoanalytic and reader-response critics, formalists and feminists and deconstructors, might conceivably overlook.

Although a number of influential critics working between 1920 and 1950 wrote about literature from a psychoanalytic perspective, the majority of critics took what might generally be referred to as the historical approach. With the advent of the New Criticism, or formalism, however, historically oriented critics almost seemed to disappear from the face of the earth. Jerome McGann writes: "a text-only approach has been so vigorously promoted during the last thirty-five years that most historical critics have been driven from the field, and have raised the flag of their surrender by yielding the title 'critic' to the victor, and accepting the title 'scholar' for themselves" (*Inflections* 17). Of course, the title "victor" has been vied for by a new kind of psychoanalytic critic, by reader-response critics, by so-called deconstructors, and by feminists since the New Critics of the 1950s lost it during the following decade. But historical scholars have not been in the field, seriously competing to become a dominant critical influence.

At least they haven't until quite recently. In his essay "Toward a New History in Literary Study" (1984), Herbert Lindenberger writes: "It comes as something of a surprise to find that history is making a powerful comeback" (16). E. D. Hirsch, Jr., has also predicted a comeback. He suggested in 1984 that various avant-garde positions (such as deconstruction) have been overrated and that it is time to turn back to history and to historical criticism:

> We should not be disconcerted by its imposing claims, or made to think that we are being naive when we try to pursue historical study. Far from being naive, historically based criticism is the newest and most valuable kind . . . for our students (and our culture) at the present time. (Hirsch 197)

McGann obviously agrees. In *Historical Studies and Literary Criticism* (1985), he speaks approvingly of recent attempts to make sociohistorical subjects and methods central to literary studies once again.

As the word *sociohistorical* suggests, the new historicism is not the same as the historical criticism practiced forty years ago. For one thing, it is informed by recent critical theory: by psychoanalytic criticism, reader-response criticism, feminist criticism, and perhaps especially by deconstruction. The new historicist critics are less fact- and event-oriented than historical critics used to be, perhaps because they have come to wonder whether the truth about what really happened can ever be purely and objectively known. They are less likely to see history as linear and progressive, as something developing toward the present.

As the word "sociohistorical" also suggests, the new historicists view history as a social science and the social sciences as being properly historical. McGann most often alludes to sociology when discussing the future of literary studies. "A sociological poetics must be recognized not only as relevant to the analysis of poetry, but in fact as central to the analysis" (*Inflections* 62). Lindenberger cites anthropology as particularly useful in the new historical analysis of literature, especially anthropology as practiced by Victor Turner and Clifford Geertz. Geertz, who has related theatrical traditions in nineteenth-century Bali to forms of political organization that developed during the same period, has influenced some of the most important critics writing the new kind of historical criticism. Due in large part to Geertz's influence, new historicists such as Stephen Greenblatt have asserted that literature is not a sphere apart or distinct from the history that is relevant to it. That is what old historical criticism tended to do, to present history as information you needed to know before you could fully appreciate the separate world of art. Thus the new historicists have discarded old distinctions between literature, history, and the social sciences, while blurring other boundaries. They have erased the line dividing historical and literary materials, showing that the production of one of Shakespeare's plays was a political act and that the coronation of Elizabeth I was carried out with the same care for staging and symbol lavished on a work of dramatic art.

In addition to breaking down barriers that separate literature and history, history and the social sciences, new historicists have reminded us that it is treacherously difficult to reconstruct the past as it really was—rather than as we have been conditioned by our own place and time to believe that it was. And they know that the job is utterly impossible for anyone who is unaware of the difficulty and of the nature of his or her own historical vantage point. "Historical criticism can no longer make any part of [its] sweeping picture unselfconsciously, or treat any of its details in an untheorized way," McGann wrote in 1985 (*Historical Studies* 11). *Unselfconsciously* and *untheorized* are key words here; when the new historicist critics of literature describe a historical change, they are highly conscious of, and even likely to discuss, the *theory* of historical change that informs their account. They know that the changes they happen to see and describe are the ones that their theory of change allows or helps them to see and describe. And they know, too, that their theory of change is historically determined. They seek to minimize the distortion inherent in their perceptions and representations by admitting that they see through preconceived notions; in other words, they learn and reveal the color of the lenses in the glasses that they wear.

All three of the critics whose recent writings on the so-called back-to-history movement have been quoted thus far—Hirsch, Lindenberger, and McGann—mention the name of the late Michel Foucault. As much an archaeologist as a historian and as much a philosopher as either, Foucault in his writings brought together incidents and phenomena from areas of inquiry and orders of life that we normally regard as unconnected. As much as anyone, he encouraged the new historicist critic of literature outwardly to redefine the boundaries of historical inquiry.

Foucault's views of history were influenced by Friedrich Nietzsche's concept of a *wirkliche* ("real" or "true") history that is neither melioristic nor metaphysical. Foucault, like Nietzsche, didn't understand history as development, as a forward movement toward the present. Neither did he view history as an abstraction, idea, or ideal, as something that began "In the beginning" and that will come to THE END, a moment of definite closure, a Day of Judgment. In his own words, Foucault "abandoned [the old history's] attempts to understand events in terms of . . . some great evolutionary process" (*Discipline and Punish* 129). He warned new historians to be aware of the fact that investigators are themselves "situated." It is difficult, he reminded them, to see present cultural practices critically from within them, and on account of the same cultural practices, it is almost impossible to enter bygone ages. In *Discipline and Punish: The Birth of the Prison* (1975), Foucault admitted that his own interest in the past was fueled by a passion to write the history of the present.

Like Marx, Foucault saw history in terms of power, but his view of power owed more perhaps to Nietzsche than to Marx. Foucault seldom viewed power as a repressive force. Certainly, he did not view it as a tool of conspiracy used by one specific individual or institution against another. Rather, power represents a whole complex of forces; it is that which produces what happens. Thus, even a tyrannical aristocrat does not simply wield power, because he is formed and empowered by discourses and practices that constitute power. Viewed by Foucault, power is "positive and productive," not "repressive" and "prohibitive" (Smart 63). Furthermore, no historical event, according to Foucault, has a single cause; rather, it is intricately connected with a vast web of economic, social, and political factors.

A brief sketch of one of Foucault's major works may help clarify some of his ideas. *Discipline and Punish* begins with a shocking but accurate description of the public drawing and quartering of a Frenchman who had botched his attempt to assassinate King Louis XV. Foucault proceeds, then, by describing rules governing the daily life of modern Parisian felons. What happened to torture, to punishment as public spectacle? he asks. What complex network of forces made it disappear? In working toward a picture of this "power," Foucault turns up many interesting puzzle pieces, such as that in the early revolutionary years of the nineteenth century, crowds would sometimes identify with the prisoner and treat the executioner as if *he* were the guilty party. But Foucault sets forth a related reason for keeping prisoners alive, moving punishment indoors, and changing discipline from physical torture into mental rehabilitation: colonization. In this historical period, people were needed to establish colonies and trade, and prisoners could be used for that purpose. Also, because these were politically unsettled times, governments needed infiltrators and informers. Who better to fill those roles than prisoners pardoned or released early for showing a willingness to be rehabilitated? As for rehabilitation itself, Foucault compares it to the old form of punishment, which began with a torturer extracting a confession. In more modern, "reasonable" times, psychologists probe the minds of prisoners with a scientific rigor that Foucault sees as a different kind of torture, a kind that our modern perspective does not allow us to see as such.

Thus, a change took place, but perhaps not so great a change as we generally assume. It may have been for the better or for the worse; the point is that agents of power didn't make the change because mankind is evolving and, therefore, more prone to perform good-hearted deeds. Rather, different objectives arose, including those of a new class of doctors and scientists bent on studying aberrant examples of the human mind.

Foucault's type of analysis has recently been practiced by a number of literary critics at the vanguard of the back-to-history movement. One of these critics, Stephen Greenblatt, has written on Renaissance changes in the development of both literary characters and real people. Like Foucault, he is careful to point out that any one change is connected with a host of others, no one of which may simply be identified as the cause or the effect. Greenblatt, like Foucault, insists on interpreting literary devices as if they were continuous with other representational devices in a culture; he turns, therefore, to scholars in other fields in order to better understand the workings of literature. "We wall off literary symbolism from the symbolic structures operative elsewhere," he writes, "as if art alone were a human creation, as if humans themselves were not, in Clifford Geertz's phrase, cultural artifacts." Following Geertz, Greenblatt sets out to practice what he calls "anthropological or cultural criticism." Anthropological literary criticism, he continues, addresses itself "to the interpretive constructions the members of a society apply to their experience," since a work of literature is itself an interpretive construction, "part of the system of signs that constitutes a given culture." He suggests that criticism must never interpret the past without at least being "conscious of its own status as interpretation" (Greenblatt 4).

Not all of the critics trying to lead students of literature back to history are as "Foucauldian" as Greenblatt. Some of these new historicists owe more to Marx than to Foucault. Others, like Jerome McGann, have followed the lead of Soviet critic M. M. Bakhtin, who was less likely than Marx to emphasize social class as a determining factor. (Bakhtin was more interested in the way that one language or style is the parody of an older one.) Still other new historicists, like Brook Thomas, have clearly been more influenced by Walter Benjamin, best known for essays such as "Theses on the Philosophy of History" and "The Work of Art in the Age of Mechanical Reproduction."

Moreover, there are other reasons not to declare that Foucault has been the central influence on the new historicism. Some new historicist critics would argue that Foucault critiqued old-style historicism to such an extent that he ended up being antihistorical or, at least, nonhistorical. As for his commitment to a radical remapping of relations of power and influence, cause and effect, in the view of some critics, Foucault consequently adopted too cavalier an attitude toward chronology and facts. In the minds of other critics, identifying and labeling a single master or central influence goes against the very grain of the new historicism. Practitioners of the new historicism have sought to decenter the study of literature and move toward the point where literary studies overlap with anthropological and sociological studies. They have also struggled to see history from a decentered perspective, both by recognizing that their own cultural and historical position may not afford the best understanding of other cultures and times and by realizing that events seldom have any single or central cause. At this point, then, it is appropriate to pause and suggest that Foucault shouldn't be seen as *the* cause of the new historicism, but as one of several powerful, interactive influences.

It is equally useful to suggest that the debate over the sources of the movement, the differences of opinion about Foucault, and even my own need to assert his importance may be historically contingent; that is to say, they may all result from the very *newness* of the new historicism itself. New intellectual movements often cannot be summed up or represented by a key figure, any more than they can easily be summed up or represented by an introduction or a single essay. They respond to disparate influences and almost inevitably include thinkers who represent a wide range of backgrounds. Like movements that are disintegrating, new movements embrace a broad spectrum of opinions and positions.

But just as differences within a new school of criticism cannot be overlooked, neither should they be exaggerated, since it is the similarity among a number of different approaches that makes us aware of a new movement under way. Greenblatt, Hirsch, McGann, and Thomas all started with the assumption that works of literature are simultaneously influenced by and influencing reality, broadly defined. Thus, whatever their disagreements, they share a belief in referentiality—a belief that literature refers to and is referred to by things outside itself—that is fainter in the works of formalist, poststructuralist, and even reader-response critics. They believe with Greenblatt that the "central concerns" of criticism "should prevent it from permanently sealing off one type of discourse from another or decisively separating works of art from the minds and lives of their creators and their audiences" (5).

McGann, in his introduction to *Historical Studies and Literary Criticism,* turns referentiality into a rallying cry:

> What will not be found in these essays . . . is the assumption, so common in text-centered studies of every type, that literary works are self-enclosed verbal constructs, or looped intertextual fields of autonomous signifiers and signifieds. In these essays, the question of referentiality is once again brought to the fore. (3)

In "Keats and the Historical Method in Literary Criticism," he outlines a program for those who have rallied to the cry. These procedures, which he claims are "practical derivatives of the Bakhtin school," assume that historicist critics, who must be interested in a work's point of origin and in its point of reception, will understand the former by studying biography and bibliography. After mastering these details, the critic must then consider the expressed intentions of the author, because, if printed, these intentions have also modified the developing history of the work. Next, the new historicist must learn the history of the work's reception, as that body of opinion has become part of the platform on which we are situated when we study the book. Finally, McGann urges the new historicist critic to point toward the future, toward his or her *own* audience, defining for its members the aims and limits of the critical project and injecting the analysis with a degree of self-consciousness that alone can give it credibility (*Inflections* 62).

In "Genius, Degeneration, and the Panopticon," a new historicist reading of *Portrait* that follows this introduction, R. Brandon Kershner begins by speaking of the need to see Joyce's novel as part of a "network of cultural forces," as a representation of society that cannot be disengaged "from other such representations." After mentioning a number of "social and historical resonances," Kershner concentrates on two: the idea of surveillance and the conception of genius that were prevalent at the time the novel was written.

Kershner openly avows his indebtedness to Michel Foucault; indeed, he begins his discussion of surveillance by citing Foucault's reference, in *Discipline and Punish,* to the "'Panopticon'—an architectural model for a prison in which a central, unseen observer can watch each prisoner at will." Foucault used the Panopticon "as his own model for the technologies of regulation that arose after the eighteenth century in Europe"; for Kershner, it serves as a model for what Church and state—and society in general—seem to the young Stephen we meet at the beginning of *Portrait.* Power and power relationships have become faceless, "disindividualized," in the late nineteenth-century Ireland in which Stephen struggles to grow up. Such power tends to have, in Foucault's words, "its principles not so much in a person as in a certain concerted distribution of bodies, surfaces, lights, gazes."

So powerful is the sense of being watched in Stephen's—and Joyce's—historical time and place that Stephen's very habits of thought are governed by the principles and discourses of observation. At first thinking that his sin has "covered him from the sight of God," he quickly reverts to the opinion that in all he does he is watched:

> But after the first retreat sermon he imagines that he has merely exchanged God's gaze for one more demonic; he sees himself as a beastly body "gazing out of darkened eyes, helpless, perturbed, and human for a bovine god to stare upon." (p. 376).

Kershner, following Foucault, explores the seemingly paradoxical connection between surveillance and discipline and the rise of "the ideology of individualism." He finds the apparent contradiction illustrated in Stephen's confession, an act of revealing "the secret thoughts and actions that [Stephen] believes have made him uniquely damned,'' an act that at the same time proves the weakness of the individual and the complementary power of authority. Stephen's various attempts at self-liberation are consequently viewed by Kershner as what Michel de Certeau has called the ''practices'' and ''tactics'' whereby people attempt to resist the totalizing tendencies of modern culture.

Among Stephen's tactics is his attempt to fashion himself into a kind of Celtic artist-aristocrat, an Irish genius beyond the limits of his culture's fixing, deadening gaze. The trouble is, Kershner points out, that the nineteenth-century notion of genius informing the novel is a ''racialist'' one associating the people of Ireland, among others, with the very *opposite* of genius. To complicate matters further, it is tightly intertwined with the oppressive idea of the priesthood; and the concept of ''class'' is not only in transition but also deeply suspect in the Irish mind. Thus, Kershner suggests, Stephen's decision to attempt to disentangle and distinguish himself by trying to become an Irish artistic genius is jeopardized, if not doomed, from the start.

Kershner goes on to place all of these ideas in a still wider context of fearful, late nineteenth-century discourses about familial and racial degeneration, but to summarize these in detail would be to spoil not only his fun but that of his reader as well. Suffice it to say here that Kershner's portrait of *Portrait* is a dense canvas. It makes sense of things like ''Stephen's guilt and terror at his sexual self-indulgence'' by rooting out not only their religious and ethical sources but also their sources in contemporary views of sexuality and, especially, masturbation, which was connected in the popular mind with the decline of genius and the devolution of the race. The result, to use Clifford Geertz's phrase, is a ''thick description''—not just of Joyce's text and its many, nonliterary intertexts but also of our own world and way of reading.

Ross C Murfin

THE NEW HISTORICISM: A SELECTED BIBLIOGRAPHY

The New Historicism: Further Reading

American Literary History. A journal devoted to new historicist and cultural criticism; the first issue was Spring 1989. New York: Oxford UP.

Brown, Gillian. *Domestic Individualism: Imagining Self in Nineteenth-Century America.* Berkeley: U of California P, 1990.

Dollimore, Jonathan, and Alan Sinfield, eds. *Political Shakespeare: New Essays in Cultural Materialism.* Manchester, Eng.: Manchester UP, 1985. See especially the essays by Dollimore, Greenblatt, and Tennenhouse.

———. *Radical Tragedy: Religion, Ideology and Power in the Drama of Shakespeare and His Contemporaries.* Brighton, Eng.: Harvester, 1984.

Goldberg, Jonathan. *James I and the Politics of Literature.* Baltimore: Johns Hopkins UP, 1983.

Graff, Gerald, and Reginald Gibbons, eds. *Criticism in the University.* Evanston: Northwestern UP, 1985. This volume includes sections devoted to the historical backgrounds of academic criticism; the influence of Marxism, feminism, and critical theory in general on the new historicism; changing pedagogies; and varieties of cultural criticism.

Greenblatt, Stephen. *Renaissance Self-Fashioning from More to Shakespeare.* Chicago: U of Chicago P, 1980. See Chapter 1.

Hirsch, E. D., Jr. "Back to History," Graff, 189–97.

History and. . . . Special number issue of *New Literary History* 21 (1990). See especially the essays by Carolyn Porter, Rena Fraden, Clifford Geertz, and Renato Rosaldo.

Lindenberger, Herbert. *The History in Literature: On Value, Genre, Institutions.* New York: Columbia UP, 1990.

———. "Toward a New History in Literary Study." *Profession: Selected Articles from the Bulletins of the Association of Departments of English and the Association of Departments of Foreign Languages.* New York: MLA, 1984. 16–23.

McGann, Jerome. *The Beauty of Inflections: Literary Investigations in Historical Method and Theory.* Oxford: Clarendon Press-Oxford UP, 1985. See especially the introduction and Chapter 1, "Keats and the Historical Method in Literary Criticism."

———. *Historical Studies and Literary Criticism.* Madison: U of Wisconsin P, 1985. See especially the introduction and the essays in the following sections: "Historical Methods and Literary Interpretations" and "Biographical Contexts and the Critical Object."

Michaels, Walter Benn. *The Gold Standard and the Logic of Naturalism.* Berkeley: U of California P, 1987.

Morris, Wesley. *Toward a New Historicism.* Princeton: Princeton UP, 1972.

Thomas, Brook. "The Historical Necessity for—and Difficulties with—New Historical Analysis in Introductory Literature Courses." *College English* 49 (1987): 509–22.

Veeser, H. Aram, ed. *The New Historicism.* New York: Routledge, 1989.

Foucault and His Influence

As is pointed out in the introduction to the new historicism, some new historicists question the "privileging" of Foucault implicit in this section heading ("Foucault and His Influence") and the one following ("Other Writers and Works of Interest . . . "). They might argue for the greater importance of one of these other writers or point out that to cite a central influence or a definitive cause defies the very spirit of the movement.

Foucault, Michel, *Discipline and Punish: The Birth of the Prison.* 1975. Trans. Alan Sheridan. New York: Pantheon, 1978.

———. *The History of Sexuality.* Trans. Robert Hurley, Vol. 1. New York: Pantheon, 1978. 2 vols.

———. *Language, Counter-Memory, Practice.* Ed. Donald F. Bouchard. Trans. Bouchard and Sherry Simon. Ithaca: Cornell UP, 1977. Consists of selected essays and interviews.

Dreyfus, Hubert L., and Paul Rabinow. *Michel Foucault: Beyond Structuralism and Hermeneutics.* Chicago: U of Chicago P, 1983.

Sheridan, Alan. *Michel Foucault: The Will to Truth.* New York: Tavistock, 1980.

Smart, Barry. *Michel Foucault.* New York: Horwood and Tavistock, 1985.

Other Writers and Works of Interest to New Historicist Critics

Bakhtin, M. M. *The Dialogic Imagination: Four Essays.* Ed. Michael Holquist. Trans. Caryl Emerson. Austin: U of Texas P, 1981. Bakhtin authored many influential studies of subjects as varied as Dostoyevski, Rabelais, and formalist criticism. But this book, in part due to Holquist's helpful introduction, is probably the best place to begin reading Bakhtin.

Benjamin, Walter. "The Work of Art in the Age of Mechanical Reproduction." 1936. *Illuminations.* Trans. Harry Zohn. New York: Schocken, 1969.

Fried, Michael. *Absorption and Theatricality: Painting and Beholder in the Works of Diderot.* Berkeley: U of California P, 1980.

Geertz, Clifford. *The Interpretation of Cultures.* New York: Basic, 1973.

———. *Negara: The Theatre State in Nineteenth-Century Bali.* Princeton: Princeton UP, 1980.

Goffman, Erving. *Frame Analysis.* New York: Harper, 1974.

Jameson, Fredric. *The Political Unconscious.* Ithaca: Cornell UP, 1981.

Koselleck, Reinhart. *Futures Past.* Trans. Keith Tribe. Cambridge: MIT P, 1985.

Representations. Published by the University of California Press, this quarterly journal regularly contains New Historicist studies and cultural criticism.

Studies of Joyce with New Historicist Elements

Brown, Richard. *James Joyce and Sexuality.* Cambridge: Cambridge UP, 1985.

Herr, Cheryl. *Joyce's Anatomy of Culture.* Urbana: U of Illinois P, 1986.

Kershner, R. B. *Joyce, Bakhtin, and Popular Literature.* Chapel Hill: U of North Carolina P, 1989.

Lowe-Evans, Mary. *Crimes Against Fecundity: Joyce and Population Control.* Syracuse: Syracuse UP, 1989.

Manganiello, Dominic. *Joyce's Politics.* London and Boston: Routledge, 1980.

Osteen, Mark. "The Intertextual Economy in 'Scylla and Charybdis.'" *James Joyce Quarterly* 28 (Fall 1990): 197–208.

Williams, Trevor. "Dominant Ideologies: The Production of Stephen Dedalus." *James Joyce: The Augmented Ninth.* Ed. Bernard Benstock. Syracuse: Syracuse UP, 1988. 312–22.

A NEW HISTORICIST PERSPECTIVE

R. B. KERSHNER

Genius, Degeneration, and the Panopticon

Genius is the ability to recall your childhood at will.
–BAUDELAIRE

Frank O'Connor tells the story of a picture hanging in Joyce's Paris apartment: a city scene, surrounded by an unusual flat wooden frame. Visitors would sometimes ask about it, and Joyce would reply, "That's Cork." If they explained that they really meant to inquire about the frame, Joyce would assure them, "Oh, that's cork, too" (O'Connor 609). The story is generally told to illustrate Joyce's notorious fondness for puns, but here I would like to stress his interest in frames and contexts, and the difficulty of disengaging them from what we imagine we can distinguish as the subject of art. *A Portrait of the Artist as a Young Man,* for example, should alert us to a frame in its very title, yet over the past fifty years or so we have become expert in disengaging the book's text from its intertexts, its peculiar representation of a society from other such representations, and the novel itself as literary production from the network of cultural forces surrounding and traversing it. Like most modernist texts, *Portrait* seems to dictate the terms of its own reception; and like most modernist heroes, Stephen Dedalus rather convincingly appears before us bathed in an aura of uniqueness—as if he were himself the sole copy, the traditional work of art that, as Walter Benjamin points out, "withers in the age of mechanical reproduction" (221).

Stephen has been the object of intense critical scrutiny for so long not only because of the prestige of Joyce's novel but because of the force and density of his construction as subject. In a sense, he is all there is to look at. Throughout the book he is the focus of a remarkable number and variety of authoritative gazes, while he in turn struggles to become the only perfect watcher, the observer whose privilege is to be set apart from all others. Because of the way in which his perceptions dominate the novel, Stephen comes to fill all the narrative space that Joyce makes available. Not coincidentally, his aesthetic mode of evaluation at the same time gradually displaces all others in the book's value system.

Stephen's apparent uniqueness and his aesthetic elevation are not disembodied artistic phenomena; they both reflect and contest broader historical currents in Joyce's society and in ours as well. In approaching such problems, a number of possible "frames" present themselves: the situation of Joyce as a colonial writer in the waning years of the British empire; the situation of Stephen as a young, artistically inclined intellectual at the time of the greatest prestige of positivistic science; the situation of the book as an example of "high culture" literary production during a period when "popular literature" had developed fully but was not yet transmuted into an aspect of "mass culture." But for now, I would like to explore some of *Portrait's* social and historical resonances by concentrating on two major patterns: Stephen's attempt to move from observed to observing subject and his deployment of the popular myth of the Genius, linked to images of the superhuman and the subhuman, in his effort to alter his social positioning.

I

In *Discipline and Punish: The Birth of the Prison,* Michel Foucault adapts the eighteenth-century philosopher Jeremy Bentham's invention of the "Panopticon"—an architectural model for a prison in which a central, unseen observer can watch each prisoner at will—as his own model for the technologies of regulation that arose after the eighteenth century in Europe. Before this time, punishment was public and somewhat random; afterward, the idea of ritualistic punishment was gradually replaced by the concept of individual rehabilitation, a process that would be continuously monitored. As Foucault notes, the Panopticon model applies not only to prisons but to schools, hospitals, factories, sanatoriums, and by extension, to the whole of European society as it becomes increasingly bureaucratic. Without itself embodying power, it models the pathways through which power must flow. The effects upon the participants, Foucault suggests, are basic. "The Panopticon is a machine for dissociating the see/being seen dyad: in the peripheral ring, one is totally seen, without ever seeing; in the central tower, one sees everything without being seen" (201–02).

In the late nineteenth-century Dublin of which Joyce writes, the Church somewhat anachronistically sits at the Panopticon's center, although it shares that location with more formal representatives of the state. At the beginning of *Portrait* all sources of authority blend together for Stephen—his family, other adults, the Church, the state, books, even older children, all of whom seem to know the rules of which he is ignorant. Gradually, he learns to distinguish among these sources and their varying ideologies. For instance, the state rather paradoxically combines Britain's colonial administration with local "Nationalist" authorities who both represent and contest Britain's power (Parnell is the prime example here). Similarly, while the Church formally claims no temporal power, in popular mythology it is associated with the independence movement; this is the tradition to which Dante appeals when she asserts that "the priests were always the true friends of Ireland" (p. 45). At the same time, popular wisdom notes that it appears intimately involved with the colonial administration. As Simon Dedalus says of the Jesuits, "Those are the fellows that can get you a position" (p. 72).

But while Stephen comes to master these distinctions intellectually, on a more fundamental level he is coming to realize that what constantly observes him is no individual or group of individuals, but a faceless "They" whose identities, motivations, and sources of authority are finally irrelevant. Foucault notes that the mechanism of the Panopticon "automatizes and disindividualizes power. Power has its principle not so much in a person as in a certain concerted distribution of bodies, surfaces, lights, gazes." Finally, the observation is internalized by the one observed, who "inscribes in himself the power relation in which he simultaneously plays both roles; he becomes the principle of his own subjection" (Foucault 202–03). As Stephen announces much later in *Ulysses,* tapping his brow, "In here it is I must kill the priest and the king" (*Ulysses* 15: 4436–37).

An observing but somehow distant or disembodied eye haunts Stephen throughout *Portrait.* First is his father, who "looked at him through a glass" (p. 19), immediately followed by the sharp-eyed eagles who threaten to "pull out his eyes" if he does not apologize for his (unconscious) error of wishing to marry a Protestant girl. The peculiar turn that the mechanism of observation and discipline takes in *Portrait* is that it is often Stephen's own sight that is threatened or brought into question. As he grows more conscious of the watching authorities he is correspondingly more aware that "his eyes were weak and watery" (p. 20). When Father Dolan arrives in the classroom the students are displayed in organized rows, all easily visible from his position of authority. He knows that particular boys deserve punishment not only because he can immediately see that they are not doing their lesson but because, as he warns a child, "I can see it in your eye" (p. 54). The eye of authority *sees,* while

Stephen's eye only *betrays.* Dolan's "nocoloured eyes behind the steel-rimmed spectacles" (p. 57) are invulnerable, but after his punishment, myopic Stephen is further blinded by tears.

As Stephen grows, his sins become more substantial: first masturbation, then consorting with prostitutes. His initial reaction is disengagement, as he sees that no immediate retribution has come. Indeed, he thinks that his sin has "covered him from the sight of God" (p. 99), whose cosmic, sleepless eye has superseded all others. But after the first retreat sermon he imagines that he has merely exchanged God's gaze for one more demonic; he sees himself as a beastly body, "gazing out of darkened eyes, helpless, perturbed, and human for a bovine god to stare upon" (p. 104). And the text of the final sermon, *"I am cast away from the sight of Thine eyes"* (Psalms 30:23; p. 116) makes it clear to him that to be removed from God's sight means to cease to exist in any familiar sense. He will be cast into utter darkness, "not even able to remove from the eye a worm that gnaws it" (p. 140). Unseen by God—or by His representative, the Church—the sinner no longer exists as human. Or will he be unseen? The hellfire sermon's whole point is to visually display the sufferings sinners like Stephen will undergo; in it, Father Arnall creates an eye—the "eye of the narrative"—that sadistically notes every nuance of the pain of the damned.

From the emphasis on sight, it might seem that what is in question here is the transgressor's actions, or even appearance, but this is not so. As Foucault makes clear, the Panopticon model is a technology of selfhood. "It is no longer the body, but the soul" that is addressed by authority (Foucault 101). Foucault articulates a central paradox of modern societies: that the ideology of individualism, which purports to assign value to people "in themselves," is an effect of the Panopticon model of surveillance and discipline. The individual must be known—in effect, socially created in distinction to others—in order to be educated, policed, healed, and generally categorized. The confessional to which Stephen resorts neatly embodies this contradiction, because here Stephen will confess the secret thoughts and actions that he believes have made him uniquely damned, and here the priest will assign him to the proper category of sinners and set him the approved penance for his case. Here, as Marxist critics argue is generally the case, the ideology of individualism is easily appropriated by authority.

As is usual in Romantic novels—and *Portrait* shares many characteristics with the Romantic variety of *Bildungsroman*—the protagonist's response to the totalizing power of social institutions is not to abandon the ideology of individualism on which those institutions rest but to assert even more forcefully his unique selfhood. Nor is this necessarily entirely ineffectual. Michel de Certeau has discussed ways in which people in modern societies are able to resist their cultures' totalizing tendencies through what he calls "practices" or "tactics":

> *A way of using* imposed systems constitutes the resistance to the historical law of a state of affairs and its dogmatic legitimations. A practice of the order constructed by others redistributes its space; it creates at least a certain play in that order, a space for maneuvers of unequal forces and for utopian points of reference. (18)

Popular culture, de Certeau asserts, can be one such practice. Unlike Theodor Adorno, who sees modern mass culture as merely a repressive part of the "ideological state apparatus" (Horkheimer and Adorno), de Certeau sees ways in which examples of mass culture can be liberating.

Certainly this is the way in which Stephen attempts to use his reading of Alexandre Dumas's *The Count of Monte Cristo*. The hero of the novel, Edmond Dantes, is betrayed by his friends on the day he was to wed the beautiful Mercedes and unjustly thrown into an island prison; there, with the help of a fellow prisoner, he transforms himself into a master of all arts and sciences. After his escape he retrieves the lost treasure of the Borgias, whose location his fellow prisoner has entrusted to him, and returns to France, unrecognizable, as the Count of Monte Cristo. There, shrouded in mystery, with almost superhuman powers and endless wealth, he takes his revenge on his former friends. He also coldly rejects Mercedes, who abandoned hope of his return too soon for Dantes's liking, with the words, "Madam, I never eat muscatel grapes" (p. 65). The count's weapons throughout are those that Stephen claims: silence, exile, and cunning (Kershner 1989, 204).

As Dantes himself explains in an extended speech, the real source of his power is the fact that he *belongs to no country;* indeed, he has no identity. We might say he has stepped outside the Panopticon, or has discovered an invisible location within it. Throughout the book he adopts different disguises and sets a variety of elaborate plots in motion, then quite literally sits back and watches their denouement like a spectator at a drama. His mastery of the social forms—for example, his cold politeness—masks the fact that he no longer belongs to French society and is immune to its claims upon him. Although he and his Oriental slave-girl are a spectacle in Paris, in a fundamental sense he *cannot be seen* by others and has usurped the position of author-observer. Indeed, all the literary figures with whom Stephen identifies in the second chapter, such as Claude Melnotte (from Bulwer-Lytton's *Lady of Lyons*) or Ingomar (from Maria Lovell's *Ingomar the Barbarian*) are disguised outsiders who gain power by virtue of that fact (Kershner 1989, 221–27).

II

But what is actually happening when Stephen attempts to construct himself as subject with the aid of such fantasies? And what are their roots and implications? I would argue that these are important questions for the book, because the "aristocracy of art" (Harper) to which Stephen lays claim, the particular language in which he expresses his sense of superiority, the imagery with which he portrays those around him, and even his final decision to conjoin exile with authorship are all aspects of his attempt at social "self-fashioning" (Greenblatt). I want to suggest that Stephen's defensive tactic, his ascent to the sphere of art, is entangled with a number of formations in the nineteenth-century popular mind, many of which have their genesis in scientific conceptions of the period. It should not be overlooked that the methodology of positivistic science is itself a mode of subject-formation, in that it places the scientist-observer at the center of his own Panopticon. Indeed, nineteenth-century medical scientists and psychologists with their clinical studies and pathological taxonomies are major contributors to Foucault's conception. Yet on the other hand, each scientist or pseudoscientist, insofar as he feels able to "step outside" his society in order to view humanity with detachment, can make some weak claim to having regained the center of the universe.

Many scientific approaches to humanity in the late nineteenth century, for all their vaunted objectivity, seem from our contemporary perspective to be rather transparently structured by the social norms from which they declare their independence. Most versions of sociology and anthropology, for instance, were heavily "racialist" (we would say, pejoratively, "racist") in their foundations. Beginning with de Gobineau's influential *Essay on the Inequality of the Human Races* (1853–55), which proposed the idea of an Aryan race, a host of books elaborated the idea of a spectrum of races, which was in fact a disguised hierarchy, each with different "essential" qualities. Following Darwin, the idea that different races represent different biological stages in the development of modern man soon gained general acceptance, with the Anglo-Saxon race, at least in British books, often placed at the summit. Otherwise, the crown was usually awarded to de Gobineau's synthetic "Aryan race," which unsurprisingly happened to include strains from most politically dominant European nations.

Even so firm a believer in the determining force of culture as Matthew Arnold adopted a racial rhetoric when he codified the characteristics of the Celtic and English peoples in his 1867 *Study of Celtic Literature*. In the essay, Seamus Deane observes, "Of course, every virtue of the Celt was matched by a vice of the British bourgeoisie; everything the philistine middle classes of England needed, the Celt could supply. (The reverse was also true)" (25). Arnold's binary opposition, which George Bernard Shaw parodically reversed in his 1907 play *John Bull's Other Island,* pictured the Celt as dreamy, imaginative, and ineffectual, full of primitive vigor and sensuality, while presenting the Anglo-Saxon as pragmatic, hardworking but anemic and overcivilized, yet filled with the virtues of intellectual force and organization. Less sympathetic English portraitists, enraged by the increasing political agitation of the late nineteenth century in Ireland, filled the Sunday press with cartoons of barely civilized, apelike Irishmen. No wonder Stephen fears that the peasant woman he once saw in a doorway, a "batlike soul," is "a type of her race and his own" (pp. 160–61). He knows that "this race . . . produced me" (p. 177) and can only hope that by superhuman effort and some miraculous personal transformation he may be able to "forge in the smithy of [his] soul the uncreated conscience of [his] race" (p. 218).

But race was a particularly vexed question in late nineteenth-century Ireland, where indigenous racial myths collided with political realities. When Stephen describes the statue of the Irish national poet Thomas Moore as "a Firbolg in the borrowed cloak of a Milesian," he refers to an Irish belief that the original rude, dwarfish inhabitants of Ireland, called Firbolgs, intermixed with a tall, "aristocratic" race that originated in Spain. From the condescension he shows his peasant friend Davin, whom he calls "Firbolg" (p. 158), there is no doubt that Stephen considers himself the true Milesian. When Davin questions whether he is Irish at all, Stephen offers to show his friend the Dedalus family crest and family tree in the Office of Arms (p. 176). Indeed, one of the first things we hear him tell a schoolfellow is that his father is "a gentleman" (p. 21). In reality, of course, Simon Dedalus could at best consider himself a member of the bourgeoisie fallen on hard times.

Racial myths aside, the social structure of Ireland at the time virtually guaranteed that claims to true social distinction were reserved for members of the Protestant "Anglo-Irish Ascendancy" rather than Catholic families like the Dedaluses (or the Joyces, for that matter). Still, aristocracy was a slippery concept at the turn of the century, when commoners could earn British peerages by conspicuous merit, or even indirectly purchase them. The originally Celtic Irish, whose traditional systems of class distinction had been destroyed, by default considered themselves "all kings' sons," somewhat as Americans came to consider descent from Mayflower families a kind of de facto claim to aristocracy. The fact that many of the Irish national leaders such as Parnell were from old Protestant Anglo-Irish families was tactfully ignored. The conflicting claims of political and racial nationalism further complicated the issue. In the 1870s the Irish parliamentary leader Isaac Butt and the radical Nationalist John Mitchel had both argued for greater Irish self-determination on the grounds that the Irish should join the British in administering the Empire of lesser breeds; fifteen years later, Parnell and others were speaking out for the rights of Irish, Indians, Chinese, and other victims of British oppression (Brasted). The shift in political identification entailed a change in the contextualizing of racial identity as well, underlining the fact that the concept of race had always had an unacknowledged political element.

Stephen's growing sense of his own aristocracy is paradoxical, confused, and heavily overdetermined, that is, it has a multitude of contributing causes. On the level of personal psychology, Stephen is engaged in what Freud called the "family romance," the fantasy shared by many prepubescent children of the period that they were not really the children of their own parents but actually the offspring of nobility, for unknown reasons being raised in ordinary households. On a social level, his confused sense of election reflects a general confusion about what could constitute aristocracy in modern Ireland. Stephen invokes his family's ancient lineage in Ireland, but then so could the Murphys and Dolans whom he scorns. Formal titles of aristocracy were mostly reserved for the Anglo-Irish families who had been imported into the country starting in the Tudor period; and though many of these families considered themselves as Irish as any Celt, their titles were a function of empire, and thus (for Stephen) were tainted. The old aristocracy of lineage was gradually giving way during the nineteenth century to an aristocracy of capital; and indeed during the brief period when his family is better off than his neighbors Stephen is happy enough to consider this a sign of election. When the Dedaluses fall on hard times, however, he decides that they are still noble, but distressed.

III

But overriding these conflicting paradigms of racial and personal distinction was the doctrine of racial and familial *degeneration*, which by the turn of the century had blossomed from a hypothesis suggested by a few clinical psychologists and anthropologists into an article of popular faith and a cause for general alarm throughout Great Britain and Europe (Gilman; Kershner 1986). In his 1857 *Treatise on the Physical, Intellectual, and Moral Degeneration on the Human Species,* the French physician B. A. Morel hypothesized that an organism's necessary but costly adaptation to pathological circumstances could include dangerous modifications that would be exaggerated in later generations, leading to sterility and death. Valentin Magnan's *The Degenerates* (1895) extended this idea, arguing that a weakening of the "psychophysical resistance" of certain species, or indeed human families or inbred groups, would be progressive. Since most scientists up through the turn of the century were Lamarckian—that is, they believed that acquired characteristics in an organism would be passed on to later generations—this process was seen as more rapid and unopposed than would be the case with the slower modifications produced by Darwinian selection. Social commentators, such as Max Nordau in his highly influential *Degeneration,* translated in 1895, extended the idea to the realms of politics and art: everything of which Nordau disapproved in modern society—from Impressionist painting, Wagnerism, and Ibsenism to Marxism and women's education—was for him a sign of physical and mental degeneration. Impressionist paintings were fuzzy, he asserted, because the painters were victims of "nystagmus," a trembling of the eyeball. Feminists were really masculine females, Ibsenites hysterics, and so on through his personal list of modern evils.

Nordau, a physician, claimed that his argument was neither political nor aesthetic but merely a scientific diagnosis. Meanwhile, Darwin's demonstration that humanity had evolved from animal species lent a nightmarish coloration to the popularization of the idea of degeneration: under primitive conditions, or indeed under the pathological conditions of lower-class urban life, might not humans physically regress, becoming increasingly animal? The general tendency of late nineteenth-century scientific and sociological thinking was to look for overt physical signs of "bestiality" that would mirror an individual's degenerate inner state. One of the most honored scientists of the time, Cesare Lombroso, published a book in 1878 that purported to distinguish subhuman "criminal types" from the population as a whole on the basis of facial and bodily appearance. The "born criminal," he concluded, was an atavism, a reversion to an ancestral type who "reproduces in his person the ferocious instincts of primitive humanity and the inferior animals," especially the apes.

British and European thinkers around the turn of the century were increasingly worried by various forms of the idea of degeneration. The British in particular feared the urban underclass, then called the "residuum," whose members lived in conditions that liberal reformers called "subhuman"; it was an easy step even for liberals like Lombroso to see the people themselves as less than human, through no fault of their own. The dubious performance by the British army in the Boer War and the disturbing statistics on physical fitness that emerged from the army's examinations of potential recruits fed popular fears that the Empire was in a decline that was not only spiritual but biological. Racism fed these fears, inasmuch as the expansion of the British Empire had led to a certain amount of miscegenation, and mixing of races was widely held to lead to degeneration. The distinguished biologist Louis Agassiz argued that "interbreeding" was catastrophic: "Let anyone who doubts the evil of this mixture of races . . . come to Brazil. He cannot deny the deterioration consequent upon the amalgamation of races" (Holmes 248–49).

Another focus of the fears of degeneration was sexual license, especially masturbation, which was thought to be a clear sign of degeneracy. J. H. Kellogg, a physician and director of the American cereal company, argued that an obsession with sensual matters would be inherited, leading to a decline in the race. Indeed, even the lawfully married could not be too careful about the spirit in which they approached sexuality.

> It is an established physiological fact that the character of offspring is influenced by the mental as well as the physical conditions of the parents at the moment of the performance of the generative act. In view of this fact, how many parents can regard the precocious—or even mature—manifestations of sexual depravity in their children without painful smitings of conscience at seeing the legitimate results of their own voluptuousness? (Walters 152)

Many Victorian convictions about sexuality, such as the belief that masturbation could lead to idiocy, arose against the backdrop of racial degeneration.

The two themes—the sexual and the racial—were, of course, commonly intertwined, in that the "lesser" races were believed to be prone to sexual indulgence. Such a belief, a classic example of the projection of repressed desires onto the "Other," applied even to the Irish, with their extremely low birthrate, their late marriages, and their rigid social separation of the sexes in youth. Stephen's guilt and terror at his sexual self-indulgence arises from religious and ethical sources, but the imagery in which his unease expresses itself is rooted in degeneration theory.

Stephen sees beasts all around him, and in despair sees himself also as an animal: "he rose and went to the window, clearing the thick scum from his mouth with his tongue and licking it with his lips. So he had sunk to the state of a beast that licks his chaps after meat" (p. 104). If Stephen is sometimes an animal, his friends are almost invariably so. Lynch is reptilian, Davin brutish, Temple gnomish. His erotic dreams are populated by "apelike creatures" (p. 107), perhaps recalling the "feeble creature like a monkey" who turns out to be a senile relative of his and who mistakes him for "Josephine" (p. 69). In his hallucinatory vision following the sermon he sees "goatish creatures with human faces, hornybrowed, . . . trailing their long tails behind them," one of which is clutching around his ribs a torn waistcoat (pp. 124–25).

Perhaps the most vivid such example is the old "captain," the library attendant with monkey's eyes whose "blackish monkey-puckered face pursed its human mouth with gentle pleasure" (p. 197). Stephen immediately thinks of the rumor that the man is the product of an incestuous union (one of the surest routes to degeneration), and he elaborately envisions the seduction scene: a couple lie beside a pond slimed by swans and embrace "without joy or passion." Stephen notes that the man's hand is Davin's and is angry with himself at the thought. Perhaps a part of his anger expresses his unarticulated fear that the true Irish peasant race has incestuously bred itself backward along the evolutionary path. He does not *want* to see the peasantry as subhuman but does so despite himself, fearing that they are himself, or at least the paradoxically subhuman angel with whom he must wrestle. In his diary he notes dreaming of struggling with an ignorant old peasant with "red-rimmed horny eyes," recalling the "hornybrowed" Pan figures of his vision (as well as Jacob wrestling with his angel [Genesis 32]).

Stephen hopes to be his race's savior, and oddly enough he expresses this hope in terms of a kind of Lamarckian spiritual eugenics: how, he asks, could he "cast his shadow over the imagination of their daughters, before their squires began upon them, that they might breed a race less ignoble than their own?" (p. 205) And just as Stephen imagines an alternative future for his race, so he imagines alternative versions of its past. In his diary he notes a pair of dreams, in the first of which he visits a gallery "peopled by the images of fabulous kings" whose eyes are "darkened by the errors of men"; in the second he sees "strange figures" who are "not as tall as men" advancing from a cave, their faces "phosphorescent, with darker streaks" (p. 215). These silent creatures stare at him as if to ask him something. Is he the son of eternal kings, or the offspring of something subhuman? Or are the creatures, like H. G. Wells's degenerate Morlocks in *The Time Machine,* not his race's past but its future?

Clearly, Joyce's representation of Stephen is shot through with ambivalences, ambiguities, and contradictions with respect to race and, more generally, with respect to the young man's status. Is he a Milesian among Firbolgs, or a Firbolg himself? Are all the Irish a brutish race—as Goethe put it, like dogs always baying around some noble stag—or are they, as Davin believes, a noble alternative to the brutal English? Is Stephen in some sense an aristocrat, and if so, in what sense? From about the end of the first chapter, Stephen is continually judging his own superiority or inferiority to others, and his judgment vacillates wildly with his mood and experiences. But very seldom does he view himself as basically *like* his schoolmates. More often, he feels infinitely their superior or else far beneath them, but in either case he sees himself as different in kind. Certainly this is a matter of character, and certainly it has to do with his sense of uniqueness as an aspiring artist, but both Stephen's character and his sense of election are greatly dependent on social formations of the time. The particular form of Stephen's self-exaltation depends upon a complex of ideas and images at the turn of the century that derive from the patterns of degeneration and progressive evolution and that cluster around the term *genius*.

IV

The word *genius* did not begin to take on its modern sense of a uniquely talented man—the word was almost invariably reserved for males—until the eighteenth century (Battersby 2). But it was the Romantics who impressed the concept with their logic of exclusion, creating the genius not simply as a person with a greater talent than others but as a man different in kind from other men, and superior to them. As Christine Battersby explains, genius "had been transformed from a kind of talent into a superior type of *being* who walked a 'sublime' path between 'sanity' and 'madness', between the 'monstrous' and the 'superhuman,'" and the focus had shifted toward the *personality* of the creative individual (103). Byron, the poet Stephen defends from his schoolfellows' mockery, was the most famous "type" of the genius. His unconventional life, his notorious affairs, and even the rumors of incest in his life all fed his legend. Even the Count of Monte Cristo, with all his sinister uniqueness, is seen by Parisian society as Byronic. On the other hand, in *On Heroes and Hero-Worship* (1840), the essayist Thomas Carlyle stressed the divine quality of the genius, the "most precious gift that Heaven can give to the Earth; a man of 'genius' as we call it; the Soul of Man actually sent down from the skies, with a God's–message to us." At the least the genius was a sort of secular saint. Indeed, the poetic genius in particular was held up as being himself a sort of God; as early as the eighteenth century the Earl of Shaftesbury claimed in *Characteristics* that "a poet is indeed a second *Maker;* a just Prometheus under Jove."

Thus Stephen's final goal, to become a "priest of the eternal imagination, transmuting the daily bread of experience into the radiant body of everliving life" (p. 192), merely restates in slightly less blasphemous terms the divine mission of the genius. The genius was the carrier of the *logos spermatikos,* the engendering "word" discussed by St. John and by the Stoics; much of the rhetoric surrounding the genius during the nineteenth century put equal emphasis on the sexual and the transcendent qualities of this extraordinary being. In his 1767 *Essay on Original Genius,* William Duff reported that the ardor of a genius makes him "particularly susceptible of the charms of the fair sex," but warned that the youthful genius might waste his powers in "dangerous passion" (Battersby 79). Others took a less morally rigid view, arguing that the sexual athleticism of a figure like Balzac was simply another expression of his superhuman potency. In this light Stephen's sexual precociousness, whatever its personal cost to him, is but one more sign of his potential genius.

But perhaps the most bizarre transmutation of the genius figure resulted from its insertion into the myth of degeneration. Lombroso was responding to this strange linkage when he followed his book on criminal types with one on hereditary genius. Late in the nineteenth century a number of medical observers, inspired by the period's mania for finding physiological and biological correlates for "spiritual" qualities, underwrote the popular view that genius, rebelliousness, and madness were closely allied. Reversing the polarity of Max Nordau's judgments in his book *Degeneration,* they argued that the reason so many of the artistic and intellectual figures he discussed displayed "degenerate" qualities was because genius was itself a possible aspect of degeneration. In 1895 W. L. Babcock discussed the possible patterns of life for what he termed a biological "throwback":

> First, and most prominent in the order of frequency is an early death. Second, he may swell the criminal ranks. Third, he may become mentally deranged and ultimately find his way into a hospital for the insane. Fourth, and least frequently, he startles the

> world by an invention or discovery in science or by an original composition of great merit in art, music, or literature. He is then styled a genius. (Becker 38–39)

This version of the genius, of course, is directly opposed to the more common variant in which he is the next evolutionary step in a vaguely Darwinian model.

The figure of the genius-degenerate does neatly capture a fundamental ambivalence about the superman figure that was to play itself out later in science-fiction treatments: a man sufficiently superior to ordinary mortals becomes not only a hope for the race (or the species) but a threat to it as well. Many of the genius figures of literary High Modernism, such as Stephen or D. H. Lawrence's Rupert Birkin, are strongly ambivalent in their attitude to ordinary humanity. Even the Count of Monte Cristo, in good Faustian fashion, has purchased his remarkable abilities at the cost of his common humanity, and as Dumas's novel draws to a close he frequently agonizes over whether he has become a diabolic figure rather than the agent of Providence. At least in the popular mind, these extremes tend to meet: the superman and the throwback, the genius and the degenerate are similar in that they owe little allegiance to the rest of humanity, that crowd whom the young Joyce called "the rabblement." Again, aspects of this pattern pervade *Portrait.* By the Church's standards, Stephen is indeed a moral criminal. Around the time of his experience with the prostitute, he feels totally removed from the rest of mankind, and looks on it coldly. "He had known neither the pleasure of companionship with others nor the vigour of rude male health nor filial piety. Nothing stirred within his soul but a cold and cruel and loveless lust" (p. 92). Even his sanity is in question: we should realize that during the retreat sermon he literally hears voices and sees visions—visions even more compelling than those he sees in moments of inspiration.

In some respects, the Romantic genius figure only reached full flower at the end of the nineteenth century, when science and pseudoscience lent their authority to ideas of a superior being. As late as 1903 Joyce's famous contemporary, the Austrian writer Otto Weininger, twenty-three years old and the author of an influential study of genius, sought out the room in which Beethoven had died in order to commit suicide; he believed that it was better to die than to live with mere talent and convinced himself by racialist arguments that Jews like himself could not be geniuses. Perhaps without intending to do so, Francis Galton, the founder of modern eugenics and the cousin of Darwin, encouraged such a radical view in his study *Hereditary Genius* (1869). Galton's assumption, which he claims to defend logically, is that "high reputation is a pretty accurate test of high ability" in any field (Galton 2), and his thesis is that men of the most exceptional "natural gifts" more often than not are genetically related to others; he is particularly interested in "famous families" such as the Adamses in America and the Russells and Darwins in England.

It soon becomes clear, however, that Galton's ostensibly objective, scientific study is actually legitimizing an aristocracy. His tacit assumptions are made clear in his casual note that France would be a poor subject for study because "the Revolution and the guillotine made sad havoc among the progeny of her abler races" (4). As the phrase "abler races" makes explicit, Galton's approach is actually a microscopic version of a racialist argument, and indeed his project occurred to him during an examination of the characteristics and abilities of various races. In his preface to the book's 1898 edition, Galton admits that he is concerned by "the striking effects of an evil inheritance" that are shown in "the yearly output by unfit parents of weakly children who are constitutionally incapable of growing up into serviceable citizens" (xx). On the other hand, it is now possible to breed a superior race:

> The improvement of the natural gifts of future generations of the human race is largely, though indirectly, under our control. . . . The processes of evolution are in constant and spontaneous activity, some pushing towards the bad, some towards the good. Our part is to watch for opportunities to intervene. . . . (xxvi–xxvii)

By the turn of the century, such ideas were in the air even in Ireland and seemed all the more crucial because of widespread fears of racial degeneration. Because most scientists had been Lamarckian until well after the turn of the century, few people understood that Darwinian selection was an effective corrective to such minor instances of biological degeneration as actually occurred (and that these invariably happened among very primitive organisms). Even in 1921, the physician Samuel Holmes could announce that "everywhere the nemesis of degeneracy hangs threateningly over the organic world" (4–5). Yet this spectre was not enough to rally people to Galton's eugenic program. Whatever millennial hope the idea of positive evolution held out was counterbalanced by a certain fear of the evolution of a "master race." Some observers wondered just who was to implement programs like Galton's, and on what basis. On a less conscious level, popular myths articulated deep fears of the superman. Dracula, for example, is identified in the

Irishman Bram Stoker's 1897 novel as a degenerate and criminal type; the character who realizes this makes formal, scholarly allusions to Lombroso and Nordau. Indeed, it is because they can identify him as a degenerate that the band of heroes are able to outsmart the vampire despite his superhuman powers. We can only wonder at the nineteenth-century faith in taxonomy that allows a creature who is dead and drinks blood to be subsumed so easily into a physiological-psychological category.

Meanwhile, a more fundamental if less likely threat had been articulated in imaginative literature. Since about midcentury, increasingly alienated artists had been envisioning new and superior types of men, such as the poet Arthur Rimbaud's "assassins," who would have no truck with the bourgeois rabblement. In a well-known essay, Hugh Kenner pointed out the affinity between the innately superior figure of the dandy and aesthete, such as Yeats's Owen Aherne, and the "superbrain," whose most popular version was Sherlock Holmes; both these are reflected in Stephen Dedalus (Kenner 158–78). Friedrich Nietzsche's *Übermensch* is the most famous of these conceptions, a superior creature who is beyond ordinary morality and is, by the Christian standards that Nietzsche deplored, a monster of egotism. In *Ulysses* Stephen's friend Mulligan, feeling his side, claims that his twelfth rib is gone, and exclaims, "I'm the *Übermensch*. [Stephen] and I, the supermen" (*Ulysses* 1:708–09). Mulligan is being facetious, but towards the climax of *Portrait,* when Stephen envisions the mysterious host who "call to me, their kinsman, making ready to go, shaking the wings of their exultant and terrible youth" (p. 218), he is fully serious.

"A man of genius," says Stephen in *Ulysses,* "makes no mistakes. His errors are volitional and are the portals of discovery" (*Ulysses* 9:228–29). Shortly afterward, he announces: "His own image to a man with that queer thing genius is the standard of all experience, material and moral" (*Ulysses* 9:432–33). One implication of these rather obscure pronouncements is that the genius makes his own rules and cannot fail—if he were to fail, he would be no genius. And if his "own image" is the "standard of all experience" then he is outside the Panopticon entirely. He cannot be identified and judged by "Them" because he is literally incomparable to those around him. The genius, the superman, the aristocrat of art—all these are attempts to recenter the subject, the "I," in a world grown maddeningly regimented and restricted. For Stephen, his own transformation into some vaguely imagined winged being, an aesthete high above the multitude, is bound up mysteriously with the idea of escape; because he is Irish, he can briefly convince himself that in France they order these things better, or at least less. Later he will return, his wings clipped.

The interlocking cultural constructions of genius and degeneration, I have tried to show, inform *Portrait,* and function as oppositional structures—"tactics," in de Certeau's terms—to the social Panopticon. Naturally I have adopted a faintly parodic tone in discussing these constructions: we know better now than to invest our energies in such outmoded and scientifically invalid terms. And yet the occasion of this essay, and of the entire volume, is Joyce's "genius," which was first perversely recognized as a sort of degeneracy, as a glance at *Portrait*'s early reviews will show. Although I have tried to demonstrate ways in which genius and degeneracy pervade late nineteenth-century writing as a whole, including literary, subliterary, and nonliterary works, the unacknowledged point of my demonstration has been, paradoxically, that this pervasiveness is significant because it exists also in Joyce. If our common humanity is a fundamental tenet of contemporary Western culture, it would seem that we are equally committed to a fascination with the uncommon strains that play within it, at a cost we do not usually recognize or assess.

WORKS CITED

Battersby, Christine. *Gender and Genius.* London: The Women's Press, 1989.

Becker, George. *The Mad Genius Controversy: A Study in the Sociology of Deviance.* London: Sage, 1978.

Benjamin, Walter. *Illuminations.* Trans. Harry Zohn. New York: Schocken, 1969.

Brasted, H. V. "Irish Nationalism and the British Empire in the Late Nineteenth Century." *Irish Culture and Nationalism, 1750–1950.* Ed. Oliver MacDonagh et al. New York: St. Martin's, 1983. 83–103.

Certeau, Michel de. *The Practice of Everyday Life.* Trans. Steven Randall. Berkeley: U of California P, 1988.

Deane, Seamus. *Celtic Revivals.* London: Faber and Faber, 1985.

Foucault, Michel. *Discipline and Punish: The Birth of the Prison.* Trans. Alan Sheridan. New York: Vintage, 1979.

Galton, Francis. *Hereditary Genius: An Inquiry into Its Laws and Consequences.* New York: St. Martin's, 1978 [1869].

Gilman, Sandor, ed. *Degeneration.* New York: Columbia UP, 1986.

Greenblatt, Stephen. *Renaissance Self-Fashioning: From More to Shakespeare.* Chicago: U of Chicago P, 1984.

Harper, Margaret Mills. *The Aristocracy of Art in Joyce and Woolf.* Baton Rouge: Louisiana State UP, 1990.

Holmes, Samuel J. *The Trend of the Race: A Study of Present Tendencies in the Biological Development of Civilized Mankind.* New York: Harcourt, 1921.

Horkheimer, Max, and Theodor Adorno. "The Culture Industry: Enlightenment as Mass Deception." *The Dialectic of Enlightenment.* New York: Continuum, 1985.

Joyce, James. *Ulysses.* Ed. Hans Walter Gabler, et al. New York: Random House, 1986.

Kenner, Hugh. *Dublin's Joyce.* Boston: Beacon, 1962.

Kershner, R. B. "Degeneration: The Explanatory Nightmare." *Georgia Review* 40 (Summer 1986), 416–44.

———. *Joyce, Bakhtin, and Popular Literature: Chronicles of Disorder.* Chapel Hill: U of North Carolina P, 1989.

O'Connor, Frank. "Egotism in Irish Literature." *The Listener* 31 (1 June 1944), 603, 609.

Walters, Ronald G., ed. *Primers for Prudery: Sexual Advice to Victorian America.* Englewood Cliffs: Prentice, 1974.

Glossary of Critical and Theoretical Terms

Most terms have been glossed parenthetically where they first appear in the text. Mainly, the glossary lists terms that are too complex to define in a phrase or a sentence or two. A few of the terms listed are discussed at greater length elsewhere (feminist criticism, for instance); these terms are defined succinctly and a page reference to the longer discussion is provided.

AFFECTIVE FALLACY First used by William K. Wimsatt and Monroe C. Beardsley to refer to what they regarded as the erroneous practice of interpreting texts according to the psychological responses of readers. "The Affective Fallacy," they wrote in a 1946 essay later republished in the *Verbal Icon* (1954), "is a confusion between the poem and its *results* (what it *is* and what it *does*). . . . It begins by trying to derive the standards of criticism from the psychological effects of a poem and ends in impressionism and relativism." The affective fallacy, like the intentional fallacy (confusing the meaning of a work with the author's expressly intended meaning), was one of the main tenets of the New Criticism, or formalism. The affective fallacy has recently been contested by reader-response critics, who have deliberately dedicated their efforts to describing the way individual readers and "interpretive communities" go about "making sense" of texts.

See also: Authorial Intention, Formalism, Reader-Response Criticism.

AUTHORIAL INTENTION Defined narrowly, an author's intention in writing a work, as expressed in letters, diaries, interviews, and conversations. Defined more broadly, "intentionality" involves unexpressed motivations, designs, and purposes, some of which may have remained unconscious.

The debate over whether critics should try to discern an author's intentions (conscious or otherwise) is an old one. William K. Wimsatt and Monroe C.

Beardsley, in an essay first published in the 1940s, coined the term "intentional fallacy" to refer to the practice of basing interpretations on the expressed or implied intentions of authors, a practice they judged to be erroneous. As proponents of the New Criticism, or formalism, they argued that a work of literature is an object in itself and should be studied as such. They believed that it is sometimes helpful to learn what an author intended, but the critic's real purpose is to show what is actually in the text, not what an author intended to put there.

See also: Affective Fallacy, Formalism.

BASE *See* Marxist Criticism.

BINARY OPPOSITIONS *See* Oppositions.

BLANKS *See* Gaps.

CANON Since the fourth century, used to refer to those books of the Bible that the Christian church accepts as being Holy Scripture. The term has come to be applied more generally to those literary works given special status, or "privileged," by a culture. Works we tend to think of as "classics" or the "Great Books" produced by Western culture — texts that are found in every anthology of American, British, and world literature — would be among those that constitute the canon.

Recently, Marxist, feminist, minority, and Third World critics have argued that, for political reasons, many excellent works never enter the canon. Canonized works, they claim, are those that reflect — and respect — the culture's dominant ideology and/or perform some socially acceptable or even necessary form of "cultural work." Attempts have been made to broaden or redefine the canon by discovering valuable texts, or versions of texts, that were repressed or ignored for political reasons. These have been published both in traditional and in nontraditional anthologies. The more outspoken critics of the canon, especially radical critics practicing cultural criticism, have called into question the whole concept of canon or "canonicity." Privileging no form of artistic expression that reflects and revises the culture, these critics treat cartoons, comics, and soap operas with the same cogency and respect they accord novels, poems, and plays.

See also: Cultural Criticism, Feminist Criticism, Ideology, Marxist Criticism.

CONFLICTS, CONTRADICTIONS *See* Gaps.

CULTURAL CRITICISM A critical approach that is sometimes referred to as "cultural studies" or "cultural critique." Practitioners of cultural criticism oppose "high" definitions of culture and take seriously popular cultural forms. Grounded in a variety of continental European influences, cultural criticism nonetheless gained institutional force in England, in 1964, with the founding of the Centre for Contemporary Cultural Studies at Birmingham University. Broadly interdisciplinary in its scope and approach, cultural criticism views the text as the locus and catalyst of a complex network of political and economic discourses. Cultural critics share with Marxist critics an interest in the ideological contexts of cultural forms.

DECONSTRUCTION A poststructuralist approach to literature that is strongly influenced by the writings of the French philosopher Jacques Derrida. Deconstruction, partly in response to structuralism and formalism, posits the undecidability of meaning for all texts. In fact, as the deconstructionist critic J. Hillis Miller points out, "deconstruction is not a dismantling of the structure of a text but a demonstration that it has already dismantled itself." See "What Is Deconstruction?" pp. 326–38.

DIALECTIC Originally developed by Greek philosophers, mainly Socrates and Plato, as a form and method of logical argumentation; the term later came to denote a philosophical notion of evolution. The German philosopher G. W. F. Hegel described dialectic as a process whereby a thesis, when countered by an antithesis, leads to the synthesis of a new idea. Karl Marx and Friedrich Engels, adapting Hegel's idealist theory, used the phrase "dialectical materialism" to discuss the way in which a revolutionary class war might lead to the synthesis of a new social economic order. The American Marxist critic Fredric Jameson has coined the phrase "dialectical criticism" to refer to a Marxist critical approach that synthesizes structuralist and poststructuralist methodologies.

See also: Marxist Criticism, Structuralism, Poststructuralism.

DIALOGIC *See* Discourse.

DISCOURSE Used specifically, can refer to (1) spoken or written discussion of a subject or area of knowledge; (2) the words in, or text of, a narrative as opposed to its story line; or (3) a "strand" within a given narrative that argues a certain point or defends a given value system.

More generally, "discourse" refers to the language in which a subject or area of knowledge is discussed or a certain kind of business is transacted. Human knowledge is collected and structured in discourses. Theology and medicine are defined by their discourses, as are politics, sexuality, and literary criticism.

A society is generally made up of a number of different discourses or "discourse communities," one or more of which may be dominant or serve the dominant ideology. Each discourse has its own vocabulary, concepts, and rules, knowledge of which constitutes power. The psychoanalyst and psychoanalytic critic Jacques Lacan has treated the unconscious as a form of discourse, the patterns of which are repeated in literature. Cultural critics, following Mikhail Bakhtin, use the word "dialogic" to discuss the dialogue *between* discourses that takes place within language or, more specifically, a literary text.

See also: Cultural Criticism, Ideology, Narrative, Psychoanalytic Criticism.

FEMINIST CRITICISM An aspect of the feminist movement whose primary goals include critiquing masculine-dominated language and literature by showing how they reflect a masculine ideology; writing the history of unknown or undervalued women writers, thereby earning them their rightful place in the literary canon; and helping create a climate in which women's creativity may be fully realized and appreciated. See "What Is Feminist Criticism?" pp. 295–307.

FIGURE *See* Metaphor, Metonymy, Symbol.

FORMALISM Also referred to as the New Criticism, formalism reached its height during the 1940s and 1950s but it is still practiced today. Formalists treat a work of literary art as if it were a self-contained, self-referential object. Rather than basing their interpretations of a text on the reader's response, the author's stated intentions, or parallels between the text and historical contexts (such as the author's life), formalists concentrate on the relationships *within* the text that give it its own distinctive character or form. Special attention is paid to repetition, particularly of images or symbols, but also of sound effects and rhythms in poetry.

Because of the importance placed on close analysis and the stress on the text as a carefully crafted, orderly object containing observable formal patterns, formalism has often been seen as an attack on Romanticism and impressionism, particularly impressionistic criticism. It has sometimes even been called an "objective" approach to literature. Formalists are more likely than certain other critics to believe and say that the meaning of a text can be known objectively. For instance, reader-response critics see meaning as a function either of each reader's experience or of the norms that govern a particular "interpretive community," and deconstructors argue that texts mean opposite things at the same time.

Formalism was originally based on essays written during the 1920s and 1930s by T. S. Eliot, I. A. Richards, and William Empson. It was significantly developed later by a group of American poets and critics, including R. P. Blackmur, Cleanth Brooks, John Crowe Ransom, Allen Tate, Robert Penn Warren, and William K. Wimsatt. Although we associate formalism with certain principles and terms (such as the "Affective Fallacy" and the "Intentional Fallacy" as defined by Wimsatt and Monroe C. Beardsley), formalists were trying to make a cultural statement rather than establish a critical dogma. Generally Southern, religious, and culturally conservative, they advocated the inherent value of literary works (particularly of literary works regarded as beautiful art objects) because they were sick of the growing ugliness of modern life and contemporary events. Some recent theorists even suggest that the rising popularity of formalism after World War II was a feature of American isolationism, the formalist tendency to isolate literature from biography and history being a manifestation of the American fatigue with wider involvements.

See also: Affective Fallacy, Authorial Intention, Deconstruction, Reader-Response Criticism, Symbol.

GAPS When used by reader-response critics familiar with the theories of Wolfgang Iser, refers to "blanks" in texts that must be filled in by readers. A gap may be said to exist whenever and wherever a reader perceives something to be missing between words, sentences, paragraphs, stanzas, or chapters. Readers respond to gaps actively and creatively, explaining apparent inconsistencies in point of view, accounting for jumps in chronology, speculatively supplying information missing from plots, and resolving problems or issues left ambiguous or "indeterminate" in the text.

Reader-response critics sometimes speak as if a gap actually exists in a text; a gap is, of course, to some extent a product of readers' perceptions. Different readers may find gaps in different texts, and different gaps in the same text. Furthermore, they may fill these gaps in in different ways, which is why, a reader-response critic might argue, works are interpreted in different ways.

Although the concept of the gap has been used mainly by reader-response critics, it has also been used by critics taking other theoretical approaches. Practitioners of deconstruction might use "gap" when speaking of the radical contradictoriness of a text. Marxists have used the term to speak of everything from the gap that opens up between economic base and cultural superstructure to the two kinds of conflicts or contradictions to be found in literary texts. The first of these, they would argue, results from the fact that texts reflect ideology, within which certain subjects cannot be covered, things that cannot be said, contradictory views that cannot be recognized as contradictory. The second kind of conflict, contradiction, or gap within a text results from the fact that works don't just reflect ideology: they are also fictions that, consciously or unconsciously, distance themselves from the same ideology.

See also: Deconstruction, Ideology, Marxist Criticism, Reader-Response Criticism.

GENRE A French word referring to a kind or type of literature. Individual works within a genre may exhibit a distinctive form, be governed by certain conventions, and/or represent characteristic subjects. Tragedy, epic, and romance are all genres.

Perhaps inevitably, the term "genre" is used loosely. Lyric poetry is a genre, but so are characteristic *types* of the lyric, such as the sonnet, the ode, and the elegy. Fiction is a genre, as are detective fiction and science fiction. The list of genres grows constantly as critics establish new lines of connection between individual works and discern new categories of works with common characteristics. Moreover, some writers form hybrid genres by combining the characteristics of several in a single work.

Knowledge of genres helps critics to understand and explain what is conventional and unconventional, borrowed and original, in a work.

HEGEMONY Given intellectual currency by the Italian communist Antonio Gramsci, the word (a translation of *egemonia*) refers to the pervasive system of assumptions, meanings, and values — the web of ideologies, in other words — that shapes the way things look, what they mean, and therefore what reality *is* for the majority of people within a given culture.

See also: Ideology, Marxist Criticism.

IDEOLOGY A set of beliefs underlying the customs, habits, and/or practices common to a given social group. To members of that group, the beliefs seem obviously true, natural, and even universally applicable. They may seem just as obviously arbitrary, idiosyncratic, and even false to outsiders or members of another group who adhere to another ideology. Within a society, several ideologies may coexist, or one or more may be dominant.

Ideologies may be forcefully imposed or willingly subscribed to. Their component beliefs may be held consciously or unconsciously. In either case, they come to form what Johanna M. Smith has called "the unexamined ground of our experience." Ideology governs our perceptions, judgments, and prejudices — our sense of what is acceptable, normal, and deviant. Ideology may cause a revolution; it may also allow discrimination and even exploitation.

Ideologies are of special interest to sociologically oriented critics of literature because of the way in which authors reflect or resist prevailing views in their texts. Some Marxist critics have argued that literary texts reflect and reproduce the ideologies that produced them; most, however, have shown how ideologies are riven with contradictions that works of literature manage to expose and widen. Still other Marxists have focused on the way in which texts themselves are characterized by gaps, conflicts, and contradictions between their ideological and anti-ideological functions.

Feminist critics have addressed the question of ideology by seeking to expose (and thereby call into question) the patriarchal ideology mirrored or inscribed in works written by men — even men who have sought to counter sexism and break down sexual stereotypes. New historicists have been interested in demonstrating the ideological underpinnings not only of literary representations but also of our interpretations of them. Fredric Jameson, an American Marxist critic, argues that all thought is ideological, but that ideological thought that knows itself as such stands the chance of seeing through and transcending ideology.

See also: Cultural Criticism, Feminist Criticism, Marxist Criticism, New Historicism.

IMAGINARY STAGE According to Lacanian psychoanalytic theory, the pre-oedipal, prelinguistic stage of child development that precedes the Symbolic stage. During the Imaginary stage, also called the mirror stage, the child conceives of the mother and indeed of the entire world as being indistinguishable from the self.

See also: Psychoanalytic Criticism, Symbolic Stage.

IMPLIED READER A phrase used by some reader-response critics in place of the phrase "the reader." Whereas "the reader" could refer to any idiosyncratic individual who happens to have read or to be reading the text, "the implied reader" is *the* reader intended, even created, by the text. Other reader-response critics seeking to describe this more generally conceived reader have spoken of the "informed reader" or the "narratee," who is "the necessary counterpart of a given narrator."

See Reader-Response Criticism.

INTENTIONAL FALLACY *See* Authorial Intention.

INTENTIONALITY *See* Authorial Intention.

INTERTEXTUALITY The condition of interconnectedness among texts. Every author has been influenced by others, and every work contains explicit and implicit references to other works. Writers may consciously or unconsciously echo a predecessor or precursor; they may also consciously or unconsciously disguise their indebtedness, making intertextual relationships difficult for the critic to trace.

Reacting against the formalist tendency to view each work as a free-standing object, some poststructuralist critics suggested that the meaning of a work only emerges intertextually, that is, within the context provided by other works. But there has been a reaction, too, against this type of intertextual criticism. Some new historicist critics suggest that literary history is itself too narrow a context and that works should be interpreted in light of a larger set of cultural contexts.

There is, however, a broader definition of intertextuality, one that refers to the relationship between works of literature and a wide range of narratives and discourses that we don't usually consider literary. Thus defined, intertextuality could be used by a new historicist to refer to the significant interconnectedness between a literary text and nonliterary discussions of or discourses about contemporary culture. Or it could be used by a poststructuralist to suggest that a work can only be recognized and read within a vast field of signs and tropes that is *like* a text and that makes any single text self-contradictory and "undecidable."

See also: Discourse, Formalism, Narrative, New Historicism, Poststructuralism, Trope.

MARXIST CRITICISM An approach that treats literary texts as material products, describing them in broadly historical terms. In Marxist criticism, the text is viewed in terms of its production and consumption, as a product *of* work that does identifiable cultural work of its own. Following Karl Marx, the founder of communism, Marxist critics have used the terms "base" to refer to economic reality and "superstructure" to refer to the corresponding or "homologous" infrastructure consisting of politics, law, philosophy, religion, and the arts. Also following Marx, they have used the word "ideology" to refer to that set of cultural beliefs that literary works at once reproduce, resist, and revise.

METAPHOR The representation of one thing by another related or similar thing. The image (or activity or concept) used to represent or "figure" something else is known as the "vehicle" of the metaphor; the thing represented is called the "tenor." In other words, the vehicle is what we substitute for the tenor. The relationship between vehicle and tenor can provide much additional meaning. Thus, instead of saying, "Last night I read a book," we might say, "Last night I plowed through a book." "Plowed through" (or the activity of plowing) is the vehicle of our metaphor; "read" (or the act of reading) is the tenor, the thing being figured. The increment in meaning through metaphor is fairly obvious. Our audience knows not only *that* we read but also *how* we read, because to read a book in the way that a plow rips through earth is surely to read in a relentless, unreflective way. Note that in the sentence above, a new metaphor – "rips through" – has been used to explain an old one. This serves (which is a metaphor) as an example of just how thick (another metaphor) language is with metaphors!

Metaphor is a kind of "trope" (literally, a "turning," i.e., a figure that alters or "turns" the meaning of a word or phrase). Other tropes include allegory, conceit, metonymy, personification, simile, symbol, and synecdoche. Traditionally, metaphor and symbol have been viewed as the principal tropes; minor tropes have been categorized as *types* of these two major ones. Similes, for instance, are usually defined as simple metaphors that usually employ "like" or "as" and state the tenor outright, as in "My love is like a red, red rose." Synecdoche involves a vehicle that is a *part* of the tenor, as in "I see a sail" meaning "I see a boat." Metonymy is viewed as a metaphor involving two terms commonly if arbitrarily associated with (but not fundamentally or intrinsically related to) each other. Recently, however, deconstructors such as Paul de Man and J. Hillis Miller have questioned the "privilege" granted to metaphor and the metaphor/metonymy distinction or "opposition." They have suggested that all metaphors are really metonyms and that all figuration is arbitrary.

See also: Deconstruction, Metonymy, Oppositions, Symbol.

METONYMY The representation of one thing by another that is commonly and often physically associated with it. To refer to a writer's handwriting as his or her "hand" is to use a metonymic "figure" or "trope." The image or thing used to represent something else is known as the "vehicle" of the metonym; the thing represented is called the "tenor."

Like other tropes (such as metaphor), metonymy involves the replacement of one word or phrase by another. Liquor may be referred to as "the bottle," a monarch as "the crown." Narrowly defined, the vehicle of a metonym is arbitrarily, not intrinsically, associated with the tenor. In other words, the bottle just happens to be what liquor is stored in and poured from in our culture. The hand may be involved in the production of handwriting, but so are the brain and the pen. There is no special, intrinsic likeness between a crown and a monarch; it's just that crowns traditionally sit on monarchs' heads and not on the heads of university professors. More broadly, "metonym" and "metonymy" have been used by recent critics to refer to a wide range of figures and tropes. Deconstructors have questioned the distinction between metaphor and metonymy.

See also: Deconstruction, Metaphor, Trope.

NARRATIVE A story or a telling of a story, or an account of a situation or of events. A novel and a biography of a novelist are both narratives, as are Freud's case histories.

Some critics use the word "narrative" even more generally; Brook Thomas, a new historicist, has critiqued "narratives of human history that neglect the role human labor has played."

NEW CRITICISM *See* Formalism.

NEW HISTORICISM One of the most recent developments in contemporary critical theory, its practitioners share certain convictions, the major ones being that literary critics need to develop a high degree of historical consciousness and that literature should not be viewed apart from other human creations, artistic or otherwise. See "What Is the New Historicism?" pp. 361–72.

See also: Authorial Intention, Deconstruction, Formalism, Ideology, Poststructuralism, Psychoanalytic Criticism.

OPPOSITIONS A concept highly relevant to linguistics, since linguists maintain that words (such as "black" and "death") have meaning not in themselves, but in relation to other words ("white" and "life"). Jacques Derrida, a poststructuralist philosopher of language, has suggested that in the West we think in terms of these "binary oppositions" or dichotomies, which on examination turn out to be evaluative hierarchies. In other words, each opposition — beginning / end, presence / absence, or consciousness / unconsciousness — contains one term that our culture views as superior and one term that we view as negative or inferior.

Derrida has "deconstructed" a number of these binary oppositions, including two — speech / writing and signifier / signified — that he believes to be central to linguistics in particular and Western culture in general. He has concurrently critiqued the "law" of noncontradiction, which is fundamental to Western logic. He and other deconstructors have argued that a text can contain opposed strands of discourse and, therefore, mean opposite things: reason *and* passion, life *and* death, hope *and* despair, black *and* white. Traditionally, criticism has involved choosing between opposed or contradictory meanings and arguing that one is present in the text and the other absent.

French feminists have adopted the ideas of Derrida and other deconstructors, showing not only that we think in terms of such binary oppositions as male / female, reason / emotion, and active / passive, but that we also associate reason and activity with masculinity and emotion and passivity with femininity. Because of this, they have concluded that language is "phallocentric," or masculine-dominated.

See also: Deconstruction, Discourse, Feminist Criticism, Poststructuralism.

POSTSTRUCTURALISM The general attempt to contest and subvert structuralism initiated by deconstructors and certain other critics associated with psychoanalytic, Marxist, and feminist theory. Structuralists, using linguistics as a model and employing semiotic (sign) theory, posit the possibility of knowing a text systematically and revealing the "grammar" behind its form and meaning. Poststructuralists argue against the possibility of such knowledge and description. They counter that texts can be shown to contradict not only structuralist accounts of them but also themselves. In making their adversarial claims, they rely on close readings of texts and on the work of theorists such as Jacques Derrida and Jacques Lacan.

Poststructuralists have suggested that structuralism rests on distinctions between "signifier" and "signified" (signs and the things they point toward), "self" and "language" (or "text"), texts and other texts, and text and world that are overly simplistic, if not patently inaccurate. Poststructuralists have shown how all signifieds are also signifiers, and they have treated texts as "intertexts." They have viewed the world as if it *were* a text (we desire a certain car because it *symbolizes* achievement) and the self as the subject, as well as the user, of language; for example, we may shape and speak through language, but it also shapes and speaks through us.

See also: Deconstruction, Feminist Criticism, Intertextuality, Psychoanalytic Criticism, Semiotics, Structuralism.

PSYCHOANALYTIC CRITICISM Grounded in the psychoanalytic theories of Sigmund Freud, it is one of the oldest critical methodologies still in use. Freud's view that works of literature, like dreams, express secret, unconscious desires led to criticism that interpreted literary works as manifestations of the authors' neuroses. More recently, psychoanalytic critics have come to see literary works as skillfully crafted artifacts that may appeal to *our* neuroses by tapping into our repressed wishes and fantasies. Other forms of psychological criticism that diverge from Freud, although they ultimately derive from his insights, include those based on the theories of Carl Jung and Jacques Lacan. See "What Is Psychoanalytic Criticism?" pp. 235–51.

READER-RESPONSE CRITICISM An approach to literature that, as its name implies, considers the way readers respond to texts, as they read. Stanley Fish describes the method by saying that it substitutes for one question, "What does this sentence mean?" a more operational question, "What does this sentence do?" Reader-response criticism shares with deconstruction a strong textual orientation and a reluctance to define a single meaning for a work. Along with psychoanalytic criticism, it shares an interest in the dynamics of mental response to textual cues. See "What Is Reader-Response Criticism?" pp. 268–78.

SEMIOLOGY, SEMIOTIC *See* Semiotics.

SEMIOTICS The study of signs and sign systems and the way meaning is derived from them. Structuralist anthropologists, psychoanalysts, and literary critics developed semiotics during the decades following 1950, but much of the pioneering work had been done at the turn of the century by the founder of modern linguistics, Ferdinand de Saussure, and the American philosopher Charles Sanders Peirce.

Semiotics is based on several important distinctions, including the distinction between "signifier" and "signified" (the sign and what it points toward) and the distinction between "langue" and "parole." *Langue* (French for "tongue," as in "native tongue," meaning language) refers to the entire system within which individual utterances or usages of language have meaning; *parole* (French for "word") refers to the particular utterances or usages. A principal tenet of semiotics is that signs, like words, are not significant in themselves, but instead have meaning only in relation to other signs and the entire system of signs, or langue.

The affinity between semiotics and structuralist literary criticism derives from this emphasis placed on langue, or system. Structuralist critics, after all, were reacting against formalists and their procedure of focusing on individual words as if meanings didn't depend on anything external to the text.

Poststructuralists have used semiotics but questioned some of its underlying assumptions, including the opposition between signifier and signified. The feminist poststructuralist Julia Kristeva, for instance, has used the word "semiotic" to describe feminine language, a highly figurative, fluid form of discourse that she sets in opposition to rigid, symbolic masculine language.

See also: Deconstruction, Feminist Criticism, Formalism, Poststructuralism, Oppositions, Structuralism, Symbol.

SIMILE *See* Metaphor.

SOCIOHISTORICAL CRITICISM *See* New Historicism.

STRUCTURALISM A science of humankind whose proponents attempted to show that all elements of human culture, including literature, may be understood as parts of a system of signs. Structuralism, according to Robert Scholes, was a reaction to "'modernist' alienation and despair."

Using Ferdinand de Saussure's linguistic theory, European structuralists such as Roman Jakobson, Claude Lévi-Strauss, and Roland Barthes (before his shift toward poststructuralism) attempted to develop a "semiology" or "semiotics" (science of signs). Barthes, among others, sought to recover literature and even language from the isolation in which they had been studied and to show that the laws that govern them govern all signs, from road signs to articles of clothing.

Particularly useful to structuralists were two of Saussure's concepts: the idea of "phoneme" in language and the idea that phonemes exist in two kinds of relationships: "synchronic" and "diachronic." A phoneme is the smallest consistently significant unit in language; thus, both "a" and "an" are phonemes, but "n" is not. A diachronic relationship is that which a phoneme has with those that have preceded it in time and those that will follow it. These "horizontal" relationships produce what we might call discourse or narrative and what Saussure called "parole." The synchronic relationship is the "vertical" one that a word has in a given instant with the entire system of language ("langue") in which it may generate meaning. "An" means what it means in English because those of us who speak the language are using it in the same way at a given time.

Following Saussure, Lévi-Strauss studied hundreds of myths, breaking them into their smallest meaningful units, which he called "mythemes." Removing each from its diachronic relations with other mythemes in a single myth (such as the myth of Oedipus and his mother), he vertically aligned those mythemes that he found to be homologous (structurally correspondent). He then studied the relationships within as well as between vertically aligned columns, in an attempt to understand scientifically, through ratios and proportions, those thoughts and processes that humankind has shared, both at one particular time and across time. One could say, then, that structuralists followed Saussure in preferring to think about the overriding langue or language of myth, in which each mytheme and mytheme-constituted myth fits meaningfully, rather than about isolated individual paroles or narratives. Structuralists followed Saussure's lead in believing what the poststructuralist Jacques Derrida later decided he could not subscribe to — that sign systems must be understood in terms of binary oppositions. In analyzing myths and texts to find basic structures, structuralists tended to find that opposite terms modulate until they are finally resolved or reconciled by some intermediary third term. Thus, a structuralist reading of *Paradise Lost* would show that the war between God and the bad angels becomes a rift between God and sinful, fallen man, the rift then being healed by the Son of God, the mediating third term.

See also: Deconstruction, Discourse, Narrative, Poststructuralism, Semiotics.

SUPERSTRUCTURE *See* Marxist Criticism.

SYMBOL A thing, image, or action that, although it is of interest in its own right, stands for or suggests something larger and more complex — often an idea or a range of interrelated ideas, attitudes, and practices.

Within a given culture, some things are understood to be symbols: the flag of the United States is an obvious example. More subtle cultural symbols might be the river as a symbol of time and the journey as a symbol of life and its manifold experiences.

Instead of appropriating symbols generally used and understood within their culture, writers often create symbols by setting up, in their works, a complex but identifiable web of associations. As a result, one object, image, or action suggests others, and often, ultimately, a range of ideas.

A symbol may thus be defined as a metaphor in which the "vehicle," the thing, image, or action used to represent something else, represents many related things (or "tenors") or is broadly suggestive. The urn in Keats's "Ode on a Grecian Urn" suggests many interrelated concepts, including art, truth, beauty, and timelessness.

Symbols have been of particular interest to formalists, who study how meanings emerge from the complex, patterned relationships between images in a work, and psychoanalytic critics, who are interested in how individual authors and the larger culture both disguise and reveal unconscious fears and desires through symbols. Recently, French feminists have also focused on the symbolic. They have suggested that, as wide-ranging as it seems, symbolic language is ultimately rigid and restrictive. They favor semiotic language and writing, which, they contend, is at once more rhythmic, unifying, and feminine.

See also: Feminist Criticism, Metaphor, Psychoanalytic Criticism, Trope.

SYMBOLIC STAGE According to Lacanian psychoanalytic theory, the stage in which the child (especially the male child) learns that what had seemed wholly his and even undistinguishable from himself (i.e., the mother) is in fact someone else's: something to be desired only in the form of socially acceptable substitutes. That recognition, according to Jacques Lacan, facilitates the child's entrance into language, for words themselves are not the things they stand for but, rather, are substitutes for those things. The Symbolic stage, which corresponds with what Freud called the oedipal stage, follows a pre-oedipal stage that Lacan termed the "Imaginary stage."

See also: Psychoanalytic Criticism.

SYNECDOCHE *See* Metaphor, Metonymy.

TENOR *See* Metaphor, Metonymy, Symbol.

TROPE A figure, as in "figure of speech." Literally a "turning," i.e., a turning or twisting of a word or phrase to make it mean something else. Principal tropes include metaphor, metonymy, simile, personification, and synecdoche.

See also: Metaphor, Metonymy.

VEHICLE *See* Metaphor, Metonymy, Symbol.

About the Contributors

THE VOLUME EDITOR

R. B. Kershner is a professor of English at the University of Florida, where he teaches twentieth-century literature and poetry writing. In addition to numerous articles, he has published *Dylan Thomas: The Poet and His Critics* (1977) and *Joyce, Bakhtin, and Popular Literature* (1989); the latter won the 1990 American Conference for Irish Studies award as the best work of literary criticism in the field. He is a member of the Board of Advisory Editors of the *James Joyce Quarterly*.

THE TEXTUAL EDITOR

Chester G. Anderson is a professor of English at the University of Minnesota, where he heads the Celtic Studies program. He was editor of the corrected text of Joyce's *Portrait* in 1964 and editor of the Viking Critical Edition of *Portrait* ("Text, Criticism, and Notes") in 1968. He is the author of *James Joyce and His World* (1968) and of the chapter "Joyce's Verses" in the 1984 *Companion to Joyce Studies*.

THE CRITICS

Sheldon Brivic is a professor of English at Temple University. He has published *Joyce Between Freud and Jung* (1980), *Joyce the Creator* (1985), and *The Veil of Signs: Joyce, Lacan, and Perception* (1991). He was recently guest co-editor of a special issue of the *James Joyce Quarterly* on "Joyce Between Genders: Lacanian Views." He is beginning a study of ALP, the heroine of *Finnegans Wake.*

Suzette Henke is Morton Professor of Literary Studies at the University of Louisville. She is the author of *Joyce's Moraculous Sindbook: A Study of "Ulysses"* (1978), co-editor of *Women in Joyce* (1982), and author of *James Joyce and the Politics of Desire* (1990). She has published articles on Virginia Woolf, Anaïs Nin, Dorothy Richardson, Linda Brent, Janet Frame, and others; and she is currently working on a study of women's "life-writing" in the twentieth century.

Cheryl Herr is an associate professor of English at the University of Iowa. She is the author of *Joyce's Anatomy of Culture* (1986) and editor of *For the Land They Loved: Irish Political Melodramas, 1890–1925* (1991). She spent 1992 in the Irish Republic and Northern Ireland as a Guggenheim Fellow, researching numerous aspects of Irish culture and preparing the manuscripts of two books.

Norman N. Holland is Marston-Milbauer Eminent Scholar at the University of Florida. Among his eleven books on reader-response and psychoanalytic criticism are *Five Readers Reading* (1975), *The I* (1985), *The Brain of Robert Frost* (1988), and *The Critical I* (1992).

THE SERIES EDITOR

Ross C Murfin, general editor of *Case Studies in Contemporary Criticism*, is dean of the College of Arts and Sciences and professor of English at the University of Miami. He has taught at Yale University and the University of Virginia and has published scholarly studies on Joseph Conrad, Thomas Hardy, and D. H. Lawrence.